ALL

FICTION BLENDED
WITH
NON-FICTION

By

Sandra L. LaVaughn

©2019 by Sandra L. LaVaughn

All rights reserved. No part of this book may be reproduced, stored in a retrieval system, or transmitted in any form or by any means without the prior written permission of the author or publisher. The exception is by a reviewer who may quote brief passages in a review to be printed in a newspaper, online, blog, magazine, video review, or journal.

Printed in the United States of America

All characters and events are fiction. Any resemblance to real people or incidents is purely coincidental.

Published by LaVauri Publishing House

Edited by Ricky LaVaughn
Revised editing by Esther L. Truth

Sandra L LaVaughn has written another book on the process of writing, producing, and directing a feature-length independent film titled: "How I Produced A Movie with Eight Thousand Dollars."

Sandra L LaVaughn has a feature film that is available entitled: "The Blue Room."

A documentary entitled: "A Walk On The Wild Side."

A WORD FROM THE AUTHOR

All But One is not a religious book, it is an adventuresome story about everyday life's victories and failures, whether the characters believe in God or not. This imaginative tale follows their connection with each other through their religious belief, respect, jealousy, love, and hate. The story shadows the characters struggle with overcoming abuse as they wrestle with the decision to make the right choice. Occasionally, they make mistakes when deciding. Unfortunately, too often, several of the characters elect to go down the wrong path, in the state of mine that they do not care.

Sometimes, they are happy with life, so they rejoice, other times, quick as a wink, life will serve them a green tomato, a few become confused. Others are pitched a rotten tomato, they feel cursed, get angry and lash out. A few of the characters developed a relationship with God, while others take the wrong path.

    All But One,
       All About Life,
          All About Choices

God can hear the prayers of His people, generations away.

ACKNOWLEDGMENT

All But One could not have been possible without the untiring efforts of my son, Elder Ricky LaVaughn. Rick was an encouraging supporter and prayer partner as this book took on a life of its own. He is a great accomplished author; he's written six books and is working on his seventh. Rick supplied me with the jots and tittles that I never knew were needed for a work of this kind. Son, thank you for taking time away from completing your book, to help finish mine. Rick spearheaded the creation of the book cover with a professional artist.

Thank you, Sonny, from the bottom of my heart, for being what I and this book needed. I am grateful for your executive skills and hard work to make All But One a reality.
    You're wonderful.

Without my daughter, Esther "Missy" L. Truth, professionalism as the editor of All But One, the story would have been factually incorrect. Missy like myself, is a historian, unlike me, she is a teacher. She thoroughly read the book, even did research to make sure the historical satire was accurate according to the time-period; thus, her critique of the manuscript was on point. While I was writing, Missy called asking, "how's the book coming?" I was so happy to finally say, it's done.

Thank you, Missy, for the encouragement, prayers, and being my cheerleader. In addition, through your editing skills, the story is kept precise according to its time.
    You're wonderful.

God blessed me with children that believe in the power of prayer.

Thank You, Jesus, for Your blessings and my little family.

TABLE OF CONTENTS

Prologue: 8

PART I
Chapter I: Moe's Escape ... 12
Chapter II: Help From The Underground Railroad Stations ... 24
Chapter III: The Beginning ... 38
Chapter IV: Harry's True Color ... 55
Chapter V: H.B. Metropolis ... 72
Chapter VI: The Hired Hands ... 85
Chapter VII: Last Phase of HB Metropolis ... 105
Chapter VIII: Moses ... 119
Chapter IX: Charles Brown ... 132
Chapter X: MacCall Family Lies ... 137
Chapter XI: Paula ... 143
Chapter XII: Happy Harry ... 148
Chapter XIII: Hoodwinked ... 151
Chapter XIV: Back To Boston ... 165
Chapter XV: Forever Apart ... 177
Chapter XVI: Two Slaves and One Friend Got Away ... 187

PART II
Chapter XVII: Paula and Moses Offspring ... 196
Chapter XVIII: Donovan Victor Bright ... 215
Chapter XIX: Ogville and MacCall ... 226
Chapter XX: The Magazine That Changed Lives ... 236
Chapter XXI: Valentine Day ... 251
Chapter XXII: Valentine Night ... 267
Chapter XXIII: Becky Lou Brown ... 276
Chapter XXIV: The First Meeting ... 282
Chapter XXV: After The Storm ... 288
Chapter XXVI: NAACP ... 296
Chapter XXVII: Hidden Gates ... 303
Chapter XXVIII: Becky Lou Brown – Discovery ... 316
Chapter XXIX: Smarter Than ... 323
Chapter XXX: Harry's Prayer ... 332
Chapter XXXI: Easter Sunday ... 344
Chapter XXXII: The Day After ... 365
Chapter XXXIII: Trouble ... 377
Chapter XXXIV: Theenda's Mom ... 391
Chapter XXXV: A Place To Meet ... 406
Chapter XXXVI: Haze Return ... 420

Chapter XXXVII: The Day Before	436
Chapter XXXVIII: Night Of The Escape	451
Chapter XXXIX: Save The Children	469
Chapter XL: Harry, It's Over	475
Chapter XLI: All But One	488
Chapter XLII: Jeff Brown Return To Ogville	499
Chapter XLIII: Freedom Home	521
Chapter XLIV: March 2018	528

Epilogue: 535

LaVaughn

A MAP OF THE PLANTATION

Below is a map that Donovan received and used to help the slaves. It was created by the nurses and teachers' over time.

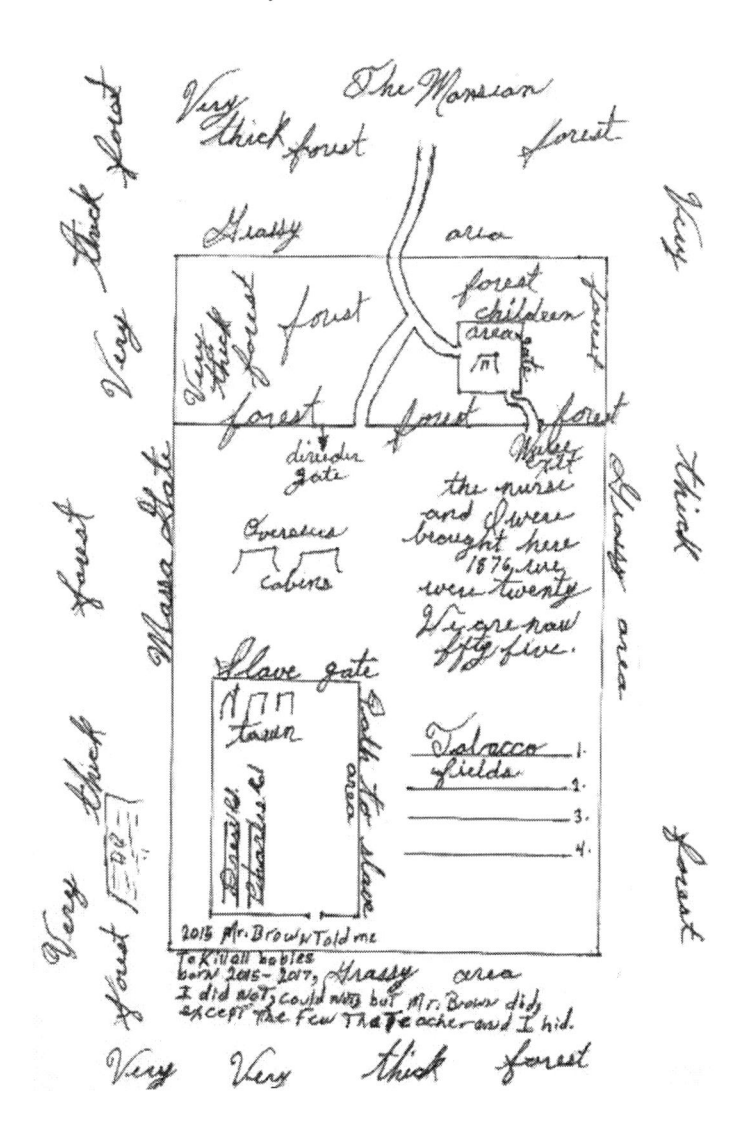

PROLOGUE

January 1865, the Confederacy was on a decline, yet during the war the Southern Officials boldly sought-after power and control. They desperately wanted to keep America divided.

February of that year, Confederate President Jefferson Davis agreed to send delegates to a Peace Conference with President Lincoln, and Secretary of State William Seward. At this meeting, President Davis strategy was to resolve the South weakening structure by insisting on President Lincoln's resignation. However, Lincoln refused to attend, thus the Conference never occurred. Lincoln being President of America, did away with the Southern states determination to divide. Davis Peace Conference did not help his cause, it backfired, he was accused of treason and stripped of his Presidential position.

Abraham Lincoln won the Presidential nomination, November 6, 1860. The Civil War broke out on April 12, 1861. On March 25, 1865, General Lee unsuccessfully attacked General Grant forces near Petersburg. In the South East, General Gorden and Johnson surrendered to the Yankees on April 26, 1865, the Civil War officially ended in April 1865.

Many of the slaves joined the Union or Confederate army to get off the plantation compound. The Civil War was a personal vendetta for the slaves, they fought to be free and to end the chattel of slavery. They fought for trade tariffs, states' rights, industry vs. farming, Abraham Lincoln, and many other reasons the Civil War broke out. The freedmen and women did not understand all the details for the Civil War; however, they totally grasped that part of the war was for their freedom.

By the early 1900s, slavery supposedly ended across America, in most southern states freedmen and women could go about their way without a threat of being forced back into slavery. Regrettably, the Indians were forced on reservations throughout the country, where even today several live and work.

Harry V. Brown, like tornado winds blended with a volcano eruption, vaulted into a sequestered course of hostile combat, to keep slaves on his plantation forever. His plan and twisted plot were a nauseating success, from 1865, until the twenty-first century.

Harry lived deep in the heart of Dixie where the land was spectacular, and the gleaming bright yellow sun hung brilliantly in the beautiful alabaster sky. The vivid green grass blanketed the Deltas lustrous land, the trees grew thick and dramatic with leaves that gracefully bowed down to their maker. Harry loved the Delta and all its loveliness. He was aggravated that the South had lost, and the Southern Generals were surrendering to the Yankees. However, Harry had great hope in a Cherokee Indian fellow, named Stand Waite, he learned that Waite was born in Oothcaloa and fought with the Confederates. Harry admired that the young Indian did not back down from the Yankees. Watie was promoted to the position of Brigadier General, of the Cherokee Brigade. Nevertheless, on June 23, 1865, with no one by his side, Watie was the last Confederate general to lay down his arms. Harry's ignited hope in the last man standing, ended.

In 1865, Harry heard of a man named Nathan Bedford Forrest, he was a Confederate Army General during the American Civil War, and the founder and leader of the Ku Klux Klan. Before the war, General Forrest gained his wealth as a cotton planter, horse and cattle trader, real estate broker, and selling slaves. He was a crude malicious man, whose campaign of intimidation and violence against Southern blacks and whites, who worked to end slavery were atrocious. Harry sat amidst powerful wealthy slave owners, that joined General Forrest wicked craving to keep the institution of slavery. General Forrest began his speech with, "get their first with the most."

General Forrest was a self-made millionaire. Harry loved the guy, the KKK founder quote became Harry's favorite, he heard, "get rich more than the most." Though it was not the quotation of the General, Harry believed that he heard and recited the General verbatim. One evening Harry was in his bedroom, he looked in the mirror and quoted what he thought Forest had said, "get rich more than the most." Harry smiled at himself, he pointed at his face in the mirror and continued, "that is your plan." Harry became a loyal follower and supporter of the General.

The KKK founder, spoke loud and hard to get his point across at a rally that was held in his honor. General Forest and the men were angry, the north was winning the war, he ended his speech with the way he began only louder and more forceful with revulsion and rage, "Get there first with the most!" He sat down.

Though most of the men did not get the full meaning of the General's quote, still they stood and cheered, Harry's heart burst with excitement. He adored the man and thought General Forest was right about slavery and their loyalist. If the north didn't allow the south to maintain their ways, Harry yelled out, "I will acquire wealth then fight the fight as an individual." He then chanted, "get rich more than the most." Harry's bass voice roared with eagerness.

Harry attended General Forest meetings, though personally, he was not a fan of the KKK's outfits, Harry fancied wearing suits that made him look prosperous. When they insisted that he wear their attire he stopped attending the meetings but maintain their hateful philosophies. The KKK hostility ignited within the soul and spirit of Harry, he allowed hate and anger to be the energy that propelled his cruel deceptive plan. He concocted an odious decision to keep slaves unendingly.

Harry's outrageous strategy lasted until his nemesis, Donovan Victor Bright, born 1993, discovered Harry's secret plantation.

Harry's harrowing journey began as a ten-year-old boy, named Moe

LaVaughn

ALL BUT ONE

Part I

I

Moe's Escape

In 1825, Moe turned ten-years-old, his birthday fell on a Sunday. Jeb's colored and white slaves worked side by side in the sugarcane fields. To him they were the same, Jeb simply believed that poor people were better off being a slave, after all, they had housing, a job, and food. One day Jeb said to himself as he galloped from the sugarcane field to home, "what more could a slave want. On my land, I give them everything," he said out loud before entering his house.

Jeb had twelve slaves working at the shoe factory. Moe was one of Jeb's trusted slaves that could work in the factory. In the sugarcane fields, the twelve slaves worked from five o'clock in the morning to noon, then walked to town to work in the shoe factory for five hours. At the end of the month, the slaves were paid three dollars. Out of their hard-earned money, Jeb gave them a nickel and kept the rest. The slaves received the nickel due to the manager insisting that Jeb pay his property for their work.

Moe was happy, he saved his nickels over the years in a small tin can, that he buried in the woods at the base of a tree. He had worked at the factory for twenty-eight months, Moe said to himself, I's rich."

However, out of the twelve, only Moe worked on Sunday's. On his birthday, Moe entered the factory doors just before it started raining. Buckets of rain poured out of the sky, giving Moe a reason to stay the night. Moe said to himself, "perfect." He asked the manager if he could stay all night in the factory and be back on the plantation in the morning.

The manager said, "yes, you may stay."

To make time go faster Moe swept, mopped, took all the trash out back, dumped it in the pit, set it on fire, went back inside, and straighten up. The guard that stayed there in the evenings saw Moe working hard, he said, "my wife packed extra food, would you like to eat with me?" Moe had hard bread he'd stolen from his mom, the guard had fresh bread and meat, "yes Sir." Moe's eyes shined as the guard unwrapped the food, he even had a big piece of cake. Moe got two tin cups sitting on a nearby table, he said, "I's gits' us some water." He ran out back and filled the cups from the well. The two sat talking and laughing, Moe wished the man was his father.

At 11:00 PM, Moe was in that great big factory with only the guard who after they ate, stayed to himself. Moe thought, "I need more food to take with me."

Moe had planned to escape his Massa and mom; he was running away. He remembered the company's owner always had nuts, candy, and cookies in his office. He entered the manager's office and saw a half-eaten cake, dried beef, and other snacks. As Moe wrapped the food in a newspaper that was lying on the desk, he saw sitting in a corner his boss black business case leaning against the wall. Moe smiled as he put the food in the case, he went out back and filled his flask.

He looked around the shoe factory, everything was clean and in place, he was ready to head north. He looked at the clock, it read 11:15. For two years, Moe had returned to the plantation in the dark all by himself. At that time, he was going to a familiar place. Fright encased Moe's nerves, he was running away from what and who he knew, he was going alone to an unknown. Moe stepped outside into the dark, it had stopped raining, the frogs and crickets sounded louder than normal, the dark was darker, the sky blacker, his heartbeat so hard it felt like it was trying to escape his chest. When the door closed the latch click echoed in the night, the noise startled Moe. Then Moe had an idea, he thought, maybe I'll go home and tomorrow escape with my brothers. He took off running fast as he could, then quick as a wink stopped.

It was as if he ran into a wall of flashbacks. Moe stood frozen, remembering earlier that day.

Instead of getting cake and ice-cream for his birthday, that morning, Moe's mother was drunk and in a fussing mood. She lied yelling that she had saved money to get a shack for them, and no longer work for their Massa. She told Moe that it was his fault that their Massa swapped his brother and sister, Bo and Jo, for a slave cook. His mom ranted and raved for hours. Moe's brothers ran out the slave shack, since this time it wasn't one of them that she chose to beat with her vocals. That morning, it was their little brother's turn.

Moe's mom walked towards him with her fist balled up and punched him in his face. Moe stumbled back towards the door, she grabbed him, bent low to his level, held him close to her face as she spouted, "Massa be giben' me yo' nickel from da' shoe factree," she heaved Moe towards the door, he fell to the floor with a loud thump.

He mumbled under his breath as he got off the floor, but loud enough for her to hear, "you's be an evil bugger."

She slapped Moe hard.

Moe kicked at his mom but missed, she yanked the door open and pushed him out, he fell on his back partially on the stoop and ground. As she closed the door she said looking down at Moe, "I's git yo' nickel, it be da' end of da' month."

Normally on Sundays, Moe would leave early going to the shoe factory, he would take his time and play along the way. But not on his tenth birthday, Moe had a plan.

Picking himself off the ground, Moe watched her disappear out of sight. He ran back in the shack and grabbed his quilt, his other pair of pants and shirt. He looked around the room for anything else he could take. On the table was a big piece of bread Massa had given his mom, he took it, and wrapped it in his dirty handkerchief. Hanging on the wall was his father's flask with a strap, he grabbed that as well. When realizing there was nothing more to take, Moe put everything in the middle of the quilt and tied the four corners together. He had seen pictures of runaways with a makeshift pack, tied together with a stick going through the top. He quickly went outside and found a long stick. The quilt and stick were too big and heavy for him to carry. He put the quilt and flask over his head and shoulder like a crossover purse. Moe went deep into the woods; at the base of a tree he had buried his nickels for the past two years in a small tin can.

Every Sunday, Moe had to be at work by one o'clock. On that morning, he was going to visit Elijah an old slave that was in his nineties. Oftentimes, he had saved Moe and his brothers from their drunken mom.

Moe remembered a conversation he had with Elijah. Two months before his birthday, Elijah said, "I's know you's be leavin." He looked at the little boy sitting on the stoop of his shack, and said, "da' moss and moon can be mighty confusin,' dis here pantation' ain't fer' from da' ocean. West be Massa house, you's gotta' go throw he's land, and piece way from dat' be's da ocean, den' go right ta' norf."

Elijah taught Moe how to run and be free. It normally took Moe not quite an hour to walk to the shoe factory. Moe said to himself, "plenty of time." He ran to say goodbye to Elijah, he found the man sitting in his shabby chair, in front of his shack, Moe sat on the stoop where he normally sat.

Without looking at Moe, Elijah asked, "ta'night?"

The two sat a few minutes with knowing peaceful smiles on their faces. Moe asked, "how'd ja' know?"

"Well," Elijah began, "yo' mama' was round here sayin' she gets yo' money." He looked at Moe, and nodded before saying, "good thang' you's keep it, she'd drank it up. You be ten-year-old, dat' be old nuff' ta' go."

"I's leavin' from da' factory ta' night."

"I's know son, I's know. You's big nuff' ta' make it whars' ya goin. Git' free foe' both of us, while you still be alive, I's gonna' be free soon."

Moe asked," whad'' ja' mean, you be free?"

"I's old, ain't got long ta' lib." By this time Elijah was ninety-two.

Moe began crying, the old man reached for the young boy. Moe sat on Elijah's lap and cried. He rocked Moe and told him his story. He shared with the ten-year-old, that their Massa was his little brother. He told Moe that when he was a boy, his mama was a maid in Massa house.

Elijah explained, "mama had deep brown skin, big bright eyes, long white teeth, and thick black hair down to her shoulders." He smiled as the memory of his mother flashed before him. He mumbled, "I's ain't thank bout' her foe' a long time."

Moe buried his head on Elijah's chest as the old slave talked, he said, "when I turned six Massa put me in da' field, he had a son dat' be older dan' me, he teach' me ta' read, writs', and cipher' numba'. He told me not to tell cause' it be agin' da' law. Mercy me child, we had fun breakin' da' law, he teach me fo' five years, and den' he be gone. I's neva' seed' him again, my learnin' stopped." Sharing his past with Moe brought back memories of his mother and the days of long ago. Sadness filled Elijah as he thought about old Massa first son left, and now little Moe going to a new life. Elijah said, "Naw son, I won't be round long." Lonesomeness and gut-wrenching sadness caused a few tears to roll down Elijah's cheeks. He wiped his face with one hand as he squeezed Moe a little closer with the other.

Moe sat up and said, "you's teach me ta' write and read, whys it agin' da' law?"

"Massa all ova' say, slave or servant git uppity, and start thankin' when dey' git learnin."

"How's Massa yo' brother? He be white - you ain't."

"Well Moe," Elijah began, "Massa did somethin' bad to my mama, den' I's be born. I's be pert' near' forty when Massa married a young wild gal' dat' git's wid' child, and gib' life to our Massa, Massa and me got da' same daddy."

"Life be hard foe' us. Did ja' run?" Moe asked.

"Yep, Massa sold my mama, I took off runnin' behind he's' house. I didn't wanna' be here wid' out my mama."

Elijah's mama saw her son running with an overseer on horseback going after him. Seeing her child in trouble, she jumped down off the cart and ran trying to save him from the overseer's. The man that purchased her had a gun, he shot her in the back as she was running. She died instantly. He tried to sue her previous Massa, but the judge said, "you didn't have to shoot."

Elijah paused, he was deep in thought before saying, "I's knows we's close to da' ocean cause I's seed' it, da' sky and water met."

He looked at Moe and smiled, he held up his right hand, his thumb was missing. "Massa cut my thumb off foe' running, cause he's thanks I's right hand, I's be left hand. I's memba' da pain, I should run right foe' norf.' All I's do is stand der,' dat' ocean, stars, moon be da' prettiest thang' I's eva' seed. I's shoulda' kept runnin, but I's stopped." He looked down at Moe sitting on his lap and said, "don't stop, keep runnin."

Elijah sent Moe in his slave shack to get a box and bring it out to him, Moe obeyed, when he returned, he handed Elijah the box. Inside were black shoes perfect for working in the fields and factory. The shoes were a little too big for Moe. It didn't matter, they were his first pair of shoes. Moe hugged Elijah tight and said, "thank you, dad, thank you."

Elijah said, "happy birthday, son."

Moe cried, he had never received a gift, and Elijah was the only one that remembered Moe's birthday.

Elijah looked up and saw Moe's mom coming their way, he said, "son, trouble be a' comin,' when I's run, I be twelve, nobody tells' me what's ta' do. You child, do as I tells' ya." He stood next to Moe.

Moe said, "thank you foe' eva'thang." He watched his mother totter towards them, looking at her dirty wide feet, Moe said, "mom ain't got no shoes." He looked down at Elijah's feet and smiled, he said, "you always be' wearin' shoes."

Elijah bent down to Moe's level, turned the boy to face him, he cradled Moe's head in his hands and whispered, "out da' factory doe,' go left foe' long while, straight down through da' woods to da' Ocean, den' go right. Dat' take yah' norf."

His mother grabbed Moe by the ear and pushed him in the direction of the shoe factory, "git ta' work, ta' night yous' git's paid, Massa already gib' me yo' nickel." She looked at Elijah, "you's stop fillin' he's head wid' foolishness." She saw the shoes Moe was holding, she continued, "put dem' on my bed, I's be sellin' dem', whad' you need shoes fer'?"

Moe turned facing Elijah, he ran to him and gave Elijah a hug, and then took off running. His mother did not follow, instead, she stopped to talk with a friend that was sitting on his stoop drinking. She showed him her shiny nickel.

Elijah stood watching Moe run. He went to his chair, sat, looked down at the stoop where Moe always sat. He looked up and saw Moe waving, he waved back. Moe turned and ran, he watched Moe leave, Elijah wept as the little boy he called, "son," disappeared out of his sight. Sadness was so strong in Elijah that the pit of his stomach felt like it was tied in knots. He tried to stand, but his heart was too heavy with grief, he flopped back

All But One

down in his chair. He cried hard and squeezed his stomach to end the pain of sorrow.

Moe got his things out the woods, put his shoes in the quilt. As he was on the path to work, the realization that he may never see Elijah again, made him cry, he fell on his knees and wept.

Whenever Moe thought of Elijah, he felt sadness from his stomach traveling up to his heart, escaping out as tears that rolled down his cheeks. Moe stood to ponder whether to return to the plantation or run, a memory of his older brother and sister, Bo and Jo, were sold for a young cook. He remembered Betsy the old cook telling him and Elijah that she had cooked for Massa daddy when she was a teen, but now she was old and tired.

Moe liked Betsy, but he missed Bo and Jo, so much so, he got sick. Even though he was ill, his mom made him go to the sugarcane field in the hot sun. While working he fainted, an overseer thought Moe had fallen asleep, he ran and got Jeb, who ran in the field, using his whip, Jeb hit the child twice. Moe did not move. Jeb had the overseer to check Moe, who was still lying on the ground, the overseer said, "Sir, the boy is sick."

Jeb said pointing at Moe's mom, "fifteen lashes."

Elijah had Moe to stay in his cabin, he knew Moe's mom was not fit to care for a cockroach. It took three overseers to tie Moe's mom to a tree, she kicked, spit, twisted, scratched, and clawed. She received ten lashes on top of the fifteen, the slaves stopped work to watch the spectacle. The overseers were irritated and tired from dealing with the wild woman.

Moe's flashbacks ended. He looked around at the factory and faced his dilemma. He slumped when he realized that the supervisor of the shoe factory had not paid him. The thought of his mom getting his money, pushing him down, punching, and slapping him around, jackknifed in his head. Moe stilled his storm and repeated Elijah, out da' factory doe,' go left foe' long while, straight down through da' woods to da' Ocean, den' go right. Dat' take you norf."

He turned and ran back to the factory, the doors were locked, so he stood in front of the door and went left. He followed Elijah's instructions. Once he reached the ocean, it was just as Elijah had said, the sky and Ocean met. The blackness of the sky made the moon look like it was sitting on top of the ocean, the stars sparkled on the water like floating diamonds. Moe stood in admiration of the view. He was tired and hungry, he sat on the bank and ate a piece of the cake, some of the dried beef, and took a sip of water. An additional recollection popped in Moe's memory, his older brother Bo told him that early one morning before sunrise, their dad woke up and left his kids and wife, with a young slave girl. Before their dad left, he was the one that fed and bathe his kids, at the time, Moe was only a few months old. With their dad gone, Bo and Jo, the eldest of the children became parents to their younger siblings. Moe said to himself, "he left us, he was nothin' but another' useless person in my life."

One last time, Moe stared at the ocean and its beauty, he heard Elijah's words, "do not stop."

Moe slow jogged north, stopping periodically to catch his breath.

****

On the plantation, Moe's mom anger surged, her youngest child had not returned. She tried to hide from her Massa among the tall sugarcane. Her anger subsided, and fright took over when he was near her. She stood immobilized when Jeb said, "git over here," then asked, "what happened to the boys?"
Her eyes followed where Jeb was looking, then back at Jeb and said about her sons, Toe and So, "dey' be clean."

Elijah and Betsy had cleaned the boys. Betsy had the house slave, to give Toe and So something to wear from the teenagers that had outgrown their clothes. Fortunately, for the boy's sake, their cuts, black eyes, and bruises were more prevalent due to their cleanliness.

Jeb asked a second time, "what happened, to my property?" He nodded towards the boys.

Their mom looked at her sons and had a flashback of the evening before. The memory slapped her in the head so hard she almost fainted. The woman had spent the nickel on booze and gave her friend the penny for a piece of meat. She remembered entering the shack seeing her sons eating vegetables. She snatched their food, most of it fell on the floor, she said, "pick dat' up, eat it."

She began eating their vegetable with her meat, Toe and So ignored her and was leaving, she grabbed an iron rod from the fireplace and beat them both. Her older son ran to the door, she grabbed him by the hair. She yanked him so hard that a big clump of his hair came out with pieces of his scalp. Blood splattered all over his face and clothes. Out of breath their mom stopped and looked around the room, the straw in their mattress was coming out, the table and food had spilled on the floor. She threw her son's clump of hair on the floor, it landed by the food. She swung the iron rod at the boys again, this time they were quicker than their mom, the oldest boy opened the door and ran fast with the younger brother close behind. They made it to Elijah's shack, huffing and puffing and bleeding.

Jeb was waiting for their mother to answer his question, the oldest boy said, "Massa," he pointed to his mom, "she did dis' ta' us. Unk Lijah clean us up."

"I want my nickel back by days end," Jeb said to the boy's mom, then asked, "where's Moe?"

Moe's mom quickly answered, "he be at Lijah's shack all da' time."

The older boy said, "Massa, Lijah don't know whars' Moe be gone," he pointed to his brother and said, "afta' mom beat us, we's sleep in he's shack."

Jeb said, "you will stay with him from now own. Never go back to her."

"Yaw, Sir," both boys said in unison.

Jeb glanced at the older boy and said, "you old enough to work with the animals, go now and talk with my slave that take care of my animals."

The boy was excited, he said, "thank yous' Sir." He ran to the animal farm.

Jeb studied the boy's mother before he said, "I want you to experience what living with you feel like."

When Jeb left, Moe's mom said to her son, "you's thank Massa punish me, he ain't, we be sleepin ta'gather. I's kill yah' ta' night. I's hate ja' both."

Her son replied, "we's stay wid' you' no mo,' Massa says."

Jeb went to Elijah's, who was sitting in the raggedy chair in front of his shack. Jeb asked Elijah if he had seen Moe. Elijah answered, "Yes'day' I's seed him, he be on he's' way to dat' fac'tree."

"He did not come home last night; do you know where he went?" Jeb asked.

Elijah lied as he answered, "Moe talk bout' boats, iffen' he ain't at da' fac'tree dat's whars' he be goin', south ta' git on a boat. Dat' boy loves boats, Massa Jeb."

"Has he ever seen a boat?"

"Naw Sir, Moe say, one of yo' friend tells him bout boats. Ever since den,' dat' boy talk bout' boat"

Betsy was sitting outside in front of her shack talking with Elijah when Jeb stopped by. She said, "mornin' Massa."

Jeb nodded towards her, he said to Elijah, "those boys that stayed with you last night, is moving in."

Elijah smiled and waved to Jeb as he left.

Since Jeb had put his old cook in the slave quarters to die, she occupied her days by preparing Elijah's meals and extra for the children he fed. She joined the little band of Christians, they didn't have a church building to worship in, so they gathered around an old oak tree. A great number of the coloreds attended the service with only a few whites worshiping with them. The slaves sang, prayed, Elijah preached.

Elijah learned to read the Bible with his Massa first son. During that time, he memorized twenty Bible verses and taught another man in his sixties the verses, and how to apply them to their situation and ask God for help.

Betsy and Elijah watched Jeb gallop away. Betsy looked at Elijah and asked, "how you goin' take care doe' boys?

Elijah said, "Massa silly, he thank' dat' cause' he say so, it gonna' happen. No matta' how's we's be fillin."

"Wha'd' ja talkin' bout."

"Massa say, do dis,' he say do dat,' we's posed' ta do what he say, don't matta' iffen' we's be sick. We's work til' we's die."

"We's he's' property, "Betsy held her head down sorrowfully as she continued, "owned like da' chickens."

He looked at Betsy and said, "you be yongen' me, I's be dying soon, take good care of da' boys. Dey' had it hard. You be up in da' big house, you's don't know what be goin' on down here in da' slave quarters."

Betsy replied, "I's bout's ta' learn."

Jeb went into the fields and asked the slaves and overseers about Moe's mom. They all told him, what he knew and had seen, the slaves said that she was a despicable drunken woman that beat her children. One of the slaves, looking down at the ground said, "you's a mighty fine Massa, none us slaves got nonthin' ta' runs fer.' Dat woman be awful Massa Jeb."

Jeb thought about Moe's brothers' cuts, bruises and the big opened sore in the middle of the older boys' head, made Jeb shiver. He went ballistic, he ordered Moe's mom to receive thirty lashes, he told the overseers to pull her hair out by the roots, just like she did her older son.

The overseers were happy, they all hated the woman. That day, her beating and hair pulling ordeal was atrocious. Moe's mom went home. She crawled in the door, laid on the floor and shivered from the pain that was all over her body. Moe's mom scooted to her bed; she moved the mattress over. A floorboard was loose, she struggled to lift it, she reached in and pulled out a handkerchief that had two dollars in change. Holding it in her hands, she spotted the small chest that sat in a corner. She opened it; her husband's knife was there. She pulled herself in a sitting position and leaned against the wall. Her motivation to end her life was Jeb's words, "I want you to experience what living with you feel like."

Her scalp was burning, her back, face, and legs were in pain. After the overseers had seen what she had done to her oldest son head, they snatched clumps of hair with skin attached from all over her head. Moe's mom wiped her brow with the back of her dirty arm, blood smeared on it. She leaned forward, the opened gashes on her back, left traces of blood on the wall. She looked at her feet that were filthy, big, and had spread wide from never wearing shoes. She realized that a great number of the other slaves wore shoes. She said, "I's do't not won't' ta' lib' wid' me."

She held the knife with both hands and rammed it through her throat. She did not die right away; the pain was excruciating as she pulled the knife out. Her body shook violently in pain, she cried, changed her mind about dying, she wanted to run, she wanted to be free. She had a strong desire to one day work in the shoe factory and see other people, beyond the plantation.

Moe's mom had been a slave all her life and never been off the plantation. One time, she snuck around to see the front of

LaVaughn

Massa house, she saw further than she had ever seen before. It was wide opened space and the front of Massa house was grand. A noise frightened her, she quickly and unseen ran back to the slave quarters. That was the last time she saw a glimpse outside the slave area and fields.

The blood in her esophagus was suffocating, she could not talk or yell for help. She laid on the floor gasping for air, crawling towards the door to get help was tough. Moe's mom made it across the floor only, two paces. Unable to go any further, she laid flat on her stomach, in front of her, was the rod she used to beat her sons. She squeezed her eyes shut; she did not want to remember the day before. Gasping for air triggered her eyes to open, laying behind the rod was the clump of hair she pulled from her oldest boy's head. The meaty part from his scalp was filled with dry blood. Looking at the site caused her to revisit her hatefulness towards her children.

She struggled to breathe through her nose, her eyes were stretched wide open as she gazed at the items on the floor. A tear dripped out her eyes, she inhaled and died at the same time.

An overseer entered the cabin, on the floor he saw the opened handkerchief that held the coins. He took the money, stuffed it in his pocket. He looked at Moe's mom closer, she was still holding the knife, the slit in her throat was barely visible due to the blood clotting. He left, to report that the boy's mom had killed herself.

II

Help From The Underground Railroad Stations

Six o'clock the following morning, while Moe's mom was killing herself, Moe stood in front of a small pretty cabin that had a candle burning in the window. He remembered Elijah telling him, "fire in da' window is help fo' run-a-way."

Moe knocked on the door. A man with a kind face opened the door and yelled, "hon, it's a white runaway child."

She came to the door and said, "Hello little one," she looked at her husband and continued, "let's see what he's all about."

The couple in the cabin were friends with Jeb, Moe's Massa. If the runaway appeared to one day be an asset to America, they would help them on their way to the next station. On the other hand, if they were loud, boisterous, and was going to be a menace to society, the wife prepared stew or soup, laced with an herb that would put them to sleep, her husband sold them to Jeb.

Moe's nature was that of a person the abolitionist would help. The woman bathed Moe and gave him the pants and his shirt that were wrapped in his quilt, though they were dirty, the clothes were cleaner than what he had on. After cleaning him up, Moe ate breakfast with the husband and wife. He asked the man, "how'd you know I's be a slave?"

"Most runaways have the same pack over their shoulder or tied to a stick."

On his travels north, Moe lost the case that held his food, the boy was famished. He scraped his plate clean and asked for more.

The man asked which plantation Moe was running from, Moe told him. His wife said, "you're only eight miles from where you run." She looked at her husband, then Moe, who had fallen asleep face down on the table.

Her husband said, "let's take a chance. He will stay here for two days, when I get off work, I will take the boy to the next county."

"North, right? Not back to..." She was asking.

"Yes, North," he replied before she could finish talking.

Before leaving, the man took Moe to a room and laid him on a cot. He entered the kitchen, looked at his wife and said, "he's the son of the man that was with a young woman we helped ten years ago."

His wife asked, "how do you know?"

"He said, he had a newborn. That boy looks just like that man. Short, stocky, round head, and clubbed fingers."

The woman said, "he's not far from here, should we tell him."

The man thought first before answering, "no, they have too many kids." He left for work.

Moe woke up a little after lunchtime, the woman asked how he slept. Moe said, "very fine ma'am." He asked if he could stay with them.

She explained the plantation he had run from, was too near her home. She comforted him by saying, "you're a sweet kid, if I lived further away, I would keep you." She lightly pinched his cheeks and gave him a hug, she then said, "you can stay for the next two days, you have a long journey going north."

The two talked and laughed, Moe told her about his evil mom, his two brothers. Being in her presence made him miss Elijah. Moe told her all about him, and how sometimes he called Elijah, dad. He showed her the shoes Elijah bought for him. Though he did not understand, he shared with her that Elijah and their Massa were brothers. While Moe talked, the woman washed his clothes, his hankie, with Moe's permission she threw his dirty quilt away and gave him a clean one.

Tired Moe napped while the abolitionist woman prepared dinner. Her husband returned home at five o'clock, together the three ate and talked like he and Elijah use to do. Moe could not seem to get full, he slurped his food down fast, sopped the juice with his bread, then asked for more. When they finished dinner, the woman of the house told Moe to keep his money close because someone could steal it.

Two days later her husband took Moe to the next county as promised. He told Moe to look for a candle in the window, travel at night, trust the Amish and colored abolitionists, some whites are friendly while many may work for his master." He put his hand on Moe's shoulder and continued, "young man, be careful,"

With Moe on his way north, the male abolitionist went to see Jeb. When he arrived, Moe's brother took his horse around back where it received care. The man only knew that Moe was from the plantation, he did not know of Moe's relatives. He simply said to the young boy, "thank you."

The abolitionist entered the house and was escorted to a room where Jeb was waiting for him. Before the man could sit down, Jeb asked, "have you seen a little boy. The man lied and told Jeb a simple, "no," he sat.

Jeb complained that he had lost three slaves and his father never had a runaway. Jeb said, "my father told me that before I was born, my brother took fifteen of his slaves, he never heard from my brother again." Jeb deduced the slaves did not run; they were taken."

Jeb father did not know that his son and the slaves made it safe to the north. Jeb's brother married a pretty slave colored girl, they lived in Cincinnati across the Ohio River with their six children. The whole family was abolitionist, one of Jeb's nephew became a spokesman for the equality of all Americans. Jeb's brother, nor his brother's wife told their children, that their uncle was a slave master.

After listening to Jeb share his story about his family, the man told Jeb that he believed one of his overseers was helping the slaves escape. Jeb asked, "one of my men?"

"Yes, one of your overseer's. You told me that a man and woman escaped years ago, which way did they go, and when?"

Jeb answered, "I don't know where they went, they left early in the morning."

"Did they find the couple?"

"No," Jeb answered.

"Who told you early in the morning? How would they know the time?" The man asked.

Jeb looked at the man with alarm and said, "the same bounty hunter and overseer, I sent to find Moe."

"How old is Moe."

Jeb answered, "ten."

The man said, "Two people on horseback, cannot catch a little boy on foot. It sounds like you need to handle one or both."

"If they return without my property," Jeb began saying, he stopped talking as though he was thinking and then continued, "I will take care of both."

Jeb walked the man outside; he was going to the sugar cane field to check on the slaves and ask about the over-seer he trusted. He said to the man, "watch for a ten-year-old."

The man smiled as Jeb hurriedly left, Moe's brother brought the man's horse around, he got on his horse and asked, "is there a slave named Elijah?"

"Yaw, Sir."

"Tell him, a boy named Moe, is safely on his way north."

The boy said, "I's tell um' Sir."

As the man rode off, Moe's brother ran to tell Elijah who had become very ill. Still, he sat outside in his chair, hoping to hear a word about Moe before he passed away. When the boy reached Elijah he whispered, "Moe made it Norf. He be safe." He hugged Elijah.

Elijah asked, "how's you know?"

"Dis man dat' knows Massa tells' me."

Elijah said, "I's knows who you be talkin' bout."

"How's ya' know?" Moe's brother asked Elijah.

"Run along, git' back ta' work child."

Elijah relaxed when he got the news about Moe, he was worried that the boy may get caught and treated crudely. He used his chair as a walker to get to Betsy's cabin. He knocked on the door, she answered, he said, "it be time foe' me ta' go."

Elijah had prayed that Moe would escape before he died. On his and Moe's last day together, Elijah was sad and happy, Moe was going to freedom before Elijah's time on earth ended. He had become feeble in health but strong in mind. The day Moe left hurt him deep in his soul, but Elijah believed with his whole heart that God had special plans for the little boy. Elijah believed that Moe was the chosen one to end slavery.

Betsy helped Elijah to his shack, she cried as she bathed and dressed him in a suit of clothes he purchased when he turned sixty, it still fit. When he was dressed, he said barely above a whisper, "dat' made me tied."

The year a businessman from New York, opened a shoe factory near Jeb's father's plantation, Elijah was twenty. His Massa got several of his slaves a job there, on payday, their Massa went to the factory and collected their money. However, the owner of the shoe factory snuck and gave the slaves a penny. One of the slaves told their Massa about receiving money. Furiously, their Massa went to the factory and shouted at the northerner, he yelled, "I have the means and power to shut this company down!"

The owner of the factory stopped giving the slaves money. When the slaves found out the reason the penny stopped, they beat the man to death. The employed slaves received thirty lashes, including Elijah who was not a part of the murder.

Elijah was determined to make some money, after the beating, twenty-year-old Elijah pulled the owner of the company aside and said, "I's not tell Massa." From that day forward Elijah received one penny a month. Elijah worked in the factory until he turned seventy-five. Every three years, Elijah bought new shoes and saved his money. His other purchases were the suit and Moe's shoes.

After his bath, Elijah dressed, hobbled to his bed, and laid down as Betsy cleaned his shack. Elijah's heart was beating irregular, his breathing was shallow. When Betsy finished the housework for Elijah, she sat next to his bed and held his hand, Elijah whispered, "my boy got away."

Betsy asked, "the abolitionist that will save or sell ya' sent word?"

"Yes, he did." Elijah tried to sit up, Betsy helped him up, Elijah said, "da' boys can stay in dis' slave shack since dey' mama unfit. Pleeze' care foe' dem."

Crying Betsy said, "yes Lijah, I's care foe' dem boys."

He asked her to let them stay in her shack for that night. Betsy said, "yes, I will."

Elijah pointed to the clothes he had on and said, "bury me in dis."

"I will do as you ax."

Elijah said, "Betsy, thank you foe' all you did ova' da' years. Go now, time foe' me ta' rest."

Before leaving Betsy gave him a hug and kissed him on the cheek. She left crying.

The following morning, Betsy fed the boys and sent them off to work. She entered Elijah's shack and found him dead and still neatly dressed in his new clothes. Elijah was lying on his back with a smile on his face. Betsy said, "rest now Lijah." She left to tell Jeb.

Betsy went to Massa house to talk with the head of the house slaves. She said, "Lijah gone. He got news of dat' boy, he be free in da norf."

The head of the house slaves said, "he missed and worried bout' dat' lil' boy so deep, he died from a' sad heavy heart."

Betsy said thoughtfully, "Yeah, dat's right. I's glad he got good news bout' da' boy, afo' leavin' us." Betsy cried.

The head of the house slaves pat Betsy on the back and said, "me to Betsy."

Wiping her eyes, Betsy said, "I's glad does' boys mama be gone, she ain't hurt dem' eva' again. Wished I'd know yesta'day,' Lijah would like dat' news."

After leaving the abolitionist home, Moe traveled two nights in the dark. He could not see where he was going, to him everything was scary, the shadows in the woods looked like a ghost. The animal sounds caused him to jump, the second night Moe felt something touch his feet, he took off running. The third day, he gave going by the light a try, he loved it. Hence, he ignored the man's advice to travel by night, during the day he felt safe.

Not quite two months after leaving his first stop, he made it to Virginia. Moe was tired, hungry, and his feet hurt from walking barefoot. The shoes that Elijah had given him were too big. Even so, the following morning with a little rest and an empty stomach, Moe put leaves in the shoes to create a cushion which made the shoes fit better and his journey easier.

An hour after he put his shoes on, he saw a white family riding in a wagon, they were going in the same direction as himself. They waved for him to join them, Moe thought it was safe, they had kids around his age, and they were white. For several hours they laughed and talked as they traveled. The rocking of the wagon was like a sleeping pill to exhausted Moe, he fell fast to sleep. Their oldest child was thirteen, while Moe slept, he went through Moe's belongings and found the tin of money. The boy pushed Moe out the wagon and kept his things and the money. Moe hit the ground hard, at first, he was dazed and confused then realized what had happened. He ran after the wagon as fast as he could. The boy held up the tin and jiggled it. The family laughed loud and hard. Moe running at top speed got a little too close. The father made a clicking noise, he said, "yah," and snapped the harnesses making the horse gallop. The family was poor and only had ten cents, they had stolen the horse and wagon, two states over.

    They rode out of sight, Moe stood watching them disappear. All he had were the clothes on his back, and shoes from Elijah. Had he left them in the quilt, he would be without his first gift from anyone, more important, something from the only person he loved.

    Moe walked and cried, he was not thinking about the sun setting, normally before dark, Moe would find a bush and shake it hard, to see if there were any creatures hiding. If there were, they would scurry out and Moe would go in. On the night Moe was robbed he was infuriated, feeling sorry for himself, and exhausted, he fell asleep on the ground shivering. Moe had a dream about finding the family that took his money and belongings, he made them his slave. He would be mean and evil, he visualized beating them until they bled.

    The next morning before daybreak, he woke up still angry. He got up and began his journey north in the darkness of the morning hours. He was furious, hungry, filthy, and broke. Moe sought retaliation. As he walked north, Moe kicked anything that was in his site as he with deep seeded anger, strode through the woods. Walking past a wide pathway, behind trees he saw a light flicker. Moe turned around and walked down the pathway. Looming from behind the trees was a massive size house that was bigger than his Massa. In two windows were candles burning, due to the size of the house and its grandeur, Moe was reluctant to enter, truly he thought the people inside were white, just like the folk that stole his money.

    He stood looking down the long path that led to the house, then a plan popped in his head. Moe was going to take his revenge out on the family inside. A question sprung in his head like flowers in spring, what if the family that robbed him lived in the house? Moe picked up the biggest stick he could carry and ran up the path to the house, he slowly walked up to the twelve steps that led to a massive size porch. Using a lion's head knocker, he banged on the door as hard as he could. He held the stick like a baseball bat, ready to whack anyone that answered.

To his surprise, a well-dressed black man answered the door, Moe angrily asked, "yo Massa home?"

Mr. Evans said, "this is my house young man, are you in need of help."

Mr. Evans oldest son, who was the same age as Moe, joined his dad at the door, he looked out and asked, "who is it, dad?"

Moe was totally outdone, it was a black family, husband, wife, and three boys, they were the Evans. Moe dropped his stick.

Inside the house was as lavish as the outside. Moe told them about the robbery. Just like the first abolitionist woman, Mrs. Evans bathe and fed Moe. Their oldest son was Moe's size, only a little taller. At first, Moe was afraid to go up the steps to the sleeping area, with coaxing from the Evans boys, he got the courage. That evening Moe slept extremely well, he had his own room and a real bed with a mattress. He avowed, "I's neva' sleep on straw again." The next morning, he woke up rested and smelling something, he had never smelt before. Holding onto the banister, he slowly eased down the steps and found his way into the kitchen.

Mrs. Evans was cooking bacon and biscuits. Moe asked, "what dat you be cookin?"

Mrs. Evans said, "good morning Moe, how'd you sleep last night?"

"Mighty fine ma'am." His mouth watered heavy. He finished saying, "I's neva sleep on a bed dat' soft."

She handed Moe a bacon strip. He took a bite; the bacon was so scrumptious his taste buds danced a jig in his mouth. Mr. Evans entered the house carrying a pale of milk and the oldest boy a basket of eggs. Mrs. Evans got a skillet to cook the eggs. Moe wanted to live with this family, he fancied calling himself Moe Evans. He asked where he was. Mr. Evans said, "Maryland."

He asked if the house was a castle, Mrs. Evans said, "it's our castle." She looked at her husband then back at Moe and said, "your castle, small or big is not the house, it's where you make your home."

Moe did not hear a word she said, he marveled at the entryway of the house. The porch was huge, it was made of smooth stone, there were eight stoned columns that stretched across the massive house. the vestibule was made of evened shiny stones that had hues of gray, white, and sprinkle with black. Hanging from the tall ceiling was a beautiful candle chandelier. Everything about the house was stunning and brightly decorated.

Moe told Mr. and Mrs. Evans about the husband and wife he stayed with. The family that stole his things, and the long ride he had with them. he said, "afo' I's git's in Virginee' I's walks' many days. The sun went up and down, den' up and down, I's be walkin' a long time."

Mrs. Evans said, "so, you had God and the devil after you. But God won, look at how far you come, you stopped at one station, and none of the others to get this far. "

The Evans were serious farmers, they had over five hundred chickens that were constantly producing babies and eggs, over fifty hogs, twenty-five piglets, twenty cows, and seventeen calves. In their garden, they grew all kinds of vegetables and a vineyard that was acres deep.

****

In the 1700s, Mr. Evans great-great grand-dad was stolen from Africa. He was sold to a family in the most Southern Virginia county, that bordered North Carolina. The man that purchased the African, discovered his new slave knew how to make wine. The plantation owner put him on land that had wild grapes growing. The Massa had two of his trusted slaves to assist the winemaker, though they continued to live on the plantation. Their Massa let them ride a mule to and from the distillery. The door was wide open for the two male slaves to escape, but the winemaker told them his plan.

They agreed to stay. Together the three men build the winemaker a one-room shack, and a barn with two rooms, one large the other small. The barrels of wine were warehoused in the larger room, the men built several five-tier shelves to hold the barrels. The smaller room was the distillery, where the wine was made. Though the two men help build the room, the winemaker, designed and put the machines together. When both rooms were finished the Massa gave the winemaker his smartest female slave, as his wife. Their job was to make wine and babies, instead, the winemaker told her, his plan. She agreed to work with him, they did not have children. It took the winemaker, his two helpers three months to build and turn the wild grapes into an orchard. As the men did the hard work, the winemaker's woman prepared their meals. The four worked together like a smooth-running machine.

The winemaker kept sixty barrels of wine; he gave his helpers twenty each. Deep in the woods, the winemaker built two covered wagons with high sides to carry his barrels. His helpers stole two of their master wagons. Eight months after the distillery was built the winemaker and his helper's escaped slavery. One helper ended up in Ohio, another Chica-go, the winemaker married the woman, they bought land in Maryland near the Chesapeake Bay area. The husband and wife duo first started a vineyard, then a farm. His Massa had named him Joe, but once free the winemaker returned to his African name, Abu.

****

On the farm, Moe learned how to milk a cow, gather eggs, he had fun with the boys running after the chickens. They laughed, fell, and got extremely dirty. Mr. Evans and his wife were standing by the window watching, Mrs. Evans said, "they are doing more playing than catching the chickens."

Laughing, Mr. Evans said, "I and my brothers did the same thing when dad told us to catch chickens to take to town.

One of the boys fell flat on his face in the mud, Mr. and Mrs. Evans laughed.

Moe always stood wide leg, they laughed when a chicken ran between Moe's legs, followed by the youngest boy that slid through to catch the chicken. He caught the bird, rolled on his back and yelled, "I got one."

When the boy stood up holding the chicken, Moe sat down and laughed until his stomach hurt.

During the holidays, Evans made over six hundred barrels of wine, to be divided between the states of Maryland, Ohio, New Jersey, New York, Michigan, Pennsylvania, and Virginia. At the time there was no prohibition, making and selling wine was not against the law. Mr. Evans maintained Abu's cleanliness and Abu's three wines.

One year after moving to Maryland, Abu heard about Moon Drop grapes grown in Boston, Gewurztraminer, red, and green grapes. However, Mr. Evans discovered a plethora of grapes that did not exist when his grandpa, Abu, started the vineyard in the 1700s. Though he kept his granddad's original wine recipes, Mr. Evans made new wine with the grapes he had learned about, younger people loved the taste, while the older Americans appreciated the old wine.

Moe enjoyed living with the Evans, he wanted to stay but something in his blood was urging him to go further north. The morning Moe was leaving, Mrs. Evans fixed a big breakfast and bacon that Moe loved. She packed Moe seven biscuits, five sweet rolls, extra bacon, and three boiled whole potatoes, she wrapped the food in a towel, neatly folded the new clothes that she had made for him, his shoes and laid them in the new quilt she had made. She asked the reason Moe didn't wear the shoes that Elijah had given him. He said, "they are too big and hard to walk in." He put the food wrapped in a towel on top of his shoes. She let Moe keep her oldest son's extra pair of shoes and clothes he was wearing, they were a little too long, otherwise, the clothes fit.

Mr. Evans said, "be careful, only trust abolitionist, coloreds, and the Amish." He told Moe pretty much what the first man said.

Mrs. Evans gave Moe a hug, held his face between her hands and said, "grow to be a good man."

She and the boys stood outside and waved Moe off. Moe's heart hurt just like it did when he left Elijah behind. She held his face between her hands just like Elijah had, Moe cried. To calm the boy, Mr. Evans asked Moe where he was going, the boy said, "norf."

Mr. Evans took him to where Maryland crossed over to Pennsylvania. He told Moe, "if you run into any trouble come back, I could use the extra help on the farm."

Moe gave Mr. Evans a hug then said, "I wish you was my dad." he jumped off the carriage and waved good-bye.

Mr. Evans sat a few minutes watching the young boy leave. Moe got so far, turned and waved, then ran on.

The day Moe left the Evans, the bounty hunters returned to Moe's Massa plantation. They had gone as far as the tip of Florida. Surly, Jeb thought the men would have Moe with them, they had been gone for over three months. Instead, they returned with a message from several ship captains saying, "if the boy is found on my ship, I will bring him back when I return."

Jeb could smell alcohol on the men, they smelt as though they had gone swimming in it. Jeb's rifle was cradled in his arms, he pointed it at the men. The overseer said, "we tried our best."

"No, you did not," Jeb said.

The bounty hunter said in a matter-of-fact tone, "I believe the ship captains lied to us."

Jeb shot and killed his overseer, the bounty hunter tried to gallop away. Jeb aimed, and shot, the man fell to the ground, dead.

The remaining of Moe's journey was rough, he never ran into people as nice as the first two Underground Railroad Stations. Moe met three additional families that gave him water to clean his face and hands, wipe the dirt off his clothes, a little food and water to drink. To rest, they allowed him to stay one night in a barn or on their porch.

One-year after running away, eleven-year-old Moe, entered the city limits of Boston, Massachusetts, he was too tired and hungry to continue. The clothes that Mrs. Evans had made for him were too small, and the shoes, too tight. The Evans oldest sons' pants and shirt finally fitted Moe perfectly. When he arrived in the city, Moe put on a clean pair of socks that Mrs. Evans made, and the shoes from Elijah were a perfect fit. He applied for employment at several establishments, only to be laughed at, due to his thick unintelligible southern drawl. Moe was too young for city jobs and smelt awful. He lived on the streets and ate garbage for one month. Moe didn't know where he was, he wanted to continue north but could not find anyone to help him. His luck changed when he met Billy, who hired Moe to work at The Brown Steel Mill.

Though Billy was a colored man, he was the supervisor of the company. Billy saw himself in Moe. It was six years ago that he and his wife, Liza, had run away from the chattels of slavery. Billy was twenty and Liza eighteen when they escaped.

Billy and Liza went through the states by the Atlantic Ocean, the Carolina's, Virginia, through Pennsylvania, and New York. They hid in bushes and tall grass, unlike Moe, they had bounty hunters hot on their trail. An Amish family hid them in a small hiding place, that was under their pigs' trough. The bounty hunters entered the families house and overturned their furniture and knocked dishes off the shelves. And in their bedrooms, ripped up their mattresses that were stuffed with cotton. Outside in the backyard, the bounty hunters set the Amish family chickens free.

When the unethical men were gone, Billy and Liza came out their hiding place, they tried to wash the pig smell off their bodies. Unfortunately, the pigs' odor had gone in their nose straight to their brain cells. Be that as it may, the runaways stayed a few more days to help get the family's home back in order and helped catch most of the chickens.

Billy and Liza ran the rest of their journey wearing Amish clothes. When they entered Boston, Massachusetts the couple changed their names to Billy and Liza. Billy said to Liza, "here we's die ta'gather 'free, and not slaves."

One cold day, Billy and Liza were huddled together trying to keep each other warm and live long as they could. Billy looked up and saw a kind face man coming towards them. He stepped in front of the man, he asked, "kind Sir, would you have a morsel of bread foe' my wife?"

The man looked down at the woman sitting on the ground quivering, he noticed that Billy was just as cold but was concerned for someone other than himself. The man said, "my name is Henry Vincent Brown, I own the Brown Steel Mill."

That day, he hired Billy to work at his Steel Mill and sent him to school. Billy finished twelve years of schooling, in four years. Every year, Billy would send the Amish family two dollars. He and Liza purchased a German-language book, to improve the language they had begun with the Amish family.

Together Billy and Moe cleaned one of the backrooms which became Moe's home. Moe asked Billy if he could stay forever in the back room. Billy said, "until you turn sixteen, then together we'll find you a place to live."

Moe thought of the Evans family and chasing chickens. He laughed until he cried as he remembered young Evans sliding between his leg to catch the chicken. But his tears of joy turned to sorrow, he said, "I's gotta' make nough' money to go back and lib' wid' dem." He buried his face in his cover and while crying mumbled, "I's shoulda' neva' left." He fell asleep.

Moe met Billy's wife, he admired her from the first time they met. She was kind, had a caring face, and was a good cook. The Brown Steel Mill company's uniforms were too big for the young boy, so Liza adjusted two uniforms to fit Moe's big bone skinny frame. She was determined to fatten Moe up; his bones were too big for him to be so lean.

She and Billy were the same when they ran to Boston. Skin and bones, very little muscle and no fat.

Billy and his wife third year living in Boston purchased a house in a better neighborhood. They tried to have children, but Liza womb was destroyed. Liza was a pretty house slave, her Massa allowed multiple men at the same time have their way with her. Frighten, Liza retaliated and tried to escape. The men and her Massa became angry which the outcome was always a whipping, kicking, and stomping.

Billy was a field hand, one day he saw Liza standing by a weeping willow tree with one of the branches around her neck. She was tired of the Massa and his male friends, Billy went to her and said, "let's run now."

Liza said, "we's git caught. I's gotta' kill me, to have peace."

He grabbed Liza's hand and ran.

Living with the Amish family was a preacher, who married the runaway slaves. The woman of the house and Liza planned an Amish wedding which made Liza a happy bride. Standing next to Billy, lighting bolts of flashbacks of her life on the plantation seemed to take over her emotion. Liza looked at Billy, she took a deep breath and smiled, an overwhelming feeling of peace and joy of her future caused her to smile.

Billy looked at his beautiful bride and fell in love, he smiled.

III

The Beginning

Moe absolutely treasured his home in the back room of The Brown Steel Mill, he could finally rest mentally and physically. Not even with the Evans could Moe totally relax. Unsettling quiet thoughts screamed in his mind, yelling he was going to be caught, thrashed, sent back to his mom, and the sugar cane field. Moe loved his freedom in the North. In his little area, he could freely come and go as he wanted and practice saying words correctly, sometimes he rehearsed with Billy and Liza.

Billy and Liza had lived in Boston for years, Moe thought that their dialect was perfect, at least they did not sound like him. One night in his little room, he practiced enunciating his words, "dis, dat, dem, does, ain't. Yes," he said out loud, "I's," he corrected himself and said, "I will change how's I's talk." He let out a sigh, shook his head then said, "dis' ain't gonna be easy." He laughed.

In the evenings, Liza cooked dinner for her two men, Billy and Moe always came in hungry and tired. After eating and cleaning the kitchen, the three retired to the sitting room where they talked about being free. Moe told Billy and Liza about his life as a slave on Jeb's plantation.

Billy and Liza reminded Moe of Mr. and Mrs. Evans, they were full of joy and love. Moe shared that he wanted to save his two brothers and return to the Evans to become their sons.

One evening after dinner, Moe told them all about the Evans massive house, their animals, garden, and grapevines. Billy said, "I'll ask Mr. Brown if I can take you back, shortly I am going to visit my Amish friends. Maybe Mr. Brown will help get your brothers."

When Moe left, Billy said to Liza, "ain't no colored rich like that. I have to find them and see for myself."

"Naw," Liza said, "I believe him. He described everything perfectly. Me a writer of short stories, you an educated supervisor of a big company. Six years ago, we were owned like," she pointed to a picture hanging on the wall and said, "like that picture we bought from the artist."

"Hum," Billy said thoughtfully, he continued, "all I know is, I have to meet the Evans." Liza said with a smile in her voice, "they will be easy to find, rich coloreds in the south, with slavery all around."

Billy laughed and said, "it's probably the wine that white folk doesn't want to get rid of. They are protecting him."

While Billy and Liza were laughing and talking, Moe was on his way home, he stopped past the general store to buy candy. He put a piece in his mouth, "yummy," he said. He joyously skipped down the street humming, and then stopped and said loud to himself, "me and my brothers gonna' be Mr. Evans sons. Der' be six of us boys." He was thinking and laughing about catching chickens, picking grapes, milking the cows, and eating delicious bacon. Moe was so engrossed in his thoughts that he walked past the Steel Mill. He looked around and realized what he had done, Moe bent over, put his hands on his knees, and laughed hard.

In the Evans household, he had learned to say his prayers before going to bed. That night, he prayed for his brothers, and the Evans, Billy, and Liza. After his prayer, he laid on his back thinking and remembering, Bo the eldest, his sister Jo, and two brothers So and Toe, he whispered softly, "Lord take care of my brothers and sister."

Moe lived a happy carefree life in the back room for two weeks. He had everything he needed, someone to feed, care, and love him. Liza took him shopping to buy clothes, shoes, he bought a slingshot. She taught him to save a portion of the money he made.

Being raised by a drunken mom and cruel Massa, Moe did not accept authority from anyone. On the other hand, he obeyed Billy and Liza because they simply guided him the way he should go. Just like the Evans family, they didn't yank their boys by the hair or beat them, knock them down, or slap them in the face. He remembered when Mr. Evans told him and the boys to clean the chicken coops. Moe decided he was not going to clean those stinking things, Mr. Evans said, "young boy, you will do as I say, or get a whipping." He folded his arms looked down at Moe and said in a calm baritone voice, "you choose."

Moe laughed as he remembered running outside to help with the chore. His reason to obey was not that Mr. Evans was tall and threatening, instead, his orders were in love. Moe got under his covers and dreamed about arriving at the Evans home with his brothers and Billy by his side.

The following morning, Moe woke up crying when he had to say goodbye to Billy. He rubbed his eyes, looked around the room and said, "it's only a dream."

On the last day of his second week, Moe's life flipped flopped and stopped. Henry V. Brown, the owner of the company and his wife had returned from their trip to Europe. Henry took his wife home and then went to the Steel Mill. While there, one of his workers told him about Moe sleeping in the backroom. He informed Henry, that Billy and his wife were taking good care of the child, who was a hard worker.

Henry quietly went to the back room and saw Moe fast asleep. He noticed the young boy kept his little space clean and cozy, he allowed Moe to continue sleeping.

Henry rushed home to talk with his wife about taking Moe on as their son. The Browns were childless, so they thought raising an eleven-year-old as their own would make them happy and add laughter in their home. But first, before making their final decision, Henry asked Billy about the young boy, who had only good things to say about Moe.

Since Mr. Brown was in a chatty mood, Billy asked him if he could take a trip with Moe to see his Amish friends and take Moe to visit the Evans family, who were abolitionists. Billy told Henry about the family that helped Moe escape. He shared Moe's concern for his brothers living on a plantation with a mean hateful mother and owner.

Billy thought his kind-hearted employer would understand and offer help that he could not. The thought of attempting to save Moe's brothers from a plantation was frightening yet exhilarating at the same time.

Henry said, "I am going to make the child my son, give him my name." He began to walk away but changed his mind, he turned towards Billy and continued, "you may go see your friends, the boy stays here with me."

"His brothers' Sir?" Billy asked.

"Are no concern of mine." Mr. Brown left.

The day Billy was leaving to visit the Amish family and the Evans, Mr. Brown delivered legal documents to Billy in his home. The papers stated that Billy was a free colored that worked for him at The Brown Steel Mill. Included in the papers was written permission for Billy to use his horse and buggy. Billy was smart and thought above the law, he asked Mr. Brown to write the letters twice, in case one was stolen from him, and he was taken to court or the auction block. Billy asked, "Moe want to return to a family named Evans, while I'm traveling, he could go with me, I will bring him back. What do you think Mr. Brown?"

Henry said "no, that boy will make new memories." then left.

Liza said as she closed the door behind Henry, "that man cannot erase Moe's memory."

While Harry was In his carriage on his way to the Steel Mill, Moe ran at top speed to Billy's home to say goodbye. Billy and Liza were on the porch, Moe ran up to them and said, "I's wanna' go wid' you."

Liza said, "Mr. Henry Brown has a surprise for you, he has something to discuss with you."

Billy said, "yes, you are getting a new home." He kissed Liza and hugged Moe.

When Billy pulled off on his month-long trip, he waved bye to the two standing on the porch. Billy was sad, he was leaving his wife behind, and happy because he had saved six dollars for his Amish friends. Moe stood next to Liza crying as he watched Billy disappear out of sight. It was just like his dream, only Moe thought he would be at the Evans with his brothers by his side, waving to Billy as he returned to Boston. He gazed at Liza and said, "I have a home, what is he talking about?"

"In a few days, Mr. Brown will speak with you?"

"I hate Mr. Brown, wish he'd stay away," Moe said.

Liza said, "You may like what Mr. Brown is going to tell you."

Liza smiled and kissed Moe's forehead. Moe almost fainted, no one had ever kissed him, he smiled big.

Henry and his wife made Moe their son and changed his name to Harry Victor Brown. Henry told his wife, "Billy is dependable and a good hire for my company. He took good care of our son." Mr. Henry Brown was moved with joy, he finally had a son to teach the steel mill business.

In the Brown's home Moe's anger began to germinate, although he liked his new name, he said out loud, "Harry Victor Brown," it sounded stately. Ill-advisedly, he did not like the people that he had to call, mom and dad. Even though Harry could read a little and cipher numbers, it was good enough for human chattel, but not in the world of freedom. For that reason, Mrs. Brown took it upon herself to teach and train Harry, to get him up to speed before sending him off to school. Once he was caught up scholastically, she planned to send him to a private school. Henry's wife was excited about her mission to teach a child.

Regrettably, Harry did not like the posh lady, he was rebellious and disturbingly nasty, so much so, that Mrs. Brown thought seriously about returning him to the backroom. Harry was only eleven years old, still, he stayed out late, slammed the door when he came in past midnight. Whenever he became angry, he threw dishes, broke windows, dumped food on the floor instead of the garbage. He wrote on the walls, cleaned his hands on the drapery, or use them to blow his nose; through it all, he kept his room clean.

On too many occasions Harry and Mrs. Brown got into heated arguments. He yelled that he was tired of her hovering over him and watching his every move. One day he yelled, "I's know how ta' read and cipher numbers."

Mrs. Brown said arrogantly with great annoyance, "we do not say, cipher." She looked at Harry to explain but decided he wasn't worth it. He was not her child, he was unqualified to be called human, he was nothing but a savage beast. She was irritated when she said, "Moe, you are not worth my time."
Harry slapped her hard and walked out. The side of Mrs. Brown's face was black and blue for weeks before the bruising began to leave. Every time Harry saw her, he flinched.

****

Billy's trip was remarkable. He did not run into any trouble with the law, slave catchers, or weather. His first stop was in Virginia with the Amish family that hid him and Liza under the pig's trough. He was happy to see that there was a whole Amish community that had developed over the years. The man of the family that had helped Billy and his wife said, "let me show you what we did with the money you sent every year. They had built a schoolhouse for their children, a recreation building, and a church. Billy was introduced to the people that had joined the community. They thanked him for the six dollars. He said to the family that he knew before leaving, "I'm glad to see that you're not alone out here."

The preacher that married the couple inquired about Liza and her wellbeing. Billy told him they were happy, working, how much they can do as a free man and woman, and about Moe. The preacher said, "May God bless you for sharing your profits. Billy, that was very good of you, and the whole community appreciates it."

"Vielen Dank," said the husband, translated, "thank you very much."

Billy waved and said as he was leaving, "Tachuss," meaning, "goodbye."

The husband yelled out, "komm wieder," in English "come again."

His wife said in English, "next time bring Liza, I want to introduce her to the women in our community."

"I will," Billy said with confidence.

His next stop was the Evans family, in Maryland. As Liza said, the family was easy to find, everybody in town knew them. A few of the townspeople asked if he was a new hire for the Evans. A white woman ran out one of the stores and said to Billy, "tell Mrs. Evans the material she ordered is in."

"Yes ma'am," Billy replied a little confused. When he saw a few men that looked like bounty hunters, he prayed his way through town. His heart raced hard and fast, it caused him to cough, he prayed, "Lord, help me please." He relaxed when he got through town and on the road to the Evans house.

When Billy arrived, he stopped on the path that led to the Evans home, he was amazed, "wow, rich colored folk," Billy said to himself.

As Billy pulled closer to the house, Mr. Evans came out and stood on the massive porch, and asked Billy, "May I help you?"

Since Billy was riding a horse and buggy, Mr. Evans figured he was not a runaway.

Billy said, "My name is Billy, Sir." Thoughts plowed through Billy's mind; how can this be? Colored this rich, in the south, with slavery all around us, no wonder Moe wanted to stay with the Evans. Billy smiled as he thought, *I want to stay with the Evans.*

Mrs. Evans came to the door and said, "bring him in, honey."

Billy thought, what a pretty colored woman with a soft voice.

Inside the Evans home, Mrs. Evans asked, "how may we help you?"

Billy said, "I come to tell you about the little boy you helped, Sir."

Mr. Evans asked, "can you be more specific?"

"Yes, Sir." Billy replied then said, "his name is, Moe," he thought, why do I keep saying Sir to this man, he's colored like me.

Mrs. Evans asked Billy how the boy was getting along. They shared with Billy that Moe gravitated to the family. Their three sons entered the room, like mom and dad they were good looking clean-cut articulate boys. They giggled through telling Billy about Moe, sometimes speaking at the same time. Their mother would say, "boys-boys, one at a time."

Mr. Evans took Billy around their farm and in the winery. He had over twenty people, a mixture of coloreds and whites that worked for him. When Mr. Evans went to speak with one of his workers, a colored man pulled Billy aside and said, "if you be lookin' foe' a job, Mr. Evan's be a good man ta' work foe.' He built some houses on da' west end of town foe' all us."

Billy smiled and said, "thank you."

Billy told Mr. and Mrs. Evans about Moe's concern for his brothers, Mr. Evans said he'd see what he could do. Billy stayed with the family for two nights three days, he got to taste the bacon Moe loved. Early in the morning on the third day, Billy was packed and ready to go. Like Moe had mentioned, the Evans were the kindest people in the world. Mrs. Evans made Billy a lunch and gave him extra food to eat on his way home, and a pound of smoked bacon for Billy's wife to cook. She said, "bacon is Moe's favorite food."

He said, "thank you, Miss."

Mr. Evans and his boys put a barrel of red wine on Billy's wagon. Before getting on the wagon, Billy stood in front of Mr. Evans and bowed, he said, "thank you, Sir."

On his way home Billy seriously thought about returning with Liza and work for the Evans family, "like Moe, I want to come back."

As he rode through town, Billy saw one of the men that looked like a bounty hunter, this time Billy waved at the man, he in turn waved and said, "howdy."

Billy was almost home when he said to himself, "did I bow to that man? He must think I'm stupid."

Back home, Billy went straight to the Mill, he gave the barrel of wine to Mr. Brown, they rolled the barrel into his office. He told him about Evan's family, and about the plantation that still had Moe's siblings. Henry said, "thank you for the wine, my son's name is Harry, not Moe, and you're to say nothing to my son, about that family or his brothers." He abruptly dismissed Billy with a wave of his hand.

Billy mumbled under his breath once he was outside Henry's office, "how rude and ungrateful, I should have kept the wine and shared it with the men in the plant."

Billy couldn't wait to get home and share with Liza his trip and tell her about stately, Mr. Evans.

****

Harry was home when Henry entered the house to tell his wife about Billy's trip and learning which plantation Harry was from. Mrs. Brown said, "good, I'm sending Moe, the worthless thing back to where he belongs, a filthy brainless slave on a plantation."

The minute she said that Harry's face turned red.

Since Harry had slapped Mrs. Brown, she spent most of the time in her bedroom. She emerged when Henry was home, but as soon as he left, she went straight to her bedroom and locked the door.

Her husband got irritated with his wife, he did not agree with her decision. He was going to take it upon his-self to put the boy in school and let the teachers handle him. Henry shouted at his wife, "slaves are not brainless, Billy was a slave and until I hired him, my mill was doing little business."

Harry joined in the conversation, he said hatefully, "yes, send me to school, get me out the house with this witch." He stormed out of the room.

One week after Billy's return from his trip, Harry skipped school and went to see Billy. They talked about the Evans, Liza sliced the bacon and cooked several pieces. The flavor burst in her mouth, Moe sat back and enjoyed the memory of living with the Evans as he ate the bacon. Billy said, "this is delicious," as he chewed on the bacon.

Billy asked Moe, "which name do you prefer, Moe or Harry? The name you choose is what I will call you."

He answered, "I like Harry."

At work, Harry noticed that too often some of the boys came to work with black eyes, cuts, and bruises. They stood around bragging about the gang fights the night before. Harry wanted no part of that lifestyle. He said to himself, "they are just like mom, and many of the slaves on Massa Jed plantation." He noticed that only a handful of the Steel Mill's employees had a home and lived good lives, just like on the plantation.

Even though Harry was behind in school he caught on quick, he studied hard and worked even harder to lose his southern drawl. Harry watched and learned from the rich boys that attended his school. He copied their mannerism which was similar to his dads, they had confidence and charm that Harry lacked. They made fun of his dialect, slow talking, and country ways. Harry had been through much worst, so he let their negative words roll out his mind like water on a duck's back. He continued to imitate the boy's superiority. Though Harry started school in late November, he academically sailed beyond the superior boys, like airstream in a windstorm.

Harry desired elegance, insight, and the glory of everyone looking upon him as a demigod, just like Henry. Harry also noticed that since Billy's three-day visit with the Evans, there was a certain change in his friend. Billy's characteristic was different, along with the way he moved, talked, his gestures, how he watched the employees, even his dress, Billy went shopping and began wearing suits, ties, and dress shoes. He took a greater interest in the operations and finances of the Brown Steel Mill. Billy went from being an employee of the company to a businessman. The men respected this new Billy. The sales of steel increased with Billy's drastic change.

During summer break, Harry calmed down and became a better son for the Browns. He listened to his parents and imitated his dad's dialect, he asked Henry to help him with his enunciation. He noticed that there was a difference between the wealthy and working-class way of speaking and what they talked about. There was something else he observed, when Henry entered the Steel Mill, the workers were more professional, and addressed him as Mister, and said yes Sir, and no Sir. What Harry did not see, was the employees respected Henry because of his kindness towards them. Henry cared for their wellbeing by making the Steel Mill a safe place to work.

During Harry's summer break, Henry took his son around the Steel Mill, to train him on the business side of the company. Henry wanted Harry to be the next owner. Harry thought to himself, *I have to change from country to city elegant.*

Summer vacation ended, Harry returned to school, he nailed it. He changed how he walked, talked, dressed, Harry obliterated the plantation boy and became an affluent cultured teen. He sounded like, looked like, and acted like blueblood royalty, Bostonian born and bred. Except there were that growing anger and hate that festered in his inner soul.

When Harry was a senior in high school, his visits with Billy and Liza had tapered off. Though whenever Harry went to their home, Liza prepared a meal for her two boys. One day when Harry visited Billy and Liza, he asked Billy about his brothers. He said it's been years since you returned. When is my father going to…"?

Billy cut Harry off and said, "I talked to him about your brothers upon my return home."

"What did he say?" Harry asked.

"It's not his problem."

When Harry left, Liza said, "Billy, that was eight years ago, didn't you tell Harry when you returned."

Billy said, "I tried but he cut me off, he wanted to know more about the Evans, and not his brothers."

Liza commented, "I notice a change in Harry, did you see it?"

Harry went home and yelled at his dad about his brothers, he said, "I just came from Billy he said…"

Henry refuted loudly, "I told you to stay away from those people."

Harry yelled, "I do as I please." He slammed the door as he left.

Henry was extremely jealous of the friendship between Billy and Harry, so much so, two weeks before Harry's graduation, Henry demoted Billy to the assembly line.

Billy went home and calmly shared with Liza how Henry had humiliated him in front of the workers. Liza asked, "what will we do."

Billy said, "you'll see. He hired a new supervisor that's a drunk."

Liza worried about their new situation and for her husband. She developed a small boil in her stomach, her worries subsequently were bottomless.

On the day of Harry's graduation, Henry visited Billy in his home, he said to Billy, "I am giving you your position back."

Billy challenged Henry, he said, "Mr. Brown, I need more money."

Henry said, "no," and left.

As Henry was leaving Billy said, "see you at the graduation."

Harry received the highest honors in his class. Mrs. Brown could feel that something was not quite right with the boy. Henry, on the other hand, was proud of his son. He told Harry that upon his death he was leaving everything to him. Henry's wife

saw an evil smirk spread across Harry's face, he said, "I'm going to be rich, but first..." he looked at Mrs. Brown.
She asked softly, "but first what, Harry?"
"I'm still working it out."
She backed away from him, Henry said, "leave the boy alone."
Inaptly, Henry thought his new hire would add revenue and respect to his company. After all, he was white and educated. For his bad decision and inappropriate way of handling Billy, Henry underwent a rude awakening. He learned running a company had nothing to do with the color of a person's skin. Henry's new hire incompetence caused the steel mill to miss out on a multimillion-dollar business deal that Billy had set up. Henry had a fit and then fired the man.

Billy and Liza attended Harry's graduation; they were proud of the young man. Harry had begun hanging out with his friends, that thought highly of themselves. He had taken on their distinguishing flaw of superiority. When he saw Billy and Liza wave, he turned his back and snubbed the couple, he joined his friends that were talking on the school steps.
Liza watching Harry's conceit asked Billy, "what did he just do?"
Billy grabbed her elbow and said, "let's go."
Harry saw them leaving. A theater-size memory caused him to flinch, watching them walk away, reminded him of Billy alone in the wagon pulling off to visit the Evans. He realized that he never thanked Billy or Liza for the food, friendship, a time they spent together, their love, his home in the back room. Harry ran calling, "Billy! Liza!" When he reached them, he gave Liza a hug first then Billy. He said breathless, "I'm sorry."
Liza said, "boy, do that again, I'll beat you good." She laughed as she hugged him a second time. Henry and his wife joined the small group, Henry said to Billy, "I am going to triple the salary you made as a supervisor. Will, you come back as the manager?"
Billy laughed and said, "I'll take it." He looked at Liza and grinned.
Liza smiled back and said, "I see."

All But One

****

Harry graduated from college when he was twenty-two which is where he met Stella, a beautiful young woman that had a year left to graduate. Harry got a job working at the Brown Steel Mill, on weekends Harry met Stella, he took her on carriage rides, they walked hand in hand in the park. On Sundays, Stella made them a picnic lunch where they sat on blankets and talked. Stella talked about becoming a teacher, Harry just wanted to be the richest man in Boston. Stella desired to have children; Harry pretended he wanted them. Stella said, "Oh, Harry life would not be worth living if we're not together."

Harry scratched his head and wondered how rich her parents were. Stella asked Harry about his family, he could not talk in detail about the Browns, only the mill. Stella, on the other hand, talked about her mother being from England, and her father from Vermont, her family alternated their travels between England and Vermont every two years. She talked about her grandparents, aunts, uncles, and cousins. Harry sat listening as he remembered his family on Jeb plantation.

After Stella's graduation from college, her parents discussed, with the Browns, their daughter marrying Harry. Mrs. Brown wanted to tell Stella's mother that Harry was dangerous, he was a slave, he had a temper, he hit her, he was not her child. She began to say to Stella's parents, "that boy is not fit…"

Henry stopped her and said, "ignore my wife, she doesn't want to lose her son." He then agreed with Stella's parents, "they would make a fine couple."

Mrs. Brown stood shaking her head, no. Stella's parents and Henry ignored her. Leaving Mrs. Brown out of the preparations, the three planned an elaborate engagement party to be held the following year on Harry's birthday. But first, before the festivities, Henry sent Harry and Stella, with two chaperones to England where they stayed for two months. Stella introduced him to her British relatives. They were not impressed with the young man; however, Harry was flabbergasted and awe-struck. He never thought he would get off the plantation, let alone out the country.

Harry hated the Browns but loved their money, in England he flaunted it everywhere he went. He noted that the British manufactured steel in tons, while the US was at a much lower base. He listened and learned from the British companies; he saturated every instruction he received. He asked questions about their machinery, their workers, their profit and loss. While Harry was learning to better The Brown Steel Mill, Stella spoke with college professors about their teaching methods.

On several occasions, the couple visited Harry's favorite place, standing outside looking at the King's palace. He treasured history and historical buildings, such as the structure that housed the King. Harry said, "the first palace was built in 1703. It was rebuilt and named Buckingham Palace by King Charles, for his wife Charlotte in 1761." Harry looked at Stella and said, "I am going to build you a castle, and name it, The Boston Palace."

Stella said, "a hundred years from now, people will visit and say, Harry Victor Brown built the palace for his wife, Mrs. Stella Brown," she giggled like a young schoolgirl.

Upon their return home, Harry's gained knowledge tripled The Brown Steel Mill's capital. Within a year he raised the company's year-end profit to over a million dollars through the increased steel that was being manufactured. Harry and Billy worked closely to turn The Brown Steel Mill into the largest in the north.

Harry argued with his father; he wanted the company to grow beyond Boston. Henry said aloud resounding, "no."

Henry was disappointed in his son, he went home and told his wife, she simply said, "still want him to marry Stella?" Mrs. Brown could see that Henry was filled with rage, even so, she continued, "he will destroy her like he's doing you."

Henry was angry with his wife and son. Meantime, Harry took matters in his own greedy hands. He literally caused two small companies, that was in another county, to go out of business. Harry paid the men wives twenty dollars, to tell him anything about their husbands. The women were bought and purchased with pocket change. Though the women did not know each other, they told Harry the same lie. They claimed that their husbands used inferior material and sold the steel for top dollar. Within a few months, he owned their company.

Henry hired a lawyer to undo Harry's treachery and returned the money to the two company owners. The men took the

All But One

money, kicked the women out their home, gave them nothing, the women were penniless.

After the incident, Henry told Harry that he was going to cut him out his will, leaving him nothing. Harry boiled, he told his mother who said, "now son, your father will never do that. He loves you more than I do."

Harry said through clenched teeth, "you think I care how you feel about me." He left the house.

A criminal plan brewed in Harry's heart. He hushed his rebellion for a while, he was waiting for the right time. Until then, he lived in a world of pretense around his parents. Henry and Harry became fake friends, father and son would have won an Oscar for their performance. It was all perfect hate; love was absent in their feelings for each other. Henry began the paperwork to omit Harry out of his will, the day after the birthday and engagement party Henry was going to sign the final papers. He was also, going to empty Harry's bank account.

On Harry's birthday and engagement party, which was to be a happy occasion, turned out to be a horrific night. The party was held in an elaborate hotel ballroom. The Governor, Mayor, and all the socialites from surrounding counties were invited. That evening, Harry was working at the mill to finish auditing the books; at five o'clock, he changed into his fancy dress suit.

Harry's parents were picking him up at six o'clock. Harry's mother was dressed in all black, instead of going to a celebration she looked as if she was going to attend a funeral. Henry, on the other hand, looked handsome in his tux with bright silver buttons, dark red cumberbund, and bowtie. Henry planned to announce at the party that on Monday morning he was signing the papers to cut Harry out his will. He looked at his wife sad face and said, "cheer up my lovely wife, after we drop Harry off at the party," he paused before continuing, "I asked the bank manager to open the bank tonight."

"Why?" She asked annoyed and confused. Henry's wife was not in agreement with Harry marrying Stella or her husband giving the white slave thing that lived in her home, so much money. She said, "I am against this whole evening."

"But my dear," Harry began and finished saying, "tonight I am emptying out his bank account."

Harry's wife looked at him in total astonishment and joy, she asked, "you don't want this wedding either?"

Before he could answer the wheel on the carriage fell off. Harry's wife shouted several times, "Harry did this!"

Within thirty minutes Harry was dressed and working on the books again. An hour later, "finished," he said to himself as he looked up at the clock, it was six thirty. He ran around his office and blew the candles out, and then sprinted outside only to run into two police officers. They were coming towards the door of the Steel Mill; one of the officers told Harry that his parents had been killed in a horse and buggy accident. The other asked Harry to accompany them to the morgue to identify the bodies.

When they arrived Harry could not believe the state of his parents, some of their body parts were ripped off, their faces slashed, his father's forehead was bust open, one of his mother's eyes had popped out. "What happened?" Harry inquired.

A police officer told him that one of the wheels came off, the buggy flipped over, which spooked the horse making it run faster dragging his parents on the ground. "The carriage should have dislodged," an officer said more to himself.

To everyone standing around it appeared that Harry's world had stopped.

At the funeral, Harry put on a good show, he cried that he was downtrodden, he wanted his mom and dad back, he wanted happiness. Harry screamed, "please pluck these weeds of sorrow." He sobbed loudly. After the funeral, he said to the minister that officiated the funeral, "I am so sorry."

"It's not your fault young man," the minister replied.

While Harry put on a good show at the funeral, a man went to the police station and reported that he had seen the wheel come off. He claimed that Mrs. Brown yelled, "Harry did this. Harry did..." "And then the carriage flipped over, it was all over." He stood in silence before stating, "I'm thinking the horse and carriage should have dislodged. Maybe saved their lives."

An officer said, "you are correct Sir."

The police and several other men went out to the scene where the man claimed, he had seen where the accident had taken place.

All But One

The day after Harry's parent's funeral, he broke up with his fiancé, whom she thought he was as close to her as her heartbeat. Stella tried to salvage their love and fill the void in Harry's heart. She fixed his meals, played the piano for him, took him to museums, even carriage rides, be that as it may, Harry broke off their engagement.

Harry met with his father's solicitors to check if Henry had carried out his plan to take him off the will. Henry V. Brown was in the beginning stage of removing Harry but had not completed the process. For that reason, his adopted son got everything. Harry received the money and ownership of the Steel Mill; he and Billy were in one mind to make the company a huge success. Billy said, "I want to try to produce tons of steel every year." He looked at Harry and asked, "what do you think?"

Harry was awe-struck, he grasped that Henry had a muzzle on Billy's capabilities. Harry trained Billy as Henry had him, thus, Billy's increased knowledge about the operation of the Steel Mill, increased the incoming revenue. Harry wanted Billy to soar as high as he wanted to go, the company and his pockets would be better for it.

IV

Harry's True Color

By 1843, The Brown Steel Mill had increased in size and was on the verge of making four and a half tons of steel that year. Twenty-eight-year-old Harry constructed two new wings on the Steel Mill to handle the work. He left Billy in charge of the Mill and moved to a southern state, that was not of his birth.

****

Back in the South, Harry did not want to see his family, though he inquired about their welfare. When Harry was six years old, his older brother and sister, Bo and Jo, was sold to another plantation owner for a cook. However, with the aid of an overseer, they escaped slavery. Three months later Bo and Jo arrived in Miami, Florida, they could go no further because there was the largest body of water, they had ever seen blocking their journey. For several weeks they hid in bushes and ate garbage. Fright, loneliness, being so far from home made them closer, it shoved them in each other's arms. If only they could read, they would have seen a sign that would have welcomed them in the person's home.

Harry learned that Bo and Jo made it to Florida, changed their names to Tom and Sally. Seeking a better life, they got jobs, Tom became a janitor in one of the city schools, Sally a housemaid for a wealthy woman. With a little cash in their pocket, they rented a little shack in the outer skirts of town, and then decided to do the unthinkable, they got married. Out of the union, two babies were born three years apart, both had serious birth defects, they died within two years of being born. John and Sally believed it was because of their secret and not due to them being so closely related. The couple lived childfree, maintained their jobs, and stayed together as husband and wife.

    Harry's two remaining brothers, Toe and So, got married to women on Jed's plantation, they and their wives worked full time at the shoe factory. Jed had not changed, out of their hard-earned wages he paid them a dollar. On the plantation, Jed gave each of Harry's brothers a cabin to make their home, he wanted them to have plenty of children. In town, their wives went to a woman who fixes them. The female's botched job made the women unable to conceive and unfortunately, very ill. Both women hemorrhaged for days. To take time off to heal, they told Jeb that they had a woman disease and it was contagious for the first three days. Jeb backed away and let the women take a week off. He knew it was true because his wife had told him that she got the disease three times a year. The women laughed at Jeb's ignorance.

    Harry's brothers and their wives were happy, they had a home, and worked in town at the shoe factory. Though slaves, they were free to go to the store to buy food, shoes, and material for clothes. They even purchased furniture and curtains for their shack. They were not working in the hot sun, nor concerned about bringing a baby into slavery. Harry often wondered the reason they didn't run, but then he remembered Elijah telling him, "when the slave gets learning, dey get uppity."

    He learned that Elijah died a few days after he ran away and his mother killed herself on the day he ran. For the first time since his Bostonian parent's death, Harry smiled. He never contacted his siblings.

    In the eyes of the townspeople, Harry's Boston accent, elegant behavior, and expensive clothes made him someone to be revered. It was as though, they worshiped him in everything he did, Harry had become a demigod. According to the townspeople, Harry could do no wrong, they embraced his every word. He was short, stocky, and affluent. The women swarmed around him like honeybees around flowers, they treated him like he was a rock star. Harry ignored them. The men idolized him, they invited Harry to join their club; he was a guest speaker for special occasions. Of all the women that flirted and lapped after Harry like a dog in heat, he chose quiet, refined beautiful extremely rich, Baerbel MacCall. Her father owned most of the stores, houses, the refinery, and buildings in the small town of MacCall. Harry's heart belonged to Stella; his pockets wanted to be filled with the MacCall money. Two years after moving to MacCall, Harry married Baerbel.

In Boston, Mr. Henry V. Brown had a picture of eleven-year-old Moe sitting on his desk. When Mr. Brown died, Billy took the picture without Harry's knowledge. He left the two of the family together, something about the pictures looked strange. Mrs. Brown appeared to be very angry, Henry indifferent, and Harry stood off to himself. The family's facial expression and stance looked as though they were enemies being made to take a picture together. Billy said to himself, "three adversaries."

In 1846, Billy's wife wrote a book titled, "Then and Now." It was to debut that year. One of the stories was about Moe, she titled that chapter, *Little Moe*. Liza added the photo of Moe in the middle of his section. On the front cover of the book was a picture of a slave shack, the back was a picture of their new eleven room house, new furniture, and an indoor bathroom. Liza paid for everything with the large sum of money, she received to write the book.

Billy wrote a letter to Harry with the updates on the Steel Mill, he also told Harry about Liza's book. Harry wrote back asking Billy to have the book debut` after his wedding, June 1845.

In August, Harry left his new bride behind as he traveled to Boston. While there he'd heard that Stella had married the Mayor of Boston. "She married well," he said to himself.

Both couples had gotten married the same year. In addition to the news, Billy shared with Harry that a company in New York had put in an order for three tons of steel. With that purchase, the Brown Steel Mill would have produced seven tons of steel within the year of 1845.

Harry threw an elaborate successful book signing party for Liza. His guest list included reporters from different counties. Harry was a genius, Liza's book sold like wildfire in and around the United States. Harry was hoping to see Stella, but she was in Europe on her honeymoon.

Before returning to the south, Harry allowed Billy to continue running the business. He didn't want Henry Brown's house, so he put it up for sale and left Billy in charge.

Harry returned home in November the richest man in MacCall. By hook or crook, Harry was going to get his hands-on Baerbel's father's money and businesses.

March 1846, Baerbel was four months pregnant. Harry had not returned to Boston since his trip in 1845, he packed his bags and returned. By March, The Brown Steel Mill sold six tons of steel across America. Harry was pleased with Billy's business skills.

While in Boston, Harry visited his parents' grave site, he looked around and saw people attending a funeral that was close to where his parents were buried. Harry smiled and drew attention to himself; he fell on his knees and in fake sorrow cried fervently, "mama, daddy, I love you, I miss you." Adding to his drama, he laid on his stomach and stretched over their graves. And cried aloud, "come back, mom come back."

Billy had followed Harry to the graveyard, when he saw Harry lay down, Billy went to him and said, "I'm here for you big brother."

Harry's first child was born in August 1846, while he was in Boston. Baerbel named her son after her father, with Harry's last name, William MacCall Brown. When Harry returned home, the baby was two months old. He changed his son's name to, Charles Brown.

****

As a wedding gift, Baerbel's father built the newlyweds a huge house on seven thousand acres. Harry bought two hundred and fifty slaves, coloreds and whites. To keep them happy he built a little church that doubled as a school on the plantation. He had two sons that were one year apart, at first, he raised his boys to be kind slave owners. He did not want to be mean like Jeb. Harry lived in a fantasy world; he believed that a church, a school, and being kind to the slaves would make them happy and satisfied. The slaves did not share Harry's love for the delta or slavery.

Harry appreciated the beautiful shimmering sun; it burned the backs of the slaves. Harry's favorite tree was the weeping willow that swayed gracefully in the wind, to the slaves the branches were used as a whip. No, a church, a school, and kindness were not enough for them; they wanted freedom, equality, they wanted to go back to Africa or Europe. All Harry had to do was remember his days as a slave, but greed blocked his memory and money corroded his heart.

During the Civil War, Harry did all that was in his power and finances to aid the Independent Southern States to win the Civil War. He met with the public officials, he attended KKK meetings, supplied clothes, shoes, food, anything the troops needed.

In 1863, His oldest son Charles was seventeen and Drew the youngest sixteen. He was taking them to town to enlist. Baerbel protested profusely, so much so she threw an adult size temper tantrum. She broke the mirror on her vanity, then went into Harry's bedroom and broke his mirror, using scissors she ruined most of his clothes.

Harry did not flinch; he had his trusted slave, Joe to take him and his sons' downtown. Once they reached their destination, Harry signed Charles and Drew up to serve and protect his beloved south. He made sure the regiment that his sons were a part of received two sets of clean uniforms, boots, four pairs of socks, clean underwear, and all the ammunition and guns they could carry. He stood proudly as he watched them march off to victory. Once they were out of sight, he told Joe, "return the horse and buggy, tell the misses nothing. Tell Clara to clean my bedroom, I will return when I am ready."

"Yaw Sir, Massa," Joe replied.

Harry caught a train going to Boston. To bring the railroad to his small town, Harry donated millions of dollars, he rejoiced when the town named the station after him. The naming ceremony was a big festivity, downtown MacCall was crowded with people attending the program. There were speakers, and singers, and food, all for Harry.

While in Boston Harry went to the mill and met with his good friend Billy, who was about to retire from the company.

Harry asked Billy to give the company a few more years and during that time train his predecessor.

Harry visited his parent's gravesite, as he stood next to them, he looked around and in a short distance saw a very elegant woman standing in front of a grave. She looked familiar to him, to get her attention he cleared his throat. When she looked over, he gasped in surprise, for it was his fiancé, Stella. He wondered who had died? Whose grave was she visiting? One year after Harry's parent's funeral, Stella's mother and father were on their way to England, but a storm came and sunk the ship, there were no survivors.

Twenty years after losing her parents, Stella's husband became ill with pneumonia and never recovered, he died in the hospital. Like Harry, she had two children, a boy, and a girl, that were teenagers.

They left the graveyard, Harry took Stella to their favorite park, they became a couple again. Harry lied and told her that his wife had died giving birth to their third child, who after living for thirty minutes passed away in his arms. Stella was touched; she gently rubbed Harry's brow with her gloved hand, and then cupped his chin in the palm of her hands and softly said, "all is well, I'm here for you."

To Stella, he was the same soft gentle loving man she knew so long ago. With time passing, she had forgiven him, her love for Harry was etched in stone, never to fade.

Harry apologized for leaving her behind, he claimed his parent's death was too much for him to bare. Harry assured Stella that he was back for good, he took her out to eat on several occasions, she prepared picnic lunches, they went to the beach and took trips to the mountains in Vermont. Harry promised to purchase land, he said, "I want to build you the castle I promised years ago."

Stella was happy to have Harry back in her life, but Harry's mind and motive salivated at the thought as to how much money she was worth. He sweet talked her into marrying him, he bought her a ring with a large solitaire diamond rock. Stella was impressed and without thought said a soft resounding, "yes."

In the back of Harry's mind, he was thinking he had to return to MacCall and eliminate his wife.

Harry told her that he had to go back south to sell his house and pack his things, then after the war, he would return. Before Harry left, they began planning their wedding. Stella was excited, she clasped her hands in total joy. "When is the war over?" she asked.

Stella was thrilled about the wedding and being with Harry forever. Harry was pleased that he had made Stella happy, he adored watching her, she was beautiful, sophisticated, and fashionable. "I hope soon my darling," he smiled and gently kissed her, "very soon my darling." Harry was excited about their combined richness. His dream to build Stella a castle was becoming a reality.

Poor Harry did not know that Stella's parents were not as rich as he was thinking. Nor did he realize that the title Mayor was a prestigious privilege that did not pay millions of dollars, though they lived well. Harry confused his love of money with a person, he did not love Stella, he adored her wealth.

Before leaving Boston, Harry visited Billy and Liza. They talked about the success of Liza's book, Henry's insane jealousy of their friendship. Harry asked Billy to make round iron rods twenty-two feet long and six inches thick. He placed an order for thirteen by thirteen feet solid iron plates that were to be six inches thick. He did not tell Billy the reason, he knew if he had, their friendship would be over. While Billy and Harry talked, Liza was in the kitchen singing and cooking. Her Moe was visiting and was staying the night in one of their guest bedrooms. It was an amusing time for the threesome, they reminisced about their first meeting when Harry was a child, the backroom, and the Evans. Harry paused for a brief moment; he had a flashback of Mr. Evans big beautiful house. He looked at Billy and asked, "did you see their house, what was the porch and entranceway made of?"

Billy answered remembering the biggest house he had ever seen and how well it was constructed, he answered Harry with deep pride, "the porch and vestibule were made of smooth stone from Africa."

Harry commented, "it was massive and beautiful."

Harry's visit was tense, but each played through the moment and made it comfortable.

All But One

Billy and Liza stood on the porch waving Harry off as he returned home. When Harry was out of hearing, Liza said to Billy, "you did not tell him about our new house in Vermont."

Billy said, "something was different about him."

"I noticed that also," Liza said.

"What are the thousands upon thousands of thousands of rods and plates for, why does he need so many?" Billy said in a confused tone.

Liza said, "so tall and gigantic."

"I guess we will eventually find out," Billy said as he and Liza entered the house.

Harry was at the train station when he realized he did not ask if Billy had heard from the Evans. Harry was young when he was at their home, he had no idea which way to go and find them. Harry remembered their house, kindness, and how much fun he had. If Harry had asked Billy about the Evans family and not just the house, he would have learned, that Mr. Evans youngest son ran the farm with his dad. His older boy became a doctor, the middle boy moved to Indiana, opened a store, sold his father's wine, hired several dressmakers, he sold rack ready clothes for men, women, and children. In addition, he retailed shoes, perfume, purses, hats, and undergarments. The Evans boys had done well.

Harry returned to the south in March 1865, a deliriously happy man. The train stopped in New York, while there, Harry bought Baerbel a gift; after all, he had been away for two years.

Whenever Harry had memories of his childhood days as Moe, his mother yelling at him, and Massa beating him, he thought of the color gray. He bought Baerbel a gray drawstring armlet, a matching parasol, and shawl. He also bought her gray silk material to have a new dress made for her funeral. He sent a telegraph asking someone to tell Joe his return date and time to MacCall.

Gaining Property

April 1865, the Civil War had ended. An outraged Harry, for the second and last time, disappointed his fiancé. Harry with his whole heart expected the South to win; he had plans to eliminate Baerbel and leave the plantation to Charles. He was going to return to Boston, where he would run the Steel Mill with Billy and marry Stella. His tactics took a detour in July 1865.

Harry became a dogmatic determined man to preserve slavery on his plantation through the endlessness of time. His plan, aspiration, and hope were to get his precious chattel back. The south losing the war turned Harry into a dominating demon that ruled with an iron fist. Without any remorse, Harry in this insolent egocentric culture, broke the law like a devious thief, in broad daylight, which turned out to be his death trap.

Billy had begun designing the molds for the rods and plates, Harry's plan had commenced, and he was satisfied. If the south won the war, there would be no need for the iron rods, he would try and sell them. However, before taking his son's downtown and signing them up to fight in the war, then going to Boston, Harry barricade himself in his room and formatted a plan. In essence, he was prepared for victory or defeat.

The South may have lost its authority over their valuable human property, "I will not," he whispered aloud to himself. On Harry's plantation, only eight slaves stayed behind, his other two hundred and forty-two had run away or joined the army. On the train, Harry's thoughts got the better of him. Harry was no different than his wife, they both had their tantrum moments. If Harry wanted something bad enough, he had no qualms going after it by thievery or murder. Baerbel simply threw things.

Joe met Harry at the train station, before going home he had Joe to first stop past the MacCall's home. Lining the pathway to the stately house were trees filled with Spanish moss, Jo did not like the hairy matter, he thought it was haunting. He was glad Harry did not like Baerbel's parents, since their wedding, this was Harry's second time visiting. When they pulled in front of the house, Harry jumped down, went on the porch and knocked on the door. A female house slave let Harry in, she escorted him to the room where Mr. and Mrs. MacCall were drinking tea and eating tea cake.

It was a quiet Sunday afternoon; all the house slaves were in the slave quarters. The main color in the room was silver gray. Harry loath the room and it's dull gray furnishings.

Harry sat next to Mr. MacCall, his wife began pouring Harry a cup of tea, "no let me do that," Harry said as he reached to pour himself a cup. He hit her hand and the tea spilled all over the table. Harry jumped up and said, "I'll get your help." He took the fancy tea kettle with him.

The train had arrived in MacCall earlier than Harry anticipated, which was in his favor. While waiting for Joe he went into a store and purchased a vial of poison, he put it in his pocket.

Harry saw the slave girl coming out of another room, he told her about the incident and that he would start another kettle. While in the kitchen, Harry noticed that the wood burning stove was still hot, he put more water in the kettle and poured the poison in the water. On the counter were two containers that had tea and sugar written on them, using his hand he put tea and sugar in the kettle. When the slave girl entered the kitchen carrying the items from the tearoom, he told her that the tea was ready. She sat the things she was carrying on the counter, Harry saw a strainer in one of the cups, he got it. The slave girl got out three clean cups. Harry poured the girl a cup of tea, she smiled and said, "da' cup foe' you, Massa, Mistress."

Harry said, "just drink," he held the cup to her mouth and watched her sip until it was gone. When Harry took the tea to the MacCall's, the slave girl went to the window and waved at Joe, he smiled and waved back, she returned to the kitchen and died.

Harry entered the tearoom with two clean cups and the tea, he poured the MacCall's a cup, apologized for the mess he made, and then sat watching the husband and wife sip their tea until the cup was empty. Mrs. MacCall said, "this tea is delicious."

Mr. MacCall said, "sweet and tasteful."

Harry smiled as he left the tearoom and the mansion, he got on the buggy and sat next to Joe and asked, "did you see anyone?"

"Naw' Sir." Joe lied.

When the slave girl waved, Joe thought she had a strange look on her face.

Two weeks after Baerbel's parent's memorial service, Harry was happy because his wife, the only child of the MacCall's, got everything.

Harry was jogging up the porch steps when he detected, out of the corner of his eye, he saw someone coming. He turned, it was his sons slowly meandering up the long pathway, "they look like ragamuffins," he said to himself.

Harry's defiant outburst against the South losing the Civil War, confused many southern executives since he was from the North. Charles and Drew stood at the bottom of the porch steps and looked up at their father.

"Hi pops," Drew said. "We've been gone for a long while."

Charles stuttered, "The war is-is over, and it's good-good to be-be home."

"And you idiots lost," Harry barked before entering the house.

After the Civil War, several slaves struggled to attain employment and regenerate their sense of self-worth. For too many years, they had been stripped naked and treated less than an object. Upon their freedom, they desired to regain family value, confidence, and self-respect, much of which was destroyed upon their abduction from the arms of mother Africa. The poor whites could not understand the reason they were treated like they were equal to the darkies. After the Civil War, all slaves entered the battle of hatred that was thrashed upon them. Still, the newly freedmen and women clung to the firm belief that America was home, and they would survive. Although free, the doors of opportunity were slammed shut in their faces. Several white slaves left MacCall seeking employment out of the South, while others remained and joined the KKK.

Letter from Stella

The stagecoach carrying mail entered the town of MacCall and dropped off the parcels and mail at a store that doubled as a post office. As the storekeeper assorted the envelopes, he came across a letter from Boston, Massachusetts for Harry V. Brown. An employee in the store ran out and told a few others about the Bostonian letter, the news spread like wildfire. The small town had never received mail from a northern state. Fortunately, for the storekeeper a crowd of people stacked in the shop just to see the return address. Many made purchases, in hopes it would help them to see the address. A male onlooker told the storekeeper that he would deliver Harry's mail that had come in. The storekeeper looked around and spotted the other employee at

All But One

the store, he said to the man, "take my horse and deliver this letter to Mr. Brown."

The storekeeper looked at the gentleman that offered to deliver Harry's mail and said, "I am sorry Sir, Mr. Brown will not take too kindly to strangers going to his home."

Paula a young slave girl, entered the drawing-room carrying a tray of food for Harry when someone knocked at the door. Paula answered, when Harry heard a male voice, he stood next to his young slave. Harry recognized the man from the store instantly, he asked, "what bring you out this way?"

He handed Harry the letter and left, Harry called him back and gave him a few coins.

Harry whistled as he took two steps at a time going to his room. He read the letter and then laid the letter on the top of his chest-of-drawers. He was going to answer the letter after his workers were hired.

Baerbel was in her room that was down another wing of the house, even so, she heard Harry whistling as he rummaged around his room and then went back downstairs. She tiptoed through the hall, peeked down the stairs and saw Harry going into the drawing-room. When he was out of sight, she went into his room where she saw Stella's letter. Baerbel read the letter, Stella wrote how much she loved and missed him, his tux was ready, her dress would be finished by their wedding day. Baerbel continued reading how sorry Stella was about his wife's death and his three children, she ended the letter stating they were about to start a new family with each other. After reading the letter and hearing Harry whistling, the hairs on the nape of Baerbel's neck stood straight up. All the years they had been married she had never seen or heard Harry so happy. She put the letter back in the envelope and laid it on the chest.

She went to her room and wrote to Stella, *"I's not dead, I's neva' had three babies, only two and they's be alive."* She signed, *"Harry's wife, Baerbel."* She got dressed and had Joe to take her to town, where she mailed the letter. The very next day Baerbel was nervous, she wanted to stop the letter from reaching the woman. she had no idea what was going to happen, her mind raced a hundred miles an hour, what if the woman wrote Harry back? What if she came to the house? Did she speak proper like Harry?

On a hot day in July, Harry, his wife Baerbel, and sons were finishing lunch when he scooted back from the table and said, "boys, follow me into the drawing-room, Vance is coming over for a meeting."

The Brown's home décor was a Gothic theme; all the woodwork throughout the mansion was dark mahogany, even the furniture. In the high ceiling of the dining room were mahogany wood paneling that surrounded the base of the ceiling. A built-in mahogany and metal stand were positioned in four corners of the room, on each stand sat a three-foot gargoyle made of stone. Their wings spread up and out, knees bent, their torso leaned forward as though they were about to leap down on the family. Baerbel was extremely frightened of their big sharp off-white polished teeth, and their glassy piercing eyes that seared her bloodcurdling soul.

Harry, in contrast, was mesmerized by the beast apparent strength. He looked up at one of the gargoyles, took in a deep breath and exhaled slowly. It was as though his strength derived from the stone beast. A movement in the dining room caused him to jump, he looked at his wife with contempt, hate spewed out of his mouth, "Vance is coming over, clean this mess up."

Baerbel was short, she had soft tired blue eyes. Her heart-shaped face, untanned pale white skin, perfectly petite keen nose, and thin narrow chin was not the reason Harry married her. The capital that followed her in the union was his gluttony. Baerbel, answered back in a strong singsong southern dialect, "whys' Harry, you's talkin' ta' me likes' I's' one of the darkies."

Harry shouted, "woman, mind your place, tell Bella to fix something for Vance to eat, he will arrive soon."

Looking around he saw his sons still in the dining room, Harry shouted, "why, are you still here?"

Charles and Drew at a run-walk pace hustled out the kitchen, down the long hallway, into the drawing-room. If it were possible, steam would spew from the top of Harry's head. His anger had grown to the strength of a volcano erupting if anyone challenged his views, he mushroomed.

In the drawing-room, he joined his sons. He said, "Charles, Drew when Vance arrived, I'll start the meeting." He looked away from the young men, glanced around the room as though he was seeing it for the first time.

He motioned for them to take a seat. Harry walked by the big picture window, that went from the ceiling to just above the floor, he was looking for Vance to arrive. He turned and sat in his favorite chair; the headrest was the gargoyles' opened mouth. One armrest was its tail, holding the chair was the beast claws and feet. Dark red and hints of brown upholstery covered the Gothic chairs and couch in the room. The medieval era was Harry's favorite historical period.

Harry had no idea what the Gothic historical era was all about, except when he was a boy living in Boston, the Brown's had a picture book of old English drawings of a gargoyle. The pictures in the book were black and white, Harry deduced they had to have been brown and dark red velvet, they were his favorite colors and material.

As the three men sat quietly, Bella, Harry's cook, backed through the double doors that led into the drawing-room. She was carrying a tray filled with sandwiches, cake, and lemonade. Drew yelled, "Why'd you bring so much food?"

Drew was tall and handsome with blond hair, he had big blue eyes, perfect white straight teeth, and a flawless physique. His good looks were from his mother's side of the family. Unfortunately, he inherited his father's rotten character and evil personality, so much so he was wicked. Drew was eighteen years old at the time of the meeting. To prove his manhood, he had killed seven Union soldiers, five Confederate, and shot at his brother, Drew claimed they were weak and useless.

Bella nervously answered Drew, while looking a Harry, "Massa Brown tells me ta' bring food."

"Leave it niggra," Drew shouted.

Bella sat the tray down and slowly began to back out the room. Ignoring the encounter, Harry walked over to the picture window again. This time he saw Vance old mare, sluggishly coming down the long driveway at a snail's pace. He looked around at his sons, "Vance is coming." To Bella, he said, "no disturbance, close the doors behind you, tell the Misses to be, soundless.

"Yaw' Sir, Massa." She left closing the double doors gently behind her.

Charles looked at his dad with deep concern, and asked, "Dad, want me to let Mr. Vance in?"

Charles was taller than Harry and better looking than his dad and brother. Though Charles inherited his father's big bones. Charles even had a proud walk and expensive taste like his dad. He had black straight hair and big green eyes with eyelashes that women dreamed of having. He had inherited his grandpa William MacCall Italian features and deep velvet voice that was smooth as silk, he drove women crazy. In addition, to his already elegant voice, Charles added a little zest, he practiced Harry's Bostonian accent. His personality echoed his grandpa, he was kind, loving, and caring. Drew had the height; Charles the good heart.

Drew hated poor people and slaves. Charles silently worked with and funded the abolitionist tasks, to set the slaves free. Slaves that had children, he would give the parents money from his allowance, so once free, they would have means to begin a new life. He also had connections in Canada.

Drew was brassy, Charles was as sweet as apple pie, the women adored him. He was a teenage heartthrob and player, Charles had a new girlfriend, just about every other week. Harry absolutely loved it. One evening before the meeting, Harry looked in the mirror and said to his reflection, "wish I had been like Charles when I was younger." Harry turned from the mirror laughing and continued, "that boy knows what to do."

In the drawing-room, Harry paced the floor as Vance aged dawdling mule poked alone. "Naw' I'll go out to meet him," Harry said in answering Charles request to let Vance in.

As Harry began going toward the front door, he heard Baerbel's loud voice coming down the hall into the drawing-room. She was screaming in an ear-piercing foolhardy sound.

In the kitchen, Baerbel was taking her frustration out on old Bella. Baerbel slapped Bella in the face and then pushed her on the floor. Bella fell to her knees and pretended to cry. Baerbel loveless marriage, Drew's disrespect, accompanied by an abundance of self-love was the high-flying vulture that ate holes into the core of her lonely solitary soul. "Cain't you move faster niggra," Baerbel yelled. "You move slower than a sick old mule."

She was going to slap Bella again, Paula ran in and instantly helped Bella off the floor. Baerbel was yelling so loud she did not hear Harry entered the kitchen, he studied the scene for a moment. Baerbel yelled, "both you's ain't nothin' but stankin' pigs wid' legs." She spun around to leave but fell right into Harry.

Harry said through clenched teeth, "iffen' you don't keep the noise down, I'll put you out and make you live in one of the empty slave shacks, I will not repeat myself."

He said to Bella and Paula, "I am getting you help." He grabbed Baerbel's skinny arm and squeezed hard, he said, "I am a man of my word, I am a man of action."

Baerbel said not a mumbling word.

Harry hurriedly walked down the hall, burst through the drawing-room doors, "I'll meet Vance," Harry said as he rushed past his sons, and went straight out the front door.

Vance was climbing down off the wagon as Harry was exiting the house. Vance was a short skinny man of little means, he and his wife lived in a two-room shack close to Titleburk. Unknown to Harry, Vance and his wife were abolitionists; Charles had financed several of their missions.

Harry tolerated the little man because he would do anything for a small price. Harry walked off his porch to meet his friend and said, "hello Vance, glad you could come," he reached out and shook Vance's hand. "My boys are waiting inside."

Once inside, Harry had the men to pull their chairs in a circle; leaving enough room in the middle for Harry to spread out his map.

"Hold all questions; listen to what I have to say first. So, boys, Shut-up."

Harry opened the map and laid it in the middle of the circle. Drew sat on the edge of his seat; questions yelled in his head. Knowing his father, he chewed on his bottom lip, squeezed his knees together and held his peace.

Charles and Vance caught each other's eye and said not a word.

"I bought the three properties that conjoined mine," Harry began, "I now own sixteen thousand two hundred and fifty acres. That equates to approximately twenty-seven square miles. I am calling it, the H. B. Metropolis. On the MacCall property, my new home The Castle will be built." He looked at the three men, "before you say anything, I am tearing down the MacCall house." Harry radiated with excitement, he shifted in his chair before

continuing, "understand this; I will be talking in mileages. He looked at his sons and Vance. "That's important information for your understanding," he continued.
Drew couldn't keep quiet any longer, "why pops?"
"Shut-up," Harry snapped. "When I'm finished, you'll appreciate what I'm doing." Harry pointed at the map. Charles shifted in his seat. Vance sat so still; he resembled a mannequin posed in a store window.

As Harry described his plan, his thoughts were on the iron rods and plates. He stopped talking, got up and walked over to the big picture window, he stood frozen in place. He exhaled, faintly asked himself in a soft whisper, "will I get caught?" Harry pulled himself together, turned facing the men and said, "I'll continue."

V

H.B. Metropolis

Harry eased down into his chair; thoughts pounded in his head like a jackhammer trying to break through a steel wall. He knew his plan was wrong, inhuman, and against the American Government. Still, he continued, he started the meeting by saying, "this house, the barn, the small cabin that's in a distance from here, and the slave quarter sits on seven thousand acres." He pointed at the map and said, "adding to my property I purchased the three adjoining plantations providing me," Harry chuckled then boasted, "with the largest plantation known to man."

To keep his illegal slaves at bay, Harry installed four sets of gates and planted a forest all around his property. The gates stood sixteen feet above the ground and were firmly entrenched six feet deep. Surrounding the gates was miles of forest to keep his illegal plantation concealed and invisible. The walls of steel and impenetrable forest were meant to be imposing.

The Gates

The main gate was in the shape of a rectangle, it began seven miles behind Harry's mansion. This gate was installed twelve miles going north and south, and ten miles east and west. The massive iron bars made the gate look like a gigantic outdoors jail cell. This gate was called the main gate, the slaves called it Massa gate.

Inside the main gate were three different gates that were installed the same depth and height as the main gate. The first gate was called the divider gate. It was installed one mile south of the main gate and ran east and west for ten miles, attaching to either end of the main gate. This gate separated the children from their parents.

The second gate sat between the outer gate and the divider gate. Living in the two squared acres gate was where the children were raised. A four-room cabin was built in the middle of their area. Inside was a room for the boys, one for the girls, the nurse and teacher shared a room, and a large gathering room. Outside was the cooking area. In the 1900s a kitchen and full bathroom were added in the cabin. This gate was called the children gate.

On the southern side of the divider gate, the overseers lived six and a half miles from this gate. Two three room cabins were constructed for the overseers and their women. A barn with four stalls for their horses was built. The horses grazed on the land around the overseers' cabins. The oversees women were responsible for keeping the land clean and free of manure, they roped off the horses' grazing area.

The third and final gate was installed four miles south of the overseer's, Harry wanted his slaves to be happy and comfortable in their compound. The slaves living area was a one-square-mile. This gate was called the slave gate. Inside the slave complex were sixty small cabins that lined up in rows of fifteen across from each other, on two different dirt roads. Harry named them Charles and Drew Road. The cabins had four rooms, two on the lower level and two upstairs. Harry's slaves were a mixture of whites and coloreds. He tried to treat both groups the same, in some instances, the whites were treated worst. His experience with his own race was too often brutal.

Within the slave gate and a half mile from their cabins, was a church that gave the slaves hope. A bar with watered down liquor, to keep them mindless and comfortable with their confinement, yet alert enough to keep working. Lastly, there was a general store where they received their ration of food, material to make clothes for themselves, children, nurse, teacher, and the overseers. They also made beautiful quilts, for the Brown family to sell in town. The men designed and made furniture, that was sold to merchants across the state.

Outside the slave gate, were gargantuan tobacco fields that were separated into four half-mile square. Every four years, the crops were rotated which allowed three fields several years to rest. The tobacco was on the eastern side of the slave gate.

A half mile from the slave gate was the southern region of the outer gate.

The Forest

Completely wrapping around the outer gate, Harry left a half mile of an opened field. At the end of the half-mile, an eight-inch-wide ditch was dug thirteen and a half feet deep, six-inch steel plates were placed against the wall of the dugout. The ditch encompassed the twelve-mile outer gate. wherever a forest was planted, steel plates were installed. Harry hoped the steel plates would stop the tree roots from going under the clearing into the slave area, and perchance up the massive slave gate. Thus, enabling the slaves to climb up and over. He had an understanding, that nature had a way of sometimes interfering with plans but knew that his ingenuity would outmaneuver nature. Directly behind Harry's mansion, there was nothing but the barn. Harry planted a garden of wildflowers; behind the floral garden, he had a row of multiple trees put in. The scenery made a beautiful view that hid what was behind it. Even though the illegal plantation was built seven miles away, Harry did not want to take a chance on it being discovered. He left room for a hidden path, that led to the outer gate.

On the outside of the ditch, a seven-mile-thick forest was planted twenty-seven miles north and south and twenty miles east and west. For his own peace of mind and to keep from feeling claustrophobic, in the front of his mansion Harry left six acres of land opened and free from all the trees and gates. He also, increase the width of the long dirt road that led up to his home.

Inside the outer gate, a dense row of trees was planted on both sides of the divider gate. A forest was thickly planted around the outside of the children area. When they were outside the kids, nurse, and teacher had to look up to see out.

A clearing was left between the outer gate and the divider gate for Harry to get through. Between the divider and outer gate, another forest was planted behind the outer gate's opening all the way to the main gate, stopping at the plates.

The slaves' main labor was working in the tobacco fields. When they became older in their late fifties the men made furniture and women sewed. Harry realized that it was possible for someone to question where he was getting his crops and that the tobacco had to be inspected periodically. He learned how to cover his tracks through one of his KKK friends. The man had a made-up company to conceal his illegal activities. He died in a terrible fire accident that was set by his son who was also a member of the KKK organization. Unfortunately, the boy could not split his heart into two parts, hate people who were different from him and love everyone like him. Still, Harry used the man's theory and practice for H. B. Metropolis. He built a tobacco farm between MacCall and Titleburk, far enough away for his illegal plantation to stay hidden.

Outfox the American Government

Harry sat back in his chair exhausted, he had talked almost none stop. He said, "boy's, Vance, I am going to need your help to make all this happen."

Charles couldn't hold it in any longer. "Pop why are you doing this?"

Harry's answer shocked his son's but not Vance. He knew that Harry was a ruthless man. Vance put up with Harry because he was poor and needed the money.

Harry explained that the gate surrounded two acres of land was where children were going to be reared and taught a skill until they turned fourteen. And then given to a family of similar skills. The four-room cabin was going to be built for the kids and caretakers. I will hire two trusting women one a nurse the other a teacher, to raise the little monkeys," Harry said to proudly.

Drew cut in, "who's going to do all the work?"

"Good question," Harry said with a chuckle, "Since slavery is over, I'll hire those coloreds and whites walking around looking for work."

Vance finally got up the nerve to say something, he nervously cleared his throat, "Harry it sounds like you're going to lock yourself in with the slaves."

"No, not at all my good friend, I am going to build me a magnificent castle, not the size of Buckingham, but just as grand on the MacCall's land."

Charles asked, "are you tearing down this house?"

Harry stood up and went to the big picture window, he gazed down the long driveway before saying, "no, this is the house for the plantation, my castle will be built so I can get away, hold parties, and socials events without being detected." A few tears rolled down Harry's cheek, he wiped his eyes and sorrowfully whispered. "A place for me to feel normal."

It was as though Harry knew that he was destroying his family, from one generation to the next. The plantation master life would be wrapped in the secret so tight; they would cease to exist. Harry thought of Stella, he would never see her again, he thought, *who will get her money?"* His desire was to get H.B. Metropolis up and running, kill Baerbel, and marry Stella, he believed she would keep his secret.

Drew cut into Harry's thoughts when he asked, "When are you going to hire these people."

Harry turned and briefly looked at Charles, he went to Charles and patted his shoulder before answering Drew's question. Harry went to his seat and answered, "We'll get an early start tomorrow morning," he looked at Vance and said, "Vance you're staying here tonight."

Vance argued, "Harry, I got a wife, she will be worried and mad iffen' I ain't home ta' night."

Harry replied in an authoritative tone, "that was not a question." He went to the snacks that Bella had brought in earlier and grabbed a hand full of grapes.

Harry knew if he continued to live in his current home while developing his plantation, this would create a certain doom and gloom against the project. Harry foresaw, that keeping slaves on his property, would cause a catastrophic constitutional issue, that would land him in prison and destroy his plot to outfox the American Government. And then a lightbulb went off in Harry's head, he said softly to himself, "I'm building a museum." He looked around at his sons and Vance with a great big smile, he proudly said with a topmost lie, "I am building a museum." Satisfied with his fib, he stuffed three grapes in his mouth and smiled.

Baerbel's Letter

On the day of Harry's meeting about the plantation, Stella received Baerbel's letter. She was confused, distraught, in disbelief. At first, Stella thought a jealous crazed woman was trying to destroy her wedding. On the day of Harry's meeting, Stella took the letter to Billy who was at the Steel Mill. She figured he would know if Harry was married since they were good friends. When she arrived, a worker took her to Billy's office. After their greetings, she asked, "is Harry married? Are his children alive?"

Billy inquired of the reason she was asking, she handed him the letter from Baerbel. Billy froze before asking, "why did his wife send you this letter?"

Stella said, "Then, his wife is alive."

"Yes, they have two sons." Billy handed Stella the letter and asked, "why are you asking about Harry's family."

Stella said in sorrow, "it doesn't matter."

She left. Billy was in a state of confusion but had enough clarity to recognize that Stella was extremely distraught. As she walked out of the building, her shoulders were slumped, upper torso bent at the waist, her head lowered, when she got to the exit she cried. Billy wrote a note to Stella's children, he had one of the workers to deliver them the message. Her children attended a local college where they lived in the dorms. Stella's daughter, Matilda, received the note from Billy, she showed it to her brother, Morris, from the urgency of the note they left school immediately.

Three hours later when they arrived home, Stella had committed suicide. She was lying on her bed face up, holding the letter from Baerbel. Stella's son, Morris sent a servant to get Billy. They tried to read the letter their mother was holding but was afraid to touch the dead body. When Billy arrived, he was taken to Stella's bedroom. Billy entered the room, out of the corner of his eye, he saw a wedding dress and what looked like a tux hanging on the closet door. He asked, "was your mother getting married?"

Matilda answered, "yes, to a man from the south."

Billy looked at the name on the tux, it read, Harry V. Brown. That's when he knew the reason Baerbel had written the short note. Billy gently eased the letter out of Stella's hand, at the bottom of Baerbel's message, he wrote, "*She killed herself because of your lies. Our friendship died with her.*"

Billy said, "I will have my wife help you with the arrangements. He looked at Stella's sad face children and asked, "are you okay? You're welcome to stay with us if you like."

Billy went home and let Liza read the letter, he told her about Stella's suicide. Liza said, "we both said, that Harry was acting differently when he was here."

Billy said sadly, "And now we know what it was. He told Stella that his wife and children were dead."

"We opened our home and hearts to that man," Liza said before going to Stella's home to prep the body.

Billy mailed the letter to Harry with no return address, he went to the Brown Still Mill and resigned as the manager. A worker asked, "when are we shipping these plates and rods?"

Billy answered, "a few years. Harry requested over forty thousand rods and the same number of plates."

The worker asked, "are you staying that long?"

Billy thought long and hard before replying, "I always finish a job, yes I'm staying."

When Billy returned home, Liza was in the sitting room crying, she asked, "how could Harry do such a thing? Those kids are only nineteen and eighteen."

Billy looked at his wife and said, "he killed Stella with lies and his parents with hate."

"What did you say about Mr. and Mrs. Brown?"

Billy ignored Liza's question and said, "I quit the job, we're leaving after the rods are mailed to Harry. I always complete what I start."

"A few years gives you time to fix this Billy, you always do, we don't have to leave."

"No, my dear, I want nothing to do with a lying murderer, we'll move to our home in Vermont when the rods are made."

Liza asked, "did you ever find out what they are for?"

Their conversation was cut short when someone knocked on the door. Liza went to the door and opened it, it was Morris and Matilda, with suitcases.

Harry was still munching on grapes, his sons, and Vance had joined him. Harry said, "I'll get Bella to prepare us something to eat."

Charles said, "this is good pops," he grabbed a sandwich and took a big bite.

Meanwhile, Bella was in Baerbel's bedroom turning the covers back for her to slide between. Baerbel whispered to Bella as she got in bed, "Keep yo Massa away from me ta'night. When he's mad likes dis,' he be too rough foe' tiny me. Offer him yo' Susie, she be ten and of age. Being a slave make her tough nough' to handle yo' Massa. I's delicate."

Bella stopped tucking her mistress in and stood straight and tall. Harsh memories rushed through her mind. She remembered being slapped only an hour ago in the kitchen. When her grand-daughter, Susie, was a two-month-old baby, Massa used her naked body as a foot warmer. Her husband was beaten to death, her twelve-year-old daughter died from Massa and four of his friends raped her. Clara, her only living child was crippled from Drew pushing her down hardwood stairs. At the time Clara was twenty-seven and Drew fifteen. Mistress and Massa thought it was funny, Baerbel said, "she need ta' watch where she goin."

Bella went over to help Clara off the floor, Mr. Brown told Bella to mind her business and that Clara was strong enough to care for herself. Bella could still see her daughter crawling down the hall, into the kitchen. Bella went over to the door to open it, Drew pushed her out the way and said, "she can do it herself. It's entertaining to watch her slide on the floor." He laughed.

Clara slowly crawled off the porch into the yard where she passed out. The Brown's kept Bella working for three hours longer that night, and Drew locked her son-in-law, Joe, in the barn so he could not help his wife. Before leaving her duties on that evening, Bella fixed the Brown's lemonade with water, spit, sugar, and her urine, and then she went home to nurse her daughter back to good health. If only Charles had been at home that evening, he would have stopped the ordeal. Charles had no qualm defending the ill-treated.

All But One

Bella's memories ended, she looked at her mistress. "I-will-not-allow yo' evil huz'ban to touch any of us ever again," Bella said through clenched teeth. "This ends ta'day."

Baerbel said hatefully, "whad' you say ta' me? Evil woman."

Without saying a word, she left Baerbel's bedroom, went down the stairs, quickly walked down the long hall, through the kitchen, and out the back door where she saw her son-in-law, and said, "follow me."

The whole time Baerbel screamed over and over, "whad' you say ta' me?!"

From upstairs, a muffled sound of Baerbel's voice seeped down the steps through the double doors into the drawing-room. "I'll be right back," Harry said calmly. A few minutes later Harry had Baerbel by the arm dragging her down the steps, through the hallway, into the kitchen, out the back door straight to the slave shacks.

While Clara was washing clothes, Bella was telling her and Joe about leaving, when Mr. Brown rushed past them dragging his protesting wife. Joe left, but Bella and Clara watched the calamity. Harry pushed Baerbel into a shack, closed the door and fastened it so Baerbel was trapped inside.

The mother and daughter duo froze as Harry walked towards them. He said to Bella, "get some of her things and put them in front of the shack's door. I will check on her in the morning."

Bella smiled as she said, "Yaw Sir." She and Clara watched him leap on the porch and enter the house.

Bella said laughing, "he said he'd put her in a slave shack iffen' she didn't Shut-up."

Clara remarked, "and so's he did."

Both women laughed until they cried.

Bella began to leave; she looked back and said, "Follow me." She and Clara found Joe by the barn getting a wagon ready for a trip to town. Bella said to Joe, "hitch up the good horse and wagon, we's leavin' ta'day." To Clara, Bella said, "Go fetch da kids, dey' help us pack."

"But mama whar's we's gonna' go? me and you cain't walk far."

"Slavery be ova' child. Why's we's still here? Everybody else be gone. Iffen yah' don't come, me and my grand chil'ren leave wid' out ja."

Joe asked, "I's agree we need to leave, but how we gone go, mama?"

"Ain't you going to town fo' Massa di'reckly."

"Yes, ma'am."

"Go ax Massa iffen he be ready foe' you ta' go. Massa don't likes runnin' up a bill wid' da' shops, so he gib' you money."

"So's we's got a chance ta' run mama?" Clara asked.

"Sho's looks like it."

"Massa gonna here us going in and out da house," Joe said in a matter of fact tone.

Clara told Joe, "he gib' mama a reason to go up and down da' stairs."

"Yes, he did, we's goin' ta Saint Louie, I's like's da name. Sounds like's good church folk lib' der." Bella said daydreaming. She continued, "now Joe, put da horse and buggy on side da' house." She looked at Clara, "go git da chil'ren', we be leavin' soon. I's got a couple of thangs' ta' git out da' house."

Joe asked, "whad" iffen' Massa hear us."

"He ain't, Massa and dem' in da middle room, we's by da' kitchen and da' liberry."

When Bella left, Clara said to Joe, "hitch up two horses, we's got's a long way ta' go."

Before entering the house, Bella removed her shoes, and had her grandsons to do the same, they left them on the porch. Since Baerbel was in a slave shack, Bella went to Baerbel's room and helped herself to bed sheets, spreads, quilts, blankets, plus clothes and coats for the female, she also found fifty dollars. She took the things from Baerbel's room to the bottom of the steps, handed them to her grandsons who took the items to the wagon. Joe, Susie, and Paula packed them on the wagon, while the boys went back to the bottom of the steps, where Bella had laid more things. She went to Harry's bedroom and found seven hundred dollars in his drawer, and ten dollars lying on top of the dresser. She also took several of Harry's shirts, pants, shoes, coats, and his bedding. In Drew's room, she took several of his pants, shirts, and shoes for her grandsons, all he had was five dollars, she took it. She went to Charles room and found two hundred and fifty dollars,

All But One

she only took his money and put it in her apron pockets with the other money. Charles wore expensive fancy clothes and shoes specifically designed for him; he did not ware ready-made clothes. Bella and her family worked together in an assembly line until Bella had what they needed.

While Bella was upstairs, her daughter was in the kitchen, preparing food for their trip, she also took pots, pans, and silverware. When the boys finished assisting Bella, they helped their dad fill two big barrels with water from the well.

It took Bella, her family, and Paula, six trips carrying the things from the back porch to the wagon. Harry gave Joe seventy-five cents to buy the items he needed. "Paula, you should come wid' us," Bella suggested.

"Massa say he git' me help, so's I's stayin' foe' dat," Paula replied, "y'all family, maybe I's meet me a huz'ban, git's married, have chil'ren' of my own, be a family." She smiled, "den' I's leave."

"You be da' only slave here. God be wid' you young lass. When you leave, come ta' Saint Louie." Bella said to Paula as she and the kids laid down in the back of the wagon. Paula helped Joe cover everything over except the two barrels.

Paula stood on the side of the house, so Harry would not see her waving bye. Joe nervously road down the long driveway. When Joe was around the bend in the road and could no longer be seen by Harry or his sons, Joe exhaled, and said, "we made it."

Paula stood watching until Bella's family was safely out of sight, sadness sweltered through her. Her heart felt like it was going to stop, she pushed through and returned to the back of the house where she had chores to do. Bella had already prepared dinner for that evening's meal, all Paula had to do was warm everything up. She could barely see as she set the dining room dinner table, tears flowed from her eyes like a waterfall. For the first time in her seventeen years on earth, Paula was all alone, it was suffocating

In the drawing-room, the snacks were gone, and the meeting had resumed. Harry was so deep into his explanation of the H. B. Metropolis layout, that neither he nor the three men heard Bella's family escape. Unbeknown to nervous Joe, from where the men and Harry were sitting, they could not see out the big picture window. Bella's plan worked, she and her family escaped Harry Vincent Brown in style.

With slavery being over, Joe, Clara, Susie, Bella, and her two grandsons, drove through town without a fuss. When they got outside of town Bella looked back and said, "look yonder,' Massa ain't knows we be gone." She looked up at the sky, "everythang' be bigga' in freedom. Looking back at people going in and out the shops, she asked, "Massa own all dat?"'

"Yes ma'am, since he killed mistress folk," Joe said as though it was an everyday occurrence.

Everyone on the wagon was quiet, only the sound of the horses trotting and the wheels crunching on the dirt road was heard.

Joe said, "mama, Massa won't's you ta' fix breakfast in da' mornin, he won't's grits, bacon, ham, biscuits, gravy, and eggs. He won't's a big breakfast."

They all laugh except Bella, she asked, "Joe, whad' you say bout' da' MacCall?"

They sat in silence for a while, Joe said, "Massa killed da' MacCall's and dey' slave girl."

"What?" Bella asked.

"Dey slave girl had a strange look on her face when she looked out da' window, now I's' knows it be da' look of deaf"'

Bella asked, "Lawdy Joe, you seed deaf in da' face?"

Again, they road awhile in silence.

Bella broke the quiet when she said, "I took over one thousand dollars from Massa house." Bella hushed for a moment, and then said, "I's be feelin' guilty but since Massa be a killin' folk, I's ain't no moe.'"

Joe said, "I's glad you got dat' money, cause' Massa gib me, change."

"I's thanks da' Massa foe' learnin' us to read, write, and cipher, we's rich. "Bella said with great Joy.

Her daughter said, "Saint Louie here we's come."

Susie asked, "Whar's we's stayin' grandma?"

"Baby girl, in a nice house, wid' da money I's buy us a place we can call home." Bella began humming, she stopped and said, I's neva seed past da' pantation.' Slave go from dey' shack to da' field, back to da' shack."

"We's gots' da' church and school grandma."

"Still on da' pantation' child."

Bella began singing, "Swang' low, sweet cherry-out."

Joe, Clara, and their children responded, "Comin' foe' ta' carry me home."

Bella said, "Our chariot be comin' and we's goin' ta freedom land. Mistress goes ta' town she come back happy, Massa goes ta' a Bostin' he comes back happy, we's' goin' ta' Saint Louie,' we's' ain't comin' back, we stay der,' be happy."

Clara said, "We's be free body, mind, and soul."

"Amen." Joe and Bella said together.

One of Bella's grandsons said, "thank you grandma foe' savin' us.

"You welcome my child. It be God dat' save us." Bella replied.

Bella and her family followed the sun going west; oftentimes they received help, food, and direction on their journey. A couple of times they assisted the Underground Railroad Conductors by giving runaways a ride to the next station. For her kindness, God blessed Bella and her family as they traveled westward.

VI

The Hired Hands

The night after the meeting Drew was in his room snoring. Charles was with a girl in his room, Vance was wide awake worrying about his wife. While Baerbel was frightened in the slave shack with only a raggedy chair to sit in and straw to lay on, Bella was on her way to St. Louis.

Harry was awake in his room, frightening questions and nightmares were keeping him up, the same two queries fluttered in his mind. Will I get caught? If so, what will the government do to me? Harry was determined not to be defeated, he sat up in bed, clenched his teeth tight together, and heatedly muddled, "this plan has to be designed so no-one will ever find out." He laid down, He looked at the clock, it was three o'clock, he finished by murmuring, "I'll see to it."

Harry laid down, pulled the covers over his shoulder and said, "they are poor people, this is good for them." Harry tossed and turned and finally said, "Yes," they will have a home, food, job, and each other. Yes, this is the right thing to do." Harry settled the matter by claiming, "it's the Yankees fault."Harry's conscience was ripping him apart, he could not sleep. He pushed the covers back, leaped out of bed, and claimed as if there was truth behind his decree, "I am building a museum." Satisfied, Harry returned to bed and had one bad dream after the other. The nightmare that woke him up, were teary eyes dripping like raindrops, he ran so he would not get wet. One big eye was catching up with him with a thousand smaller ones trailing behind. The big eye grew the closer it got to Harry, it was dripping blood and tears, the faster he ran the slower he moved. Harry looked up at the enormous eye, it was his. The eye hovered over Harry and his twenty-seven-mile plantation, he became stationary in a frozen posture, the eye blinked and darkness overpowered the light of day. When the eye opened, an oversized drop of blood was oozing down towards him and his property. Harry woke up screaming and covered in sweat. He leaped out of bed, looked at the clock it was three-thirty, Harry had a small bar in his room, he poured himself a glass of alcohol and studied his chart.

To keep track of H. B Metropolis, Harry developed a phase chart that he kept in his room. Phase one, hire ex-slaves. Two, build slave shacks and his barn. Three, hire builders from Europe to build his castle and plant the forest. Four, install the gates and plates. Five, keep the hired hands kids ages newborn to three-year-old in the children's area, poison the rest and Baerbel. His biggest problem was how to poison a large group of people, the MacCall's were easy, it was only three of them. Six, hire a nurse and teacher to care for his hired hands children. Harry laid down and went to sleep.

A few hours later he woke up tired but excited, he put a check mark next to hire ex-slaves. He exited his room and locked the door. He gaily strolled down the upstairs hallway, knocked on both of his sons' bedroom doors as he went past. And the door of the bedroom where Vance got little sleep due to worrying about his wife. Harry whistled merrily as he lightly bounced down the stairs and cheerfully strolled along the long hallway to the kitchen. He pushed the kitchen door wide, closed his eyes, and took in a big gulp of air to smell the deliciousness of a big breakfast cooking. Mentally he tasted the fried eggs, bacon, ham, grits, and Bella's biscuits were light and fluffy on the inside and just crispy enough on the outside. His mouth watered as he thought of dipping the biscuits in Bella's homemade gravy. "Hum-hum good eating," Harry mumbled to himself, he loved Bella's cooking. He opened his eyes, what a disappointment, the kitchen was clean, tidy, and void of Bella and food cooking. What he smelt was a memory etched in his imagination.

"Bella!" He shouted, then bellowed in an ear-shattering deep throat, "Bel-llaaaa!" His stomach was empty, his face beet red, and his temper was on the rise, if he had a chimney on top his head, fire and lava would erupt.

Paula ran from another room into the kitchen. Harry was standing in the middle of the room when Paula entered, she nervously asked, "what be wrong Massa."

"Where is Bella?"

"I's thank' dey' gone, Massa."

Paula was four feet eleven and small, Harry bent down to her level and asked, "Why do you think that?"

"I's cain't' find dem' no whar's Massa."

"Git breakfast ready," he snapped before storming out the Kitchen, he leaped off the porch and ran into Charles and the girl.

Charles and the girl were kissing. The girl got on her horse, reached down and ruffled Charles' hair. Charles lifted her dress to her knee, and kissed the side of her leg, she giggled. Harry watched the two in horror. Charles slapped the horse backside and said, giddy-up. Harry stood in disbelief. When the girl galloped off, he asked Charles, "what time did she come here?"

Charles said, "last night, pops."

Harry could not believe his son answer was so candid. He said, "Young man stop bringing your women in my house."

"Okay pops." Charles leaped up the porch stairs two at a time, he turned and winked at Harry, and then said, "I'm hungry, where's Bella?"

As Harry wrestled with the raggedy barn doors, he said out loud, "did that silly boy just wink at me." Once inside he saw that two horses and his largest wagon were gone. Anger surged through his twisted mind, he was leveled to a silent mad man, his wide chest heaved up and down as though he had just run a twenty-six-mile marathon. Harry did something that he had not done since running away and leaving Elijah behind. He did slave work, got the horses and wagons ready. He went to the slave quarters and let Baerbel out the shack. "Clean up and help Paula with breakfast," Harry demanded.

Baerbel sprinted past Harry, she ran up the porch steps and landed heavy. She ran into the house breathless. When she entered the kitchen she humbly said, "Paula, I's be back down ta' help."

Paula was so shocked she froze for a few seconds. She was already sad and lonely, now she had to put up with the mean mistress. "I should'a gone wid' dem." Paula whispered to herself.

Harry stumbled in the house like a drunkard, he looked at Paula who was cooking and said, "I'm getting you help."

Paula slumped. When Harry left the kitchen, she said under her breath, "is da' misses my help, I's hoppin' ta git' a huz'ban." She delicately cried, wiping the tears away she prepared breakfast.

Bella had taught Paula how to cook but being only seventeen years old, her culinary skills were no match to her trainer. Paula felt so alone, it was overpowering, so much so, it felt like someone was holding her under water. Charles saw Paula working around the house with tears rolling down her cheek, he had seen her use her apron hem to dry her face. Charles thought she looked so sad and hapless; he wondered the reason Bella left her behind. He went to Paula and said, "when we get back from town, we will have several people to help you." He began to leave but turned and said, "you are going to get paid and no longer work for free."

Paula looked up at Charles and sheepishly said, "thank you sir."

"Cheer up little one, life is going to get better for you." Charles said before going outside.

He pulled the horses and flatbed wagons that his father had gotten together, around the front of the house where he met his dad, Drew, and Vance. Harry told the men, "It's six in the morning, make your last round to town no later than five o'clock this evening, I want all hired hands standing in the back of the house. Baerbel and Paula are preparing food for us, eat between drop off if you get hungry. Leave the hired hands and return to town and pick up any stragglers. If we find Bella and her family, they'll be beaten unmercifully and returned to the plantation."

Harry looked at Vance and said, "I need your wife's help, after your last run, go get her and return tomorrow with all your things. You'll be staying for a while."

Before Vance could reply, Harry pulled off saying, "let's go."

Vance watched Drew and Harry's forms grow smaller, as their horses trotted down the long pathway with their empty wagons noisily rumbling behind them. He wondered if Harry recognized him as a grown man. Vance whispered to himself, "my wife will not be a part of this." Vance's heart was heavy as a sack of bricks, something didn't feel right to him. Still, he began to pull off.

Charles saw the expression on Vance's face, he rode over to him and asked, "are you feeling okay?"

Vance replied, "No."

"If I see Bella, I shall wish her well," Charles said.

"Me too." Vance said and then asked, "How do you feel about your father's plans? Building a museum like slavery was a good thing." He paused for a moment before continuing, "Something's not right. All the gates, so tall and thick."

Charles asked, "I wonder, why?"

"Yeah, why? I never been to a museum, do they have gates?" Vance asked.

"No, they have doors not gates."

"I feel like I need to escape like Bella."

"Me too," Charles looked at Vance and continued, "at first dad said he was keeping slaves in the gates, then he changed and said they're not actually slaves only actors."

"If they're actors, he won't need the gates."

"Well," Charles began before continuing, "dad said nothing about locking the gates."

"Hum, no he did not. We'll see." Vance looked at Charles and said, "let's go."

Despite their disagreement with Harry, the two men pulled off towards town.

By the end of the day Harry, Charles, Drew, and Vance had collected over three hundred freed men and women. Harry called them his hired hands. Harry, Baerbel, Charles, Drew, Vance, and Paula standing next to Baerbel, stood on the back porch while the hired hands were in the yard looking up at them. Anticipation flowed through their thoughts, each hoped to be employed and not returned to slavery.

Harry answered their unasked question, "I have a job for all of you, it will take about eleven years to complete at which time...."

Before Harry could finish, the coloreds and whites hollered with joy, the men danced all over the back yard, some of the women did a little holy dance, the young children and babies didn't understand the reason for the loud commotion, so they cried. Except for one white male that thought he was better than the rest, asked proudly, "will I's haft' ta' work wid' dem?" he nodded towards the coloreds.

Harry had a flashback of the family that stole his money. His Bostonian accent was so thick when he hissed, "if you want to get paid, you will," Harry sounded like he was from England.

Through the noise, Harry screamed and yelled out of control, he couldn't get them to quiet down. The louder Harry yelled the more deafening sound they made. Baerbel ran into the kitchen and grabbed two heavy cast-iron skillets. She returned carrying them, her arms tremble as she held the hefty skillets beyond her waistline. She banged the skillets together which caused her to vibrate. Even so, she got everyone's attention and quiet, even Harry. He looked at her and yelled, "was that necessary?"

Still trying to gather her composure, Baerbel said smugly, "dey quiet ain't dey?"

With Drew by his side, Harry looked down at the large crowd standing before him. He whispered to Drew, "they look like different types of monkeys."

Drew laughed as he agreed with Harry and said, "they do dad."

Harry said to his hired hands, "I brought you here because I am employing you to work for me, you will be given a weekly salary."

The hired hands became silent, "sir how much money are you going to pay us?" Though a black man, he did not sound like the others.

Harry whispered to Drew, "he asked like he's used to making money and trying to talk proper like an affluent white man." Harry then looked down at the man and said, "thirty-five cents a week."

Cheers from the crowd thundered in Harry's back yard.

In 1865, thirty-five cents could purchase the same amount of groceries that forty dollars would in 2017.

The proper speaking man said, "thank you, sir, I use to make six cents a week, you see sir," he lied and told the truth all at the same time, "I was born free and attended school, still I was unable to get a job. Sir, thirty-five cents is very generous of you, thank you." He looked at Paula and smiled.

Cheers rolled through the crowd, Harry looked at Baerbel, she hit the skillets together, except, not quite as hard this time. They quieted down, Harry continued, "the pay scale is like this, the men twenty to fifty years of age salary is thirty-five cents a week, the older men and women fifty-one and older will receive twenty-five cents a week, male and females fourteen years old to nineteen will receive fifteen cents per week, payday is every Friday."

One of the old slaves yelled out, "fine by me sir, cause I's' neva' make a cent in my life," he danced a jig.

Harry continued, "If you can count, you know that you're about to be rich slav-ah, I mean…," Harry cleared his throat retraced his words and shuddered, "you-you're going to be ric-rich pep-folk-people."

Harry choked trying to say the words.

A colored woman said, "thank you sir, foe' the jobs, and foe' callin' us people, humans."

She looked at the white woman standing next to her and whispered, "he almost choked ta' deaf' tryin' ta' git' it out."

Both women put their hands over their mouth and giggled softly.

The white woman said, "Sir. I's got no place ta' stay."

"I'll get to that." Harry told the woman.

The man that was dancing stopped, took in a deep gulp of air and whispered, "glory, glory, glory," he said, "sir my name be, Zeek."

Harry sheepishly smiled and said, "let me introduce myself, I am Harry V. Brown, standing next to me is my youngest son Drew Brown." He looked around for Charles, who was standing by the door, Harry motioned for him to come over. Charles stood next to his mother, "this is my eldest son Charles, standing next to Charles is my wife Baerbel, and next to her is our ex-slave, Paula. She will show you to your new home. You may clean and fix them up as you please, soon we will build new cabins."

Paula stepped forward with a big smile plastered on her face, she had become emancipated with the others. She was free, she was going to make money like Massa Charles said, and she liked the educated colored man. Her tears dried up, Massa Charles was right, he brought back a lot of help. A feeling of joy and peace caused her heart to flutter.

Harry looked around and spotted Vance standing all alone, he introduced his best friend, "over there by the door is my good friend, Vance."

Vance was deep in thought, he did not hear Harry call the first time, Harry called a second time, "Vance."

It startled Vance, he looked at Harry, who waved, then Vance waved to the crowd. He looked down and saw Moses standing in the front of the crowd. When Moses got on his wagon, he showed Vance, his graduation certificate from an architect school. Vance could not believe his luck, Harry was going to pay him very well, and he would get Moses to build him a house in Titleburk. Vance was ready to go home and tell his wife that God had answered their prayers.

The arrogant white male asked, "what kind of work is we doin' sir?"

"I am turning this place into a huge memorial, a museum showing the joy of the good old South. Years from now, people will come to see our history, the beautiful rolling hills, shimmering sun, glorious green grass and trees, everyone happy and working together."

One of the women from the crowd commented, "that's mighty nice of you sir, this is work I believe we all be proud of."

One of the men yelled out, "I agree wid' her, I's' mighty proud to work foe' yo' sir, I's' thought we be pickin' cotton or sugarcane." He then turned and said to the man standing behind him, "I don't know 'bout da good old souf, rollin' hills, and happy.'

A white male whispered, "he should say, beat till you die, starve to death, chopped off limbs, sale yo' chil'ren." The man held up his hand and showed his two missing fingers.

A woman that was standing next to the men said, "Dat's what I member bout da' good old souf."

While the hired hands deliberated softly among themselves, Harry pushed Drew in front of him, and said yelling, "my son Drew, will explain the work you'll be doing."

Drew stammered and stuttered as he made a clumsy attempt to give them their instructions. "Grou-gro-group on-on-one."

Harry softly whispered in Drew's ear, "calm yourself, son, they are nothing but animals, talk to them like you talk to the horses."

Drew looked over the crowd and smiled, he remembered how he talked to the animals, he pulled his shoulders back, held his head high, closed his eyes and bellowed in a rough voice, "I'm dividing you up into five working groups." He opened his eyes and gave them their instructions according to Harry's plan. Afterward Drew told them that it will take about nine to eleven years to complete the job.

Another hired hand asked, "afta dat, den' what?"

Charles stepped forward and said, "dad, may I?"

"Sure son." Harry scratched his head, pulled Charles close to him and chuckled, "leave the woman alone."

Charles whispered. "not my kind pops," he laughed. "I like them clean and rich."

Harry pat Charles on the back and said, "son after my own heart."

Drew listening said, "everybody knows Charles has women stretched from one end of the county to the next, let's get on with this."

Charles unique deep soft velvet voice caused everyone to pay attention, especially the women. Harry looked on with pride and a smile plastered on his face. Charles said, "You can leave, so save most of your money, after all, you're staying on this land for free. When the work is completed, you can go anywhere you want." He looked throughout the group and said to the coloreds, "To all the coloreds, slavery is over, you too can go anywhere you want."

They mumble among themselves, then one of them stepped forward and said, "Mr. Charles, sir. I speak foe' all us, we's gonna' stay and work foe' you sir. You's got's a find family."

Harry noticed they addressed Charles, not him or Drew. He decided; he was going to hand the plantation over to ruthless Drew. He wanted Charles to live and enjoy life. Which was something he nor Drew knew how to do.

Another slave asked, "how much of our money will we have ta' payback to you?"

All But One

This time Drew jumped ahead of his brother, he pushed Charles aside and hollered in an agitating raspy voice, "none, the money is all yours."

Harry watched the hired hands ignore Drew, they looked at Charles, Harry got their attention when he asked, "can any of you build furniture? Are there ladies that can sew?"

One woman yelled out, "I'm a candle-maker."

Other hired hands raised their hands in answer to Harry's question.

The man who spoke so eloquently and was born free said, "sir my name is Moses, thank you for your generosity."

Harry dismissed them, "you're dismissed, you may start cleaning the old cabins. Tomorrow I'll give you some money to purchase supplies for your different tasks."

The white arrogant white man asked, "do I have to stay with them?" He pointed at the coloreds.

Charles looked at the man and said, "we do not want your kind here, leave now." He looked over the crowd and said, "you are asking too many questions, follow Paula," he gently took Paula's elbow and led her to the porch steps, he concluded by saying, "she will take you to the shacks where you're staying."

Paula took the lead, Harry's hired hands followed her, Moses ran past the others and caught up with Paula. He wanted to get to know her better, in his mind she was important, she stood on the porch with the family, and a white man helped her off the porch. As soon as he saw her standing with them, he began making plans to woo Paula and make her his wife. She was introduced like she was one of the family. The fact that Paula was petite with a sparkling personality and very beautiful, was not what he was looking for. Moses wanted to rise above all others, he wanted power, he wanted to stand on the porch with the family and be introduced. Paula was his ticket to make it happen.

As the hired hands were on their way to the slave shacks, the arrogant man was following them, Charles jumped off the porch and stood in front of the man and said, "you're going the wrong way."

Several males, coloreds and whites, stood united on Charles side. The man looked around and saw that he was outnumbered, he left.

Charles said, "thank you all." As they were going to the shacks, he shook their hands.

Harry and Drew joined Charles in the yard, Harry said to Charles, "normally, men with many women, are not fighters, you have bravery I've never seen before."

Charles said, "It's no big deal pops."

Vance was still standing on the porch in a happy daze. He was hoping Harry would let him use a small wagon and horse to go get his wife, Deb.

Harry said watching the hired hands, "there's no difference between race's when poor."

Charles replied saying, "there's no difference no matter the situation. If a colored, Chinese, white, or any person cut themselves, we all bleed red blood. When we're hungry and our stomach growl, it's in the exact same place, our hearts are in the same place, legs, arms, eyes, ears, nose all in the same place. Only the skin color is different, God created mankind in an array of colors like a beautiful rainbow."

"Hum, I never looked at it like that Charles," Drew commented as he cut Charles off before asking, "What's next?"

Harry said, "I am going to teach them to read."

Charles asked, "why."

Harry replied, "It will build their minds to be thinkers, a little education will make them better workers. Boy, before this war none of my slaves left because I would teach them." Harry paused for a moment, he saw Moses talking to Paula, he smiled, and continued, "they don't mind being a slave as long as they can learn to read and write, make them feel equal to their Master." Harry got caught up lying and said, "my daddy's slaves ran all the time..."

Charles looked confused and cut in asking, "your daddy had slaves? I thought he owned a steel mill."

Harry walked-ran from his boys towards the house, when he leaped on the porch, Vance asked if he could use one of his horses and a small carriage. Harry consented.

Drew and Charles watched Harry run to the house, "Hum," Drew muttered to himself before saying, "Charles, I remember dad talking about a mill. That might be something we should look into."

"Why did he call his hired hands, slaves?" Charles asked and concluded, "another matter to investigate."

The next day early in the morning, Vance entered his lopsided shack, bursting with joy. Deb, his wife, went ballistic, she bombarded him with questions. "Where have you been? Was it with a woman? Did you get too drunk to come home? Did you get lost? Where were you? You know I don't like staying in these woods by myself." She slapped him, she calmed down and asked, "why didn't you come home last night. I was worried."

Vance went over to the table and emptied out his pocket. Harry had paid Vance in dollars and not change. Vance spread the money on the table.

Deb stood silently as Vance talked. When Vance took a breath, Deb ran into the askew bedroom her husband had built and got her two dresses and another pair of undergarments. The rest of her belongings, she had on. Vance went into the bedroom and grabbed his other pair of pants and shirt. Deb asked as she put their clothes in the frayed bag her mother had made for her, "how are we going to get there?"

She looked around the cabin and got the tea set her mother had given them, it was still in the box. there was nothing else Deb wanted to take. They had two each, tin plate, forks, cups, and one pot. Vance said, "let me show you." Vance took the bag and tea set and placed them next to the door.

He grabbed Deb's hand and took her outside. Vance said, "in Harry's carriage."

Deb marveled at the carriage, then went to the horse and rubbed its head. She looked at Vance and said, "honey, you're the best."

Vance and Deb fed and brushed the horse down, Deb ran in the cabin got the extra cover, she returned outside where Vance helped her spread it over the horse.

Eight o'clock that morning they took one last look at the shack then pulled off, Deb said, "we've lived in this cabin for twenty years." She looked back and watched their home disappear, then said, "I hope we stay humble and never forget our modest beginning."

Vance looked at Deb and said, "we will."

Deb suggested, "let's give it five years and not stay the full eleven."

"I was thankin' the same "

Deb was excited about their adventure she asked, "how long will it take to get there?"

"With this horse, we will arrive in town by four o'clock."

Deb said, "I packed us a lunch."

Deb was from Indianapolis. She ran away from home the night her stepdad entered her room and tried to have his way. sixteen-year-old Deb surprised him, she clawed, kicked, scratched, then her knee got him right in the growing. She leaped out of bed and ran to her mom's bedroom with him limping behind her. She told her mom what he tried to do. He called Deb a liar. Her mom said, "go back to bed child and stop fibbing."

Deb was not about to let him get away with what he tried to do, she yelled, "those scratches, bite marks, is proof I had to defend myself from this wasted pieced of trash you married."

When she turned to leave her stepdad slapped her hard in the back of the head. Her mom asked the man, "why did you do that?" She got up and followed her daughter.

The stepdad yelled, "she nothing but a troubling liar."

Deb had a big bag in her room that her mom had made a few years back. Deb said, "I have to get out of this house."

"You're sixteen now," her mom said as she helped Deb pack the bag, then said, "by the time I was your age I had two boys and pregnant with you."

Deb half hazard dumped stuff in the bag; her mom would take it out, fold everything neatly then put it back. Deb stopped and watched her mom undo the mess she was doing, she looked at the bag and said, "you made me this when I went to see grandma."

Deb's mom had made the bag out of potato sacks, she took yellow, red, and green yarn and made two large sunflowers, she sewed one on the front, and the other on the back. She made the handles out of pine wood and the interior lining from an old dress she could no longer wear. When the bag was all packed, Deb and her mom went to the kitchen, she gave her daughter the jar filled with change and said there's about twenty dollars in the jar. Deb's mom looked around the room, went to the bottom of the stairs and looked up, then tiptoed back to the kitchen. Deb watched her in confusion and asked, "what're you doing."

Her mom opened a drawer, reached in the back and pulled out one hundred dollars and handed it to Deb. She said, "make a better life for yourself."

Deb hugged her mom tight. The woman waved as her daughter was leaving, she said, "Deb, write."

Deb began walking south. The only thing Deb knew how to do was make alcoholic drinks. Her mom had taught Deb how to make inebriating beverages. On her journey south, the young girl lied about her age to secure bar jobs. She never stayed in a town longer than four months, Deb wrote to her mother about her adventures as she traveled deeper into the South. After three years going from one town to the next, Deb tired of being homeless, she wanted stability. She landed a barmaid job in Ogville where she met Vance. He was a short unassuming gentle twenty-year-old man. Deb, in contrast, was a loud rough nineteen-year-old. Yet, something clicked when they met.

A few months after the meeting, Deb and Vance got married, Deb wrote to her mother announcing that she was married and had an address. Over the years being with Vance, his loud rowdy wife calmed down and became a loving caring spouse.

On their fifth anniversary, Vance asked Deb to tell her mom to come for a visit or move in, since her husband had passed away. After Deb wrote the letter, Vance got busy and began building a back room for her mom. A few months later, her mother sent a letter stating that she was on the way.

Deb's mom packed her things and was on the next stagecoach going to live with her daughter and her son-in-law. She had purchased a gift for the couple. It was a tea set with sunflowers painted on the cup and saucer. She couldn't wait to see her daughter's happy face when she opened the box. Deb's mom was so excited to see her daughter, she was overly talkative to anyone that was close enough to hear.

A month later, a stranger knocked on Deb and Vance door, he had bad news. The man told her that the stagecoach driver was going too fast around a mountain, the coach flipped over and crashed at the bottom. He sadly looked at Deb and said, "your mother was in the stagecoach," he looked at Vance then back at Deb and said, "Ma'am I am very sorry, there were no survivors."

Deb asked, "how you know it was my mother."

He handed Deb a package and an envelope, her mother wrote that she was happy to see her daughter after so many years. At the last minute she decided to bring the letter and package, she wanted to be the one to hand them their gift. Deb opened the box, not one dish had cracked or broke. Deb fainted. Fifteen years later, she was going to meet Harry for the first time and start a new life. Deb was happy, every time a run-a-way knocked at the door, she relived the man standing in the doorway giving her bad news about her mom.

Harry's carriage road smooth as they traveled down the dirt road, Deb smiled and said, "this is nice," she looked at Vance and asked, "where are we staying?"

"You'll see." Vance smiled proudly.

Around five, Deb was giddy when they road through town, and astonished when she saw Harry's mansion, Deb said, "It's big and beautiful."

Vance went around back where a hired hand took the horse to the barn, a second man took their bag. When Deb saw the cabin, she loved it even though it was rustic and old, it stood upright and was larger than their two-room small shack that leaned to the side. Vance smiled as he watched her eyes light up with joy.

Deb said, "It's perfect." She looked back to see how close they were to Harry's mansion, she said, "I cannot see it."

A forest separated the cabin from the mansion, a line of trees stood like toy soldiers along the path that led to Harry's home. A shabby fence went around the cabin, the back yard had enough room to grow a big garden and to raise chickens. Deb looked at Vance and said, "we will have chicken, fresh eggs in the morning. We will repair the fence."

Vance said, "don't have to, Harry is building a two-story cabin for us."

"Brand new," Deb asked in excitement.

When they went inside Deb loved the four-room cabin, it was furnished and had a bed with a store-bought mattress. In their old cabin, Deb and Vance slept on a straw mattress. She went through the cabin that had soft furniture, real dishes, silverware, pots and pans, curtains at the window and not paper.

She looked at Vance and said, "it's going to be a little hard for me to be humble in this cabin. I'm feeling a little proud."

Laughing, Vance said, "you will."

As she ran from room to room the man and Vance just stood in the living room, waiting for her to calm down, when she did, she said, "I love it. I wish mom was here."

Harry began watching Moses closely, he was different from the others. One day when Charles was in the hired hands living area, he saw Moses working on his cabin, he went inside to see Moses handy work, he asked, "Moses, what type of work did you do?"

"I'm an architect, sir." He showed Charles his certificate.

Charles returned home and told his dad about Moses handy work. Harry went to Moses shack to see for himself. He looked around the interior of the shack, Harry saw skills in Moses that he wanted to use. He did not want to suffocate Moses capacities like Henry did Billy. Moses showed Harry his graduation certificate. Harry returned home, sitting in the library looking at the H.B. Metropolis plans, he said to himself, "I am a blessed man, two coloreds making me rich. But little do they know." The paperwork that held Harry's final plan, had the names of all the people that had to die. Billy and the workers at The Brown Steel Mill names were on the list. They made the iron bars and plates, Harry planned to eliminate anyone that had anything to do with the construction of the love of his life, H. B. Metropolis. Only his sons would live.

One day, Moses got his wish, he was invited inside Harry's home, where he saw Paula planning a social event with Mrs. Brown. When he entered the kitchen, he paused and watched the women for a fleeting moment. Harry said, "Moses follow me."

Paula almost jumped out of her skin, she was embarrassed that Moses had seen her, she gave him a cute shy smile. Harry and Baerbel looked at each other then back at Paula and Moses, when the couple eyes met, they engaged in an unspoken admiration for each other. Harry cleared his throat to get Moses attention. He took Moses to his library when they entered, Harry showed Moses the map of his metropolis, and they talked about Moses designing a castle.

Although Harry had hired an architect from Europe as the designer, he was going to have Moses and the hired hands to assist the European construction crew. After the meeting, Harry said, "Moses I want to see your complete layout of my museum."

The two men had several disagreeable meetings about the design of the cabin. Moses wanted four rooms and Harry one. To win the battle, Moses decided to play around with Harry's ego. He explained that the four rooms would show that Harry was a loving caring master. Harry agreed with Moses and believed in his professional skills. From that day forward Harry made Moses the commander of designing H. B. Metropolis.

Harry had several of his hired hands to scatter and go to different forest throughout the south. They gather wood to build a new barn and sixty cabins for the slave complex, a new cabin for Vance and his wife Deb, two for the overseers, one for children, and sixty for the slaves.

Moses designed the interior and exterior of the cabin, Vance cabin had five rooms, two upstairs and three down. The outside of the cabin was painted white, with dark gray exterior plantation shutters accenting the cabin.

Inside the overseer's cabin were three rooms, all on one floor. The children cabin was big, it had four rooms, one for the boys, the girls, the nurse, and the teacher slept in the same room. There was a great room for everyone to gather. The children's rooms had fifty pallets on the floor. Harry wanted to always have one hundred children being raised as the next generation of slaves. These cabins were painted white.

Though, in the 1900s, a kitchen and two indoor bathrooms were added to the children cabin.

The slave cabins had four rooms, two upstairs and two downstairs. The outside of their cabin was painted white with a dark gray accent painted around the windows, which matched the gray tin roof.

All the cabins had a tin roof, wood floors, a porch in the front, and wood foundations. Moses with his training refused to build any building, flat on the ground.

For the cabins, omitting Vance, the men made furniture and real beds, Harry ordered mattresses and glass for the windows. The women made curtains, quilts, bedspreads, and throw rugs for the floor. Moses designed all the cabin as the same inside and out. Though the women decorations for the cabins were different yet similar.

Vance and Deb purchased their furniture and household items in town. The children had furniture but the slept-on mats.

Moses recommended that Harry spruce up his house and remodel a few rooms to make it elegant for his family.

The old horse stable behind Harry's house was torn down, a more durable and larger stable, that held fifteen horses, made from oak was built. Inside of Harry's house, Moses walking around noted that the floor would give and where heavy furniture sat, was sinking in. In the dining room, the gargoyles stands were pulling away from the wall.

For the renovation of Harry's mansion, he had to move out. He took his family to live, temporarily, in the MacCall mansion, that was several rooms larger than Harry's. Baerbel was happy to be home again, Harry was determined to build a humongous castle.

Moses and his crew took everything out of Harry's home and stored it in the empty slave shacks and barn. When they ripped out the floors, the mansion was sitting on a tree trunk in the four corners of the mansion, with several in the middle. Moses asked Harry about it, he said, "I thought that was good enough."

"Hum," Moses said, he asked, "what did the builders say."

Harry answered saying, "They claimed it would not hold."

When Harry was not around Moses said to himself, "no wonder the foundation was a shoddy job."

Moses had the men to remove the twelve tree trunks that were holding up the house. Working on buildings in New York, Chicago, and Washington D.C. Moses had learned how to make and use concrete. The whole mansion was renovated from the roof down to the foundation inside and out. Moses gathered that Harry liked dark reds and brown, he took a chance and ordered mahogany wood planks for the mansion floors. He purchased the wood from a New York company that he had worked with.

The outside of the mansion was painted white all over, Moses was in a chance-taking mood, he purchased black plantation shutters for every window on the house. He had the men to paint the post on all the porches black. They stood back and looked up at their handy work, it was spectacular. When Harry and his family returned, they thought the same.

While the gargoyles were off the wall, the women waxed and shined what they called, the ugly beast. The furnishings were returned inside the mansion, the women made new curtains, quilts, and fancy frilly bedspreads out of expensive materials. A crew of women cleaned and polished the chandeliers.

The first thing Harry noticed was the mahogany floors, he absolutely loved them. Moses bold chance paid off.

Harry strutted proudly around his house inside and out, several times a day.

A few times a month he took carriage rides through the hired hands area, he fantasized about the children section, the big black gleaming gates that were going to be installed. He chuckled when he remembered hearing a woman refer to a cabin as a house.

When the hired hand compound was complete. Harry gave everyone a week off. He told them to get away for a little while. However, to entice them to return and complete H. B. Metropolis, he called them all to where it all began, to the back of his newly renovated mansion. Over sixty new people had joined the hired hands. Zeek yelled out, "dis be whar's we start long ago."

Harry said looking at the man, "that is correct," he looked at the group and said, "all who return from their weeklong trip, men and women will be paid a silver dollar the first and third week of the month. Children six to fourteen pay is a quarter.

They all shouted. A woman asked, "you be tearin' down da' shack, whar's we stay?"

Harry replied, "in the new cabins when you return."

With the hired hands gone, Harry went to see the new cabins. He entered one and said, "wow, this is nice."

Separating the two rooms downstairs was a ceiling beam, and two steps that led down into the cooking and eating area. Harry went up to the second floor, the bedrooms sat on either side of a narrow hallway. The rooms did not have doors, the women had made curtains to cover the entrance for privacy. Harry was extremely pleased with their work. "No wonder they call this a house," he said to himself as he looked around. Each bedroom had a closet, dresser, and chest-of-drawers. The only thing missing was mirrors, Harry purchased one for each bedroom in all the cabins.

He had received a letter that he thought was from Billy, before leaving his home Harry put the letter in his pocket and went to the slave compound. He returned downstairs and made himself comfortable in one of the living room cushioned chairs to read the letter.

The last time Harry heard from Billy was when he wrote that Stella's kids found their mother dead. Entirely, due to Baerbel's letter. Harry was hoping to hear from his friend again, this time apologizing for quitting and severing their friendship. Instead, it was from a third person that had taken over Billy's job. The letter informed Harry that the steel rods and plates were complete. Harry was happy and sad at the same time; he had no idea where Billy had gone. The Brown Steel Mill was folding, Harry wanted the money it generated but to make that happen, he needed Billy.

VII

Last Phase of H.B. Metropolis

The forest, cabins, and ditches were planted, dug, and built; it took the hired hands seven years to complete the projects according to Moses' designs. The steel plates and rods took longer than Harry anticipated. While Harry irritably waited, he took a stroll among the cabins. They sat in rolls of fifteen across from each other on two different roads. A light bulb went off, he had the men to make two clearings thus creating a wide path for Charles and Drew Road.

He had them to build a cabin that sat by itself, with its front door facing the two roads.

One day Harry was sitting on the side of his bed, reviewing the letter from Billy about Stella killing herself. He cried, he no longer had a friend, and the possibility of being with someone that was wealthy was gone.

Baerbel was walking past his room, she entered, and was surprised to see him in such a tormented state, she asked, "are you crying?"

Harry did something he did not believe in, he punched Baerbel so hard it knocked her out.

Years ago, when Harry hit his adoptive mom, he walked away feeling guilty. It was as though he had slapped himself, he wanted to say sorry but did not believe she would accept his apology. Harry didn't want her to like him, he wanted her to not be afraid in her home. Every time his adoptive mother locked her bedroom door, Harry cringed with sorrow. Whenever Henry was home, she emerged from her room, and halfway hide behind her husband. Looking at her apparent fright of him, Harry vowed he

All But One

would never hit a woman again. He taught his son's to never put their hands on a woman, he said, "they are too fragile."

He looked down at Baerbel, stepped over her and left the mansion. Outside on the porch, he said to himself, "Baerbel is no woman, she's an evil beast." He got on his horse and slow galloped to the slave area.

When Baerbel came too, one eye was the color and size of a plum.

There was one last building for the men to build while waiting on the iron rods and plates. It was a huge edifice, the size of an airplane hangar. The outside walls of the building were tin sheets and wood walls inside. The construction of this building was in the Southwest corner of the plantation, in the center of the forest. Once all the trees and bushes became like a wall, the massive structure would be hidden. While waiting for the rods, Harry had received several castle designs from the designer in Europe, he didn't like them. For that reason, he asked Moses to design a castle. Harry liked Moses because he didn't ask questions, he simply got the work done.

Moses went home to his new cabin that was tastefully decorated. He had the women to make him seat covers stuffed with cotton. The coloreds nor a great number of the poor whites had ever heard of a slave having seat covers. The women made seat covers for all the cabins. Two white women that had been indentured servants/slaves for a candlestick maker had acquired the skill. They taught some of the other women. Moses trained a few of the young teenage boys how to carve candlestick holders. These were skills that followed from one generation to the next.

Moses had never seen or heard of a castle, he got a book on European castles from a shop in town, the wife of the storekeeper allowed him to use the book for a few days. From the pictures Moses drew several ideas, he returned the book to the shop on the day agreed. Moses took his drawings to Harry, one castle was round, another square, the one Harry loved the most was in the shape of a V. Still, Harry was not satisfied, he told Moses the design he wanted, inside and out.

Two weeks later Moses took his drawing to Harry, he was flabbergasted at Moses skills, he shared the drawings with Charles and Drew. Charles fell in love with the castle, Drew liked the plantation house that he called the Brown Mansion, Harry smiled at the difference in his sons. Charles had gigantic size dreams, while Drew took after the MacCall's, who were rich but comfortable with the status quo.

Harry sent the blueprint of his favorite castle to Europe. Months later the company traveled to America with a small crew, as the administrators of the construction. Harry had sixty of his best men with Moses to be the construction crew.

Finally, the gate rods and plates arrived. Over a hundred men dug thirteen by thirteen and a half foot trenches, while another group placed the plates against the wall. Then concealed the plates by covering them over with dirt. Harry had another large group of men to dig six-foot holes a half inch apart, to install the rods. Each rod was placed a half inch apart and stood six feet into the ground and sixteen feet above. When the men finished with the trench they helped dig and install the outer gate, dividing gate, slave gate, and children gate.

One day, Moses got his wish, he was invited inside Harry's home, where he saw Paula planning a social event with Mrs. Brown. When he entered the kitchen, he paused and watched the women for a fleeting moment. Harry said, "Moses follow me."

Paula almost jumped out of her skin, she was embarrassed that Moses had seen her, she gave him a cute shy smile. Harry and Baerbel looked at each other then back at Paula and Moses, when the couple eyes met, they engaged in an unspoken admiration for each other. Harry cleared his throat to get Moses attention. He took Moses to his library when they entered, Harry showed Moses the map of his metropolis. The two men had several disagreeable meetings about the design of the cabin. Moses wanted four rooms and Harry one. To win the battle, Moses decided to play around with Harry's ego. He explained that the four rooms would show that Harry was a loving caring master. Harry agreed with Moses and believed in his professional skills. From that day forward Harry made Moses the commander of designing H. B. Metropolis.

Harry had several of his hired hands to scatter and go to different forest throughout the south. They gather wood to build a new barn and sixty cabins for the slave complex, a new cabin for Vance and his wife Deb, two for the overseer's, one for children, and sixty for the slaves.

Moses designed the interior and exterior of the cabin, Vance cabin had five rooms, two upstairs and three down. The outside of the cabin was painted white, with dark gray exterior plantation shutters accenting the cabin.

The overseers' cabins had three rooms on one floor. The children cabin was big, it had four rooms, one for the boys, the girls, the nurse, and the teacher slept in the same room. There was a great room for everyone to gather. The children's rooms had fifty pallets on the floor. Harry wanted to always have one hundred children being raised as the next generation of slaves. These cabins were painted white.

Though, in the 1900s, a kitchen and two indoor bathrooms were added to the children cabin.

The slave cabins had four rooms, two upstairs and two downstairs. The outside of their cabin was painted white with a dark gray accent painted around the windows, which matched the gray tin roof.

All the cabins had a tin roof, wood floors, a porch in the front, and wood foundations. Moses with his training refused to build any building, flat on the ground.

Omitting Vance, the men made furniture and real beds for the slave cabins, Harry ordered mattresses and glass for the windows. The women made curtains, quilts, bedspreads, and throw rugs for the floor. Moses designed all the cabin as the same inside and out. Though the women decorations for the cabins were different yet similar. The hired hands dreamed of staying in the cabins, but they knew it was for the museum.

Vance and Deb's five-room cabin were fully built and the old one torn down, Deb's humility started to dwindle. She wanted to travel north to New York to purchase their furniture. Vance had Baerbel to talk to her, she told Deb about a big city east of Titleburk. She said, "dat's where we got our furniture."

Deb said, "thank you." Deb traveled to the city and purchased their furniture, plus new expensive fancy dresses.

The children had furniture but they slept-on mats.

Moses recommended that Harry spruce up his house and remodel a few rooms to make it elegant for his family.

The old horse stable behind Harry's house was torn down, a more durable and larger stable was built. Inside Harry's house, Moses walking around noted that the floor would give and where heavy furniture sat, was sinking. In the dining room, the gargoyles stands were pulling away from the wall.

When renovations began on Harry's mansion, he had to move out. He took his family to live, temporarily, in the MacCall mansion, that was several rooms larger than Harry's. Baerbel was happy to be home again, Harry was determined to build a humongous castle, and tear down the MacCall house.

Moses and his crew took everything out of Harry's home and stored it in the empty slave shacks and barn. When they ripped out the floors, the mansion was sitting on a tree trunk in the four corners of the mansion, with several in the middle. Moses asked Harry about it, he said, "I thought that was good enough."

"Hum," Moses said, he asked, "what did the builders say."

Harry answered saying, "They claimed it would not hold."

When Harry was not around Moses said to himself, "no wonder the foundation was a shoddy job, and an ignorant man was in charge."

Moses had the men to remove the twelve tree trunks that were holding up the house. Working on buildings in New York, Chicago, and Washington D.C., Moses had learned how to make and use concrete. The whole mansion was renovated from the roof down to the foundation inside and out. Moses gathered that Harry liked dark reds and brown, he took a chance and ordered mahogany wood planks for the mansion floors. He purchased the wood from a New York company that he had worked with.

The outside of the mansion was painted white all over, Moses was in a chance-taking mood, he purchased black plantation shutters for every window on the house. He had the men to paint the post on all the porches black. They stood back and looked up at their handy work, it was spectacular. When Harry and his family returned, they thought the same.

While the gargoyles were off the wall, the women waxed and shined what they called, the ugly beast. The furnishings were returned inside the mansion, the women made new curtains, quilts, and fancy frilly bedspreads out of expensive materials. A crew of women cleaned and polished the chandeliers.

All But One

The first thing Harry noticed was the mahogany floors, he absolutely loved them. Moses bold chance paid off.

Several times a day, Harry strutted proudly around his house inside and out.

A few times a month he took carriage rides through the hired hands area, he fantasized about the children section, the big black gleaming gates that were going to be installed. He chuckled when he remembered hearing a woman refer to a cabin as a house.

As the completion of the hired hand compound came to an end, Harry gave everyone a week off. He told them to get away for a little while. However, to entice them to return and install the gates and plates, he called them all to where it all began, to the back of his newly renovated mansion. Over sixty new people had joined Harry's original hired hands. Zeek yelled out, "dis be whar's we start long ago."

Harry said looking at the man, "that is correct," he looked at the group and said, "all adults that return from their weeklong trip will be paid a silver dollar every Friday, children six to fourteen pay is a quarter. I need you to install the gates, plates, and tear down the cabins.

They all shouted. A woman asked, "you be tearin' down da' shacks, whar's we stay?"

Harry replied, "in the new cabins when you return."

Several of the hired hands shouted aloud, "thank you, Mr. Brown."

Moses said, "we'll be back."

With the hired hands gone, Harry went to see the new cabins. He entered one and said, "wow, this is nice."

Separating the two rooms downstairs was a ceiling beam, and two steps that led down into the cooking and eating area. Harry went up to the second floor, the bedrooms sat on either side of a narrow hallway. The rooms did not have doors, the women made curtains to cover the entrance for privacy. Harry was extremely pleased with their work. "No wonder they call this a house," he said to himself as he looked around. Each bedroom had a closet, dresser, and chest-of-drawers. The only thing missing were mirrors, Harry purchased one for each bedroom in all the cabins.

He had received a letter that he thought was from Billy, before leaving his home Harry put the letter in his pocket and went to the slave compound. He returned downstairs and made himself comfortable in one of the living room cushioned chairs to read the letter.

The last time Harry heard from Billy was when he wrote that Stella's kids found their mother dead. Entirely, due to Baerbel's letter. Harry was hoping to hear from his friend again, this time apologizing for quitting and severing their friendship. The letter was not from Billy, it was from a third person that had taken over Billy's job. The letter informed Harry that the steel rods and plates were complete. Harry was happy and sad at the same time; he had no idea where Billy had gone. Unfortunately, the Brown Steel Mill was folding, Harry wanted the money it generated but to make that happen, he needed Billy. One day while Harry and Charles were walking by the workers, Charles asked, "why are you putting in metal plates?"

Harry impatiently said roughly, "to keep the forest roots from growing anywhere near the gate. Otherwise the slaves, I mean, thieves will be able to grab a branch and climb over. I can't have that."

"I see," Charles said confused. He thought to himself, pops said, "slaves."

Harry adored his hired hands, he wanted to keep them building his Metropolis, and pay them top dollar. With money not flowing in from the steel mill, Harry was afraid he would need to stop work or pay his workers a lot less money. He began to worry. Through the years, out of the original three hundred plus, twenty-seven saved their money and left Harry's employment. The remaining original hired hands stayed the full eleven years to bank as much money as they could. In place of the ones that moved on, Harry always gained twenty to fifty more people looking for work.

One day, Harry was walking around his second-floor porch rejoicing, thinking, and looking through his binoculars. He was happy to see poor whites and coloreds save their money for a better life. He understood what Charles was talking about, we are all the same from our brain down to our toenails. Harry said out loud, "it's not the color of skin, it's the ambition of the person." Harry leaned on the porch railings, smiled and continued, "that's what Charles was explaining." He thought about Moses, who didn't look like the coloreds or whites. Moses had told Harry that he was half Egyptian and Indian. Harry had never seen either race, though often, Moses reminded him of Mr. Evans.

In the adult slave area, they had one square mile to move about. A half mile on the southwest corner of the cabins, the men-built a bar, general store, and a large pretty church close to the western area of the outer gate. Harry asked them to build it big enough to hold two hundred people. One of the men carved a cross made from walnut wood to be placed on top of the church. A female slave asked Harry if they could put round glass windows around the walls. Harry consented. They also built wood pews for the two hundred people to sit, a pulpit, and podium for the preacher. When Harry saw the church, he was angry and yelled, "it's too close to the gate, I should make you tear it all down." He stormed off because it would cost him more money and take extra months to cut down a few trees, cut up the wood to replace any wood that would be destroyed while dismantling the church. He did not have the money to buy wood that was cut professionally.

Harry was irritated because the Brown Steel Mill was losing money, no one at the mill knew where Billy had gone. The lack of cash flow was making his pockets thinner than his patients. To make extra cash, he sold items from the MacCall house that brought in a nice sum of money. It was mostly the northerners that made the purchases. Harry put in the newspaper that he was having a sell, the news spread north.

Moses got what he wanted, he and Paula had a church wedding, Harry attended with his family and friends. Baerbel and Paula became close, they were more like mother and daughter than slave and mistress. Baerbel traveled to Titleburk with Paula, to purchase a wedding dress. Paula was excited, even though she had to stay in the lower level of the hotel with the other slaves, she did not care. In the basement, the coloreds ate well and had a dance party. Paula had fun that night. And now, Like Moses, she had traveled. On their way back to the plantation, Paula said, "mistress, da' world be, mighty big and a whole lot of fun."

"Yes, it is," Baerbel said as she thought about her travels. She was rich and had only been to MacCall and Titleburk. She sat thinking. She reached over and grabbed Paula's hand and said, "you are so right, my little girl."

Baerbel's parents lied royally to her. She was told that her dad was from London, England, he told her that his sister was an assistant to a Knight, that was related to the Queen. Her mother expressed her upbringing as an aristocrat. She raised Baerbel to be a debutant, just like she was raised in Baltimore, Maryland. The MacCall's never thought that their grandson or daughter would one day, travel to find their important relatives.

Traveling with Paula ignited a longing, to go further than the two towns. Baerbel was on a mission to find her aunt that was close to the Royal family. She had excited jitters running through her vain. As she and Paula were heading back to the mansion, Baerbel thought of attending parties in the castle. She was going to ask Charles for money so that she could purchase three beautiful gowns for the elaborate parties at the Queen's palace, spending money, and her trip across the ocean. Baerbel was full of excitement, it was like living with her parents again.

When she thought of Drew, Baerbel's smile turned upside down. Drew looked like Harry's hired hands, the only different, Drew wore wrinkled suits, and sometimes stunk of alcohol. And never had money. She thought asking Drew for money would be no different from asking little Paula.

She looked at Paula with a big smile and said, "I am going to travel."

Paula had no idea what Baerbel was talking about, she was excited about her wedding to the best-looking man she had ever seen, and her pretty store-bought wedding dress.

The reception was held in Harry's backyard, several guests arrived for the food and drink. The slave women made it look festive, though, Harry's friends thought it looked a little primitive and plain. Paula gasp at the beautiful decorations, and Moses felt like a king. He was escorted on the porch to be introduced, Moses stood tall and proud with the Brown Family, and his beautiful bride by his side. The moment was exactly what he envisioned so many years ago.

Harry looked over at Moses, he watched Moses raise his chest, square his shoulders, point his nose skyward. Harry shook his head when seeing Moses looking beyond the crowd as though he was above and better than everyone. Harry looked down at the paper that Moses had given him with his full name written, *Mr. Moses Berhanu*. He crumbled the paper and said as he looked out at the crowd, "I introduce to you, Mr. and Mrs. Moses." He quickly glanced at Moses to see his reaction.

Everything about Moses deflated. Harry's purposeful blunder made Moses angry, it instantly showed in his face. Moses pushed Paula to the side, ran off the porch, and rushed through the crowd knocking them out of his way. He had been insulted and shamed.

Harry smiled as he watched the proud niggra ego burst in front of everybody. Paula stood all alone on the porch confused and embarrassed. It didn't matter to the crowd, no one knew his last name, and the whites did not know that coloreds had two names, only their owner's name. Still, Moses rough exit did not hinder the party. There was plenty of food, good music, and dancing, Harry had hired a band from Titleburk.

Paula went home to Moses, when she got there, he was gone. She changed clothes and cried.

A few weeks after their wedding, Harry noticed that sometimes Paula had a bruise or two. "Hum," Harry said to himself, "good job keeping her in place."

Baerbel said to Paula, "run before it's too late." Baerbel looked around to see if anyone was listening, she whispered so low that Paula had to read her lips to see what she was saying. "I am planning my escape; you do the same. It may take years but start planning, now."

Charles had noticed the bruises as well, on one occasion he pulled Moses aside and beat him good and hard. Moses told Harry about his beating, he did not have to tell, Harry could see Moses swollen face with black and purple bruises. Harry halfheartedly reprimanded Charles, he was proud of his son. He went to his room and chuckled, "I love that boy."

During the time the church was being built, Zeek had had an epiphany. Five whites and four colored men were completing their work on the church. The nine men stood back and said it was very pretty. During lunch they were sitting on the ground in the churchyard, Zeek said, "I have a strange feelin."

A builder said, "nothin' strange bout' dis' place, God gonna' be in here."

A white hired hand asked, "what ja' mean, strange?"

"We's need ta' build a small Backroom," Zeek answered.

"Why?" another man asked.

"Don't know, but we's need ta' add a room wid' dirt flo,'" Zeek answered. He went inside the church to the back wall.

The others followed him inside. He looked at the wall and said as he used his hands to put an emphasis on his idea, "cut out a doe' right here."

"We can use the wood to lay the flo," one of the men mentioned.

Zeek said in a fixed tone, "No, we's got's ta' leave the flo' as is, dirt only. I's' know it sound strange but it's what we hafta' do."

"That ain't how Moses drew it," chimed Dan one of the white men, "and he be close ta' Mr. Brown."

"I don't care, it's what we got's ta' do." Zeek insisted.

Dan said to the white men, "let's go." As they were leaving, he said, "we'll let the niggra's finish what dey' be doin' den' tell Mr. Brown."

It was agreed, among the five.

One of the men said, "why's don't we's tell da' other whites ta' leave and let da' niggra's' do da' rest of da' work."

Dan said, "we's gots' plenty money ta' go."

Again, the five agreed and put their plan in motion.

While the coloreds were discussing on restructuring the church back wall, the five white men petitioned the whites to leave. They told them what the four men were doing, as though they could not see since they all lived and worked inside the slave area.

Moses was in his cabin, he heard the men stirring up trouble, he went to the church. When he arrived Zeek explained that the church was not complete, he said, "der' be no room foe' da' cleanin' thangs."

Moses agreed it was a good plan, he said, "I'm on my way to see Mr. Brown, I will let him know that you are doing a good deed for his museum." He began to leave, but turned around and said, "allow me to show you how to cut the wood, so it can be used again, it won't be enough to build a room, which is okay, I have plenty of wood to give you."

The men were happy to have Moses help. When he left the men said together, "Thank you."

Zeek said, "you's a kind man, Mr. Berhanu."

Moses waved as he left.

One of the coloreds asked, "Zeek, why you's call him Mr. he be colored like us."

"I's just gittin' him on our side."

One of the coloreds said, "You know, Zeek be right."

The four men laughed.

Zeek continued, "iffen' Massa ask why we build da small room, we say da' church need stuff ta' clean it, dis' be a good place ta' hold dat' stuff."

One of the men said, "it work foe' Moses."

Another one agreed, he said, "show 'nuff did."

It was settled and agreed between the four coloreds, as to what to say, if asked. One of the men asked Zeek, "why is we makin' a small room."

Zeek answered, "I don't know. We's just hafta."

Jim, the leader of four men that tried to betray Zeek over the church backroom, liked a woman named Jane, he said, "git yo' thangs ready to leave. We's got's nuff' money to git' married."

She gave Jim a hug and kiss, and then said, "it's bout' time you' ax' me." She ran in her shack and packed her things.

Jim and the other four men went around to the other white men and women, they told them to let the coloreds finish all the jobs. Jim told a group of men, "I's leavin' y'all needs to come."

It took three days to complete the backroom in the church. Moses went to the church to inspect the extra room, he told them, "job well done."

Jim, Jane, with the four white men went to Harry's mansion to report the colored building an extra room in the church. They said nothing about Moses. Harry told the men; I will handle it. He asked if they wanted something to eat, "of course we do," Jane answered. Harry took them to the drawing-room, Jim said, "I like this animal chair."

Harry replied as he was leaving, "it's a gargoyle, I'll ask my cook to get you some plates ready." He saw Drew coming down the stairs, he said, "follow me."

When they entered the kitchen, Harry told Paula to set the dining room table for six, and Baerbel to warm some food. When the two women were done, he sent them out and told them not to return until evening. Harry asked Drew, "is Charles here."

Laughing Drew answered, "he's with his latest girlfriend, we won't see him until morning."

Harry smiled and shook his head before saying, "that boy knows how to live."

Drew said with jealousy in his voice, as he mixed the food with poison, "so you say, pops."

Harry escorted Jim and his friends in the dining room. they laughed and talked as they were eating; it was Jane that realized they had been poisoned. With all the slaves in their compound, Vance and Deb was gone, Harry and Drew used a wheelbarrow to take the six bodies to an old well, they dumped them down.

The following morning, Harry went to the slave area to speak with Zeek. The four men stuck to their story like crazy glue.

Harry agreed with Zeek and his men, creating extra space for cleaning supplies was a great idea. He told the men, "this shows you have initiative." He looked around the church then said, "you men did a fine job."

Harry asked if they were going to add a door to the new room, Zeek answered, "naw Sir. We're goin' ta' hang a curtain."

Harry sent them on their way. Several hired hands saw Harry, they asked about Jim, Jane, and the others. Harry said, "they came to my home and accused me of treating them unfairly, I fired them."

A male said, "they will not get the rest of their pay."

One of the women that was friends with Jane said, "dey were tryin' ta' get us ta' leave and let the coloreds finish the work. I told them no. I won't's all my money."

Another person said, "Me too, I got's plans."

Harry chuckled as he galloped home when he exited through the divider gate, Drew saw him, he said, "pops come here." Drew was walking among the new plants between the divider and main gate.

Harry dismounted his horse and joined his son. Drew said, "when this forest between the divider and main gate grow and fill in, it will make a good burial ground."

Harry agreed. 1872, Father and son had committed their first murder four years before the completion of H. B. Metropolis. Jim and his crew were the first to die for the sake of Harry's unlawful setup.

The following morning, Harry and his sons were laughing, talking, and eating breakfast in the kitchen, Charles announced that he wanted to go to Boston and investigate The Brown Steel Mill operations. He was unaware that his father and brother had killed six people.

Charles liked melted butter in a saucer, he dipped his bread, then spread apple butter on top. He stuffed the bread in his mouth.

Harry asked as Charles as he prepared another piece of bread, "are you going to marry that girl?"

Charles put the food in his mouth then asked, "which one?"

While the Browns were having supper, Paula was in hers and Moses bedroom trying to mend her new bruise that was on her chest. Moses was sitting at the table looking at a letter he received from a building company in New York. The company had sent him instructions on how to open a branch in MacCall. Moses dream was to start his own company, and not be a branch. The company would be owned by him and his children. Moses sat back and imagined himself wealthy, he smiled and said in confidence, "Harry will give me the money, he like everything I do.

VIII

Moses

1854, Moses was born a slave on a New York horse farm, to a man that raised, raced horses. Little Moses was raised by his parents until a tragedy happened. It was a misfortune that caused the couple to lose their two-year-old son for a little while, yet it saved the husband and wife duo from a debasing situation.

The child's dad, Thaddeus Berhanu, trained the farms' racehorses, his mother Dakota was an upstairs house slave. Their Massa liked the couple a little too much. Thaddeus was an Egyptian and Dakota and American Indian, their Massa called Moses, "the beautiful one."

Moses looks were very striking, he had inherited his father's Egyptian features.

The plantation master enjoyed wild parties. He would put Thaddeus and Dakota in a room, where they were made to disrobe. His company not only viewed the couple but in a wicked state of mine felt and grope with their mouth and hands the couple from their face down to their feet. After the dehumanizing ordeal, Thaddeus and Dakota returned to their slave shack, feeling shamed and brutalized.

But all changed when Thaddeus and Dakota tried to escape from their Massa wild sex crazed gatherings. Early one morning they devised a plan to run. Their Massa was leaving the plantation and was not returning until the following night. Thaddeus said to his wife, "this is our time to go."

At eleven thirty that night, Dakota fed two-year-old Moses, to get him full and quiet. At midnight, the husband and wife duo, with their sleeping toddler quietly ran out their cabin only to get caught within an hour of their flight. Two-year-old

All But One

Moses was taken to the mistress. Two overseers pushed Thaddeus and Dakota in the barn and locked the doors. They gagged the couple and beat them for an hour. Then slammed Thaddeus and Dakota down on their stomach, Thaddeus' face hit the cement floor so hard his nose was broken, and lip busted. His handsome face was severely bruised.

God in His mercy put blameless Thaddeus and Dakota in a deep sleep. At three thirty that morning, the grueling rape, beatings, and urinating on the couple ended. Thaddeus and his wife experience nothing, they were out cold.

The overseer that had Thaddeus, tied his left leg to his right arm, and right leg to his left arm. The other overseer did the same to Dakota. They were left in that position and laid in their blood until their Massa returned that evening at nine o'clock. The male slave that took his Massa's horse, told him about the couple in the barn.

The plantation owner stood in the barn looking down at his beautiful property. He thought of the money he was going to lose, hostile anger surged through his heart, mind, and soul. The owner called a meeting with all the overseers. When they were gathered, the owner asked, who was responsible for his slaves' condition. He stood back and had each man look at Thaddeus and Dakota. The two that maimed his stunning slaves, told him how the coupled tried to run. The owner asked, "so you did, this?" He pointed down at the couple, to emphasize his question.

One of the men that were responsible for the deplorable condition of the two slaves, said haughtily, "dey' cain't run no moe."

The owner had four of the guiltless overseers to untie Thaddeus and Dakota, at which time, they woke up. It was as though God in His mercy protected them.

A male slave helped Thaddeus; a female was with Dakota. The two slaves took the couple to their cabin, where they bathe and tended to their wombs.

The master of the plantation with four overseers', tortured the two *guilty* men to death. The master went home, as he entered his house, he heard two-year-old Moses crying. He quickly went to the room where they were and stopped his wife from beating on the child. He said, "I'm saving him when he gets older, we'll show him off." He began to leave but turned back and said, "he look just like his dad, people will pay as they did for his parents." He left the room.

One week after their torment in the barn, Thaddeus held Dakota's hand and said, "I'm sorry what you went through Kota, it…"

Dakota said, before he finished talking, "saved us both from Massa's terrible parties."

Thaddeus said, "I thank God for knocking us out during the barn torment."

"Me to, God through their hate, protected us from the overseers' venom."

"Yes, it was brutal and left my nose crooked, it will never be the same which is good protection from the parties."

Dakota said, "I got this scar from my hairline to my chin."

Thaddeus said, "another blessing."

"It was God, we had to be broken." Dakota paused before continuing, "I'd rather be a cripple than…" Dakota began to cry.

"Massa parties." Thaddeus went to her and held her as he said, "we're safe now."

Dakota said, "Our baby boy is with those horrible people."

Thaddeus said, "God protected us, He will do the same for our son."

Thaddeus and Dakota's facial scares keloid as to accentuate their deformity according to the plantation master. Their faith in God was unwavering and more pronounced.

One day in the plantation house, two-year-old Moses saw his mother and ran up to her, out of habit she picked him up, gave him a hug, and a kiss. The Mistress yelled, as she in anger snatched the child from his mother, "he is yours no more, keep your filthy hands off this child."

She walked away carrying Moses kicking, hitting, pulling his mistress' hair, crying, and yelling, "mama."

The mistress punched the two-year-old with her fist, he hit and kicked her back. The hurt in Dakota's heart was greater than the ordeal in the barn. She fell on her knees crying profusely.

The Massa had plans for the child, but his wife evilness was about to destroy his beautiful precious property. He allowed

Moses to visit his parents on weekends, hoping it would calm the child down which it did not. As a matter of fact, the longer Moses was with the plantation owner, the little boy became more hostile. Moses was so destructive, a month before his third birthday he was permanently returned to his parent's shack. In his parent's home, little Moses calmed down.

One evening Thaddeus watched Moses sleep peacefully, he looked at Dakota and said, "they will do to him…"
"That cannot happen," Dakota said before Thaddeus finished talking. "It will not happen; you will see to it." She demanded. "God through you and your African markings will save our son, just like you said last year. God will save our child."
Thaddeus began, "I said…"
Dakota cut him off and said, "I don't care what you said. Do something!"
Dakota knew all about herbs, she had one that would put the person in a deep sleep nor would or could they feel pain.
For her son, Dakota hummed a tune of her native heritage as she mixed the medicine. While Dakota prepared the herb, Thaddeus woke Moses up and began playing with him. when the mixture cooled down Dakota, made a tea and gave Moses a few drops.
When little Moses fell in a deep sleep, Dakota did her native ceremonial Sun Dance. Thaddeus used a small sharp knife to carve a cross on his sons right and left cheek, next to his ears. And a larger cross on his back and chest. With the carving over, Dakota stopped the bleeding, she put a salve she made on the opened sores and patched them up. The sores healed within a week.
When the Massa saw the scar on Moses' face, he asked, "what happened?"
Even though the scares were in the shape of a cross, Thaddeus and Dakota answered together, "he fell."
Thaddeus said to his wife as Moses played, "God has saved little Adlai, our baby boy."

When Moses turned six, he worked with his father training the horses. Thaddeus taught Moses how to ride. Two new overseers were hired, one of them noticed that Moses seemed to have a gift with the horses. He shared this information with his boss. For two years the owner watched Moses posture when he was riding. On Moses eighth birthday he hired a man from Kentucky that trained jockeys to work with Moses. The young boy was so good that when he turned ten-years-old, the owner signed him up to compete. Moses won races from New York down to Kentucky. He made his Massa a very wealthy man, regrettably, Moses did not receive a cent.

While traveling Moses noticed in Ohio that coloreds were free, there was a colored family that owned a horse farm. He wanted to grow up and be just like them. At the races, the family had three jockey's, two coloreds one white. Moses returned home joyously telling his parents that one day they would move to Ohio. He said, "dad we can have our own farm and horses." He shared with them how big the world really was

The Massa observed that as Moses grew, he had a keen eye for building structures like an architect. When Moses got too big to be a jockey, he sent the young man to school. He planned to make money off this slave in more ways than one. When Moses was a child, he entered him in horse races, when he was a young teen, he hired him out as a building contractor. And later sent him to a two-year architect school. After Moses graduated, his Massa got him jobs in New York, New Jersey, Chicago, and Washington DC. Moses never saw a penny of his wages

April 1861, the Civil War broke out, a job that Moses was working on stopped due to the war. Moses and the three, gun-toting overseers returned to the plantation. Several slaves had run away and joined the army along with two overseers. This left numerous empty shacks. Moses asked the Massa if he could move in one of the shacks, he refused. Moses was put back in his parent's shack.

Early one morning, in 1863, Moses entered the shack, he was clean, dressed, and ready to do a small job his Massa had for him on the plantation. Dakota was up making a fire in the fireplace, as Moses entered. She said, "Good morning son,"

Moses said, "hope I didn't wake you."

"No, I was awake."

Thaddeus heard them stirring around, he called Moses to his bedside and said, "I want to tell you about who I am." He sat up in bed.

Moses said, "I have two hours before I have to leave." He got a chair and set it next to his father's bedside, and said, "I have plenty of time."

When Moses was seated Thaddeus began, "your birth name is Adlai, it means ornament of God, our name Berhanu means, light. I am from West Africa. My father's people are from an old ancient country that no longer exist."

"What country is that?" Moses asked.

"The Kingdom of Kush in Eastern Africa. When war broke out my family went to Egypt, he met my mom. A family conflict broke out between dad's brothers, he went to West Africa with several others. In our small community dad was the leader. I was born 1812 when I turned eighteen, father sent me with several guards to Egypt. where I was to find an Egyptian wife and return home. Sixteen months later I returned home with a beautiful wife. Within three years of marriage, I had two sons, they were born in 1831 and 1833."

Moses was elated, he said, "I have brothers."

Thaddeus laid down, and said, "listen, son." He then verbally spelled his last name, B-E-R-H-A-N-U, he asked Moses to repeat the spelling. Thaddeus knew he was dying so had nothing to lose. He reached for Moses' hand and said, "I wished I had told you about our family long ago."

Moses said, "it's okay pops, you would have been beaten to death."

Thaddeus held tight to Moses' hand as he told his son about their history. He asked for water, Dakota brought him a tin cup filled with water. She held the cup for him and said softly, "drink up."

When he finished drinking, she wiped his mouth and helped him lay back down.

Thaddeus winked at his wife and said, "your mother is from the western part of this country. That's where we were going when you were two years old." He stopped and moaned as he stirred around to get comfortable.

Dakota sat on the bed next to him and said, "enough talking for one day." As she rubbed his head with a damp cloth, she looked a Moses and said, "we were caught, you took from us, we were beaten and left to die."

She kissed Thaddeus on the forehead and returned to her chair in front of the fireplace.

Thaddeus reached for his son's hand and said, "go on to work now, I'll be alright."

Moses said, "how did you end up in this country" Where's your wife and son's." He paused for a moment before whispering more to himself, "my brothers?"

Thaddeus explained, "our little African community was nowhere near the ocean. We were on the mountaintop living in houses, not mud huts or under a grass shelter." He repeated himself, "houses son, my father's house was bigger than Massa's. You see, most of us were from Egypt, others Sudan. My mother and father were Egyptian, we worshiped the Egyptian god, wore Egyptian clothing, the architect of our buildings was Egyptian. We were a thriving peaceful community. High on the mountain, we had heard about these big boats filled with white skinned people from a new country that talked funny. Father said we were safe because we were far-far away from the Ocean." Thaddeus stopped talking, closed his eyes.

Dakota was setting the table for them to eat breakfast, she ran over to Thaddeus and shook him, she screamed, "Thaddeus!"

When Thaddeus opened his eyes, Moses exhaled, Dakota said, "don't you ever do that again," she began to leave, stopped, looked at Thaddeus and Moses and said serenely, "breakfast is ready."

Thaddeus sat up, looked at Moses and said, "father was wrong, those white skinned people kicked us out our homes and took over our village. They killed my dad, mom, and anyone over forty years of age. They beat and shackled the rest of the males young and old, even my sons who were six and eight years old."

Moses said with tears in his voice, "I'm so sorry dad."

Dakota sat in a chair in front of the fire, breakfast food was on the table getting cold. Silence filled the one-room shack, only the sound of fire crackling in the fireplace was heard. All was so still until Thaddeus cleared his throat which made Moses and Dakota jump. Laughing, Thaddeus asked, "what's wrong with you two?" he continued, "don't be sorry, son, you were not born."

He looked at Moses who was listening and hanging on every word. Thaddeus continued, "about fourteen of those men chose our best-looking women and raped them so many times that most died. Our women were not accustomed to harsh treatments. Four white-skinned men had my wife, she put up a good fight, she kicked, bit, and spit all over them. One of the men grabbed her and pushed my wife to the ground. Her head hit a rock that had a jagged point, the impact busted the side of her face wide opened, so much blood flowed out they left her alone." Thaddeus zoned out for a second, he could see the whole tribulation happening all over again. He continued, "She found a way to turn her head toward me, our eyes met, and then her eyes went blank. She was not raped nor were her clothes torn from her body, she died with her dignity intact. I thanked the god Montu for answering my prayer."

Moses asked, "Montu?"

"Yes, he is the falcon-god of war. He is the god of my…" He looked at Moses and said, "our people."

Dakota said, "tell him how you got here from Africa."

Thaddeus continued, "my youngest son's leg was shackled to my leg and his arm mine. My oldest son was killed, the men were telling him what to do, but none of us understood their language, they killed my boy and several others. The white-skinned men marched us down the mountain, to the ocean and dumped us in the belly of that big boat. It stunk so bad, it was years before the smell was gone out of my nose and memory. When we got to this country my son shackles were removed when he was purchased. My boy looked at me, he kissed the back of my hand, looked up at me and smiled, he said, "I love you, dad." He jumped off the auction block headfirst, he died like his mother, head bust wide open. "A big oversized man kicked my baby boy to the side like he was trash."

Moses cried.

Dakota said, "how do people that think they are better, more intelligent, and believe they are privileged to do such evilness to others. When I was taken, that is the first thing they did to me, removed my clothes and raped me."

Moses handed his father a towel, using the cloth to wipe his face Thaddeus said, "Koda, tell him your story."

Moses stood, before leaving his father's bedside, kissed him on the forehead, squeezed his hand and said, "I love you pops. Just like my brother loved you." He kissed the back of Thaddeus' hand.

He went to his mom; she was sitting in a chair by the fire. Moses asked about her health. She said, "I'm doing fine."

He knelt next to her and said, "Dad mentioned that you were already in this country, how did they take you?"

Dakota said, "I am from the Rocky mountain area of this country. Like your father, I was married, had two daughters and one son. I am eleven years older than Thad; my children were teenagers. My husband was at work, my kids were with friends, I was out for a walk enjoying the warm sun and nature. You see son, I taught my tribal community how to use the herbs of the land for illnesses. I often walked looking for herbs." She looked at Thaddeus and said, "we both are from a tribe that functioned and lived peacefully together, as one unit."

"Yes, we were," Thaddeus responded as he sat on the side of the bed.

Dakota continued, "our Massa was an Army Captain, he had gotten shot in his leg and shoulder, a caravan was returning him home to New York. I should have run, but I stopped to watch them go by, big mistake on my part. Massa said something to a few of the men on horseback, they came after me, I took off running fast as I could which was not fast enough, they caught me. The men stood me next to a covered wagon, Massa came around instructed the men to remove all my clothing. He inspected me, then violated me. Afterward, he said, "she'll be a good house slave." Dakota stopped talking and cried. She ended by saying, "How sick is people."

Moses looked around, and saw his dad walking towards them, he asked, "what are you doing pops?"

"Help me next to your mother."

When he was sitting next to Dakota, Thaddeus reached over and took her hand in his, then said, "she was here for two years before I arrived, after I was purchased in 1841, I was put in this shack, my name was changed to Sam, only Massa call me that."

Dakota said, "he changed my name to Rebecca, we never used those names. Your father calls me Koda, I call him, Thad."

Still holding Thaddeus' hand, she squeezed it, then continued, "when I was brought here, Massa put me in the loft of the barn, close to the house. Two years later, he bought Thad and put us together, like animals we were to begin breeding. We did not touch each other until we were legally married, in that slave church not far from here." She smiled before continuing, "we both, was introduced to God and His Son, Jesus."

Moses asked, "did you tell each other about where you came from?"

"Yes, we did," Dakota answered, "we were escaping to my home."

"Mom, how were you going to explain to your husband, dad and me?"

"We were only thinking about being free," Thaddeus said.

Dakota said, "we were caught, you were taken from us"

Moses said laughing to break the sadness that had consumed the shack, "I must have been an awful child because they gave me back to you."

Thaddeus and Dakota laughed out loud. Finally, Moses thought, joy had returned to the family.

Dakota said, "child you tore that place up, when Massa brought you back, he said, you bite, hit, kicked him and his wife, broke windows, dishes, and knocked over a very expensive vase."

Laughing, Thaddeus said, "the vase was from another country."

Thaddeus and Dakota had a good laugh as they told Moses about his seven months stay with their Massa. Thaddeus said laughing, "Massa showed us where you had bitten him that day."

Dakota said, "those tiny little teeth marks." She and Thaddeus laughter out loud and hard.

Moses said, "let's keep this moment going, filled with laughter and joy. On my way home from work, I will stop past the garden and get some vegetables and herbs, then ask the cook for a chicken. Will, you teach me how to cook a dish from my Indian and African heritage?"

"Yes son, we'll end the day on a high note," Dakota said.

She began singing a tribal song as Moses left.

Watching Moses leave, Thaddeus said, "I'm glad we told him."

"Yes, he took it well." Dakota replied as she looked around at the table filled with breakfast, she said, "let's eat."

Outside, Moses ran to the field, fell on his knees, and cried. He felt the scars on the side of his face, he said aloud, "thanks dad for saving me."

True to his word, Moses returned home that evening with a whole chicken, vegetables, herbs, Massa's cook had given him corn, salt, sugar, oil, meal, and flour. Thaddeus, Dakota, and Moses had fun preparing that evening's meal together, and an even greater time as they sat at the table enjoying the delicious food. During supper, Thaddeus and Dakota reviewed that morning discussion and shared more of their story. Thaddeus said, "Adlai, one day write our history." That evening Moses jotted down talking points of what his parents had told him.

The next morning Thaddeus had a burst of energy, while Dakoda prepared breakfast, Thaddeus and Moses went to the horse barn. It had been a few years since Thaddeus had been further than the front of the cabin, he was shocked to see how dilapidated the barn had become, and the condition of the horses. He was even more surprised, that there were only four horses. The owner of the plantation had gotten old and was no longer involved in horse racing. Together father and son washed and brushed the horses, then fed them, and cleaned their stalls. One of the horse's name was Rocky, Thaddeus told Moses to take care of the horse. He explained that Rocky was the grandson of the fastest horse their Massa ever raced. Two hours later they returned and ate everything that Dakota had prepared. Moses left to see what the Massa had for him to do.

While Moses was away, Thaddeus and Dakota talked for a little bit, he said, "I am tired." She helped him to bed. He smiled, held Dakota's hand next to his heart, and said just above a whisper, "my beautiful wife, thank you for my son and a good life."

Dakota said, "I am joining you soon Thad. First, I have to get our son off this plantation."

Thaddeus said, "please do, tell our son, I love him." He kissed Dakota's hand, closed his eyes, and whispered, "I love you." He peacefully passed away.

Thaddeus funeral was held the next day.

All But One

Moses had his mother with him for two days after his father passed. He and his mother sat in front of the fire, they cooked meals together, they talked. Dakota pleaded with Moses to leave the plantation. Their third day together, early in the morning, Moses stood by his mother's bedside. She said, "your father and I love you dearly, it is time for me to go. Adlai, I need for you to escape this place and be free."

Moses laid his head on his mother's chest and cried, he said, "I cannot lose you both."

Dakota said very softly as she rubbed Moses head," use your jockey training, run to Ohio and join the army, run son, run."

Moses heard and felt his mother's heart stop. He jumped up and yelled, "mom!"

The next day she was buried next to Thaddeus.

It took Moses a week to finally leave. Though he knew his parents would soon leave him, he had not prepared his heart for their departure. Moses became lethargic, he stopped eating, for several days he sat in his father's chair, rocking and crying. The sadness was thicker than syrup and bitter than sour grape.

His last night in the shack, he was awakened by his parent's laughter, he smelt food cooking, he heard his mother say, "run."

Twenty-year-old Moses jumped out of bed called out, "dad, mom, you here?" he lit a candle no one was in the shack. He said to himself, "it was a dream, I have to go, and I know how." Twenty minutes later he left the cabin.

Both of Moses parents died in April 1863, three days apart.

Moses brushed Rocky down, fed and saddled the horse. The few remaining overseers thought Moses was doing his chore. But when Moses jumped on Rocky's back and galloped off, they learned differently. Being a professional jockey, the overseers could not keep up.

On his flight away from the plantation, he was happy that he and his father had gone to the barn, one last time together. After his dad's funeral, he and his mom went to their shack and prepared a few meals together. She told him to run and join the American Army.

To keep his slaves from escaping, Moses Massa told his slaves, that people with candles in their window were evil, and to stay from them. When he arrived in Philadelphia, he saw a tiny house with a candle in the window, Moses and his horse was tired and hungry, so he knocked on the door. He figured they could be no worse than his Massa. The couple were nice and accommodating. He made two more stops before landing in Ohio which took him five weeks to reach. In Ohio, he joined the army and fought gallantly for the freedom for his mom, dad, brothers, and sisters he would never meet.

Coloreds during the Civil War could not arm themselves with guns or swords, Moses found a big thick stick and was better with that stick, than most whites that carried weapons.

Moses unit went south and fought in Chickamauga on top of Look Out Mountain, and Chattanooga at the foot of a mountain, his unit fought in several southern states until the end of the war. Through it all, his unit only lost one man.

After the Civil War, officially ending on April 1865, Moses was a homeless recluse that worked odd jobs, he searched for something stable.

Moses job search ended when he found himself in MacCall. In the middle of town, he saw four men riding on flatbed wagons, hiring people, Moses walked up to one of the wagons, and said, "Sir I am filthy, I stink, I need a job."

Vance said, "hop on the back."

Moses jumped on the back of Vance wagon, he reached in his pocket and pulled out the papers with his family history and his graduation certificate.

IX

Charles Brown

Charles Moved To Boston 1872

    The day Charles was moving to Boston, Drew and Baerbel stood on the front porch waving bye. Harry watched his favorite son leave from the drawing-room window, he whispered, "going to miss you son, wish I was more like you."
    Baerbel would not stop crying so Drew sent her back in the mansion, when she entered Harry left and went to the library. When Charles carriage got to the end of the driveway, he turned and waved, and then the carriage disappeared out of Drew's site when it went around the bend. Silently, Drew cried. They were one year apart, they were like twins, they had fought, argued, talked, planned, played, even went to war together. Drew like Harry admired Charles free spirit. Drew went to the side of the mansion, fell on his knees and cried.
    When Charles arrived in Boston, the first person he inquired about was Billy, the new manager at the Steel Mill gave him Billy's Vermont address. Charles went to Billy's home, he was old and sad, but doing well. Due to Harry's treachery, his employees lost respect for him, they never gave Harry, Billy's new address. Billy's wife was diagnosed with a stomach ulcer early on from stress. Her husband and Harry splitting their ways, disappointment in the little boy called Moe, permanently leaving her home in Boston were reasons the ulcers hemorrhaged. He tried to make his wife last days fun and peaceful. He bought a carriage and two horses, he took her on long rides, she enjoyed the warm wind blowing in her face. Her favorite was a walk in the park, when the ulcers worsened, the extracurricular activity

stopped. Soon, she faded away looking into Billy's eyes, she saw that they began to water, she said, "no-no, none of that. We had a good life, from slavery to I wrote a book, you were the manager of a big company, we bought two big houses."

Billy laid his forehead on hers, eyes to eyes he said, "I love you." Being so close to Liza, he could see his wife was declining, her warm breath on his face was weakening each time she exhaled.

She smiled and said, "thank you for grabbing my hand and running us to freedom, it was a beautiful wedding, perfect marriage, good life." Her pupils shut, one long breath emitted as she whispered, "I love you." She was gone with a smile on her face.

Billy closed her eyes and cried. He rattled around the house for two years, feeling lonely and sorry for himself until Charles showed up. Billy told Charles about the wrong his father had done, he studied Charles facial expressions and mannerisms, he was better looking and refined. Billy thought, he must have received it from his mother's side. He told Charles, "I have no reason to hold a grudge against you, young man."

Charles had no idea what Billy was talking about, he simply replied with an innocent, "okay."

Billy left no stone unturned, he told Charles about his father from Mo to Harry, and about Mr. and Mrs. Brown that adopted him when he was eleven years old. Charles responded, "the MacCall's are old money, so dad is-is..."

"Pathetic. You see Charles, Mr. Henry Brown had a family member, who was one of the Pilgrims that came over here from England. He was one of the ones to help set up colonies."

"What a history," Charles remarked.

Billy gave Charles a copy of his wife book, which had the picture of Harry when the Browns took him in. "Harry is everything old money is not," Billy said.

"When he's not around, mom calls him butt lips, because of how his mouth is round and poke out."

Billy laughed, and said, "our thoughts exactly."

"Our?"

"Yes, me and the guys at the mill claim Harry's nothing but a goofball."

All But One

They laughed so hard Charles held his stomach from the pain. Billy wiped tears off his cheeks from laughing. "I am so happy I met you," Charles said wiping his eyes then continued, "I haven't laughed like this since, never."

Billy liked Charles, he thought he would be a good match with a female he knew. Billy went back to Boston with Charles. He showed him the house Harry was raised in, he took him around the steel mill and presented him as the owner of the company. Many of the men shook Charles' hand, the manager asked if Billy was coming back. Billy answered, "no, enjoying relaxing too much."

Charles said, "when I get settled, I will meet with you and the accountant."

The manager said, "I am the accountant."

Confused, Charles asked, "who's the manager?" He looked at Billy.

Billy said, "it's how Harry set it up, I was the manager and accountant." Billy nodded towards the new manager and said, "Harry made him the same."

"Okay," Charles began asking several questions, with the manager answering as best he could.

"That will change," Charles commented.

As Charles was thinking and pacing, Billy and the new manager looked sideways at each other, then hunched their shoulders, as if to say, "don't know."

Charles asked, "you're the manager of all the different departments?

"Yes, Sir." The man answered.

"How many supervisors do you have?"

"I'm the manager."

Charles asked, "You're both? How many shop foremen do you have?"

"Shop what, Sir?"

"How about office staff?"

"I'm it, Sir."

"How much steel do you process yearly?"

Billy answered the question, "when Mr. Henry Brown was alive, we sold a little under a half ton per year.

When Harry returned from England, he had learned how to manufacture over two tons per year. Eventually, we got up to seven tons a year. When Harry ordered the steel rods and plates that jumped us up to over twenty tons. Then Harry and I broke up, I moved and stopped generating business through sales." He looked at the new manager and asked, "do you do sales."

The man answered, "no."

Billy said, I come down occasionally to check the books, I believe you're doing maybe two to three hundred pounds per year."

Charles bellowed, "that's not acceptable, no wonder pops want to shut this down." He looked at Billy and said, "I refuse to shut down." He looked at the manager and continued, "give me a week, then we will meet."

Outside Charles asked Billy, "how many departments are there?"

Billy looked at Charles and said, "one I guess, we all work together."

"How many different jobs are there?"

"About twenty."

Charles said, "we'll meet first, come to my hotel room tomorrow?"

Billy looked at Charles confused. Charles asked, "where are you staying? I will pay for your room?"

Billy said, "we can stay at my house."

When they got to Billy's Bostonian home, Charles was amazed, he looked up at the house and said, "wow, how much did pops pay you?"

Billy laughed and said, "we Bought this with the money from my wife's book."

Charles said, "I'm impressed, you own two huge houses."

Three months after Charles arrival in Boston, Billy presented him to a beautiful young woman, that had dark brown hair and big green eyes. She captivated Charles heart the first time he saw her. Before Matilda, when Charles moved to Boston there was a fresh new field of women, Charles was having fun.

Billy noted that Charles was a hard worker and lover, to slow him down and get him focus, he introduced Charles to Stella's gorgeous daughter. Billy's plan was to get Charles to settle down, the strategy worked, Charles fell in love at first

All But One

sight. Matilda's eyes and big beautiful sunshine smile won his heart.

With Charles focused and in control, The Brown Steel Mill production increased to one ton his first year in Boston. Charles told Billy he wanted to triple sales the following year. Eighteen months after meeting Matilda, Charles asked her to marry him. She said yes, for the next six months she planned the wedding with her father's sister. At first, Matilda's family were reluctant, after all, Charles was the progeny of Harry. But Charles was over the top handsome, charming, and charismatic, he could talk a lion to eat a carrot out of his hand, and not harm him. Matilda's American and European family adored the young man.

Six months before the wedding Charles mailed three separate invitations to the mansion. Baerbel collected the mail, she kept hers and gave the other two to Harry. One month later, Baerbel sent a letter to Charles asking for money, she wanted to travel to Europe to her father's home. She complained that Harry only gave her fifty dollars every month and that was not enough to travel.

One month later Baerbel received a letter from Charles asking her to attend the wedding and meet his bride. Baerbel replied through a telegram, just send da' money, I am leavin' yo' father and ain't got time foe' a weddin."

Charles told Billy about his mother's message, Billy said, "send her the money. Don't try to make people do what they don't want to do. You'll only irritate the person."

Charles sent the money.

Four months before Harry's shindig, Baerbel was on a ship going to Europe. Baerbel had written a letter to her father's sister stating she was on her way. she had written that she wanted to see where the queen lived, purchase new party dresses and fancy hats, to wear to the British Balls. Baerbel had planned to travel and see all of England.

X

MacCall Family Lies

On the ship heading towards England, Baerbel boasted about being related to the queen through her father's family. She had never been beyond her little country town, seeing all the elegant people, ladies dressed in the latest fashion she had never seen, and the men were dashing. She was happy that Charles had given her thousands of dollars, she was planning to purchase all new clothes. She envisioned going shopping with her aunt, she would purchase the latest fashions.

Baerbel was failing at trying to fit in. When she was born, everyone in Titleburk and MacCall, rejoiced. She, after all, was the daughter of a wealthy prominent man, whom the town was named after. Baerbel never had to make friends, because everyone rallied around her. On the ship, away from home was another experience.

Baerbel styled, she smiled, she walked with the fingers on her right hand gently resting on her collarbone, as she nodded and smiled at each passerby. She perched her lips, walked with her head held high, her nose pointed towards the sky, she squinted and fluttered her eyes. In her mind, she resembled a high-class woman, no one, was greater than she.

When the boat docked, she departed with the flair of what she thought made her look superior. And then, she looked over and saw two toothless dirty people holding a sign with her name written on it. She turned and said to the people behind her, "the queen must have sent them."

Baerbel father's people were not rich, they lived down a wet rat-infested alley. Eleven people lived in a four-room flat. A

All But One

pot sat in the corner of the room as the toilet. There was no well or water to bathe. Her family took her money, sold her jewelry, and all her clothes, excluding one dress. In the matter of a month, Baerbel was dirty, sticky, stinky, and broke. Her second month in England, she was bitten by a rat, she became very ill. Lying in bed, she said to her aunt, "I should have gone to Boston."

Her aunt said, "you were a fool for coming here alone. Didn't your dad tell you about us, and where he was raised."

Baerbel said, "father had a thick southern dialect."

Her aunt said, "so, he didn't tell you about his home."

****

Charles and his new bride went to New York to visit his mother's people. He learned that she lied to him from a storekeeper where her father worked. Charles grandma was raised in a New York slum. A high bridge was the dividing line, coloreds on one side and whites on the other. Charles grandma met his grandpa one week after he got off the boat from Europe. They met, got married, moved to Vermont, bought a house, and in a few years sold it and moved south to a town without a name. Within a few months and lots of practice, the MacCall's had a deep southern drawl. Charles said, "Tilda, my grandma is nothing but a lie, she said she was from a rich family."

Charles and Matilda stayed in New York for two weeks and shopped after learning about Charles grandma. They mailed their purchases home and got on a boat to Europe, where they first visited Matilda's relatives, who were doctors, professors, or business owners. Matilda's family were successful people. The older ones remembered meeting Harry when he traveled to Europe with Stella. They had nothing good or positive to say about Harry. Charles apologized for his father's misgivings, his wife family liked Charles, he was excepted as one of them.

Matilda's brother, Morris had moved to Europe, he took them around to the different sites, the threesome had a grand time together. Charles shared with him what was going on with Billy and the Steel Mill. Morris told Charles that he was tired of being away from home, America. He said, "I plan on moving back soon."

Charles said, "join me at the Steel Mill."

Morris said, "done. I'll return in a few months."

Charles said, "you have a job."

After spending two weeks with Matilda's family, the couple's next stop was Charles grandpa family.

Before leaving Morris told Charles, "meet them in a park, not in their home."

Charles said, "I was going to invite them to our hotel room."

Morris replied, "not a good idea."

Charles asked, "how do you know about my family."

"When you sent the itinerary of your visit, I went to see them for myself." He paused before saying, "not good."

When they left, Charles wife said, "I know what you're thinking, do not do it. Get word to them and let's meet them in the park." She looked at him sternly and said in a demanding tone, "hide your money."

Charles took his wife and Morris advice; it was a good thing. William MacCall relatives were prostitutes, drug addicts, and alcoholics that resided down a rat-infested alley, where people threw their waste and garbage out the windows. Their hair was matted and dirty, their teeth were yellow or missing, they and their clothes were filthy. Charles inquired about his mom, he looked at one of the women strangely, she had squeezed in a dress he had seen his mom ware. One of the men said, "she was weak and sickly."

Charles asked, "sick from what?"

The woman wearing his mom's dress said, "she got bit by a rat."

His aunt said, "young man I am your aunt, we git bit by rats all the time, we okay."

Charles asked, "did you call a doctor?"

A man said, "I am your father's older brother, he always send us money, do you have any money."

The woman wearing Baerbel's dress said, "We ain't got no money for a doctor."

"She had money," Charles said.

Another female said, "that was gone before she died."

Charles looked at his wife and said as he grabbed her hand, "I've heard enough, let's go."

A female asked, "You got money for us."

Charles turned beet red and yelled, "mom had enough money to get you out the slums. You chose to be stupid and spend it all." He saw a police officer in the park. He looked at his filthy poor relatives and yelled, "officer!"

Charles looked around; his relatives had scattered. Matilda said, "call the police again, let's follow them with the police by our side."

Three policemen went with Charles and Matilda down the filthy alley. When Charles saw where his mother stayed, he cried and said, "she should have come to Boston."

Charles had given his mother five thousand dollars, her family spent it faster than lighting flash, on booze, drugs, and gambling. When Charles, his wife, and the three policemen arrived at the rundown apartment, Charles aunt was the only one home. Standing outside trying to see in he asked, "take me to see my mother."

His aunt said, "she's dead."

Charles was stunned. His heart his mind became blank, like an empty barrel. Charles wife said, "she died because you did not call a doctor."

Charles aunt said, "we didn't have the money."

"My husband gave his mother five thousand American dollars," she yelled so loud the police had to calm Charles wife down, she said softer, "you could have gotten a bigger cleaner place to live."

Charles spoke up, he looked at the police officers and said, "Sir, you'll find drugs in there."

His aunt protested profusely, Charles and his wife left, the police officers entered the apartment, they found the drugs. Also, the officers were glad that Charles had left, otherwise he would have learned that his mother was not bitten by a rat, instead she was raped several times.

Before Baerbel died, she recalled hearing the house slave women crying for help when Harry's friends had their way with them. She yelled when the memory of laughing at Bella's daughter crawling on the floor and out the kitchen door struck in her mind. She cried hard because it was her idea to lock Jo in the barn and keep Bella working late. Baerbel sat up and pushed the man off her, she yelled, "no!"

    Charles aunt grabbed a pan and hit Baerbel in the head. Right before dying, she had visions, she saw a young teenage girl face as though the child was standing there. Baerbel's last memory was of sending an elderly man out to the girl. When she heard the girl screaming, Baerbel left and joined the others in another room. When the man was finished with the girl, he joined the others. As he entered the room Baerbel winked at him. Baerbel last words were a loud babble, "dey be slaves, I's a rich white woman." Unbeknown to Baerbel, when the man joined the others, the girl entered the kitchen got a glass, went outside. She and young Bo chopped the glass up until it looked like grains of sugar. Bella made lemonade.

    She remembered the telegram that she sent to Charles, she wrote, *I's should have come to Boston to be wid' you.* She asked her uncle to get the note to Charles. He sent it to Charles because he felt sorry for his niece. Within six weeks Baerbel was skin and bones, she refused to eat the slop they called food, and would not wash in the same water others had cleaned themselves. She was raped and slapped around several times a day. Lying on an overly stained mattress, several tears rolled down Baerbel cheek, she died angry at her father for lying to her. She was mad at Charles for not being more persistent and order her to move to Boston, she had hostile thoughts about Drew whom she felt loathed her, but most of all she hated Harry who was the reason she was living in filth. Baerbel died raging mad at everyone but herself, her tears originated from self-pity.

    Her aunt and the others went to Baerbel bedside, for a moment they stared down at her. The aunt said, "she looks surprised."

    Baerbel died during her third month in Europe. From the ship to the rat-infested alley Baerbel never saw beyond the slums. Her dreams never materialized.

    Upon Baerbel's death, the family did not have enough money to pay for a funeral. Her aunt gave the crematory

Baerbel's pearl bracelet, she was cremated, and ashes were thrown in the trash.

XI

Paula

April 5, 1876

On the day Vance dropped his last load of men and women off in the back of Harry's mansion, Moses jumped off the wagon. He bombarded his way through the freedmen and women to the front. Twenty-two-year-old Moses looked up at the Browns and saw, seventeen-year-old Paula standing with the family. He was determined to use her and rise above coloreds across the nation.

Unlike Thaddeus and Dakota, who were nice and kind, their son Moses was mean and hostile towards his wife and sons. His parents would have been disappointed with their son. Moses had an anger issue that subsided when he lived with his parents. It was as though they were the glue that held the rage at bay. Living with anyone else he spiraled out of control.

One week before Harry's shindig for his hired hands, Moses entered his cabin and saw his boys cleaning. The oldest boy had inherited his father's flair to make anything out of wood. He had proudly made two toy horses, one for himself the other for his younger brother. His carvings left wood shavings all over the floor. When Moses entered the house, the older boy was sweeping, his little brother was gathering the pile of wood shavings and threw them in the fire. The older boy saw his dad standing in the doorway, he stopped what he was doing and ran to his father showing him what he had made. Moses pushed him aside, he went straight to Paula, who was cooking. Moses yelled, "housework is for women only!"

When He began beating Paula, the boys ran upstairs to hide. They did not come down the steps until Moses was gone. The oldest boy said, "one day, I's kill em' foe' our mom."

He helped Paula off the floor onto a chair, she laid her head on the table. The youngest boy ran and got an old hired hand named, Mama Faye. She walked in the cabin looked at Paula and said, Lawdy child, what happen ta' ya."

That same day Harry sent Vance to deliver a few digging tools and fetch and bring Moses to the mansion. When Paula got word that Vance was on his way to the slave compound, even though she could barely walk and was sore and bruised, she begged Moses to let her and the boys go with him. She promised that they would stay outside and sleep in the barn with the horses. Moses said yes, with one thing that Paula had to agree to do, she agreed. Vance drove the horse pulling the flatbed cart filled with digging tools for the big shindig that was being held inside the slave gate. Moses and a few other men helped Vance unload the things off the cart. When they finished unloading, Vance stayed the night on the cart. Paula asked Moses if she could take food out to Vance, he said yes.

When Vance saw Paula, he flinched then asked, "what happened to you?"

"Can you please help me leave Mr. Vance?" She whispered as she handed Vance a plate of food, she also gave him and his horses' water. She asked him to help her to the church.

Before eating, he took Paula to the slave church. Inside the church were two books under the podium, Paula got the first book, on the last page there was just enough room for her to write her name, the date Bella said she was brought to the plantation, the dates of her son's birth,1866 and 1869, and their names, Boy One and Boy Two. She also wrote a message, *April 1876, I am running away from my husband Moses with my two boys.* Paula and her sons were the last to have their names written down in the book.

She opened the second book, it was empty. She said, "I am the last of Harry's original slaves, it's all over," she placed the books in their place.

Paula went out to Vance and said, "I would like to come back in a few years to see the museum," she looked at Vance and asked, "how about you?"

Vance said, "I need time away from this place." He handed her the empty plate.

When they pulled in front of Paula's cabin, Moses came out and yelled, "where have you been, git in here and fix my boys plates."

The next morning, Vance was in the driver's seat with Moses sitting next to him. Vance looked at Moses then jumped down off the wagon, he entered the cabin to see if Paula needed help. She had new cuts and bruises, and the oldest boy had a black eye. Paula gave Vance a hug and then sent the boys out. As the boys were leaving, Vance watched Moses scoot over to the driver's seat. Mama Faye going to Paula's cabin saw the oldest boy eye. She entered the cabin, and said, "y'all stayin' wid' me from now own." She went to Paula and continued, "he beat ja' agin?"

Moses did not like the way Paula was raising his sons, he felt she was training them to be loyal slaves and not independent, as himself. For that reason, he got her to agree to help clean the debris around the newly built building in the woods, he had planned to cause her accidental death. With her out-of-the-way, he and his boys would start an architect company. He looked where Vance had sat, scooted over and took the reins.

What Moses did not know was that Paula had a plan as well. She was snatching the opportunity to run with her sons that were, ten and seven.

Paula was in more pain but calmer when she asked Vance to help her, she said, "please help me hitch up Massa smallest wagon when we get to his house."

Mama Faye asked, "can I's go wid' ja'?"

"Yes ma'am, mama Faye," Paula answered.

Mama Faye said, "Gib me one moment." She hurried out of the cabin.

When she was returning, Paula and the kids were on the cart, Moses still in the driver's seat began to pull off. Paula said, "Mama Faye is coming."

Moses ignored Paula and kept going, Vance reached over and grabbed the reins, the two horses stopped. Mama Faye climbed on huffing and puffing. Vance told Moses to move when Moses got down and went around to the passenger side, Vance scooted to the driver's seat.

Once they reached Harry's mansion, Paula, the kids, and mama Faye got off the flatbed cart. Standing in the backyard looking up at the porch, mama Faye said, "five years ago I came here, my life changed." She took a deep breath and released slowly, she looked at Paula and continued, "from slavery, ta' freedom."

Moses pointed towards the porch, and said, "boys that's where I saw your mama, standing with the family like she was one of them. I thought she was going to be my equal, intelligent. She turned out to be, dumb and useless."

Vance caught Paula's eye and inconspicuously nodded towards the side of the house, but said, "I'll take the horses in." Inside the barn, he got a small wagon and one horse ready for Paula and her family.

Before entering Harry's house, Moses turned to his sons and said, "I have big plans for you two." His oldest boy looked just like Paula while the youngest resembled his handsome Egyptian dad. Moses asked, "what's our family name?"

The older boy said nothing, he balled his fist, his body grew tense, seeing that her son was in a position to hit his father. Paula gently put her hand on his shoulder to calm him.

Moses looked at the other boy, he asked, "what is our name little boy?"

"Berhanu, daddy," his youngest son said proudly.

"What does it mean?"

"Light, daddy."

Moses said, "Good job son." He looked at his oldest boy and punched him hard, and said, "our name is who we are, a proud family from Africa."

He said nothing to Paula nor looked her way, he leaped up the porch steps and entered the kitchen.

Moses was expecting Harry to give him good recommendations, and money so he could start his business.

Moses entered the library with a proud swag, he said, "good morning Mr. Brown, how's your day?"

Harry said, "sit down Moses."

Paula, her sons, and Mama Faye stood nervously on the side of the house. Vance pulled up and told them to get in and lay down, he placed a cover over them. When they were a few paces down the road away from Harry's mansion, Vance stopped and jumped off the wagon.

Vance said to Paula, "I understand your reason for leaving, and then asked, "do you have enough money."

"I believe so, Sir," Paula replied, "I took Moses money and the remainder of mine."

Mama Faye said, "I's save all my money, dat's what's I's go gits.'"

They pulled off, with Paula driving the horse and buggy. Paula looked at the old lady and said, "I am going to Saint Louis to find a friend of mine, where would you like to go."

"May I's go wid' you. I's got no famly' 'cept you and da' boys. My chil'ren be sold some twenty years ago." She paused before saying, "my huz'ban ran away."

"Will it be okay to call you mama?" Paula asked.

"I's like dat." She smiled; the worried look melted from Mama Faye's face.

Paula said, "boys, meet your grandma."

The youngest boy said, "hi grandma."

The old woman cried and laughed at the same time; tears of happiness flowed down her cheeks.

Paula said, "I was sold to the Brown's when I was a baby, never knew my mama or daddy. Miss. Bella said that I was a tiny baby, brought from another plantation."

"Who be Miz. Bella?"

"Mr. Brown's favorite cook, she raised me."

"She teach you ta' talk."

Paula chuckled, "no ma'am, too many years with my husband, Moses."

XII

Happy Harry

April 10, 1876,

    The eleventh year of employing the hired hands, Harry's H.B. Metropolis was ready for visitors to come and admire the museum. Over the span of the years, many more people joined the hired hands. Three days before Harry's shindig, he had several of the men put digging tools, and enough food to feed six hundred people on the back of a wagon. The hired hands drove the wagon with Harry following on horseback, to the slave area. When they arrived, Harry said, standing next to the western side of the slave gate, "dig a hole large enough to bury six elephants?"

    Well, the men had only heard of elephants and had never seen one, they stood beholding Harry with blank faces. Harry had only seen a picture of an elephant, he said, "dig a hole large enough to bury eight one-room slave shacks."

    One of the white men asked, "why we do dis' boss?"

    Harry lied, he looked at the men that expected him to give a rational reason, instead, he said, "the burial will symbolize the end of slavery in America. After you finish digging, on April 13, I am going to have a down-home foot-stomping farewell shindig by the hole."

    Moses asked, "What do you want me to do?"

    "Dig," Harry said in a demanding tone.

    One of the hired hands asked, "tonight Sir?"

    "No, go home get some rest, tomorrow began digging. A hole that size will take a few days. While you're digging another group of men will tear down a few old slave shacks that I left standing."

The men were tired, they began to leave, Harry said, "wait, on the day of the shindig I want all of you to be there, I am giving everyone two shiny new silver dollars, and your last payment." Over the years Harry increased his hired hands pay to a dollar and twenty-five cents.

One of the men said, "dat' be pert' near two-dollar…"

"Naw dat' be ova' two dollar." Another man corrected, then continued, "dat be three-dollar we's gits."

One of the men asked, "it be all right iffen' we's' make a barrel of rum?"

"That's a great idea," Harry said thoughtfully with excitement. "A great idea, indeed," he repeated to himself, as he galloped home.

They exploded with joy.

Moses, on the other hand, was not as joyous. His dream had come true, he had become Harry's right-hand man, and on several occasions met with Harry in his home. He had explained the architect of the buildings to be built and the layout of Harry's Metropolis. On his wedding day, he stood on the porch with the family and looked down at the slaves with Paula by his side. A dream he'd had on the day he was hired.

Paula had taken his boys, Moses had no idea where she had gone, he was so angry had Paula returned he would have killed her. He was miserable without his sons by his side and insulted that Harry had suggested he dig. He felt that he was above digging, and terrified, he would never see his boys again. Moses went to his cabin, up to his bedroom, pulled up a loose floorboard where he kept a gun, the papers with his family history, and his college graduation certificate.

He laid the gun on his bed, then went downstairs, the documents were old, soiled, and barely legible, Moses cried as he read what he had written so many years ago. The sting of his parent's death revisited him. He pulled himself together, got several pieces of paper and wrote his family history a second time. He also included his birthday, his parents' birthdays, and the date of their passing. He wrote a message reading, *dad, mom, you have two grandboys, they are seven and ten. You would love them as much as I do. Dad, I have so much anger, I cannot control it. That is not how you raised me. It's like, I'm back on the plantation in*

Massa house. I don't remember being there but what you told me about my stay, I was a very angry baby in their house and calm with you. I need your mom-dad, I need you.

He put the pen down, went upstairs, laid across his bed and cried hard. He eventually sat up and lit a candle. He looked at the bedspread and saw a splatter of Paula's blood. He ran down the stairs crying. He wrote, *my wife was a beautiful soft speaking young woman, I was mean to her, sorry dad, sorry mom, sorry Paula. I will do better.*

Moses' heart was heavy with grief, he had to keep wiping tears away that would not stop rolling out his eyes. In a sad state of mind, Moses made one small box out of a piece of tin that was left from the roofs of the cabins, and a larger box with wood. He put his family history, certificate, and the message he had written in the tin. He placed the tin in the larger wood box.

Moses ran to the church; in the back room, he dug a hole in the dirt floor and buried the box. On his way home, he asked himself, "why did I do that?" He started to turn back and dig the box up. A plan emerged in his brain; his lack of conscience agreed with the thought. After the shindig, Moses was going to take the hired hands money, if they protested, shoot them. He decided to ask Paula to take him back for his sons' sake, he wanted to be, a better man. Moses entered his shack and locked the door, he got his gun and all the bullets he could find, then stuffed everything in his pockets.

While Moses was spiraling out of control like a runaway locomotive, happy Harry was in a hurry to get home. He had a way to commit his homicidal quest.

XIII

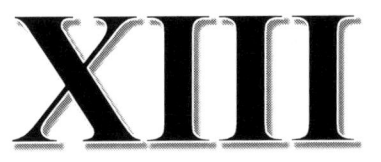

Hoodwinked

Charles was in his office at The Brown Steel Mill, Billy entered with an emergency message from Harry. Charles thought the letter was a late response from his dad, about his mother's death. When Charles returned to Boston, he wrote a letter about the filth the MacCall's were raised in. He wrote that his grandma was from the slums in New York and his grandpa was raised in a rat-infested alley, he said which is where Baerbel died. And then, on the lighter side, he told them about his wife clean, educated, successful family. As Billy was walking out of the office, Charles said, "they did not attend my wedding or responded to the picture of my first child."

Billy said, "Boston is a long way, away."

Charles said, "Europe is further, and mom been dead for years. Dad is just now writing. I never heard from my brother."

He opened the urgent mail. Harry was requesting Charles attendance at the shindig; he balled the letter up and threw it in the trash.

****

The money was so good, that Vance and Deb stayed until H. B. Metropolis was completely built. Deb looked at Vance and said, "let's stay to get the last payment then leave."

Vance said, "we have enough money, I want to leave, now."

Deb said, "Harry's giving us two silver dollars, I will frame one to be our first picture on the wall, in our new big house."

Vance said as he packed, "we have thousands of dollars, I am leaving."

Deb pleaded, "just a few more days, please wait with me."

Moses was still angry, he stayed because he planned to follow through with his plan to steal the hired hands money. He was determined to find his sons, and sweet talk Paula to be his wife again. During his travels from one city to the next, Moses had read signs with the family last name and son, Hertz and Son, or Stance and Sons. Moses could see a big white sign with big black letters reading, "Berhanu and Sons." He smiled.

Charles arrived in MacCall, the day before the shindig. He entered the front door and went straight to his bedroom. It was the same, it had been seven years since he was last in his room. He decided not to unpack, Charles was ready to go home, he missed his wife and son. Matilda got pregnant with their first child while on their honeymoon. They named the baby Drew after Charles brother.

Charles went out on the back porch. Harry, Vance, and Moses were talking when he stepped out the door. Charles looked, quite dapper and extremely prosperous. He was rested and not haggard looking. The clothes he wore were expensive and fashionable, he looked like he had stepped out a fashion magazine. Harry said surprised to see Charles, "look at you." He stood and asked, "when did you get here."

Vance and Harry rallied around Charles, but Drew, sat on the other side of the porch mad. Moses left; he never forgave Charles for the thrashing he received. With Charles back in town, Moses moved out of the slave quarters and rented a hotel room in town. Harry gave Moses a horse for his commute. Moses ego had grown excessively, instead of wearing work clothes on the plantation, he bought three suits, dress shirts, ties, and shoes. One-day Harry said to Drew, "Moses is an arrogant worthless thing."

Charles left Vance and Harry; he went to where Drew was sitting. Drew furiously said, "you got married, had a baby, and did not tell me, your brother."

"That is a lie."

That was the wrong thing to say, Drew blew up like a match being dropped in a gas can. Boom! Harry and Vance went quiet. Drew grabbed Charles by the collar and slammed him against the house. Before Drew could speak Charles grabbed Drews' arms and twisted them outward, he squeezed so tight Drew wanted to cry. Charles spun him around and slammed Drew against the house wall so hard, it almost knocked Drew out. Charles said, "wait here," he began to walk away, turned facing Drew and said, "don't you ever attack me again." Charles entered the house.

Harry said as he watched Charles go inside, "my boy is back." He laughed before asking Drew, "everything all right son?"

Drew pulled his shirt sleeve up, on his forearm bruises had begun to set. Harry went to Drew to see, he said, "wow, he really roughed you up. What are you going to do about it?"

Drew yanked his arm from his dad. "I'm fine," Drew replied. He was shocked at how strong Charles was.

Harry went back to his seat smiling.

Charles ran out of the house, grabbed Drew's arm and said, "come with me, got something to show you."

They walked over to the barn far enough away, so Harry could not hear them, but close enough so Charles could keep an eye on him. Drew said pulling up his sleeve, "you hurt me."

Charles ignored his brother, he told Drew he had sent an invitation to the wedding and the baby blessing. He handed him Liza's book. While Drew flipped through the pages, he argued, "no you didn't," and handed the book back to Charles.

"Yeah, I did. Now, look at this." Charles said.

He opened to the chapter with Harry's picture. Drew asked, "who is Moe?"

Charles answered, "Dad."

"Dad?" Drew repeated, he read the caption under the picture, *Eleven-year-old Moe, once a slave on Jeb's plantation. Now free in Boston.* Drew asked, "you sent the invitations?"

"Yeah, and a letter about mom."

"Mom is in England and she won't write?" Drew said.

Charles stood in shock, all this time, years, his brother did not know their mom was dead. He asked in disbelief, "did dad show you a letter I wrote about mom's death?"

"Mom's dead?" Drew asked confused. Drew fell on his knees crying, Charles was lost for words, a few tears rolled down his cheeks, not for his mother, but for his brother who did not know that the person who gave him life, was no longer alive.

Drew stood and said, "I am going to his room and find what you sent. Keep Moe out here."

Charles said, "Bring everything tomorrow, I'll bring the book, we'll confront Moe at the shindig."

"I like your idea, big brother." He left sniffing and wiping his eyes.

Before the crack of dawn on April 13, 1876, the hired hands joyfully prepared for their exodus shindig and their new life. Harry had all the hired hands to leave their children three years and younger, all ninety-three of them, in the children's area. The kids four and older stayed with their parents.

Over the eleven-year span, Harry had over five hundred hired hands, they were proud of their work. Harry strutted around his Metropolis like a colorful peacock, he was king of his city. He planned to become the tobacco monarch; nobody could stop him. Harry's tobacco on the fake field was thriving and doing so well that it was going to keep any suspicion away from H.B.

The Brown Steel Mill was prosperous, Charles was sending Harry a very healthy check every month. "I'm invincible," he said to himself as he proudly strolled around with his hands clasped behind his back.

Early in the morning, on the day of the shindig, Harry's hired hands prepared for the big celebration, while the silver moon shimmered in the darkness of the navy-blue sky.

Charles and Drew had left out at three o'clock that morning. On their way to the slave area, "Charles said, "I wrote several letters about mom, my wedding, little Drew."

"Who is little Drew?" Drew asked.

Charles laughed, "your nephew."

Drew said, "I saw the picture of the little tyke, he's my namesake." Drew road the remaining way to the slave quarters with a smile plastered on his face. When they arrived in the slave compound, Drew said, "I'm going back to Boston with you, to introduce him to his uncle." They got off their horse, Drew said, "grandma and grandpa were poor. Mom thought they were rich."

He leaned his head on the horse and said, "mom's dead." Drew cried.

    Charles could not think of anything to say to comfort his brother, he stood in silence until Drew moved. He could not imagine how a person could be so evil, empty of caring, void of feelings, barren of love. Charles could only see the top of Drews' head that was leaning on the horse. The horse stood motionless like a mannequin, as though it understood its owner was grieving and needed a moment of silence, of stillness.

    When Harry arrived in the slave area with Vance and Deb, he walked around smelling the food. He made sure the five hundred tin cups he had purchased were on the table and sitting next to the ditch the men had dug. He had purchased one hundred bottles of liquor, only forty was on the table. "Perfect" Harry snickered, "they're already drunk," he claimed.

    Harry had three forty-ounce bottles of poison in a pouch that was on his horse. He took two bottles out and stood by the rum, he slightly lifted the lid and pour the first bottle in. A noise spooked him, he stopped, turned facing so no one would see him put the bottles down his shirt. Zeek said standing behind Harry, "dis' ain't cool nough ta' drank boss."

    Harry turned around and said, "I know, it smelled so good, I had to take a sniff."

    Zeek laughed hard, while Harry lightly chuckled. One of the hired hands yelled for Zeek's help, Harry watched him leave. When no one was watching he took the second bottle out his shirt and poured the poison in. He went to his horse and put the two empty bottles in the pouch and took the third bottle out. He looked around at his hired hands, they were busy fixing plates, talking, eating, drinking, and having fun. Zeek back was toward Harry, a burst of loud laughter emitted from Zeek, and his friends Harry quickly poured the third bottle in the rum, he walked ran to his horse and put the bottle in the pouch. He tied the pouch tight and in knots, he made it difficult for anyone to open it.

    Vance saw everything his good friend was doing. He looked at Deb and said, "don't drink the rum."

    Drew was dancing with a pretty hired hand, Charles went to him and said, "need to ask you something."

    Drew said, "in a minute."

Charles walked away. He was irritated with his family, all he thought about was getting home to his wife and son. Before he left, Charles had a strong desire to slap Harry. Drew caught up with him and said, "what do you want."

"Did you get the invitations and letter?"

"Yes, the invitations were unopened, when I opened them pictures fell out. The letter about mom was opened," Drew shook his head, then said, "just think, had Harry opened the invitations he would have seen his grandson, my nephew, named after his uncle." He playfully punched Charles in the arm and said, "thank you, Charles." Laughing he said, "he looks just like his uncle."

"No, he does not," Charles said laughing. He looked at Drew, sadness had settled on his face. Charles continued, "you know Drew, he kind of do look like his uncle."

Drew said, "I know," he smiled then continued, "all these years he knew mom was dead."

Just think, Charles said, "had pops opened the invitations he would have recognized Stella's daughter, she looks just like her mom."

Drew asked, "who is Stella?"

Charles told Drew all about Harry's adulterous deceitful rumble in the hay.

Drew asked in the most downhearted tone Charles had ever heard, "Harry did not tell me about my mom, why?'

"He's an evil old crow," Charles replied, he put his arm around Drew shoulder. "He will pay," Charles said.

Late in the evening, when the sun was setting, everyone was tired and drunk from cheap wine, except Harry, Charles, Drew, and Vance. Deb looked up at Vance and said, "it's almost over, we leave here and start our lives together in the new house." She was drunk and giddy with excitement.

Vance looked at Deb and said, "don't drink the rum.

Deb didn't listen, she continued talking, "I want to get two big chairs with cushions and set them in front of the fireplace. In the evenings before retiring, we'll sit there and talk about our day. We'll invite only important people over."

The rum had cooled off and was ready to be served, several women filled the cups full, everyone got in line to receive their drink even the children. Harry yelled out asking everyone not to drink because they were going to drink together, he said, "we began this project together, we will end it together."

Zeek asked, "where's da' cabins we need ta' bury?"

The question threw Harry for a moment, being a professional liar, he recuperated and said, "my boys and Vance will bring them, tomorrow."

Moses stood by Zeek and said, "something doesn't feel right."

While the women poured the rum, Harry went to his boys that were standing together. He pulled them aside and said, "do not drink the rum, pretend."

Drew said, "naw pops, I am going…"

"You will die," Harry said.

Charles gasped and said, "those three bottles of poison on the kitchen counter, is in the rum?"

"You are a smart child Charles." Charles slapped Harry so hard he fell to his knees. While Harry was on his knees Charles said, "you failed to tell Drew, mom is dead."

Harry tried to stand, Charles, knocked him back down and said in a gangster tone, "you will pay."

Drew grabbed Charles' arm and said, "hold on brother."

Harry got up and walked away. Everyone stopped, the hired hands watched in shock. Harry pulled himself together, straighten his clothes and gave his goodbye speech. He got the hired hands attention by banging a metal cup on the gate and said, "well, it's time for you to go your way," to his sons and Vance he said, "boys and Vance after we drink this fine rum together, give everyone two silver dollar and their last pay." He turned back to the hired hands, and said, "God be with you on your new journey."

One of the freedmen said, "Mr. Brown we thank you foe' what you's' done foe' us."

Harry said, "Thank you for your hard work. I am not an easy man to please, but all of you did better than my expectations." As he talked his face grew redder and stung from the slap he received from Charles. Harry continued, "I thought it would take much longer, but you finished in eleven years, thank you." Harry held up his cup and said, "a toast to your new life, let us drink together."

Everyone drank. Charles looked at Drew and whispered, "what if this do not work."

Vance and his wife were next to the money table, that was close to the slave gate exit.

Without anyone seeing him, Vance turned sideways to pour his drink out, then held his cup as though it was full. Vance looked at Deb and said, "don't drink."

It was too late, she quickly slurped down the liquor, Vance wiped his mouth as though he had just finished drinking.

Several of the hired hands using their cups got more rum, others went to the table where Vance was handing out the money. Deb turned to him and said like a kid in a candy store, "give me one, give me one."

Vance gave her a silver dollar. She smiled, laid her head on his shoulder and slid down his body to her death. Vance stood watching her, he knelt next to her, he shook and said, "Deb, get up." He stood and saw most of the hired hands began dropping dead like flies being sprayed with a can of industrial insecticide, Vance fell as though he was dead, he was in a good spot, hidden behind the table.

Zeek dropped to his knees and softly prayed just above a whisper, "I unnastan' Lawd, foe' da' reason, foe' da' room wid' da' dirt flo, and da' church close to da' gate.' I's pray Lawd, foe' dey' safe journee." He slowly exhaled saying, "tank ya Lawd, fo' eleven years free," his breath slowly released as his head bowed lower. Zeek died on his knees in a prayer position.

Several tears that rolled down Zeek's cheeks as he prayed, dropped on the ground.

Moses approached Harry and his sons, and said, "it was never your plan to let us go, I watched you, you didn't drink so I didn't drink, and guess what."

Moses pulled out a gun, Charles jumped in front of his father, Drew pushed Charles out the way, the bullet struck Harry in the arm. Drew whipped out his own gun and shot Moses in the shoulder, Moses dropped his gun, Charles ran over and picked it up. Moses said, "I should have been nicer to Paula and my boys, I should have gone with them."

"Shut-up fool," Drew standing close to Moses pointed the gun, pulled the trigger, and missed.

Getting out of Drew's way, Moses fell to the ground and rolled. He stood and said, "I was raised in hate but not to hate. My mom and dad taught me to love, when they died, I became the boy raised in hate."

Charles said, "good speech." He pointed the gun, shot, the bullet went straight to his heart.

Falling, Moses had a surprised look on his face. When he hit the ground, he was dead.

Harry stood next to his sons, the three looked down at Moses body, "Good job Charles, I still think you are a disgusting child. How dare you hit your father."

Charles' eyes glowed with rage, he gave Harry a look that was so evil it frightened him, Harry stood behind Drew.

Drew turned and pointed his gun at Harry, and said, "you had me angry at Charles because he didn't invite us to his wedding, I found the letters and invitations, there are pictures in the letters, had you opened them you would have seen your grandson." Drews' voice became soft, "why didn't you tell me mom was dead. Been dead for years." He cried.

Charles said, "Listen to this Drew, I only told you half the story," he told Drew about Harry's life as a slave and his four siblings. Charles ended by saying, "He ran away, landed in Boston and was taken in by a rich family, that he killed."

Harry said sarcastically, "are you finished?"

Charles continued, "Moe is nothing but a white slave." Charles handed the book to Harry and asked, "look familiar Moe?"

With his good arm, Harry tried to punch Charles, "You been talking to Billy."

"Billy is a kind honorable man," Charles commented.

Harry shouted, "he left me to rot."

"No Moe. He quit because you killed your parents in Boston, while married to our mom, and you told another woman that you were going to marry her." Charles looked at Drew and said, "show him the pictures of my wife and his grandbaby."

Looking at the picture Harry said softly, "that's Stella."

"No, that's her daughter, who is my wife. You and your lies are responsible for my mother-in-law killing herself."

Harry tried to kick Charles; Drew pushed Harry back. Drew laughed as he said, "Charles told me your names were Bo, Jo, So, Toe, and you the youngest, Moe. Excuse me as I become a religious man, thank You God for letting him marry my mother, whom you did not tell me was dead."

Harry looked at Charles and said, "I will kill you, something I should have done years ago. It will not be a merciful death Charles, you're an ungrateful twit."

Charles frowned as he said, "kill me like you did your parents in Boston, who were celebrating your engagement and birthday. Billie told me that the police found a few of the bolts, they showed them to him, he confirmed they had been tampered with. He was going to take everything to his grave but decided to unburden himself, by regurgitating to me, what you had done."

Harry put his hand on Drew's shoulder and softly said, "Drew, you're my favorite son, are you going to let him talk to your father like that? Look what he did to my face."

Drew yanked away from Harry and said, "you strut around here like you come from royalty. You're nothing but a white slave raised in hate just like Moses."

Using Moses gun, Charles stood like a marksman, pointed Moses gun at Harry and said, "it's time for you to go Moe." He pulled the trigger, the bullet struck dead center Harry's eyebrows, he fell instantly to the ground. Charles looked at Drew and said, "little brother, let's clean this mess up."

Drew stood in awe of his brother, he simply said, "Dad had no favorite, we all slaves to him, you, me, ma, Vance, the rest of America, niggers, and whites. Charles, me and you can run this place together."

Vance stood and said, "with all, I just heard, you can shoot me now or let me live."

Charles and Drew thinking everybody was dead, Vance terrified the brothers. Charles said as he got himself together, "you can help us dump the bodies in the grave Moe had them to dig."

The three men laid Harry's and Deb's body on one of the carts. They worked into early morning dumping over five hundred hired hands, in the grave and covered them over with dirt.

Drew stopped to take a breather, he asked, "Think they thought they were digging their grave?"

Vance said, "no, they did not know, they grew ta' luv' and trust Harry."

Drew said, "the tobacco in this area is going to be vibrant green and healthy."

"Tobacco?" Charles asked.

"Yes, tobacco and sugarcane."

Charles said, "Drew, we're inside the slave's quarters, they will plant their vegetables here."

Charles went over to his father and found a key in his pant pocket.

Drew said, "we have at least seventeen years before the children are between the ages of eighteen and twenty-one, a time when they will move to their new home." He looked down at the massive grave and said, "I will not eat anything that's grown on this plot of land." He laughed hard.

Vance asked, "are you going to let me live?"

Charles and Drew said to gather, "yeah."

Charles smiled and said, "I'm tired, let's stay in one of the cabins, then take Harry's body home tomorrow morning," Charles looked around at Vance wife, then over at Moses.

Vance followed Charles' eyes, he said, "I'll take her and bury her behind our cabin. And be on my way." He picked her body up and laid Deb across the horse she had ridden.

Charles asked, "why didn't you tell her about the poison?"

Vance said, "I did, she would not believe me. I even suggested that we leave a few days ago. She got caught up in money and things."

Drew said, "she did change."

"She made a drastic change," Charles admitted.

Vance left riding on the horse he had ridden on, with Deb draped across her horse. Vance took her to the well and dropped her body down. In his pockets were several silver dollars he had stolen off the table, he went into the house and got the money they were saving." He changed horses and left.

"Drew looking down at Moses and asked, "what are we going to do with his body?"

Charles suggested, "Moses shot dad, we killed Moses. Justice served."

Drew agreed with Charles and then asked, "what do we do about Vance."

Laughing, Charles said, "we will never see him again."

"How you know?"

"I know Vance."

All But One

Before sunrise, the brothers took the two bodies out of the slave area, they locked the gates behind them. Harry had hired a teacher and nurse to care for the children, they were locked in the children area. Before going to the mansion, Drew went straight to Vance cabin, he was gone.

The next morning, while Charles and Drew were leaving the plantation, Vance was on a train going west. He was never seen again.

Drew asked Charles, "why did mom go to Europe?"

Charles answered truthfully, "she was leaving dad, she thought the family in Europe were rich. I asked her to come to Boston and live with me, she turned me down."

Drew pushed Charles again then said, "you could have told me," he punched Charles a second, by the third time the punch was hard, Drew was growing angrier at the whole situation.

Charles said, "let's not fight."

Drew swung a fourth time. One punch from Charles and Drew was knocked out cold. Charles dumped water on his brother's face. When Drew came too and was standing, Charles said, "stop hitting me. I know you feel deceived and sad, hitting me is not the solution."

Drew asked, "where did you learn to fight and shoot."

"Grandpa," Charles answered.

Drew said, "tell me about the MacCall's."

Charles told Drew about their grandma and grandpa birthplace and lives before they became rich. He finished by saying, "so, we are from a slave and very poor people."

Charles and Drew brought a table into the drawing-room and laid Harry's body on top. They took Moses body and dumped him in front of the police station. The brothers went inside the station where Charles did the talking. He told the authorities that their mom had left his dad, she was living in Europe. Charles showed them the letter she sent asking him for money. The officer acknowledged that they had not seen her around in a while.

The five openings to the gates had the same lock, Harry had six keys made. One key he kept in his room, an extra key in the kitchen. He had a chest in the attic where he put his H. B. Metropolis complete plan, drawings, maps, the four extra keys, and the newspaper article Charles had written about him.

Before the funeral, Charles put a key down Harry's shirt next to his heart. Drew asked, "why."

"In hell, he will have a piece of his Metropolis."

Drew said, "you are nothing that you look like."

"What do you mean," Charles asked.

"You look soft, easy, flyboy. But you're not, you fight, lie, and kill without a flinch."

Charles smiled and said, "I learned that from grandpa before Harry killed him and grandma. And when we were in the army."

"What do you mean he killed them?" Drew asked.

Charles looked at Drew, he thought he was either ignorant or innocent he didn't know which. Charles said, "Baerbel told me that Harry threw her in a slave shack. Did you know about that?"

"Yes."

"The best thing Harry did for me was to hire someone to kill me. Why do you think I went to Boston? And the best thing you did for me, shot me when we were in the army. I was tired of combat. Did you know that?"

"No," Drew answered. Drew smiled saying, "the soldiers liked you best, they respected you, you were full of strategies."

To ease Drew jealousy, Charles said, "Harry left all this to you. I don't know what you are going to do with the children, how you are going to care for them, who's going to raise them, why do you need overseer's, tiny houses, all the gates, and the forest. It looks illegal to me, but you know exactly what to do, how, and when. I am going to stick with the steel mill."

Drew stood taller, shoulders back, he resembled a soldier when he said, "dad left all this to me, and the Steel Mill to you. We'll see who's going to be the richer brother."

"It's not a contest Drew."

Drew said, "I am making it a contest."

Charles said, "I have a few hours before my train leave, let's take a look at the castle Harry built."

"Good Idea."

Charles and Drew went to see the castle for the first time. It was spectacular. Looking at the monstrous size building, Drew said, "I thought it was supposed to be V shape."

Charles replied, "I'm glad it's not."

The castle was four stories high, had fifty rooms, thirty thousand square feet, with an east and west wing. It was not the size of Buckingham Palace, not even close, it was, however, the largest house in MacCall. The Brothers proceeded up the twelve steps that led onto the marble porch. Twelve marble columns spread from one end of the porch to the other. They entered the castle through double doors made of pure brass and gold. The knocker on the door was a big lion's head with a ring going through its nose.

Inside the castle the vestibule was like non-other, it was bedazzling to behold. The decor was gold, crystal, and ivory, the floor was made of smooth stone with splashes of grays, white, and black. A beautiful huge chandelier hung from the high ceiling. Charles was breathless, he continuously repeated a breathy, "wow."

Watching Charles reaction, Drew said, "I can see you living here. The mansion is mine."

Charles said, "yeah, gargoyles, deep dark colors dad liked. But this place is bright, airy, it's happy. Who is this Harry? I would like him," Charles laughed, then said as they went from room to room, "no wonder pops was low on cash."

"What did you say?" Drew asked.

In Harry's will, he left the plantation to Drew and Steel Mill to Charles. He had asked Charles for money to give to Drew. Charles sent him thirty-five thousand dollars.

Harry had spent every dollar he had on the castle. Charles answered Drew's question by saying, "Dad left us thirty-five thousand dollars, the mansion, and the castle."

Drew said, "dad left you the castle and mill, me the mansion and plantation, we'll see which brother will be the richest."

Charles said again, "little brother, it's not a contest."

XIV

Back To Boston

Charles and Drew returned to the mansion where Charles had hired a stagecoach to take him to the train station. Drew stood on the porch watching Charles leave for the second time. History repeated itself. When the carriage was out of sight, it hit Drew, Charles had a wife and child, he had no one. Laughing, Drew remembered he was supposed to return to Boston with Charles and meet his namesake.

Drew jumped off the porch and sprinted down the long path after Charles. This time Charles did not turn around to wave bye, he was on his way home to see his wife his son. When the stagecoach turned out of the mansion's yard, Drew stopped running, he stepped out of the yard and watched the stagecoach, he waved hoping his brother would see him. inside the coach Charles remembered he did not wave goodbye, he leaned out the window and saw Drew, the brothers shouted, "goodbye," several times to each other.

When the stagecoach was out of Drew's site, he said, "he left me." As Drew entered the mansion yard, a question popped into his head, "who would watch the slaves?" He flopped to the ground crying.

A pain of seclusion hit Drew in his gut so hard, it took his breath away. Drew pulled his self together, went to the barn and hitched a wagon and two horses. He checked the children and caretaker water and food supply. He left and was gone a week. Between Titleburk and MacCall he purchased enough food to last the babies, nurse, and teacher for several months. He even purchased three chickens, a hen, a chicken house, hay, and four extra barrels. He overflowed the barrels with water, which gave

All But One

them eight barrels. Drew told the nurse and teacher to make the food and water last for at least two months, he said to them, "all the children need to be alive when I return. If any is missing or dead, I will kill you." He left going to Harry's old homestead to get a wife, he wanted to see if the plantation Moe escaped from, was still there.

Drew went to the shoe factory where Moe worked when he was a kid, the company had gone out of business. Drew was leaving to visit the plantation where his dad was a slave when he saw a woman coming down the street. She and her clothes were filthy dirty, Drew asked her name, she said, "BB"

She was poor, dirty, homeless and wanted to get out of poverty, so, it was easy for Drew to woo her. Drew asked, "what does the B's stand for."

"Dat's' my name Sir, BB."

For several weeks, Drew bought her new clothes, got her hair done, cleaned her up. He told her he had to visit a place, he asked her to wait in town for him.

Drew visited the plantation where Moe was a slave. It was still in operation, some of the buildings were old and worn, there were only a few people working the land, they were called, sharecroppers. There were no overseers to keep the workers in line. Drew asked an old man if he knew where a little boy named Moe lived. The man took him to the shack and said, "da woman kill herself in der.' Nobody lib' in it since dat' day.

Drew stepped inside the shack; his foot went through the floor. He was getting ready to run, but from the light that came through the open door and holes in the roof, he saw bones lying on the floor.

He went back outside found the old man and asked about the bones he had seen.

Moe's brother heard Drew ask the question. He was the younger of the two that stayed behind. He went to Drew and said, "young man, dat' be my mom, she be an evil drunk. Massa beat her good for beating on us kids. She kill herself da' day my little brother left."

Drew asked, "what is your name?"

"Toe Sir. I had three brothers and one sista."

"Where are your, brothers and sister?"

"Da' oldest two and Moe I ain't knowin' whar's dey' be, my brother dat' worked the farm died years ago, both our wifes' died from a surgery dey' had. I's da' only one left. I's an old man son."

Drew allowed his uncle to talk, he said, "I's like a little place wid' a porch, I's sit out der' all da' day long. No worry bout' food, nonthin."

Toe slowly turned to leave, Drew watched him go to a shack that leaned so low it looked like at any minute, it would fall over. After Elijah died, Toe and his brother moved into the cabin. When they married his brother moved into another shake and Toe remained in Elijah's shack until the day, he met Drew. Drew went with him and said, "I know of a place like that, it's far from here, I am going back today, you can come if you like."

Seventeen other sharecroppers said that they wanted to go. Their ages ranged from twenty to over seventy.

Drews luck changed, he needed slaves to begin the tobacco growing on H. B. Metropolis. All the cabins were empty since Harry's hired hands children were still babies. Drew said to them, "I will find a way to get you there."

A woman said, "Sir. we's got a wagon ta' carry us all, and foe' horses."

Drew asked, "where's your Massa."

Toe answered, "Mr. Jeb be old and cain't see."

Another worker said, "he wonts' know we be gone."

Drew said, "we're all set, follow me to town, I am going to ask a woman to marry me, then we will go home."

They silently trailed behind Drew; in town, he asked BB to marry him, she said, yes," before he finished asking.

When they arrived at H.B. Metropolis, the eighteen thought the mansion was spectacular, Drew took them down to the slave area and told them to pick a cabin. Drew was proud, most of them chose Drew Road. While they were looking for a home, Drew returned to the mansion. He left all the gates opened. They stayed put, they had a job, town to go to, plenty of food, and beautifully clean home, what more could Drews hired hands desire. Drew went to Titleburk and purchased vegetable seeds for the garden, food, and wine, he returned to the slave compound. On the plantation where they were sharecroppers, most of the workers from Jeb's plantation lived in the raggedy shacks or slept on the ground, they never went further than the slave quarters. Jeb who was old and cranky gave them a small piece of bread. they collected rainwater for their thirst. They stayed true to Drew because life on H.B. Metropolis was exquisite, nor did they ask about the large building sitting alone.

Drew never told Toe, that he was his nephew, still, he bought the man a rocker, and sat it on his porch. Regrettably, BB became Drew's punching bag and drinking buddy.

When his new workers were settled, Drew went to Ogville and hired a locksmith to come to his home and change the locks on the outer and divider gates. The man asked too many questions for Drews comfort. When the locks were changed, and he had eight new keys to the two new locks, Drew killed the locksmith and threw his body down the well.

None of the men knew how to make furniture, though they were experts in the tobacco fields. Drew had them plant tobacco in the four sections, some of the men suggested to Drew to let the land rest for a year. They explained that the fields were divided into sections of four, giving three segments time to rest and renew to its healthy state. Drew told them that they were to do as he said.

The women made quilts, clothing, and planted a garden over the grave of Harry's hired hands.

To keep their home and peace, the eighteen obeyed Drew. Drew's plantation ran like a well-oiled machine, even though it was slowly going downhill. Seeing the plantation and meeting his uncle drove him to drink heavily. He was nothing but the son of a slave.

Drew's uncle made him cry when he said, "young man, all my life be rough and hard, tank' you's foe' savin' me from dying da' way I's born, a slave, dirty clothes, unbathed, no shoes." He smiled as he continued, "I's got new clothes, foe' pairs of shoes, bathe eva'day, beautiful clean house, a porch and dis' chair to rock in. Tank' you, young man foe' carin' foe' me."

Drew took Toe's calloused hands that were covered in warts in his, and said, "you are very welcome Sir." He smiled and lovingly squeezed Toe's hand.

Toe's favorite part living on the compound was working in the vegetable garden, especially since the food was for him and the others. In the general store Drew supplied meat, baking items, and material. A few men built a smokehouse to preserve the meat.

On weekends they all went to the bar and had a good time. Life was good for the workers. Even though the gates were not locked, male nor female on no occasion ventured away from H.B., they never expected to live so well, they had everything they needed and more.

****

  Charles first son died of measles. Two years later, in 1883, their second son was born, they named him Duke. Life was good for the little family. Billy spoiled Duke, who adored him. They took family trips, and park outings together. Traveling on trains in the north Billy could sit with the family and enjoy the sites with little Duke. But going South was another issue. One summer, they were taking their first trip to see Drew.
  Billy had to get off and go in a boxcar with the animals where the coloreds sat on the floor. Charles took his family off the train with Billy and went back home. Charles wrote a letter to Drew, explaining the reason the trip was momentarily canceled. Billy felt bad because he knew that Charles wanted him to meet his brother.
  A month later, Charles was at the steel mill in his office, on his desk he had a picture of his wife holding Duke, one of Drew in front of the mansion, another of Mr. and Mrs. Brown. Charles had received a letter from Drew, what he had written made hairs stand on his back. Charles read *darkies should not ride with white folk, they ain't nothing but animals that can walk on two legs. They ain't free, they still slave and will always be.*
  Charles picked up Drew's picture, it never dawned on him that his brother felt so harshly towards coloreds. He sat Drew's picture back on the desk, and said softly to himself, "it's a good thing we didn't make it to MacCall. Drew would have put Billy in the slave area."
  Another tragedy took place in Charles life, in 1885, his wife died giving birth to their third son. Charles named the child Cody, after his dead father-in-law, Mayor Cody. Charles was lonely and thought about returning to MacCall. He hired a nursemaid to care for his sons, so he could continue his duties in the steel mill which he had grown weary of. He did not want the company any longer, he talked to Billy about selling, for several

years Billy had helped Charles run the mill. Unfortunately, in 1892, Billy fell ill and was not going to get better. Charles told Billy, "I will not run this company without you, I want to sell."

Through his illness, Billy helped Charles sale the Brown Steel Mill, at the time the company was selling over thirty thousand tons of steel every year. With the new locomotive transportation, the Brown Steel Mill sales skyrocketed. The steel was used to build every part of the train and tracks, for that reason the business sold for a very high price. Charles sold Brown Steel Mill to Morris, his brother-in-law.

1893, Billy died a very rich man, due to investing and saving most of his money. In his will, Billy left everything to Charles, his money and two houses.

Morris also purchased Charles mansion that sat on a hill. He kept Charles workers, but to serve in the managerial position, he hired some of his relatives from Europe to work for him. Charles closed Billy's two houses and returned to MacCall enormously wealthy. With Billy's money, the funds he saved, the selling of his mansion, and the Brown Steel Mill, Charles left Boston a multimillionaire.

His inheritance from Harry and his mother put together was like a penny in a wheel barrel compared to his prosperity. His son Duke was ten, and Cody eight years old when they moved back to MacCall.

Billy and Harry Epic

Two men, one Black, one White. They were close comrades that became distant enemies. Both born a slave, both ran to freedom, both became rich. Both were rags to riches saga. One died contented and surrounded by friends and Charles. The other died a criminal surrounded by hundreds he executed and his sons. One enjoyed his riches; it was a blessing to him. The other fixated over being rich, it was a curse to him.

****

1893

The children of Harry's hired hands were between the ages of eighteen and twenty-one, it was time for them to move to the slave area. Their caregivers, the teacher, and the nurse taught the girls how to sew and Drew taught the boys and girls how to plant tobacco. Before leaving the children area to the slave compound, Drew coupled them together. He had the young slaves stand in the middle of the yard; Drew had one mass wedding with himself officiating as the pastor. The nurse and teacher stood watching the debacle.

The teacher looked around at the thick trees that blocked their view, she said to the nurse, "I never paid this any attention, but we cannot see beyond the trees."

The nurse said, "I use to wonder what that great big building was that sat away from everything. It's covered by trees."

The teacher said, "and all the gates," she asked, "what are they for? We can only see up, not out."

Looking up the nurse whispered, "we're going to die."

Drew heard the women, he said nothing. What he did not know is the teacher had drawn a picture of what she could see from the children area before the thick forest filled in. Her picture was of the land, gates that she could see, although miles away she drew a building sitting alone.

After the wedding, there were four single girls, Drew believed the older men in the slave complex would marry them and have children. The young adults had outgrown the cabin and small yard and were ready to leave, the nurse and teacher desired to go home to their family. Inside the cabin, they all packed their things and were ready to face the world.

The teacher went into the room she and the nurse slept in and got the drawing of the plantation. When the nurse entered the teacher said, "I'm taking this with me and show to the officials."

The nurse said, "for now, hide it with what I wrote about this place."

The teacher asked, "where?"

"Help me," the nurse said.

The two women struggled to pull a heavy chest-of-drawer from the wall and using a metal object they loosened two boards on the floor. The teacher took the covers off a large schoolbook, she put the nurse's writings and her picture between the hardbacks then placed it under the floorboard. Together they returned the chest-of-drawers to its place.

With everyone packed and ready to go, the nurse, teacher, and their students sat around and talked about their future. The nurse looked at the teacher and said, "that building is miles away, how could we see it?"

One of the twenty-year-old male students answered, "God. Before the woods grew, we all could see far."

A female student said, "yes, it was God. There is something wrong about this place."

"God is going to fix it," said the twenty-year-old male student.

While the students and their caregivers were talking, Drew went to Ogville and found two drunks, he hired them to be the overseers. The men stayed in the mansion; they received a five-day training on their job duties. At the end of the instructions, Drew paid them. He took the men to H.B. Metropolis and showed them where they were going to stay. One of the overseers asked, "this house foe' when we be workin?"

Drew said, "yes."

The other overseer asked, "Sir. may I go home and gib da' money to my wife, and come back in da' mornin?"

Drew replied, "do this one thing for me, then you may go."

The overseers on horseback escorted the young slaves to the cabins. Over the eighteen years, only thirteen of the original eighteen from Jeb's plantation was still alive. Drew's uncle Toe was a very happy man in the slave compound. On one of the days that Drew visited his uncle, Toe was sitting on the porch rocking, Drew sat on the step.

It was a similar scene of Moe sitting on the stoop listening to Elijah.

Toe said talking to Drew, "young man if mama be a slave foe' you, I's believin' dat' mama would not drank da liquor and be so mean."

Drew turned his head away from his uncle when he felt a few tears roll out of his eyes.

Nine years after moving to H.B. Toe became ill, he could no longer go to the upstairs bedrooms, he slept downstairs. He was going to sleep on the floor but Drew bought him a bed and had the nurse to come once a week and care for him. Early one morning before sunrise, Toe got up and dressed, he sat on the porch. As the sun rose Toe watched most of the workers go to the tobacco field and a few in the garden. He waved at all the passerby's, they waved back and said, "mornin' Toe."

Toe yelled back, "mornin, find day ta'day." the warm morning sun was shining on Toe, it was like sitting in front of a fireplace on a chilly wintry day. Toe smiled as he said, dis' be perfect," he laid his head on the high back rocking chair, closed his eyes and died with a big satisfied smile. Drew wept. He had softened a little, but when his uncle died, he returned to being mean and bitter.

The thirteen remaining workers helped the young folk to settle in their new homes. They were happy to see new faces and young people; after the young adults joined the thirteen inside the slave compound, Drew locked the gates.

The overseers returned to the divider gate to go home, they were locked in. Drew had killed and buried the nurse and teacher that Harry hired from the local hospital and school to care for the children. The families of the two women searched years for their lost relatives, unfortunately, without any success. As a souvenir, Drew kept the newspaper article about the two lost women.

Charles Returned to MacCall

After selling everything except Billy's two houses, Charles and his boys arrived in MacCall. He went to Harry's mansion to see Drew; Harry's well-kept mansion and an exquisite yard were in disarray, even the long path was overgrown with weeds.

When Charles arrived, Drew and his wife were sloppy drunk, Drew opened the door and was surprised to see Charles and his boys. Drew said, "hello brother. Come in," he looked down at the boys and playfully asked, "who are these little people?"

Drew worked his wife like she was a horse, he promised her an easy carefree life but only gave her a hard time. Charles told Drew, "I'll be back in the morning. I'm taking the boys to pops castle to rest tonight."

Drew said, "you can stay here."

Charles backed out the door with his boys, when he was standing on the porch he said, "see you in the morning." He and his boys left.

Due to no one living in the castle, dust and dirt had taken over. He cleared a section for them to stay until he hired a cleaning crew.

Drew was spending the money as fast as it came in. He had no business or people skills. On the other tobacco field that Harry started as a cover-up, was a wasteland. The four tobacco sections had been used and misused, instead of letting the fields rest for a period, Drew worked all the land at the same time, just as the workers told Drew, the fields stopped yielding healthy tobacco. Drew had no farming skills; he was a lousy salesperson with a mean personality. Harry's H. B. Metropolis was falling apart. Charles never visited or had anything to do with the plantation, it was not his profession.

It took two weeks for Charles to find eight women from town to clean the castle from top to bottom, and twelve men to clean and shine the outside and work in the yard, it took them six months to complete their task. When the castle was immaculate, Charles hired six men and eight women as the castle staff. The castle attic had bedrooms, a male and female lavatory which is where his staff lived. In the basement was where they worked except the outside employees who kept the grounds of the castle in perfect condition. Even so, the basement also had a sitting area with chairs arranged in front of a fireplace, for the staff to sit and take a break.

Drew complained that people would discover the plantation. Charles argued that Harry had the castle built, to have a place to freely live without anyone finding the mansion.

There was only one way to H. B. Metropolis, the road dead end at the forest, it led from or to Harry's mansion. Everyone else lived on the other side of town. H. B. Metropolis was several miles away from the castle, Harry built his castle to be his haven, have his social events, and live in disguise a normal life.

When Charles returned to MacCall, he went around visiting his old friends and acquaintances. The townspeople gravitated towards Charles like he was Moses that parted the red sea. Drew, as usual, was ignored by everyone, he and his wife were the town's drunks. With Charles back in town, Drew went to his favorite bar, once Drew was drunk, he said to anyone that would listen, "my brother moved far away, he did nothing for you or this town, he returned, and everybody loves Charles. I stayed here to help this town grow, I poured money in this town to help it out, I paid money to get a hospital in this town, I created jobs for some of you, what did the almighty Charles do?" He looked around, no one said anything, nor were they paying him any attention. Drew shouted, "nothing! Charles did nothing, he left town, he left you!" Only the walls were listening, Drew angrily stumbled out the bar.

The clothes that Charles and boys wore were sophisticated and posh, Charles velvet voice was deep and smooth. Women loved Charles, unlike Harry, the playboy in Charles took advantage. The men respected him, and the KKK wanted him to join them. Charles was not about hate and degrading people, he wanted to uplift and aid those who needed help.

One evening Drew was having a memorable moment, he thought about a pretty slave girl, one of Harry's friends had his way with her in the back of the barn. At the time he was young and outside playing, he heard the girl yelling. The man came around the barn straightening his clothes before entering the house.

The girl asked Drew to bring a glass and towel from the kitchen. Drew ran into the house and got the items, before leaving out Bella said, "when she gib' it back ta' you, bring it ta' me."

The girl rolled the glass in the towel and beat the glass with all her strength. Drew had no idea what she was doing but it looked fun, so when she paused to take a breath, he grabbed the stick and beat the glass until it was as fine as salt. The girl said, "Thank you." She bent down and whispered, "gib' dis' to Miz' Bella, plez.'"

Bella filled the man's lemonade with the finely chopped glass and a lot of sugar. The man died two days later.

Drew's wife entering the room startled him, "what do you want woman?" Drew yelled.

All But One

BB stood in the dining room looking at Drew, trying to figure how to rip him off and leave. She asked Drew, "what are you thinking about, you be in a deep daze."

Drew said, "I was thinking about the day I asked you to marry me, it was a mistake." He looked around the room, and said to himself, "I have an idea, he ran into the kitchen and got a glass out the cupboard."

He asked, "what's for dinner?"

"Fried chicken, and..."

Drew cut her off and said, "I have a taste for soup, cook some soup."

"That will take me…"

"Just do it!"

That evening Charles and his sons were enjoying their weekly visit with Drew. Laughter and talking filled the room. BB was not allowed to sit with them, she sat in the kitchen eating alone. Although Drew was mean to her and often time beat her, still, she stayed. BB was mistress of a big house, had a comfortable bed to sleep in, she took long baths, had plenty of food to eat, and all the alcohol she could drink. She stayed because one day when the opportunity allowed, she planned to take his money and leave the state. She took the soup and bread out for them to eat and set the food on the buffet, Drew told her to leave it, he would serve the food.

Drew fixed Charles a big generous bowl of soup, he sprinkled a wee bit of crushed glass on top. The glass was so fine it looked like salt, Charles stirred his soup around and took a big gulp. After two dinner visits at Drews, Charles began having stomach pains, chest pains, and regurgitated blood.

The doctor had him to stay in bed for a long period of time. And gave him a big dose of medicine that made him defecate. Charles began to heal, he and his boys stopped having dinner with his brother. Drew did not want to kill Charles quick; he would sprinkle only a few grains of glass at a time, it was going to be a long slow death. Drew wanted his brother's life, his boys, his fancy clothes, his accent. Charles did not look like the son of a slave. He looked, sounded, and acted like a child of an educated affluent man.

Jealousy corroded Drews' heart.

XV

Forever Apart

One year of not eating or drinking food or beverages from Drew's home made his stomach pain to go away. Feeling much better, Charles could perform as normal. He took the boys for walks in the park where he swung them around and around until all three would fall on the ground laughing. He took them to museums and long buggy rides. He did not like the clothes in the three towns, they took train rides to New York, Pennsylvania, New Jersey, and Boston to see the boy's uncle Morris and his family. Anywhere the train went, Charles took his sons to sightsee and shop. Wanting to visit another country, Charles took his sons across the border to Canada which was a great experience. A large number of slaves had escaped to the country, there were schools, stores, and businesses that fugitive slaves' owned.

Charles wanted his boys to have and feel the love of a parent, which was missing from his and Drew's life. Harry took him and Drew no place, not even church. Their mother's headache was too painful for them to travel to Titleburk with her. Drew stayed home, but when Charles turned fourteen, he got on a horse and would go to his grandpa's, Ogville, Titleburk and sometimes further. Charles was always in trouble with his parents. Oftentimes, he stayed gone all night or came in past midnight.

To take a greater interest in is boys, Charles gave up being a woman's man and became the father his boys required.

Whenever they were in town, Duke still visited Drew, sometimes three times a week. When he turned thirteen, Duke began spending the night. On Duke's fourteenth birthday he told his dad that he was going to live with his uncle Drew, and they were going to fix the house to look as fine as the castle. Duke had grown close to Drew and had become just as mean, he said, "Uncle Drew took me to see the slaves. I even met some, they are happy and like their area, grandpa was a genius."

That was exactly what Charles did not want to happen. Duke's reason for wanting to move out of his father's house was spearhead by Drew, who covertly desired to destroy Charles. Duke was young and impressionable; he fell right into Drew's hands.

His uncle Drew promised that one day the slaves would be his. Duke went home to get his things to permanently move out of the castle and in the mansion. Charles had a fit and told Duke that he was going to move him back to Boston, Duke stormed out leaving his things. Charles stopped him and said, "don't tell your brother about the slaves."

"Never." Duke said, "or he'll take them away from me."

Duke told his uncle about his dad's threat. This was good news to Drew, laughing to himself he said, "Charles is jealous of my relationship with his son." Drew was happy, he said to Duke, "I can handle him for you, but it has to be my way."

"Do it, uncle," Duke said with laughter in his voice.

Drew thought, his plan was soundproof, he was finally going to get both of Charles boys and make them hate each other, the way Henry raised him and Charles. Two men that were on Drew's payroll, carried out any dirty work Drew needed to be done. This time, it was to kill Charles and bring him, Cody.

Two evenings after Duke moved out the castle, Drew's two hitmen used the key that Drew gave them to enter Charles home. Cody was downstairs, when he heard someone enter, he ran up the steps to Charles bedroom. The men followed Cody. One of them grabbed Cody, the other got in a fight with Charles. Cody broke out the man's grip and fought a good fight. What Drew had forgotten, Charles could fight and refused to be bullied. Charles held his ground and beat both men. He stood back, he gave them a moment to recuperate then said, "I can end this."

One of the men asked, "how?"

Charles reached for Cody, he had the boy to stand behind him, Charles asked, "how much is my brother paying you."

The other man responded in surprise, "brother, you're Mr. Drew's brother?"

"Yes, how much is he paying you."

"Two quarters each." One of the men said proudly.

"Hum," Charles moaned.

"But Sir, we will only get the money if we kill you and take your son to him."

Cody said, "I will not live like a pig. And you are not killing my dad." He got in a fighting stance.

Charles said, "this son is staying with me." He looked at Cody, then at the two men and said, "I will give you something, then you will leave us alone."

Both men agreed, one of the men said, "we be leavin' town iffen' you's pay more den' Mr. Drew.

Charles said, "go downstairs to the library, I'll bring it to you."

The men rushed out of the room so fast they stumbled over each other, Charles watched them go down the steps. When they were gone Cody whispered, "you're paying them? they came to kill us."

Charles shook his head, he went to his chest and pulled out a gun, and said, "I said I was giving them something."

"I don't understand, dad."

"Killing is something. I am giving them, death." He put the gun behind his back, went downstairs, stood in the doorway of the library and shot each man like he did Harry, right between their eyebrows. He looked at Cody and said, "let's pack and leave."

Cody said surprised, "dad, you can fight and shoot, wow. Who taught you?"

In MacCall, the following day, when the men did not return Drew was livid, he and Duke went to the castle to see what had happened, they found nothing but a rumbled mess. Drew had no idea where the men or Charles had gotten off to. Duke entered the library, he called for Drew. When Drew entered the library, he recognized Charles marksmanship. Drew and Duke searched through the house looking for Cody and Charles.

Like Harry, evilness wrapped itself around Drew's heart, he stormed out the castle angry, he was going to turn the brothers against each other like his dad did him and Charles. Drew was enraged he broke out several windows, tried to kick the door down, but only hurt his foot. Charles had beaten him again.

All But One

Duke said, "I didn't know dad could shoot."

He watched his uncle Drew, angrily storm out the castle. when he was gone Duke said, "go, dad." Duke went to his father's suite and looked around, he found several pictures, his favorite was of him, with his dad and Cody. He took them all. He went to Cody's room, Cody still played with toys, he took a few of the toys. Duke went to his room, he fell across his bed and cried. He pulled himself together, got the remaining of his clothes and left.

****

Charles bought property on the outskirts of Ogville and changed their last names to Paddleton. The father and son duo cut all ties to the Brown family and never saw Drew or Duke ever again. They became abolitionists, even though slavery was illegal and over, there were a few plantations that broke the law, so slaves were still escaping and needed help. Charles built a huge house on his property, a carbon copy of the castle Harry built which was a larger model of the Evan's house. Charles castle was the exact replica and size of the Evans castle. Fortunately, the Evans used crushed stone, not Ivory.

Charles castle had twenty rooms and not fifty, and a basement with two extra rooms to hide slaves. The castle porch and vestibule were made from tons of ivory.

During those years it was not against the law to kill an elephant for his tusk.

****

On H.B. Metropolis the young slaves got pregnant. The four single girls, who on the day of the mass wedding in the children area had no one to marry, married men from Jeb's plantation. Drew went to Titleburk and kidnapped a nurse, teacher, and two overseers, he locked them in. He killed the two original overseers. Duke suggested hiring young women from another state that was newly graduated from college, one a nurse the other a teacher. Fourteen-year-old Duke proposed to get the overseers from out of state towns. He told his uncle, "when I turn twenty, we will get rid of the people you hired, and I will travel to hire new and younger folk."

Drew agreed with his nephew. Even though young, Duke went to town and met with the administrators of the MacCall companies, Duke had his father's business flair. By the time Duke was sixteen, the failing companies were making a profit.

Before Duke's twentieth birthday, H.B. Metropolis was generating so much tobacco, the government was asking questions. For that reason, Duke cultivated the second field Harry purchased years ago, he bought another field going towards Ogville. The employees did not live on the plantations, they were free coloreds, whites, anyone that needed a job. As promised, Duke told Drew to kill the nurse, teacher, and two overseers upon his return, he traveled to another state and shanghaied a graduating nurse and teacher. Duke looked like his dad, had a deep velvet voice like him, but could lie like Harry, he did not take the young women against their will, he sweet talked them to travel back with him to MacCall. He was gone for one month, on his way back home, he stopped in a city outside Titleburk, where he saw two men sitting on a street corner, he hired them. When the four new employees came down the long path that led up to the house, they thought it was spectacular. They oohed, and awed as they entered the mansion, Duke took his four new employees to his home office. The four-talked and agreed to work for young Mr. Duke Brown. Duke fabricated great lies and made offers that the nurse, teacher, and two overseers could not turn down.

Drew had seen Duke return with four people. He entered the mansion and said, "everything is ready."

Duke took the teacher and nurse to the children area, on the way Duke lied. He said, "the children are orphans. The coloreds left their babies in town to fend for themselves, the sheriff brought them here."

The nurse said, "that is so sad."

Duke said, "when you return to the mansion, the maid will show you to your rooms. On Holidays you're allowed to go home and see your families."

Drew took the overseers as far as the cabins, he said, "clean these two cabins for me, when you're done. Come to the

All But One

mansion and I'll pay you." Drew left and locked the divider gate behind him.

Duke took the nurse and Teacher to the children cabin when they saw the children the women became excited to work with the kids. Duke left and locked the children gate.

Drew thought of Duke as a young genius, he was like Harry and Charles, think of something then make it happen.

Duke studied Harry's plans thoroughly, he moved everyone out of the plantation house, into the castle, as Harry had originally planned. Duke never called Drew's wife anything, he thought she was too common to live with them.

Duke married a pretty refined girl; he built his wife a big beautiful house in Titleburk. They had three children; he taught his oldest son about the plantation operations. Duke was riddled with guilt, about agreeing to kill his brother and father, he named his first-born, Cody Charles Brown.

Duke's wife nor his other two children learned about the plantations' existence. He and Cody stayed in the Titleburk home on weekends, Duke's wife didn't mind nor asked questions. She was a socialite if Duke was home for her social events or an important dinner, she was content.

When Charles moved into the castle, he made the main section home, he closed the east and west wings. In the castle, Duke put his uncle in the west wing. He stayed where his father lived in the main corridors. He even slept in Charles suite.

One-day, Drew had gone to the plantation alone, Duke took that moment to reminisce. In his nightstand drawer he kept a picture of his father, brother, and the three of them together in New York, he took the pictures out his drawer. He smiled remembering Charles taking them to the park, swinging them around until they could not stand. Duke looked away from the picture and up at the ceiling, he closed his eyes and rocked back and forth as though he was a kid again going around and around, his favorite part was when the warm sun beamed on his face, and the wind blowing his hair. Then all three fell to the ground, Duke laughed out loud, he said to himself, "I was happy." He looked at the pictures again, in each one they looked happy and was smiling, "I use to smile," he said.

Duke never saw his father or brother again, it was as though they had vanished, he knew they were alive but where. Duke whined, "Dad where are you, I'm so sorry dad and Cody, I am truly sorry." He buried his face in his pillow, his voice was muffled when he said, "I wish I was with you; uncle Drew is an idiot, he thinks he knows everything." He cried himself to sleep.

While Duke was in the castle reminiscing about his childhood, Drew was doing the same in the mansion where he and his brother were raised. Inside the house screamed memories, to get fresh air he went on the back porch, he relived the slave standing in the yard looking up at him and his family. He smiled remembering Charles telling the hired hands that Paula was going to show them to their new home and helping Paula off the porch. "Always a gentleman," Drew said. It was too much, he went back inside and headed for the front porch. As soon as he exited the house, he had a vision of him and Charles coming up the long driveway, returning from the Civil War after being away for years. He could still hear Harry shout, "you lost." Drew look down the long road and said, "like it was my fault."

Before entering the house, he remembered waving goodbye to Charles as he left for a new life in Boston. Sadness overwhelmed Drew. He entered the house, standing in the doorway of the drawing-room, he looked around and said, "this is where it all began."

Drew sat in Harry's gargoyle chair and cried. Duke nor Drew spoke of Charles or Cody, ever again.

Duke grew to look and sound just like Charles, it was as though they were identical twins.

On a bright sunny day, Duke was talking to his son in the mansion drawing-room, Drew heard Duke but thought it was Charles. A spark of joy that he did not know existed, leaped in his heart, He opened the double doors and yelled in a joyful manner, "Charles!"

Duke's heart pumped with happiness, he asked in excitement, "is my dad here?"

Silence filled the room. Duke and Drew stared at each other for a moment, Drew left and Duke said, "let's go to the slave compound."

It was at that moment that uncle and nephew knew, they both missed Charles.

BB was sick and tired of living with a person that did not speak to her, she threatened Drew, she said, "iffen' you's don't tell me what's yo' work be, I's go to da' sheriff. Drew calmly said, "walk with me, I want to show you what my pops built."

He took her to the outer gate and shot her, she was buried in the divider gate forest.

At age seventy, Drew left H. B. Metropolis to Duke. He got a hotel room in MacCall that was over a bar, where he ate little and drank a lot. When Drew left, Duke was already lonely in that big castle, he became depressed. Every evening, before going to bed, Duke would take the pictures out of his drawer, he lined them on his nightstand and said, "Goodnight dad, goodnight Cody. I love you both." He placed the pictures in his drawer and tried to fall asleep. Duke muddled through life in an isolated depressed state of mind.

Charles youngest son Cody grew too looked like a handsome Italian. Cody graduated from college, a few years later he got married. His first born was born 1914, he named the baby, Duke. Like his brother, Cody had three children and carried a permanent sorrow in his chest due to the division of his family. Cody's wife was a lawyer, his three children attended college. Charles was proud of his son, Cody ran for Mayor in the city of Ogville, and won.

In MacCall, Duke had a meeting with the Brown family company's, he saw Cody's picture in an Ogville newspaper that a boy was selling. The article was about Cody winning the election, Duke recognized Cody's face but not the name. Duke said to himself, "Good job dad, you started a whole new life." He took a second look at Cody's picture that included his family. Duke laughed out loud when he read that Cody had named his first born after him, Duke Paddleton. He said, "I love you too little brother." Duke never showed the article to Drew, he took the newspaper to the mansion attic and locked it in the chest.

Cody's, children grew to be successful. His son Duke Paddleton became a senator. His middle child, Mark a lawyer, and his baby girl, Gwen became a doctor. Charles remarried, and lived a long happy prosperous life, despite losing half his family. His new wife was a medical doctor, she desired to care for people of all races, Charles gave her money to open a clinic.

He wrote a memoir about his escape from his brother and the history of H. B. Metropolis. To keep the papers safe, he put them in a chest that was kept in the basement with the two keys to the gates.

When Charles returned to MacCall from Boston, and before Drew tried to kill him, Charles waited until Drew and his wife were in town at a bar. In the castle, Duke and Cody were fast asleep. Charles took his fastest horse and galloped to the mansion, he entered Harry's room and got the key to the chest.

Charles went up to the attic, in the chest he dug through newspaper articles about how wonderful Harry was, even the article he had written. He found the keys, Drew had put them on separate key rings and labeled them, master and divider. Charles took one each, and a copy of Harry's plan. He also took his son's and his birth certificates. He shut the chest and locked it, returned the key in Harry's room, and returned to the castle.

Several years after escaping from his brother and son, Charles searched for Duke, he missed his first born. Had Charles approached Duke, he would have learned that his son loved him deeply, suffered from depression and loneliness. Duke would have accepted Charles with opened arms. His grandson Cody would not, Cody reached back three generations and was meaner than Harry's mom. If Harry was alive, he would be afraid of his grandson.

Charles went to Titleburk, while there he learned that Duke had three children, he named his first born, Cody. Charles was amazed that his sons named their first born after each other. He said to himself, "that's love." Charles never looked for Duke again. His heart was breaking with every breath he took, but he had to let his first-born go.

Harry's sons, Charles and Drew at no time saw each other again, yet, they both died at eleven o'clock on September 29, 1929. Charles was eighty-two and Drew eighty-one. Charles caught the flu and did not recover, he died in the hospital. Drew died of alcohol poison in his hotel room.

1960, Duke was diagnosed with heart cancer, he was eighty-five. His wife died in 1958 of breast cancer. While Duke was in the hospital his children came to visit, yet, the night he passed, Duke was alone. He sat up in bed and said, "finally, it's over." He thought the cancer was going to stop his heart, he would close his eyes, and his life would be over. Instead of dying peacefully, cancer pain was agonizing, and he had a heart attack. The ache caused him to convulse. His face was distorted, he slobbered, his eyes rolled back in his head, he tried to call out but was unable, he panted for air, fifteen minutes later, it was over. After the second shift nurses' reports, a nurse entered his room. Duke and his bed looked like a karate fight had taken place, and Duke lost.

Cody and his wife lived in the castle Charles built. On Cody's seventy-fifth birthday, he hired a full-time chauffeur to drive him and his wife around. He stayed busy, they attended the Governor's Ball, Mayors parties, his wife was an executive on the hospital board, they held social events and attended them as well. The husband and wife duo held fundraisers for the clinic that Charles second wife opened.

Sadly, 1970, Duke's brother, Cody Paddleton, was killed by a drunk driver, he was ninety-three. One evening they were on their way home from a social event, a car full of drunk teenagers were speeding on the wrong side of the road. The collision killed all but the teenage driver.
Donovan Bright discovered H. B. Metropolis in 2017, he was twenty-three years old. Charles Brown was the plantation master when Donovan made his discovery, he was fifty-five.

XVI

Two Slaves and One Friend Got Away

Vance took a train going west, traveling through all the different states and cities, he chose to make his home in Oklahoma, Oklahoma, the double name intrigued him. Harry had paid Vance and his wife thousands of dollars, plus he had the money he stole during the shindig. Vance settled down and bought a house in a wealthy region of town, as he walked around the house, he knew that his wife would fall in love with it. He said to himself, "she would be, too proud." Thinking about his wife, Vance moaned softly, the house had ten rooms and not the six his wife desired. He bowed his head and said, 'yes this would be too much for her.'

After purchasing his house, he met a pretty single woman that was a few years younger than him. Her husband was killed while in combat during the Civil War, he left his wife with two young children.

Vance began dating the widowed woman, her children, twelve and ten loved and respected him. The woman's parents threw the couple a big wedding, for their honeymoon he took his new bride to Dallas, Texas. His new wife was kind and loving, she liked to travel, yet had never been outside the city. She was a caring wife, an excellent cook, and housekeeper.

His father-in-law owned a motel, Vance wife said one day, "my father is happy I married again, being a female and his only child, he was going to close down the motel when he got too old to run the business."

Vance asked, "why?"

All But One

"Father doesn't feel that a woman should own a business, nor know how to run one. My mother feels differently. Once when dad became ill, mom ran the motel, successfully."

Vance said, "I will run the motel for him if he teaches me."

"That is exactly what dad wanted you to say, but you teach me and the kids."

"I will because life is not guaranteed."

His wife father trained Vance in the motel business. Easy going Vance got along with his wife's mother and father splendidly. Twice a year, Vance took his family on train rides to visit other states, the children called him pops. Vance and his wife lived a long happy life.

Sometimes Vance wondered about H.B. Metropolis and the two brothers, he hoped Charles was doing fine and living in Boston with his wife and son.

Like Charles told Drew long ago, they would never see or hear from Vance again, and they did not.

****

Bella and family made it to St. Louis, she purchased her dream home, a three-bedroom house, with a kitchen, living room, and an extra room she turned into a sewing area. Her new home had a big yard for her garden, a front porch that went across the house, and a back porch. In the backyard, she had a grapevine, vegetables, and an herb garden. Bella joined a group called, We Made It, the group consisted of elderly women that had escaped from slavery. Their slogan was, *We's made it out of slavery, we's free to help others now and always.*

The women made clothes for school children and homemade bread that they sold to a local grocery store. The women used that money to purchase children of all age's shoes and coats. Joe, a carpenter made their furniture, Bella and Clara made soft seat cushions for the chairs that Joe made. They slept on store-bought beds and mattresses. A local store owner saw Joe's work, loved it and hired him as a furniture maker. Clara got a job working in a dress shop while Bella stayed home to raise the children, she saw to it that they received an education. They flourished, all three became medical doctors and started a clinic in their neighborhood. Bella's grandchildren married and blessed her with great-grandchildren.

In June 1900, Bella turned one hundred years old, her daughter, Clara, threw her mother a big house birthday party, Bella helped to cook a feast. church members and the choir that Bella sang with attended. Bella stood and sang in her second alto voice, *Just As I Am*, written 1835 by Charlotte Elliott. After which they cut the cake.

Bella told the group, "I'm a little tied,' she went to her bedroom, where she had a pitcher of water and a basin, she washed up and changed clothes. Bella put on a satin black dress on with lace color and sleeves, a black hat with black feathers, black lace gloves, black shoes with a pearl on top, and her pearl necklace. She wrote a note that read, *I was born a slave, I die a free woman, I have lived a Blessed life serving God. To my loving daughter, thank you for a wonderful send-off. To my grandchildren, great-grandchildren, Joe, church family and friends I love you all.* She laid down with her face pointed towards Heaven, closed her eyes never to wake again.

Clara entered her mother's room; she saw that Bella was dressed in a brand-new outfit from head to toe. She went to her bedside, pulled up a chair and held Bella's hand. She looked at her mother's peaceful face and asked, "how did you know." She wept.

****

Paula didn't fare as well. She left H. B. Metropolis hoping to join Bella in St. Louis, her trip took over two years. Paula was under the influence of Mama Faye; they wasted and flaunted their money. A man called the women whores, Mama Faye said to the boys, "you neva' let nobody talk's ta' yo' mama like's dat, git' dat man. Paula's older son got into a fight with the man. Mama Faye pushed the youngest boy off the wagon and said, "hep' yo' brother."

The youngest son was the carbon copy of Moses in appearance and temper, he gave Mama Fay a defiant look and said in his child deep throat voice, "don't touch me," as he got back on the wagon.

Mama Faye backed away from the boy, she said to Paula. "he ain't nothin' but trouble."

The remaining of the trip, Paula's younger son faded to black, he didn't speak, he ate when they had food, he collected rainwater to quench his thirst, he shared with his mother and brother. He told Mama Faye, get ja' own wata."

She did and left the young boy alone.

To help finance their journey north, Paula sold the horse and buggy. They walked the remaining two hundred miles, unknown to Paula, to New York. Along their way, Paula asked individuals for directions to St. Louis, since she was on the east coast, she was given directions to New York. When she learned that they were in New York, and not St. Louis, she cried.

They arrived in New York City with just enough cash to acquire a cheap four-room apartment in the red-light district. As soon as they settled down, Paula's youngest son asked her to enroll him in school.

Paula couldn't get a job, so the old woman turned their apartment into a harlot house and added two extra women. Paula became a drunken depressed slut. On the plantation Paula had lived a clean life, she was in church every Wednesday night and Sunday morning. Often times Paula exited outside to pray, unfortunately, one of Mama Faye's men introduced her to drugs. Paula's prayer life ended.

Her oldest son joined a gang and adopted their personality, he was rough, vulgar and embarrassed by his mom lifestyle. His crew went to war with their adversary, sadly, his gang lost the battle, many were brutally injured, and a few did not recover. Paula's son was one of the boys that died, he was fourteen. Paula signed her youngest son up for school, she wrote his name down as *Son 1*. On their way to what Paula thought was St. Louis, a man that had given her directions to New York, his name was John.

Paula youngest son asked the teacher to call him John. The young boy excelled in the colored school, even though the schoolhouse was a shabby dilapidated building, and lessons were inferior to whites. John desired to get away from the alcohol, parties and opened erotic acts in their apartment. He left at age eleven and got a job selling newspapers on a street corner.

After classes, he sold the papers, ran errors for the owner of the paper, and for a while lived on the street. When winter came a janitor that worked in the colored high school, saw the boy shivering in front of a store, he cleaned out a backroom for the young boy. Paula's son could not remember how to pronounce his father's African name, though he remembered it had something to do with light. Paula never called either of her sons by their African last name. She did not talk about Moses or the plantation. Unfortunately, the memory of John's father and their home was slowly fading. The few things he could remember was the place was very green, they lived in a clean pretty house, and his mother cried late at night.

John's teacher asked the young boy his name last, he knew his dad's name meant light or bright. He said, "John Bright."

John graduated from college with a doctorate in history and became a professor at an upstate New York University, where he met and married a high school teacher. Within the course of five years, he and his wife had two children.

The day John left home, he did not look back, he never saw Paula again until he was married and had kids. John for the first time since he was eleven went to visit his mother. He had learned that she had syphilis and was living in the same filthy apartment that John used to call home. He knocked on the door, the Janitor answered and recognized the young man as soon as he walked in the apartment, he said, "hey young man, look at you Mr. College Graduate wearing a suit and tie." He felt the material of the suit then said, "it ain't cheap neither."

John was very surprised to see the janitor. He shook the man's hand before either could say anything, Paula laying on the couch raised her head and yelled, "Who is it?"

"The little boy I took care of years ago."

"Tell em' I have no money."

"Hello, mama."

Paula sat up in total surprise.

"Mama," the janitor said.

She slid over, so John could sit on the couch. The couch was disgustingly filthy, he smelt the stench of vomit, blood, and alcohol, and other smells he didn't recognize, he said, "it's okay, I'm not staying long." He remained standing, and said, "I stopped by to give you this." He handed Paula two twenty-dollar bills.

She snatched the money and did not say thank you, she blamed John for his older brother's death, made fun of his new name, John Bright. Paula told him that she wished they had never left the plantation because she and her boys would have fared better. John disagreed with her, he told her that he had a college degree, was teaching at a university, owned his home, and was not living in the slums. She blamed John for her messed up life and accused the boy of her mistakes. John looked at the man and said, "thank you for giving me a place to stay and food to eat." He handed the janitor two five-dollar bills.

"Son this is not necessary, you already thanked me," he said as he took the money. The janitor reached out and gave John a hug, and continued, "you grew to be a fine successful young man. I hope I had something to do with that."

Smiling John said, "you did, had I stayed here," John looked back at his mother...

"I understand, son." The janitor replied softly.

Paula stood as though she was in pain, she said, "wait, stay right there, got something to give you," she walked funny and held onto the wall, as she slowly went into another room.

While Paula was gone, John asked the janitor if he was sick as well. He answered, "naw' son, I never slept with the women, I make sure she has everything she needs until the end. Mama Faye was the first to die, then the other women, that's when I start taking care of Paula. I think yo' mama hanged on to see you." He scratched his head and said, "why didn't you tell me she was your mama?"

"Would you have told me to go home."

The janitor thought for a moment before saying, "no, I would have her to meet us in a park. I disagreed with her lifestyle."

John said, "thank you."

Paula entered the room carrying a picture and piece of paper, she slowly eased down onto the couch. On the paper, she wrote a message and her name on the back of the picture. She wrapped the picture in the paper and handed it to John, "something to remember me by." She looked at John and said, "sorry for the way I brought you up."

"It's okay mama," he kissed her on the forehead.

Paula watched her son exit her home, she could not fathom how one son could be so evil and the other like an angel, when they both were raised by the same sinful unfit mom. The janitor closed the door behind John. Crying out loud Paula said, "it's another part of me gone."

Paula had a twin sister; the baby girls were sold separately on plantations that were in different States. Paula survived the trip, but her sister died on the road to her new master. The twins were one month old when they were sold. The janitor asked, "what ja' talking about?"

Paula said, "all my life, it felt like some of me was missing. Massa told Miss. Bella about my sister."

In the next five months, John mailed two twenty-dollar bills to his mother. She wrote him a thank you letter and apologized for blaming him for his brother's murder, place her lack of parenting when he was young.

Six months after John's visit, Paula was taken to the hospital. Her third day in the hospital the janitor went to see her. She said to him, "I should have left Mama Faye on the plantation."

The Janitor said, "she was an old woman, I understand the reason for bringing her, why did you allow her to make you sell your body and turn your apartment into…"

Paula cut in to correct the janitor, "she did not make me, I chose over my boys, alcohol, men, wild parties, my body barely covered. The shame of it." She handed him the key to her apartment and said, "when I die, run my obituary in the newspaper. My son will read it, and know I am gone."

The Janitor asked, "how will I pay for it?"

Paula smiled and said, "each month my son sends me two twenty-dollar bills, I only spent one and put the other in the top drawer in my bureau. The money in the drawer will be more than enough to pay to have my obituary in the newspaper. He will read it, and know his unfit mom is gone."

The janitor asked, "what do I write?"

"Paula said faintly, "look in that nightstand and get the note out."

The janitor opened the drawer and got the obituary that Paula had written. As he read Paula said, "thank you for saving my baby boy. He is who he is, because of you." While he was reading what Paula had written, she turned her head and cried, in the midst of weeping she quietly passed away.

The janitor said, "Paula this is beautiful." He shook her to get her attention. She did not move, he rolled her on her back, her face was still wet from the tears. He pushed the call button. Before the nurse entered the room, he said, "thank you, Paula, for being a good friend." When a nurse entered, he was crying.

The janitor left the hospital, went home got a pen and added a message at the bottom of her obituary.

Every morning John Bright would read the obituaries, one morning his mom was in there she had written, *"Paula, runway-slave from Massa Brown Plantation. I died free from slavery, but not free from myself."* Under her obituary, the janitor wrote, *"from being owned to trying to make it on your own, ain't easy. She did not die alone. Your son and I love you, Paula. Rest in peace."*

His wife entered the room, John was crying, she asked, "what's wrong honey?"

"My mother died."

John handed her the newspaper and pointed to Paula's obituary. His wife said, "we'll keep this for the children."

"No," John answered, he got the paper and threw it in the fireplace, he later realized that was a huge mistake.

LaVaughn

ALL BUT ONE

Part II

XVII

Paula and Moses Offspring

John Bright got married and had two children, his daughter, Jo Ann Bright was born 1893, and son John Bright Jr. born 1895. On Jo Ann's tenth birthday, her mother took her daughter shopping. She wanted Jo Ann to choose her own birthday gift. Instead of getting something for herself, she got a leather wallet for her father, a silk scarf for her mother, and a wood whistle for her brother. Her mother was so impressed with her daughter's selflessness, the next day she went back to town and bought Jo Ann a beautiful very expensive already made dress, and material to make Jo Ann a doll. John Sr. tried to argue about his wife shopping spree but was shut down when she reminded him about their daughter's kindheartedness, and the wallet he had in his pocket. Realizing he'd lost the argument, he hushed.

From that day forward John Sr. always purchased the same wallet and put Paula's picture and note in the slot. He only showed the items to his wife; it was his personal secret. John's plan was to put the wallet in his pocket, it was to be buried with him.

On Jo Ann's twentieth birthday, John took her to hear Ida B. Wells Barnett speak which was an exhilarating experience for his daughter. John thought his vivacious daughter would enjoy hearing the crusader since the majority of Jo Ann's conversations were about equality for all. After hearing the speaker, Jo Ann was chatty on their way home. She said, "dad you're a genius for studying history. When I finish college, I am going to teach history to change America's mindset."

John Sr. and Jo Ann arrived home in the early hours of the morning. Still, a few hours later Jo Ann was up, she had prepared breakfast, eaten and was dashing out the door to class. Her mother entered the kitchen and asked, "did you enjoy hearing Mrs. Barnett?"

Jo Ann gave her mom a hug and said, "she was wonderful, history is our way out." She left.

****

Two years later, Jo Ann graduated from college, against her parent's demanding her not to go, she packed her bags and moved to Mississippi, a state where lynching was a norm. She hungered, to make a difference by teaching history about coloreds and whites in America. Jo Ann wrote an article titled, *No Longer Divided*. She ended it stating, *in this country, there are poor coloreds and poor whites, rich coloreds and rich whites, some coloreds are educated, some whites are educated – we are all the same. No longer divided.* Jo Ann's paper won several awards, she was invited to speak at two engagements, each time she got too excited and lost focus on her topic. Thus, she was never asked to speak again. However, her writings about America and its lack of justice for all was published in Colored American newspapers and magazines.

Within a year of moving to Mississippi, Jo Ann married a man that was an eloquent speaker. She traveled with him throughout the south as he addressed the audience on rights and justice for all men. Jo Ann and her husband made a perfect couple, she wrote his speeches, he articulated her writing with pure conviction. He was handsome, cool, calm and suave. On the other hand, Jo Ann was beautiful, spunky, and determined to change America. Her husband loved her beauty and enjoyed her attitude towards life. One day, three years after their wedding, he was reviewing a speech that he was going to give that evening in a small town that sat on the edge of the Mississippi River. Jo Ann and her husband were in the pastor's home for the weekend. Whenever they traveled, they stayed with the pastor of the local church.

While reviewing his speech, Jo Ann and her husband got into an argument about her wandering off alone, she wanted to go to the general store that was down the road to get a little snack. He said, "no, it's too dangerous, we'll go later with others."

All But One

Jo Ann argued, "it's just down the road where coloreds walk up and down all day." She opened the door to the room they were sleeping in, then turned and said, "I'm hungry." She left closing the door behind her.

Her husband followed her outside, he grabbed her arm and said, "baby, it's not safe."

She yanked her arm away and said, "it's just up the road." She hurriedly walked away.

Her husband saw a little boy playing. He called the boy over and gave him a few coins to walk with his wife.

The little boy ran and caught up with Jo Ann, he asked, "lady, may's I walk wid' ja?"

"Yes, you may," was her amused reply.

They walked along laughing and talking. Jo Ann asked the boy about his mom, who was a sharecropper, dad was gone, he had five siblings. His answer to Jo Ann's question about school, "naw ma'am, I's cain't tend' school cause' I's work in da' field all day."

On their way back to the pastor's house, five teenage white boys had come to the colored section of town, they watched Jo Ann and the boy exit the store. One of the boys said, "we's gonna' git's a nigga' ta'day."

The boys followed behind them, Jo Ann turned and saw them coming, she said, "run."

She and the boy took off running down the dirt road. The teenagers caught Jo Ann, they beat her with their fist, sticks, stones, laughing one of them said, "you's ain't welcome here nigga."

The boys threw their sticks and stones down and proceeded to kick her several times in the head, chest, stomach, and back. The little boy Jo Ann walked with ran for help, two colored men were coming down the road, he went up to them and said, "please help."

The two men heard the commotion, one of the men told the boy to run ahead and tell the pastor. The men ran the boys away, one of them picked Jo Ann up and carried her to the pastor's house, he took her in the front room and laid her on the couch. A colored hospital or doctor was not around, the pastor's wife tried the best she could to nurse Jo Ann. Her husband knelt by her side, her face was so swollen and bruised she was unrecognizable, she said, "I should have listened."

Her husband kneeling next to his wife was crying, JoAnn put her hand on his cheek, she whispered, "look at me."

He looked into her swollen eyes, JoAnn whispered, "never give up," her hand fell to her side. She closed her eyes and died grimacing from the pain that exploded through her body.

Jo Ann always carried in her purse the phone number to her parent's home. The two men that brought her to the pastor's home, walked with Jo Ann's husband down the road to the country store. On their way, Jo Ann's husband knelt on the ground where he saw his wife blood. He picked up several small stones and wrapped them in his handkerchief. Once in the store, he made the sad call to her parents, when her husband hung up, he cried uncontrollably.

****

The news sent her father into a deep depression. John, his wife, and son took a train to Mississippi for the funeral, John did not cry. For two years his wife, who was heartbroken as well, and John Jr., did all they could, to get him out of his depressed state.

1919, John Jr. became a professor of mathematics in the same New York University his father attended. John Jr. got married, and in 1923, his wife was pregnant with twins. John Sr. had never heard of a woman carrying two children in her belly, he thought that was astonishing and dangerous. He asked his son, "how can a woman carry two people at one time?"

When it was close to their daughter in law's due date, they packed their bags and drove to his son's home. "How can a woman carry two babies at one time," John Sr. asked his wife as he drove down the street.

Though still gloomy and depressed, becoming a grandpa temporarily quieted his pain from losing his vivacious daughter.

When the couple arrived at John Jr.'s home, his mother was astonished at how big her daughter in-law's stomach was. She clapped her hands out of sheer joy, gave her daughter-in-law a hug and until the baby's birth she cooked, clean, washed, dust, swept, simply pampered the mother of her future grandchildren.

All But One

The day John Jr. went to the hospital to bring his wife and babies home, John Sr. and his wife stayed at the house. he looked at her and said, "I was born in slavery and you were born in slavery. That little baby in the hospital is the second generation of our offspring, born free."

His wife said, "you weren't born in slavery. I was because my mom didn't leave the plantation. After the war, she stayed and died on the plantation. After her funeral, I walked and walked from Delaware to New York. I stopped on the college campus in Rochester. Mama was a field hand; I was born right there in the field."

"Field, in Delaware?"

"Yeah, they grow crops. For years I was a slave."

John Sr. said, "I remember a big black gate that was all over the place. In the evening us kids would play outside, we didn't go near those gates," he stopped as though he was thinking, then continued. "I'm not sure why we didn't. Maybe because there was this rough looking man, some coloreds called him boss others, Massa. There was a man that stayed in our house, he had a strange accent, sometimes he would say words I didn't understand. My mother cried a lot, she'd fall or run into things, I prayed that mom would stop hurting herself. I just now remembered that." He said more to himself.

John Sr. reached for his wife's hand and held it as he said, "here's how I know I was born a slave. Mama, grandma, my brother, and I road on a wagon to this great big house, we got off that wagon. We got on the back of another wagon, we laid down, this white man covered us over. He took us so far, then stopped, he removed the covers, talked to mama, then off we went with mama driving. I watched that man walk away until he disappeared. I was seven my brother was ten, when we arrived in New York, I was nine. I asked mama to send me to school." His mind trailed off for a moment before continuing, "I have no idea how I knew I could go to school. I didn't know what school was."

His wife said, "that was God. He has something for you to do, ask Him what it is." She squeezed John Sr.'s hand and continued, "if you were free, you would not need to hide in the back of a wagon."

"That's right," he said not really listening.

"Now that you are a grown man, you do know that that man was...?

"Beating on my mother? Yes, I realize that, and my daddy, he wasn't around a lot."

John's wife said, "yes, could have been, one day you said that a man took you and your brother to town, you never talk about him."

"We did go to town, several times, I never knew the name of the town or state. When we got to New York my brother was killed in a gang fight when he was fourteen."

"Your mother could have run from your father, not slavery, especially since a white man helped her. Slaves did not randomly go to town, or anywhere without our papers."

"That's that psychology you studied in school." John Sr. said laughing. He stood and paced.

His wife asked, "Do you remember your dad showing white folk papers?"

"No, he did not," John replied.

His wife said, "you were not a slave. I wish we'd had this conversation when Jo Ann was with us, she would have loved to talk with you about your family."

"I was not ready then, now, something has awakened in me, I don't know what it is but it's building as though it's going to explode." John sat down and said, "what if it's not me God wants to use, but our son or his offspring."

His wife said, "when I met you, I thought there was something different about you. Your aura, John Jr. has the same thing. Jo Ann did not, she was like me, neutral, regular so to speak."

John Sr. flinched. She was talking about his baby girl not being special, JoAnn was his world.

Still holding his hands, she continued, "you had to go see your mother, that was deemed by God, she was very articulate, she only misspelled four words on the note she wrote to you, I am sure that they were words she had never seen written. Again, ordained by God. This too is of God, you keep that note and picture in your wallet, you've never shown it to anyone, except me," she pointed to herself then continued, "one day, someone with your genetic factor, is going to reach into that little slit, pull out your mothers note, and the picture will fall out. That person is going to do something, extraordinary."

John Sr. said, "you say my genes, baby, you carried the children. So, the combination of our genes will do what you claim is ordained by God." Irritated he said, "stop saying that."

She yanked her hands away, got up, and sat in a chair. As soon as she did, John Jr. and his wife entered the house with John Jr., carrying the twins that they named Donald and Rachel.

His mother went to the family, hugged her daughter-in-law, kissed the babies, and hugged and kissed her son. She grabbed her daughter-in-laws' arm and helped her to a chair. John Jr. took the twins to his dad who was on the couch, he placed the twins in each of his father's arms.

John Sr. held the babies close to his chest. He looked at his wife and said, "our second generation, born free." As he rocked and cried, his wife tried to take the twins, but he would not let them go. He remembered seeing Jo Ann's badly beaten face and body, he cried for Jo Ann's husband, for his wife who lost her shopping buddy, he cried for losing someone that was a part of his body and now they were gone. He looked at his two grandbabies lying still in his arms, though not from him, yet they were a part of him. Through teary eyes, and wet face he looked at his son and whispered, "thank you." He held the babies closer, buried his face in their blankets, and cried.

Watching his grand twins grow up, was exactly what John Sr. needed to completely heal out of his depression. He never forgot his daughter, but over a short while, his depression melted away as the twins grew. John Bright, Sr. never again talked about his mother, brother, or life on H.B. Metropolis, the memory of it all slowly began to fade away with age. John kept the picture of his mother and the note hidden in a slot inside the wallet. Just in case his wife said, "it's ordained by God."

1953, John Sr. grandson, Donald Bright, became a Lawyer with the National Association for the Advancement of Colored People, NAACP. John Sr. was eighty-four years old; he was so proud of his grandson; he thought his heart would burst. He never expected his family to excel as they were doing. He believed, being born of a woman that was a prostitute his blood was tainted with her bad blood, and his children would be ruined.

Through his son and daughter's success and his grandchildren becoming prominent citizens, John Sr. grasped the notion that it is not the blood running through a person's vain that ruin their lives. Instead, it is the choice they choose to make. John Sr. stopped blaming others for Jo Ann's death, because like his wife said years ago, "Jo Ann was warned, she did not listen, she chose, wrong."

At the time, John Sr. did not like his wife harsh words, he knew they were true. He realized; Jo Ann was a grown woman that elected to walk down that road alone.

John Sr. died in 1955, a happy fulfilled man and glad his mother brought her boys to New York. His wife died in 1956, before her death she gave her son, his father's wallet. She said nothing about the content. She died believing, when it's time, God will reveal the contents of the wallet to whom He's chosen.

John Jr. kept the wallet in a flat tin can, that he purchased in a department store.

Donald's twin sister Rachel moved high in the New York mountains, where she and her husband lived a solitary life, in a small two-room cabin that they built. Twice a year during spring and fall, they would come down to the city to purchase sugar, flour, salt, other cooking items, hygiene, and personal things. Rachel nor her husband worked so they relied upon Donald to give them the money to purchase the items. The couple lived off vegetables planted in their garden, and animals her husband hunted and killed. Rachel taught herself how to preserve the meat, from her mother she learned how to can vegetables.

On a cool fall cloudy afternoon, in 1957, a year after her grandmother's funeral. Rachel was out gathering blackberries, she was storing them up for the cold winter months. It was canning season, she was making, wine, Jelly, and preserve the rest. Sadly, she was picking the berries so fast that she accidentally put in her basket a few deep red berries that were toxic, they had begun to grow among the blackberries. She picked a basketful of the berries and just enough of the dark red to be lethal. Maybe, had it been a bright sunny day, instead of a cloud-covered sky, she would have seen the difference in colors.

In the cabin, with only candlelight, Rachel began the process of preserving the berries. She washed a few and put them in a bowl to have as a dessert after dinner. While she prepared dinner, her husband was out back cleaning a bear that he had shot. He cleaned the meat and put it in the smoker, he was happy because they were going to have meat during the harsh winter months. Unfortunately, that night after dessert, they both became very sick. Her husband looked in the bowl and saw the poisoned red berries. He did not tell her the reason they were ill. Rachel became unwell before her husband. As she cleaned the berries, she had eaten one of the red berries, it was bitter, she added sugar and stirred them around. Her husband took her hand and laid her down on the bed. He went back to the other room, using a knife he carved on the table, *it was the red berries.* He returned to the bedroom, laid next to Rachel, who had died. Not long after her, he was gone.

  Near the end of the fall season, Donald panicked, Rachel and her husband always came down a little early, to stay a week or two with him and purchase their needed things for the winter. Something felt wrong, he felt a loss, yet no one was sick or died, he had not heard from his sister or her husband. He took some of his buddies up the mountain to his sister's cabin. When Donald opened the door, the smell caused him to stumble back. Donald and his friends entered the two-room cabin, they found the couple peacefully lying on the bed. their decaying bodies, clothes, and bed covers had dried vomit stains. Donald was relieved that his grandpa, John Sr., had already passed away, because this would have sent him over the edge, all over again.

  Donald requested an autopsy to confirm that the couple had eaten poison berries, as written on the wood table in his sister's cabin. His father was appalled and said no. Donald put the funeral on hold. He wanted his father to calm down and think with a clear head. John Jr. blamed his son Donald, he said, "you were twins, it was up to you to care for your sister." He accused his son of not visiting his sister more often. Donald told his wife, "dad accuse me of not seeing Rachel, neither did he."

  John Jr. did not stop at his accusations against his son, he also pointed his finger, at his son-in-law. But then, he was dead as well. He went back to his son and blamed him a second time because Donald did not check on his sister often enough. He tried to sue the State of New York and hold them responsible for allowing people to live in the mountains. John Jr. wanted anyone to be accountable for his daughter's death, he was so traumatized that he became ill.

Donald walked in his aunt JoAnn Bright disobedient shoes, he ignored his father and had the autopsy done. A few weeks after receiving the report, Donald visited his father's home, and said to his dad, "think about it dad, Rachel knows nothing about the wilderness, with no training she decided to move in the mountains and live a life she was not familiar."

John Jr. slapped Donald hard. At which time, Donald said, "I had the autopsy done, they died from eating poison berries."

John Jr. was going to slap his son again, but Donald blocked the lick and left his dad's home.

A few weeks later, John Bright Jr. died, he was eighty years old.

After John Jr, funeral, Donald's wife asked how he was holding up. Donald said, "this may sound harsh, I am relieved. Dad did not accept Rachel was responsible for her death. At least grandpa finally realize that it was his daughter's fault."

"You didn't know that woman."

"No, dad told me all about it. He said, grandpa told her not to go to Mississippi, and her husband told her not to go to the store. She did anyway." He looked at his wife and asked, "whose fault was it."

"Sounds like hers."

"And my sister? Even though everyone told her not to live like a recluse."

"Her choice." His wife answered.

"I was a little boy when grandpa said to Rachel and me, "God got coloreds out of slavery, if we ain't careful, He will put us back." He paused before saying, "I agree with grandpa to a point, maybe not as it was in the past, I do believe slavery can be a form of self-enslavement."

His wife asked, "is that a word?"

Donald replied angrily, "It is now." He looked at his wife and said, "I'm not angry with you, I'm just mad at the stupidity of my family."

She smiled and said, "your father told you not to have the autopsy."

They laughed as Donald said, "disobedience runs in the family."

His wife said, "be glad you did, it confirmed your suspicion."

Donald replied, "yes, it explained the carving on the table, that simply read, *it was the red berries*." He looked at his wife and said, "did I mention they were holding hands."

She reached over and took Donald's hand in hers, he cried and said, "my sis and dad gone, pointlessly."

She wrapped her arms around Donald and held him tight.

The next day, Donald went to visit his mother, who was doing a whole lot better than what he expected. She was calm and at peace. She said to Donald, "your sister's death is not your fault."

"I know mom."

Donald and his mother talked and laughed for a long while that day. She handed him the tin that held the wallet, then said, "your grandma gave this to your father before your grandpa passed. I don't know the importance of it, but it's a part of the Bright family history."

Donald opened the tin and said, "it's a wallet. What am I supposed to do with this?"

"Pass it down to your son."

Donald put the wallet back in the tin, and said, "most families pass down an heirloom, this family an empty wallet."

His mother laughing said, "and a tin, don't forget that." They had a good laugh, Donald's mom said, "the wallet and tin are expensive items. Take the wallet out the tin and look at it again."

Donald opened the wallet, while he was inspecting it, his mother said, "your grandma and grandpa were professors at an all-white university, they went from being slaves to being professors." She took the wallet and tin from Donald and laid them down. She asked, "do you remember going to their home."

"That great big house? Rachel and I use to run all around the house, inside and out." He laughed at the memory.

His mom said, "your father never told you, your grandpa left the house to you."

"Me, why not dad? Didn't he sell it?"

Donald's mom said, "your father was mean, your aunt Jo Ann, I am told by your grandmother, that she was kind and caring.

She wanted world peace, kind of like what you're doing as a lawyer. When you were hired on with the NAACP, your grandpa cried like a baby."

"Why."

"He said you have Jo Ann's spirit."

"What about Rachel?"

"He loved her, but she was different like something was missing."

Donald asked, "Is that what you think?"

"Don't you? Your sister quit school at age sixteen, ran away from home, moved up in the Mountains. Think about it, when she and her husband came to visit your home, you brought the boys over here." She got the tin with the wallet and held it in her hand then said, "you did think she was a little strange." Donald's mother concluded.

Donald laughed and said, "she was wild, like her husband. I didn't want her around my children. Though I believe she was happy."

"Yes, she was, twice a month Rachel and her husband would find a way to give us a call, she spoke only to me, her voice was happy. Her husband loved visiting you, he had no family, we were it."

"He was white."

"Sometimes race is not a factor, in your sister's case, it was a blessing." His mother answered.

Donald asked, "was dad mean to you? he was hateful to me and Rachel, I felt we were in his way. That's why sis and I liked going to grandpa's, it was peaceful at their home. "

Donald's mom handed her son the tin, and said, "your dad paid sixty dollars for the tin and the wallet is very expensive, purchased in the 1800s by your aunt Jo Ann." She looked at the shock on Donald's face, then said, "I guess, you do have an heirloom. What are you going to do about your grandpa's house?"

"Keep it, maybe one of the boys will want to live there, I like New York City better than Rochester."

His mom smiled and said, "your father and I felt the same. Although, every other month we would drive up there and stay for a few weeks. He hired a company to clean, paint, varnish the wood, we bought new furniture and kept some of the older pieces that were beautiful. It's a big house and cost a lot of money to redo."

"It was fourteen rooms, I think," Donald said.

"Seventeen rooms, I had to pick out the furniture for every room." She smiled and said, "in answer to your question, yes, your father was mean and hateful, he never hit me. He put his value in expensive things and not his family or character." She looked at Donald and asked, "does that make sense?"

"Yes ma'am, I'm not sure what dad was so mad about, but he always had a chip of some kind on his shoulder, he drove Rachel insane."

His mother responded, "yes, he called her a wild child. He used to tell me that Jo Ann was just like her."

Donald said, "I don't believe dad, grandpa said, aunt Jo Ann had a purpose in life. Rachel, on the other hand, was animal wild."

His mother said, "don't say that about your sister."

Donald and his wife had two sons, Donald John Bright born 1947, and James Dan Bright 1948. When Donald's dad died, the family of four visited Donald's mom once a week. They got closer with John Jr. gone, his mom had an aura of contentment that surrounded her. Donald's mom died peacefully in 1957, two years after John Jr.

Standing by his mother's bedside before she took her last breath, she said to Donald, "thank you, son, for making my last year's pleasant. I love you and my grandboys." She passed away peacefully, unlike his dad who had died angry at the world.

Straight out of high school Donald John Bright attended college, James Dan Bright, unfortunately, moved to Harlem, New York where he became the lead singer for a jazz band. His dad thought, at least he finished high school, unlike his aunt Rachel.

One of the band members introduced James to a pretty girl that was a prostitute and addicted to drugs. The band played in nightclubs from ten o'clock at night to sunrise, they could play for long hours without getting tired because they were taking drugs. James' voice got worn-out and he grew tired. James girlfriend introduced him to uppers, at first, he was vehement with her for suggesting that he take a substance that would alter his life.

Regrettably, he continued to travel and sing with the band, eventually, he began taking drugs, to wake up, sing, and sleep. Taking uppers, James would perform beyond quitting time. One year later, nineteen-year-old James became a father, he was addicted to drugs that were destroying his heart. James was born with a heart valve disease that he was aware of, he had spent most of his childhood in doctors' offices or the hospital. Though he was mindful of his heart problem, he continued to sing and take drugs to keep up.

One evening, James was performing, during his routine, he was barefoot, his feet had swollen too big for his shoes to fit. He was confused and dizzy, he got out of breath while singing, he stumbled through the lyrics, during his last song James fainted on stage.

He was rushed to the hospital and received treatment; the doctors told him there was nothing they could do. They advised him to stop taking drugs, stop smoking, stay away from liquor, and slow down. He did not listen. James girlfriend had a boy in a hospital that was across town. His buddy picked him up from the hospital and took him to get his girlfriend and baby. James knew that he nor his girlfriend were fit to be parents. he gave her money, Donald's address, and phone number then told her to take the child to his brother in upstate New York. He told her in the car, "I cannot go to my brothers with you, my family is very successful."

The Driver said, "he's right, I've heard a lot about the Bright family."

When they arrived home in their hotel room, his girlfriend took the baby to their room while James used the office telephone to call his brother. James told Donald about the baby and his girlfriend, he asked, "would you please raise my son for me, the baby is three days old. My girlfriend will be there soon." He did not give his brother time to reply, James quickly ended the call by saying, "thank you, Donald, I love you brother."

James and his girlfriend lived in a hotel that was two doors down from where Paula stayed in the red-light district, and across the bridge from where Baerbel's mother was raised.

When James entered his hotel room his girlfriend was gone, the baby was lying on the bed crying. A colored nurse at the hospital could see that the couple had nothing. She purchased two bottles, powdered milk, three diapers, safety pins, two blankets,

All But One

baby lotion, Vaseline, and three gowns. When they were leaving the hospital, James said to the nurse. "truly, you're my son's angel. Thank you, ma'am."

    James made two half bottles of milk out of the powdered milk, and then fed the baby. He sat the other bottle in a bucket of ice. After the baby ate, James patted the baby's back and sang a lullaby, until it let a loud three-day-old belch. James laughed and said, "you're excused." He bathed the baby and dressed him in his new clothes. When the baby was dressed James said, "you are my handsome baby boy. You will love your uncle; he will love you. He is a kind gentleman." James hugged his son before laying him down. James took his regular dose of the drug, laid next to his son, kissed his little forehead and said, "daddy loves you." James fell asleep and never woke up.

    The money that James had given to his child's mother, was spent on maintaining her drug habit. The baby cried all the time, he was skinny, dirty, had a bad diaper rash, and constant cold. She was a cheap hooker strung out seven days a week. Three days after James died, the babies luck changed when his mom's pimp offered a solution. He said, "I will drive you to James brother's house if you make two hundred and fifty dollars tonight.

    That prostitute left at six o'clock that evening. While she was out working the streets, her pimp looked around the room to see if they had anything for the baby. The two bottles were filled with water, he found the powdered milk, read the directions and made the child milk and fed it. When he began to undress the baby, the baby belched and threw up some of the milk. The pimp said laughing, "you are excused."

    The Pimp removed the gown and diaper that James had dressed his son in. The pimp almost cried at the site of the little boy, it ribs protruded where fat should have, he had a diaper rash, his skin was dirty like he had been outside playing. He ran warm water in the sink and using the hotel soap, washcloth, and towel, he gently washed the baby. He wrapped the baby in a towel and looked around for something other than the dirty diaper and clothes to put on the baby. On a stand was the bag of thing from the nurse. The pimp rubbed Vaseline all over the baby, extra on his backside. He dressed the baby and wrapped the six-day-old in one of the new baby blankets. He laid the baby on the bed and pulled the covers over the tiny little shoulder. Using the hotel soap, he washed the little boys' gown and diaper then hung them up to dry.

The pimp said, "your daddy loved you very much," watching the baby suck his tongue as he slept made the pimp smile. He began seriously thinking about settling down and start a family, he wanted a normal life. The pimp had never seen anybody black or white, living a regular lifestyle. The people he knew including his family were thugs, gangsters, pimps, drug addicts or dealers. He laid down next to the little boy and fell asleep. Unlike the child's father, he woke up the next morning.

When the maid entered, he asked for a clean towel and washcloth. He got the baby up and said, "good morning little Tyke. The pimp washed the baby, rubbed him down with Vaseline, changed its diaper, dressed the child in a clean gown, wrapped him in his blanket, and fed him.

The tiny baby's mother returned at eight thirty that morning, she entered the room beaming, she had made four hundred and seventy-five dollars. She showed it to the pimp, his response was not what she expected. He said, "you're nothing but a filthy whore that cares only for drugs."

She said, "but I made a lot of money."

He took the money and said, "we leave tomorrow morning, be ready."

That night at ten o'clock, she called James brother and asked if she could bring the baby in the morning, she told Donald the truth about everything. Donald was devastated, he had no idea that his brother was dead, cremated, and ashes were thrown in a park without his knowledge. He slammed the receiver down so hard, it made his wife, who was in the other room jump. She asked, "Don, everything all right?"

Before sunrise the next day, the pimp pulled up in front of the hotel, he was kind of happy to see Little Tyke. When James girlfriend got in the car with the baby, it was crying and stunk. The pimp punched her hard, like Mike Tyson one punch knockout on Michael Spinks. She had done nothing for the baby, he had on the same clothes and diaper that the pimp had put on him in a little over twenty-four hours. The pimp was enraged. He asked if she had fed the child, she got the bottles out her purse, both were filled with dirty water. The pimp took a bottle, ran to her room, got the powdered milk and prepared the bottle. He went back out to the car, handed the bottle to the mother. Finally, the baby stopped crying as it hungrily gulped the milk down.

****

At eleven o'clock that morning, James girlfriend was standing on Donald John Bright's porch, she handed the nameless baby to him, and said, "it has no name, "it has no name, it's seven days old." She gave Naomi the baby's birth certificate, then left. Naomi read the certificate, it read *Father, James Bright, Mom, is Nameless*.

The baby had puked on the blanket and his clothes several times, his diaper was full of poop and pee. Donald handed the baby to Naomi, it stunk to high heaven. WOW! They stood on the porch gasping for air as they waved to the couple driving off. Naomi said in the baby talk, "come on little one, I'll clean you up."

Donald said, "yeah, you do that, I have to go to work." Holding his nose, he kissed Naomi, said bye to the baby and left.

Donald and his wife Naomi had no children, due to an accident she had when she was young. Naomi was a tomboy growing up, she was raised with five brothers that climbed trees and jumped off their barn rooftop, anything they did she followed. One day, Naomi fell out of a tree and crushed her pelvic bone and bruised a few of her internal organs. She was in constant pain, the doctors wanted to let her heal on her own, but the pain was too excruciating. They did a laparotomy and discovered her female organs were badly damaged, so they removed her damaged parts. She told Donald the whole ordeal when they started dating, he said it was okay, they came to terms that parenthood was not for them.

The Pimp dropped the Little Tyke's mom off on a street corner, and went home, he had several thousand dollars locked in a hidden chest in his three-room apartment. He did not own a suitcase since he never traveled, he had two grocery bags, he put the money in one and clothes in the other. He looked out the window and saw that no one was watching him. The syndicate that he worked for, often snooped on their guys. He figured they probably thought he was still in Rochester.

When the pimp pulled up in front of Donald's house, he was surprised to see black folk living so rich. He said to himself, "that house is huge." He admired Donald and his wife standing on the porch, they looked prosperous. They looked free from crime; they did not appear to be people that hid from the police. The pimp's kindness and deep concern for James baby spearhead a positive change within him. When he saw the house and the child's aunt and uncle, he decided to make a change in his life. He asked himself, "how did James leave all that he had, and chose to live with a drug addict prostitute and become a druggie himself. He had a choice, I didn't."

Standing in the middle of his bedroom, the pimp looked out the window one last time, no one was there. The pimp was nervous, he had never been outside the state of New York, he was frightened, would the syndicate catch and kill him for sneaking off. Even so, he left. Hours later when he saw the sign that read, *Welcome To Pennsylvania,* he said," I choose to change who I am, and my name."

Several months later he settled down in Denver, Colorado, changed his name, opened a bank account, no one asked where the money came from. He landed a job with a construction company. He loved his new life, he had regular people that were his friend. During tax season, he did the guys taxes. As a side gig, the pimp landed a job with H&R Block where he had to take training on tax preparation. After the class ended, he worked for H&R Block for one month and then quit, the ex-pimp was responsible for his Boss taxes, he had to make unlawful, lawful.

Two years after moving to Colorado, the pimp married a woman that was a hairdresser, he bought his wife a lovely house. They had three children and one on the way, he named his first child, Tyke. The pimp was thirty years old when he left New York running from his life of corruption.

One day he was home alone, his wife had taken the kids shopping to purchase new school clothes. Looking out the living room window, an overwhelming flush of peace filled within him, he whispered softly, "Thank You, God, for helping me to become, a normal man. Thank You, Father, for the baby that changed my life." When he finished talking to God, his pregnant wife pulled up in the driveway, their children rushed into the house to show him their new school clothes.

    The ex-pimp smiled.

XVIII

Donovan Victor Bright

With the baby's mom, the pimp, and her husband gone, Naomi cleaned the baby, dressed the child in its new gown and diaper. She threw the two filthy gowns and diapers in the outdoors trash, and then took the baby shopping.

Donald and Naomi named his brother's son, a combination of names, James Donald Paul Bright. They incorporated Naomi father's first name, which was Paul. Donald wanted to tell James that his parents died in a car accident. Naomi asked, "what if he learns the truth?" She looked at the baby and said, "we may have to contend with the drugs in his system."

Donald groaned saying, "I didn't think about that."

When James Donald Paul Bright turned seven-years-old, he asked about his parents. Donald told him the whole truth and that was that James never asked again. From that day forward, he called his uncle and aunt, dad and mom. The drugs from his biological parents did not affect the little boy.

James Donald Paul Bright grew up and seemed to be in a hurry to do everything, he graduated from high school when he was eleven, got his doctorate at the age of eighteen, and married his college sweetheart after his graduation. Donald gave James his great-great-great-great grandpa's wallet, that was still in the tin can as one of his college graduation gifts.

Out of John Bright Sr. offspring, both James had children at the age of nineteen and seemed to be in a hurry to grow up. James Donald Paul Bright and his wife, Sara named their first child Paul, born 1986. They had two other children John 1987, and

Donovan Victor Bright 1994. Donovan was a chubby spoiled baby. Paul acted like he was the father, and John just cried a lot. When Donovan turned two, he became the ruler of the house, if it didn't go his way, he would pick up something and throw it at the person which he would get an old fashion spanking.

Donovan Bright inherited Thaddeus Berhanu personality and Moses looks.

James noticed out of his three son's that Donovan, throughout his school years was voted as President of his class or chairman of the board. He was never an assistant or vice; he was always the head. Donovan's demand to be the leader of everyone made his brothers, John and Paul angry, they planned conspiracies to keep Donovan in trouble. However, at the age of six, Donovan watched and erudite his older brother plots, before they knew anything, their little brother turned their scheme around and got them in trouble.

One evening when the Bright boys were grown, James wife, Sara, was in the bedroom putting lotion on her hand and preparing to retire for the night. James entered and said, "I thought our boys would never get along. But they did."

Sara asked, "what brought that on."

"Dinner time this evening, watching them at the table laughing and joking."

Sara said, "I noticed that as well." Laughing she said, "it was rough going when they were little."

James commented, "poor John, I thought he would never like Donovan, or stop crying."

Sara looked at James and said, "he pulled through, I am proud of him." She smiled and continued, "I am proud of all three."

"Me too," James said in agreement.

James was fascinated with his family history, John Bright Sr., had started a book with the family tree, beginning with himself, though he didn't have a birth certificate or knew where he was born. James tried to find John Bright's birth records, he contacted as many hospitals in New York but to no avail. It was as though John Bright just materialized. All James had was his grandpa's wallet and stories about his aunt JoAnn, John had written in the book how JoAnn was killed. Each generation continued to log births, accomplishments, and deaths in the book.

Like his father, Donovan studied history, got his master's degree at a Manhattan college where he met his beautiful wife, Theenda Carboy. She was shy, he was aggressive, she was quiet, he was outgoing and president of his class. They both were smart and studied hard. Theenda had seen him dashing around campus, on the day they met, Donovan was speedily walking towards her. She didn't know what to do, she began to run away, but Donovan yelled, "stay where you are," in a demanding voice.

Theenda stopped and with shaky legs, she tried to stand still, her heart raced, she was shaking so hard her pressed hair flopped in her face. She whispered, "if I move, I'll fall." She left the hair in her face and shook. The closer he got she said softly, "my goodness, he's beautiful." When Donovan got close, Theenda lost control of her breathing, and a silly smile she could not get rid of was plastered on her face.

Donovan had only seen her at a distance, her figure and long pressed hair blowing in the wind caused him to miss a class, he had followed her to her class. When Donovan got closer to Theenda, the ridiculous smile, hair in her face and shaking did not run him away, instead, he fell in love. Theenda had kindness in her voice that gently rung in his heart. Though her mannerism was frayed with shyness and fright, he saw potential that he knew she had. One year after meeting, they got married.

Donovan had a strong desire to get away from the fast pace hustle and bustle of New York. Theenda wanted to go anyplace her abusive mother was not. Since she and her sister had become adults, her mother verbally abused her children and beat her sister's children when she babysat. Theenda was all for leaving.

On a map Donovan and Theenda found three small towns to visit. In 2016, during Christmas break, they flew south to the two states where the towns were located. Ogville was their last town, it was perfect for them. The town was small, slow, the people were over the top friendly, exactly what they were looking for. Ogville had three schools, Ogville Elementary, Ogville Middle School, and Ogville High. Donovan landed a job as the high school's history teacher and Theenda got a job in Ogville Elementary as a first-grade teacher.

Theenda treasured young minds, she wanted to develop them into something great, teach them critical thinking from the beginning of their learning.
The Bright's returned home and reported that they found a small town and had chosen a house to purchase.
Theenda suggested they stop past her mother first, to get it over with. When they arrived, as expected, Theenda's mother did not disappoint. She opened the door cursing and fussing, that it was too late in the day to visit and without alerting her they were coming over. She went on and on about trivial things without hearing the reason they were visiting. Donovan and Theenda stood on the porch in the cold waiting to be invited in. They were not. Theenda said while her mother was quarreling, "we're moving out of New York."
Mrs. Carboy cursed Donovan out for taking her daughter away, she called Theenda names that were only approved by the devil and not God. "You're a fool for running around chasing after this thing." She said pointing at Donovan.
Theenda turned and ran to the car with Donovan behind her. Before they got in the car, Mrs. Carboy slammed the door shut. As Donovan pulled off Theenda waved and said to her mother, who was looking out a window, "bye forever."
They drove straight to Donovan's parents' home without saying a word to each other. Standing on his parents' porch, Donovan said, "I'm sorry Baby Girl."
"I'm used to it Sweetie," Theenda said softly with sorrow in her voice.
Donovan had the key to his parents' home when the key rattled his mother opened the door. Opposite Theenda's mom, Donovan's parents were happy to see them back, they wanted to hear all about their trip, the town they picked. His parents ordered pizza and called Donovan's brothers to the house.
Tears rolled down Theenda's cheek. She could not remember a time when the Carboy's sat around talking. She wiped the tear away.

Sara looked over and saw Theenda's watery eyes, Sara said, "Theenda come with me." She took Theenda by the hand, and said, "I want to show you my garden." Sara took Theenda outside in the backyard where she had honeysuckle trees, roses, and tulips all buried under snow. Sara turned Theenda to face her and said, "tell me about it."

Theenda said, "My mom," the tears flowed like a waterfall after a hard rain.

James had seen Theenda's sad eyes, he looked at Donovan and asked, "what's wrong with your wife."

Donovan said, "her mother."

His brother Paul asked, "is she ill."

"No, just mean," Donovan said.

John said, "I remember her from the wedding."

James said, "yep, that's right, I remember, she is an angry loud tyrant."

December 29, 2016, James and Sara held a goodbye party in their home for Donovan and Theenda. Attending the farewell party was Donovan's two brothers, his older brother's wife, and two kids. Over a hundred people attended despite the bitter cold. Everyone went to bid the young Bright's farewell, it was a happy, gloomy occasion.

No one from Theenda's family attended, not even her sister, whom she had invited.

That evening Donovan and Theenda stayed their last night in their apartment, on the floor. Theenda said, "this was our first home together, I am going to miss it."

Laughing, Donovan said, "you have taken a thousand pictures of the place outside and in when you get a little teary-eyed, look at the pictures."

They left their keys on the counter as instructed, hand in hand they left. The couple's furniture and Theenda's Honda had been shipped to Ogville. With only overnight luggage they were driving down in Donovan's sports car.

Before getting on the road, Donovan and Theenda visited his parents to say goodbye, Donovan said, "mom, dad, when you get too old to care for yourselves, you're coming to live with Thee and me." He gave them both a hug and asked, "okay?"

Donovan's mom had tears in her eyes when she looked at the young couple. Theenda reached for Sara's hand and said, "we talked it over, it's okay by me."

Donovan said, "we found a house with a big room downstairs," he looked at Theenda and said, "Thee has deemed that room, yours."

Sara gave Theenda and Donovan a hug and said, "thank you both, but that will be a long time from now."

Donovan said, "Okay, maybe not now, when you and dad come down to visit. "

James gave Donovan the tin box with the wallet inside. Donovan looked at it and said, "Paul's the oldest."

James replied, "you're my child that love history."

Donovan said, "thanks, dad. This means a lot to me."

James and Sara stood on the porch waving as Donovan drove off. Crying, Sara whimpered, "there go, my baby."

James said, "that's a grown man." They stood quietly watching Donovan car mingle in with the others. James continued, "I'll miss him. That boy can get in more devilment than most." He looked at Sara and said, "Lord help us, he's going south."

****

The further south Donovan and Theenda got the warmer the air. At the time Theenda was driving, she said, "this is spectacular." She opened her window then continued, "feel the warmth."

Donovan was fiddling with the tin box, he responded, "it is nice." He opened the tin and took the wallet out.

Theenda asked, "what's that?"

Donovan said, "my great-great long time ago-grandpa, born in 1869."

"Good grief Sweetie, most folk only know their grandparents, your family can go all the way back to the 1800's?" Theenda said.

Donovan opened the wallet, put his fingers in the tiny slot and felt something. He pulled it out and froze when he opened the note a picture fell out, he called his dad. Theenda said, "put the phone on speaker."

Donovan turned the speaker on, his father said, "Hello son. Everything okay?"

"Yes, Sir. "Donovan answered then asked, "who's the woman in the picture?"

"What picture?" James asked.

"The one in the wallet you gave me. On the back, it reads, Paula. Who's that?"

"You mean the wallet in the tin? There's no Picture there."

"I'm looking at it, there's also a note"

"Are you kidding me, read it," James said confused.

Donovan read the note, *we came to New York in 1878, I did everything wrong. My oldest child was killed in a gang fight, I blamed my baby-boy, in 1880, age eleven he left and became in'pendent. I didn't see him till now. He stands before me a grown man and coll'age gad'u'ate like his dad. He grew to look like his dad who was an Egiptan' from Afreeca.' I had nothing to do with my Egiptan son's success, he's smart like his dad. He named himself, John Bright.*

Long pause before James said, "I'm speechless."

Theenda said in a demanding tone, "hold on you two, I'm pulling over," She insisted they say nothing more, "this is too much history you're talking about. Just wait, stop talking."

Donovan and his dad hushed for a bit, then James whispered, "your wife pulled over son."

Donovan whispered, "yes Sir," he looked at Theenda and said in his normal voice, "dad she can hear us."

Theenda cut the car off and said, "that's why you look the way you do. You're an Egyptian, true African Egyptian, and you know it. What I wouldn't give to know where I come from."

"Ah, you're part Asian, Baby Girl, so Asia."

Theenda rolled her eyes, and said, "not funny."

Laughing James said, "yeah, it's a little bit funny." He stopped laughing and continued, "son, no one ever looked in the wallet, we passed it down from one generation to the next," James paused and said proudly, "my boy."

"When I get to Ogville, I'll scan the note and picture to you."

All But One

"Let's do the dates first," James suggested. "John Bright was born in 1869."

"Right." Donovan agreed.

"1878, would make him nine when they got to New York. In 1880 he was eleven." James paused for a while.

Donovan asked softly, "dad, still there?"

"Give me a minute to think son." All was quiet until James said, "my dad told me, his grandfather told him, that his grandpa ran away from his mom, when he was eleven years old," James burst out laughing before saying, "boy, that's our grandma from the eighteen hundred, and we have a picture of her. She's from another state, no wonder I could not find her."

"Dad, they got to New York in 1878, where did they come from? What happened to his dad?"

James said," Now, there's the unsolved mystery."

It was ironic that the sixth generation of Moses and Paula was going back to where it all began, as a historian.

God Blessed Donovan and Theenda to get a job teaching, January 2017, in the middle of the school year. Ogville school district was not looking for a teacher, they simply liked the young couple and made a place for them in the school system.

Donovan's grandma that was married to Paula's son, John Bright, predicted as she said, "one day, someone with your genetic factor, is going to reach into that little slit, pull out your mothers note, and the picture will fall out. That person is going to do something, extraordinary."

****

Donovan and Theenda were out for a walk in sunny warm Ogville, they were getting acquainted with their neighbors and neighborhood. Donovan said, "I called mom and told her it's eighty-five degrees in January."

"What did she say?"

"Shut-up boy, it's twenty here."

They laughed. Theenda said, "that sounds like her."

He said, "dad, mom, my brothers are astonished by the picture and note I sent."

Theenda said, "it really is unbelievable."

Donovan and Theenda's first day in class after the holidays, was January 4, 2017. Donovan was a tall handsome drop dead gorgeous black man, his perfect physique looked like he was artistically designed by Elijah Pierce, a sculptor that lived in Columbus, Ohio. In looks he was duplicate Moses, his personality paralleled Thaddeus. The male students wanted to dress and be like him. The females just wanted him.

Theenda, was classy, sophisticated, and gorgeous, she was Black American mixed with a hint of Asian and American Indian, the mixture gave her a striking appearance. She resembled the pictures of Cleopatra in looks and figure. Theenda had a good laugh when a fifth grader told her to leave her husband and marry him. During dinner, she told Donovan about the boy's proposal, he did not think it was funny.

In New York there were thousands of beautiful people of all shapes and sizes, that resembled fashion models. in Ogville, not so, they weren't ugly just country decent. The clothes in the stores appeared to be from the 1950's era.

Even so, Theenda enjoyed the slow quiet small-town lifestyle. After dinner, she and Donovan took long peaceful walks, no rush hour, no school buses, one beautiful park, only three small city buses. The sidewalks were free from being jam-packed with heavy traffic of people coming and going in different directions. One evening, the happy couple drove downtown, and walked along the main street where Theenda saw beautiful wood furniture in a store window, they went inside and purchased a dining room set, plus kitchen table and chairs.

After making their purchase, they quickly walked back towards their car, Theenda stopped so abruptly she almost pulled Donovan's arm out of its socket. He said, "ouch," then asked as he yanked his hand out of hers, "what's wrong with you?"

She said softly, "I can see the sidewalk, and we're downtown." She looked around and continued, "look at the bareness of people, cars, buildings." She looked at Donovan and whispered, "listen, "she pointed to her ear, and continued, "to the quiet."

Donovan was lost for words, he nodded in agreement, then said, "peaceful."

All But One

Theenda stopped to look in a clothing store window, she said in a matter of fact voice, "we'll fly to New York to shop."

"I thought you liked it here."

She hunched Donovan, who was looking in another direction, and pointed at a suit on a mannequin and asked, "like that suit."

He looked at the suit in the store window and said, "yep, we'll spend a few weeks in New York, to shop and visit the fam."

They left the shops and walked to Mall Street, where a statue of Paula's Massa, Harry V. Brown stood. He was standing in the center of a triangle shaped island, that was in a downtown park. The statue was fifty feet tall and stood on a ten feet pedestal. It was donated to the city by Harry's great-great-great grandson, Charles Brown. He thought of Harry as being more important than Christ the Redeemer. An exact replica of Harry's statue was in downtown Titleburk and MacCall, only the statues in those towns stood one hundred and twenty feet tall, it stood on a twenty-five feet pedestal. Charles had total control of all businesses and the police departments in Titleburk and MacCall. In the two towns, Charles commanded that no building could be built, as tall or taller than Harry's statue. Ogville remained nonaligned to H.B. Metropolis, though the town commission allowed Charles Brown to build the statue. Being Independent of Charles and the Browns rulebooks, Ogville was free to mandate their regulations as a small town. They were free to follow States Laws like other cities.

Donovan said, "let's get to the car."

"I think we're lost." Theenda giggled softly.

"I know where the car is, there are only one street and one parking lot," Donovan remarked.

****

Ogville was a party town, the residence celebrated every holiday downtown around Harry's statue. Latino, Asian, Black American, German, Easter, Memorial Day, Fourth of July, Labor Day, and Christmas. Though the commemorative holiday that Blacks did not participate, was the Confederate Memorial Holiday, nor did they attend parades, or shop. They were unanimous in their unspoken united defiance that was incognito during the holiday.

The residents and businesses kept their Christmas decorations up through Dr. Martin Luther King birthday. The week of his celebration, whether it fell on the weekend or weekday, the white residence planned a grand gospel gala Performing were local choirs and quartet groups, the triangle was the stage.

XIX

Ogville and MacCall

    Charles Brown II served as the twenty and twenty-first century Master of H.B. Metropolis, he adored his grandpa Harry the originator of H.B. His admiration for Harry was due to the article written by his uncle Charles in 1876. He wanted to know more about his uncle, Charles searched in the attic chest and saw the article about Cody Paddleton winning the Mayor's Office, he asked himself, "why is this in here?" He read the article but did not see anything about the Browns, he threw it away not realizing, Cody was his great-great-great uncle and the son of whom he was searching for. To Charles, it was as though the man he was named after, disappeared off the planet.

    For many years, Charles continued his search for his namesake throughout the mansion and Castle. He searched in Ogville, MacCall, and Titleburk libraries, sadly, Charles only found the same article that his uncle had written long ago. In the mid 2000's Charles gave up hope of ever finding the man he was named after, he became restless, he wanted to travel and see the world. January 2017, he fashioned a plot to escape H.B. Metropolis secrets.

****

    Donovan, the history teacher at Ogville High School, had his senior class to work on a special historical research project. He thought since he was in the south, it would be interesting to see the student's topics. Donovan wondered how many would research plantations, or the Underground Railroad Stations, or Ogville historical figures. His purpose for giving his students the assignment was twofold. Through their research, he would learn more about the town he chose to live in. His students, that seemed to know little about where they were born, would gain knowledge of their hometown.

To Donovan's surprise, his four senior classes enjoyed doing the research, they compared notes, and class discussions continued after the bell had rung for them to go to their next class or go home. Donovan had to literally put them out of his classroom. There was a black student whose family lived in an Underground Railroad house that sat by the river. The student's parents invited all of Donovan's classes to tour their home and learn its history. The teacher assistants, students, and Donovan had a great time learning about their town, instead of research they called it, Mr. Donovan's Students Discovery. And then, it came to an end when a student, made a historical discovery that got his family murdered.

On January 17, 2017, the third week of researching, one of Donovan's students handed him a piece of paper with only a few words written on it, the student found the paper in the basement of his home. Donovan had no idea what the note meant; the students showed the paper to his father he did not understand the message. The next day in class, Donovan asked if the student had learned the meaning of the message, the student had not. Donovan encouraged his students to dig deep, and don't give up.

After class, on January 18, 2017, the student went to the library and asked Becky Lou the Librarian if there was a microfiche machine. Becky Lou showed him the machine's location. The other Librarian was leaving for the day, she said, "Becky, leaving out, see you in the morning."

Becky Lou replied, "Alright, I'm locking up in a few minutes."

The student could not find what he was looking for on the microfiche, he asked Becky Lou if they had information on a plantation with people still living there. Becky Lou said, "very interesting." Then she asked, "why do you need this info?"

The student ignored her question and asked, "Do you have anything about the plantation in the library."

"I need to know," Becky Lou began, she looked in the curious boy's eyes then continued, "I need to know the reason."

"It's for my class research."

Becky Lou asked confused, "what teacher is asking you to do this?"

"Mr. Donovan Bright, the history teacher. My class is researching Ogville history. We call it, Mr. Donovan's Students Discovery." The teen laughed.

"He's from New York, right?" Becky Lou asked.

"Yes, ma'am." The student answered.

Becky Lou asked, "can you keep a secret?"

The student answered, "yes ma'am."

Becky quickly went to the door, pulled the blinds, that read *Closed,* and locked the door. "Be right back." On her way down into the basement, Becky Lou whispered to herself, "I have to let her know." She returned to the student carrying a dusty hand-drawn map, and two sheets of papers with just enough information about H.B. plantation to dampen his young mind. When Becky Lou handed the items from the basement to the student, he said, "I found a piece of paper that read, *an illegal plantation still exist*s."

Becky Lou asked to see the paper, he pulled it out of his pocket and showed it to her, as she was reading, he said, "if it's illegal then slaves are there, right?"

Becky Lou unlocked the door and said, "share what I gave you and the note with your teacher. The people in this house are very dangerous. Tell no one else about what I gave you or the note you found."

Becky Lou watched the teenager run down the street, she whispered as she closed the door and locked it, "he lives in Stacey's house." She got her purse and left, running to her car she said, "I have to tell Mrs. Paddleton I know Mr. Bright's location."

The student ran all the way home from the Library, as he entered the house his eyes shined with eagerness and joy, he had found a dangerous place. He said as he ran up the stairs to his room, "wait till I tell Mr. Donovan." He went to his room and wrote his report. When he finished, he printed the report and gave it and the items from the library to his dad, who was intrigued by his son's discovery. He said, "dad the Librarian whispered, tell no one, it's a dangerous place."

His father said, "she was teasing you." He read the report.

The next day the teen's father took off work at lunchtime, he drove to MacCall to discuss his son's finding with, Sam

Stevens the Chief of Police. When he entered Stevens office, he realized the papers were in his briefcase, that was in the trunk of his car. He had planned to bring it in and show the papers to the police. The teen's father sat talking at first about the hot weather, he wanted to get the feel of Stevens which was not working. He became nervous as he sat before the Chief who was standoffish. Different thoughts rumbled in the man's head, what if the Librarian was right? What if the Chief was part of the secret? Sweat ball formed on the man's forehead. The teen's father decided not to tell the police about his son's discovery. Instead, the extremely nervous man said, "I hear there's a plantation in town, I would like to take my family to see it, would you happen to know the location?"

Chief Stevens sat motionlessly, his deep-set eyes pierced the man through and through. Stevens said, "excuse me," he left. When the Chief returned, he said, "sorry about that." He assured the teen's father that no such house existed, then abruptly dismissed the man.

Relieved to be out of the police station, the man walked ran out the door. When he got to his car, he was met with a surprise, two of his tires were slashed. He was confused when an officer came out, he asked the man, "how did this happen in a police parking lot?"

The officer hunched his shoulders and asked, "need help?"

"Yes Sir, I only have one extra tire."

The officer returned inside the police station, when he came out, Stevens was with him, he told the officer to go on his rounds. The two men stood in silence as they watched the officer pull off. When he was out of site Stevens inquired about the year, make, and model of the man's vehicle. With the info, Stevens returned inside and called the used tire company.

That evening when the teen's dad arrived home, he was nervous and frightened. He called his family together and said, "we have to leave this weekend, pack a few items, Saturday morning, we're leaving everything behind."

The teen said, "but my report. I'm hoping to get an A."

"What's so urgent honey?" His wife asked.

All But One

The teen's father told them about the two flat tires. And the men from the used tire company, he said, "they told me if I don't keep my mouth shut about the Brown family, I will be eliminated."

"They literally said that dad?" His adult daughter asked.

"Not out loud, they whispered like they were afraid."

"Afraid of what?" His wife asked.

"Not what, who."

"I don't understand dad." His son said.

"Maybe you'll understand this. After they got my tires on, one of the men got in the truck and turned it on, the engine was loud. The other stood in front of me with his back to the police station. He talked fast as he was taking the money, "when the Chief finds out who is talking about the Browns, they end up dead. Be careful." He ran to the truck.

His wife said flippantly, "you went straight to the police, that's who you were supposed to tell, you told the boss, so I don't see the problem. I will not leave my things behind."

His daughter said with a strange angry tone that emitted from her throat, "weren't you listening, the Chief is in on it."

The following day after class, the student handed his report, note, and papers to Donovan and then whispered in his ear, "investigate in secret, the place is very dangerous." He turned and ran.

Friday morning, January 20, 2017, the student and his family were found dead in their home. The newspaper caption was, "A Mysterious Death."

****

In his home office, Donovan sat quite at his desk remembering the most bizarre funeral that he had ever attended, on January 21, 2017. Ogville residence arranged the family's funeral, it was nothing fancy. When Donovan arrived at the funeral home chapel, there were five compose wood crates of different sizes lined up in front of the room. Donovan walked down to see the body of his student and his family. He stood looking down in the crates, there was no pillow, no cushion, no cover, no satin, just plain blank boxes. A little baby was in a tiny box, Donovan had to stifle a chuckle, the baby had on a pamper and tee-shirt, lying next to the child's little head was a pacifier. Saturday morning, the whole family was dead, on the day of their escape from Chief Stevens.

The chapel was full, not a sound was made, no one spoke, not even a pastor, no music played, only thick suffocating stillness smothered the air. Ten minutes later a police officer stood, raised his hand, everyone left. All was quiet in the parking lot; everyone got in their cars and drove off. Donovan went home to tell Theenda about the oddest funeral he had ever attended, she was not home.

He looked at the clock, it was ten thirty in the morning. Taking precautions, Donovan drove one hundred miles north. He went to a Target and purchased ten pay-as-you-go phones, and cards to add minutes. When he got home five hours later, Theenda was there. He told her about the funeral but not the phones. At the time Donovan had no idea of the reason he purchased so many phones or drove so far. He locked nine phones in his office file cabinet. In his desk was the student's map, on the pay-as-you-go phone he entered H. B. Metropolis in google maps, Donovan found Harry's plantation. Had it not been for the student, he would have been oblivious of the plantation.

Monday, January 23, 2017, Donovan went to the library to see if he could find more information on the microfiche machine. When Donovan entered the library, Becky Lou saw the best-looking man she had ever seen. The Library had a stack of old Essence Magazines on a rack, the other Liberian hunched Beck Lou and asked, "is he a model out of a magazine?"

Becky Lou said, "he sho'nuff look like it."

Donovan found nothing in the library.

****

The following Sunday, Donovan returned home from H. B. Metropolis. The sun was beginning to set as he pulled into his driveway, he jumped out the car, ran on the porch and stopped. His thoughts were muddled and confused, he wanted to tell Theenda what he had seen, he waited for a moment and wondered if she would believe him or simply think he had lost his mind.

All But One

When Donovan stepped inside the house, he could smell food cooking, he followed his nose. He went through the family room, past the home library, the den where Theenda's book club sometimes met, the room for his parents, through the dining room, and into the kitchen. "Hello Baby Girl," he kissed her cheek, "I think I saw slaves today," he sat down.

Theenda turned from the stove and said, "what?"

He was slumped over the table liked he had run a marathon, Donovan normally sat tall, proud, and ready to eat. She went to him and asked, "are you okay?" She studied him before asking, "where you've been? You're filthy." She stepped back and continued, "you stink."

Donovan laid the notes from the library and the map of MacCall on the table. He looked at her through sad eyes and said, "I don't know," he pushed the papers towards her.

"You don't know where you've been? Give me a second," Theenda said. She cut the food that was cooking off and put it in serving dishes, she sat the dishes on the counter. She went back to the table, sat down and opened the map, looking around at the food she said, "dinner's ready." She returned her attention to the map and asked, "what am I looking at?"

"Don't think I'm crazy Baby Girl," Donovan said before trying to explain, he watched her reading the notes and said, "this is going to be a hard pill to swallow."

Theenda looked at Donovan and said, "just say it."

Donovan said out, "we may have moved to the wrong town."

"Explain," she said and pushed the papers aside and gave him her undivided attention.

"Well," Donovan started, he looked at his wife, he knew she loved the school, her kids, the town, and had made friends. Donovan lowered his head and said, "Baby Girl, I think I saw slaves today." He waited for Theenda's response.

She got up from the table and began making their plates. She asked, "hungry?" she sat his plate in front of him, then said, "you're filthy and stink, go clean up before we eat."

Donovan said, "before you have me shipped off to the funny farm," he watched her busy herself around the stove, he continued, "I have no other way to say this except, I walked fifteen or more miles today, through a forest. I-I-I saw through my binoculars people were dressed like slaves walking around, and shacks all lined up in a row."

"Theenda sat down, said her grace and began to eat. "I'll eat without you then."

"Imagine how I felt when I made the discovery, there was a huge giant tall gate, I left an Essence Magazine and a note."

A little irritated Theenda asked, "which one of my magazines did you leave?"

"The one with President Barack Obama."

She stopped eating and glared at Donovan before saying, "There were several, I was saving those."

"Baby Girl, I'm trying to explain."

"Okay, I'll calm down, did you talk to anybody?"

"No, I didn't," he got up and began to leave, "I'll clean up." He left.

With him gone, Theenda went into the library and looked through her magazines, she said quietly to herself, "he gave the one titled, President Barack Obama, my favorite," she exhaled and said, "I'll be okay." As she was going back to the kitchen, she said under her breath, "gave my favorite one away."

When Donovan returned to the kitchen, Theenda was sitting in the same spot, mad.

Donovan sat down. Theenda said, "your food's cold." Donovan looked down at his plate, then at her, she said, "yeah, I could have warmed it up. I chose not to as you chose to give my favorite Essence away."

He stuffed his mouth with food and said, "not that cold." He took a bite of the roll, looked at Theenda and continued, "Yes, I saw a plantation, no I did not speak to anyone, but I did see people walking around. Remember when we visited the plantation in New Orleans? We walked through the Massa house and the slave shacks, that's what I saw, only there were people inside this tall giant size gate, I couldn't get in." Donovan looked troubled and confused before saying, "I have no idea why I took your magazine. I just knew that's what I was supposed to do. I put it in a freezer bag and left it between the gate's tight prongs." He looked dejectedly at his wife and sadly said, "Baby Girl, I don't know why I did it, I am sorry."

"Maybe, we should go visit," Theenda suggested.

Donovan stuffed more food in his mouth before saying, "we can't get in."

"Why?"

Donovan said a little irritated, "the gate."

"Don't get upset with me, I'm trying to forgive you. Isn't there a house?"

Donovan checked himself and said, "sorry. There are gates and forest that wraps around the whole property. Yes, there's a big house in front." Donovan said and then took a bite of bread.

"So, the owner locked themselves in?"

"Seems like," Donovan said as he ate a bit of food, then continued, "It was like looking in a kaleidoscope." He put more food in his mouth before he swallowed and said, "everything was nice and in order. The forest, the gates, the house, all of it was well thought out."

Theenda said, "Sweetie, if you're not mad, or crazy, and telling the truth, we need to report this." She took a breath and said, "How did you find out about it?"

Donovan ate in silence for a moment. Theenda pushed her plate aside and read through the notes. She noticed a rough draft of a huge building sitting alone, "what's this?" she showed the drawing to Donovan.

"Wood furniture was in there, you would love it," he looked at their table and chairs and said, "as a matter of fact it looked sort of like this set." He paused when he remembered the furniture in the store downtown. He said, "like both our sets." He looked down at the table and said, "this and our dining room furniture." He pointed to the drawing Theenda was looking at and said, "I drew that."

Theenda said, "I know."

"The building was huge," Donovan said as he watched Theenda flip through the papers.

"I think the police should hear about this," Theenda said.

"No, we can't," Donovan replied as he finished eating.

Theenda asked, "why not?"

On the table were toothpicks in a clear glass holder, Donovan grabbed one, slid his plate aside and said, "remember the family that mysteriously died a few weeks ago."

"Yeah."

"The teenager was my student, he's the one that told me about the plantation in MacCall. He said something about it being dangerous, the next morning his whole family was found dead."

"I don't understand." Theenda began, "did you report he was missing from class?"

"The article appeared in the paper before classes begun."

As Donovan twirled the toothpick between his fingers, Theenda sat watching him before asking, "someone randomly went to the house? Just out of the blue killed a whole family, then wrote an article."

"If you think that's strange, you should have gone to the funeral."

Theenda said, "what would happen if the FBI found out that someone still has slaves."

Donovan said, "somebody is being paid to keep it quiet. My student's whole family was killed." Donovan stood up then sat down and said, "gone Baby Girl, and nobody is doing nothing, five people died in their home. And nobody is doing nothing." He stood and took their plates to the sink. He looked at Theenda and said, "the police should be over there, yellow tape around the house, why aren't they?"

"Where did they bury them?" Theenda asked.

"Cremated, after the strangest funeral, ever."

Theenda suggested, "maybe it was a random murder."

"The boy's father drove to MacCall and spoke with the police about it. Are you listening?"

Theenda got defensive and said, "don't talk to me like I'm the crazy one." She shifted in her chair to see Donovan who was by the sink, she asked," are you saying, the police are keeping it quiet?"

Donovan went back to the table, sat across from Theenda, the two were quiet, as though they were in deep thought. Theenda looked at the table and chairs, then at Donovan and asked, "if this is true, what're we do?"

"Good question," he reached across the table, put her hand in his, and said, "good question Baby Girl."

XX

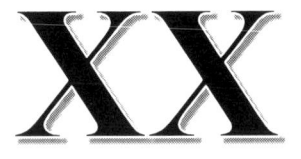

The Magazine That Changed Lives

While Donovan was at home trying to explain what he may have seen to Theenda, on the plantation, a fourteen-year-old boy, named Cush, found the Essence Magazine. Cush showed it to his father, Lee, and grandma, Lillie.

****

The slaves worked twelve hours six days a week. The two overseer's, Roy and Fred, began work before the slaves since they had to get up, get dressed, go to the slave quarters ring a bell and yell wake up, and open the slave gate. The slaves were always up, they wanted to see the overseers do more than sit on their horses watching them.

Usually, the two overseers sat quiet, but in February 2017, they were happy and chatty, that year was their last year being held hostage on the plantation. They were being released off the plantation January 2018. Fred said, "we've been here thirty-seven' years, we were hired 1980, man we worst' twenty years old. Can you magine' how da' world look now?" Fred asked.

Roy said, "they can keep my woman that Massa's daddy, pick for me."

Fred shook his head in agreement, "mine too. She neva' got pregnant, I wonder why."

Roy said, "we white men, treated like the niggras. When we get out of here, I'm telling the authorities."

Fred said, "I remember those two old guys face when we arrived, they jumped down off their horse and ran out da' dividing gate past us, likes dey' on fire."

Laughing Roy said, "old Massa Brown said, "Hey boys, not so fast, we are going to feed you. My son and cook are in the kitchen waiting for you."

Fred said, "dey' were runnin' fast ta' freedom"

Roy said, "now we know why," he jumped down off his horse and said, "Freedom going to feel mighty nice. I don't want Massa food; I just want to go home."

"Yeah," Fred said, "too many years locked up, we ain't seed' nobody," he looked at the gate and shook his head and continued, "why we locked in?"

Roy said, "oh God." He held his head down in disgust.

Fred asked, "what's wrong?"

"This plantation is not legal; those two old men were killed," Roy commented.

"What are you talking about?"

Roy said, "I'm talking about, I believe my girlfriend is married, probably have children. My mama and daddy probably dead and buried. But I will never find out." He cried.

Fred looked at Roy and said, "you'll see yo' gurl' friend, maybe she wait fo' ya."

Roy pulled himself together, he wiped his face. The slaves stopped to watch Roy cry. Lee, one of the slaves working in the tobacco field said to another slave, "dey' ain't no better dan' us."

The slave said, "you be right Lee, dey' cain't git out either."

Fred said, "I's got three women pregnant,' naw I's thank' foe." He looked at Roy and said, "I's could be a grandpappy."

Roy said sadly, "don't you see, you'll never see them. I was supposed to graduate from college in 1982. My dad is a chemical engineer, I was studying to be an electrical engineer. My mom a nurse. I have two sisters and a brother." Roy smiled and continued, "I may be an uncle, but I'll never see any of my family."

"Wow man," Fred said, "you be from a smart family.' My sista' git to da' sixth-grade afo' she git' knocked up. The rest of us, third grade, man, mom and dad didn't go at all, dey' cain't read."

Roy said thoughtfully, "I wonder why nobody come get us, those two overseers had to have told somebody about this setup."

All But One

Fred said, "knowing the Brown famly' like you say, dey killed does' men." He paused as though he was deep in thought before continuing, "when dey open dat' gate, Roy run fast as you can, yellin' and hollerin."

"Honestly Fred, that's a good idea."

Fred said, "Mr. Brown ride over to our cabins on a motorbike, we take it, no matta' who be driving, we jump on and leave dis' place."

Roy said, "that's our only way out." He slapped Fred on the shoulder and continued, "good job Fred, we have a plan."

The overseers' wives were not allowed to go by the divider gate or near the slaves. Someone in the Brown family was always watching. Roy's first year locked on the plantation, his woman jumped on a horse, and thinking she was going to get out, galloped to the divider gate where she was shot to death. The next day Roy had a new woman, Charles told Roy that his first woman ran away. Roy and Fred knew what happened, they heard the gunfire, still, they said nothing.

After Charles father hired Roy and Fred, Charles changed the overseer's exit off the plantation. While Charles father, Ben, was living, he told his dad, "I don't feel like dragging four dead bodies back to where they came from."

Ben asked, "what'd you mean son?"

"Out the gates, in the house, kill all four, then back through the divider gate, and bury them." Charles continued as he held up four fingers, "two overseers two women, dad that's a lot." He ran his fingers through his hair and continued, "when Roy, Fred, and their women get too old, why don't we walk them through the divider gate, shoot them, then bury them in the divider gate forest. That would be a whole lot easier."

His father said, "son, run Metropolis your way."

Ben Brown born in 1935, died in 2016 of heart failure.

The slaves stopped producing tobacco since the overseers were always sleeping on the job. The overseers had grown old and tired, it got harder for them to stay awake, sitting around doing nothing. They came up with a strategy, one would sleep on the ground for thirty minutes while the other kept watch, and then switch. Sometimes that worked, other times they both fell asleep, one on the ground the other sitting on his horse.

Ben, Charles father built mini-malls in MacCall, Ogville, and Titleburk to sell his products. The slave women sixty years and older made quilts, bedspreads, curtains, and throw rugs which were sold in the mall's stores and shops around the country. For the slave compound, the women made candles for their cabins, women and men clothes for the slaves, children, the nurse, and the teacher. Men sixty and older made the dining room and kitchen sets that were sold in the malls and across the country.

In 2017, there were seventy-five adult slaves, twenty children ranging between the ages of two to thirteen. Charles assigned the fourteen-year-olds in homes with the same skills, he gave the overseers detail instructions on where to place the teens. The nurse and teacher were fifty-five years old. Charles had the women to train Helen, a slave, how to take care of the children. Helen received a minimal nurse's aide and teacher's training as the nurse and teacher prepared to leave. Charles told the women that soon they were going to get their freedom. He said, "you have to promise to keep the plantation a secret, and not tell anyone."

The two women said together, "I promise."

The teacher said to the nurse when no one was around, "we'll keep our mouths shut as we hand over our memoirs to the police."

The nurse laughed and said, "our promise kept."

Throughout the years, each set of teachers and nurses found the memoirs hidden under the loose floorboards, since the Browns or children never entered the sleeping room, the papers were safe. The women wrote in the memoir changes made during their time, from the first nurse and teacher in 1876, to the last in 2017, each recorded the date they were locked in with the children. They wrote in detail what they had seen and heard, if the overseer was not looking or for a moment walked away, a slave whispered to the nurse an atrocity that took place in their area. The nurse recorded everything she saw as she walked from the children area to the slave compound. The nurses had empathy for the mother, who wanted to at least see their baby but could not. With the overseers watching closely, the nurse wrapped the baby in a blanket and took the newborn to the children area.

All But One

In the early 1900s a nurse allowed a weeping mother to hold her baby, the overseer killed the mother, baby, and nurse. He told the master of H.B., who had the three taken to the divider gate area. When the nurse did not return the teacher knew what had happened, she heard three gun shots. She quickly wrote in the memoir the tragedy; she also wrote that she was going to be killed. An overseer stood outside the children cabin and called for the teacher to join him. She said, "children it's going to be okay, stay inside." She hugged each child and left.

The teacher was escorted out of the children gate to the divider burial grounds, she looked down and saw the three bodies, she looked up and saw a gun aimed at her. She closed her eyes and prayed for the children.

Helen stayed in the children area to learn how to take care of the kids' aches and pains and teach them reading, and writing. The boys that were trained to make and design furniture were placed in a furniture maker home as their son. While learning how to make furniture, they would also work in the fields until they turned sixty. Charles taught all the children how to grow and care for the tobacco plants.

Helen was permitted to join the other slaves on the second and fourth weekends. She walked non-stop eleven and a half miles to the adult slave area as the overseer rode horseback. Sometimes, on her way home, the trip was halted, they would rape or beat her, after which she limped the remaining miles home.

The slave's enemy was one of their own, Helen's husband, Bo. He protected himself from beatings, and hunger, by supplying his owner incriminating information about the slaves. In his peahen tiny brain, he assumed that he was a cut above the rest because twice in his life he had been off the plantation with Harry II. Both times in the same club where he saw, who he thought, were other slaves dressed up. One day after an outing, Bo and Harry II were on their way home, Bo asked Harry if he could get clothes like the other slaves he had seen, he especially liked the one colored man that looked more elegant than Massa Charles. That was Bo's last time off the plantation.

I's Neva' Seed

At the end of the working day, the tired overworked slaves left the tobacco field at 6:00 pm. Their stride took on the appearance of an ape locked behind bars, their heads hung down, arms loosely dangled by their side, shoulders bent towards the ground, their bodies were tired, their spirit was severely fragmented. The overseers had gone into the slave town area, wherein the bar they got two bottles of watered-down liquor.

Just before entering the slave gate a young fourteen-year-old named Cush, saw something sticking between the gate rods. He looked around for the overseer's, they were not there. He ran over and snatched the item. His Dad, Lee, yelled in a loud whisper, "git back here boy!"

Cush looked at the item and yelled, "Daaad," he stuffed his finding in his shirt and joined his dad before the overseers saw him. As the overseers left, they locked the slave gate and galloped home.

Cush and his father entered the cabin, Cush took his finding out of his shirt and laid it on the table. He said, "look, dad."

Lee's mom, Lillie asked, "look at what?"

Lee and Cush were standing by the table gazing down at the Essence Magazine in a confused state. Lillie was by the fireplace when she asked, "Lee, what ja' lookin' at?"

"I 'don't know maw," Lee answered.

Cush said, "I found it, grandma, by da' outer gate."

"You let dat' child go by the outer gate?" Lillie went to the table, pulled a chair out and sat down, "Massa will beat him."

"Mama, da' overseer' didn't see him," Lee pushed the magazine in front of her, "look at dis."

Even though the slaves made the candles, they received only two the first of the month, one for upstairs and the other for the first floor. On this evening Lee was burning both candles downstairs. Lee was a good-looking rugged man in his mid-thirties. Lillie was a short heavy-set woman with few wrinkles, salt and pepper hair, and a kind face. She looked at Lee then at the magazine and said, "I's neva seed' nonthin' likes' dis." She looked at Cush and asked, "whad' dis' be?"

Lee grabbed the magazine and tried to take it out of the freezer bag but could not.

All But One

"Let me try dad," Cush tried to get the magazine out, but failed.

Lee said to Lillie, "look at da people on dis thang."

"Who dey be, dey brown likes us," Lillie said.

Lee had a confused expression on his face, he said, "I's' don't know mama. Look at dis' colored man, look at all des' pretty bright colors on dis' here thang. Feel da' paper. Mamma dis' be strange." A second time he tried to get the magazine out the bag.

Cush reached for the magazine, he fiddled with the freezer bag. Lee and Lillie watched him intensely, Lillie said, "don't rip dat strange paperboy,"

Cush looked at the little blue button on top, he asked, "what dis' be?" He slid the button on top to one side, when the bag opened, he reached in and pulled the magazine out.

Lee took the magazine and flipped through it, he was amazed, he read the caption on the cover, "Prezdent Ba-rack Ob-am-man."

Lillie got the freezer bag and asked, "what kind of name dat be?" she held up the bag and looked through it.

"Listen to dis mama, it says Prezdent Back Ob-am-man."

"Prezdent' of what? Dat' man be slave likes us." Lillie said in a matter of fact tone.

"Hum," Lee said, "He don't look likes it."

Looking at the picture Lillie said, "Dat's cause' he be a dressed-up slave."

Cush said, "da Prezdent of Southern States be Prezdent' Nixon. Ain't no slave be Prezdent."

Lillie snapped, "boy hush up, you's' git' us in trouble goin' by dat' outta' gate."

Lee said, "I won't's ta' tell uncle Glaidous," he looked at Cush and said, "run and git' unk."

Cush dashed out the door, Lillie yelled, "don't let the door slam..." The door slammed shut. Shaking her head, she said, "Lee you need to teach dat' boy manners fo' he become a man."

Ignoring his mom, he said, "ma look a note on dis' here paper." He looked confused and asked, "whar's git yellow paper?"

Lillie held the freezer bag up, with a puzzled look on her face asked, "what kind of paper dis' be?" she put it up to her face and looked through it a second time, she said, "I's' see through it."

She looked at the note Lee was holding and said, "dat' be pretty paper."

Lee said, "dis be strange mama, paper be white, not yellow."

Lillie held the freezer bag up to her face and said, "and not see through."

Lee said, "dis' paper be sticky on da' back."

"Let me see," Lillie said as she reached for the sticky note and handed Lee the freezer bag. He instantly put the bag up to his face and said, "I can see through it."

Lillie read the note, then without moving her head looked up at Lee and asked, "whad' dat' mean."

****

While Lillie and Lee tried to figure out the message Donovan had written, Donovan and Theenda were cleaning the kitchen and dishes. Donovan was rinsing the dishes and putting them in the dishwasher, while Theenda was cleaning the countertops, table, and stove, she said, "your mother called today, sorry I forgot to tell you."

"What did she want?"

"Your father tried to find Paula's birth certificate, your mother bought me a present, I'm so happy she and I don't have the usual crazy relationship, of I hate-mother-in-law-hate-daughter-in-law thing happening, know what I mean?" She laid her head on Donovan, and continued, "makes my life easier."

Donovan chuckled when he said, "and mine. I'll call dad to see if he found anything."

Theenda deep thought said, "uhm, Sweetie?"

"Yeah Baby Girl."

"If there are, I mean a big if slaves are on the plantation, how many were there? That's assuming there are slaves."

"I don't know," Donovan answered.

"Have you told Timpkin and Haze?"

"Not yet."

"Are you going to tell them."

"Tonight, at a restaurant."

"So, you're leaving here and going to eat again."

"No, I'll have a coke or something."

Donovan met with Timpkin Linwood and Haze Day in McDonald. Timpkin was a short, muscular good-looking man in his mid-fifties. He was a manager for a government division, he wore Jeans, sports jacket, dress shirt with a tie. Haze, in his thirties, was not happy to be meeting in McDonald. He was a pretty boy know it all, with an all-American apple pie face. He owned a janitorial company that he claimed made him rich. Haze being a savvy talker, confident, and all-knowing business ethics landed him contracts with large corporations within the whole state.

Mild-mannered Timpkin was a quiet peaceful kind-a-guy, on the other hand, Haze was fiery, hot-tempered, fast pace I-ain't-got-time thirty-year-old man. Donovan was smooth as evening blues, just don't push the wrong buttons. Donovan tried to share with his friends his discovery of slaves. Haze blatantly blared out, "Don-man why we here?"

Donovan looking confused said, "I need to tell you something..."

Haze Day said, "naw man, why we here so late at McDonald, of all places."

Timpkin was wondering the same thing when he commented, "yeah, why? KayKay is going to be mad I'm out so late?"

"Listen, I have something to share with you," Donovan took a deep breath looked around the empty McDonald and whispered, "I found slaves, living, breathing, walking, talking, not in a play or a book, but in a nearby town."

Timpkin looked confused, "in a book."

"He just said," Haze turned to Donovan and asked, "wait, what did you just say?"

"I didn't stutter," then whispered, "I said I found, note the word, found."

Haze checked his attitude made a U-turn and followed what Donovan was claiming. "Mm' hum, so Don-man you found slaves, 2017, well'um, where?" Haze asked.

"Forty-five miles North West of here, a family has owned them since 1865."

Timpkin being the only one born and raised in Ogville, defended his town, "no such place exists!" Timpkin began to get agitated said, "saying, "note the word," proves nothing."

Haze lost patience with Timpkin, shouted, "Shut-up Tim-man."

The employees stopped and looked at the three men, the supervisor went over and asked, "everythang' alright?"

Donovan said, "sorry, yes, we're okay." When he left, Donovan said, "Shh, quiet," Donovan commanded, "keep it down."

"Don't yell at me," Timpkin whispered through clenched teeth.

"Guy's keep your voices down. People have died," Donovan whispered very softly. "Don't make me regret telling you."

Timpkin said in a loud whisper, "I don't believe that my town could do such a thing."

"Then why don't you come with me," Donovan suggested.

"I am not interested in hearing more of your condemnation accusation of my town committing such a hideous crime." He stormed out.

Haze watched Timpkin leave and said, "now that was a lot of big words, he worked for the Government too long." He tried to comfort Donovan and continued, "don't worry 'bout him Don-man, he'll come around."

"I don't know Haze; it was hard for me to believe."

"You said some people died over this, so...?"

"So," Donovan cut Haze off and continued, why am I telling you? Don't know."

They sat quietly for a while, Haze broke the silence when he said, "misery loves company, I'm miserable." He looked at Donovan and asked, "are you miserable?"

Donovan clasped his hands together, looked down at the table and said, "yea. No, I am concerned people are being made modern day slaves. I pray I'm wrong."

"So, you should be miserable, because, in 2017, America still has slaves." Haze said.

Donovan looked at Haze and said, "I get it, no one is free until we're all free. Until that happens, we're in a state, of misery."

Haze said, "you and Tim-man throw words together better than I do. You said what I said only better."

"As long as we're on the same page my brother," Donovan said.

All But One

****

Outside Lillie's shack Cush returned with uncle Glaidous, "come on unk I's' got somethin' ta' show ya."

"Stop pullin' on me boy," Glaidous said. "Iffen' you's don't I's gonna tan yo' hide."

Lillie was standing in the doorway and whispered, "Glaidous, cut that noise out, git' in here, we's got business ta' tend to."

"What ja' talkin' bout woman? You da' one keepin' up a ruckus."

Inside the house, Lee was still looking at the Essence, he said, "unk look at dis'. Cush close da' doe."

"But dad it be hot in here."

"Boy iffen you's don't close dat' doe' you's gonna' feel hot hands on the seat of yo' britches."

Lillie said, "then it be my turn ta' gib' ya' a lil' heat in the seat." She said to Glaidous, "look at da book Lee gots', and look at dis' seehre paper."

Cush closed the door, then said, "I's' find it unk by da' outer gate."

Glaidous looked at the cover of the Essence and asked, "who des' pretty brown people," he flipped through the Essence and asked, "what dis be?" He closed the book and looked at the cover again, then at Lee and asked, "what kind of slave dey' be?"

Lee tried to pronounce the book, "Eas-send mar-ja-zine."

Glaidous threw the book onto the floor, jumped back, and said, "you be speakin' devil talk."

Lillie said, "read dat' pretty paper son."

Cush picked the magazine off the floor. Lee began to read, "my name is Doo-noo-in."

Frighten Lillie nervously said, "let's pray first."

Glaidous in response, "hush-up woman, Lee read."

"What be wrong askin' God to help us? Yous' say it be of da' devil," Lillie said.

Lee began to read but Cush cut in, "dis' be exciten' ain't it dad..."

Simultaneously Lee and Glaidous yelled softly at Cush, "Boy hush."

"I's prayin." Lillie began praying, "Lord-a-mercy on us po' creatures…"

Glaidous said, "woman pray to yo'self."

Lee said, "everybody quiet please, let me read, Mr. Doo-noo-vin wrote, I am a black American."

The three asked in unison, "a what?"

Lee stopped reading and said, "member Massa say strange people from other contree' come ta' America, he be one dem." Lee showed Glaidous and Lillie the note and said, "see he spell America wrong.", he put an n at da' end.

Glaidous and Lillie looked closer at the note, Lillie said, "show nuff' did." She took the magazine and said, "look at dem coloreds, dey be from another America dat' end wid' n. Mr. O-bam-man be da' Prezdent of dat' country."

Glaidous said, "maybe he a slave who git' out he's outer gate, he sees on da' other side of da' trees."

Lillie did not accept Glaidous explanation, she said, "no white man gonna' let us, slaves out, keep readin' Lee."

Instead of reading, Lee said, "maybe he be a slave from Africa, dat's whars' our family come from years ago."

Everyone went silent in the little cabin, the two flickering candles cast mysterious shadows on the rough wood walls. The crickets outside were loud, the crunch of someone running on the dirt road past Lee's cabin caused them to jump back to reality.

Glaidous asked, "Why ain't dey' in da' cabin?"

Muffled laughter from outside slipped through Lee's cabin windows and crunch from people walking on the dirt path. And then, silence saturated the outside and inside of Lillie's cabin. Lee cleared his throat, Lillie jumped. Glaidous chuckled softly, and said, "almost jumped out yo' seat old woman."

"Shut-up Glaidous," Lillie whispered.

Lee continued to read, "I would like to meet wid' you, pick a time and date, leave a note, and I will come." Lee gasped and said, "tell me unk, he be out da gate, tell me plez,' how he do dat,' what dat' called?" Lee said too loud for Lillie.

She whispered in a soft light roar, "boy iffen you's' don't be quiet Massa will hear ya,' den we's all be in trouble."

Glaidous hands didn't know which direction to go as he paced back and forth, eyes rolled around, he said, "dis' cain't be,

All But One

I's' won't out dis' pantation. He ain't from another country, he be right here. I's won't off dis' pantation, a 'foe I's die."

Cush jumping up and down, exclaimed with joy, "what dis' mean daddy!? What dis' mean?"

Lee quieted down and said, "I don't know son," he looked at his mother, and asked, "what dat' called mama? when a man can git' out and walk about. What da' called?"

Glaidous stopped and stared at his baby sister with great intensity, "what dat' be call Sis?"

Lillie thought a moment before saying, "it be called, ah' walk-about, hum um, he be ah' walkin' about ain't he. So's," she said matter factually, "he be, ah' walk-about."

Glaidous looked at his sister, and said, "how you know an old woman."

Lee looked at his mother as though she was the smartest human alive and said, "mama, I's' wanna' be a walk-about."

"Me too daddy, me to," Cush walked around the cabin and said, "likes dis, cept' out der."

Ignoring Cush, Lillie asked, "we's gone tell da others?"

Lee answered, "naw not yet. What iffen' dis' be Massa son."

Glaidous said, "naw, dat' boy too dumb ta' read a book like dis." He took the magazine from Lee.

Lillie said, "da ova seer cain't git out, it ain't dem."

Cush asked, "So's, who left it, daddy?"

Glaidous said, "I's ain't a knowin' who, I's do know we's cain't tell Sophie," he looked at Lillie and continued, "I know she yo' friend and all, she cain't be trusted."

Lee, agreed with his uncle, "unk is right mom, please don't tell aunt Sophie."

Glaidous rejoiced a little too loud, he said, "I's' know when we's meet da' walk-about."

Lee asked, "When unk?"

Easta' Sunday, three months from now,' the overseers don't come over here on holidays."

Lee said, "unk you right, dat' be a good time, no body work on dat' day, Massa like Easta, he don't come round."

Lillie said, "Glaidous, Lee you's crazy, dey' be here iffen' we..."

Lee talked over her, "unk the walk-about cain't git' in da' gate."

Glaidous said, "we have Easta' in ta'bacco field two, it be away from da' outer gate."

Lee thoughtfully answered, "yeah, dat' a good spot."

Glaidous said, "We's gonna meet a walk-about."

Lillie said, "Glaidous you might have somethin,' but what 'bout da overseer's, dey' be comin' ta' git' food."

Lee said with a chuckle in his voice, "I know, I'll ask Bo to ask Massa iffen' we's can have Esta' Sunday in da' ta'bacco field, den' suggest he be da' one ta' watch us, he can tell Massa iffen we's do anythang' wrong."

Lillie looked at her son, "Lee you thankin' bout doin' somethin' I's' see's it on yo' face."

"Mama, what if slavery be ova,' I's got's ta' know. Da' overseers come git' dey' food and leave, dey' always do, we gits' Bo drunk, he fall sleep, he always do."

"Yeah, Bo will thank he da' boss of us. He ask Massa." Lillie said.

Glaidous said, mm 'hum, I's' wonda' whad' da' walk-about gonna' say when he sees us."

Lillie said, "what we gonna' say when we sees him."

Lee said, "I's' thank' I's' got' it."

Glaidous asked, "got what?"

"The gate and the forest - we cain't see out or get out and nobody cain't..."

Glaidous finish Lees sentence, "see in or git' in."

Lee looked at his son, then at his mother, at his uncle, at the magazine, and said "Cush, mama, unk, we's locked up slaves, and it be agin' da' law. And dis brown skin man likes us, be da' Prezdent of da' Souf. And Mr. Doo-noo-man come ta' set us free."

Lillie took the magazine and laid the freezer bag next to it. she said, "glory be, Lee say slavery be ova,' and nobody knows we's here on dis' pantation."

Cush ask, "I wonder iffen' da' walk-about will help us, I's wont' ta' walk-about..."

Glaidous cut in, "Lawd child, what ja' talkin' bout,' we lib' off dis' pantation like des' brown people in dis' here mar-ja-zine."

Lilly agreed with her brother and said, "we's won't know how," Looking at a sofa in the magazine she asked, "what dat' dey' sittin' on?" Looking at a car, she asked, "what des' round thangs,' and dis' thang sittin' on top of." She turned the page and saw a house, she asked, "is des' big clean beautify shacks, cabins? We's don't know how ta' lib' likes' des' walk-about."

With deep sorry in his voice, Lee softly said, "mama, I's' willin' ta' learn how ta' lib' likes da' walk-about. Maybe da' walk-about teach us how ta' walk-about." Lee examined the magazine, and asked, "I's' wonder how dis walk-about find us?"

The candles burned low as the four slaves sat deep in their own thoughts.

"Glory be," Lillie said. "We may be doin' what Massa planned. Mr. Doo-noo-man may be a trap fo' us, we's meet him, Massa beat us good."

"We's neva' be da' same," Lee said softly. "We's gotta try."

Glaidous started leaving, when he got to the door he looked back and said, "you's right Lee, we's neva be da' same, Massa wanna' beat me, dat' ain't he's first time it won't be he's last." He opened the door turned and said, "We's neva' be da' same." He left.

Lilley watched him leave, she sat silently staring at the door. Lee asked, "whad' ja' lookin' at mama?"

Lillie answered, "he ain't gone no whar's. He just stand der' tryin' ta figure it out."

"Yes, mama, unk Glaidous right, I's neva' be da' same. I's got ta' know, beaten or no beaten."

Cush stood next to his dad nodding in agreement and said, "gotta' no grandma." He sat in a chair next to Lee.

The three sat around the table, in front of them was the Essence Magazine laying on top of the freezer bag. Glaidous opened the cabin door, grabbed a chair, and sat next to Lillie, she reached over and gave his hand a squeeze. The four slaves sat quietly around the table. Cush laid his head on Lee's shoulder. A muffled moan escaped through Lee's lips.

Tears slid down Glaidous cheeks as he stared at the magazine, he said, "I's not da' same."
Lillie cried.

XXI

Valentine Day

Donovan was up at six o'clock in the morning, he had prepared a delicious breakfast for his sweetheart. During the weekdays before work, the couple normally took a morning jog through the park. But on Valentine Day, after breakfast, Donovan had planned for them to run through their neighborhood. That evening, he was driving her to Titleburk to dine in the city's finest restaurant.

For Theenda's Valentine Day surprised breakfast, Donovan had set the table for his prissy wife, he thought it was a little girly but then, so was Theenda. The centerpiece on the kitchen table was an arrangement of a dozen pink roses, as an extra surprise he purchased online pink placemats and cloth napkins, with a white rose embroidered in the middle.

Theenda entered the kitchen wearing a pink jogging suit trimmed in white, her glance fell on the table, the expression on her face made Donovan feel proud of his effort to please her. "Sweetie, this is beautiful," she ran into Donovan's arms and gave him a big hug and kiss, "perfect," she said as she turned and went to the table, she sniffed the roses. "My favorite color and flower," she said, "thank you." She went to the counter to see what Donovan had cooked. In one serving dish was raisin pancakes, in the other turkey bacon, two omelets, and toast lightly buttered, she stood next to Donovan put his hands in hers and said, "let's forgo jogging today and eat this delicious breakfast later." She led him upstairs.

****

Benjamin "Breeze" Wood was born and lived in Ogville where he was extremely unhappy. He had dreams of getting into the music industry, instead, he was stuck running his dead father's construction company. Under his father, the company was a booming success, unfortunately, he fell off a scaffold and died. Two days after the funeral, Breeze mom moved north with the foreman of the company. Even though Breeze was thirty years old he was inept to run the family construction business. Still, Breeze mother put him in control, he was supposed to send her a large sum of money once a month. Under her son's unprofessional clutches, the company failed, and she got nothing. He was a scheming lying untrustworthy entrepreneur; his deceitful unsympathetic attitude drove good workers away from his employ.

Apart from the construction business that he loath, three evenings a week, Breeze played his tenor saxophone, which was his first love at the Blues Night Club. He felt that the construction company interfered with his progress of becoming a professional musician. Breeze yearned to be emancipated from the entrapment of dust and dirt. He was determined to one day become a music writer and producer. It was the thirst that kept him alive, it was his motivation that made his spirit thrive, the audience applause was his Rose of Sharon, his Lilly of the valley. Breeze was going out of business and moving to Los Angeles. He had a friend that was a filmmaker out there, who had asked Breeze to come and write a score for the movie he was producing. Breeze said yes, it was a big break and opportunity for himself and his band.

He was working on his last and final construction projects, which was renovating the Brown Family three Mini Malls located in Ogville, Titleburk, and MacCall. It was the job Harriet, Charles Brown daughter, had hired him to do. Breeze took the job; the money was more than enough to move himself and his band out west.

Outside in the middle of each mall on the walkway, was a bust of Harry V. Brown. By 2017, Charles Brown owned ninety percent of everything in MacCall and Titleburk, even Sam Stevens, the Chief of Police. In Ogville, Charles only owned the Mini Mall and Harry's statue. Harry would have been proud of his offspring.

****

Ogville Chief Of Police, Giddion, was good friends with Inez Paddleton, she was the wife of Charles Paddleton great-grandson, Conley Paddleton. He was named after Charles youngest son. Conley and Inez had two sons, David and Morgan. David moved to New York married and had children. Morgan stayed in Ogville, he married and had three children. Sadly, his oldest son was born with a birth defect and died. Morgan's youngest children Phillip and Phillipa were twins born 1977. The twins attended The Ohio State University, Phillip was in the medical field, and Phillipa got a law degree. While they were in college, their parents moved to New York. After Phillipa graduated from OSU, she moved to Ogville to be with her grandmother. Seven years later, Phillip completed his internship and joined his sister and grandmother in Ogville, they lived in the castle Charles built in the 1800s. Though in 2005, Conley using one million dollars of the family money, had the castle renovated and restored.

Conley rented a house while the restoration took place on his castle. One year later, Paddleton castle was grand and ready for the family to move in. Conley had been diagnosed with cancer the year before the renovation began, he made the decision to keep his illness from his family. However, he shared with Ogville's Chief Gideon that he knew he was dying, he asked the Chief to look after his family once he had died. Conley departed the world ten days after moving back into the castle, his death was a throbbing shock to his family. Conley never complained or appeared ill, he said nothing about doctor's visits, he had energy, ate a lot, nor did he lose weight.

The week the family moved back into the castle; Conley was overjoyed. He helped Inez cook a big dinner, the family sat around the table laughing and talking. Two days later, he said to his family, "I have a doctor's appointment." Cancer had spread throughout Conley's body, he was immediately admitted to the hospital, the next day he expired. Mrs. Paddleton, Phillip, and Phillipa were devastated after Conley's death. Losing her grandpa hit Phillipa the hardest, she was his little princess. In the hospital, Conley said goodbye to his family, to Phillipa he said, "be good my little princess."

All But One

The Paddleton's became an extended family to Chief Gideon and his wife and grandchildren. Except, Mrs. Paddleton only shared with Gideon the secret about the slaves. She and Gideon began working on a plan to free the men and women wrapped tightly in bondage. Their search for a trustworthy person ended when Donovan moved to town.

****

Charles Brown music preference was the fusion of Blues, Jazz, and country. Charles preferred shows was the Cosby's, and the Voice, the main judge was his favorite country singer. He also watched the news to keep up with the world and the travel channel. When he saw on the news that his favorite TV character was accused of drugging women and having his way with them, Charles sided with the actor, his respect for women was nonexistent. The love for his wife was because she ensued what he wouldn't.

His reading consisted of multiple newspapers and travel magazines, as Harry had said in 1865, "the master of the plantation would be bound to H. B. Metropolis for life."

Charles wanted to escape the confinement of the plantation. His wife Barbara shared his dream, she was her husband doormat, hitman, housekeeper, cook, slave, lover, and mother of his children who he did not like, though he used them as well.

Charles first two children were daughters, this broke his heart, however, in 1993, he had a son. He christened the boy Harry V. Brown II. At first, he kept the family business a secret from his wife and daughters, only the boy was trained. Before getting married Charles renovated his uncle Duke's home in Titleburk, which was where he was living when he got married.

Charles was the most successful of all the plantation masters, he focused only on the tobacco plants on the plantation and one other tobacco field. He sold the field near Ogville and started a cigarette and cigar company, the cigars were manufactured in Cuba though written on the package was, made in America. His cigars were expensive, each one was wrapped in gold foil and came in wood boxes made from African Blackwood or Sandalwood. He made one thousand boxes on even years, each box held forty cigars, the cost per box was fifteen thousand dollars, the cigars were not sold individually. The tobacco field that he kept, had several acres of land which Charles purchased. On the new property, he built two buildings for manufacturing his cigarettes.

The slaves were not having enough children, so the mass production of furniture and tobacco picking was dwindling. Thus, in 1985, Charles illegally apprehended over eighty children of different races ranging in the ages of four and three-year-old, from across the country. They were put in the children area when they turned fourteen, Charles personally delivered them to the slaves, who had never seen an Asian, Indian, or Latino. Being a slave, they had no rights or choices, they nervously took the strange child given to them and believed that God had cursed their home. Fortunately, as time passed by, the adults learned that everyone is Gods people, thus they grew to love the new addition in their family.

Charles needed help running the plantation and mini-malls, his son was no assistant. Out of desperation in 2008, he brought his wife, Barbara, a blond with light blue eyes, and his two daughters to the plantation house. Charles walked in his uncle Duke's shoes who had also married a poor woman, he traveled to Ogville to find his wife. Against his father's wish, Charles married a girl who had nothing. Before they married, he changed her name from Mable to Barbara. In Titleburk was a school that taught proper decorum, when she learned to be a woman of his taste, he sent her to the city community college.

Barbara knew they were rich but was not aware of where the money came from. Charles showed her the accounting books; she had an associate degree in accounting. The first thing she noticed were several flaws, Charles made her the accountant of H. B. Metropolis. His youngest daughter Harriett turned out to be interested in preserving H. B. Metropolis and the malls, it was Harriett's idea to shut down and renovate the malls outside and in. Unfortunately, his oldest daughter was against the secret and had threatened to report the whole family. Barbara picked up on her husband's stress, she told him that she would take care of their daughter. Charles told her about Chief Stevens.

Barbara got her scarcity of feelings and restricted emotion from being raised by a drug addict mother and a non-existing father. She had taken six months of karate classes, she worked in a shady hotel where too often she had to fight off pimps, drunks, and drug dealers. She also loved watching movies about the Mafia which she gained knowledge on how to terminate a person. But her all-time favorite movie was Hoodlum; she adored the smooth ease of the main character. He never allowed his emotion to get ruffled out of control, he calmed his people, thought things through, turned his decisions into a strategy. Barbara took on his character, she stayed calm, even when things got out of hand. Watching the main character of Hoodlum, she learned how to create a solution. Craving to get out of poverty and away from her life, she said, "yes," to all of Charles demands. She loved her new life and fell deeply in love with smooth talking handsome Charles.

Barbara had the opportunity to copy the Hoodlum character, excitement stirred within her. She gave Chief Stevens a call, she talked and listened. That evening she arranged to have a barbecue but didn't have the sauce, she sent her oldest daughter to the store. She knew exactly what her daughter was going to do.

She stopped at the store first then went to MacCall Police Station. Four of the deputies did Chief Stevens dirty work, though he did not tell them about the plantation, Stevens had one of the officers to cut Barbara's daughter gas line. Driving up and around the mountain that led to H. B. Metropolis, she had a fatal accident. Charles was calm again, the Brown family secret, still intact.

Harriett had shopped at the malls but never knew the bronze bust was her granddad. She hired another group of men to polish and shine the bust. Harriett and her father made a perfect team, she was over the malls and plantation general store, he took care of the slaves and tobacco fields.

Charles took Barbara to the castle; he was hoping she would like it. Even though it needed work, weeds, leaves, and trees had taken over, the big beautiful structure blew her mind. Barber spent five million dollars on renovations and furniture, the work took fourteen months, after which the family moved in. Harry II was beginning to show and interested in the family business since they were together. That's when Charles realized the reason his son was acting out, he wanted the family working on the business together. Barbara, on the other hand, kept a close watch on her son. Something about him she did not trust.

The inaudible deception that enclosed around Harry V. Brown twenty-seven-square-mile Metropolis, was affecting Barbara, her devious heart grew rigid.

Charles could see that she was turning into something evil, he said to her, "this place is wrapped around the rule of Satan's selfishness, hate, lies, strife, seditions, heresies, envy, murder," he paused for a moment before continuing, "Barb, we just killed our daughter and thought nothing of it."

She said, "I like the castle it's peaceful here, the mansion has an evil spirit, like scary movies on TV."

****

In Titleburk, Breeze crew was completing the work in the mall. The malls in MacCall and Ogville was completed and ready to open.

One afternoon, Breeze was preparing to check on the mall in Ogville; he was excited, in one week the malls were going to open and he was leaving. Before leaving, Breeze was outside talking to the Foremen about the Titleburk mall, while they were talking a construction worker ran up to him and said, "Breeze, a section of the mall's roof caved in, two workers got hurt."

Breeze said, "we're so close to being finished, what happened?"

The construction worker said, "the roof caved in, several of the men got injured." Breeze took a deep breath, then said, "the Browns will blame me for this mishap," he started to leave.

The worker said, Breeze, "what about the workers that got hurt."

"Do what you can! I have to call my lawyers." Breeze quickly went towards the construction trailer.

The foreman still standing in place, yelled at Breeze, "are you going to the collapsed building to check on the men?"

Before entering the trailer, Breeze said, "call their families."

The foreman said to the construction worker, "I'll go with you. Call an ambulance as Breeze instructed. I'll call their families."

All But One

****

  At the turn of the century, Charles had two buildings in the slave town torn down and rebuilt. At first, Charles was going to destroy the Church, fortunately, the building was well preserved, it received a paint job inside and out, plus a new roof. He had the shacks repainted, brand-new poles made for the porch, and they received a new roof.

  The slave's toilets had not been updated since 1920, some of the male slaves tore down the old outdoor toilet and filled the hole in with dirt and weeds from the tobacco fields, while several other men dug deep holes for the new toilets. Ben, Charles father, traveled to the partying town of Ogville where he purchased new outhouses from a company that supplied toilets for big events. Ben rented a big flatbed truck to haul the toilets, he hired two homeless men to deliver the outhouses to H.B. Charles, Ben, and Harry watched the slaves and the two homeless men struggle to get the toilets over the deep holes the slaves had dug the day before. The women bathroom had six stalls and four sinks, the men had three urinal, three stalls, and three sinks. The running water for the sinks was from a five-hundred-gallon rain harvesting tank. The sinks had mirrors above them. Once a month Charles supplied paper towels, toilet paper, and large containers of hand sanitizer. For the men, Charles purchased lemon or lime scent, the women strawberry or roses. Too often after washing up the slaves would spread the hand sanitizer on their arms and clothes as a perfumed lotion. Charles also purchased three one thousand gallons of rain harvesting tanks for the slaves to have water to take care of their daily needs, water their garden, and tobacco fields. They were overjoyed with their new modern-day water supply, and toilets. Ben put the two homeless men in a cabin on Charles Road and made them his slaves.

  In the General Store were powdered milk, powdered eggs, lard, flour, beans, sugar, salt, meal, yeast, corn, and vegetables from their garden, and clothing that the women made. The store opened every first and third weekend. Originally the overseers ran the store, but Barbara found flaws in the overseers bookkeeping. The slaves purchased supplies from the store with their work performance and quality of work. If the slave's labor was sufficient, according to the overseer's, they received enough ration to last two weeks. If not, they received nothing. Sometimes the overseers would tell the truth, too often they lied just to have an opportunity to beat a slave or watch them struggle as they worked in the tobacco field hungry. Still, the less the slaves got the more food the overseers took for themselves.

Barbara noted that the weight of the tobacco that Charles wrote down, and what the overseers recorded did not match. She sent her son and daughter to investigate. Together, Harriett and Harry took over running the store, Harriett immediately knew what the overseers were doing. From that point on, for two months, the overseers received a fraction of a one-week ration that was to last them for two weeks.

Charles was all about running the tobacco business, so he let Harriett and his wife take care of the overseers. One day, Harriett left the castle to go shopping, she was a resurrected Duke from the dead. She went to other cities in search of new overseer's, she also studied the women for their personality and looked for possible slaves of all races. In a city twenty miles outside Ogville, she met a young man that was all alone on Valentine Day. Harry II went to Titleburk, with both kids gone for the day, Charles said to his wife, "I want to take you to California."

Barbara ran into Charles' arms and said with joy, "you have hundreds of millions of dollars, let's burn this place down and go."

Charles asked, "what about the slaves."

"Burn them up," Barbara replied.

During Valentine's Day, folk from across American shopped for Valentine Day cards, flowers, and chocolates; Harriett was people shopping, her mother was ready to kill folk, Charles wanted to abandon the plantation, and Harry was getting drunk.

The only holiday the slaves knew about was New Years, Easter, and Christmas. On the day violence was brewing in the Brown family household, Lillie and her sister-in-law, Sophie, was relaxing, talking, and making quilts on the general store porch. Lillie said to Sophie, "mighty nice of Massa let us come ta' town ta'day," One of the male slaves walked past, Lillie spoke to him, "good afta' noon Harvey."

Harvey lifted his hand in a wave, and said, "afta' noon Miss. Lillie."

All But One

Sophie looking in the opposite direction, said to Lillie, "yonder comes Bo."

Lillie said, "I's' sees him a 'comin,' he be old Massa tall-tail slave, his mouth always yappin' tellin' Massa what us slaves done. Likes we's doin' somethin' wrong."

Sophie smiled and said, "yeah, I's' hears' yah' talkin,' but old Massa treat him good."

Lillie said a little too loud, "Massa don't know how ta' treat nobody good or bad."

Sophie bellowed, "God made us ta' obey Massa and Massa obey the Good Book."

Lillie said, "dat what Massa say, I's' cain't find it in the Good Book, I's' thank' Massa lie ta' us."

Sophie said, "I's' thank' we's need ta' leave dis' alone Lillie, a foe' Bo hears us."

"Did God create white folk to walk about? Did God create colored folk to be locked behind gates until we die?" Lillie asked.

Bo walked up to the ladies and said, "hi ladies, you's keepin' out of trouble?"

Lillie unable to contain herself, and powerless to get control of her trembling voice said, "you's' thirty years younger den' me, you's askin' me iffen' I's' keepin' outta' trouble, I's' gotta' go." She walked away in a huff leaving Sophie behind.

Sitting at a booth at the bar was Lee, Glaidous, and Ben. Lee had told Ben about their findings of the Essence Magazine. Glaidous asked Lee, "you's git' da' note by da' outer gate fo' Mr. Doo-noo-van?"

Lee answered his uncle nervously, "not yet unk I's' git nervous 'bout meetin' a walk-about. One-minute I's' feel brave, next minute I's' nervous."

"I's' won't ta' meet dis' man, git' da' note by da' gate."

Ben, a short, chunky man said, "der' be slaves dat' ain't locked behind gates, yaw' sho'nuff know bout' dat?"

Lee whispered, "unk, keep it down, dis be a secret," he looked at Ben and said, "so's keep hushed."

Ben said, "you's' thank' I's' crazy? My mouth shut tight."

Glaidous quieted down and said, "a foe' I's' die I's' wanna' hear what it be like to lib' on da' other side of dat' gate, whad' be out dare."

"Dat book da' walk-about gib' us, gib' me new feelin' I's' neva' had afo,' it changed me, mama, Cush, and you unk, Ben it gonna' change you too. I's' tankin' what iffen da' walk-about wanna help us off dis' here pantation?" Lee said and asked all in one breath.

"I's' tank the same thang," Glaidous said, "but I's' scared to say anythang."

Ben looked at the two men, "whad' it feel like to be outside da' gate? What's out der?"

"Come by my shack ta'night, I's' show ya da' mar-ja-zine, you sees' how dey lib' out der."

****

While Lee and his family were confused and slowly altered from being caged into desiring freedom, Donovan and Theenda were relaxed in their home library. Donovan was reading the sports section in the newspaper, Theenda was playing the piano. The Bright's home was quiet with only the peaceful sound of the ivories being tickled by Theenda's gentle touch, and occasional noise from Donovan turning the pages of the newspaper. Peace girdled the atmosphere in their home.

Outside the beautiful deep blue sky was the backdrop for the incandescent sun. Not a cloud in the sky. The lush green grass blanketed and soften the land. The laughter of children playing sifted through the Bright's closed windows. Donovan laid the newspaper down, and asked, "Baby Girl we've been married for two years, when are we going to start our family?"

Theenda abruptly stopped playing and stared straight ahead, without looking at Donovan, said, "I don't know, where is this coming from?"

Donovan replied with a question, "you don't know?"

Theenda stammered, "I-I-I, ahh, I..."

"Do you want children or not?" Donovan asked then continued, "It's a simple question."

Theenda replied, "not."

Donovan yelled out, "not! What do you mean? Not! Before we married, I assumed that you wanted children. I want one or two, maybe three little me running around the house."

Theenda stood and nervously paced back and forth, anxiously she rubbed her hands together. Her face was tense and tight, chill bumps ran up and down her arm. She bent over as pain erupted in her stomach, sweat broke out on her forehead. Theenda was jarred from peace and tranquility to having an anxiety attack. She whispered, "I can't have children."

"What? What did you say? Stop pacing, sit down."

Theenda sat in a chair opposite Donovan, she rested her head in her hands, as though it was too heavy for her neck to hold up, she let out a long deep, "ahh." With her head still in her hands, her eyes closed, she remembered the abuse that she and her sister suffered from the hands of their mother. Theenda remembered her mother pushing her eldest sister down the basement stairs, her hip broke, it never healed correctly. Now she walked with a limp. After her sister thumps and bumps down to the bottom of the stairs, her mother pushed her down the steps, Theenda remembered landing on top of her crying sister. Their mother closed the basement door, leaving them down there for hours, Theenda suffered from mental and physical scars from the incident. Theenda and her sister made a solemn vow to never bring a child into this world of hate. Her sister broke the promise they made.

In the background of Theenda's thoughts, Donovan was asking her a question, she said, "I'm sorry, I didn't hear you, what did you say?"

Irritated Donovan, replied, "stop daydreaming, I was saying, I would like to start a family asap."

Theenda looked at Donovan, and then away when more bad memories flooded through. She blared out, "I can't have children."

"Why not?"

Her voice was shaky as she very quietly said, "I've had an abortion."

At first, silence submerged in the chilly frost of nothingness. Then all hell broke loose, Donovan's anger mushroomed like a megaton bomb. The Bright's quiet peaceful home turned into a center of heated discussion, Donovan shouted, "it better be before we got married." At this point, his chest expanded to its fullest as he inhaled a room full of air. Frost escaped when he growled, "you said that you always used safe sex precautions, now you tell me you've had an abortion."

Sweat profusely flowed in a steady stream down Theenda's brow like a middle age woman having an intense hot flash. Her hair became limp from the perspiration that seeped through the pores of her scalp, it trickled down her face, her neck, her blouse.

Donovan stared at her through boiling anger as he thundered the question, "what's wrong with you?"

Theenda stood, she sat, she stood, she sat. She looked nervously around, she rubbed her hands together, she rubbed her chin, her forehead, her cheek, she stood. She cried, "it wasn't before we got married," she sat.

Silence.

A roar louder than a lion rumbled out of Donovan's mouth, "my baby you aborted?!"

He stormed out of the library, through the vestibule, out the front door, when the door slammed, Theenda cried uncontrollably.

Instead of taking Theenda to the fancy restaurant, Donovan went to the Blue Night Club. He entered the club, quickly went through the restaurant to the bar. He ordered a vodka on ice. The bartender said, "hum, you come here a lot but not for alcohol, sure you want…" he stopped and looked at Donovan, his complexion was a mixture of red and brown, his hair uncombed, he gnawed on his bottom lip and his nails, the bartender changed his question to a comment, "vodka it is."

Haze had seen Donovan enter the nightclub, he waved for Donovan to join them at their table, Donovan ignored Haze and went to the bar. Haze and Timpkin joined Donovan, Haze asked, "why are you here?"

Timpkin apologized to Donovan, he said, "Donovan the other day I was angry, I'm sorry for walking out, Haze set me straight."

Haze said to Donovan, "we have a table in the restaurant my friend Breeze is playing tonight. For my own peace of mind, I need…"

Before Haze finished talking the bartender handed Donovan the vodka and said, "here you go."

All But One

Timpkin said, "he doesn't drink."

As Donovan reached for the drink, he looked at Timpkin and Haze, then said, "go away."

Haze said, "no you're going to the restaurant with us." Haze grabbed Donovan by the arm and said to Timpkin, "grab his other arm."

Donovan tried to pull away from the two men, he said, "I am not drunk, leave me alone!"

Ignoring him, Timpkin and Haze forced Donovan off the bar stool into the restaurant and slammed him into a chair at the table.

Timpkin said, "what's up with you."

"None of your business," Donovan said.

Haze yelled, "you sit at a bar ordering vodka, a drink you've never had in your life, that drink will blow your brain out."

Timpkin said calmer than Haze, "your lip is bleeding, tears are rolling down your eyes, did you know that?" He handed Donovan a napkin and continued, "if not, I'm making it my business."

Donovan took a deep breath and said, "I was thinking about the slaves." He looked a Haze and noticed he had a black eye then asked, "how did you get the shiner?"

Timpkin said a little too loud, "I don't buy there are slaves!" He calmed down and continued, "no slaves in my hometown."

Donovan said, "well, I'm going to talk about the slaves, had no business dragging me over here." He pulled himself together by stretching, wiped his eyes, blew his nose on a napkin, took a deep breath, and said, "thank you from rescuing me from a night of drunkenness."

Timpkin and Haze simultaneously responded, "you're welcome."

Haze asked, "what's wrong with you Don-man?"

"Honestly Haze, I really don't know myself," Donovan answered, "but I do know this, I want to help the slaves on the plantation to escape."

Haze said, "okay if it will make you feel better, let's talk about the slaves, all right with you Timpkin?"

Timpkin reluctantly said, "Mm' hum, I guess."

Donovan told the two men that he's going back out to the plantation the weekend.

Haze said, "I'll go with you," he looked at Timpkin and asked, "Tim-man how bout' you?"

Timpkin looked around the restaurant, Breeze and his band were about to play, he said, "Haze, there's your friend."

Haze looked across the table, directly into Timpkin's eyes, and ask, "how 'bout you? Are you going out there with us?"

Timpkin looked at Donovan, and said, "why don't you mention your find at the next NAACP meeting first."

Donovan said, "I will, hopefully, they will help more than you."

Haze commented, "I agree," he looked at Timpkin and said, "looser."

The three men listened to Breeze and his band, Donovan said, "he ain't half bad, how do you know him Haze?"

"I met him at a Black Business Conference about a year ago in New York. He told me that his hometown had only one janitorial service and they were lousy. He said that the job opportunity was great, so I packed my bags and here I am. Day by Day Janitorial Company is a whopping success. Breeze and I have been friends ever since."

Still avoiding Haze question, Timpkin mumble, "a stupid name for a company."

Haze looked at him, and said, "Day is my last name, got a problem with that, take it up with my daddy, no take it up with me," Haze pushed his chair back as he violently stood, and said, "outside old man."

Donovan cut in, and said, "yelp, we need a big sip of vodka to calm our nerves."

Timpkin stood up, the two men stared each other down then looked at Donovan, and together said, "you don't drink."

Donovan sat up and put both elbows on the table, he balanced his head between his hands, and said, "I'm going home."

As he stood, he looked across the room and saw a black man coming in the door with a well-dressed mousy little white man. The black man was dressed like pictures of slaves that were in his history books.

Donovan said softly, "he looked like a slave from a history book."

All But One

Timpkin asked, "what're you looking at?"

Donovan nodded toward the men that had just come in the bar, Timpkin and Haze looked in that direction. As Donovan, Timpkin, and Haze stood to leave, Harry Brown and the slave Bo, passed by the three men. Harry accidentally bumped into Donovan, Harry said, "excuse me, Sir."

Donovan replied, "no problem."

Bo bowed as he passed by Donovan.

Even though Bo's eyes remained downward, he saw in detailed the three men clothes and shoes. He looked at his Massa's clothes, and then his raggedy dirty clothes, his shoulders slumped even lower. He didn't only notice the brown men like himself were oh so clean, and his Massa said "Sir," to the well-dressed colored man, like they were equals.

While passing the men, Bo got a good look at Donovan out the corner of his eye. He wanted to be the young man in looks, dress, and smell. Bo watched the three men leave the club, he longed to go with them, he wondered, *where was their Massa?* He looked around the club, there were coloreds and whites laughing and talking. A feathery thought fluttered in his head, *"is slavery ova?"*

Outside the club, Haze asked, "did that black man look like a slave or was it just me."

Donovan said, "I was thinking the same thing."

Timpkin argued, "slavery is over, he was probably a very poor black man and the white dude is helping him. Your imaginations are running wild."

Donovan said, "helping him how to stay drunk and poor?"

Haze took the conversation a step further, "did you smell the black guy?"

Donovan asked, "did you see the emptiness in his eyes?"

Timpkin said, "they both smelt different, a smell I'm not familiar with."

Donovan said, "something is not quite right with either of the two men."

Haze asked, "you mean with their mind,"

Donovan replied, "no, I don't know what I mean."

He and his buddies left, Donovan was sad and mad as he drove home.

XXII

Valentine Night

Donovan entered the house slamming the door behind him, he went down the basement stairs like an out of control madman. After locating his suitcase, he ran back up the steps to the master bedroom. He yanked the closet door open and began pulling out his clothes, he haphazardly stuffed them into the suitcase. Theenda, quietly, stood in the doorway and watched as silent tears slowly rolled down her cheeks. She whispered, "I'm sorry."

She turned and left. As she was going down the steps, Donovan yelled, "why an abortion?! Why the coward way out?"

Theenda continued down the stairs without saying a word, Donovan insisted on getting an answer, he yelled even louder, "why an abortion Theenda?!"

She went into the living room, Donovan was close on her heel, when she stopped walking, he bumped into her almost knocking her down and falling himself, he grabbed her arms, spun her around, he stood close to her and yelled, "why?!"

Theenda whimpered softly, "have a seat, I'll tell you why."

Donovan sat in his favorite chair, he looked around the expensively furnished room, he remembered picking the couch and love seat out with her. His favorite chair, a lazy boy was a late wedding present from her. Theenda had written across the huge bow that was wrapped around the chair, "for your buns only, my love." The memory caused him to smile.

He glanced at the pictures on the wall, the drapery, the phone that matched the decor, the plants that added completeness, "this is home", he thought and said, "I don't want to leave my

All But One

home, I don't want to leave you." He sat on the edge of the lazy boy, and said, "give me a reason to stay."

Theenda told her story, "when I was a little girl my..."

Donovan said angrily, "Thee I am talking about now, not when you were little, you said you aborted my babies, I didn't know you as a little girl."

Ignoring Donovan, Theenda continues, "my daddy left my mom, he blamed us girls for their problems. He said my brother was all the children he wanted. During this time, I was five, my sister ten, and my brother thirteen. When daddy left, the beatings started." Theenda showed Donovan her neck, and said, "see this scare here?"

Donovan said, "yeah I've wondered how you got that and a few other scares on your body."

Theenda continued, "mama was cooking chicken, I walked in the kitchen, I don't remember what I said or did, she didn't need a reason, she swung at me with the cooking fork, it was hot and covered with hot grease, the fork hit my neck. I was eight years old." She opened her blouse, and showed Donovan another scare, and said, "see this scare on my breast?"

Donovan said, "yes, I've seen it." By now Donovan had calmed down, feelings of sorrow flood within his heart.

Theenda continued, "mom's boyfriend slugged me with a wrench. I was six years old. You've seen my sister and asked the reason she limp; out of embarrassment, I didn't tell you. She limps because mom pushed her down the basement stairs, she landed hard on the cement floor and broke her hip, sis was twelve. When she turned thirteen, she had the first hip replacement, she grew the new hip didn't. She's had five replacements to keep up. Know how I broke my left arm?"

Very softly Donovan asked, "how?"

"Mama pushed me down the basement stairs after she pushed my sister, I landed on top of her, I got multiple cuts and bruises and a broken arm. I don't remember what we were doing, I remember we were too young to be treated like that. I can have the hospital in New York send my medical records if you need to verify that I am telling the truth."

Donovan said, "you don't need to do that." A question pounded within his head, what does this have to do with Theenda not wanting children? But from the colorless look on Theenda's face, he asked, "why didn't you tell me that you were an abused child."

Theenda said, "child? The abuse never stopped, it altered from physical abuse to verbal. I may be grown, but the abuse continues in a different form. The insults are about my looks, my cooking, my dress, my hair, our home, you, she talked about me to her friends, my friends. I'm not sure what she said about me, but her church friends will have nothing to do with me. Not even a hello. And my relatives don't come around because of whatever fell out of her mouth. That's why I said yes to moving far away from New York. A new start, new church, new friends."

Theenda looked at Donovan, he had become squeamish and was looking uncomfortable, she stared out the window as though she was lost in her thoughts before saying, "I have to hand it to my brother, when he turned sixteen, he beat the crap out of mom, took cash, her bank card, credit card, and her driver's license out her purse. He went into her room and found her checkbook." She looked at Donovan who was looking as though he was someplace else, Theenda asked, ""still with me Donovan?"

"Yes, yes, I'm listening, what does this have to do with a baby?"

"I'm getting to that. My brother used mom's credit card to run, he bought two thousand dollars in clothes. Mom and dad tried to find him but could not. Dad said he changed his name, he could be here in the states, he could be in New York, he could be anywhere," she paused for a moment before continuing, "he could be dead." She smiled when she said, "mom claimed she had twenty-two thousand dollars in the bank, my brother left her, one dollar."

"How?" Donovan asked.

"He wrote a letter stating she had a medical emergency and needed the cash, he signed the letter and check, his handwriting and signature were carbon copy moms. The bank teller pulled mom's signature card; it was a perfect match."

Donovan was speechless and uncomfortable, he shifted several times in the chair before he said softly, "I'm sorry. But your father is home."

"Sweetie, I am not telling you this for pity, you asked why an abortion, I do *not* want to be that woman to any child, absolute evil hate. People perceive my mother as a saint, her drinking and

All But One

partying days are over. The minister and the church members see a lonely sweet elderly lady, whose no-good daughters abandoned her." She looked at Donovan and said, "even you thought she was perfect until our wedding day, all the beatings and verbal abuse that my sister and I endured, I should be crazy, a drug addict," Theenda folded her arms and shouted, "and an alcoholic to forget my childhood!"

All Donovan said was, "ahh." Then cleared his throat.

Theenda inhaled and seethe through gritted teeth, "my father returned home when my sister and I left, I went to college, sis went to having babies."

Donovan said calmly and cautiously "I thought the beatings stopped when you were seven."

"I only told you a few, you looked uncomfortable like you do now." She walked around the room and said, "Oh yeah, at our wedding, mom punched your three-year-old niece with her fist. I thought your aunt had lost it."

Donovan said, "yeah, I heard about that. Where were you?"

"I was crying in my pretty white wedding gown. While my sister and your aunt yelled at mom, your mother took me out the room, during this fiasco you, the groomsmen, and bridesmaid was outside waiting for me to come out and throw the flowers."

"I remember that you came out with mom, she kept wiping your face, I thought the tears were because of your happiness."

"On our wedding day, your mom became mine."

Donovan chuckled as he said, "I think my aunt beat the crap out your mom. When they came outside, your mom's hat was sideways, suit messed up, and…"

"She gave mom two black eyes," Theenda laughed softly, "your aunt apologized a few weeks later. I gave her a hug and said, thank you. Your family is awesome."

"People say the Bright's are educated, sophisticated, yeah right, we can get pretty ghetto when we need to," Donovan said laughing.

Donovan gazed into his beautiful wife's watery eyes. It broke his heart to see tracks of dried salt on her cheeks from the tears she'd shed earlier. Still, he had to know, he must know, so he swallowed, clenched his teeth and ask, "why don't you want to have children? Your sister did."

"You would walk out on me like daddy and my brother did. I would beat our child just like mama and my sister. I don't want to put anyone through the same ordeal. I suffered child abuse, now I am going through prolonged anguish of character annihilation by my mother. When does it end?" She shook her head, and dismissed the matter by saying, "I will not put anyone through my trauma."

"Where did you get the hair brain idea that if we have children, I'll leave, and what's character annihilation?"

Complete destruction of a person's character, their personality, and the media say battered children abuse their children, and women marry men like their daddies."

"Thee, that's not completely true, there are several adults who were abused as children. Now they have kids and they don't abuse their little ones, because they remember how the abuse made them feel. Too many people are abusers because that's what society and the news media tell us. They expound on the anger in our country and blame the leaders, and poverty, for that reason, many acts upon what they hear and do not turn to God, Who is the only one that knows what lies within us.

A few people see a psychologist, some will seek God's presence, people find ways to ward off the evils of ill-treatment. There are others who still receive affliction from their parents like yourself, they learn to love them from a distance like what you're doing."

It all sounds good, but it won't work for me. It's in my blood, you're leaving me, we don't even have children, mom was not poor. Abuse is not a thing, it's what lodges in a person's heart, it knows no race or color of skin, or what's in a bank account, or education. It's a choice."

Donovan thought about his sloppy half packed suitcase upstairs. He knelt at Theenda's knees and said, "you've given me a reason to stay."

"Your bags are packed."

"I was angry, and not thinking, Baby Girl you thought you were saving babies from your experience as a child. I can't condone abortions, but I will forgive."

Theenda asked, "you know why I'm so skinny?"

"You don't eat much, and you run all the time."

"Correct, I don't have an appetite because I can't forgive myself for having the abortions, I can't have a child cause my mother's destructive hateful ways will seep out. Like mother, like daughter, like a sister. How can you forgive me? I can't forgive myself?"

****

On the plantation in the early evening, the sunset turned the sky into multiple shades of pink, purple, orange, and blue. Several slave teens sat under a tree discussing the hopelessness of their future on the plantation. Cush was with the group of teens, he fought against all that was in him to keep his mouth shut about the walk-about. He squirmed around like he had to use the bathroom, one of the teens asked, "whad' be wrong wid' ja' Cush?"

Cush answered, "nothin."

One of the girls spoke up and said, "yesta'day old Massa say it be time that I's' git married and start havin' babies, cause I's' turn sixteen on ta'morrow."

Another teen asked, "what yo' mama say?"

She said," I's' guess Massa right."

Cush said in anger and deep intensity, "we have da' babies' den Massa take da' babies, he say slave too dumb ta' raise babies."

Another slave teen said, "I's' sick and tired of Massa yelling at us every other Sunday."

One of the slave girls said, "Cush I's' like it when yo' uncle preach."

All the teens agree with a unanimous, "me too."

A seventeen-year-old male talked about the beating he received a few weeks ago. He said, "I's' memba' like it be yesta'day, da' overseers beat me likes' dey' won't's me dead. Den' dey pored salt on my back where dey' beat me. Ohh dat' hurt powerfully bad."

One of the female teens said, I's' memba dat,' nobody could help you not even yo' mama, not until the sun had set."

Cush said, den' we all come out da' house to get you, likes' we did when dey' beat my daddy last week."

"Dis week my last week livin' wid' mama, cause it be time I's git' married." The teen that was beaten said.

"Whars' dey' gonna' put you?" Cush asked.

"Ova on Charles Road."

The sixteen-year-old girl asked, "who you be' marrin?"

The young male teen said, "I's don't know, who eva' dey' put in my house, we be married."

The sixteen-year-old said, "I's wonda' iffen it be me?" she looked around the group and asked, "anybody else be told dey' need ta' have babies?"

Silence swept over the young group. Cush said, "iffen sixteen be da age, I's got two moe' years."

A female said softly, "I's turned sixteen yesta'day, Massa ain't said."

Cush asked, "I's' wonder iffen' it be easier on other pantation?"

One of the other teens replied, "I's' wonder dat' meself, do you eva' wish you could leave here and walk and walk..."

Another teen cut in, and said, "I won't ta' ride a horse likes' da' overseers."

Cush looked at the teen and said, "I's' neva' thought 'bout dat, ride a horse sit up high, I's' wonder iffen' dey' see ova' da' gate."

At that moment Bo stormed across the field, he looked like an angry rhino charging towards the teens. Undisciplined hostility ignited deep within Bo's soul. He yelled to a degree that was unreasonably loud at the teens, who peacefully sat under the whipping tree on a quiet evening. Bo pulled out his whip and yelled, "what yaw' doin' here?!"

The teens scooted back from Bo, Cush spoke up, "we just talkin' bout..."

But before Cush could finish speaking Bo said, "you's thanks' just cause you's Lee's boy you can talk back ta' me."

An older teen spoke up, "we's just be talkin' bout our future."

Bo screamed in a voice internalized by Satan, "what future!" He growled, "I's' thank all yaw' ain't nothin' but a waste of space," Bo began to swing his whip towards the unsuspecting teens, they jumped up and run towards their cabins, Bo yelled at them, "git home, I's boss round dis' parts!"

All But One

The teens were not hurt physically, only emotionally. They wanted to talk and discuss their feelings, which was their only form of therapy.

Inside the church, Lee and Glaidous had finished cleaning. Lee took the broom and dust cloth to the Backroom. Lee returned to the chapel and said, "looks good in here."

Glaidous said joyfully, "Lawdy, Lawdy we's gonna' meet a walk-about."

Lee went to the podium and got the book filled with names of the slaves. He flipped through the book, the last names listed was Paula and her boys. He read what Paula had written. He said more to himself, "how'd she get out da gate?"

Glaidous sat on the front pew, he looked wonderingly at Lee, his mind in deep thought as he said, "Mr. Doo-noo-van comin' ta' meet us, I feel' it in these old bones."

Lee muttered, "I's wanna stretch wide, see beyond da' trees."

Glaidous asked, "you's git da' note by da' gate?"

Lee said, "I's did, bout six days later it be gone."

Glaidous stood and said, "Glory be to God I's hope Mr. Doo-no-van got it."

Lee said, "Amen, uncle." He looked at Paula's notation again, then asked, "I's wonda' where she run to, how she git out da' gate"

Glaidous looked at Lee and asked, "who?"

"Paula, Unk."

Confused, Glaidous asked, "who dat?"

****

Still talking with Theenda, Donovan tried to fix the mess and said, "you, my precious reached inside yourself and drew out virtue, so everyone loves and sees a virtuous woman. On the other hand, I reached inside myself and yanked out anger. Both of us will go to counseling, we will have children and you will be a wonderful mother and wife. I will be a good father and husband. You understand?"

Theenda sighed deeply before saying, "I don't want to repeat this day, I want this day gone forever, I don't want to have

LaVaughn

this conversation ever again, I don't want the word abortion mention in this house. It already crowds my mind."

"And so, it is. You promise me, no more abortions."

Theenda exhaled and said, "I promise, she asked Donovan, "you promise you won't leave me?"

"I promise. You see Thee, your family issues are all over the place, mine is hidden. My granddad died of a drug overdose, he gave his son to his brother to raise as his own, and not nephew. My grandpa is my uncle.

Theenda said, "changing the subject, a few days ago, I tried to find the Brown plantation but there are over six thousand plantations with that family name here in the south. With sixty-seven being in this state, counting the one you went to."

Donovan laughed, "you are kidding me? She could be from any place. But wouldn't it be funny if she was from that particular plantation." He laughed even harder.

Donovan had no idea that his grandma, was from the very plantation he had left the Essence Magazine.

XXIII

Becky Lou Brown

Week After Valentine

    Becky Lou was from the line of Harry's grandson Duke Brown, who named his first son Cody, after his brother he tried to kill. Cody Brown, Charles Paddleton first grandchild, married an Irish woman with red hair and green eyes, all their children took after their mother. Cody named his first son Tom, who had a son named Ben, he married a beautiful Italian woman with cold black hair. Ben named his firstborn, Sam, born 1960, his second son Charles born in 1962, who became the plantation master. When Ben was thirty-eight his wife gave birth to a baby girl, they named her Becky Lou, she was born 1970. She was the only family member Charles was close to.
    Charles and his brother had dark hair with amber eyes, Becky Lou was a carbon copy of her Irish grandma, she was a redhead with freckles and green eyes. Her brothers called her carrot top. Becky Lou's dad and grandpa Tom spoiled her rotten, she was the apple of their eye, the beat in their hearts, she was the first girl to be born in the brown family in years. Becky Lou turned out to be spoiled, loud, wild, rowdy, and pregnant at age fourteen. She was an embarrassment to the family, Ben sent his precious daughter to a home for girls in Florida where she had the baby, she named him Anthony Brown. Ben paid a woman to raise the child in a far western state. The only contact the Browns had was through the woman, who every year on Anthony's birthday sent the family a picture. Anthony's fifth birthday Becky did not receive a picture.

Ben wrote a letter to the woman, the letter was returned, Ben did some investigation, he learned a burglar broke into the home and killed the woman and Anthony as they slept. During this time, Tom, Ben, and Charles were the only family members that knew about Becky's baby and the hidden plantation. However, only Charles and his grandpa Tom knew the murderer. Tom was proud of his tall handsome grandson; he sat his son Ben down and made Charles master of H. B. Metropolis. Tom claimed that Ben was too soft.

Since the child was an undisclosed being, Becky Lou could not attend her son's funeral or travel to see his body.

1982, Ben moved to Titleburk and let the overseers run the plantation. Without his father's approval, Ben hired five men to guard the gates and forest, they lived in Vance old cabin, they were given everything Ben thought they needed, alcohol, food, cable TV, and women. Tom was outraged. Summer of 1983, Charles turned twenty-one, he and his grandpa moved to the plantation house.

Between MacCall and Titleburk, Charles hired eight homeless men to clean the yard, and paint inside and outside the plantation mansion. He hired three homeless women to clean and polish everything that was of metal or wood. He let the homeless men and women stay in Vance cabin, since they were homeless Charles figured they would go nowhere, and they didn't. He promised them after their task was done, he would pay each five hundred dollars. Their last day, Charles threw a party for the homeless and his father's five guards. The party was held in Vance cabin, using streamer's and Christmas lights, Charles had the women to decorate the cabin, the men hung the lights.

Tom was a mean ruthless plantation master, and Charles was a cool ruthless man. He could smile in the person's face, shoot them or slice their neck, slip on his shades, and stroll away like it was just another day. Tom admired his grandson.

Harry wanted to be like his son Charles, Tom wanted to be like his grandson Charles II.

It was Tom's idea for them to move into the mansion, then kill everyone after their work was done. Charles went in town and picked up twelve pizza, and two kegs of beer, before taking them to the cabin, Tom poisoned the beer, Charles stirred each keg for five minutes. Charles called the cabin and had a few of the men to push the kegs and pizzas in a wheel barrel to the cabin. At the party, Charles danced with the three women. He laughed, talked, and joked around; Charles was the bell of the party.

They did not die right-a-way, the party continued for a few hours. Charles sat down and thanked them for being good workers, he said, "I am going to miss you."

As the guards and homeless men and women were talking, they quietly and peacefully passed away.

Charles had three cans of gasoline hidden in the woods, he poured the liquid inside the cabin, and on the dead bodies. When Charles got on the porch, he left the door opened. He removed his shoes and jumped on the ground, he struck a book of matches and threw it in the opened door. Charles stood watching the cabin that Vance wife loved too much, go up in flames with the bodies inside. He picked up his shoes and threw them inside the cabin.

The families of the murdered victims had no idea where they worked, hence, their absence did not lead back to the Browns. A year after the manslaughters, Tom became very ill. Before Tom's death, Charles shared with his grandpa his plans to manufacture cigarettes and cigars. Tom said, "go for it grandson. I am so happy to see a real man in charge."

Shortly after Tom's funeral, Becky Lou was out with a friend shopping in Titleburk, the friend stole jewelry. She and Becky Lou were put in prison, Charles hired a lawyer named Phillipa Paddleton to represent his sister, Charles nor Becky Lou knew that they were Phillipa's cousins.

Charles Paddleton's offsprings were teachers, speakers, doctors, Government Officials, they held social events to raise money for a good cause. Charles loved to travel; he raised his family to go beyond their imagination. Charles would be proud of his offspring, they toured the USA and the world, sometimes together. The family was close, they were the Paddleton's, a name Charles Brown made up when he ran from his brother Drew and son Duke.

On the other hand, Charles brother Drew and son Duke side of the family was social oddballs, they maintain life as status quo. A few were high school graduate's other dropped out, they were poor, except Charles brother Sam. He went to night school to get an accounting certificate. The whole family lived in Titleburk and was not aware of the plantation. Except for the ones that became H. B. Metropolis Master.

Becky Lou was different than Duke's line of misfits. She liked people; she got a job working as a file clerk for a local company but got fired after the arrest. Charles was proud of his little sister, she attended college, it did not matter that she had completed one quarter. After losing the file clerk job, Charles got his sister a job working in the Ogville library and part-time for him in the children's area.

The nurse and the teacher in the children area were close to fifty-five, they were fresh graduates from college with a degree in nursing and education. On their hire date, both women were twenty-three years old. On their last day, they were invited to the plantation house, Charles wife and Harriett had prepared a feast for the women. When they entered the house, they noticed that the furnishings had changed, everything in the kitchen was modern and digital, they could not believe their eyes.

The nurse and teacher ate, laughed, and talk but in the back of their minds, they were going to report H.B. Metropolis to the authorities. They knew everything that went on in the slave compounds through Helen, and the nurse who delivered the slaves babies. The teacher had drawn a crude picture of the plantation from what she was told by the nurse and Helen.

There was one problem, they left the memoir in the children cabin.

In the kitchen the nurse and Teacher listen to Charles explain how much the world had changed, he talked and watched the nurses' eyes become droopy with sleep, he talked until their faces fell in their plates. He and Harry II carried their bodies to the grave that was already dug. Next to the nurses, were fresh graves for the aging overseers. He was not going to find new overseers and anyone to work with the children, Charles had planned from an early age to end H. B. Metropolis and travel.

Charles hired his sister, Becky Lou to be Helen's relief. When Helen saw Becky Lou lack of clothes, painted face, and loud personality, she suggested that Becky Lou wear the nurse or teacher dresses. Becky Lou clothes were way above the knee, the young boys' eyes almost popped out their heads. Becky Lou showed her gratitude by wearing the clothes while she was on the complex. On every other weekend, Helen went home to the slave complex.

The children liked it when Becky Lou came, she would bring big bags filled with donuts, cupcakes, pies, candy, and chips. Harry II, her nephew, told her not to give any to Helen. He did not trust Becky; Harry kept a close watch on all her comings and goings. He argued with his father, Harry blared out, "Pops, she should be locked up like the nurse and teacher."

"Harry, you forget I am a part of this family, I got this," Harriett said confidently.

"I'm not talking to you," Harry said as he scowled at Harriett. He looked at his dad and said, "I'll go to town and find someone to be the overseer."

Harriet said, "I found two overseers,' a nurse, and a teacher a few counties away."

Charles said, "that is not necessary." He walked out of the room.

In the slave town area, Lillie and Sophie were leaving the general store porch, Sophie asked Lillie, "who foe' you's makin' does dress."

"Helen say's dey fo' a white woman dat' watch da' kids."

"Do you know what be wrong wid' Glaidous?" Sophia asked.

"Wad' ja' mean Sophie?"

"Don't know, he be happy now days. He's sermon be different," she looked at Lillie, "you's change to, like yah' know somethin."

They walked on a little further, Sophie asked, "Lee changed to, why y'all change and not me?"

Lillie had taken all she could and said, "cause you's talk too much."

Sophie said, "I's tells Massa."

"Zaxctly," Lillie said crossly as she quickly walked away. She saw Glaidous coming down the road, she motioned for him to go to her cabin.

Glaidous had known his sister for over sixty years, he recognized the look on her face, and it wasn't a come to coffee big brother look. Only three people made his sister mad, Bo, Harry, and his wife, Sophie.

In the castle, and Still, in the midst of arguing with his children and wife, Charles said, "Becky is my little sister, I will talk to her."

"I believe..." Barbara began saying.

"She's my sister, discussion over." He looked at them and shouted, "over!" and left slamming the door behind him.

XXIV

The First Meeting

February 15, 2017

    Wednesday, the day before the NAACP meeting, Haze, his wife Tess, Timpkin, his wife KayKay were visiting the Bright's. Theenda invited the couples over for the first true meeting about the slaves. It was the wives first time hearing about the illegal plantation. Donovan shared his discovery of slaves in a nearby town. Tess was shocked, but KayKay was appalled that she was just finding out. KayKay was a social worker and a self-important woman. In looks she matched Timpkin perfectly, she wore plaid pleated skirts and a blouse that matched perfectly with a color in the plaid. Her hair was permed, she wore it in a bun with a ribbon that matched the blouse.

    Tess was a registered nurse, she was pretty but had a hard look, she was twenty-six-year-old with soft smooth skin. Tess had Indian like features; her cold black hair hung down to her waist. At the meeting, Tess was trying to hide her face with her hair. She looked like she was playing peek-a-boo, a small portion of her forehead, the tip of her nose, and her lips were visible. Tess and Haze were sitting on the loveseat, her body was turned away from him. Haze was sitting on the opposite corner of the loveseat. Tess asked very softly, "how did this happen? Poor Timpkin, KayKay was a quarrelsome belligerent individual that knew everything. At the time of the meeting she argued with Donovan, she said, "me of all people you could have talked to about this matter, I'm a social worker and fixing problems is my job." She violently crossed her leg, roll her eyes and jerked her head in the opposite direction of Donovan and stared at Timpkin. Her chest heaved up

and down with each breath she inhaled and exhaled. She looked at Timpkin and snapped, "you should have told me." She folded her arms in anger, she looked at Theenda and barked, "you knew."
Twenty-two-year-old Theenda said to a sixty-three-year-old woman, "don't start with me, I'm not the one."
Timpkin looked at his wife and tried to figure out why he married such a hot-tempered, overly confident unnecessary woman. He flashed back to the first time he saw her, she was tall, thin, paper sack brown pretty girl. She cut into his thoughts and ask, "why didn't you tell me?"
Theenda tried to calm the moment by saying, "Timpkin thought Donovan was lying about slaves," she looked at Timpkin and said, "right Timpkin."
"Right Thee. It's still hard for me to conceive that slaves exist in my hometown; how could such a thing happen?"
While talking he remembered the reason, he married her, the memory popped in his head so quick he jumped. When they were dating, she was all over him like a bad habit, after the wedding she was cured. It's been a downhill ride ever since and now he was ready to get off the ride. He looked at KayKay and frowned.
KayKay looked at Timpkin with remorse and asked. "what're you frowning about?"
"How can there be slaves in America?" he asked.
Donovan looked around the room at each person and said, "I don't know, but it happened."
Theenda said, "according to the memoirs of the nurses and teachers dating back to 1876, they are real."
"Would you like to read the memoir?" Donovan asked the group.
"I'll get it, Sweetie," Theenda left.
Donovan continued, "April 13, 1876, Mr. Brown held a party for the slaves after construction was complete, he told them that they were free, he was going to give them some money and let them go. But he poisoned their drink killing the slaves from ages four years and above. On the same day, Mr. Browns youngest son shot, and killed his father. It's believed that he also killed his older brother years later."
Haze said, "a whole lot of killing going around."

All But One

Timpkin asked, "what happened to the nurse and teacher? And how do you know the memoir is authentic."

Donovan said as he paced, "the dates, details. The gates and tiny houses that I saw is mentioned in the memoir."

KayKay asked, "the children three and under what happened to them?"

"They were raised by the nurse and teacher. At age fourteen they were given to a husband and wife to raise as their own. when the male turned seventeen or eighteen, they were put in a cabin with a sixteen-year-old girl. That's how they became husband and wife, though each generation of ministers secretively married the couple in a religious ceremony. The two women wrote that they never told the children about freedom or their past, if a child would have said anything about the world outside the plantation, the overseers would have killed the child and them."

KayKay replied, "so it is possible that the slaves living now really don't know a thing about freedom."

Still standing, Donovan answered, "you got it."

Haze said, "so, we may be the first people they will see outside the plantation."

KayKay asked, "I wonder if they know about Africa or the Civil War?"

Donovan answered a simple, "no."

"Not really," Theenda said returning to the room carrying a thick notebook filled with stacks of papers, she said, "just think at the time of the Civil War there were a little over four million slaves in existence not just in the south. She adjusted the memoir in her arms and continued, New York. Pennsylvania. Maryland, New Jersey, Delaware, and so on. Harriett Tubman made her last freedom run to the south in the early 1900s before she got ill."

Timpkin asked, "so, the Civil War didn't end slavery."

"That's what she just said, ignorant man," KayKay said belligerently.

Ignoring KayKay, Theenda said, "there were a number of reasons for the Civil War that did not include freeing a bunch of black folks, though it was a small part which was the beginning of our freedom. It allotted thousands of slaves to join the army or just run like crazy to Canada."

Donovan questioned, "I wonder how many slaves exist now?"

"Do you know how ludicrous you people sound?" Timpkin asked uneasily.

Donovan said, "I think we're talking about becoming a modern-day abolitionist."

Timpkin chimed, "that's ridiculous."

Theenda said, "here's the memoir." She handed them to Timpkin, he did not take the folder.

KayKay took the memoir and asked, "where did you get these."

"A secret source," Donovan answered quickly in the tone of, none-of-your-business.

****

On the first and third weekend of the month, Becky Lou was Helen's relief. One day, Becky Lou made a discovery when she stepped on a loose floorboard, she bounced her foot on the board several times, the disconnection seemed to be under the dresser. She pulled the chest out, lifted the board and there were the memoirs. She took them to Mrs. Paddleton, who suggested that she make copies and give a copy to Donovan. Becky Lou went to the Library and made two copies. She met Mrs. Paddleton through Phillipa her lawyer. From that day forward, Becky Lou did odd jobs for the kind elderly woman

On the day Becky Lou was in the library, Donovan was there developing a different project for his class. He told his class, "do not write or research topics about slavery, plantations, or the Underground Railroad."

Becky Lou was going to take the papers to his school, but there he sat. She was nervous as she walked over to the table where Donovan was sitting. She wondered, what should I say, she stood in front of him and said. "Mr. Bright this is my report, you said that I could ask you to edit." She laid the large stack of papers in front of him.

He said, "yes, I will look it over for you."

"Thank you, Mr. Bright."

Becky Lou was several years older than Donovan, but she was acting like he was her senior. She returned to her post that was behind the desk. She watched the confused look on Donovan's face as he flipped through the pages. The more he read, he realized what they were.

Becky Lou gave Mrs. Paddleton the original memoir, Donovan a copy, she placed the second copy under the floorboards.

Ten o'clock that evening after the first meeting, Tess and Haze were at odds in their house. Tess was upstairs preparing for bed, while Haze was in his home office reviewing his companies accounts. Tess went downstairs, and asked, "what do you think about the meeting?"

Haze turned and looked at her said, "let me finish these figures, I'll be up in a minute."

Tess left the room and ran back upstairs, jumped in bed and pulled the covers over her head. Haze finished working and went upstairs to their bedroom. "Tess," he said, she pretended like she was asleep. He shook her and call out, "Tess"

She rolled over and said, "what?" In a hateful way.

"You asked me a question earlier. I think it's disgusting to keep someone against their will." He removed his shirt and was going towards their en-suite to shower.

She had an ornament on her nightstand, she picked it up and threw it at him, she missed.

He went to the closet and grabbed some of his things, on his way out the bedroom he asked, "can't we have a conversation without fighting?"

Tess said, "never." She threw the clock that was on her nightstand at Haze. Around the bottom of the clock was a decorative silver hard metal stand, with a sharp edge. Haze bent down to get out of the way of the clock, the metal part slammed and skidded across his back.

Tess was sitting up in bed, Haze ran over and knocked her into a laying position, then smashed his fist into her stomach. With each hit, he said, "git out my house, git out my house."

Tess struggled without success to escape his fists, so she fought back. She slapped and kicked like a wild woman. Haze walked away from the bed, he picked up his things and went towards the door, before leaving he said, "get out my house."

Tess pulled herself on the side and shuffled to the bathroom. When she looked in the mirror, she realized that Haze's fist found more than her stomach, Tess already bruised face looked like a swollen eggplant. She whispered to herself, "One day I will get him, so help me God, this house will be mine." She whispered to herself.

In another bedroom, Haze looked in the mirror, Tess fingernails had scratched the side of his face, his back was hurting. He turned to see his back in the mirror, his tee shirt was bloody. He slowly pulled it off, looking in the mirror the scar was a long opened wound bleeding heavily. He sat on the side of the bed and said, "I'm sick of this."

Haze was losing too much blood and the pain was excruciating. He put on a clean shirt and drove himself to the emergency room.

XXV

After The Storm

    Tess woke up the next morning in great pain. The Day's home had three bedrooms, each had an ensuite. Tess cleaned up as best she could, her chest and abdomen area were black and blue. She had a black eye, and a few gashes on her forehead where Haze used his right hand, all four fingers had rings. He had never beat her that bad, "next time he'll kill me," she smiled at her reflection in the mirror and said, "not unless I get him first."

    She got dressed and called Theenda, no answer, she did not take time to leave a message. It was six o'clock in the morning and still dark outside, she got in her car and pulled off. One of her tires was flat. Out of fright, she drove the wobbling car six blocks destroying the rims. She called Theenda again, this time she left a hair-raising message. She knew Haze was gone; his car was not in the garage. She looked around cautiously just in case he was watching and catch her off-guard. She said as she walked quickly to the bus stop, "for him to flatten my tire he's really mad." She began running to the bus stop looking continuously over her shoulders.

    A passenger on the bus saw a woman running and waving her arms, they alerted the driver to stop and let her on. Tess only had her phone that was in a protective cover with slots, where she kept her driver's license, social security card, and a dollar, she had left her purse in the car. The bus ride was two dollars. Tess looked like she needed an ambulance, one of the passengers paid the rest of her bus fare. When Tess saw the people on the bus looking sadly at her, she put on an acting hat and overemphasized her pain. The closest stop to the hospital was six blocks away. The driver pulled to the stop, he said, "from here is a long walk."

Tess eased off the seat like she was a little old lady, the driver said, "ma'am I'll drive you to the hospital," he stood and said to the passengers, "if you don't want me to take her, I will let her off here."

Tess was standing by the door bent over in abysmal fake pain. The passengers agreed the driver should take her to the hospital. "Thank you all," Tess said feebly, she eased down on the seat and pretended to pass out. Two female passengers went to Tess to help her. One of the women pulled Tess hair off her face, she gasped in horror. The other woman said, "poor baby, she was running from him."

The bus driver called his boss to make him aware of what was happening, while several passengers called the hospital alarming them that they were on the way. Many of the passengers went up front to see Tess freshly beaten face and the large handprints around her neck. One of the men on the bus said, "next time, he'll kill her."

When they arrived at the hospital a few of the passengers helped her off the bus. An orderly was waiting with a wheelchair.

Tess cuts and bruises were attended to and two hours later, she was able to go home. At 10:30 am, Tess called Theenda a third time. Theenda answered. Tess asked if Theenda would meet her at the Mall, due to the desperateness in Tess' voice, Theenda agreed. It was Saturday and Donovan was out, Theenda jotted down where she was going and left.

Tess was born and raised in Oxford, Mississippi, she graduated with a degree in nursing from the University of Mississippi known as Ole Miss. Before graduation Tess sent out job applications all over the south, Ogville Hospital hired her on the spot. A few months after moving to Ogville Tess and Haze met in 2016 and began dating. Donovan, Theenda, Tess, and Haze met at an NAACP meeting in January 2017.

Theenda noticed that Haze kept pulling away from Tess, every time she touched him, he flinched. So, when Tess whispered and giggled that they were getting married, Theenda pointed out that Haze appeared to not be interested. Tess got mad and stopped talking to the Bright's, she scooted closer towards Haze and turned her back to Theenda. Out of the corner of her eye, Theenda saw Haze pull away.

When Tess was single, she desperately wanted to get married. She pushed Theenda's suggestion to the side and married Haze at the courthouse. Tess moved into Haze home, she loved it, the house was big, pretty, and well kept, Tess wanted it for herself.

One morning, Tess was cooking breakfast, Haze entered the kitchen sat down and said, "I'll be in late this evening, have a lot to do at the office."

Tess yelled, "you mean with other women."

Haze innocently asked, "what other women?"

Tess had a plate in her hand, she threw it at him, it crashed against the wall, she picked up another and threw it, Haze jumped out the way. He said, "I paid a lot of money for those dishes."

Tess was cooking eggs for breakfast, she threw the skillet at Haze, he jumped out the way, the skillet clipped his elbow. He rushed out of his once peaceful home without saying goodbye to his new bride.

Theenda arrived at the mall, she saw Tess slumped on the bust of Harry V. Brown, she was wearing her nurses' uniform, her hair was crumpled, her stockings were covered in runs and holes. The closer Theenda got to Tess, she noticed that her eyes were blood red, bandages were on her head, all the joy, happiness, and peace had departed from her new-found friend. Tess' eye was badly swollen and bruised, and there were finger impressions around her throat. From the looks of Tess, all hope was gone.

While at the hospital, Tess heard that Haze was admitted, she caught a cab to where she left her car and then called AAA. She lied and told them that her husband was on his way home to kill her, she had to get away, but her tires were slashed. They believed her. When the man, from AAA, saw her, he rushed to change the tire. When he left, she drove home, rubbed an emery board on her white nurses' stockings. Out of the dirty clothes, she got a nurse's uniform, ripped the pockets, put it on, ruffled her hair, then called Theenda a third time.

Tess saw Theenda coming, she said, "thank you for coming, I-I-I need to talk, I'm so sorry for..." She broke down crying.

Theenda looked around for a place to sit, she reached out to Tess, and said, "there's a restaurant on the bottom floor." With Tess leaning heavily against Theenda, the two women walked with a faulty dexterity to the mini mall's restaurant. Once they were seated, Theenda asked, "what happened?"

"Haze"

"Is there anything I can do?"

Tess answered, "I need a place to stay for a few hours, I need someone to listen. Please help me," Tess cried.

Theenda "KayKay is a professional counselor, I can call her."

"She's too stuck on herself, she won't listen."

"I'll listen, I'm here for you," Theenda said mournfully.

"You may disrespect me for what I am about to share with you, I have no one to turn to." At this point, Tess was sobbing and talking.

Theenda reached across the table, and asked, "what could be this bad." She looked around and saw that other people were staring at them, a waiter walked over and asked Theenda, "is everything okay?"

"Please bring her a cup of mint tea." The waiter left.

Tess pulled herself together and said, "Thee, a few hours ago I had an abortion, I know it's a bad thing, but-but I had a reason to-to..."

Theenda smiled to herself and remembered only a few days ago she had made the same confession to Donovan. She said, "girl do I have a story to tell you, when you finish drinking your tea let's go to my house, you can rest there."

"Thanks, Thee, you're a true friend."

Theenda studied Tess bruised swollen face, raggedy uncombed hair, her wrinkled uniform, she asked, "is the abortion the reason for the bruises?"

Tess looked into Theenda's eyes, she saw compassion and concern, she lowered her eyes, shook her head and answered, "no, the bruises are the reason for the abortion."

Three o'clock PM, two employees of Haze picked him up at the hospital. One drove his car to the job, the other drove Haze. The man driving Haze said, "boss, you need to go home and rest." He pulled out the hospital parking lot, and continued, "Sir, you're not a violent man, she will kill you. Then what will your employees do?"

Haze said, "I'm working on it." He' looked at the man and continued, "I'm staying at a hotel tonight."

The driver said, "I hate to say this boss, but you need to man up."

Haze said, "I saw enough fighting between my parents, I was and still is determined to be a lover and not a fighter. I am done with her."

"Good." The man said, "it just ain't right you come to work looking like you lost a boxing match to Mike Tyson."

Haze laughed and said, "thank you for your concern." He sat thinking, pulled the visor down looked in the mirror and said, "you're right, I'm losing the battle of peace to chaos."

The driver said, "in one month, that woman brought you down low." He looked at Haze and said, "you can ask me."

Confused Haze asked, "What are you talking about? Ask you what?"

The driver said, "yes, I know a good lawyer."

Laughing, Haze said, "good answer."

****

On the plantation Harry II, was in the slave's area causing trouble, he had the overseers to grab Saul and physically yank him out the tobacco field and tie him to the whipping tree. Saul was going to be used as an example of what the slaves would receive if their work was not as superior as their neighboring plantations. Saul said, "you choose me cause' I's cain't tell any bad on da' slaves, dey ain't doin' nonthin,' I's ain't Bo, he make up thangs."

Harry's face got beat red. Saul continued, "iffen you's wanna' beat me," he pushed the overseers away and went to the whipping tree and finished by saying, "do whad' you's gotta' do."

The overseers tied his hands to the tree, Saul received his beating while Bo proudly stood guard holding a long stick, to keep the slaves from trying to save Saul. He used the stick to pock at them on intervals. Lee was in the group, sadly he asked, "Bo, why you doin' dis? You be one us."

Words seethe through Bo's teeth, "git' back to work or you'll be next." The slaves returned to the fields, but they looked at Bo and the overseers with intense hate. After the beating Saul was left alone and hanging from the tree by his wrist. That evening Lee and Ben returned to the whipping tree for Saul, together the two men untied the ropes off Saul's hands. Lee told Ben, "mama be waitin' at Saul's place, "she got somethin' ta' gib' him.

Ben asked, "thank we should tell Saul bout feedom?"

"Yeah, let's do dat." Lee replied.

Saul had fainted, so Lee and Ben carried him to his shack. When they reached Saul's place, several slaves were standing outside complaining about the many beatings that had taken place since Harry moved in with their Massa. One of the male slaves yelled out when he saw Lee and Ben walking towards the group, "dis' gots' ta' stop, since Massa Harry come lib' wid he's maw and paw, he be da' devil foe' us."

One of the women spoke up and said, "it be like he tryin' ta' kill us."

Lee and Ben said nothing, they walked past the crowd and entered Saul's shack where Lillie had prepared, tea.

Lee said to his mom, "what's dey' won't's me ta' do bout' Massa."

One of the female slaves entered Saul's shack, and said, "I's' help you, Miss. Lillie, what ja' need me ta' do."

"Lee and Ben gonna' hold Saul up in dis' chair so's I's' gib' him dis' tea I's made." She held the spoon up to Saul's lips, and said, "swallow dis, Saul." Then she looked at the woman and said, "make a pallet on da flo' he cain't make it up dem' steps ta'night."

The slave woman looked at Lillie and said as she made the pallet, "Miss. Lillie somethin' gots ta' be done bout young Massa Brown, us slaves ain't gonna' work iffen thangs' don't git' better round here."

Lee looked at the woman, "you's' thank' dat'll make thangs better foe' you, foe' us?"

We's gotta' do somethin," the slave woman rebuttal.

Saul shook his head no as he said, "no we cain't stop workin,' that will make Massa, moe angry."

Lillie said to Saul, "I knew dis' tea would work."

In a corner of the room, Lillie was washing out the spoon and dishes wishing the crazy chatty woman would leave, so they could talk about Donovan. Lee and Ben gently laid Saul on the pallet, Lillie said, "I's can stay wid' Saul."

All But One

Lee said, "naw, go on home, I's take care of Saul."

Bo and a man gathered in Saul's shack insisting they all agree to stop working. Lee noticed that Bo was the ringleader of the bunch, Bo also whipped an alluring smile on the woman that was doing so much talking.

Lee said, "I's' cain't stop workin,' it be a few weeks ago dat' I git' a beatin,' dat' be painful. No, I's' cain't stop workin."

Lillie also caught the look between the slave woman and Bo, she said, "der' be a sick man in here, y'all git' out of here now!" She walked toward them fanning her hands for them to leave. She got behind the slave woman and push her towards the door.

The slave woman said, "Miss. Lillie I's' stay wid you."

Irritated Lillie said, "naw' missy, you's' go home git' plenty rest foe' ta' morrow."

"Iffen you's' don't need my help, I's' be goin," said the slave woman, with great annoyance as she left.

When the woman, Bo and his crew had left, Lillie said to Lee and Ben after she closed the door, "somethin' not right."

"Bo tryin' ta' start somethin', I's not sure, why?" Lee asked

Jethro said, "he ain't neva' had people wid' him."

Glaidous walked into Saul's shack and said, "did y'all hear da' news?"

"What news?" Lillie asked.

"Young Massa Brown says he's gonna' kill off us old'um' and keep the young'uns."

Lee asked his uncle, "dat's whad' young Massa say, whad' Massa say?"

"We don't know yet," Glaidous commented as he scratched his head. He looked around at his sister, and said, "maybe we's find out soon."

"Maybe dat's da' reason Bo tryin' ta start trouble."

"Happy Easta wid' da' walk-about, gone," Lillie cried.

"Naw mama, I's see to it we meet dis' walk-about."

Ben whispered, "maybe dis' time next year we be free."

"Whad' y'all talkin bout, Jethro asked.

"I's hope dis' here year we's'fee." Glaidous responded.

"Me too." Lillie agreed.

They told Jethro about the walk-about and how they were going to meet him on Easter Sunday. Lee commented, "I feel da' Bo be workin' wid' young Massa Harry."

"If Mr. Doo-noo-vin don't help us quick," Glaidous said as he pointed to Ben but looked at Lee, "y'all life will be livin' hell, Lillie and me be dead."

"Whad ja' thank' bout' dat' woman dat talk too much?" Ben asked.

Lee responded, "she be on Bo's side, they be just like us, slave."

"I agree Lee," Glaidous said, "after all dis' be ova' and young Massa be da' boss, he won't need Bo."

Lee began to pace, he stopped and said, "unk I's thank dey' plan ta' kill us all in da' adult area and keep da' chil'ren."

"He won't's ta' rule da' chil'ren," Ben uttered.

"Save us Mr. Doo-noo-vin," Lee and his uncle murmured together.

XXVI

National Association for the Advancement of Colored People

February 16, 2017

    It was a stormy Thursday night, Donovan, Haze, and Timpkin were at the NAACP meeting that was being held in one of the High School's classrooms. Due to the rain, only a handful of people had attended. The Committee Head said, "we didn't get much done this evening, most of our members had other things to do so they stayed home. The main speaker's flight was canceled because they had a snowstorm up norf,' we're ending the meeting."

    As the speaker continued to speak Donovan's mind trailed off into the distance of the plantation, he wondered if the people at the meeting knew about the plantation. Outside the winds howled like a pack of wolves, big drops of rain pulsated against the windows, heavy thick clouds slowly sailed past the silvery moon. Inside the school was warm and dry; the secretary was about to close the meeting when Donovan stood and asked if he may say a word.

    The secretary said, "Mr. Bright would like to have a moment of our time." She motioned for him to come down front.

    One of the NAACP members, mumbled, "I gotta' go, the rain is pouring down out there."

    Donovan said, "I only need a quick second of your time," he looked around and everyone was waiting for him to continue, he said, "a few weeks ago I visited a plantation..."

Before he could say another word a flurry of mumbles filled the room as people began to leave. Donovan tried to continue, "if you would let me finish you will know exactly what I'm going to say."

A woman from the audience said, "I know exactly what you're going to say, you better leave it alone." She left.

A middle age man said, "we know about the plantation, you're a newcomer to this town, the plantation exists but nobody lives there." He left and several others with him.

The secretary added, "eleven years ago a man name Phil started up the same old mess about slaves on some plantation," she cleared her throat and then said, "Phil is dead."

An elderly man said, "ah-um that's right, that's right, if you got children and a wife, they will kill them too, there was a family that was new in this town, they arrived about three years ago." He looked around the room and ask, "y'all remember them?"

From across the room someone yelled out, "they were the Stacey family, the whole family was killed six months after they came."

Haze said, "we're the NAACP, we help people." Haze was trying to look as though he was doing fine but his back was killing him, he had two new bruises on his face, to cover them over his secretary had applied foundation.

One of the women got up to leave, she walked to the door turned around and said, "I have children that I want to see become adults, and a husband that I want to grow old with." She left.

Donovan said to the people as they were leaving, "we can't let people own other people as if they are objects."

An elderly stately gentleman walked up to Donovan and said, "if there are slaves out there keep quiet, somebody is killing folk, a family was killed just last month." He looked at Donovan and said, "I saw you at the family's funeral."

Haze asked the gentleman, "will you help us?"

"No, I'm too old, besides you hang out together, no one will be the wiser."

Donovan asked the elderly gentlemen, "is this a warning?"

The man said, "we all know about it but don't want to believe it, we know of the family in MacCall. That statue in the

All But One

middle of downtown," he looked around to see if anyone was listening. Only Timpkin and the Janitor was left. The man said, "is Harry V. Brown. I heard he built that plantation." He left.

As the man was leaving Timpkin joined Donovan and Haze, "What'd that old man have to say about your claim."

"He said everybody knows about the slaves," Donovan said.

Haze said, "so why don't you?"

Sheepishly Timpkin said, "we know there's a plantation, no people are there."

Donovan looked around, only the janitor was left, he looked at Timpkin and said, "prove me wrong and go with us."

Haze said, "yeah, do that."

Timpkin looked at Donovan and ask, "how do you know it was slaves that left you the note? Maybe it's a trap."

Donovan answered, "the spelling of the words, the language, a feeling within me. I know they exist," he nodded towards Haze and said, "we're going to meet them, come with."

Haze said, "I read the note, they wrote, "meetin' ta' take place "Easta' Sunday, by outer gate." He took in a deep breath and said, "made me feel funny all over."

Donovan watched Haze, with every move he wrenched in pain, he asked, "are you okay Haze."

"Yeah, I pulled a muscle."

Timpkin said still talking about the slaves, "you don't understand, whenever I or my brother or sister acted out, mama would tell us she was going to take us to a plantation that had slave ghosts and leave us. Most parents would scare their children with that tale. Too many still do."

Donovan asked Timpkin, "did you tell your children that?"

Timpkin answered, "no, it scared me, so I decided that I didn't want my children to go through what I went through."

Haze said, "sounds like a form of abuse."

"Donovan asked, "were you abused as a child, Haze?"

"Naw man, my old man just used the strap on us boys a few times a day, he wanted the best from us, we were hard head and bad. We deserved it."

Donovan asked Haze, "do you have any sisters?"

LaVaughn

"One, she is nine years older than me, she ran away when she was fifteen, why all the questions?"

Timpkin asked, "why did she run away?"

"Was your father in her bedroom on occasion?" Donovan asked.

"Man, I was only six years old, I guess sometimes I'd see him coming out of her room, but then he'd leave me and my brother's room after beating us senseless. Why you ask?"

"Just asking," Donovan said, "although, I wonder if child abuse is more prevalent than we think." Donovan got a little too philosophical for Haze.

The conversation irritated Haze, he said, "be more specific, what are you talking about Don-man."

The janitor came over to the three men, he said, "Mr. Bright may I interrupt?"

Donovan knew the janitor; he said, "Ron, meet Timpkin and Haze, guys Ron."

Ron said, "please to meet you, gentlemen. About that plantation, it does exist, I've never seen it but," he apologetically looked at the men and then asked, "may I tell you my story?"

Donovan and Timpkin said at the same time, "sure."

Haze said, "go for it."

The Janitor said, "back in 2000, my wife and I had a baby, when he turned four, someone came to the door and asked to purchase our son. We said no, we may be poor, but my son was mine, and not for sale. My wife was a teacher's aide in the elementary school, I work here, we took our son to daycare. After work, he was gone. We never saw him again."

Timpkin said, "I remember that several children went missing from that daycare."

"Yes," the janitor replied, "the daycare didn't call any of us about our missing babies."

Donovan asked, "what year did you say?"

"Back in 2004, is when my boy went missing."

"I read that's the year kids were taken from daycares across the country," Donovan looked at the man and asked, "you don't think it was the family that owns the slaves, do you?"

"Don't know, he could be there, could be anywhere, could be dead." The janitor answered.

Timpkin said, "Naw, no way. There are no slaves in 2017."

"We'll never know." The janitor replied as he began to walk away, he turned and said, "it's closing time gentlemen."

The rain had stopped, the air was warm and muggy. In the parking lot, Haze said, "Don, Tim, both of you insinuated that I was abused as a child. Well, I was."

"I'm no expert on the subject, so I might be wrong," Donovan said.

Timpkin looked at Haze then at Donovan, and said, "you might be right, yep, yep you might-be-right."

Haze asked roughly "What are you talking about Tim-man?"

Donovan said, "Yeah." He looked at Timpkin.

"The plantation, what're you two talking about?"

Haze said, "Me. Trying to figure out if I was abused or not."

"Where's your brother?" Donovan asked.

"You're still on that Don-man?" Haze asked before he said, "In jail with my dad. Why?"

"Your mom?" Donovan asked without answering Haze's question.

"Mom died years ago."

Timpkin asked, "how did she die?"

"Dad said she fell down some steps."

Haze asked, "what about your home life Don-man?"

Donovan said, "we need to leave, Theenda will be worried," he turned to leave.

Haze grabbed Donovan's arm, and said, "answer the question Don-man."

Donovan said, "I'm embarrassed to say."

Timpkin asked, "why?"

"Well, my mom is a lawyer, my father, a history professor at a University in New York City, my brother, Paul Bright, is a medical doctor, and my brother John, I'm thinking he should be an architect, but he is a history professor. And then there's me, I'm the baby, my parents' failure, the black sheep."

"What are you talking about?" Haze asked.

"The abuse that went on in my home," Donovan continued, "is educational abuse. My parents pushed us to be superior, think superior, act superior, walk superior, only choose superior friends, buy big houses. We were forced to get our Ph.D., John didn't want to, but he did, his passion is building things, he graduated from Harvard. Paul graduated from Yale, he always wanted to be a doctor. I graduated from Morehouse and got a master's degree from a university in Brooklyn. I got sick and tired of school, study, school, study, no life - no life. While I'm on a date, I'm thinking I should be studying, while I'm studying, I'm thinking about being on a date. After getting my masters, I didn't go back to school. My mom called me the black sheep, so on graduation day I wrote, in white letters on my black graduation cap in big bold letters, "black sheep." Donovan laughed saying, "Paul told my parents, "you spoiled him, what did you expect." Donovan chuckled saying, "mom and dad didn't speak to me for a month."

Timpkin said, "but you took after your father, both of you teach history."

"You see, I don't teach at the university level or attended Harvard, Yale or an Ivy League university, that's the failure."

"I would trade families with you any day," Haze looked at Donovan and continued, "is being the baby of the family the reason everything has to go your way?"

Timpkin was deep in thought, he ignored Haze and said, "I would think that your dad is proud of you Donovan, you're a Morehouse man, they also teach men how to be, gentleman."

Donovan said, "gentlemen? Yeah-right, all we thought about was the girls at Spellman."

Haze watching the two men felt left out because he knew nothing about college, he had never heard of Morehouse and did not know the difference between a University and College, to get back in the conversation he asked, "Timpkin what about you?"

"Well Haze, I attended the college in Titleburk, my parents threaten to put me on a plantation with slave ghost that frightens me, but my abuse is my marriage."

Donovan asked, "don't you make more than her?"

"Yes. She's even slapped me a couple of times."

"Wow," Haze said, he looked at Timpkin and said, "I walk in your shoes."

"Don't you ever hit your wife, Tess is a shy sweet woman and my wife friend. Thee will kick you from one end of town to the other." Donovan said.

"Okay, so what do we have here," Haze said, "we're a couple of abused misfits attempting to help somebody when we can't help ourselves. Donovan, your family is in New York, can't depend on them, mine is in jail, don't know where my sister is, Timpkin are your parents living?"

Timpkin answered, "yes, they are a healthy ninety-year-old couple."

"Okay, not much help there," Haze said, "I guess you two are right I'm physically abused, my dad raped my sister and killed my mother. Donovan, you're an overly educated young fool, Timpkin your parents frighten you stupid and is old, you're a fifty-year-old man, and Don-man you think you know Tess, you believe what you think you see." He grimaced in pain before saying, "so what good are we to anybody?"

Donovan said "Haze you miss the point; we are successful men despite our childhood traumas. We don't need nobody else; we have our wives and the three of us, that's six people, what we need is a plan."

Timpkin said, "I'll go with you, to prove you're wrong."

XXVII

Hidden Gates

March 5, 2017

    Donovan and Theenda had a backyard cookout for their friends, only Haze and Tess attended, the Linwood's were visiting their son.
    Theenda had barbecued a feast for the outing, there was barbecue chicken, and beef ribs, she wrapped several corn-on-the-cob still in its husk in aluminum foil then let them sit in milk for five minutes before she placed the cob on the grill. she grilled sliced Idaho potatoes that were steeped in Italian dressing, salt, and pepper, and grilled stuffed black bass. In aluminum foil, she put together broccoli, cauliflower, cherry tomatoes, cabbage, frozen succotash, chopped chives, green, yellow, and red bell peppers, lightly sprayed with olive oil, seasoned, and then placed on the grill. Humm good eating. For dessert, Theenda fixed dirt pie, and Donovan's favorite strawberry cake made with fresh strawberries and strawberry soda. She also prepared Tess favorite punch bowl cake, what a feast.
    When Haze and Tess entered the gate to the Bright's backyard, Haze said, "just look at you Thee, I would never believe that little itty bitty you cooked. Don-man why ain't you bigger?"
    Tess timidly said, "girlfriend you're smelling up the neighborhood."
    For the first time since Donovan met the Days, he noticed Tess. He had never seen her face; it was all ways covered with her long straggly hair. Donovan thought that she would look better if she would stop playing peek-a-boo from behind her long black locks. Tess walked over to Theenda. "She limps," Donovan

mumbled to himself. He watched Haze sit down, he looked like he was in serious agony. He asked himself, "what's with those two?"

Theenda said, "take a seat, food is almost ready."

Haze said, "I need to use the bathroom." He stood slowly like an old man with arthritis. Theenda and Donovan watched him, Donovan asked, "need help old man?"

Theenda said, "Sweetie that's not funny," she looked at Haze and asked, "what happened to you?"

He looked at Tess who yelled in a strange voice, "he's faking, all Haze want is attention and me to move back in."

Haze left. Tess asked in a child's voice, "Linwood's coming?"

"No, they are visiting their son," Theenda replied.

Tess said, "Good, I don't want her to see me looking like this."

Haze returned, slowly eased down in a chair, he asked, "are the Linwood's coming?"

"Not today," Donovan laughed.

Tess looked at Donovan and Theenda, it appeared that their attention was being lavished on Haze. Tess pulled her hair back and said to Haze, "I'm glad they're not coming, otherwise I would have to show them what you did to me."

Donovan, Theenda, and Haze looked surprised.

Theenda grabbed Donovan by the shirt, and said, "come in the kitchen with me."

Donovan was in a comfortable position and getting ready to put food in his mouth as he said, "But I..."

Theenda walked away saying, "that wasn't a choice sweetie."

Haze asked, "you let her talk to you like that Don-man?"

Theenda turned around and ran past Donovan, leaped over to Haze, POW! Like Bat Man fighting the Riddler slammed her fist dead center Hazes' face, he stood to dodge her blows. Theenda knew judo, she kicked Haze around like he was tissue paper. Staying away from Theenda's feet Donovan ran behind his wife, picked her up and ran carrying her into the kitchen.

Haze was having a hard time getting off the ground. Tess wasn't the only one with a sore body.

When they entered the house, Theenda said, "we gotta' get back out there or he'll finish Tess off."

Confused Donovan asked, "that's what's wrong with her, Haze is beating her?"

"Yes." She cried.

While Theenda and Donovan were in the kitchen, Haze asked Tess, "what happened to you?"

Laughing Tess said, "they believe you did this."

Tess was facing the house, Haze back was towards the house, he could not see what she saw, which was the Bright's coming towards them. Tess jumped up, she startled Haze, he slowly stood. Tess sat down crying. "Haze," Donovan yelled.

Haze eased into the chair.

Theenda walked up to the table and said to Haze, "you may want to call the police I have a black belt in Judo, be glad you still have-a-face."

Donovan said, "let me handle this Baby Girl."

When everyone was seated at the table Haze ask, "what did I do to you Thee?"

Donovan said, "we'll talk in private later, Haze," looking at Tess, Donovan said, "Thee and Tess have an idea or plan for the slaves' escape."

Haze said, "good." He laid his head on the table.

Theenda said, "Haze get serious, get your head off my table. You clown around too much."

Haze sat up.

Tess said, "the only time he's serious is when he's beating on me, I had to defend myself."

Donovan and Theenda looked disapproving at Haze. Tess said with a smile in her tone of voice, "I know of a way to permanently destroy the plantation."

Donovan said, "I'm listening."

"Salt the whole plantation which will destroy the land, use potassium powder to set the buildings and grass on fire."

Haze asked, "won't everybody hear the explosives,"

Theenda snapped, "potassium makes no sound."

Tess watched Theenda stand up to Haze even though she was sitting down, she marveled when she beat Haze down. Tess wanted to cheer Theenda on, she thought Theenda was gaining

All But One

strength. "That's right," Tess said enthusiastically, "it ignites quickly, burns purple which will blend in with the night sky."

"How long does it stay purple?" Haze asked.

"Not long, but long enough," Tess replied.

Haze made a sarcastic comment, "Tess who asked you to think?"

Still ignoring Haze, Donovan asked, "there are several locked gates on the complex that the slaves can't get through."

Tess said, "put the salt in burlap sacks, punch holes in the bottom then quickly walk all over the section they can."

"The locked gates?" Donovan asked.

"Someway, somehow, we need to get our hands onto a key," Theenda suggested.

Tess sat up straight and pulled her hair away from her face, revealing a swollen eye and busted lip. Donovan saw for the second time the marks on Tess face, he asked, "are you okay Tess?"

Tess full of energy and excitement answered, "Give the slaves clay, they would have to steal a key from the overseer to make a copy."

Theenda said, "Tess tell him about the plastic bags and the two groups," she looked away, she wanted Tess to hide her face again.

Tess, having a reason for living, was popping with ideas, she was going to be a modern-day abolitionist. The slaves had taken the place of her fake aborted baby. Tess was not pregnant, she lied to Theenda because she wanted sympathy, she craved attention, thus the reason she started fights.

The night before the barbecue, Tess had gone to a bar, got drunk, started an argument with a barmaid, the woman grabbed a bottle of beer off a table and smashed it in Tess face. Tess was relentless, neither women won. They both walked away with bruises and cuts, Except, Tess was no longer welcomed in the bar. The same night of the fight, Tess went to Haze home, she got out her car carrying a knife. She said softly to herself, "I'll stab him, go to the police and say he beat me. They'll kick him out the house, I'll move in."

Haze answered the door; Tess pushed her way in and surprised Haze. Using the knife, she stabbed him in his arm, when he turned to run, she sliced his back. Then went to the police station, Chief Gideon sent Officer Felix, who was friends with Haze. When he arrived, he rushed Haze to the hospital, where he learned that Haze was a regular since his marriage to Tess.

Tess could not tell the Bright's about her barroom brawl, she blamed Haze, and they were responding the way she expected. Tess was in control, she was excited and happy, she continued to come up with one idea after another. Tess was uncontrollably chatty, "or we put potassium in plastic bags and toss them over the locked gates, light several and hopefully they all will catch fire, or will wire cutters cut the gate? Can they dig out? Where are the gates opening?" After she finished talking, she was out of breath.

Theenda looked at Donovan and winked, she looked at Tess, and said, "look at my friend, little modern-day abolitionist." She said to Donovan, "I told you she was full of ideas."

Donovan laughed, "Thee what is your idea."

"My idea is to support Tess; she is a great lady."

"She's no lady," Haze said.

Theenda looked at Haze and said, "bring it."

"What're you talking about Thee?" Haze looked confused.

Donovan walked towards the house and yelled, "Haze follow me, we need to talk," he looked back at Haze who was looking at Tess. "What're you telling her?" Haze asked Tess.

"Now Haze!" Donovan said with wrath in his voice.

Haze looked at Donovan and said, "man I'm older than you, by several years."

Donovan said in a demanding voice, "Haze, you need to come now."

Haze stood like he was eight hundred years old, Tess yelled, "stop faking you're injured."

Theenda asked, "what's wrong with you Haze?"

He looked at Theenda with sad eyes and said, "you wouldn't believe me if I told you."

Theenda watched him limp away, she looked at Tess and asked, "what is he talking about."

Tess gave a flippant answered, "that man lies so much, I can't keep up."

All But One

Haze dull sad eyes pierced Theenda heart. Watching Haze enter the house, she caught a glimpse of blood on the back of his shirt. She looked around at Tess and asked, "what happened to your face?"

Tess lied and said, "Haze."

Something about Tess attitude gradually caused a changed in Theenda towards Haze. She blamed Haze for everything yet, it was he who was in bad shape. Theenda asked, "Haze, what?"

****

Glaidous, Ben, and Jethro were in the church whispering about meeting a walk-about. Glaidous asked and said, "yous' got somethin' ta' ask da' walk-about? I's been tryin ta' thank of somethin."

Ben said, "I's gonna ax iffen he hep' us offen' dis' pantation."

Jethro commented, "he be brown likes us, how he git' out hes Massa gate?"

"Dat's what I's thankin, how he git' out?" Glaidous said. He went to the podium and got the book with the slaves names, he took the book to Ben and Jethro and showed them what Paula had written. He said, "she git' out da' gate, read dis."

The three men sat back in silence. Ben asked, "how she do dat."

Glaidous asked, "where she go?"

Helen was home for the weekend, she had spent most of her time with her best friend Fanny, who knew that Helen despised Bo. The women were out walking, when Helen said, "let's stop by Miss. Lillie,"

Fanny said, "I's wanna' see cute Lee."

Helen knocked on the screen door, Lee said, "come in."

Helen walked in first and said, I'm on my way back to the chil'ren area, I's' stop by ta' holler at y'all."

Lillie came down from the sleeping area, a smile crossed her face. Lillie asked, "how you two young'uns' doin' ta'day.'"

Fanny asked, "Miss. Lillie, you's feelin' poorly ta'day.'

"My stomach hurt me powerful bad."

"We won't keep yah' Miss. Lillie, you git' better." Helen said.

Lillie said, "I's gonna' fix some tea."

Helen said I's fix it foe' you." She went in the cooking area to make the tea.

Lillie said, "you's don't need to do dat' child."

Fanny said, "Miss. Lillie, she treat ja' better dan' her mama,"

Lillie chuckled, "dat's cause she be like my child."

Once the Tea was prepared, Helen tried to cool the tea, she blew on the cup as she handed it to Miss. Lillie.

The three women sat at the table talking, Helen told them all about Becky Lou, how wild she was. She promised them that the next time she's allowed to come to the slave quarters, she would bring some candy. Lee sat listening, he thought about meeting a walk-a-bout, his leg bounced with excitement as Helen spoke about Mr. Brown's sister. Lee asked, "you have feedom food."

"Yes," Helen answered with excitement, "and it be good," she said.

before leaving Helen gave Lillie a hug, then said, "take care yoe'self, Miss. Lillie, I's bring ya' some sweet dat' Miss. Brown gets' fo' da' chil'ren."

Lee watched Helen and his mom in confusion, he said, "Helen see yah' next weekend, Fanny see you in the bar later."

"Rita comin?" Fanny asked.

"She be der," Lee answered. Helen realized that she had never been to the bar before, she asked, "I's' wonder what Massa do iffen' I's' go ta' da' bar wid' ja?"

"Beat ja' till yah' cain't stand no moe." Lee laughed.

Lillie said, "Lee shame on you," then to Helen, she suggested, "go ta' da' bar next Sat'day, when you come home."

Helen said, "I's not off till' two Sat'day from now."

Lee said, "I's take yah' den."

"I's neva' thought bout' goin." She looked at Lee with a big smile before saying, "sound like fun."

Fanny said, "den' it be settled, you's go to da' bar wid' Lee and me in two Sat'day."

Helen nodded in agreement then said, "an'dum,' I's' go wid' out Bo." The women left out happy and satisfied with their arrangement.

All But One

Fanny went back to her shack while Helen went to hers. Bo yelling at Helen was heard throughout the plantation, Bo shrieked, "woman gib' me da' spect' I's deserve.

Helen yelled back, "spect?! You have slaves beaten, you's watch us women git' raped. When da' overseer rape me on da' way here when I's' git' here you do nothin' ta' help me. We's married cause Massa put me in yo' cabin."

Bo slapped her, at that same time the two overseers walked in, behind them was Harry Brown II, he heard the argument and slap.

Harry said, "good for you Bo, treating these niggra' women the right way, gotta' slap 'em' round so's they know who's boss." Harry looked around at the overseers and laughed, they nervously laughed with him.

Bo uneasy about his young Massa being in his cabin, said, "how you doin' young Massa."

Harry II arrogantly said, "fool, don't be grinning at me, for one thing, drop and give it to me."

Confused, "Gib' yah' what Massa?" Bo asked.

The two overseers froze in place as they stared at each other. They weren't sure as to what was going to happen, but Harry had been acting strangely for the last week. Harry looked at the overseers and told one of them, "git' Bo's pants down, bend him over," he told the other overseer, "take care of her"

Fred said, "in front of y'all?"

Harry yelled extremely loud, "after I finish boy-you next!"

Fred took Helen and push her on the floor, he lightly slapped her one time, he stopped when Harry naked from waist down walked over and kick them both, then said "quiet!"

Meantime Roy was holding Bo down on his knees in a headlock, with his butt exposed. Harry walked over to Bo and raped him. Bo cried silently. Helen and the overseer turned their heads, the overseer holding Bo down closed his eyes and turned his head.

Lee went to Bo's shack to help Helen, he looked through the screen door and was shocked by what he saw. He quietly left and ran home.

When Lee entered, "Lillie said, "I's' fix Helen some tea, she be coming by."

Lee said, "not Helen dat' need da' tea." He explained what he saw, then said, "mama iffen' Massa Harry eva' do dat ta' me, kill me, iffen' he eva' do dat' ta' Cush." Lee finished with crucial contempt, "I's' kill Massa," enraged anger filled his entire soul, as he uttered, "I's' swear I will."

Lillie said, "young Massa be in a fit of rage, don't you go and git' yoe'self in da' same fit."

Lee's gasped for air as he said, "Bo is evil and dumb, but no man deserve whad' he be gettin."

They heard footsteps on their porch, then a knock, standing in the doorway was Helen. Lee opened the screen door to let her in. Helen entered the shack shivering, Lee got a blanket and wrapped it around her and said, "you be lucky."

Helen shook her head, yes, in agreement.

Lillie said to Helen, Lawd' a'mercy, whad' happened ta' you?"

"Not me, Bo. I's neva' seed Miss. Lillie, whad' I's seed' ta'day."

From that day forward to and from the children's area the overseers left Helen alone, they did not rape or beat on her, they became nicer to the slaves when the Brown's weren't around. That incident for Helen, Roy, and Fred was frightening shock therapy. Bo, on the other hand, was driven to insane anger.

****

Back at Donovan's house, he and Haze were in the kitchen as Theenda and Tess remained outside.

Without a moment's hesitation, Donovan balled up his fist and slammed Haze in the face, and ask, "how that feel?"

Haze was stunned, said, "why you hit me?"

Donovan punched him two more times with each lick he asked, "that feel good? This makes you a better person. Does this hurt? Having fun yet?"

Haze slumped to the floor and passed out. Looking down at Haze, Donovan said, "hit Tess again you'll live to regret it." He dumped a glass of water on Haze's face.

Through grunts and groans of pain, Haze collected his achy body off the floor. The stitches Haze had received, from the stabbing on his arm and back were coming loose.

All But One

Donovan asked, "what's wrong with you."

"It hurts man." Haze wobbled as he stood, he began to cry.

Donovan said, "come on, let's change your clothes."

Though Haze did not have a change of clothes, he followed Donovan.

When the men came out of the house, Theenda and Tess stood up with their mouth hanging open. Haze face was swollen to the size of a honeydew. Theenda asked, "Haze did you shower."

Donovan answered, "he could not," Donovan shook his head and said, "his back is opening up."

Haze said, "I'm okay."

Theenda asked, "what did you do to him?"

Donovan answered, "not me."

Haze said, "it's her." He pointed to Tess.

Tess said pointing her butter knife at Haze, "I know how to use a knife, I will slice you up slowly from limb to limb."

Donovan and Theenda caught each other's eyes, they became confused about the situation. Donovan cut in, "okay, so we all have our hidden gate which we will work on, we'll get them under control, so we can be effective in helping the slaves out of their visible gate. My gate is pushing the wrong button and I mushroom. But I have it under control."

Haze asked, "what does that mean." He reached into his pocket and pulled out a pill bottle.

Theenda said, "yep Sweetie, Haze face shows you're in control."

Tess laughed, too hard and loud.

Donovan saw Haze putting a pill in his mouth, "so you do drugs now?"

Haze laid his head on the table and said, "it's for my back." He slid the pill container in front of Donovan.

Tess said a little too loud, "he's faking."

Donovan said, "no, these pills are legit and the cut on his back is deep."

Theenda asked, "did you put something on it?"

Haze answered, "he poured peroxide on the stitches, and applied clean bandages."

Donovan said, "that was not a sore." He looked at Tess and asked, "name a hidden gate."

She turned her head then said, "him pretending to be in pain."

Theenda said, "I have one, my mom was a social worker, she would come home and beat her children, or push us downstairs, my brother ran away because she sliced his back with a butcher knife. She taught parenting classes."

Tess said, "getting a beating is not a hidden gate, my father was a police officer, he would come home and beat my mom, called her all kinds of names. He never hit me or my sister, he'd come home with candy in his pocket or a toy of some kind. But mom, a different story. He was a protector, of the law."

Haze said, "a woman that pretends she's innocent around others, but at home a brute," he slowly sat upright and said to Donovan, "pain pill kicking in, feeling better, I still want to go back to the hospital."

"I swear foe' God, I'll kill you," Tess spouted at Haze.

Theenda stood and said, "no more hitting."

"I believe Haze, you missed the point," Donovan said in his teacher's voice. "more like a man beating his wife, and brag about being rich."

"You still don't get it." Haze said with a depth of sadness in his voice.

"And Teachers," Theenda began, "we are supposed to train minds-challenge our students to better themselves, but too many teachers are abusive or molest their students, thus strangling the students' ability to have a fair chance in life." Theenda paused before continuing, "I recognize an abused child because of my upbringing," She looked at Tess and said, "yes, an abusive parent that pretend to be a good person is living a lie, which is what hidden gates are all about."

"Well," Haze began, "maybe their parents should have aborted them, too many abused kids grow up and become abusers." He looked sad and said pathetically, "I pray hard because I don't want to be like my parents." He looked at Tess and continued, "but here I am, living their life."

Donovan said, "yeah, an abuser just like your dad."

Haze said, "no, you don't understand"

Donovan said, "will you stop saying that."

Theenda sat quietly watching Haze, she had seen him before he married Tess. He donated to the school a basketball

All But One

stand, just the right size for elementary kids, and three small basketballs. The kids loved him. And the teachers adored him. He would come to the school once a week to teach the kids basketball technique. The one time she had seen him, Haze was energetic and happy. then he married Tess. "hum, I wonder." She said out loud.

"Wonder what?" Tess asked Theenda.

"If you told them the truth about us." Haze said.

Donovan said, "the truth about her," he got up from his seat, went over to Tess, pulled her hair back off her face and said, "in defense of her," he leaned over and got close to Haze face, he looked deep in Haze eyes and said in a growl, "this is abuse."

Donovan went back to his seat, sat down, and said, "now, let's eat."

"The last one," Haze began, "a husband and wife who in public appear to be in love, they call themselves a Christian. In church they are hard workers, but at home, it's a boxing ring." He was trying to tell Donovan his home life without really saying.

Theenda said, "that's a good one Haze."

Tess looked at Theenda curtly and said, "I can't believe you're on his side."

Looking at Haze and Tess, Theenda said to Donovan, "I think Sweetie, we have it wrong."

When the cookout was over, Donovan drove Haze to the hospital, he was admitted. The cut on his back was infected. Donovan made sure Haze was okay and had all he needed, Donovan asked, "what'd you mean when you said I don't understand."

"Don-man, if I told you the truth, you'd call me a liar. You're the kind of person that must see the truth. I pray someday you will."

"How did you get that cut on your back."

"Again, you won't believe me."

"Try me."

"Tess."

"Liar." Donovan began to leave, then turned and said, "I guess Tess sliced up her face."

Haze said, "bar fight."

Donovan yelled, "liar." He left.

While Donovan and Haze were together, Theenda helped Tess take the rest of her clothes and personal items permanently out of Haze house. Tess gave Theenda a hug and said, "Thank you."
"What for?" Theenda asked.
"For being my friend. A few months ago, you warned me. What did I do? Turned my back on you, and the next day, I married Haze. You had every right to tell me where to go."
"No, Donovan say I care too much."
"It's not you Theenda, it's the Jesus in you."
"If that's the case, who was that kicking Haze around."
"How about Haze trying to play a troubled victim." Tess Laughed she continued, "Thee, don't side with Haze, he's playing the victim for your pity."

Driving home Donovan asked himself, "how did Haze get cut on his back." When he got to a red light, he pretended he was holding a knife, he bent his arm to see if it was possible to cut his back from the top of his butt to midway his back. "hum, impossible," the light changed. He said as he drove home, "if Tess cut him that bad, absolute anger caused him to beat her."

XXVIII

Becky Lou Brown - Discovery

March 5, 2017

    Helen returned to the children cabin anxious, she had mixed feelings about what had happened to Bo. When Helen entered the cabin, Becky Lou grabbed Helen's arm and took her outside to the cooking area and said, "let's talk." Becky asked Helen about the incident on the plantation.

    Helen said, "whad' Massa do to Bo, he had it coming."

    Becky Lou was confused, she asked, "what did Harry do and who had what coming?"

    Helen explained in detail what had taken place, Becky Lou simply said, "we know he's that way."

    It was Helen's turn to be confused, she asked, "what way Miss?"

    Becky Lou stayed the night in the cabin, she went outside and called Charles, she told him to have Harry get her in the morning. Becky Lou and Helen sat up late that night talking. Becky Lou said, "Helen somebody in town is trying to help you escape from here."

    Confused, Helen responded, "ain't nobody in town but da' slave, I's don't know whad" ja' talkin' bout."'

    Disappointed, Becky Lou shoulders slump, she rubbed her head and said, "you wouldn't understand, Helen, slavery is over." At that moment the Becky Lou and Helen heard a noise in the bushes.

    Helen asked, "whad" you say?"

    Becky Lou said, "in two weeks when you return to the slave area do two things for me, one," she held up one finger, and said, "tell Lee that he has inside help," She held up two fingers, and said, "ask who's his outside help. You got that."

"I's' got it misses, I's' don't understand,' but I's' got it."

"Repeat it to me."

When Helen finished repeating, she looked at Becky Lou somberly and ask, "what iffen' he ax' me who won't's ta' know."

Becky Lou said, "give him this," she handed Helen a piece of paper with her name, phone number, and home address, then said, "tell him to get it to his outside help." Also written on the paper was, *I can help with the slaves, I know a woman who will help financially, call me after six p.m. Monday through Saturday.* As she handed the note to Helen she said, "give this to Lee. You're going to be free." Becky Lou took the message back and said, "I give it to you in two weeks."

Becky Lou looked at Helen and asked, "do you understand Helen?"

"Yes Misses."

"Good, let's get some sleep."

Helen looked out a window and saw blackness, "I's be fee? Whad' dat' mean," she whispered to herself, whad" she be talkin' bout."

Becky Lou and her niece Harriett shared a luxury apartment together in Titleburk. Harriett had become disinterested in the plantation since she began dating a man that wanted to leave the state and move out west. On Harriet's search for overseers, she met a tall handsome man, who seized her heart. She fell in love.

One evening the girls decided to visit Charles and his wife in the castle, all was going well until Harriett said she was getting married and moving to Iowa. Charles was okay with his daughter moving so far away but insisted that she keep their set up a secret. Harriett thundered that she did not want to enter a marriage with a cloak-and-dagger held over her head. She ended in the tone of a child having a temper tantrum, "daddy I will tell him and together we will keep it hush-hush.

Charles wife shot him a look, he nodded. Without saying a word, he gave her permission to handle their daughter and boyfriend. Becky Lou caught the communication between her brother and sister-in-law, she knew that Harriett was about to meet her demise. Becky Lou had driven them to MacCall, on the way home she told her niece, about Harry II incident in the slave quarters, Harriett said, "yeah, we know he prefers men over women."

"He's not having children, who will run the plantation?" Becky Lou said.

Harriett said, "there's you, and me, we'll run it."

"We are women, our names will change to our husbands, you can't run the plantation from another state." Becky Lou explained.

"No, I am named after our grandpa the originator of H.B. Metropolis. I will not change my name."

"Well, do you know your parents are going to eliminate you and your boyfriend?"

"What?" Harriett looked in disgust at Becky Lou when she said, "my parents will never hurt me."

"Who do you think ordered the murder, on your sister?"

They drove in silence for a little while, Harriette broke the quiet and said, "sis had an accident."

Becky Lou said, "think about it Harriett, your sister drove slower than a snail crawling, she could slam in the back of a semi-truck and not put a dent on the car."

Harriett said, "my parents love me."

Two days later when Becky Lou arrived home from work, she found a note from Harriett reading, *we left for Iowa,* it was written in a strange handwriting. Becky Lou went to Harriett's room, all her clothes were there, her shoes, in the chest of drawer none of her intimate apparel was missing. Becky Lou called Harriett's cell, got no answer.

Harriett personal things were on top her dresser, chest of drawer, and nightstand had not been touched. Becky Lou opened the nightstand drawer and there was Harriett's boyfriend home and cell number with his name. She called the cell and got no answer, she called the home number, a woman answered, "may I speak with Gavin please," Becky asked.

Gavin came to the phone, "hello."

"Please tell me Harriett is with you."

"She is."

Harriett came to the phone, "Becky, while you were gone, I saw a strange man coming towards the apartment, he came to the door didn't knock, he rattled the doorknob then proceeded to unlock the door. I was watching TV, I ran to my bedroom, grabbed my tennis shoes and purse, jumped out the kitchen window and ran like crazy to the apartment office, I used their phone to call Gavin."

"Throw yours and Gavin's phone away, do not call the police and do not go to Iowa."

"Becky, I am three months pregnant with a little boy. I am not keeping the Brown name."

"Harriett destroy your phones, then run."

Harriett burned their cell phones in the bathtub, one of them popped causing a small flame to ignite the shower curtain. She tried to put the fire out, but the curtain kept burning. Using the house phone, Gavin's father called the fire department, then said, "let's go." The strange man Harriett told Becky Lou about, entered the house as they were leaving.

His tall form dressed in all black was menacing. Harriet looked at her boyfriend and said, "I'm sorry."

He asked her, "who is this man?"

Going to the man Gavin's father asked him, "who are you, Sir."

The strange man shot Gavin's father and mother, using a silencer on his gun.

Harriet said, "we almost made it away from the Browns, this is my dad's doing."

Her boyfriend said, "no, not your dad. He would never do this."

Harriet answered saying, "he had my sister killed."

With that said, the man shot Harriet and her boyfriend. On the landline he entered *69, the fire department answered. He said, "I called to cancel, the fire is out." He then entered the bathroom yanked the shower curtain down, it fell in the tub, he turned the water on which put the fire out. The cell phones were useless, they had melted and wadded together.

The man looked down at the bodies, he smiled when he saw Harriet and her boyfriend. They had died face down and arm lying on each other's back. He said as he was leaving, "her father should be ashamed of himself; she was a good kid."

Having a key to the plantation house, Becky Lou let herself in, she called out to Harry but didn't receive an answer. She went out back to the barn all the horses were in their stalls. She went back into the house going through calling Harry, even upstairs she opened the bedroom doors looking for him. She had the house to herself.

Becky Lou went quietly up to the attic, she walked very carefully watching where she placed her feet on the dusty floor. She hunted for any papers regarding the beginnings of the plantation. She turned the light on, the attic was dusty and smelled of old antiquated junk. Nevertheless, she wore rubber gloves as she poked through boxes, books, and under old clothing, and piles of junk. Then, she saw a locked chest sitting in a corner with old newspapers piled on top. She removed the newspapers and with a hairpin managed to open the chest, inside she found Harry V. Brown's original plans and a map of the plantation with dates written on it, she took the plans and map. Before placing the newspapers back on top of the chest she very carefully flipped through them. To her surprise, the dates went all the way back to 1864 up to Harry's death. She kept the newspaper that had an interview with Harry telling the press that he's turning his land into a museum for future generations.

A newspaper dated in 1876, had a front-page article with a picture of her uncle Drew, he told the press due to his father's murder by one of his employees the museum was off. "And they believed him?" Becky asked out loud. The article stated that Harry paid his freedmen and women lots of money thereby making them rich coloreds. The author of the article wrote, *"no other plantation owner was kinder and gentler than Harry V. Brown, a generous man who loved his country."*

She dug deeper in the chest and felt keys, she took everything out and saw keys that were on separate chins. Each key had a tag stating the gate it unlocked. She took one each, Becky Lou kept a couple of the newspaper articles, one of them was written by Harry's son, Charles.

Becky Lou realized that she had been in the attic longer than plan. She took one of Harry's plans with the keys and put everything back, being unable to lock the trunk she hid the lock by stacking newspapers in front of the chest, and then quickly left.

She dashed outside and got into her 2017 Mercedes-Benz AMG GT and drove off with her findings. She drove to the train station, which since the 1800s had been modernized and were beautiful, there was a huge picture of H.B. Brown hanging on one of the walls. Becky Lou chose a large locker to put the things she found in the attic, she locked the newspaper articles and other items in the locker, she took the keys and Harry's plans to Mrs. Paddleton.

Becky Lou went back to the plantation house, pulled in the driveway, this time Harry's car was there, she entered the house, and yelled, "Harry!"

"Stop yelling," he said, then asked, "Why are you here?"

"My weekend to watch the kiddos for Helen."

Harry bent over in pain.

"Is there something I can do for you?" Asked Becky Lou.

He flipped his finger at her, "go away," he said.

Downstairs Charles had a half bath built; his wife called it the powder room. Harry walked down the hallway to the bathroom, he said loudly, "I'm watching you."

Becky Lou watched him disappear out of her sight as he closed the bathroom door. She sat in the drawing-room to wait for him to return. When he did, he laid down on the couch. Becky said, "I'll call you mother, and let myself in the gates."

"For your information Aunt busy body, dad and mom are on their way. Dad will let you in."

Becky Lou stood staring at Harry, she looked so sad, Harry asked, "Auntie, what's wrong?"

She could say nothing about Harriett's murder, Becky felt that her brother and his wife next target, was their son, due to his behavior with one of the slaves. She knew if she said anything, Harry would run and tell his parents, then she would be next. She said, "nephew, this has been the longest two weeks of my life."

In the slave area, Helen was excited, she was going to the bar with Lee and Fanny, plus she had four cupcakes, one of her pockets were full of candy for Lillie, and the other had the note for Lee. Becky Lou had demanded the overseers get Helen and the sweet treats to the slave quarters safely. Helen had never been in the bar; Mr. Charles had told her to stay away because it would not be good for the children. Becky Lou's free spirit had rubbed off on Helen, she decided to go despite Charles, and if Bo hit her, she was going to punch him back.

Helen felt like she was part of a big secret. She had no idea what the message on the note meant, but it made her walk proud and tall. Helen planned to do something she had never done in her life, get drunk.

XXIX

Smarter Than

March 15, 2017

Wednesday morning, soft warm air stirred smells of sweet honeysuckle, the aroma swirled ambiance of tranquility through the southern gentle wind. On that beautiful day, Donovan's plan to run through their neighborhood and meet people worked. Their neighbors sat on their porch waiting for them to run past when they did, they waved and yelled a friendly, "hello."

Many would say with a big smile on their face and in their voice, "nice day for a run."

Donovan and Theenda replied with a friendly wave and smile. Then there were those that stood by the gate waiting for the couple to stop and chit chat a bit before running on. The young people became their neighbors' favorite couple.

After their morning run, they showered and dressed for work, Theenda ate a bowl of oatmeal, Donovan poured himself a cup of coffee and said, "I haven't seen Haze since the cookout, did you speak to Tess?"

"No, it's like they both fell off the planet."

Donovan replied saying, "hum, we have a meeting in a few days, wonder if he will come?"

Laughing Theenda said, "he's probably mad at both of us for beating him senseless."

Donovan said as he sipped his coffee, "what if he's telling the truth, it's not him."

Theenda got up from the table, rinsed her bowl before putting it in the dishwasher, then said, "honestly Sweetie, I believe him. Before Tess, he was happy, played with the kids, he is actually kid like himself."

"How do you know this?"

"My first week at the school, Haze purchased basketballs and hoops age appropriate for the little kids and the fourth and fifth graders, he taught them how to play. He donated money to the middle and high schools."

"You're right Baby Girl, he bought their uniforms, I was told he attended all the school games but stopped when he got married."

Theenda said, "Tess is the cause he's trying to rid himself of."

****

Haze went to see Breeze at the business address. Sitting in Breeze office, Haze was still angry at the Bright's. He thought, "who invites a person to their home, see they are in pain, beat them anyway because they believe a slut over the truth." For that reason, he was planning on him and Breeze setting the slaves free before Easter and leave Tess to be Donovan's problem. He believed he was being smarter than Donovan.

Breeze asked Haze, "what happened to your face?"

The swelling on Haze's nose was going down, but it was taking longer for the bruises to totally leave. Haze said, "stupid happened," pointing to his face, he continued, "this is not the reason I'm here." He leaned forward and whispered. "I know where there are slaves."

"You found slaves in 2017, where? I can use extra money; did you hear about the roof caving in."

"In one of the malls?" Haze answered with a question.

"Yeah, the Browns may charge me for the cave in." Breeze sat back and took over the meeting, he said, "if you're telling the truth, tell me where the slaves are, I was born and raised in this town, you were not. I never heard of slaves being here, you claim you have, my family built most of these buildings in this town, I am important in this town. There's gotta be a lot of money to keep me-ah-us quiet about slaves in 2017."

"I'm not saying where or anything, we have to keep it hush-hush. No money will exchange hands." Haze realized he had made a mistake telling Breeze.

"I'd swear on a stack of Bibles if I had one, I will not tell a soul. Where are they? I know the person is rich, we can get rich also."

Haze asked wonderingly, "no, no money is involved. Our pay is helping others."

Breeze smiled as he said, "I don't need you; I will find them, I will get the money."

When Haze got up to leave, Breeze let out a haunting laugh as he said, "it's the Browns, no one seemed to know where they are."

****

Lillie and some of the older women were quilting. Glaidous and the older men were making furniture on the road that separated Charles and Drew Road, while at the same time the younger slaves were in the tobacco field. Usually, in the slaves' area, a yellow hew hovered above, the reason being they cooked, washed, played outside, their toilets were outdoors, and the many dirt paths kicked up a lot of dust. On that Wednesday morning, the winds had blown the yellow away. The sky was blue, not bluish yellow, the clouds were white, not beige, the air was clear, not dusty. Life was motionless, hushed, and bittersweet.

Lillie felt an uneasiness stirring about, she said to the women, "something don't feel right dis' mornin."

She got up, stepped off the porch, and looked in the direction of Massa house, she saw nothing. When she returned to the porch she said, "I's thank young Massa be' a-comin' ta do somethin' awful."

Sophie remarked, "Lillie you thank dat cause you's' thankin' bout' yesta'day at church. Massa Charles a good man, he got no grudge."

Lillie looked at Sophie and said, "sometimes I thank you have no brain in yo' head, why you trust Massa wid' all he do to us?"

"One of the slave women pause in her stitching, and commented, "Don't say that to Sophie, she bein' yo' sista' in-law."

Sophie had a downcast look on her face, her shoulders slumped, she sighed a long deep breath before saying, "young Massa ain't gonna' bother nobody, he a good man."

Lillie frowned at Sophie with unpalatable displeasure before she said, "shh, somebody comin."

Sophie looked at Lillie in a kindly way, and said, "dat's yo' mind, you's still thankin' bout young Massa..."

Before Sophie could finish, Harry and the two overseers appeared on horseback.

That morning Harry woke up displeased with his life, the plantation, and his parents. He tried to call Harriett; her phone was out of service. He wanted to take his frustration out on someone, he thought about Lillie, he said to himself, "she prances around the plantation like she's boss." Before leaving the mansion, he grabbed a bottle of liquor and left. He went to the overseers' cabin, they all got drunk, especially the overseers and their women because they were accustomed to watered-down liquor.

Harry and the overseers galloped in a drunken stupor to the slave quarter. While Lillie was looking for them, they were already in the tobacco field. As she returned to the porch and sat down, the three men had left the tobacco field and galloped towards town.

Harry sat high on his horse angrily looking down at Lillie, she turned her head away from Harry. She looked at Sophie, and said, "good man with no grudge, I feel sorry for you old fool."

Harry climbed down off his horse, and said, "ready for your beating?" He looked at the overseers and told them to take Lillie to the whipping tree. They grabbed Lillie, she tried to struggle away, but their grip got tighter.

Lillie angrily looked at Roy and Fred and said, "let me go, I's walk by myself."

The two men let her go.

Harry pulled out his whip and cracked it in the air as he followed close behind the overseers and Lillie. Without the overseers holding on to her, Lillie walked tall and strong with the knowledge that she was going to meet a walk-about, and one day be a walk-about. She smiled as she leaned against the whipping tree determined not to make a whimper, she refused to give Harry the satisfaction. Lillie thought only of the pictures in the Essence Magazine.

LaVaughn

The women, except Sophie, scattered, some ran out to the field to tell Lee and the other slaves. Another woman went in search of Glaidous. While the women were running around to get help for Lillie, Sophia did nothing. She stayed in the slave town and continued to work on the quilt.

****

While minor warfare brewed on the plantation, Breeze was at the police station, hoping to get half a million dollars for hush money, that would help him out. He proudly strutted into the police station, like regal Clydesdale's high stepping in the fourth of July parade. He demanded the secretary to get the Chief of Police.

She looked at him and asked, "who're you?"

"Never mind who I am," when she did not move, Breeze yelled loud, "get the chief, now!"

She quickly went to the chief office, returning with her was Gideon he said, "you frighten my secretary, I don't like that."

Breeze didn't apologize to the secretary, he said to the Chief, "I know about the Brown family going against the government by harboring slaves."

"I know of no such thing."

"You do know something, I see it in your eyes, I want in."

Gideon said, "slavery is over."

"Then pay me to keep my mouth shut."

"I'll go and check it out," the chief said.

"How do you know where to go?"

"I know, get back with me the day after tomorrow, if they have slaves, you'll get your money." The chief told his secretary to get one of his deputies to write up a contract, he looked at Breeze and asked, "mind waiting."

"No, do what you have to do."

"How much are you asking for?"

"Half mill."

"I'm on it."

Before leaving the Chief asked, "whose working with you?"

All But One

Breeze thought a moment before claiming, "I work alone, Chief. I got the history from working on the Brown family Mini Malls."

"Well young man, you will get paid in full."

The Chief entered his office with the secretary behind him. Breeze waited with a huge smile on his face, he was filled with greed which caused a dark foggy cloud to block his thinking. He walked into the police station, without a plan, demanding money. Fortunately, for Haze, Breeze money hoggishness saved his life. Ogville's Chief of Police called MacCall's Chief Stevens. He told Stevens about Breeze demands.

Stevens asked, "why did he come to you?"

"He's a hot head."

"I'll take care of it," Stevens said.

Gideon told Breeze that Chief Stevens want to meet with him in MacCall, "that's where you'll get paid," Gideon said with humor in his voice.

When Breeze left, the Chief secretary asked, "what slaves Sir?"

"The ones in that cocky man's head."

****

On the plantation, the slaves ran from the tobacco field towards the slave area. One of the overseers saw them coming, he ran towards the opening of the gate to close and lock it, but the slaves beat him to the opening. They ran inside their area. Both Roy and Fred had their whip out slicing in the air, Roy yelled, "git' back to work, git' back to work!"

Lee shouted back, "not without my mama."

As Harry raised his whip, he said, "you disrespected my dad in the house of God." His whip came across Lillie's back.

Lillie stood strong; she did not make a sound. Harry raised the whip again, Lee was quicker, when Harry was coming down to give Lillie the second lash, Lee grabbed the whip out of Harry's hands and said, "not ta' day." He threw the whip down.

The slaves stood by Lee. Harry pulled out his gun, Jethro a great big man-dingo built slave, chest wider than the whipping tree, arms bigger than the biggest branch, he was as tall as the highest limb, he said, "it gonna' takes' moe dan' dat' pistol' ta' kill me."

Harry jumped on his horse and galloped away.

Sophie had stopped sewing, she went to Lillie, but was pushed away. Another woman knocked Sophie down, then put her arm around Lillie and said, "come on Lillie, let's get ja' home."

Glaidous went to Lillie and asked, "yous' okay lil' sis." He looked at Sophia, "I's stayin at my sista' house ta'night." He watched Harry galloping quickly away and then said, "you can stay wid' him. Go on afta' him. You luv' him so much."

Lee looked at Roy and Fred and asked, "whad" ja' gonna do?"

Fred answered and said, "Lee, we's won't's off dis' place just like you, we's goin' to our shack and git' some rest."

"Ain't ja' goin' ta' lock da slave gate?" Lee asked.

Roy looked in the direction of Harry galloping away and said, "he took our key."

Jethro stared up at the sky, it was about two o'clock, he asked, "iffen' we take ta'day' off and sleep early, you's tell Massa."

"Iffen, we's did dat,' we's git' in trouble wid' ja'," Fred answered.

Roy and Fred left. The Slaves stood watching the two men slowly trot away. Lee said more to himself, "dey's tied' as we."

Bo decided to take over, he yelled, "git back ta' work!" He raised his whip and cracked it in the air.

Jethro calmly walked up to Bo, took the whip threw it on the ground, with one punch knocked Bo out cold, and said, "shut up fool."

Lee turned around and yelled out, "everybody, get good rest ta'night,' somethin' we's ain't neva had."

The slaves went to their cabins.

****

Chief Stevens drove up to the hidden driveway of the Brown's mansion, parked his car, went up to the mansion and rang the doorbell. Charles greeted the chief at the front door, "hot-dog lookie' here whom the cat dropped in."

The chief looking nervous, said, "Sir. I have bad news."

"Come in, have a seat."

All But One

Becky Lou was there visiting she stood outside the closed double doors to listen. She heard the chief say, "a saxophone player named Breeze, he works for you. He's snooping around your family history."

Mr. Brown slid back in his chair in dismay, and asked, "my family? There were others who snooped around, asking questions in Ogville, but they were taken care of." He stood and paced. Charles looked at the chief, and said, "they have to be silenced, get on it."

"Sir. Breeze has a little friend named Haze."

"Him too."

Chief Stevens said, "he has a wife that he uses as a punching bag. The high school history teacher got wind of Haze beating on his wife, well Sir, his little wife knows judo."

Charles laughed as he said, "she kicked Haze all over their backyard."

Both men laughed hard.

"Wait," Charles said while laughing, "and then the history teacher got in on the action, he beat Haze so bad," Steven and Charles laughed so hard tears rolled down their cheeks as Charles continued, "when the teacher finished with him, he had twelve stitches in his face, a splint on his broken nose."

Stevens said still laughing, "Oh Lord have mercy, we need him on our team."

Charles said, "husband and wife tag team."

The two men laughed and talked about Donovan and Theenda for another ten minutes.

All their lives the slaves wanted to fight back, yell out their true feelings, but they lacked the courage to stand. For the first time in their lives, Lee and the slaves stood bold and unafraid of Harry and the overseers, during Lillie's beating. Only a few slaves knew about the Essence Magazine and Donovan, but a change was taking place on the plantation. Talking to Lillie and Lee, Glaidous said, "it be da' mar-ja-zine, it bring a good spirit."

At three o'clock that evening, the slave area was quiet, even Bo was fast asleep. The next morning, they were up, working, and singing at four 'clock.

Charles had come to the mansion to stay the night since he could not reach Harry on the landline or his cell phone. He figured Harry was out with his friends getting drunk. When Harry entered the house Charles was up, Harry began fussing about the slaves, he blamed everything on them. When Harry emptied his pant pockets, he had both keys to the gates, he realized the gates were unlocked.

Charles snatched the key out of Harry's hands, ran to the garage got his motorbike, both outer and the divider gates were unlocked. As Charles went through, he locked the gates. Then Charles road at breakneck speed to the overseers' cabins, their women were home. They told Charles that the men had left only five minutes ago. Charles got one of the horses ready to ride, Roy looked around and saw Charles galloping towards him and Fred. When he caught up with the men, Charles said, "hello fellows, don't know what we'll find today. Harry left their gate opened."

Roy said, "I trust them, Sir."

When the overseers and Charles arrived in the slave compound, they were surprised to find the slaves in the field working and singing. It was a peaceful site. The overseers no longer locked the slave gate the day Harry raped Bo; they knew the slaves were trustworthy. "After all," Roy said to Fred one day, "they nor we can get out."

Six of the older slave women were on the general store porch quilting and humming. Lillie looked up and saw the three men sitting high on their horses, looking at them through the slave gate, she looked back down and continued sewing, she said, "funny what a little rest will do for you."

Charles handed Roy the key and said, "I guess they can be trusted." He went home.
Roy looked at Fred and asked, "where would they go?"
Fred asked, "as you said, how will they get out?"

On the general store porch, Sophie tried to join the women, she said, "Lillie I's sorry bout' Massa Harry, I should be der' fo' ya."

The women and Lillie continued to hum and sew.
Sophie said, "I's won't ta' help." She sat on the steps.
One of the ladies said. "Sophie, go else whars."

XXX

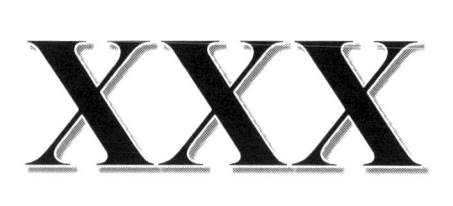

Harry's Prayer

March 26, 2017

Once or twice a month, Charles and Harry II officiated the slave church services. Normally Charles preached but for this service, Harry had prepared a sermon and Charles was proud, he imagined that his son was coming around. "Maybe," Charles mumbled to himself, "he'll travel with us." Charles clapped his hands once and claimed, "yes, we'll see the world together as a family." The slaves preferred Glaidous because he spoke on hope and a closer walk with Jesus. Charles sermons were more about the slaves behaving, he referred to them as ignorant stupid things, that should obey him and his son.

Harry V. Brown II stood on the pulpit trying to look important, or godly, he was nervous about giving his first sermon. Harry watched his father lead out, his suit fitted him perfect, hair was flawless, his skin was bronzed, Charles like his namesake had a velvet voice. Harry II, on the other hand, walked stooped over, his clothes did not fit, his hair was unkempt, he had pimples the size of a small rock, his speech was muffled. Harry II would have been a big disappointment to his namesake, Harry V. Brown I.

Charles stood on the pulpit directing his favorite song, *Bringing In the Sheaves*. He sang the song fast with a lot of energy. Most of the slaves mumbled the verse, "bringin' in da' sheep." A few of them sung loud, tasteless, wrong, and hardy when it came to the course they sang, "bringin' in da' sheep, bringin' in da' sheep, ye shall come rejoicin' bringin', innnnn, daaa' sheeeepssss."

But no one sang as energetic and dogmatic as Charles Brown, his baritone voice boomed all over the plantation, he slowed the song down to put emphasis on, "bringing innnnn, thaaa' sheeeep" and then quickly jump back in the verse singing vivaciously. Charles loved the Cosby show, but his dance steps and bouncing on stage as he sang and directed was more like George Jefferson on The Jefferson TV show.

When song service was over the slaves sat down, Charles out of breath said, "on this fine morning, my son Harry V. Brown II has prepared an excellent sermon for your wicked souls." He looked around at his son and continued, "Harry come stand by me." This is my baby boy, all of you know him, but you never heard him speak God's word. He's graduated from college; this is where white people go to become good teachers and leaders of this country. We learn to be good and kind Massa of poor people. slaves have it good. Most Massa's have their slaves live in a small gate and one room shacks, you have a big huge house and lots of lands."

"Tell em' paw," Harry encouraged his dad.

"You have a store, this beautiful church, a club to hold parties." Charles smiled at the slaves before saying, "you have it good, there are slaves out there that want to come and work for me because they've heard how good it is here." He gave Harry a pat on the back, as he said, "preach the word son."

The tired slaves, quietly sat as their minds took a stroll down memory lane, Saul's beating, Lee's beating, Lillie's, a young teen tied to the whipping tree and given forty lashes. The slave's faces were bitter sour at the thought of hearing Harry's voice.

"I'm not in the mood foe' this, not today, not tomorrow, or any other day," Lillie whispered to Rita, who was sitting next to her.

Harry gave his dad a hug, and said, "thank you paw," he turned to the slaves, and continued, "I hear that most of you insist on pretending to be sick, many of you are sloppy workers, that's why you get beatings. You ain't nothing but a bunch of lazy, thankless slobs. My family tries to teach you to be hardworking slaves. We clothe you, give you food, a nice place to live, raise-teach-train-develop your children so you don't have the hardship, that's our God-given duty."

Bo yelled out, "speak the truf" Massa, dey' lazy.

A slave woman softly muttered, "I's wanna' raise my own baby."

All But One

Harry yelled on, "It is white man duty to serve God and listen to what He tells us to do, God talks to us, He tells us how to take care of you, our property. That's why you live good, it's our duty. When we the whites, are blessed, then slave be live good."

Rita mumbled to Lillie, "talkin' bout' God, a few days ago he raped Bo."

"Sho'nuff' did," said Lillie, "I's don't thank' God approved."

Bo yelled out, "preach Massa, we lib' good."

Harry picked up his Bible and waved it in the air, he screamed, "the Bible says that your Massa is your divine being on this earth, we are your god, you must obey your Massa, work hard..."

Before he finished Lillie stood up and challenged Harry, "sho' me in da' Good Book where dat' be found."

Harry turned three shades of red, his face got so tight the slaves saw the outline of his jawbone.

Another slave kept seated but yelled out, "sho' me too Massa."

Harry slammed his Bible down on the podium, and uttered in a loud shrilling tone, "sit down woman, y'all be quiet."

Lillie said softly, "but Massa, I's' just wanna' read it foe' me."

A host of other slaves mumbled that they wanted to see that scripture.

Charles jumped up and said, "do not interrupt my son! He is preaching the word of God, you pathetic things, listen, learn, and obey what the Lord has to say."

Lee, sitting on the other side of Lillie, tugged on the back of Lillie's dress and said, "sit down mama a 'foe' you get beat."

With eyes steady on Lillie, Harry pushed his paw to the side, and agreed with Lee, "listen to your son, or I will flog you in God's house, with God watching. God in his loving mercy cain't teach or tame you heathens." He irritably looked at the slaves and said, "my daddy cain't tame you, Jesus cain't domesticate you. God gave me the power, to turn you worthless things into a human, I can, and I will. I, your lord and Massa, I will beat the devil out of all y'all."'

Charles said, "preach son, let the Word of God use you."

Sophie was sitting on the other side of the church next to Glaidous, she nervously said out loud, "only you can train us heathens, young Massa."

Glaidous kicked her foot. She rolled her eyes at him.

Harry continued to preach, "I am your inspired word from God above, don't ever question my authority again. Let us pray. When I pray, bow your heads and close your eyes." As he prayed, he held his arms outstretched and eyes opened to watch his property, they all had their eyes closed and heads bowed.

Harry prayed a prayer that angered the slaves, Harry's prayer, "Lord let these slaves obey their Massa, let them be glad that we are good to them, help them to give their evil savage hearts to my dad and me, we are their god. Help them to believe in their Massa words, follow their Massa instructions. Let these infidels obey my dad and my instructions, then they will be happy content slaves for their Massa, and not be like wild animals running free. Lord help dad and I train these wild beasts like the caretaker's train apes in a zoo. Lord plant in their satanic hearts the knowledge that you're my God, and I am theirs. Help these stumbling ungrateful sinners to truly love their Massa.

Lord God of Heaven, bless my family with richness, make us powerful, bless my family with good health, bless my family with joy, happiness, peace, and love. Guide my father to be a good god to these pagans, a good father to me, and husband to his wife. Thank you, Lord, for the financial and health blessings that you have bestowed upon my family. Amen."

Charles stood next to his son, and said, "hum-um-hum, that was a powerful sincere prayer son, didn't know you had it in you." He looked at the slaves and commented, "wasn't that the best sermon and prayer you ever heard?" He clapped his hands in praise, "glory to God, son, that was the best prayer I ever heard."

Bo yelled out, "ya' Sir Massa, best sermon, and prayer I's' eva' heard."

Sophie agreed, "ya' Sir. Massa."

The other slaves were full of anger and hate, they sat quiet and waited to be dismissed. Charles and Harry stood in the doorway of the church, Charles said, "you may leave now." He and Harry waited outside the church, to hear the slave's response as they exited the church. It was always Bo and Rita that walked up to them and claim, "dat be good service Massa."

All But One

Charles wanted the other slaves to compliment his sermons, but none never did. That Sunday he smiled and thought, *yea, I'll burn them all, their nothing but ungrateful things.* He looked at Harry and said, "let's go."

Outside Glaidous found Lillie, Rita, and Lee talking, he walked up to them, and said, "God cain't answer dat' prayer."

Lee laughing said, unk, you sinner, Massa prayed to God ta' bless hes famly, and curse us wild heathens."

Glaidous put his hand on Lees' shoulders, and through laughter said, "Shut-up you stumblin' ungrateful sinner."

Harry and his father walked past Lillie; Harry stared at her with contempt. The two men untied their horses that were tied to the stores' porch banister. Glaidous said to Lillie, "Massa gonna git' you iffen you don't be quiet."

"So, dey will," Lillie said with anger in her voice.

Watching father and son gallop home side by side, Glaidous continued, "well, der' go's our gods."

Lillie said, "so dey' say."

On their way to the plantation house, Harry was quiet. But Charles happy, he declared, "son you did a good job preaching."

Harry sat in silence, his inside was seething, his blood boiled above the normal 98.6 degrees, if it were possible, his father would see steam erupting from his ears, nose, and mouth.

Later that day, Harry's parents were in the castle sitting room. He entered, they were snuggled together, Harry saw them and got mad, "something needs to be done about Lillie," fell out Harry's tight lips.

Charles candidly said, "she was just mouthing off like she always does, I'll talk to her. Now go away."

But Harry wasn't accepting a wave of the hand dismissal, he wanted to beat Lillie until the rage within him had subsided. Harry lashed out at his father, "paw one day I will be the Massa of this plantation, I will handle Lillie my way. She struts around like she's a queen."

Charles stood, his wife blocked the door, Charles said, "Lillie wanted you to show her where it says the Lord is our God and we are theirs." He turned and began to leave then turned back and said, "we can't show them because it's not in the Bible. The fact that they want to read the verse, is quite funny when I think about it."

Harry said loudly, "So where does it say white folk rule over all the earth," if it were possible Harry's shouts would cause the walls to expand, he screamed, "the bible says no such thing! You've been on this stinking plantation so long dad; you believe that you're God's chosen one. Here's a news flash pop, you ain't!"

Barbara looked at her husband, he looked rattled, she glared at Harry, who had seen that look before. It frightened him. Even so, Harry turned towards his mother and boldly had the audacity to say, "this doesn't concern you, maw, the men in this family effectively run this place without the assistance of women."

Charles grabbed his son by the shoulders and slammed him against the wall, Harry said, "get your hand off me old man."

Charles grip tightens as he said, "You disgrace this family, sleeping with that savage beast Bo, a slave. If you weren't my son, I'd put you out there in the field with those slaves or make you a servant like your poor pathetic aunt Becky Lou. Using your words, news flash, I've never said we're their god, those were *your* words, not mine."

Harry shouted, "You, old fool, you can't see we're no better than the slaves, this family was disgraced in 1865, when Harry V. Brown set this mess up, tomorrow Lillie will learn to respect me."

Charles let Harry go and gave a quick glance at his wife.

When Harry walked towards his mother, she slapped him hard, then pushed him down on the couch. She said, "Since you come home, this plantation is rolling downhill faster than a rock heaved down the side of a mountain."

Charles took a breath before calmly saying, "it's time for you to leave while you're still breathing."

Harry stood and said, "don't worry 'bout it old man, I never wanted the job anyway." He slammed the door shut as he left. Outside he got in his car and drove like a crazed person away from the castle.

Barbara asked, "what're we to do?"

Charles answered, "I wish I knew that history teacher in Ogville."

"He'd be a good choice; I saw the man he knocked around." Barbara smiled after remembering Haze face.

Charles said, "he's going to Harriett's."

"Well, he's in for a rude awakening."

"Yes, he is," Charles said. He turned to his wife and said, "keep an eye on him."

Barbara said, "done." She left out of the room.

Charles called his older brother Sam, who was a poverty-stricken accountant. Sam's wife was diagnosed with breast cancer when she was pregnant with their son Ranch. His wife cancer went in and out of remission six times, when Ranch turned thirteen, he was diagnosed with cancer of the colon. Sam's wife died when their son turned twenty and Ranch lived to his thirtieth birthday. Medical bills had eaten up Sam's money. He was living alone in a dilapidated house. Charles normally had nothing to do with him, he had forgotten that his brother existed.

When Charles called, Sam jumped at the chance to leave. He packed his bags, put the house up for sale, and moved in the plantation house. Charles paid Sam's medical and all other bills, he bought his brother a 2017 Honda.

When Sam learned of the plantation and took over, Charles and the slaves noticed things had gotten better and their lives improved. Their work schedule changed. Monday through Friday they worked from six in the morning to four in the evening with a half hour break, Saturday, from six in the morning to noon with no breaks, and Sunday from one o'clock to five in the evening with no breaks. Though they worked seven days per week, they were working fifteen hours less. With more rest the slaves' production was greater in every job they performed, from the quilts the women made, the detailed design on the furniture was astounding, and the tobacco grew bigger and in a greater abundance.

Charles notated hiring his brother was his greatest and worst decision, his company charge more for the cigars, but the furniture, and quilts as well, he was making millions. Sam was not used to money and power, he began to drink, in town he gloated about his money and mansion. Charles was afraid that one day he would talk about the plantation. He looked at his wife and said, "Sam's gotta go."

****

Harry II

Harry discovered that his sister and her boyfriend's family was shot to death, he knew his parents were responsible. Over the years, Harry II, had killed several people associated with the plantation, and now he believed his mother was after him, he was running scared.

Harry knew when his dad got angry, his mom handled it, when he needed someone eliminated, she knew whom to call to get the job done. So, when Harry yelled at her husband, she slapped him good and hard. After Harry left slamming the door, he heard his mom ask his dad, "want me to take care of him."

Harry did not stop to gather his personal items; he ran fast as he could from his parents.

Barbara was a loyal wife, Charles saved her from poverty, sent her to a city college where she got her GED and an Associate Degree in accounting. On graduation day, she marched proud and happy. When it came to protecting Charles, no one was safe, not even her children.

Harry drove north, during his travels he noticed the further he got away from the plantation his anger was beginning to subside. At home, he'd traveled to Titleburk and back to MacCall, one time he visited Ogville. The further away he got, he noticed that people dressed different, looked different, talked differently, they appeared to be happy. Sitting in a hotel room, he realized he had been using his card and if his mother wanted to follow him, she could and would. "Oh, my goodness," Harry said out loud, "they can block my bank account."

The very next morning Harry went to the store and purchased an attaché case and legal-size manila envelopes, he went to the bank and closed out his account, he was a millionaire, so he had no worries financially. He changed his name to Jeff Brown. His ID had Harry Vincent Brown, so he slipped the teller two one-hundred-dollar bills, to allow him to close his bank account. Harry stayed at the hotel for two weeks, under the name

All But One

Jeff. Out of the million, Jeff kept fifty thousand for living expenses until he settled down, the rest he kept locked in the attaché case.

Harry's anger tapered off, he learned to break away from his family and the belief that he was a god. He thought about his first and last sermon, he fell on his knees and prayed, "Lord I am sorry for everything I did and said, Father I am no god and don't want to be, please forgive me. Amen."

Charles had gotten himself, wife, and kid's passports just in case they would have to leave the country in a hurry. Jeff kept his passport in the car glove compartment, he had two more years before it needed to be renewed. He drove to Windsor, Canada, purchased a computer and became friends with a young woman his age. Within a month he moved in with her, he was the dutiful boyfriend that bought her things, he took her out to dinner, paid her bills, and made her happy.

Jeff had a plan. He got a safety security box at a local bank and opened a bank account under the name, Jeff Brown. One day when his girlfriend left for work, he aimlessly went through her things not really knowing what he was looking for, but he would know when he found it. Their third week together he found her birth certificate, that was it. Jeff took a picture of it with his phone, and before leaving he went to her landlord and paid three months' rent, she didn't have a computer, he bought her a new laptop, and then drove to Toronto, Canada. The day he arrived, he went to a library and created a birth certificate like the image on his phone. except for Harry, had himself born as Jeffery Brown in Windsor Canada.

He stayed in a five-star hotel, he purchased a printer and paper like the birth certificate his girlfriend had. Jeff went back to the hotel got on his computer and hacked into a hospital website and created his existence as a Canadian. Online he registered to vote on the Elections Canada Office website.

It looked as though twenty-five-year-old Jeffery Brown was born a Canadian Citizen. He moved to Nova Scotia where he landed a job working as an IT technician. He bought a luxury condo, furnishings, a new sports car, and clothes. Jeff had his father's business savvy; he invested and saved his money. Jeff deduced that he could pay himself sixty thousand per year for twenty-six years, along with his salary he could live a very prosperous life. But twenty-six years was not that long, he tried to figure out what to do, he even attempted different money-making ventures. Then one-day Jeff met a man that told him how he became rich with a mop and broom. Harry started a janitorial service, he trained his workers the art of cleaning, he held seminars on good work ethics, he paid for his employees to take behavioral attitude classes.

Harry, on the plantation, had been a mean dogmatic unruly human being. He walked stooped over, rarely combed his hair, he drank heavier-than-necessary and purchased his drugs from the people that worked on the other tobacco field.

The new and improved Harry did not smoke, drink, or took drugs. Jeff remembered that Harriet had asked him about the rape, he was so strung out on drugs he did not remember the day. As a matter of fact, he said to himself, "I don't remember too much about what I did on the plantation." Harry was always drunk or drugged. His family believed he preferred men since he never dated a female, he had never dated anyone due to lack of confidence, the stagnation of his life, and always high or intoxicated.

Jeffery (Jeff) Brown, on the other hand, was smart, energetic, and charismatic, he simply imitated his father's distinctive personality and good qualities. He copied the way Charles carried himself, his smooth velvety voice without the southern accent, and Charles classic dress. One morning before leaving for work, Jeff caught a glance of himself in the mirror. He appeared to be taller than he remembered and had his father's handsome looks, except he had changed, he loved his life, he was at peace, and for the first time happy, it all glowed on his face.

Jeff stood back and looked at his full self, "hum," he thought out loud, his clothes were loose because he was thin. Jeff joined a gym to change his physical structure to match the new him.

****

Months of Planning, weeks of meetings, sleepless nights, it was the night before Easter. In less than twenty-four hours, three men were going to meet, one hundred and fifty-two years since slavery supposing ended, slaves.

Donovan held their last meeting in his home. Timpkin said, "Donovan, I don't know about you, but I am nervous."

Donovan ignored Timpkin and said to Haze, "you told Breeze, why?"

"I was mad, you and Thee beat the crap out of me, even though I was in obvious pain."

"Wait, hold up," KayKay began, "when did this happen?" she asked.

Timpkin ignored his wife, and asked Haze, "that's the reason you've missed meetings? You told Breeze?"

Theenda said, "Sweetie, I thought we were supposed to keep this quiet."

"Exactly," Donovan said looking angry at Haze.

Haze said, "okay, I was being defiant, I got beat up, blamed for Tess' face, I thought, hum, Breeze and I would free the slaves."

KayKay asked, "what happened to your face?"

Tess said, "he beat me."

"I did not." Haze said.

In his defense, one of Haze employees was at the club the night Tess got in a fight with a woman. When he learned what happened to Haze, he took him to the club, where Haze spoke with the woman, before leaving he gave the woman money to cover her medical bill.

Haze looked at Donovan and told him about Tess fight.

Tess denied it vehemently. Theenda said, "I'll call the bar."

Haze said, "yes please, they will confirm I speak the truth."

Donovan said, "Baby Girl make the call." To Timpkin and Haze, he asked, "are your bookbags packed and ready to go? We're leaving out early in the morning."

KayKay answered, "yes, I packed Timpkin's bag."

"I'll buy one and pack tonight," Haze said sheepishly.

The look on Theenda's face when she got off the phone, alerted Donovan that Haze may have told the truth.

Theenda hung the phone up and said to Haze, "we have extra bookbags, I'll pack you one."

Tess said, "well Haze, be happy someone care because I don't."

The room went quiet, Donovan said looking at Theenda, "Baby Girl."

Theenda confirmed, "he's telling the truth."

Tess went berserk, she pushed Theenda, swung at Haze but stumbled and missed, she hit Timpkin. Donovan and Timpkin physically put her out, Tess was screaming, swearing and kicking, Tess got in her car, and drove to Haze's home. She was going to break in, but an officer was in the vicinity of the neighborhood Haze lived in. She saw Haze house and the police, Tess turned around and pretended to leave the area.

When Donovan and Timpkin literally tossed Tess out the house, KayKay captured the whole thing on her phone. She texted six church ladies, who were her close friends, the pictures. The seven agreed to have Easter dinner together after Sunday service. KayKay was not stupid, unlike Haze she knew to keep her mouth shut about slaves, but everything else was good gossiping news.

After Donovan and Timpkin finished throwing Tess out, Haze asked thoughtfully, "tomorrow we're going to maybe see slaves that are locked behind a gate, we're out here, are we free?"

Donovan asked, "is anyone free?" He answered himself when he said, "I think only pure white people."

Theenda asked, "is any white American whose family was here during slavery pure white?"

Haze asked still seeking an answer, "are we free."

KayKay smacked her lips and arrogantly began speaking, "Thee that's the most uneducated thing I've ever heard anyone say."

Theenda shot kay a Queen Kung look then seethe, "shut up worthless excuse of a human being. Not one word from you." The room grew quiet, if King Kung was there, he would have swung away.

Flashback of their experience with racism stood noiseless in their memory. KayKay, on the other hand, slithered back in her chair, her neck disappeared between her shoulders that was bent forward. She looked at Theenda with soft sorrowful eyes like a puppy in trouble. In a teary whisper said, "I'm sorry." She looked at Haze and said, "no, not completely free."

XXXI

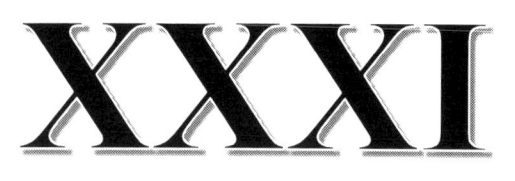

Easter Sunday

April 16, 2017

It was a dark gray early Sunday morning, puffy gray clouds hovered over Ogville. Donovan said as he opened the bedroom curtains, "I was hoping the sun would shine today.

"It still may," Theenda said as she combed her hair. She continued, "we need to get out to the car everyone will be arriving soon." As they were going down the steps Theenda said, "I wish I was going."

"You would not like it," Donovan said as they entered the kitchen, he continued, "you don't like walking through woods or the creepy things that live there."

Tess was the first to arrive, wearing the same clothes as the night before. Theenda opened the door, Tess walked in and said, "they threw me in jail last night. I just got out, came straight here."

Theenda asked, "why were you in jail."

Haze entered and said, "when she left, she went to my home and tried to break in. An officer caught her."

Tess said, "I saw the cop, so turned around and parked on a side street, I saw him drive off, I doubled back to Haze house," she looked hateful at Haze then continued, "I had to break in because Haze changed the locks, the police caught me."

Donovan walked past Tess and exited the house when he got on the porch, Donovan yelled, "come out Baby Girl, the Linwood's are coming down the street"

Before joining Donovan, Theenda said to Tess, "you have to change clothes we are going shopping, I cannot stay in this house, wondering if there are slaves."

Tess said, "I thought you were going to church."

"I went yesterday."

"Yesterday?" Tess questioned.

When Theenda and Tess exited the house, the sun burst through the clouds pushing them aside. Both Theenda and Donovan looked up at the sky and then at each other and smiled, she stood next to him and held his hand.

Tess looked at them and rolled her eyes.

Haze caught Tess action, he said to her, "I have something for you to sign,"

Before she could answer the Linwood's pulled up and parked. KayKay got out the car, Tess said, "good grief."

KayKay's black wide brim hat was as extensive as a small umbrella, she wore black lace gloves, all white silk suit, black and white stiletto heels. Theenda said, "I love this whole ensemble, girlfriend," she stood back and admired KayKay's outfit, and continued, "my my, I like that outfit." She looked around at Donovan and said, "this is how you dress for church."

KayKay said, "I thought you'd attend church today."

"I went yesterday."

"Oh, to that Advance church."

Theenda said, "no Kay, Seventh-Day Adventist, they had a play that was out of this world. If it was possible, they should get an Oscar for costumes."

Donovan said, "I agree. The music and singers were phenomenal."

Timpkin asked, "what was the play about?"

Theenda answered, "the Crucifixion of Jesus."

Donovan said without pausing, "blew my mind." He looked around at everyone then at his watch and said, "time to go."

Theenda said, "Kay it's six o'clock, aren't you early?"

KayKay said, "I'm going to the early morning service with some of my friends." She kissed Timpkin on the cheek, and continued, "see you when you get in."

She turned to leave, but saw Haze standing alone, Theenda had also seen him alone. Both Theenda and KayKay

All But One

went to him and gave Haze a group hug. Haze blushed, his reaction was like that of the shy cowardly lion, on the Wizard of Oz, before he said, "shucks ladies, thank you."

Tess stood alone watching everyone, everything they were doing.

Theenda said, "a book bag full of food, juice, and water is in Donovan's truck for you."

After their group prayer, Donovan kissed and hugged Theenda and pulled off, Timpkin sat in the front and Haze in the back. When the truck was no longer in site KayKay said, "well I'm off to church. You ladies have a blessed day."

When she drove off Tess asked, "did you really like that silly outfit."

"I loved it; she went to Bloomingdales in Atlanta."

Tess said, "hum, I thought it was silly."

Theenda said, go home shower and change, we're going shopping."

"Stores here are all closed."

"We're not going to the stores here. Go change, I'll meet you at the hotel in one hour." She ran back into the house.

Tess said to herself as she got in her car, "I am not driving three hundred miles to another state. She asked herself, what does prayer have to do with anything?"

****

In the back seat of Donovan's truck, Haze saw the stuff that Theenda had put in the seat next to him. He asked Donovan, "what is all this stuff your wife bought? She expects us to carry it?"

Timpkin said, "one of those is my bags belong."

"Okay," Haze began, he picked up Timpkin's bag and continued, "it's not as full as the ones Thee packed."

"I don't know what Thee put in our bags," Donovan began saying, he finished, "I am going to put a few bottles in my backpack and call it a day."

Timpkin said, "in case you're right and there are slaves, take the medicine Thee bought."

Haze said, "Thee is a very kind-hearted woman. You're a lucky man, Don-man."

Timpkin agreed saying, "yes she is."

Donovan said, "Haze you're going to get a good woman, I feel it in my bones."

Haze said, "that would be nice."

"Kay is not violent, she's just…" Timpkin was saying.

Donovan and Haze said together, "annoying."

Haze said, "Tim-man, she made you lunch and kissed your cheek."

"Yea, she did that," Timpkin commented.

Donovan said, "Kay is happy, she and her girls are going to talk about…"

Timpkin cut Donovan off and said, "Tess."

Haze explained, "Kay took pictures as you two, threw Tess out the house."

"Yep, they're attending the early church service, brunch to gossip," Timpkin said.

Haze said, "their minds will not be on the sermon or Jesus."

Donovan said, "their minds will be buzzing with chinwag."

Haze said, "really Donovan, couldn't just say gossip."

Timpkin said, "well, they're going to be wagging their tongues."

They laughed.

Donovan said, "to change the subject, Haze there should be a bag from a drug store. Theenda bought them medicines and Easter candy. Do you see it?"

"Yea man got it."

Timpkin commented, "that means she believes there are slaves."

Donovan replied, "what Thee said was, "I don't know what you're going to find." She handed me the bag."

Timpkin said, "we'll find nothing."

Haze asked, "is what Kay and those women planning a sin?"

"Are you asking if gossiping a sin?" Donovan replied with a question.

In the castle, Charles was in a good mood, everything was going his way. Harry had not returned since the argument; his household and plantation was running smoothly with the help of his brother, Sam. Although Sam had gotten on Charles' nerves, he was taking him to Titleburk to celebrate Easter.

Barbara could not be happier, her spy told her all about Harry's new name and his illegal Canadian birth documents. She ran and told the findings to Charles, who called Chief Stevens. He put the phone on speaker.

Chief Stevens said, "Mr. Brown when you give the word, I will make the call to the Canadian Police."

Charles said, "let's allow him to wallow in his treachery for a while, when we shut the plantation down, call the Canadian police."

Steven's asked, "when are you leaving?"

Charles answered, "soon I am giving you a few million for all your help and loyalty to this family."

Stevens replied, "thank you, Mr. Brown, with the money, I will quit my job and leave town."

After they ended the conversation with Chief Stevens, Barbara said to Charles, "that's a good plan, though there's one thing."

"What's that?"

She began, "now don't get upset Charles."

"What're you talking about woman?" Charles asked.

"You're strongly saving your sister, but your son-your flesh and blood."

"Oh, Becky will be eliminated eventually, I've taken care of that, I love little carrot top, she's exceptional. Harry, I despise. He is the Brown men weakest link."

"I concur," Barbara agreed.

On the plantation, Charles and Sam hitched a cart on the back of Charles motorbike to deliver the Easter food to the overseers. Charles noticed that when his son was around, the area was chaotic. He looked at Sam and said, "take this to the overseers."

When Sam arrived at the overseers' cabins, they had the horses and a cart ready to make the delivery in the slave area. Sam gave them twelve whole chickens, ten for the slaves. Two chickens for themselves, plus a Victrola turntable, and vinyl records. Before leaving, Sam said, "this record player was my idea."

Roy said, "thank you, Mr. Brown."

When Sam left, the overseers put two tables between the cabins, on one of the tables they set the Victrola turntable and records, Sam brought five different records, the Beatles, Michael Jackson, Lady Gaga, Conway Twitty, and Blake Shelton. The overseers' women took turns cranking it to keep the music going. Like the slaves, they did not have electric or indoor plumbing. The small group had been locked up for years, the only artist they recognized was the Beatles and The Jackson Five. The overseers took the food to the slaves while their women cooked and danced to the music.

Charles, Barbara, and Sam attended Easter Service in Titleburk. They stayed in the house Duke built years ago. Barbara wanted to sell it, but the house had been in the family for over a hundred years. Sam suggested, "when I want to take a break from the plantation house, I could stay here. You two have the castle, I'll have this." He asked Charles, "would that be okay with you?"

"Sure."

"Do you think the slaves and overseers, are responsible enough to be by themselves all day and night?"

Barbara asked impatiently, "How will they get out?"

"Don't the overseers have the key?

"Only to the slave gate," Charles answered

"Is that wise?" Sam asked.

Charles did not answer, so Sam said, "no, that is not wise when we get back, I will take the key and keep it."

Barbara could see Charles face and body language that he had had enough of Sam. She was holding Charles' arm; he could feel her get tense. He looked at her and whispered, "not now."

It was as if Charles and Barbara Brown were a restored team of Bonnie and Clyde.

Since Charles was planning on giving up the plantation, he had the slaves to plant the tobacco in fields one, two, and four. The quality of the tobacco in field number three had weakened, he decided to let the field rest for a few years.

The slaves held their party in tobacco field three. For dessert the women had baked several cakes the day before, when Roy and Fred dropped off the food, Lillie gave the men two cakes. They thanked Lillie and galloped away happy, neither of their women could bake. Roy said, "it was nice of Lillie to give us two cakes."

In Lillie's cabin was Lee, Cush, and Glaidous. Lee instructed Cush to stay with his friends and keep them away from the outer gate. Glaidous said, "Jesus is gonna save us."
"Lawd-Lawd," Lillie said. She looked at her little family and asked, "y'all be nervous? I's is."

****

Becky Lou stopped past the plantation house with treats for the kids, she had chocolate and marshmallow Easter Bunnies, bags of jellybeans, and for Helen several Almond Joys. Since Harry II was gone, Becky had begun giving treats to Helen, who shared with the slaves. Her brother Sam didn't seem to mind. Still, Becky told Helen to keep the secret between the two of them.
When Becky arrived at the house, no one was there, she went straight to where the key to the gate was always left, it was gone. She laid the sweets on the kitchen counter, and then went up to the attic to fetch a key out the trunk. As she was running up the steps, the excitement caused goosebumps on her skin, she said, "I am going to set the slaves free." But when she got to the trunk, it had a brand-new deadbolt lock. Becky gasped in fright, she muttered, "they know."
She ran down the attic stairs, out the front door, got into her car and drove to the train station to check on the things she had locked up.

****

Ten o'clock in the morning, the slave's church service ended early. They were leaving the best service they had ever had. Rita said to one of her friends, "I's ain't neva heard Mr. Glaidous speak like's dat."
The woman said, "he be full of Jesus ta'day."

Another woman walked up to them and said, "Miss. Lilly sang dat' song. Glory be child, what come ova' her?"

The slaves went to their cabins and changed out of their church clothes. They went straight to tobacco field number three, before church the men set tables and chairs up for the Easter celebration. Never had they had a rip-roaring praise God service, and so much room to party. The men made an open pit fire to cook the vegetables and meat, and to make candy for the teens.

The ladies cooked fried corn, fried green tomatoes, fried okra, an enormous pot of boiled greens with large pieces of fatback, fried chicken, and corn pong. The meal had cholesterol written all over it, still, to the slaves, it was fit for a king.

The women held a cake and pie baking contest. The men had a band that consisted of two slaves strumming away on their homemade fiddles, one of the teens had made a wooden flute, a scrub board player, and a spoon slapping musician.

In the tobacco field, several of the older ladies was working on a quilt. The older men aimed to finish a six-chair dinette set, the table's feet were going to be carved into miniature size gargoyles. They got the idea from the post on the bar and grill, Harry V. Brown had the men to design the bottom of the post, like gargoyle feet holding on to the porch.

Glaidous was so excited to meet a walk-about, he sat in a corner alone. On a large piece of art paper, that Sam sent by the overseers, Glaidous drew the scene of the slaves. Some were sewing, others making furniture, dancing, eating, cooking, standing around talking, teens running and playing, as he was drawing, Glaidous noticed all the slaves were smiling or laughing. He was drawing a happy picture.

He saw Lee quickly walking past, he yelled out, "Lee, come'mer' a minute."

Lee went to him and said, "unk, dat' be da' best sermon I's heard."

Glaidous said, "thank you, it be meetin' da walk-about." Then he asked, "what bout' Bo? Where he gonna' be while we talk ta' da' walk-about?"

"I's' got Fanny ta' keep him busy."

"Did ja' tell Fanny bout our walk-about?"

"Naw' Sir, I's' tell her we's play a trick on Bo."

"She fell foe' dat?" Glaidous asked.

"Well, I's' tell her I's' fix a big plate of food foe' her, and I's' gib' her three bottles of wine from all da' wine dat' Massa gib' us foe' da' party."

Glaidous looked puzzled and asked, "why so many bottles?"

"Two, ta' git' Bo drunk, and one fo' her."

****

10:30 a.m.

Donovan, Timpkin, and Haze arrived at the foot of the mountain, they had to climb up and through the woods.

Donovan said, "here we are."

Timpkin Looking out the window said, "where are we, I don't see a plantation, I thought coming up that road we'd eventually see more than a forest."

Impatiently Haze bellowed, "you thought it would be sitting on the side of the road?"

If it was possible Haze and Timpkin would hear Donovan's heart rapidly beat, Donovan lowered his head and took a long deep breath. He remembered when he met Theenda the first time how bad she was shaking. He smiled as he tried to hide his quivering. He said in his mind, *Don control yourself.* He looked at Timpkin and wondered how he would feel if an outsider moved to New York, claiming slaves lived in his town. He said as he parked the car, "Haze please, no arguing today." Then to Timpkin, he said, "see that metal building?" He pointed towards the building peeking through the trees, "it has furniture and tobacco in it."

When the men got out the car Donovan covered the car with limbs and weeds, Haze asked no questions he just helped. Timpkin stood watching.

Timpkin asked, "why are you doing that?"

Haze said, "Figure it out Tim-man."

"From here we walk, we should meet them soon," Donovan said.

Donovan and Haze began the long walk, while Timpkin lagged behind and argued, "do you really know where you're going? I can't imagine you just happened upon this place; did you have a map?"

Donovan looked back and said, "Timpkin we have a long way to go, come and see for yourself or stay behind." Donovan turned and caught up with Haze who never stopped walking. Haze said to Donovan, "we should have left him at home."

"I agree."

"I have to admit Don-man, I am nervous."

"We're going to be okay."

Haze asked, "did you see the paper? They killed Breeze."

"Yes, I read he entered the police station and threaten the secretary."

"I'm so sorry Don-man, I got mad at you for beating me, went to Breeze about the slaves, he asked the chief for hush money, now he's dead."

"Are they coming after you?" Donovan asked.

"I hope not. Breeze was going to take the money and run?"

"What're you two yakking about?"

"Keep up old man," Haze said.

"What were you going to do with the money?"

"I didn't want money, I wanted to get back at you."

Donovan looked around at Timpkin who looked in disbelief and sad, he said, "Tim, if this was New York, I would find it hard to believe. Who knows, maybe I'm wrong." Donovan paused before continuing, "slaves in 2017, I hope I'm wrong."

****

Lee waited by the gate where Donovan left the Essence Magazine, and where he left the note for Donovan. Lee was holding the note that Helen had given him. Ben saw a look of panic on Glaidous face, he calmly and quickly went over to Glaidous and whispered, "calm down or you gib' Lee away." Then he went over to Lillie who was looking edgy, "Miss. Lillie, would you dance wid' me?"

Lillie said, "you be years yongen' dan' me."

"I's just wanna' dance Miss. Lillie."

She stood, Ben took Lillie by her arm, and they danced.

Lee stood leaning on the gate waiting, watching. Glaidous looked around he saw Roy and Fred in the distance, he called Lee and waved him from the fence. Lee saw Rita and went to her.

All But One

Since his wife had died in 2015, a romantic link sparked between the two in 2016. Lillie believed Rita was a good match for her son, her characteristic was like Lee's dead wife, she was a good Christian woman, six years younger than Lee, so could give her more grand babies. Lillie looked over and saw Lee and Rita slow dancing to fast music. She smiled. Ben asked, "whad' you be smillin' bout, Miss. Lillie?"

Lillie nodded towards Lee and Rita. Ben said, "dey' be a perfect couple."

Roy and Fred went straight to the meat that was cooking, both overseers got off their horses, everything stopped. Fred cracked his whip in the air, "if y'all move, I'll beat ja."

Roy had a big pot, he dumped the chicken in the pot, and said, "is this all the meat that's left?" He climbed on his horse. Fred got on his horse, and said, "our women burned our meat."

Both men galloped off.

When they were out of hearing, Lillie said, "don't y'all worry, der' was' only two chickens cookin' in dat' pot, I's cookin' da' other meat back of my shack." She looked at Rita and another woman, "come on y'all help me bring da' rest out here, den' we's gonna' eat it up."

When the women returned with the remaining eight cooked chicken, the slaves ate up everything, all the vegetables, the cakes, and meat so if or when the greedy overseers returned, all they would get was chicken bones.

The band began walking towards the bar and grill. Lee looked a Jethro and nodded, Jethro, yelled, "hey everybody, let's go wid' da' band to da' bar and grill." He looked around and saw the women cleaning up the mess, he said, "first let's help our women."

With both men and women cleaning the parties clutter, everything was cleared quickly. Within the slave area, they had a pit where they burned all the trash. After the tobacco field was pristinely cleaned and trash burning, they all went to town and partied hard. If Charles ever saw disorder on his plantation, his OCD would kick in, and cause him to grab his whip and go on a flagellation fit and beat everyone. He was kind but like Donovan, don't make him mad. When the slaves were leaving, Lee looked at Fanny and nodded towards Bo.

Glaidous stood next to Lee and said softly, "I's' thank we's need ta' find another area ta' meet the walk-about, cause I's' seed' da' gate plain as day from here."

Lee looked around, all the slaves young and old was heading to the bar and grill. Lee smiled when he saw Cush in the front dancing as he led them from the outside gate. Ben eyes followed Lees, he said, "don't thank we's gots' ta' worry, dey' be leavin." Ben pointed.

Lillie said, "I's agree wid' Ben." She asked, "what time dey' be comin?"

Lee rubbed his head, and said, "I don't know. I'll leave a note iffen' dey' come when we's gotta' go in."

He sprinted to his shack to get paper and pencil. Upon leaving his cabin, he heard a muffled noise, like someone was trying to scream but couldn't. The noise was coming from Rita's cabin, Lee snuck by the cabin and peeked in the window. He saw the two overseers, Roy was holding Rita on the floor, Fred was preparing to rape her. Lee slide to the ground with his hands over his mouth, he silently cried. He quickly pulled himself together, he put the note Helen had given him, the pencil, and paper in his shirt then ran inside.

Holding Rita on the floor, he looked up and yelled, "behind you Fred."

Lee grabbed Fred and punched him hard in the mouth. Roy jumped up and ran toward Lee. Lee yelled, "run Rita!"

Rita ran out of the door. Fred ran towards Lee to knock him out, Roy went after Rita. Lee grabbed Roy and used him as a shield. Fred was too angry and out of control to stop the blows, he knocked Roy out with a left, then a right hook.

Lee let Roy go, he fell to the floor. Lee was ready to give Fred a hard right, but Jethro entered and knocked Fred out with one punch. The two men drug Roy and Fred out of the slave area and dumped their bodies dead center the tobacco.

Roy and Fred pulled themselves together, stepped out the tobacco and got on their horses. Before they left Lee said, "I's telling' Massa, I's had nough' dis."

Fred said, "you's' better not tell Mr. Brown dat' we be here, or we's tell him dat' you's' been sleepin' wid' a woman outside yo' wife.

Lee laughed and said, "my wife be' dead foe' two years."

All But One

Roy said to Fred, "yeah, where you been."

Jethro asked, "how's yah' do dis' knowin' what Massa Harry did ta' Bo?"

A dissatisfied look spread across Roy's face, then he said, "Fred we're no better than Harry."

"She be a her, not a him," Fred said uncaringly.

Roy said, "you do this again, I'll beat you myself uneducated fool."

"Who you callin' a fool," Fred asked with a vile tone.

Roy and Fred left. On the way home, Fred asked, "thank he tell Mr. Brown."

"Yes, I do. Maybe we'll get fired."

"That'd be nice. Why you yell at me in front of da' slaves."

"The slaves are Mr. Brown's precious goal. Our job is to take good care of them.

"Mr. Sam Brown seem ta' thank' of them as his property. Have you noticed dat' Roy?"

"He's the one I'm worried about. I'm more afraid of him than Harry or Mr. Charles."

Fred said, "God help us."

"No, we saw what Harry did," Roy whispered loudly, "that was disgusting, how dare us to do the same."

"It be a woman," Fred said matter factually.

Roy jumped down off his horse, grabbed Fred off his and slammed him hard on the ground. Roy stomped Fred several times in the stomach, head, and chest. He got back on his horse and rode towards home taking Fred's horse with him.

****

Donovan, Haze, and Timpkin reached the clearing out of breath, they were close to the grassy area. Donovan said, "here we are."

Timpkin asked huffing and puffing, "how far do we have from here?"

Haze asked, "hear that noise?"

"It sounds like a crude noise," Donovan said.

"Maybe music?" Haze questioned.

"Can't be music, what is that smell?" Timpkin commented and asked.

Donovan said, "It doesn't matter what the noise is, the point is that humans are making both."

Timpkin said, "I was hoping that you were wrong about there being slaves."

The three men exited the forest and began the walk across the one-fourth mile grassy area.

Donovan began to hyperventilate, he had to stop, he cupped his hands over his mouth to catch his breath.

Haze said, "pull yourself together." He looked at Timpkin. Timpkin had perspired so heavily, he was soaking wet. Haze handed him a handkerchief and said, "wipe your face." He looked at Donovan and Timpkin and said, "Really, now you fall apart."

Donovan let out a loud exhale and said, "Haze is right." He got his breath back and Timpkin stopped sweating so profusely. They continued their journey to the gate.

11:30 AM

KayKay had gone to the six o'clock service, nine o'clock she had breakfast with her six best friends. One thirty PM she entered Theenda's home wearing jeans and a blouse, she asked, "well, have you heard anything?"

Tess was there, the women discussed their commitment to the slave project. Theenda said, "once the slaves are free, they will need training, medical, and mental help," she paused and looked around the room before saying, "that covers all three of us."

Tess had her hair pulled back in a ponytail; scars were still prevalent but healing. She was a beautiful chipper confident woman. Tess leaned forward and whispered, "where will the slaves stay?

KayKay said, "they can stay – well – ah – hum, how many are there?"

Theenda said, "don't know, according to Donovan no one in this town will own up to what's going on, so we won't be able to stay here. A few days ago, they killed...."

"Breeze, a friend of Haze, I read that article," Tess said.

KayKay asked, "will we have to escape with them since we're the ones responsible for helping them?"

"I would imagine so," said Theenda thoughtfully. "Ladies," Theenda continued, "are we ready for this, fugitives for life?"

"Are you ready to leave all this," KayKay ask as she looked around the room.

"This stuff can be purchased, lives cannot. Yes, I will freely leave this house and things." Theenda said.

Tess said with great confidence, "I'm ready."

KayKay said, "you live in a hotel."

Tess stood ready to fight, Theenda said, "not today ladies, I'm not in the mood."

****

With Roy and Fred on their way home, Lee grabbed Rita's hand and said, "come with me I hope ta' meet a walk-about."

"A what?"

Lee was walking so fast, Rita had to walk run to keep up. They met up with Lillie, Glaidous, and Ben, together they began going towards the outer gate, when they reached the gate, they saw three men coming. Lee covered his face and cried, he said, "he be real."

Lille looked at Lee and said, "boy, stop dat." One thought flashed and stayed in Lillie's mind, *dey be real coloreds walkin' about. My Lord, dat's what I's wanna do.*

Glaidous said, "Lord-a-mercy. Dey' be real." He looked at Lillie and said, "all dis' time I's be a' thanking he not real, but der' be three, and real."

"What dis' be?" Rita asked.

No one was there to intervene, slave, Massa, nor overseers. All the slaves were in town, Roy was scared in his cabin, Fred was crawling to his, and the Browns were in Titleburk.

Donovan saw the five slaves standing at the gate, he inhaled, and then exhaled as he said, "like pictures in a history book." Although he thou*ght, studying and talking about slavery, is nothing like coming face to face.* He prayed, "my God, help us save them," Donovan looked at Timpkin and Haze and said, "they are actual slaves."

Haze asked, "Don-man is this what it looked like when you studied about slavery?"

"Not at all Haze."

"I think I'm going to be sick," Haze claimed, he turned around, bent over and vomited.

Timpkin said in a panic, "they are real - this can't be - not now."

Donovan looked at Haze and said, "pull yourself together."

The three men walked up to the gate and stood motionless.

As they approached the gate, Lee said, "it be more den' one of 'em.'"

Lillie replied, "sho'nuff' is."

Haze exhaled and blew his breath in no one's direction, Donovan smelt the throw-up, he said, "Haze drink some water, put a mint in your mouth."

Glaidous said, "da' youngen be in charge"

Donovan put his hand on the gate, he looked at Glaidous and uncomfortable words stumble out of his mouth, though Donovan, Timpkin, and Haze had practiced what to say, Donovan stammered, "I-I-I don't kn-know where to be-be-began."

Lillie reached up and touched his fingers, she said, "he soft."

Rita said, "dey' smell good, like morning' rain."

Donovan embarrassed ignored the comments, he slowly slid his hand away, and said, "my name is Donovan Bright, these are my friends..."

Glaidous stopped Donovan by asking, "how many walk-abouts out der, Mr. Doo-no-van?"

A puzzled look scrolled across Donovan's face, he asked, "walk-abouts?"

Lee said, "Massa say all coloreds like us be locked behind gates, how you's git out."

Haze was in such a shock, he stood frozen.

Timpkin said, "ah."

Since neither of the men answered Lee's question, he introduced the slaves, "we's don't know how ta' say yo' name Sir, my name be Lee, dis' my sweetheart Rita, my mama, my uncle Glaidous, and Ben."

All But One

Donovan looked at Rita and ask, "what happened to her?"

Lillie commented, "he talks better'n' Massa."

Without taking his eyes off Donovan, Glaidous said to Lillie, "Lillie Mr. Doo-noo-vin ax' a question."

Glaidous answered Donovan's question, "Rita be raped by da' overseers."

Haze said, "the position for overseer went out of business when slavery ended, and freedom took over."

Ben said, "slavery be ova' Sir?"

Glaidous ask, "ain't nobody slaves Sir?"

Donovan said, "everybody is supposed to be free."

"What dat' mean, fee?" Lee asked.

Haze began, "it means..."

Donovan cut in and said, "let me introduce my friends, this is Haze Day, and Timpkin Linwood, I am Donovan Bright."

Lillie said, "glory be, I's' likes yo' names."

"Me too," said Rita, I's' likes dey' clothes, what da' women look like out der?"

Donovan got his wallet and pulled out a picture of Theenda, he handed it to Rita, he said to Haze, "Haze, for real, put a mint in your mouth."

The slaves said in unison, "like the women in the picture book you leave us."

Rita said, "I's wanna meet her. She be pretty."

Haze said, "Donovan's wife is a kind woman."

Up until this point Timpkin was quiet, he said, "I will do everything in my power to get you free," he looked at Haze and Donovan, and said, "you with me."

Haze looked at Timpkin and said, "just now waking up Tim-man?" He got a bottle of water and mints out of his book bag. Haze put a mint in his mouth and drank a big gulp of water.

The slaves asked about the book bag and everything that was inside.

Lee asked as Haze drank water, "whad' dat' be?"

Haze ran back some distance from the fence and threw the waters one at a time, and the bag of medicines and candy over the gate, Lee, Ben, and Glaidous caught it all.

Theenda had also purchased three big bags of Easter Candy, a large container of tums and Aleve. Donovan, Haze, and Timpkin each had four bottles of water in their book bags, they kept one for themselves and tossed the others over the gate. Donovan showed the slaves how to open the bottle, the four slaves drank a full bottle of water none stop. The empty bottles the slaves smashed flat, to fit them through the prong of the gate.

Glaidous said, "dat' be good wata."

Lee asked Donovan, "can we's keep dis' wata?"

Donovan answered, "yes, you may."

Lee said to Lillie, Rita, and Glaidous, "I's gib' one ta' Jethro, he gonna like's dis." He looked at Donovan and said, "Jethro keep da' otha' slaves from here." He said in a pleading voice, "Mr. Bright, help us be fee."

Donovan asked Lee, "if we find a way to get you out of here, how many will leave?"

Lee answered, "all but one, dat' be Massa Brown special slave."

"So, how many?" Donovan asked again.

"Oh, der' be fitty-five of u, da' nurse say der' be twenty chil'ren in da' chil'ren gate."

Timpkin asked, "nurse."

Lillie said, "she told us that she and a teacher be lock up wid' da' chil'ren."

Rita said, "Helen da' slave girl go der' ta take care of da' chil'ren. Massa Brown sista' let Helen come home sometime."

Lee said, "oh, Mr. Bright, he reached in his shirt and handed the note to Donovan as he said, "Massa Brown sista' gib' dis' ta' Helen, she say gib' dis ta' you."

While Donovan read the note Ben asked, "what it look like through da' trees? what people likes us do out der?'"

Donovan answered, "I'm a high school history teacher, Haze owns a janitorial company, Timpkin works for the government."

The slaves stood looking at the three men in amazement and confusion.

Lee said, "we's don't unna'stand' what ja' talkin' bout Sir."

Haze asked, "do the overseers beat men and women or just rape the woman?"

Glaidous spoke up and said, "we gits' beatin' by da' whippin' tree".

Haze said, "run that by me again?"

All But One

Lillie asked, "you say you's a teacher? Massa say only rich white folk teach."

Rita said angrily, "Massa lie, he lie, he lie, he lie!" she fell to the ground crying.

Lillie helped her off the ground and said, "git up child, pull yo' self ta' gather."

Lee asked several questions, "teach us to talk better, say yo' name, git' us free."

Ben asked, "can you's do dat' ta'day?"

"Not today, we have to come up with a plan," Donovan said without much conviction.

Haze asked, "where's the whipping tree."

Lee answered, "ova' der." He pointed.

Ben said, "you can see it from here, see dat' big tree sittin' all alone, ova' der?"

Donovan and Haze said simultaneously, "I see it."

Timpkin pulled out his glasses so he could see, and then said, "the big tree standing alone."

Lillie looked at Timpkin and ask, "what dose' on yo' face?"

The other slaves waited in anticipation for his answer, Timpkin said, "glasses, they help me to see better."

Glaidous said, "I's' neva' heard such, he got extra eyes."

Donovan said, "we'll get you out of here, we'll take you to a doctor to have your eyes, ears, nose, throat, feet, and body examined."

Lee asked, "a what?"

Timpkin explained what doctors were.

Donovan put the note from Lee in his pocket and said, "tell Helen to thank Becky Lou for me."

Lee said, "yah Sir.

Lillie said, "Mr. Bright, tells yo' wife, we say thank you."

"I will Miss. Lillie."

Before leaving, Donovan had them to take the medicine out the bags, he told them what the medicine was for and how to take it.

Haze showed them how to open the bags of candy, he said, "don't eat too much, it will make you sick."

As the three men disappeared back in the forest, Lillie cried and said as she chewed on a piece of candy, "I's wanna go wid' dem."
    Rita put her arm around Lillie and said, "dey' gonna git us out. I's gotta' meet Mr. Bright wife." She reached in the bag and pulled out a piece of candy.
    Lee said, "slavery be ova," as he chewed on a jellybean.
    "Dat' da' reason foe' dat trees and gates, we be agin' da' law." Ben figured it out. He rubbed his hands together and said, "we be agin' da' law."
    "Mr. Bright ' be helpin' us," Rita said.
    "Dat's right, don't be worryin' bout' it," Glaidous said.
    They went back to the slave area, Lee said, "come on mama, it be okay," he looked around at Ben, Rita, and Glaidous, and said, "y'all come on in my cabin, we's got a lot ta' discuss. We's gotta hide whad' Mr. Bright gib' us."
    When they entered Lillie said, "I's hide dis' medsin," she looked at Glaidous and asked, "how yo' hand and knees doin?"
    Glaidous stood up, walked around, shook his hands and said, "pain be gone."
    Lillie said, "mine too."
    Ben said, "let me have some moe' dat' sweet stuff."
    Glaidous pulled up his pant leg to look at his knees, the swelling was going down. He said in complete surprise, "sis, dat' medsin, made my knee go down." He looked at her and continued, "afta Massa beat one us slaves, put one dem medsin' in da tea, all da pain go quick, like my knee and hand." He held his hands out, his knuckles had gone down."
    Ben nervously rubbed his hands, paced, and said, "I's gotta be fee." He looked at Lee and said, "how."
    Glaidous said, "dat's whad I's thankin bout."

    In Fanny's shack, dirty dishes, pots, and rags cluttered the table and floor. Upstairs two of the bottles of alcohol Lee had given Fanny was on the floor empty. Bo and Fanny were in bed snoring loud and hard. Lee was going to give Fanny and Cush four pieces of the candy. To Fanny as a sweet way to say thank you, and Cush because he loved his son, he filled his cabin with joy and laughter.

****

As Donovan, Timpkin, and Haze uncovered the car and drove off. Timpkin looked behind as they were leaving the area and said, "I just saw, real live slaves."

Haze said, "no joke."

When Donovan reached the service road, snoring was heard coming from the back seat. Timpkin turned around and saw that Haze was fast asleep, he looked at Donovan and ask, "what do you want to talk about."

"Anything."

Timpkin said, "hum." Donovan pulled onto the freeway, Timpkin continued, "see all those trees on those hills?"

"Yeah, what about them."

"There could be plantations, prison camps, anything hidden in the walls of those mountain trees, but we speed up and down the freeway dodging the highway patrol officers, admiring the beautiful scenery. When secretly entwined in the forest could be slaves, or people being tortured, exploited, or murdered.

"What a morbid thought, Timpkin."

Timpkin said, "we are coming from a plantation, with slaves, and a whipping tree."

"True." Donovan agreed.

Haze let out a loud snort.

Laughing Donovan said, "Haze agrees with you."

"I wonder why they don't just climb out."

"it's covered with grease, I got it on my hands when I touched the gate."

"Hum, I was wondering why the trees don't grow closer, did you notice that Donovan."

"I did. Did you notice the tree roots grow towards the street and not the gate? The place is over one hundred years old; vines, weeds, and trees should be all over the place."

"Something is in the ground to block the roots."

"Timpkin," Donovan whispered," this is a well-thought-out decriminalized plan."

"You're right," Timpkin stared out the window before saying, "they called us, walk-about."

XXXII

The Day After

April 17, 2017

    That evening, Theenda heard Donovan's keys rattle in the door, she ran to him hoping he would tell her what he had seen, what they did, any news. Instead, she got a missed kiss on the cheek and Donovan mumbling, I'll be back down.

    Macaroni and Cheese was Donovan's favorite dish, Theenda had prepared a meal that he loved and made his mouth water, she hoped they would talk. Instead, half asleep Donovan took a shower, got out soaking wet, put his pajama bottoms on without drying off, and laid across the bed.

    Theenda was a little disappointed as she put the food away, she had to wait until tomorrow to find out if he had seen slaves and tell him that Tess was spending the night. She went upstairs prepared for bed and was going to lie down, but the bed was damp. She thought about going to one of the guest bedrooms but decided to sleep on the chaise lounge in their room. She had no idea what he had seen if anything, she stayed just in case Donovan woke up having a nightmare. She got a blanket and laid it over him and kissed his forehead.

    She sat on the chaise lounge staring at Donovan for a few seconds, she looked at her phone, there were no calls from KayKay. She wondered if there were slaves or just sharecroppers. When Donovan let out a loud snore, she jumped to see if he was ready to talk. He was not, Theenda sat watching Donovan, she didn't want to sleep. Theenda whispered, "the moment he stirs I will ask him, what did you see." She tried to stay awake but eventually dozed off.

All But One

The next morning, Donovan woke up stretching and yawning, he looked over where Theenda usually slept but her side was empty. On the chaise lounge, Theenda was curled in a ball, wrapped in a cover and lightly snoring. Donovan woke her up, he wanted to talk.

The school was closed for spring break, so they took their time getting dressed. Donovan stood next to the chaise and asked, "did we have an argument last night?"

Theenda sat up and said as she yawned, "you took a shower and didn't bother to dry off."

Donovan disagreed and said, "I did not."

Theenda folded her arms and perched her lips, Donovan had seen that stance before, in his defense he said, "oh yeah, I remember, Baby Girl I was tired when I came in."

She asked, "did you see slaves?"

"Sure did, it was the strangest thing, they know nothing about freedom, they called us, walk-about."

"A what?" Theenda ask.

"Walk-about, they never heard the word freedom, we had to explain it to them. They had never had medicine, they didn't even know what eyeglasses were, their eyes were different, they were there but not really, they had a dull glazed stare that made me uncomfortable and sad all at the same time."

"You mean they have never been off the plantation?"

"Never."

As they talked, Theenda showered, when she finished and was getting dressed, she asked, "what're you going to do?"

"You expect me to come up with a solution right now, I've never been an abolitionist before, I've only read about them, I'm suddenly a new millennium abolitionist quick fast and in a hurry, how am I supposed to know what to do."

"Well," she began and continued, "that was a mouth full, why don't you use your wives?"

"What?"

"Tess is full of ideas, me, I have one. She stayed in the guest bedroom last night."

Donovan looked at Theenda and asked, "why is Tess here?"

"While you were at the plantation, I picked her up from work, she didn't feel like dealing with Haze."

"That still doesn't answer my question."

"Haze went to her hotel suite when you dropped him off last night."

"Why?"

"He wanted her back."

"Haze?" Donovan asked shocked.

"Yes, Haze?"

"Did he hit her again? I thought she was staying at the hotel."

"Don't think he hit her, she's still at the hotel, I have to go, Tess and I will share our idea with you later today."

"Thought we were going to I hop."

"Love yah' Sweetie." She left.

Donovan stood in the middle of the bedroom, he yelled with a smile, "back at ja' Baby Girl."

****

Tess was standing on the bottom step listening to the happy couple talk. She said softly, "one day I'll get a man like him, or I'll get him." She smiled and continued, "even better."

When Theenda came down the stairs, she asked, "what's even better?"

Tess said, "Oh, I was thinking out loud."

Theenda said, "oh, ready to go?"

Tess said, "I want a husband like Don."

"He has his moments." Was Theenda's reply.

While Donovan, Haze, and Timpkin were talking with the slaves, Tess called Theenda to ask if she could bunk at their house for the night. Still playing her games she said, "I don't want to see Haze."

Haze arrived home from the plantation, he blew Tess phone up by calling repeatedly. When it went straight to voicemail, he would hang up and call again, he did this over twenty times. Frustrated, he went to the hotel, but they were instructed by Tess to never let him up to her room if he insisted, they were to call the police. So, they did. Haze found himself locked behind bars just like the slaves he had seen. The police locked him up to calm him down, unfortunately, it didn't work because he woke up livid.

In his car were the divorce papers, he wanted her to sign them and get out his life. He was tired of fighting, Haze wanted someone he could sit down and have a conversation with, share their day, their dreams, and grow old together.

Tess had to work Easter Sunday, Hospitals cannot close, ever. Tess conjured up a lie, she told her coworkers, "Haze will come to the hotel to talk about getting back together."

One of the nurses said, "his last visit here as a patient, Haze said, he wanted a divorce."

Tess said angrily, "he lied, that's a cover-up."

Tess called Theenda crying on the phone claiming Haze wanted to get back together."

As Tess talked about Haze, in the back of Theenda's mind was the nagging memory of Haze before Tess. Theenda said, "that's hard to believe."

Tess insisted that she was afraid of Haze, Theenda met Tess at the hotel, they went shopping, ate lunch together. The ladies spent the day together.

Donovan was dressed when he went downstairs, he looked out the front room window and saw Theenda and Tess sitting in the car. He went out to see if everything was okay.

Before Theenda pulled off, Tess phone rung, it was Haze. Before answering the phone, Tess said, "I'm going to put it on speaker, so you can hear."

Theenda opened her window then cut the car off.

Haze said, "hey baby. I needed someone to talk to last night. But you didn't answer your phone, and the people at that hotel called the police."

"No more hitting, remember. Want would you like to talk about? Maybe what you saw yesterday at the plantation?"

Haze answered, "no, I have something for you to sign."

"I won't sign anything."

"When you see it, you will agree."

Tess sat quietly before saying, "meet me at the hotel."

This took Haze and Theenda off guard, Haze said, "oh, okay what time."

"Thirty minutes." She hung up.

"What does he want you to sign?"

Tess said, "He's making stuff up, he wants us to live as husband and wife. Well, I won't do that." She put the phone back in her purse and continued, "I'm taking boxing lessons, and I'm good."

"You're lifting weights also, right."

"Yes, my instructor trained me to hold fifteen-pound weights while I'm hitting the heavy bag."

From the look on Theenda's face, Tess realized she was not familiar with boxing terms. Theenda asked, "a what?"

"That thing boxers hit when they are training, you learn where to punch and how."

Donovan ran out to the car and asked, "everything okay, Thee."

"Yes, Sweetie."

Tess received a call; I was waiting for her to hang up."

"So, your car work?"

"Yes."

He poked his head in the car and gave Theenda a quick kiss, "just checking."

"I'll drop Tess off, when I return, we'll go to I h"

When they got to the hotel, Theenda asked, "want me to go in with you."

"I got this."

Theenda grabbed Tess arm before she got out, and said, "you mean to tell me that you could have beat the living daylight out Haze at the cookout."

"After watching you guys, I trained harder, today I am going to beat him all over that room, then out the door."

"Maybe, talk, ask what he wants you to sign."

Tess violently got out of the car and slammed the door hard. "you don't tell me what to do when I leave Haze, maybe I'll get your man."

She left leaving Theenda confused.

In the Linwood's' house, Timpkin and KayKay were having their morning coffee, Timpkin was so chatty that KayKay called in sick to hear what he was talking about.

"Timpkin slow down, please," KayKay said, and then continued, "now you say they didn't know about glasses, do any of them have bad eyesight."

"I would imagine so, Kay, they've never had medicine before, never seen a doctor."

"What do they do when sick."

"Don't know, figure it out, or die."

"How did Theenda know to buy them medicine?"

"Hum, I don't know." Timpkin wondered that himself.

"Could she be psychic?" KayKay asked.

"No, Theenda cares a lot about people and has a great awareness of folk needs."

KayKay was a little jealous of Theenda, it showed when she said, "you sound like you like her, you admire her a lot, I see you watching her every move."

"Do you want to hear what I saw or pick a fight?"

KayKay got up and began taking the dishes off the table. "I think I heard enough."

"Donovan invited us over tonight, to discuss..."

"Don't care what you discuss, I'm not going," KayKay said in anger.

"Alright by me, I'll drive over alone," Timpkin claimed.

"You'll go without me?"

"You're a fifty-something grown woman, what do you think?"

Exasperated she said, "Finish telling me about the slaves, maybe one day I'll go out there to meet them. It'd be interesting to see."

"What?! You talk like their animals in a zoo." Timpkin exclaimed in an annoyed tone.

"They're behind bars, aren't they?"

"One, if we're caught out there, we would get killed. Two, Donovan and I want to help them escape. Not exploit them."

"Like abolitionist? Tim, you can't do that. Not this day and time. Leave those people where they are."

"You're the one who told me to go with Donovan and Haze."

"I also told Tess and Theenda that I will leave town with those people, that was before I knew there really are slaves."

"So, you didn't mean a word of it?"

"If they can't help themselves, what can we do?" KayKay said.

Everyday Timpkin learned more about his wife in a new light, today after twenty-eight years of marriage he saw a brown skin hateful evil witch of a woman. He put her in the same order as the Ku Klux Klan, someone to be avoided. Timpkin walked out of the house without looking back nor did he say goodbye or see you later. He got in his car and drove off.

KayKay stood alone in the kitchen, "what did I do?" She asked herself. She made a phone call, "hi mom, I'm leaving Timpkin, he doesn't understand me, and he's an idiot." She listened, then said, "yes ma'am, okay I will." She hung up the phone and said, "fat lot of good she was."

That evening at the Bright's home, KayKay and Haze had not arrived. Donovan and Timpkin told Theenda and Tess about their findings. They told them about the trees not growing to the gate, the grease on the gates, they didn't have on shoes, their clothes were just like pictures in books. "It was tough seeing them," Donovan said sadly but thoughtfully. "Did you feel that way Timpkin."

"Almost overwhelming. It was like time stood still." They sat quiet, then Timpkin continued, "we want to help them escape. How do you ladies feel?" Timpkin wondered if they felt like Kay, the slaves were humans in a zoo.

"Theenda said, Tess and I were talking, if they are freed, we'll have to go with them. There's no way they could stay in this town. Nor us."

"But how to free them," Tess asked.

Timpkin was satisfied, these two women were kind and caring, unlike Kay.

A knock on the door startled them. Donovan answered the door, he let Haze in. He stared at Haze's face only for a second. As they walked down the hallway Donovan said, "we're meeting in the living room tonight."

Haze walked in front of Donovan when they got in the room, Donovan stood behind Haze and mouth to Tess, "what happened to him?"

All But One

When Haze entered the room, he stood as to not show his face to Theenda or Timpkin. Tess sat away from him. it wasn't until Haze went over to Tess and said, "I'm sorry I-I-I wasn't thinking."

When he turned around Haze had a big knot on his forehead and a black swollen eye. Tess lost it, through tear dripping laughter she said, "told you I'd get him."

Theenda asked Haze, "are you okay."

Donovan asked, "need ice?"

Theenda stood to leave, she said, "I'll get some."

Tess still laughing said, "he didn't try to defend himself. He knew that he needed an old fashion butt whipping, like what his daddy used to give him."

Donovan and Timpkin sat confused as they listened to Tess. Haze said, "she beat me really good, all because I asked her to sign the divorce papers."

Theenda entered the room carrying a sandwich bag filled with ice and a washcloth to wrap around the bag.

Seeing Haze bruises, Donovan said, "I don't get it."

Theenda said, "let me explain, Tess told me to stay out of her business if she divorces Haze, she was going to take," she looked at Donovan, "you Sweetie, from me."

"No, she won't," Donovan said sarcastically. He looked at Theenda and asked, "what did you say."

"I drove off."

Haze said, "in some cases, silence is a louder way to get your point across."

Timpkin said, "boy would Kay love to be here now."

Everyone laughed, except Tess.

Later that evening Donovan, Haze, and Timpkin went into Donovan's library, the women entered the kitchen. Haze wanted to go to the Blues Night Club, Donovan said they would be overheard while trying to plan the slaves escape. Haze wanted something strong to drink, he claimed his face hurt. Donovan asked Theenda to bring Haze some Aleve.

Theenda was about to enter the library when Donovan asked. She said, "I'm one step ahead of you Sweetie, "She sat a bottle of water, Aleve, a fresh bag of ice wrapped in a washcloth on Donovan's desk."

Haze said, "thank you Thee."

Timpkin said, "so Tess hid behind her hair because you beat her, but this time she did," he pointed to Haze's face and finished by saying, "that to you.

"No," Haze began, "Tess has stabbed me and beat me with a baseball bat, I hit her to protect myself."

Donovan said, "show him your back."

Haze said, "it just about healed."

Looking at Haze, Theenda said in a sad apologetic tone. "I'm so sorry Haze."

Haze stood up and gave Theenda a hug and said, "it's okay little lady."

Haze sat back down, Donovan said, "listen to you two, I figured out how the slaves can escape.

Timpkin asked, "How?"

"Dig their way out," Donovan said."

Timpkin said, "I was thinking the same thing, Glaidous is too old to try climbing the gate."

"The gate is so high it would take a fire truck ladder to get the people over it." Said Donovan.

The three men sat back in their seats, quietly thinking.

Theenda came in with three cans of Ginger beer. Donovan said, "thanks Baby Girl."

Haze and Timpkin said, "thanks Thee."

"No problem." She left.

Timpkin remarked, "I thought you two didn't drink."

"Dig from where? And with what?" Haze asked.

Before answering Haze question, Donovan said to Timpkin, "it's a soda." He looked at Haze and said, "The back of the church, Glaidous said that the church has a little Backroom with a dirt floor."

"Is the church the closest to the gate?" Haze asked.

"I believe so," Donovan answered.

Timpkin suggested, "it will take about a month to dig from there to under the gate."

"Maybe longer," Donovan stated, "the gates are six feet underground, they will have to dig eight feet down so the heaviest slave can crawl under."

All But One

Haze asked, "what're they do with the dirt."

"Hum," Donovan began, "here's a thought, remember the Shawshank Redemption movie, the guy put the dirt in his pockets and spread it around on the ground outside."

Both Haze and Timpkin laugh at Donovan, "Don-man," said Haze, that was a movie, the actor hauls a wall of dirt in his little pockets."

Timpkin agreed, he said, "Haze has a point, they have to dig eight feet down then right back up, they are going to need more than pockets."

"We have pants specially made, pockets that go from their waist down to the cuffs of their pants. Shirts with big pockets." Donovan suggested.

Haze rubbed his chin, looked at Timpkin from the corner of his eye, Timpkin said, "so you want pockets?" He leaned in closer to Donovan, "we buy them clothes don't you think the overseers will notice."

Donovan let out a sigh, "they'll need shovels, picks, hats with lights attached, food."

Haze frowned at Donovan, and asked, "food?"

"They need energy and a taste of freedom food," Donovan laughed and continued, "that's what they call it."

Haze said, "I wish Breeze was here, he'd let us use his equipment."

Donovan said, "no he wouldn't, or did you forget"

"That's right," Haze said quickly, "I forgot."

Timpkin asked, "where do you plan to get the construction tools?"

KayKay drove herself over to Theenda's home since Timpkin didn't bother to go home after work. When she arrived, Tess and Theenda were in the kitchen. KayKay said to Tess in an arrogant tone, "I like your hairstyle, so much better than that straggly way you normally wore it."

Theenda looked at KayKay questioningly, and asked, "Kay do you speak first then think, or do you always have diarrhea of the mouth?"

KayKay looked at Theenda in surprise, she held her arms out and turned her head from side to side, and said, "I was commenting on her new hairdo, contrary to old hair don't, what's wrong with that?" She snootily looked away.

Theenda looked at Tess, and mouth, "brain on vacation."

Tess laughed out loud, and asked, "when do you think the escape will take place Thee?"

"I suggested to Donovan during the Juneteenth celebration."

"Why?" asked KayKay angrily.

"It will draw attention from our real purpose," Theenda answered.

KayKay commented, "Hum, I had suggested to leave them alone. Periodically we could visit. Take them what they need. Give them a little freedom from the outside in."

Theenda and Tess studied Kay for a moment, then Theenda gave her a compliment, "Kay, my goodness, you are a genius." She meant it facetiously, "I was thinking you could be the chairman of the Juneteenth celebration; you know the people better than Tess or myself."

Tess said, "I'm helping Donovan, Timpkin, and Thee with the escape. Kay, you and Haze would draw the attention from us. What do you say?"

"They've never held the celebration here; you think they'll go for it?" KayKay asked.

"I think so, especially if you and Haze make it deliciously fun and the food scrumptious, it'll be an outstanding enjoyable soulful experience," Theenda said

"Yummy," said Tess, "they will be focused on the Juneteenth celebration, leaving them no time to think about what the other half is doing."

"Like a scorpion," chimed in Theenda, "it keeps you busy fighting one end, then kills you with the other, we're the other end."

"Ideas are forming in my highly developed and educated mind already, at my church in Chicago I was over the ladies' auxiliary, at a very young age. Ahh, as I think back to those days, I was good, I held excellent programs that involved the whole community. Everyone cooperated with my plans because of its perfect structure. how right you are, I am perfect for the endeavor."

Theenda said, "I thought you had the skills."

"Oh, how right you are Thee, this town is in for a good time," KayKay said with a smug smile on her face. She put her hand on her chest, stretched her neck higher, perched her lips similar to the older rich women on soap operas. KayKay said proudly then repeated herself, "how right you are darling, how right you are."

While silently laughing Tess managed to get out, "then, it's settled." Tess looked at Theenda and said, "Thee, I am sorry about the outburst."

KayKay asked, "what outburst."

The guys joined the ladies in the kitchen to get something to eat and share their ideas. When the women learned about the digging, they decided maybe June was not a reasonable time to escape. Tess said, "there's a second-hand shop not far from where I lived in Mississippi, they sell old construction equipment and materials."

Donovan said, "that work, far enough away to not be detected."

Haze said, "yeah, since people are dropping dead like flies."

A few days after the meeting, Donovan and Theenda drove two hundred miles to another southern state, they purchased fishing equipment. A friendly cashier asked, "y'all goin' fishin.'"

Donovan answered, "yes, my wife and I are going shark fishing with a group."

The cashier said, "y'all need a stronger line, honey." She told them the fishing equipment needed to catch a shark.

Timpkin had a flatbed truck with a cover. The following Thursday he and Donovan drove to Mississippi to purchase the supplies for the slave's great escape.

XXXIII

Trouble

May 5, 2017

Friday after work, Theenda, KayKay, and Tess went shopping at a second-hand store, they purchased items for the adult slaves from a size small to XXX, plus a baby, and children clothing. Excitement and compassion oozed from Theenda's happy heart, it spilled from her chatty lips into KayKay and Tess hollow ears. "I hope they like the clothes we're buying, I hope they fit. Donovan said their shoes are run over and have holes, after the escape, we'll get them shoes. We're going north, so we need to buy coats also, oh yeah and medicine, lotion, soap, I guess we need to buy everything. You two agree?" When they did not answer, she looked around at KayKay and Tess, then asked, "am I talking to myself?"

Tess said, "Haze is in trouble."

Theenda misunderstood Tess, she asked, "Did you sign the divorce papers?"

KayKay pushed Theenda aside, looked directly into Tess's face, and asked, "you're getting a divorce? When? Where? I knew something was up with you two."

Tess ignored KayKay, and lied as she corrected Theenda's assumption, "no Thee, Haze and I are doing wonderful, we're back together, the police was by the house today looking for him."

Both KayKay and Theenda gasp in shock. Theenda asked, "Haze took you back? I don't understand."

Tess got a little rattled and said, "focus Theenda." She reached out and pulled both women in closer, then said, "get this, the officer asked if I," she looked around the store and whispered, "knew about slaves."

KayKay said, "and so it begins."

Theenda asked, "What did you say to the officer? And why were you at Haze house?"

"I said sure I know about them," she laughed and said, "I asked him if he wanted to read one of my books on slave narratives."

Theenda said, "good for you," she asked, "he didn't do anything to you?"

"No," Tess said, she continued, "the officer said, no ma'am, I don't want to read anything about slaves, have a good day."

Theenda asked, "when did you two get back together?"

"Oh, a few days ago, the three beatings worked and he's afraid of Donovan."

By this time KayKay was completely outdone with her friends, she slammed the clothes on top of a rack, put her hands on her hips, and hissed, "excuse me, aren't we in this together?"

Theenda looked at Tess and said, "follow."

Tess said, "okay, where are we going?"

"So, you're not in the hotel? You and Haze are back together," Theenda paused for a moment then asked a question that caused KayKay to quiver, "what happened to you taking Donovan from me?"

KayKay was dumbfounded, she blew up like a balloon filled with helium, still, she stood silently listening to gathering information for her friends.

Theenda and Tess watched KayKay out the corner of their eyes, Tess said, "that would not work Thee, I was only kidding. Plus, Donovan said he would have nothing to do with me." Tess looked genuinely sorry when she continued, "thank you for being my friend, it was stupid of me to say such silly things."

Theenda cleared her throat and said, "I am holding off my anger right now, freeing the slaves is more important than petty backstabbing, we need your input and help on this project. Let's finish shopping, I'm famished, here lately I've been eating way too much food."

Tess asked, "why? You never have an appetite."

"I don't know."

KayKay said, "I have to go." She went to her car and called Timpkin, she asked him about Tess and Donovan, before calling her friends.

Theenda said, "now, let's get some shopping done."

Tess said, "she and her church friends are the nosiest people I've ever seen."

With sadness in her voice, Theenda said, "she's in her car calling Timpkin about you and my husband."

****

Donovan, Timpkin, and Haze trailed through the woods, they were delivering the digging equipment. Donovan and Timpkin had purchased along with the digging gear a wheelbarrow to make it easier getting everything up the hill and through the woods. The three men took turns handling the heavy container, sometimes one pushed while the other two pulled. The three men had backpacks filled with McDonald and canned sodas. Normal chatty Haze was subdued during the struggle with the equipment, Donovan said, "Haze you're awfully quiet."

Timpkin agreed, "yeah man what's wrong, you didn't speak during the drive out here, or now. What's up?"

"That's unusual for you," Donovan commented.

Haze was experiencing a large-scale dismal letdown from his friend Breeze, which shadowed his disposition, as he said, "I looked for you two for the past several days, where were you?"

"Remember Haze, I asked if you wanted to go to Mississippi with us, but you said that you couldn't take off because there was trouble with one of your workers," Donovan snapped at Haze.

Timpkin said, "we're almost to the gate. Don, do they know we're coming?"

"Yeah, remember before we left, they asked when we're coming back, I gave today's date."

Haze said, "I'm in trouble."

"What kind of trouble?" Donovan asked.

Haze suggested, "let's discuss it on the way home."

Light from the bright moon and flickering stars made their journey through the woods, a little easy.

All But One

Earlier that day Haze had learned from Tess that the police were looking for him. Thus, he had not gone home since early morning, he was grumpy, jumpy, worried, and on edge. He said, "Tess said the police are looking for me."

Donovan asked, "why?"

Timpkin said, "Breeze, right?"

"I don't have time for I told you so, what am I to do," Haze plead, "Before he was killed, I went to his house, he told me that he didn't mention my name. He had packed bags next to his living room door, he thought he was getting paid, he was taking his band to California. We argued. I told him to keep his mouth shut. But what did he do…"?

"Let's deliver the tools first," Donovan suggested, "then we'll figure out what to do with you."

"Yeah, one thing at a time." Timpkin agreed.

Donovan said, "Theenda called and said you and Tess are back together."

"No way man." Haze answered.

Donovan asked, "so Tess is not living in your house?"

Haze said, "why would I let that violent woman in my home. The last time she was there the police took her to jail, before then she busted in and stabbed me. Fool me once I learned my lesson, there's no second chance. The police went to her job at the hospital asking for me."

Donovan asked, "how do you know?"

"A nurse called and told me." Haze answered.

Timpkin asked, "how do you know the nurses?"

Haze answered, "since marrying Tess, I've been in the hospital so many times I know the staff."

When they exited the forest, it was easier pushing the wheelbarrow, Donovan heard something, his attention shifted from the perplexity of Haze situation to the sounds of horse hoofs trotting towards them. "Somebody's coming," whispered Donovan, "let's go back to the forest," he softly said."

But they had walked too far to go back, they could see the gate, they laid flat as they could on the ground, there was nothing they could do with the barrow. The men had God on their side, a big dark gray stormy cloud, covered the moon and stars. It hid the men and their equipment.

On the inside of the outer gate, the overseers were making their last round, they figured no one knew about the plantation so didn't bother to look outside the gate. They herd the men talking as they rode past, Roy said, "I don't know why Mr. Brown makes us do this every night, the slaves can't get' out."

"If we don't, we git' beat or no pay when we get out, so stop complaining."

"We made our rounds, let's go home," Roy said.

Fred said, "dis' time next year we's off dis' plantation. I's take my monies and travel."

"I'm going to find my family then report the Browns"

The men rode off out of earshot and out of sight when Donovan said, "wonder if the slaves forgot about tonight, they didn't mention them."

When the two overseers headed home, using their night vision binoculars Donovan, Timpkin, and Haze watched the two men disappear in the darkness.

"They are no better off than the slaves," Haze mumbled.

"Wonder if we should help them out of here?" Donovan asked.

Haze answered in a resounding whisper, "no, they're rapist, lying, stealing fools. You want to set them free?!"

"He's got a point." Timpkin agreed with Haze.

They began walking towards the same area where they met the slaves, "when you put it that way." Donovan said more to himself.

The cloud traveled on, the moon and stars brighten the men way to the gate. Lee saw them, he whispered, "Mr. Bright, Mr. Bright." With Lee was Glaidous, Ben, Jethro, and Saul.

Donovan said, "did you see the two men go past?"

Lee said, "yaw Sir. We seed dem."

"Dis' dey' last round," Ben explained.

"We brought the tools; Haze will explain how to use some and Timpkin will describe the rest. I'm leaving a cell phone for you Lee; I'll teach you how to use it. If you have any emergencies call me, my number is on the phone."

While Donovan was talking, the slaves stared at him in total confusion.

Glaidous said, "we's don't unnastan' walk-about talk. Slow down young man foe' us."

Pointing to the barrow Jethro asked, "whad" dat' thang' be?"

Donovan and Timpkin had put the tools in three big green army bags. Haze had hooked a bag to a fishing rod, he was struggling to lift the bag, Haze grunted, "I need help."

Timpkin helped him, Haze said, "we are going to reel this first bag over the gate when it's at your level ease it to the ground."

Saul prepared to catch the heavy bag that Timpkin and Haze were having a hard time lifting and lowering.

When the bag was over the gate Timpkin whispered, "look out it's heavy."

Saul caught it like it was a six-pack.

Watching, Haze said, "okay, that was embarrassing. Tim-man we need to man-up."

Donovan had a floodlight, he looked at Timpkin and asked, "think the overseers are far enough so they won't see the light."

"If they don't look back," Timpkin looked at Donovan's young face, he reminded him of his son, with confidence Timpkin said, "they can't see the light. Hold it low."

Donovan turned the flashlight on and laid it on the ground. The slaves jump back, Glaidous fell to the ground, Saul, ran towards the slave area. Their response to the light startled Donovan, who cut it off, he said in a calm voice, "it's all right, it's only a light, see," he switched it on and off several times."

Donovan flashed the light on the slaves and asked Lee, do you have a new person with you?"

Lee looked around for Saul and Jethro, with the aid of the flashlight Lee saw both men standing in a distance, he said, "come here Saul, Jethro." He introduced the men, "this is Saul he was beaten a few weeks ago, mama gib' him some of dat' med'cin' you gib' us. Dis' be Jethro, he be beat not long time ago." Lee said to Saul and Jethro, "dis' da' man dat's' gonna' help us off dis' pantation.'"

Saul still a little shaky said, "where we's gonna' be a slave."

"There are no more slaves Saul, you will be trained to work and get paid?" Donovan said with tears in his throat."
Glaidous said, "I's told y'all slave be ova."
Jethro asked, "what kind of work we do?"
Glaidous asked, "what's paid."
Timpkin asked Glaidous, "how old are you?"
"Near bout' sixty-eight," Glaidous responded.
"Hum, you might be able to get compensation from the government," Timpkin said.
Glaidous asked, "whad' dat' mean?"
Timpkin answered, "the government pays you money once a month for being your age."
"Money? I's' git' money foe' bein' old? Hum, what's money?"
Haze huffing and puffing as he struggled to raise a second heavy load over the gate said, "I hate to dip into your moment of education, but will somebody help me?"
Saul said, "I's likes ta' mister but I's cain't reach it," Saul had his arms outstretched as if he was helping Haze.
"Sorry," Donovan said as he reached for the rod and helped Haze lift the pole over the gate. Jethro caught the bag like it was filled with feathers, he asked, "what kind of work we's gonna do?"
Haze asked, "what kind of work are you doing now, to make you so strong."
Donovan answered Jethro's question, "whatever your heart desire."
Glaidous asked, "what my heart gotta' do wid' it."
Lee asked, "whad we do wid' money."
"Hum," Haze mumbled.
"What are you, humming about?" Donovan asked.
"They got a whole lot of questions don't they, this is not the beginning, not even the surface, these questions are less than a drop of water in a bucket." Haze rattled on.
Donovan looked at Haze for a moment before saying, "show them how to use the tools."
Haze said, "first let's get the third bag over the gate."
This time Ben caught the bag. Haze started with a construction hat with a flashlight attached, he turned the light on

then placed the hat on his head. "There are ten hats in one of those bags, grab one, turn the light on and place it on your heads."

They put the hats on backward and no light, Haze stared at them before saying, "How'd they do that?" he said looking at Donovan, "you in deep man, like over your head deep."
"Don't worry about me." Donovan disputed. He took the hat off Haze's head and slowly showed them the correct way to operate and wear the hat. He said to Haze and Timpkin, "okay guys, use baby steps to teach."
"Or, this will take all night." Haze said with a little attitude.
"They got the hat thing didn't they!" Donovan said a little too loud and rough.
"What be wrong Mr. Bright?" Lee asked.
Donovan looked at the men, they looked sad, tired, and dejected. He talked in a softer voice, "nothing gentlemen."

****

While Donovan, Haze, and Timpkin were giving equipment instructions, Charles, Barbara, and Sam were in the castle arguing about the operation of the plantation.
Charles had noticed that the slaves were getting feisty, they talked back to the overseers and Sam, they had lost respect for authority. Something had to be done before it got out of hand. Charles looked at his wife and said, "tell him, Barbara, since you're the one who manufactured the idea."
She smiled at her husband, then said, "we start another plantation without gates, twice a month fill the well water with medication that will keep them lethargic but working, they will have no mental alertness only physical."
Sam said, "they're slaves without-a-gate, why take a chance with another plantation? You already have two."
Charles explained, "we only have one plantation and a tobacco field. I'm shutting down H.B."
Barbara said, "so the IRS won't come snooping around here. The legitimate tobacco business has tiny shacks for the workers to live, but they come and go and take off sick too much.

It's not making enough money to compensate for the money the plantation is bringing in."

"We don't need another," Sam shouted.

Charles said, "We've been at this for over a hundred years. It's time to let it go."

"So, you see Sam," Barbara began, "you will still be in charge."

Sam said, "I'm the plantation Massa. I want to keep Harry Brown legacy going." Sam turned to leave.

"Wait, Sam." Charles commanded with hostility in his voice, "are you listening to me man? think lord and Massa of this plantation. We do it your way we'll all be sent to prison for tax evasion."

"I'll figure it out, I'm a professional accountant," Sam said as he stormed out the room.

Charles looked at Barbara and said, "who made him boss?" He rubbed his head which messed his hair, and said, "he is too lackadaisical with his money, he boasts about being rich, he goes to Titleburk and get drunk."

Barbara sat watching her husband grow more stressed over Sam, she stood next to Charles, kissed him on the cheek and said, "I'll alert Stevens."

Charles affirmed, "No, I'm taking care of this one."

Barbara reached up and finger-combed Charles hair back in place, she said, "I'm with you my darling."

In the slave complex their equipment training was ending, Donovan asked, "do you understand how to use the tools,"

Lee answered, "yes Sir, we do."

Donovan asked, "Lee, should we review the phone?"

"Naw' Sir. I's' got it," Lee looked at the other slaves and said, "just thank, we learnin' feedom livin'."

The men laughed and agreed with Lee, Glaidous said, Mr. Bright yo' wife talk right pretty."

Jethro said, "soft like. Dat' be da' kind of woman I's wont's."

While the slaves chuckled and agreed with Jethro, Haze said, "we brought you some McDonald's, I am hungry." He got the food out of his backpack.

Donovan and Timpkin took the food out theirs.

"What dat' be?" Saul asked, his mouth was watering like Homer on The Simpsons.

"Lawd Lawd, it smell mighty good," Glaidous said. He rubbed his hand together and asked, "nuff' foe' us."

Ben said, "I's neva' smell food like dis."

Donovan, Timpkin, and Haze tried to pass the food through the gate's bars, it didn't work. Haze put the food in his backpack with a six-pack of sodas, he put the bag on a fishing rod and hoisted it over the gate. The slaves and Donovan's crew sat on the ground and devoured the food. Donovan purchased fifteen quarter pounders and fifteen large fries. For light, they use the floodlight that terrorized the slaves. Breaking the silence Haze said, "it's a good thing we brought extra food." had

Glaidous moaned and chewed at the same time, "hum, hum dis' be good," he crammed several fries in his mouth and muddled while chewing, "what dis?"

Ben answered quickly, "feedom food good."

The only sound coming from Lee was smacking and chewing, Donovan watched him eat, then asked, "like the food Lee?"

"Mm' hum, good" mumbled Lee with his mouth full.

Jethro looked at the cans of soda and asked, "what dis?"'

Timpkin showed them how to open the can, Saul gulped it down then cough it back up said, "dis' be stronger than wine."

Laughing Glaidous said, "it fizzes in my mouth." Glaidous tried to stand and stretch but fell back down, they laugh hard. Lee asked Donovan if he could keep the food in the backpack.

Donovan said, "sure. It's yours."

Using the fishing rod, Donovan and Timpkin lowered their backpacks with food and sodas over the gate.

Jethro imitated Donovan, he said, "sure Lee."

Donovan smiled, he asked, "can you get to the cabins?"

"Yes, Sir. Mr. Bright, since somethin' happened da' overseer lev' da' gate unlocked."

"We's be waitin' out here foe' you," Ben said.

"Gentlemen, you don't have to say, Sir. or Mr. to me, Donovan is good enough."

Lee, Glaidous, Ben, and Saul said in unison, "yaw Sir. Mr. Bright."

Haze fell over laughing.

Timpkin tried to get Haze under control. "Haze pull it together." Then he snickered.

Glaidous said, "it be hard foe' usta' say Mr. Doo-noo-vin. Sir. We's say, Mr. Bright. Dat' be okay wid' you?"

"You don't need to call me Sir. or say Mr.?"

"Yes Sir.," they all said in unison as they continued to eat. Haze laughed even harder. "Give it up, Mr. Bright."

Timpkin laughed.

When they had finished eating, Donovan said, "before we leave let's clean up." He looked at the men on the other side of the gate and asked for the paper, he looked around everything was clean. The slaves had the bookbags filled with the remaining food, Lee said, "ma and Cush gonna like's dis'. Mr. Bright."

Glaidous said, "tell um' bout' da' note."

"Mr. Bright," Lee said, "I's' told to say, Miss. Becky Lou, she won't' you ta' call her."

Donovan said to Timpkin and Haze, "we have inside help, this woman is Mr. Brown's niece. She's the one that gave me the memoir."

Timpkin asked, "can we trust her."

"Yes, I believe so." Donovan said, he looked at Lee and said, "I'll call and see where her head is."

Glaidous asked innocently, "ain't her head on her body?"

****

Donovan, Timpkin, and Haze returned to Timpkin's truck. Donovan's phone rung. Theenda was calling.

Haze asked, "could that be Lee already?"

Donovan answered, "yeah baby."

"Don't take Haze home, they ram-shacked his house looking for what, I don't know. They came over here asking for him."

"Where is Tess?"

"She's at the hotel."

Haze interrupted the conversation and asked, "what about Tess?"

Donovan turned around and looked at Haze, he said, "we can't take you home. Thee said, "they're out looking for you."

Over the phone, Theenda said, "they got dogs, Sweetie."

Donovan said to Haze, "they got dogs," he said to Theenda, "Baby Girl we'll figure this out, call the school in the morning tell them I might be late coming in, tell KayKay to call Timpkin's' job in the morning." Donovan ended the call and said, "this might work out to our advantage."

Timpkin asked, "where are we taking him?"

Donovan answered, "to an airport." He pulled up Google and found an airport a hundred miles from MacCall.

Haze asked, "How does this work out to our advantage?"

They remained silent until they reached the side street that led to the freeway. Once on the side street, Haze asked, "what's going to happen to me?"

Timpkin said, "this is a mess, it won't be long before they're after all of us."

Ignoring Timpkin, Donovan said, "Haze, you will be Henry Bibb."

"Henry who?" Haze asked.

"Bibb, Henry Bibb," Donovan answered, "Henry escaped from slavery, into Canada. In four years, he completed twelve years of school, started a business, and built houses for runaways to have a place to stay and work."

"What does that have to do with Haze?" Timpkin asked.

"Yeah, what does that have to do with me."

"Henry got into the newspaper business, he bought three thousand acres of land, built a publishing house, and built houses for runaways."

"That relates to me how?"

"Find housing, land, someplace for all of us to stay."

"I have to leave my company."

Donovan said, "and your wife only for a short time."

Haze said, "tell Tess to sign the papers. And what about my anger management sessions."

"Tell me more about those sessions," Timpkin said. "What have you two been doing, and when did I miss all this?"

"They have those classes all over the country," Donovan remarked.

Haze insisted, "tell Tess to sign the papers."

"Your marriage cannot be as bad as mine," Timpkin said.

"Wanna bet." Haze said. "You've seen my face; I've had more stitches than a train track."

Donovan said, "Haze man, you're going to be okay."

"Yes, I will. Maybe I'll find a lovely lady like Theenda."

"She has her moments," Donovan said laughing.

"Don-man you're enjoying yourself, at my expense," Haze said laughing, "Thanks man for helping me."

"No problem."

Donovan and Timpkin dropped Haze off in the next largest town, over one hundred miles away. They gave Haze cash money, Donovan said, "I'll send more when you send an address."

Donovan was going to use his credit card to buy him a plane ticket. Timpkin said, "I have a Visa I bought a few weeks ago, it's never been used." He handed it to Donovan and said, "use this to get the ticket. Don't use your card."

Donovan said, "good idea," he looked at Haze and said, don't use your credit card, they'll find you."

Melancholy Haze was sad and forlorn, his heart heavy, shoulders slumped, head hung low said, "thanks for your support."

Timpkin said, "let me see your phone."

Haze handed him the phone, Timpkin dropped it on the ground and stumped it into mini pieces.

"What you do that for?"

"They can follow you."

Donovan said, "buy a pay as you go phone."

Timpkin said, "take mine." He handed Haze his phone, Donovan took it and entered his number.

Haze looked confused, Timpkin explained, "Don gave us these when we went to Mississippi."

Donovan said, "Tim will get the one I was going to give you."

Haze said, "it all worked out. Is this what people mean when they say, God is in control."

Donovan put Haze in a headlock, rubbed the top of his head and said, "you're like a big brother."

"Get off me man." Haze said laughing, "you two be careful."

"We're having the Juneteenth meeting Sunday, that should take their minds off you for a second or two."

"Call me Mr. Bibb." Haze said as he waved goodbye. He entered the tiny airport to catch his flight.

When Timpkin and Donovan got in the car, Donovan said, "a hundred miles to home."

Timpkin said, "I pray God will hold back the hostility until we're gone."

XXXIV

Theenda's Mom

May 7, 2017

There were three black churches in Ogville, the *Seventh-day Adventist Church, Second Baptist, and UpRise House of Worship*, KayKay was a member of that church, they had a string quartet, a harpist. They had a concert pianist and a brass section. KayKay and several members considered themselves to be opera singers compared to Kathleen Battle and Luciano Pavarotti, but their untrained voices sounded more like a toad with laryngitis.

The Juneteenth meeting was held in the City Library conference room. Five women and four men made up the committee, Donovan and KayKay were the only ones not born a citizen of Ogville, and it showed in their dress. One of the men wore overalls with a white t-shirt, the other two pairs of jeans with white shirts. The women wore slacks and t-shirts with the high school emblem and name written on it. Donovan was dressed business casual, he was wearing khakis and a beige silk shirt with a bolo tie, a brown belt, and shoes. KayKay had on a royal blue silk dress and matching heels and purse. She whispered to Donovan, "the proper dress attire for a meeting of this caliber is unknown to these people." KayKay handpicked the black citizens who owned businesses and attended church. She believed them to have class.

Donovan looked away disgusted with her comment, he was not concerned about how folk dressed. The group was anxious about white citizens' response to them having a three-day festival that highlighted Black American Culture. Sitting in a bemused

All But One

indifferent attitude, Donovan listened to the small group argue about the whites not appreciating the celebration. One of the women said, "white people will not come to a Juneteenth, thing."

Another woman said, "she's right, whites going to come and watch us blacks do, what?"

Donovan watched their fearless leader fold to their ignorance.

Donovan spoke up, "since I've been here, I've seen this town celebrate MLK Birthday and twenty-eight days during Black History month which was off the chain. The week we moved here, the MLK and Black History Month Committee asked my wife to sit in on the committee meetings, she was the only black. They only had two weeks to plan King Birthday. Now you're claiming that the people in this town, that make-up reasons to have a celebratory event be it Latino, Asian, German, whatever the nationality will oppose Juneteenth." Donovan stood up and said, "you have until noon tomorrow to make up your minds, we don't have time to be imprudent because we have less than six weeks to plan." He looked at KayKay and said, "if you can't lead, I'm taking over." He looked at the group, "if you can't make a decision, my wife and I will go to the whites and design a program without you. The white citizens in this town know how to throw a party." With that said, he left.

After Donovan left, the Juneteenth committee sat quietly for a few moments, one of the male committee members said to KayKay, "Kay we've never planned anything of this magnitude. It's always been the whites."

A female member said, "maybe we should plan now for next year. We'll let Mr. Bright and his wife have it this year. We'll learn from them."

KayKay spoke up as though the most wonderful meaningful inkling on how to handle Donovan popped in her head, she said, "we'll allow Donovan to do it this year with his wife and others, and next year we will go bigger, Don and his group will be as dull as the moon on a stormy night, next year our celebration will shine like the sun on a clear day."

A female laughed and said, "good idea Kay, when he falls, we won't reach down to pick him up."

KayKay said with the utmost arrogance, "yes dear, we will keep our arms folded and let Mr. big man Bright waddle in his ego."
    One of the men said, "that's not what Juneteenth is all about."
    One of the other men said as he stood, "it's about unity. Kay, you're planning a division."
    "Well, after Mr. Bright's failure," a female began, then stated with confidence, "we will unite."
    "Yes." KayKay began, our meeting will be next year, the first week of January, that gives us plenty of time to bamboozle Ogville."
    "Same place?" One of the women asked.
    "Yes," KayKay answered.
    One of the ladies said, "oh, next year is going to be fun." She looked around at the others and asked, "isn't it?"
    A male said, "you'll need to find someone else. I don't want to see that young man fail."
    Another man said, "he's right. Instead of division, we should join in with Donovan to learn, and not fight."
    The three men left.

****

    Meantime, at Donovan's house, Theenda's mom had dropped by with an unexpected visit. She opened the screen door and knocked on the front door like a demented person. Theenda panicked, she thought it was the police again, she peeked out the window it was her mother. Her heart fluttered nervously, Theenda instantly became stressed. Donovan had called saying he was on his way home with news that she would like. She was happy that Donovan was coming home, it did not matter the content of the news good or bad. Theenda stood in the middle of the sitting room hyperventilating, she placed her hands over her mouth and nose, and said to herself, "get control."
    Theenda's mother knocked on the door harder and constantly pressed on the doorbell, she yelled out, "Theenda, I'm having a panic attack out here."
    Theenda opened the door and said, "Hello mom."

"What took you so long," Mrs. Carboy yapped and pushed Theenda out of her way when entering the house.

She set her bags next to the door and went through the house like the irrational person she was. Theenda did not move from the entrance way. When Mrs. Carboy came down the stairs Theenda took her in the kitchen.

Theenda's mom was a hard-homely looking elderly woman. She was big, tall, poor, her hair was untidy, and her shoes were dirty. Her shabby look gave her the appearance of a welfare reject, yet Mrs. Carboy had the audacity to condemn her daughters immaculate clean affluently decorated home. The woman looked like she had walked to Ogville. She entered the kitchen and said, "you look awful, just like this filthy house."

Theenda was frightened of her mother, she recalled on her fourteenth birthday, all she asked was, "may I have cake and ice cream this year."

Her mother hit Theenda so hard it knocked one of Theenda's teeth out. Theenda bled profusely from her nose and mouth. She ran outside where a neighbor saw her bleeding, they rushed Theenda to the hospital. The nurse that took care of Theenda's face asked, "how did this happen."

Theenda decided it was time to report the horrible abuse that took place in her mother's home. The nurse called a social worker, she spoke with Theenda and the person that brought her to the hospital. The social worker and dentist read about Mrs. Carboy children broken limbs, cuts, and bruises. She also, discovered that Mrs. Carboy was fired from her position as a Social Worker due to child abuse allegations. Theenda was placed in a safe home.

Theenda was joggled out her total recall moment when Mrs. Carboy yelled, "are you listening to me girl, you're too old to daydream." She looked around the kitchen then said, "my church friends said, you should go to hell for treating me so poorly. The mother of the church told me at one of our Sunday dinners, we give birth to the little snot nose brats, then they turn their backs on us. And that is what you have done to me. You live in this big filthy house and don't invite me for a visit."

Theenda looked around the kitchen, all the dishes were washed and put away. "Hum," Theenda replied, on the countertop was the ingredients for a hoagie sandwich and a scented candle burning. She took in a deep breath and said, "whatever you say, mom."

"You still don't know how to cook without burning food, didn't you learn anything from me?" Her mother screamed.

Theenda replied, "nothing is burning mom, I'm not cooking."

"Don't get smart with me, I was at your sister's last week, she got smart with me, I slapped her, you're not too old for me to knock some sense into."

Theenda said, "let's take your things up to the guest room."

"What makes you think I want to stay here?"

Impatiently Theenda asked, "where would you like to stay mom?"

"You sass me, you learned to do that in that home that social worker put you in. That couple was old."

Theenda said impatiently, "they sent me to college."

Laughing Mrs. Carboy said, "they dead now, all you got is me."

"My family is Donovan and his wonderful family. Whom I love."

Mrs. Carboy reached up to slap Theenda, who took off and ran into the front room and stood behind the couch. Donovan entered the house when Mrs. Carboy was running out the kitchen, with her fist raised with the intention to hit Theenda.

Donovan yelled, "stop!" He picked up a book lying on the coffee table and threw it at her. She stopped, turned towards Donovan and leaped at him. He jumped out her way, she ran into the wall.

"Glad to see you, Sweetie," Theenda said, she came from behind the couch and stood next to Donovan. She looked at her mother and asked, "where would you like to stay mom?"

"Are you kidding me Thee," Donovan said.

Mrs. Carboy said, "you're going to stay with this man that threw a book at your mother."

All But One

Theenda stood like a mannequin in a store window, she ignored her mother's question and said, "I know of a suitable hotel, I will call them?"

Donovan said to his mother-in-law, "I believe it is time for you to leave."

Her reply, "this is my daughter's home, you can't put me out." She stood like a boxer, her non-dominant foot, and dominant foot was at shoulders width apart pointing slightly away from Donovan. Her Torso was twisted towards him, her arms were in defense mode in front of her face. Donovan trained as a boxer recognized the stance.

Theenda was on the phone making the reservation, she quietly prayed that Donovan's temper would stay at bay and not escalate. Donovan folded his arms and scrutinized the woman, he wanted to see what she was going to do, how far was she going to push him. Mrs. Carboy standing in a boxer's stance said, "try me."

Donovan tried to keep his cool, he went to the door, opened it and said, "git out." He threw her suitcases out, they landed in the driveway.

She swung at him and missed.

It was all over, Donovan grabbed the woman by the arm and pushed her out the door, then closed and locked the door.

Banging on the door she yelled, "open this door!" Pretending to cry Mrs. Carboy said, "Thee don't allow him to treat me like this, tell him to back off me, I'm only trying to help you." She opened the screen door and banged with both fists.

Donovan looked a Theenda and said, "I know how to get her away for good. If you're with me."

"I'm with you, do whatever it takes."

Donovan opened the door, and asked through the screen door, "do you know about slaves?"

"Yes, you imbecile, everyone does."

When she reached to open the screen door, Donovan slammed the main door shut and locked it.

Theenda watching said, "that's your plan?"

Her mother got an ink pen out her purse and like a mad woman began to rip the screen door, she slammed it open and shut several times. Donovan asked, "why is she so mad?"

"I don't know."

"How did she find us?"

"I sent her a birthday card, with our address on the envelope."

Donovan asked, "you did what?"

"I didn't know she would come."

Donovan called the police, he said, "pray."

When an officer answered the phone, Donovan stood by the door, he gave his name and address. He said, "my mother-in-law is here threating to take my wife to a place where there are slaves." He innocently asked, "what is she talking about?" Donovan played his part well, he said, "I have no idea what this mad woman is talking about when I came home from the Juneteenth meeting, I found my wife hiding behind our couch and her mother trying to kill her daughter. I threw her outside."

While Donovan was on the phone, Mrs. Carboy shouted, "if you don't open this door, I will burn this house down and kill you both, I read in the paper where people have been killed because of slaves, I have been here for two weeks, I know all about those slaves, LET ME IN!" She calmed down and said, "if you let me in, I will tell you all about this town's secret." Then she screamed, "I am getting a lot of money and will help you escape!"

Donovan was still on the phone with the officer when he asked Donovan, "you didn't know she was here."

"No, Sir."

Theenda peeked out the window and said, "there are about ten police cars out front."

The officer on the phone said, "I called the Police Chief in MacCall, he is on the way. His name is Chief Stevens, he'll want to talk to you and your wife."

"Yes Sir, anything to help." The call ended.

An officer knocked on the door, Donovan held the door open for him to enter. Once inside the officer said, "Mr. and Mrs. Bright, I am Officer Felix, we're taking Mrs. Carboy to the station for questioning. We will hold her until Chief Stevens from MacCall arrives to question her, he will want to talk with you, he will investigate your home and cars. You may come to the station now or wait to receive a call from us."

Donovan said, "we'll wait."

Officer Felix left.

Theenda turned to Donovan and said, "that chapter of my life is closed, Sweetie."

"I'm sorry that I wasn't here earlier."

"You didn't know she was coming; I mean that she was already here." Theenda said confused, "I didn't know. I talked to my sister yesterday, she said nothing about mom missing or coming."

"Strange," Donovan said.

Theenda asked, "How did you know she knew about the plantation?"

"I didn't." He stood shaking his head, "honestly, I have no idea where that came from."

Theenda nervously exhaled, "how about mom blaring it out, I mean loud about the slaves."

"Maybe, God had a hand in this." He stood quiet and confused, then said absentmindedly, "I don't know or understand what's going on."

The singular thought of Mrs. Carboy upcoming demise triggered an eerie feel in the room. The husband and wife duo stood side by side watching the police cars drive off. When they were gone, Donovan broke the silence by saying, "your mother come at you ready to beat you down. And you asked her, where she wanted to stay. My lovely wife, you are incredible." He chuckled as he hugged her.

Theenda said, "the hotel said she had a reservation and had been here for two weeks." She sheepishly asked, "she's not going to make it, is she?"

Donovan said, "I don't believe so."

Later that day, Chief Stevens showed up at the Bright's home. The Chief drilled Theenda about her mother, she gave the Chief the phone number to the hospital that had Theenda's and her siblings' records. Donovan took Stevens to his home office, Stevens called the hospital and gave them his name, Social Security, and badge number. While he waited to receive Theenda's records, he wandered through the house, upstairs and down. Thirty minutes later the records were faxed on Donovan's home machine. Chief Stevens sent Donovan out the office, he said, "I want to read the records and speak with the hospital alone. Not only did he speak with the hospital but also, the social worker, and the Agency that fired Mrs. Carboy, and the Police Department in New York, they faxed Stevens, Mrs. Carboy records. An hour later Chief

Stevens exited Donovan's office and said, "it will be taken care of, no need for you to go to the station." He left.

Donovan said, "the first Officer said he would do that. I don't think he was supposed to tell us what the Chief of Police was going to do."

Theenda said quietly, "he went through our closets, drawers, what was he looking for."

That evening, Mrs. Carboy was a strange fruit hanging from a tree. A picture was printed in the newspaper of her body dangling, the article claimed that she had committed suicide. Members from the church Theenda attended planned the funeral, they had her body cremated, then gave the ashes to Theenda. Everything was accomplished within two days. Nothing more was said or done, Mrs. Carboy was an outsider that accused their favorite couple of something heinous, Mrs. Carboy had to be annihilated. Theenda shipped the ashes to her dad in New York, he threw them away, sold the house, and told his daughters he was starting a new life, just like their brother that ran away, they did not hear from their dad until his death.

****

Lee, Ben, Jethro, and Saul were in Glaidous shack, he had caught a cold, Lee said to his aunt Sophie, "auntie please keep unk home this evenin."

"Dat' old fool is determined to go to the church with you boys this evening. I can't stop him." Sophie said, then asked, "what y'all be doin'?"

Glaidous said, "I's got's ta' git' out dis house." He walked ran outside and stumbled off the porch.

Outside Lee said, "Unk you ain't goin with us, we been digging foe' ten weeks, seven nights a week. We git' three' maybe foe' hours sleep per night. You's' sick, stay home and rest this evenin,' and dat' be my stand on dat," Lee said with conviction.

Glaidous said, "you need me."

"Lee, let unk Glaidous go wid' us, cain't be much harm," Saul plead.

"You need me," Glaidous repeated.

Lee told Saul, "iffen he coughs or sneeze, Bo will hear him."

Glaidous pointed, "y'all go home, look yonder"

Glaidous saw Bo, pacing back and forth, on Drew Road watching the men. "Bo, be standin' at da' end of da' row foe' a long time." Glaidous repeated, "you need me."

"Why you keep sayin' dat' unk?" Lee asked.

Glaidous whispered, "I may be old, stiff, and have a cold, I can walk and run a little bit. I's draw Bo from da' path. Y'all act likes' yah' goin' home."

Sophie stuck her head out the door and voiced softly, "Massa gonna' find out bout' what you's doin. Whad'eva' dat' be.'"

"Woman hush dat' noise," Glaidous snapped.

"Massa gonna' find out."

Glaidous told Sophie, "only iffen you tell him," he looked around at the four men, and said, "you boys head home when you see Bo followin' me, go foe' da' church."

"Unk, "you be careful out der."

Saul said, "Bo be a mean and hateful man."

"I could tell Massa bout' dis," Sophie said.

"Aunt Sophie please don't," Lee pleaded.

Glaidous peered at her before he left, and said, "you do, Massa be afta' us and you, silly woman, did ja' learn anythang' from Lillie's beatin, from yo' beatin last month?"

Lee said, "I's thank he did away wid' his children.?"

Sophie listening, said before closing the door, "Lee, I's thank' you right. Y'all go on and do whad ja' gotta do."

Saul said, "likes he did dat' wild girl, dat' help Helen. She be gone too."

"Dat's right, Helen say so," Lee said.

"He kills he kids, what he do ta' us?" Jethro asked.

Glaidous said, "stop yapping and go." He began walking slowing in the opposite direction of the church, Bo's watched the boys go to their shack, and then his eyes follow Glaidous, who was walking toward the slave gate's opening. Glaidous said, "it be a nice night, thank' I's take a walk."

Bo ran towards Glaidous and said, "oh no you don't." He caught up with Glaidous and stood in front of him.

Glaidous kept Bo engaged as Saul, Lee, Ben, and Jethro quietly ran towards the church. They were dressed in all black which Donovan had bought when he delivered the digging tools. In Haze and Donovan backpacks, they had their slave clothes to change into for their work in the tobacco field, and snack food in Timpkin's' backpack. Each night the four proudly carried their backpacks, Jethro said, "dis' bag make me feel fee.

The men laughed and agreed with Jethro.

Theenda had purchased a large container that held one hundred beef sticks, two large boxes of peanut butter and cream cheese crackers, and a big box of Gatorade and Powerade.

Bo said to Glaidous, "iffen' you don't git' home I's' beat you right-hear-and-now old man."

Glaidous looked to see where the boys were, they had disappeared in the darkness, he looked sternly at Bo and said, "you can beat me until I's blue in da' face, what do you gain?"

Bo punched Glaidous in the face, Glaidous fell. Glaidous tried to get up, Bo pushed him back down on the ground. Looking up at Bo, Glaidous uttered, "why beat on me? The Browns don't like neither one of us."

"Dey' don't like you monkeys," Bo mumbled.

The next punch Glaidous pretended to be knocked out.

Lee heard horses galloping, he asked, "y'all hear dat."

Ben said, "sound like comin' to us."

Jethro yelled softly, "crawl."

The four men dropped to the ground and began crawling towards the church. Lee whispered, "feel the ground shaking?"

"Yeah," Saul answered

Lee said, "iffen' one of us is caught don't give the others away, we's gots' ta' git' outta' here."

"Let's scatter," Ben suggested. The men roll on the ground separating themselves from each other, then laid very still. From the town area the overseers galloped towards the slave gate exit, one of their horses stepped on Lee's leg, Lee grimaced softly in pain.

"My horse stepped on a big rock," Fred claimed.

"Lazy niggas' need to clean the plantation, especially this area, they live like pigs," Roy said and continued, "I wonder what they do if they knew slavery was over?"

"Honestly," Roy began, "we ain't no better off."

All But One

"Well, when we git's out, we'll get a lot of money, and they'll still be here."

"Have you ever been outside of your hometown?" Roy asked.

Fred answered, "Naw. Dis' be da' first time."

"Have you ever owned a brand-new car or nearly new car?"

"Naw' ain't neva' owned a car," Fred answered.

"Do you have a bank account?"

"Naw."

"Do you buy new clothes?"

Fred answered, "my woman shop at da' second-hand store."

Roy kept asking Fred questions, "would you like to move back in the white ghetto?"

"Any place would be better than here. Thank' about it, we's slaves like dem," Fred answered.

Roy asked, "How'd you figure?"

Fred said, "we work for free and cain't git out da' gate, just like da' slave."

Roy responded, "we don't get beatings."

"And dat' make us free? Member when Massa Charles daughter and son gave us a little bit of food to last a month."

Glaidous and Bo heard them coming. Bo yelled, "Glaidous try's ta' run."

Roy asked, "run where Fred?"

They exited the slave area; Roy pushed the gate closed.

Fred said, "wid' dis' bottle of whiskey, me and my woman gonna' git' drunk ta'night."

Roy said, "yep, us too."

Inside the church, Lee, Ben, Saul, and Jethro discussed the overseer's conversation. Lee said, "they da' same as us."

"Iffen' dey only knew dat' we's' knows' bout' freedom," Saul chuckled.

Ben walked over to one of the church windows and muttered, "so der' be po' white people."

Lee said, "yeah, dey be slave wid' us."

Lee, Jethro, and Saul went into the Backroom of the church, where they faithfully had been digging every evening since Donovan had given them the tools. Lee asked, "Ben, you comin?" he put the hat with the flashlight on and went down in the hole.

****

Timpkin and his wife were in their family room watching television, when KayKay said, "these little pea brain townspeople have no clue about anything."

Ignoring her comment, Timpkin asked, "when are Karen and the children coming?"

"They can't, little Kay is sick, so I was thinking about going to see them."

"You have the Juneteenth celebration to plan."

"The committee is uncultured, with no idea, not a clue, yet they think that they know it all, they refuse to listen to me. And Donovan has the biggest head of all. "

"Try something different, how about listening to them or him."

"Karen needs me."

Timpkin said, "finish the project," then snapped, "try listening to the committee."

KayKay tightened her lips and muttered, "if it's a failure it's not my fault." She stalked out of the room, went upstairs to their bedroom. She slammed the door behind her. Timpkin smiled and continued watching television.

Donovan school was having a PTA meeting, the students with their parents were beginning to file in, most of the teachers were in their classroom. Donovan entered the teachers' lounge to retrieve his student roster, a few teachers were smoking cigarettes, even though it was against the law. The math teacher asked Donovan, "are you still conducting research on plantations?"

"My research was on antebellum homes," Donovan corrected the math teacher.

Another teacher asked, "did you find slaves, there was something about a woman being killed, she was connected to slaves."

"In the 1800s some of my family members were slaves, now most of them are teachers, lawyers, or doctors, not slaves."

All But One

The math teacher asked, "did you know a Mrs. Carboy, they found her body hanging from a tree, she killed herself?"

One of the teachers said, "She was from New York, aren't you from there?"

"Yeah, and nineteen million others. Why all the questions?"

"Nineteen million," the math teacher commented. He got out his phone and looked it up. "you're close, almost twenty million. No wonder you came here," he said laughing.

The teachers stood around looking at each other, a teacher asked, "what about this Juneteenth thing that is coming to our little town, you're working on that, right?"

"Yes."

"Since Kay is off the committee, I want to help." Said one of the female teachers as she smiled then continued, "sounds like fun."

Donovan chuckled when he said, "okay, we'll talk tomorrow we need all the help we can get. I have parents to see." He left.

On the pay-as-you-go phone, Lee called Donovan as he was going home from the PTA meeting, "yeah." Donovan answered.

"Mr. Bright, dat' you in here."

"Is everything okay Lee?"

"Helen say dat' white lady say she wanna talk again."

"Okay, I'll call her."

Donovan pulled in his driveway, grabbed his bags out of the car and went inside. He yelled, "Thee, I'm home."

Theenda walked up to Donovan and said, "who are you talking to," as she pecked a kiss on his lips.

Donovan whispered, "Lee."

Lee said, "We's heard da' overseer's' say Massa don't won't slave no moe,' he be killin' us. I's' don't won't ta' die Mr. Bright."

"I understand Lee, speed up the dig, I'll speed up out here. You'll be free soon."

"Thank you, Mr. Bright."

Donovan put the phone in his pocket and asked Theenda, "what's for dinner?"

"I have a taste for pizza, butter pecan ice cream, with caramel, lots of whip cream and a cherry on top, and hum, a big old fashion pickle. Like the ones they sold in the corner store in Brooklyn."

"You might need to visit a doctor Baby Girl. That sounds disgusting."

She sent Donovan out for ice cream, she called the pizza shop and ordered two pizza, then asked if they sold whole pickles. They did, she ordered five.

XXXV

A Place To Meet

May 19, 2017

Donovan's father bought him a black and silver Cadillac Escalade, he had it shipped to Ogville. Donovan piled his truck with the small band of abolitionist and drove them to Magnolia Resort in Tan Springs Alabama, population seven hundred twenty-three. Unlike Mary and Joseph, that went to Egypt to hide because of the similarity in looks and color, Donovan took them to an all-white town. Theenda said, "Sweetie, white town, in the south, hangings still going on. Is there anything in your brain that screamed, bad idea?"

When they arrived at the hotel, KayKay said, "good choice hotel Donovan."

The suite's bedroom was separated from the living room, there was a kitchen and a business area. The hotel was exquisite, five stars. It had a weight room, sauna, swimming pool, a Jazzercise program, and a five-star restaurant that sold pickles and ice cream. Theenda said, "good choice Sweetie."
Timpkin said, "I'm impressed."

Tess said, "I'm glad Haze not here, trying to get me to go back with him."

They all ignored her.

A few days before making the reservations, Donovan called his dad, James, on his home land-line. He asked his dad for a large sum of money. He and his dad had a pretend argument about Donovan wasting his money. The quarrel was for Chief Stevens, who had put a listening device on Donovan's home office phone. The day after Theenda's mom hanging, Donovan wrote a letter to his dad, he thanked him for the new truck, he told his dad about the slaves, Theenda's mom, and his bugged phone. Donovan took Theenda to a fancy restaurant in a town on the other side of Titleburk, where he mailed the letter. And then the couple prayed that God would get the letter to his father. To let Donovan know he received the letter, during the phony phone argument James was supposed to say, "why don't you write instead of call, or use your cell phone, it would be cheaper." During the conversation, James said those exact words.

Donovan ended the phone call by saying, "dad you're right, I need to do better with my money. You and mom have a blessed day."

When he got off the phone with his dad, Donovan asked Theenda, "what do you have a taste for dinner."

Theenda said, "Pizza, ice cream, and pickle."

Donovan said, "that's disgusting, let's eat out." In the car, Donovan continued, "dad got the letter."

"Cool," Theenda replied, she rubbed her belly and said, "I really do want pizza..."

Donovan cut her off and said, "let's go to the store, get the ingredients to make our own."

Theenda said, "even better."

With all the deaths that had taken place due to the hidden slaves, Donovan stayed on high alert.

Before leaving for Magnolia, Donovan told the modern-day abolitionist to leave their cell phones at home. He instructed them to only bring their pay-as-you-go phones. The hotel kitchen had closed, before going there to sign in, Donovan stopped past Kentucky Fried Chicken, and got enough food for twenty people. They went to the hotel carrying their overnight cases and food, they put the food in Donovan's suite. Once settled in the hotel, Donovan called a meeting in his suite, during the meeting KayKay complained about the lateness of the hour and long drive, she was sleepy, Timpkin eyes were droopy, Tess was chatty as usual, and Theenda was eating.

"We need to plan," Donovan began.

"Why can't we meet tomorrow?" Timpkin asked as he fixed himself a plate.

All But One

"The sister of Mr. Brown wants to help us for a small price," Donovan said ignoring everybody.

"What's the price?" Theenda asked.

"Escape with us."

By this time, everyone was piling food on their plates, then joined in on the conversation.

Theenda commented, "everybody on the run."

Donovan explained, "her name is Becky Lou, she got word to Lee that the plantation owner is going to kill the slaves and leave the country."

Tess yawned, then said, "maybe the message from Haze will help to speed things up. Haze found a trailer camp, about three thousand miles west from here, that's for sale they are high in the mountains."

Donovan looked confused, he asked, "he contacted you?"

KayKay antenna went up, she was stuffing her mouth with food, while chewing she nudged Timpkin when Theenda said, "no, I told her you got a text from him."

Donovan said, "oh," he continued saying, "those places are full of fighting hard-core poor people."

Theenda said, "think about it, where cheaper could all of us and slaves live together."

"My concern is money." KayKay chimed in.

Donovan explained, "Becky Lou knows a rich elderly white lady who is willing to finance everything, back in the day her family were abolitionist."

Tess said, "that piece of black trash Haze has not contacted me, I'm his wife." She looked at Theenda and spouted, "you didn't have to tell them."

KayKay was sitting on the edge of her seat. Theenda ignored Tess, she asked, "How many trailers are there Sweetie?"

When Timpkin began talking KayKay almost fell out her chair, he said, "Haze said the whole camp is for sale, over a hundred trailers, a park, and a little pond."

"How many are empty?" KayKay asked.

Timpkin answered, "All of them. He said it's cold, so we'll need winter clothes."

Donovan asked, "what did you talk on?"

"The pay-as-you-go phones you gave us."

Donovan said, "good."

KayKay asked, "how will we get the slaves over three thousand miles?" KayKay was proud, her husband was part of the plan and not Tess, whom she despised.

Timpkin blared out, "two school buses and use my fifteen-passenger van for the elderly."

"Tim, what are you talking about?" Theenda asked.

Timpkin said, "a few of the slaves are in their late sixties and older, the bus may be too rough for them."

Donovan looked around the room at each and said, "in a month, I would like for us to be out of Ogville, MacCall, and Titleburk."

Theenda asked, "what about Juneteenth, it's a month away? How far are the slaves in their dig?"

Donovan said, "Baby Girl, they are killing people, we have to go."

"Slow your row Sweetie, so we don't get caught, too fast we'll make mistakes. Pray, plan, go on the eighteenth of June."

Tess asked, "can we get help?"

Donovan remarked, "Thee and I have a meeting with the elderly woman when we get back. She knows people that are willing to help."

"Where will you keep the buses?" KayKay asked.

"I'm a teacher, I'll see if the owner of the junkyard that opened a few months ago let me keep them there, I'll tell them it's for my students," Donovan replied.

KayKay commented, "they couldn't be that stupid, the school supplies the buses."

"Hum, no," Donovan commented, "the bus driver is an alcoholic, I'll give him a few dollars, he'll keep his mouth shut. I'll give the junkyard man some money."

"What a waste of a human," KayKay uttered.

Timpkin studied his wife's face and said, "you should know."

The meeting went on for two hours longer, KayKay stood and said, "I'm going to my suite to sleep,"

As she was leaving Donovan said, "Wait, Kay, we'll finalize our plans at eleven in the morning."

"Where?" Theenda asked.

"The hotel serves breakfast, so eat when you can, I'm checking us out at ten thirty. There's a park not far from here, we'll get there at eleven." Donovan looked at his phone, he continued, "Haze texted me pictures of the trailers, I will show them to you tomorrow at that meeting."

KayKay said, "it's late, why is he taking pictures in the dark?"

"He's three hours behind us," Timpkin answered.

"Yeah, it's eight out there, the sun hasn't set," Donovan added.

KayKay left.

Tess asked, "what's with all the secrecy?"

Theenda said, "our homes plus Haze, is bugged."

****

May 21, 2017

The digging crew on the plantation was back in the church, Lee said with joy and a little too loud, "God Almighty, when we dig under Massa gate, we be on fee' ground." The men jump up and down, clap their hands, whooped and hollered like children playing.

Glaidous said, "fee' ground. Thank you, Jesus. You men been diggin' a long time, workin' in da' field, den' sneak ova' here and dig foe' several hours. Yaw' rest, cause ta'night, I's' dig, I's' won't ta' help us off dis' evil place. I's won't' ta' look back and say, I's help ta' dig us out."

"We's be fee." Lee said.

Glaidous said, "Mr. Bright wrote in dat' note, they be trailer homes. Big houses I's' neva' seed' Massa house, but I imagine big likes' dat."

"I agree," Lee said.

Saul stood shaking his head back and forth before saying, "I's' cain't see me livin' in a place dat' big, I's' git lost."

Jethro commented, "you's' say six rooms dem' trailer house got's?"

"Mm' hum, that's right and the toilets be inside the house," Lee said.

Ben gasp, "dat' make da' house stank."

"Dats' how dey be livin' in feedom," Jethro exclaimed.

"Dey got lots and lots of thangs' in feedom dat' we's' neva' seed afo," said Ben.

Lee looked excited at the men and said, "I won't ta' see dis' feedom, I won't ta' live fee, Mr. Bright said we get a job and get money."

"What we do wid' money," asked Jethro.

"Buy thangs," Ben answered.

"We cain't explain it but it gonna' happen," Saul commented

"Let's start digging," Lee put his hat on and said as he climbs down into the tunnel, "unk you comin?"

Before climbing down the hole, Glaidous looked around the church and said, "God Almighty, thank You's foe' feedom." He put his hat on, then turned the light on.

****

March 22, 2017

Theenda and Donovan met with Mrs. Paddleton and Becky Lou for the first time. He and Theenda's drive was not far because the Paddleton's lived north on the outskirts of Ogville. Theenda said as she got out the car, keep one eye on Becky Lou, she may be working for Mr. Brown."

"I'm not a kid Baby Girl, everything is covered."

"Sweetie, be safe."

Mrs. Paddleton lived in the castle that Charles Brown built when he ran away from his brother Drew, and son Duke in the 1800s. Her husband died of cancer and never told his family that he was sick. Donovan had no idea that he was meeting the offspring of the family for whom his ancestors were a slave. Donovan walked up on the porch, his heart thumped faster than a newborn baby, his nerves were as fragile as crystal, turbulent thoughts tread out of pace like an unrehearsed marching band. "Is this a trap," he asked himself. He looked at Theenda and asked her, "are we about to die." He reached for her hand and held it tight.

Donovan was nervous as he stood in front of the gigantic mahogany double doors. He looked at the golden lion that was holding a great big round golden knocker in its mouth. Donovan stared in the lion's eyes, and said, "I'm a dead man."

Theenda used the hand that Donovan was not squeezing and knocked, when the door opened, Becky Lou said, "hello, I'm Becky Lou, and you are?"

"Donovan and Theenda Bright," Theenda answered.

"Come in, Mrs. Paddleton is waiting for you."

Becky Lou and Mrs. Paddleton were related, though Becky Lou had no idea.

Donovan, Theenda, and Becky Lou entered the library, two walls had bookcases that ran from the high ceiling down to the floor. Mrs. Paddleton was a well-dressed, friendly ninety-seven-year-old woman. She remained seated in a chair next to a beautiful antique desk. Donovan and Theenda went to her, she held out her thin-skinned hand that had big blue veins roaming up and down, like a roadmap. Brown liver spots sprinkled from her elbow down to the back of her hand. "It's a pleasure to meet you Mrs. Paddleton," they each said.

She responded, "Mr. and Mrs. Bright, the pleasure is all mine, please, have a seat." She looked at Theenda and said, "you are as beautiful as I have heard."

Donovan sat in the antique love seat that matched the desk, he looked around at the rest of the room, the furniture dated back to when the house was built. The furnishing, the walls, the woodwork, even the pictures on the wall were meticulously cared for. Donovan remarked, "your home is lovely."

Theenda sat next to Donovan. Becky Lou had seen Donovan and Theenda pull up, sit in the car, and slowly drag up the walkway to the house. She said, "you hesitated out there."

"I thought about the many others who were killed," Donovan said looking at Mrs. Paddleton.

Theenda elbowed him and gave him a stern look.

Mrs. Paddleton caught the look but asked, "What others?"

Donovan said, "I know about Phil and the Stacy family, my student and his family, Breeze."

Becky Lou said, "that's not half the people the Browns have murdered to keep their precious plantation hushed. In the 1800s, Harry V. Brown killed his wife and best friend. His youngest son Drew killed his dad, then years later he killed his brother, Charles, and one of his nephews, and raised the other nephew. One ran away when he was sixteen, the other stayed and became Massa of the plantation, he killed a cousin that got in his way. Between 1875, and now, that's way over a hundred years, the Brown's has killed hundreds."

Partial of Becky Lou recollection about what exactly happened was missed screwed. Back in the 1800's Charles son, Duke wrote an apologetic letter as to what happened to his father and brother Cody. In the letter, he wrote in detail the events and how he was involved. Charles burned Duke's letter and rewrote that segment of the family history as Becky explained.

Donovan's eyes paused on a picture of a man with two boys, and the same man in a picture all alone. Mrs. Paddleton said, "that's Charles, my husband's great-great-grandfather." Mrs. Paddleton studied Donovan's face, and said, "When Becky Lou informed me about your dealings with the Browns slaves, I had to meet you."

Donovan said, "I read about your family's activities on the Underground Railroad stations, you have two rooms in your basement that housed runaways until it was safe for them to leave."

"The man in the picture built this house, it is a smaller replica that Harry V. Brown built. Mr. Charles used the same contractors that constructed Mr. Brown's castle. He turned his home into a station for runaways. His name was Charles Paddleton, he said that there were white Massa's who would not let their slaves go free, so they ran. Slavery is supposed to be over Mr. Bright. It isn't, is it? You see Mr. Bright, the most brilliant slave Massa in this country, Harry V. Brown, set up an unbreakable steel house. Out of all ninety-seven years of my life, there have been six people who discovered the Browns secret, none found the exact location of the plantation, and they are all dead, because of greed."

Donovan interrupted and asked, "greed?"

"Yes, they wanted money to keep their mouth shut. You, on the other hand, discovered the plantation, been to the plantation, spoken with the slaves, and promised to get them free.

All But One

Not once did you bribe the Browns or the police for money, as did the others."

Donovan looked questioningly at Mrs. Paddleton. He was amazed at her freely giving a stranger an overabundance of information. It flowed easily from her elderly lips. He wondered if she was stalling, or telling the truth, will he walk out alive.

"How do you know all this?' Theenda asked.

"All this what? My dear." Mrs. Paddleton asked.

Theenda said, "about the plantation and Donovan."

"Please, let this old woman rattle on a bit, is that okay with you two young people?"

"Yes ma'am," both Donovan and Theenda said at the same time.

Mrs. Paddleton asked, "What is your motivation?"

Donovan answered, "if it were me trapped as a slave, whether I knew about freedom or not, I'd want somebody to be doing all they could to help. The slaves are prisoners who never committed a crime."

Mrs. Paddleton looked at Theenda and asked, what's your motivation?"

Theenda said, "now that I know for a fact that there are people held as slaves, it is our God-fearing responsibility to set His people free. I feel very strong about that."

"Mr. and Mrs. Bright," Mrs. Paddleton said, "I am going to help you with money, you have to get the slaves far away from here, and I will see to it that you will not be harmed. You cannot afford to make any mistakes. When Beck told me about the memoir, it was I who told her to give you a copy."

"Thank you." Donovan said, "they were very helpful."

"Do you understand that when you save them, they cannot stay here."

"We have a place to stay, it's a trailer camp that's for sale, we need money to purchase that."

"You got it." Mrs. Paddleton said joyfully.

"Mrs. Paddleton."

"Yes, Donovan."

"How do you know so much about the plantation?"

"I read the memoirs. You see they hid them under the floorboards in the children cottage. Beck found the memoirs when she became the relief for the slave girl that watch the children."

"No, I mean before you received the memoirs.?"

"Ah," Mrs. Paddleton said, "you are clever. So, you picked up on that I know about the slaves."

"Yes, ma'am," Donovan answered.

Mrs. Paddleton looked at Becky Lou and nodded. Becky Lou said, "I am related to those people."

Theenda jumped, she grabbed Donovan's arm.

"No need to worry Mrs. Bright, the plantation owner is my brother."

"You mean to tell me, you lured us here to have us killed?" Theenda asked.

"No." Mrs. Paddleton said, "not unless they are coming here to kill me as well."

"No one is getting murdered anymore," Mrs. Paddleton said with confidence.

"What do you mean?" Theenda asked.

"My brother is tired of the plantation; he wants to travel and see the world. His first stop will be in Nova Scotia, he and his wife want to visit someone named Jeff. But before they leave, the slaves will be killed."

Donovan, Theenda, and Mrs. Paddleton gasp in shock and discuss. "What are you talking about Beck," Mrs. Paddleton asked. She looked at Donovan and said, "Mr. Bright, if you are planning on freeing the slaves, now is the time to do so."

Becky Lou told Donovan that back in the day, four men policed the outer gate, but several years ago that stopped.

"So that's why we've been able to come and go at will," said Donovan.

Mrs. Paddleton asked Donovan if he had paid close attention to the map of the plantation?"

Donovan replied, "not really, how would anyone know the exact setup."

Mrs. Paddleton said, "think about it. The nurse is stolen from her family. She's brought to the house, lied to about her position inside the house. She's taken down the path, past the forest where bodies are buried, I'm sure not six feet under. I believe anyone would know what a dead body smell like. She's taken to the children's area. To deliver a baby she's escorted to the slave area. She must walk past the slave town, the tobacco fields, to the front of the gate to the opening, into the cabin."

All But One

"I see, Theenda began. "I can only imagine, when the nurse saw the magnitude of the house and the richness of the inside. I'm thinking she may have thought, she had died and gone to heaven, she saw dollar signs, so agreed to take the job."

"And then locked in for years," Donovan said.

"Not years." Becky Lou said.

"For the rest of their lives." Mrs. Paddleton said.

Confused, Donovan said, "you lost me."

"You see Mr. Bright, the forest they walked past, becomes their grave." Becky Lou explained.

Theenda said, "you said only a nurse, the memoir has where a teacher entered notes."

"Oh, that's right. The nurse got to go to the slave quarters and back to the children area with the baby. The teacher stayed in the children compound." Becky Lou explained.

"Have either of you notice that there's a dark stillness in this area?" Mrs. Paddleton asked.

"Yes ma'am, I noticed that when we drove through MacCall, the darkness and smell is thicker," Theenda said.

She looked at Theenda and asked. "That was your mother they hung, right?"

"Yes, ma'am."

"You were smart not to try and find out what happened, they would have eliminated you. Murder and those slaves are the dark clouds that hover over these three towns death is what you smell in MacCall. You're right Mrs. Bright, that smell is stronger on the west side of MacCall." Mrs. Paddleton stood and continued, "I have something for you." She went over to a desk, pulled out a checkbook, as she wrote she said, "Beck go get the cases."

Mrs. Paddleton gave Donovan a check. She said, "the first of many."

"This is enough for the down payment for the trailer homes," Donovan said with excitement.

"You fill in the name of the real estate company."

Donovan stared at the check and said, "this is overly generous of you, I wasn't expecting anything, he asked, "how did you know the cost of the trailers?"

"I didn't, I asked the Lord, how much? Then wrote down that amount."

Theenda said, "bless you."

Mrs. Paddleton said, "I have cash that I am going to give you."

Becky Lou entered the library and sat two black cases in front of Donovan, Mrs. Paddleton said, I'll walk you out to your car," she looked at Becky Lou and said, "Beck, please fix me something to eat, I am hungry."

Becky Lou said, "yes ma'am." She turned and left.

Mrs. Paddleton got her cane and walked the Bright's to their car, standing next to the car she explained the briefcases content, she said, "one has cash, and in the other case, my husband's great-great-grandfather recorded everything, from the beginning of H.B. Metropolis, to when he ran for his life. I have a black case filled with the original documents; you have the copy of those same documents. I believe Mr. Bright that you will enjoy the content. Keep it safe."

Theenda asked, "why did Mr. Paddleton write about the plantation."

Donovan put the briefcases in the car, Mrs. Paddleton said, "Harry V. Brown was Mr. Charles father. Becky Lou has the story about the Browns wrong."

Donovan saw Becky Lou coming towards them, he quickly asked, "you're related to her? Does she know?"

"No, she does not."

Becky Lou walked up to them and said, "Mrs. Paddleton, I will take you to that Japanese Stake House you like. I'm paying."

Mrs. Paddleton said, "that sounds delicious."

Donovan asked Becky Lou, "how do you know Mrs. Paddleton?"

Becky Lou looked over at Mrs. Paddleton, then said, "on weekends I clean her home, cook enough meals to last throughout the week. I fill her in on what's happening on the plantation. Plus, her granddaughter got me out a jam."

He looked at Mrs. Paddleton and said, "Thank you Mrs. Paddleton. I am lost for words at your generosity."

"Thank you, Mr. Bright, I have always wanted to see the slaves become fugitives during my lifetime."

"Why didn't you help them escape?" Donovan asked.

"My husband used to say, it's not time, it will happen on God's time."

Donovan shook his head and said, "I was nervous about coming here." He looked at Theenda, and continued, "I thought maybe it was a setup, my thoughts were on my wife, how much I would miss her and she would miss me, I sat in my car thinking leave, run. I'm glad I didn't. Thank you both."

Theenda said, "yes, thank you."

Becky Lou said, "you haven't seen the last of me yet, I have to go with you, or brother will have me killed."

Donovan said, "If your life is in danger, let me know, I will help you escape to someplace safe; you can leave now."

Mrs. Paddleton asked, "how did you come by the name Theenda."

"My mother wanted one child, a son preferably. I'm the youngest of three when I was born, she said I am through having children, this is The End of this, pronounced, Thee-End-Da. She never had another child."

Becky Lou turned to Mrs. Paddleton and said, "I believe in this, I can't stop." She looked at Donovan and said, I have more information at the bus station."

Mrs. Paddleton said, "you said train station Beck."

"I did? Oh, I did."

"Be careful Beck." Mrs. Paddleton said frowning, "you cannot be careless, child."

"Will do," said Becky Lou. She looked at Mrs. Paddleton and asked, "do you mind if I stayed the night and leave in the morning."

"Don't mind at all, but first take me to that steak house."

Becky Lou looked at Donovan and asked, "How are you getting them out?"

"Don't ever tell anyone that info." Mrs. Paddleton said to Donovan, then looked at Becky and said, "that is none of your business."

Donovan looked at Mrs. Paddleton and said, "again, I cannot thank you enough."

"You are welcome."

"Why are you doing this?" Donovan asked.

"My family approve of what you're doing. Beck gave me two keys to the gates; they are in the case with the money."

Theenda hugged Mrs. Paddleton, she said, "you are a wonderful lady." She hugged Becky Lou and said, "thank you for introducing us to Mrs. Paddleton, and helping."

Mrs. Paddleton and Becky Lou watched them drive off, she whispered, "God be with you."
Becky Lou said, "they are very young."
"They are chosen, by God." Mrs. Paddleton said.
"Amen," Becky Lou agreed.
Mrs. Paddleton said joyfully, "I'm going to wash up and change clothes"
Becky Lou asked, "why?"
"You're taking me out to dinner."
They laughed as they entered the house.

Donovan had driven his sports car with the top down to Mrs. Paddleton, he said, "I'll have to leave my car behind."
Theenda said, "this is happening. Sweetie, we're abolitionist."
"Leaving my truck, this car, your car behind. Everything behind Baby Girl."
"Sweetie, we are saving lives, we'll buy more things. I'm sure on the other end of the world there are stores."
Donovan reply, "new car and truck. Okay. I like that."
Theenda said, "we'll have to pay our cars off and leave only the car manual in the car."
"Good idea, let's clean the cars out when we get home."

XXXVI

Haze Return

June 7, 2017

    Early one school morning, Donovan had already left for work, Theenda was moving a little slow that day because she was not feeling well. She leaped out of bed and ran to the bathroom and regurgitated, this was her third morning dashing to the bathroom. Before going to work she stopped at the drugstore and purchased a pregnancy test. The cashier who was friends with Theenda asked, "are you having a baby for our town?"

    Theenda thought before answering, she knew that Haze was returning in one week which would be just in time to help slaves escape, she answered the cashier laughing, "I'll know tonight."

    The cashier replied, "stop past in the morning and let us know."

    Another employee joined the conversation and said, "I hope you have a boy, too many girls were born this year."

    The three women laughed, Theenda said, "until tomorrow ladies." She left and drove to the school, in the parking lot she asked herself, "how am I going to be an abolitionist, expecting?" She bowed her head and prayed, "Lord, please be in total control of the abolitionist, slaves, our escape, and this child. In Jesus name, amen." As Theenda entered the school Donovan flashed in her mind, if he learned that she was pregnant he would stop the escape. At that moment, Theenda decided to not tell her husband, until it was too late.

June 15, 2017

One week after taking the pregnancy test and on the same day of Haze return, Theenda sat in the examination room twiddling her thumbs. The test was positive, so she found a doctor that combined faith, healing, spirituality, and medicine. She felt that a doctor of this sort would help her through the abusive life she suffered and overcome the fright of becoming a mother. Theenda believed that after an abortion, her system was not strong enough to carry a child. She had promised Donovan if she ever became with child, she would carry it to term. When she made that promise Theenda had no idea that she could get pregnant. And then she thought, maybe it's not a baby, maybe a cyst or fibroid tumor, she had a friend in New York that had a tumor, the doctors cut it out. Even so, there she sat anxious about questions, if she was pregnant what type of mother would she make? Will she abuse the child? "My sister does," Theenda said out-loud.

The Doctor entering the room heard Theenda, she asked, "your sister does what?"

"Abuse her children. Will I? Am I pregnant?"

"You are nine weeks, and no you will abuse this child."

"We were abused by our mother and neglected by dad."

"That's not you Mrs. Bright. Society says, all abused kids will grow to become abusers, that's a fabricated lie. Mrs. Bright, you will look on your child's tender young face, into those innocent eyes and see unconditional love. You see Mrs. Bright, the difference between a counselor and God is the doctor knows only what the patient tells him, God knows everything we suffer. Talk to Him, review with Him all-things, and God will fill in the blanks without your knowledge because maybe, what you forgot will be too much for you to bare. On the day you feel like getting a baseball bat and thrashing your child with it, most parents have those days."h

Theenda laughed.

The Doctor said, "walk away and call on Jesus, He will calm you down."

Theenda left the doctor's office with renewed sacred strength. She called Donovan and told him she had good news but did not want to share it over the phone. She asked him to meet her for lunch.

Donovan was in the teachers' lounge taking a rest between classes When Theenda called. "Baby Girl, I'm tired."

"I'll see you at 12 o'clock at our favorite bistro. Love ya." She hung up thinking, *it's too late for him to cancel the escape which is on the seventeenth, and I am carrying two little humans.* Theenda was giddy with joy, she called Donovan's mother, after telling Sara, Theenda said, "don't tell Don, I'm springing it on him at lunch today."

Sara asked, "when did you find out?"

Theenda answered, "I took a pregnancy test last week, it was positive. Today at the doctor's office, she confirmed."

Theenda and Sara were overjoyed. Theenda said, "mom, I'm carrying twin boys."

Sara asked, "why wait to tell Don?"

"He would have to cancel the escape, but now it's too late. We rescue the slave and leave out in two days."

Sara was shaken and overcome with fright, but all she said was, "I'm calling James soon as we hang up."

After purchasing a pregnancy test, two female employees asked Theenda to return the following day to let them know the result, Theenda returned as she promised. When the conversation ended with Sara, Theenda was returning to the drugstore to tell the two women that she was carrying, twin boys.

At the end of the school day, Donovan went to the junkyard to meet Haze, who was returning home. The attendant at the junkyard allowed Donovan to hide two school buses in the back of the yard. Donovan anxiously waited, he checked his watch about a hundred times and paced.

Haze had purchased a small used car to drive from the trailer park back to Ogville, over three thousand miles. Donovan heard a vehicle approaching, he ran in the direction of what he was hearing and saw Haze speeding in the driveway of the junkyard. When Haze spotted Donovan, he put the car in park and jumped out, both men ran towards each other. Haze was the first to speak, "man it's good to see you." He grabbed Donovan, they hugged.

Donovan pushed back from Haze and said, "it's been too long," He looked in Haze eyes and said, "you look good, rested. How'd you get along these few months?"

"It's lonely out there, no friends, no woman, nothing. Man, I got to get' married."

Donovan smiled, "You are."

"A new wife Don-man. Look at my face, no cuts, no bruises, my back, watch this." Haze jumped up and down and spun around. "No pain man."

"I get your drift. I have good and bad news." Donovan said.

"What's the good news."

Donovan said, "Thee and I are having twin boys."

"Shut-up, you going to be a daddy."

The two laughed for a moment.

Haze said, "congrats man."

Donovan said, as though it was an afterthought, "Haze you can't go home, Tess didn't sign the papers."

"Why?!"

Donovan answered, "the police are watching your house."

"No Don-man, why didn't she sign the papers?" Haze asked irritated.

"She says you want her back, Tess and Thee, are at Timpkins waiting to hear from you."

"Where am I staying?"

"At Mrs. Paddleton's."

"Who?"

"Call Tess so we can go," Donovan said.

Haze called Tess, anger was in his voice when he said, "Tess."

"Hello, how are you?" Tess said sweetly.

Donovan put his hand over the phone and said, "hang up."

"She needs to sign the divorce papers." Haze said as he hung up.

"I am taking you to Mrs. Paddleton, I will tell Tess to go there this evening."

"Who's Paddleton?"

"I'll explain on the way." He looked at Haze car and said, you're leaving this car here."

All But One

"I paid cash for it."

"Really Haze. You paid, what? Two maybe three dollars?"

Haze laughing said, "in the day I would not be caught in that thing. But marry a woman like Tess, the police is out to kill you, yeah, that will drive a person humble quick. I had no time to think about it. So, yeah, I bought a 1978 Ford Pinto Coupe. It made it here man."

Donovan said laughing, "we're leaving it here, let's go."

Haze handed the keys to the junkyard man, before he got in Donovan's car, he looked back at his car and said, "I took Pinto to the shop and they fixed her up, most of the parts were none existent so they made the parts, if anyone buys that car, they will become a believer in Christ."

Both men got in Donovan's car, sitting behind the wheel Donovan asked, "what'd you mean? "I prayed with the turning of the tires, Jesus please help me get home, thank you, Jesus, for helping me get home, Jesus please help me..."

Donovan laughing said, "I get it." He looked at Haze and said, "so, He got you here safe."

As Donovan pulled off, he called Theenda. "Baby Girl, I need for you and Tess to go shopping for Juneteenth celebration. I will text you when I get Haze to Mrs. Paddleton what I need."

"Gotcha Sweetie." She hung up.

Tess asked, "who was that?"

Theenda grabbed her purse and said, "We're going shopping for the Juneteenth Celebration."

She looked at KayKay and said, "we'll be back."

KayKay said, "dinner will be ready."

Theenda looked at Tess and said, let's go." She quickly walked out the door, with Tess close behind.

Tess went to her car, Theenda said, "we're taking mine." She opened the door and tossed her purse in, then got down on her hands and knees and crawled around the car looking underneath and under the chrome. Tess watched Theenda with a strong disinclination, then said, "Thee get off your knees, we're taking my car."

Theenda got up, brushed herself off and said, "get in."

"How about I drive," Tess suggested.

"Will you get in the car," Theenda yelled in a low rhythmic whisper.

Tess got in Theenda's car, but said, "something is wrong with you woman."

Theenda put a CD in, she cut the sound all the way up before yelling softly, "your car is bugged."

"Who told you?"

"Felix, the black officer told Donovan, who told me to tell you. Donovan had me to check and see if the police are watching our house. I saw one."

"I am so glad you were sitting there when Haze called, or I would have gotten diarrhea of the mouth and spilled everything."

"Me too," Theenda said,

Tess asked, "we through talking about this."

"Yep."

Tess cut the radio down when Theenda pulled off, Tess said, "girl cut this music down are you deaf?"

"You crazy."

"Where are we going?"

"To the mall in Titleburk, girl, they are having a sell like none other. You know those tweed suits that Donovan wears, they are expensive but half off at the mall, I need maternity clothes, and I am picking up a few items for the Juneteenth Celebration."

Tess's mouth gaped open wide, her face froze in a surprised look, as she asked, "you're having a baby, or are you joking around?"

"Yes, I'm having two," Theenda joyously squeaked.

"When did you find out? Have you told Donovan? What did he say?"

"Hold on girl, I will answer all questions one at a time."

The two women drove off laughing.

Donovan and Haze were on their way to Mrs. Paddleton house. Haze asked, "Everybody ready to leave?"

"Almost, we need a few more days, but only have until tomorrow."

"Since the police are watching my house, where am I sleeping?"

"Right here." Donovan parked in front of Mrs. Paddleton's castle.

All But One

"This house. Wow, it's huge."

"Yeah, her home," Donovan said.

"When am I going to see Tess."

"Tonight," he looked at Haze and asked, "are you going to be able to drive Saturday night?"

"Yea, why?"

"You drove cross country, only to drive back in a few days."

Haze said, "I'll be fine as long as I get a good night sleep."

Donovan looked at Haze and said, "thanks man, you gave up a lot, your life, your company."

Haze responded, "my top man, Doug is running it. Besides Don man, we're all giving up a lot. Our homes, cars, clothes."

Donovan's youth came out when he said, "my sports car man, dad bought me a new truck."

Haze said, "stop whining."

Donovan said, "Oh shut up, where's the trailers located?"

"In a city on top of a mountain, they are in a middle-class suburb all by themselves. The people that owned these things had a whole lot of money. I didn't know mobile homes could have seven rooms."

"Are there schools where Thee and I can teach, a place for Kay and Timpkin to work? How about you and Tess?"

"There's a high school about fifteen miles away, an elementary school a few blocks from there. Timpkin can work at the Government building. As for me, there's no janitorial service in town."

Donovan said, "you'll have to change the name of your company."

"From, Day by Day too, I don't know what."

"Hum, I don't know what, not-a-bad-name for a company."

Haze smiled and said, "You're silly Don-man."

As they got out of the car to enter Mrs. Paddleton's house, Donovan asked, "where can the slaves work?"

Haze answered, "At the glue factory."

"Is it close to the trailer court?"

"Yea, the factory is about thirteen miles away from us."

Donovan said, "Mrs. Paddleton gave us a great sum of money, if it's enough, I want to sell the trailers and build houses."

Haze perked up a little as he said, "I'm all for that. I hired a lawn company to clean up the area and take care of the yard for now when we get there the newly freed can do it. The trailers and land are all paid for."

"Good job and thinking Haze," Donovan said.

A very grateful Haze said, "thanks man for sending money for me to live off."

"When you said you got a temp job, I thought he's going to need more money to add to your pay."

Becky Lou went to the train station to get the items she took from the mansion. She kept watching for anyone that may have followed her. From a distance she looked at the locker, it appeared that no one had tampered with it. A man walking past startled her, she watched each person in the station and then escaped to the bathroom to calm herself. When she came out, she observed the area and every person as she slowly went over to the locker and grabbed the items. Feeling safe, she exhaled and ran.

Theenda and Tess finished shopping, they returned to the Linwood's where Donovan was talking to Timpkin. When they entered the house KayKay's burnt greasy food made Theenda's stomach feel queasy. Donovan watched her turn three shades of green, he jumped up and took her to the bathroom. Tess smiled while Timpkin and KayKay looked confused. "What's wrong with Thee," Kay asked before anyone could answer, she said to Tess, "it's about time we meet someplace other than their place."

Tess said to KayKay, "you're a mean vile woman."

Timpkin concurred, "yes, you are Kay."

Theenda and Donovan returned to the table.

Tess looked at Theenda and asked, "you okay?"

Timpkin said, "it doesn't matter where we meet or eat."

Donovan whispered to Timpkin, "they can hear us."

Timpkin said, "I had one and removed it."

KayKay had prepared greasy fried chicken that was hard, the cornbread had fallen and didn't get done in the middle, and whole green beans that were too salty and slimy with grease.

KayKay was busy in the kitchen putting the food in serving dishes, Theenda asked KayKay, "may I help."

"No, I'm almost finished." She entered the dining area and sat the food on the table.

Tess frowned, everything looked terrible.

KayKay looked at Donovan and said, "I went downtown today with some of my coworkers, I was surprised and had to admit, there were countless vendors from surrounding cities and states that were preparing for the three-day celebration. There's going to be four kiddy rides and three adults, looks like it's going to be a decent Juneteenth. you two is so young I didn't know you could pull it off. Juneteenth is only a one-day event."

Theenda looked at Donovan, their eyes met. Timpkin saw the exchange as though he understood, he whispered, "sorry."

KayKay sat down and said, "dig in," she looked at Theenda and said, "at least I would have had it on one day."

Theenda looked across the table at Donovan struggling to chew the chicken, she watched Tess take a small bite of a green bean and frowned. KayKay looked at Theenda's plate and said, "everything all right Thee, you haven't touched your food. Eat."

"My stomach is a little upset," Theenda replied.

Donovan said, "we're pregnant, Thee gets sick at smells and certain foods." He looked at Theenda and said, "I would imagine about now, you feel like paying the toilet another visit."

"Oh Shut-up Donovan," she said as she quickly ran to the bathroom.

Timpkin said, "lil' Don going to be a daddy."

Donovan smiled, KayKay said, "we must shop for baby things, bed, dresser," KayKay got up from the table, she continued, "I need to get a piece of paper, got lots to plan."

Tess said, "their Donovan's babies, you can't plan without them,"

Timpkin said, "Kay, sit down." He looked at Donovan and asked, "did she say, babies."

"Yes, we're having twin boys."

KayKay tried to look innocent when she said, "Thee is going to be vomiting for several months, she won't have time to plan. Besides I gave birth to three children, I know what the baby needs."

Tess said, "I'm confused, what your children have to do with theirs."

Theenda returned from the bathroom heard Tess yell at KayKay, "silly woman, I try to respect you, but sometimes Kay you make it really hard." Tess clench her teeth tightly together, balled up her fist and said, "you don't know what Theenda or Donovan want for their baby, the baby's needs are what the parents want."

Kay observed Tess's angry stance and said, "I know because I've had a few babies, you haven't been pregnant."

Tess advanced closer to Kay, Theenda stood between the women and asked, "you two okay?"

Tess did not back down, she pushed Theenda out the way, she looked in KayKay's shifty eyes and said, "you know nothing about me."

Donovan jumped up and grabbed Theenda out their way.

Finally, Timpkin grew tired of KayKay's busybody meddlesome gossiping way. After seeing the slaves for the first time, Timpkin visited his mother and asked, "should I leave KayKay?" The conversation he and KayKay had the morning after going to the plantation, caused Timpkin to have doubts about his marriage.

His mother said, "she is an awful gossiping woman, but I believe in her own selfish way, love you."

Timpkin looked at Donovan protecting his wife from his, he looked at wild Tess, he turned the television on and said in a commanding tone, "everybody sit down." He looked at Kay and said, "you will not run or ruin Theenda and Donovan's happiness by meddling in their business. Tess is right, they know what they want for their twins and for themselves."

"You side with the little brat?" KayKay asked.

Donovan yelled, "will you people be quiet!" he was watching TV, there was a picture of Becky Lou on the screen, Donovan said, "Baby Girl, Becky Lou is dead."

They all got quiet, the reporter on television said, "Another body was found at the feet of Harry V. Brown's statue, this time the dead body is an offspring of Harry's, Miss. Becky Lou Brown. She was a troublesome woman; the Brown family will be saddened from this loss."

"KayKay said, "she was nothing but a trollop."

All But One

Donovan looked at KayKay and said, "they are killing people left and right, even their own family."

Tess punched KayKay hard in her arm. KayKay tried to cry but no one was paying her any attention.

"Wasn't Becky Lou supposed to escape with us?" Timpkin asked.

"How do you know that Timpkin? you never told me," KayKay asked her husband.

"You can't keep your mouth shut long enough," Timpkin replied sharply.

"Becky made several mistakes, she did not deserve death," Theenda said.

"Mrs. Paddleton told her to be careful," Donovan replied. He looked at Theenda and ask, "are you going to be okay Saturday with those people. I can cancel this."

"No, you won't. All they want me to do is be a cook and clean the dishes," Theenda answered."

"No wonder they asked for a cook, they knew..." Tess stopped talking, then asked, "didn't Becky Lou cook for them sometimes?"

Theenda turned to Tess and said, "you know you're right, they began looking for a cook about three days ago. Becky was still alive."

"Baby Girl be careful," Donovan said with great concern.

Tess looked over at KayKay and asked, "how 'bout you take Thee's place, she has to carry a heavy sack, stand on her feet for a couple of hours, or you take my place and drive the bus, while I take Thee's placed as a cook."

KayKay looked stunned that Tess would make such a suggestion, "you hit me, my arm is sore. Besides, I portray a common domestic? My intellectual persona will beam through, there is no way the Brown's would believe that I'm a maid."

"KayKay," Timpkin yelled disgusted, "they will see a brown skinned old fool, better still, what if they put you out with the slaves." He folded his arms shook his head and said, "yeah, there's a good thought."

Donovan looked at Timpkin and said, "it's okay man."

Theenda said, "I'll be fine, I stand all day teaching and running after my students."

Donovan looked around the room and said, "everybody ready?" He looked at Theenda, and said, "Do you have the instructions on how to get to the house."

"I put them in my car, so I wouldn't forget."

"Good girl," Donovan said to his wife. To Timpkin he said, "when you get there, cover your car, then wait. Haze and I are going to the junkyard to get the buses, when we join you at the plantation, we'll park next to you."

Theenda said, "park the bus, Sweetie, you're coming up to the house to get the kids and me."

KayKay said, "when are we going to get food."

Theenda answered, "how would we explain buying enough food for over one hundred people?"

Tess said, "she only thinks of herself, no one else."

Timpkin still mad said, "Amen to that Tess." Then asked, "why is there a road that leads to the back of the house?"

Donovan said, "that was the original road before highways were built, Tom and one of his son's had a street put in the front of the house, the road in the back they stopped using."

Ignoring Timpkin and Donovan, KayKay asked, "how's it going on the plantation?"

Donovan answered, "Mr. Brown allowed Glaidous to hold midnight church services, all the slaves attend, except Bo. Mr. Brown is preaching Sunday morning service, the slaves and we will be gone.

With a confused look on her face, KayKay asked, "what night are we leaving."

"Saturday," Tess answered still angry, "where were you when he said that a second ago?"

KayKay sucked her teeth and rolled her eyes at Tess, as she held her arm like it was in a sling and constantly rubbed it.

"Well I need some rest," Theenda said as she yawned, she looked at Donovan and said, "Sweetie let's go, I'm sleepy."

"Aren't you dropping me off at Mrs. Paddleton."

"Yes," Donovan said to Tess.

"Wait, my car."

Theenda said, "I forgot we have gone around in my car today."

Donovan said, "Tess ride with Thee to our place, get your car, I'll text you the address, click on it and…"

"Yea-yea," Tess began, "my phone will tell me how to get there."

****

Lillie went to her brother's shack and banged on the door, and softly yelled, "Glaidous."

Sophie came to the door, "Lillie what's wrong."

Lillie asked, "is Glaidous in."

"I's' fetch 'em," Sophie said as she went up to the narrow stairs that led to the sleeping loft.

Glaidous came to the door and asked, "what Lillie?" He stepped outside, even though he was barefoot, so they could talk in private.

"You see Lee, Ben or Saul? I's' knocked on Ben and Saul's door, I's git's no answer. And Jethro ain't home."

Glaidous said, "those knuckled head boys be at the church digging. I's fetch' em." He started to walk with Lillie.

Lillie stopped and looked at Glaidous and said, "thanks Glaidous, but get dressed and put some shoes on."

It took Glaidous five minutes to get dressed, as he was leaving out the shack Sophia asked, "whar's you be goin'?"

"I's be back when I's gets' back." He left walking in the direction of the church, with only the moon and stars as his guiding light. Glaidous walked inside the church and found all four men sleep on the church pews. Glaidous yelled softly, "you boys better wake up, change clothes, Massa knows these ain't clothes he gib' you."

Lee, Ben, Jethro, and Saul woke up from a sleeping stupor, they had worked all day in the field, after they finished in the tobacco field, they went straight to the church and dug to four o'clock Friday morning. Lee woke up yawning, he rubbed his eyes and face, then said, Massa, need ta' leave me alone."

"Amen to dat," Ben agreed.

Glaidous said, "y'all git' up, go home, and clean up, Massa be lookin' foe' you in da' field, bout' an hour."

Jethro said, "Massa be full of da' devil."

"Amen to dat," Ben agreed again.

Yawning and stretching Lee said, "unk, my first Sunday morning out of here I want to go to a fee' church."

Ben said, "old Massa sang loud "Bringing in da' sheep. Naw' I won't miss dat."

The men took their slave clothes out of the bookbag and began to get dressed.

Saul scratching, and wiping his eyes ask, "why da' sheep gotta' join' da' church?"

Lee quickly said, "sheep, hum, I's thanks' cause' white folk take dey' sheep ta' church."

Jethro agreed, "now dat' make sense?"

Saul said, "we can't, cause we be slave."

Glaidous being the preacher answered, "Jesus be our shepherd, we da' sheep." Glaidous looked around to make sure that everything was in place, once he was satisfied, he said, "let's go." Then asked, "how far did you dig?"

"All the way up," said Jethro.

"Unk we been on freedom ground under the outer gate. We even went up on the top of the ground, it be real big on da' other side of da' gate."

Jethro grabbed Glaidous arm and said with a big smile on his face, "da' air smell clean."

Glaidous asked, "did it feel different? did the dirt smell different?"

"Nothin' we's smell afo," Lee explained. He reached in his pocket and said, "we been by a big forest where trees grow bigger dan' the whipping tree." He handed Glaidous a big leaf and continued, "look at this." Glaidous smelt the leaf. He cried, "you's been on feedom' ground. Da' leaf be biggest my hand."

Lee laughed and said, "Jethro took off runnin' to da' trees, we follow behind him. We's picked lots of leaf's." Lee said as he handed Glaidous another leaf, "I's git some foe' mama."

Jethro said, "it feel good, and I's knows why nobody can see us. Past da' grass, is lots and lots of trees, all ova."

"We's cover da hole back ova'," Saul said.

Ben said, "I's gonna' likes feedom." He looked at the guys and said, "it be big, don't it?"

Lee said, "we's bout ready ta' go."

Glaidous said, "dat' be ta'morrow night."

All But One

As they were leaving, Glaidous went in the backroom and look down in the hole and said, "feedom, glory be." He put the leaf in his pocket and closed the curtains to conceal the backroom's secret.

In Lillie's cabin, she sat down and said, "that med-dee-cin' Mr. Bright wife gib' us is powerful good. My stomach ache be gone, my hands stop hurtin,' my back, and knees stop hurtin.' Lee look at my knees," she pulled her skirt up to her knees.

Lee said, "mama, I don't won't ta see yo' knees pull yo' dress down." He handed her a bouquet of dandelion.

Lillie asked, "whars' you git dis? Dey' be pretty."

"I's been on feedom ground mama."

Lillie jumped up and said, "glory be ta' God, we's gonna be fee soon." Glaidous entered the cabin, Lillie said to him, "Lee be on feedom ground." She showed him her bouquet of dandelions.

Showing Lillie his leaves, Glaidous said, "I's know old woman. Dey' were in da' church sleep."

Lillie said, "iffen da' ovaseer seed dem."

Lee said, "dey may not tell Massa, dey' wonts' ta' leave too."

"I believe Lee be right," Glaidous said.

Lillie sat down, she folded her hands in her lap and said softly, "den' we's cain't leave."

Glaidous asked, "sis, you's got dat' whiskey Mr. Bright gib you."

Lillie brighten up and said, "sho'nuff' do."

Lee ran up the steps to his room and returned with the Essence Magazine and Cush, he laid the magazine on the table. He got a chair and sat at the table, Lillie, Glaidous, and Cush did the same. Lee said, "a few months ago we sat around dis' table and said, we's neva be da' same."

Lillie said, "glory be ta' God the Highest."

"We's learn der' be no moe' slave, we be agin' da' law. Ta'morrow, we's be fee." Lee said.

Lillie said, "no moe slave, Glory be ta' God."

Glaidous said, "let us bow down and worship God and tank' Him fo' our feedom."

The family bowed down on their knees; Lillie prayed a prayer of deliverance that she didn't know was within her.

God can hear the prayers of His people, generations away.

XXXVII

The Day Before

Friday, June 16

  The Juneteenth Committee had planned a humongous dynamite celebration. When the Government in Titleburk and MacCall, in addition to Charles Brown, and Mrs. Paddleton heard about the jubilation being held in Ogville, their donation was included with the funds raised by Ogville's citizens and its Government. The committee raised five million six hundred thousand dollars, mostly due to Charles and Mrs. Paddleton donations. No one, in either of the towns had ever raised so much money, Charles was impressed with the committee and wanted to meet Donovan.

  Mrs. Paddleton gave three million dollars, she told Donovan, "use some of the money to make Saturday programs big and eventful, everyone including the officials will be worn out."

  Donovan said, "Yes ma'am, I will."

  Charles donated one million, a friend of Donovan's dad, James, in New York, donated one million, James told the man the money was for a good cause. James donated two hundred and fifty thousand dollars.

  The committee on their own raised three hundred and fifty thousand dollars. Which would have been enough for a one-day celebration without the parade, they would have given Ogville schools a little bit of money. Donovan had the committee to agree to give each town, Ogville, Titleburk, and MacCall a portion of the funds for the renovation of their schools. The committee members thought the young handsome man from up north was a godsend. The Mayor of Ogville said, "what a brilliant idea, all the schools are old and dilapidated in our three towns."

The first day of Juneteenth was about to begin, the opening for the celebration was an immense parade. They had Clydesdale horses dressed regally, the horses pranced in unison as they led the parade, from New York Donovan had an African choir to perform in the parade, along with African drummers and dancers, there were floats, bands, singers, there were dancers and their musicians of all nationalities, and cartoon characters. Several schools from around the state, elementary to college, performed or marched in the parade. Committee members were working on different projects, others were assigned to a performer or performing group. Many of the musicians were in the parade waving, the crowd went wild when they saw the stars in person.

KayKay and her six church friends and the women that attended the first committee meeting were at the opening of Juneteenth. A woman from the first meeting said, "I don't think we'll get bigger than this." She was excited and proud; her son was playing in the college band.

KayKay rolled her eyes at the woman and walked away, she wanted to talk with Theenda, who was busy setting up the outdoor stage, and everything needed for the different performances. Timpkin was helping Donovan and some of the committee members with the parade. Timpkin said to Donovan, "this is hard work but fun," he ran off to tell the band from his college alma mater, it was time for them to begin their march. Timpkin was having the time of his life.

His wife, KayKay on the other hand, was angry and jealous, she heatedly said as she violently walked to her car, "how could those country bumpkin idiots, Thee, and Don do this." KayKay drove off, she seethed out loud in the car, "next year it'll be even bigger, I'll plan in secret, I'll do Juneteenth all by myself. Only losers need a committee." She smiled pleased with her decision.

Saturday, June 17, 2017

Donovan got up early, he was meeting with the committee members to review that day's itinerary and go over the following year's Juneteenth program. He said to Theenda, "Baby Girl rest today, we have a long night ahead of us."

She sat up and said, "okay. What time are you coming home?"

"Around one. I am so nervous for you."

"I'm going to be okay; I may need help getting the children out. Are you still helping me?"

Donovan thought for a moment and said, "change of plan, I forgot about the kids."

"What do you mean."

"You see the slaves are closer to the forest, the children are closer to the house." Donovan sat for a moment and said, "too many plans gone wrong can create our death."

Theenda said, "give me the keys, they are to the divider gate and children gate. When I finish at the house, I'll go get them."

"Hum," Donovan said, then continued, "I'll drive the bus up, while you're in the house I'll get the kids."

Theenda said, "still, put the keys in my purse."

Theenda looked at the clock, it read 6:30. She laid back down and said before going to sleep, "God knew this day would come. He needed you, a modern-day Moses to save his people."

Donovan stood with a confused look on his face, he went over to thank her for the compliment even though he was not buying he was Moses. He said, "Baby Girl."

She was fast asleep. He kissed her on the forehead and left.

Forty-five minutes later, Theenda was refreshed, rested, and ready to start her day. She was excited about the challenge of unraveling adult minds, from a slave mentality and introduce themselves to who they were and could become. As for the children, she planned to develop a curriculum to replace good with evil, and really get them ready for their new life.

That morning around nine thirty, all kinds of vendors had a booth, there were two or more selling similar products and twelve food trucks. Long lines had formed around the booths and the rides. The vendors sold books, purses, toys, clothing, art, watches, scarves, wigs, cancer awareness had a booth, a medical booth where people could get their blood pressure taken, quilts, architects, real estate agency, and two different banks from other counties had a booth, the vendors came from far and near. The committee had commandeered professional singers from Tennessee, California, and Oklahoma. Friday night Faith Hill and Tim McGraw were performing with their backup singers and band, it was standing room only. There were so many people that had attended, if the concert was not outdoors, the fire department would have put the people out. Everybody stood except for seventy VIP seats in the front.

The spirit of Ogville was over the top, the celebration was the biggest ever. Titleburk was the largest town among the three, their mayor asked Donovan to host the celebration in Titleburk in 2018. Ogville committee insisted to accompany Donovan to Titleburk and be a part of the planning committee. Ogville had over twenty thousand people to show up for the Friday event, the little town was not big enough to host such an event.

Saturday morning the crowd was growing, Ogville had to hire police officers from other cities. People were showing up to hear, country singer, Blake Shelton, and attend Sunday morning church service, which was going to be held in the park. Thousands wanted to see and hear four famous TV preachers speak, services began at seven o'clock and would end at 12:30. That evening finished the three-day festivity on a high, a gospel concert with three well-known choirs, and five top gospel quartet groups were scheduled to perform.

In order to make room for the massive crowd, the police had people park their vehicles in Titleburk and MacCall. The Juneteenth committee rented shuttle buses to transport everyone from the two towns to Ogville. The first two days of Juneteenth began as an entertainment for the public, the third day was to end celebrating God.

From Ogville to Titleburk all the hotels were full. Those who had motorhomes stayed in them, others had tents, Ogville park and amphitheater was being used for seating and a stage for the performers, MacCall beach became the campsite.

By ten o'clock on Saturday morning, a little under thirty-nine thousand people were crowded in Ogville, with the expectancy of thousands more to attend the festivities. Lunchtime Blake Sheldon was going to sing only two songs. At eight o'clock

All But One

that evening, his concert was going to be a show. Fog lights, strobe lights, the stage was going to sparkle and glow, Blake Sheldon's people were setting up Hollywood style. It was estimated that fifty thousand people planned to attend the night show. He was going to sing two songs with his girlfriend, Gwen Stefani. Donovan said to a committee member, "tonight is going to be an overcrowded exciting hullabaloo."

When the Ogville mayor heard what Titleburk mayor was trying to do, the two men got into a heated argument. Barbara loved country music. Charles brought her to hear her favorite crooner, he arranged for her to meet him and his girlfriend backstage after the concert. Nonetheless, before the program began, he stood listening to the two mayors argue.

Charles Brown, grandson of Harry Victor Brown, and Donovan Victor Bright, grandson of Paula, Harry's slave, were only a few paces from each other, they were separated by a crowd of people. When the mass dispersed, Donovan and Charles's eyes met. The men had never seen each other, yet they knew exactly who the other was. They froze as they stared in each other's eyes.

Donovan noticed that Charles appearance was commanding and in charge, he was an aristocrat, his movements were exact, not normal. He looked like a man with a dark secret, Charles emotionless eyes made Donovan shiver. Charles smiled as he observed that Donovan was a gallant strong-minded young man, he was a leader, Donovan was what Charles hoped his son would be but failed. Charles looked in Donovan's determined eyes and thought, *I have to watch him, or he'll destroy me.* Donovan looked in Charles' eye and thought *he will kill me if I don't leave.*

When their momentarily paralyzed gaze ended, Charles found his wife, he took her to the two Mayors that were quarreling. Donovan watched the stranger go over to the Mayors, he wanted to hear him speak, so in a distance followed Charles and his wife. Donovan smiled when he heard Charles unique voice, it was a baritone soft imposing, smooth velvet tone. Charles said, "MacCall is between these two towns, we have the biggest space by the river that will hold twice as many people that's currently here." He looked at Ogville mayor and asked, "which I believe I heard close to forty thousand is in attendance, correct?"

"Yes." Ogville's Mayor answered.

"Then it's settled, MacCall will host this event yearly by the MacCall River." He looked at the Mayors and asked, "do you agree?"

Both Mayors and several members of the planning committee said, "yes."

Donovan walked away but kept a close watch on Charles, he called Theenda and said, "stay home, the Browns are here." Donovan left whispering to himself as he went to his car, he said in a matter of fact tone, "he's gotta go."

Charles looked around to see if Donovan was still in the area, he did not see him, Charles exhaled and thought, *he's gotta go*, he continued speaking, "I will sit on the committee with you." He looked at the partial committee members that were around him and said, "you did a splendid job. He and his wife left.

Charles and Barbara strolled around, they purchased things from several vendors and ate, Charles got his blood pressure checked, it was high, the nurse suggested that he go to his doctor. On their way to the concert, Charles said to Barbara, "Sunday morning we'll be gone but first I have to get rid of Donovan."

Barbara asked, "how are you going to sit on the committee?"

Charles said, "it's once a year, how hard can it be, those sorry looking ragga muffins did it. Can't be that hard." He and Barbara laughed. They sat in the VIP section, Charles said, "I got a glance at Mr. Bright. He stands out from the rest." Charles looked around at the people and the decorated stage.

Barbara asked, "why kill him?"

"He will and can destroy me."

The announcer got on the stage and introduced the first performers and broadcast that Blake Shelton was performing in an hour, the crowd went berserk with cheers. Everyone knew he was there because he was in the parade on Friday. Barbara enthusiastically said, "all this is that young man's doing," she stood applauded and cheered with the crowd.

Charles beamed with satisfaction; his wife was having a good time. But deep within, he felt that something was wrong. When Barbara sat down Charles whispered, "we'll take him out before we leave."

"I'll call the chief."

Charles said, "good, let's have a good time tonight and make the call in the morning."

Barbara said, "tomorrow after you preach," they both laughed, she continued, "on our way to Canada, I'll call Stevens."

Charles put his arm around Barbara and said, "one last job."

Donovan stood and watched wall to wall people, the park was so crowded it looked like a cluster of ants scurrying about. Standing there watching, he flashed back to the meeting with KayKay and the other Ogville black residence, a woman said, "white people will not come to a Juneteenth, thing."

Donovan smiled, about eighty-five percent of the attendees were white. He left.

****

Beginning June twelve through the sixteenth, Glaidous had been holding midnight revival. Charles allowed him to have the services, however, the disclaimer was he would end the revival by preaching on Sunday morning. Holding church service at midnight was the brainstorm of Donovan, it was his suggestion to Lee in a note left by the gate. It was the only way to get the slaves together and out of their cabins.

Since the slaves work in the field ended early on Saturday, Glaidous was in Lillie and Lee's cabin, he said, "let's git' everybody to da' church after work, feed them. We'll start everythang' early."

Lee said, "dat's right unk, we make sho' we leave on time."

"Lawd a' mercy we's talkin' bout' bein' a walk-about," Lilly said as she paced the floor.

Glaidous said, "glory to God. Dis feel like a good dream."

****

Ten Fifteen

Haze had given Tess the keys to his hose, Tess walked around touching things, when she moved into the hotel, she left most of her belongings behind. She was back in the house to pack a few items of clothing, mementos her mother had given her, and a picture of her mother. Tess father killed her mother, first he strangled her then pushed her down a flight of stairs. He claimed she stumbled. Being a police officer, at first, Tess father got away with the murder. But the coroner pulled the fingerprints from around her neck, her father was put in prison. He wrote Tess an apologetic letter, that claimed her mother accidentally fell to her death. In the letter, he asked her to come to visit him, because life was hard in jail for a police officer, and to tell his lawyer that he was innocent.

Tess set the letter on fire in the kitchen sink, she said, "no dad, your finger marks were around moms' neck." She looked around the house and was satisfied she had taken all she wanted; she took nothing for Haze.

She took her wedding ring off and laid it on the coffee table. Before getting in her car, she put the key to the house in the mailbox, then drove to the Juneteenth celebration. Unfortunately, Tess strategy to humiliate Haze in front of Mrs. Paddleton, and get Donovan from Theenda, failed. She was put out of the Paddleton's home and ignored by Donovan; Tess was fuming.

****

During spring break Donovan and Theenda flew home to New York. While there, Theenda visited her sister, who was attending a secretarial school. Since their mother was hung, and father was nowhere to be found, her sister cleaned up her life, her six children, and the apartment she lived in. While Theenda was at her sister's home, a courier delivered a letter from their dad. He wrote stating, *"your brother ran to Paris France, where he worked for a construction company. Earlier this year, I returned home, I was broke and struggling in Paris, your mother wrote saying she had a guaranteed way to get lots of money, in a southern town. After your mother's death, I left again for Paris, a few months after my return, your brother was killed instantly when a scaffold he was on broke and fell to the ground. Shortly after his accident, I was diagnosed with cancer. For three years I knew something was wrong but did not go to the doctor. When I went, cancer had aggressively spread throughout my body. I apologized girls I always knew where your brother was, I apologize for not being there for you."*

He ended the letter saying, *"if you're reading this letter, I have died. There are three checks in the letter, one from your brother's insurance and his compensation for a faulty scaffold. The other is my Insurance. I saved the money for you two, I pray this makeup for my negligence."*

Staring at the checks Theenda said, "sis, between these checks, there are eight hundred thousand dollars we can split." They jumped up and down like children outside playing. Theenda stopped and asked, "wait, aren't we supposed to be crying?"

Her sister said, "girl please, let's go to the bank now before you return home."

Donovan sat with his parents and told them all about the Brown plantation, and how he, Thee, and four buddies were freeing the slaves. Sara said, "son, be careful."

James sat deep in thought and said," you can't do this alone, with just a handful of people. That doesn't sit right with me."

"Nor me," Sara agreed with her husband.

****

Ten Thirty

Theenda took their packed luggage down the steps and set them next to the door. To rest, she sat down, ate a pickle, then fell asleep. James and Sara had flown to Ogville to help with the escape. A cab dropped them off in front of the Bright's home. The doorbell rung, Theenda answered, she was surprised and happy to see them, she nor Donovan knew they were coming. Donovan's parents wanted their visit to be a surprise.

James walked in saying, "there is no way we could sit at home knowing what you two are trying to do."

"That's right," Sara agreed. "And you being pregnant and all, hum' um, I had to come."

Theenda said, "we appreciate it." She gave them a hug and said, "Donovan is at the Juneteenth celebration. I'm packing things in my car, meet Donovan there, I'm not coming back home," and then it hit her. She stood next to the sofa her mother had chased her behind, she said as tears rolled down her cheeks, "our first home together. I'm going to miss my class, I've made friends." She cried.

Sara wrapped her arms around Theenda, and said, "it's going to be all right Thee."

A very uncomfortable James said, "I'll pack the car." He grabbed two bags and took them in the garage where Theenda's car was parked.

When he entered the house Sara asked, "Jay, did you pay the cab?"

"Yes, you jumped out the car so fast it startled me and the driver."

As Theenda reached for her suitcase Sara said, "child put that down. Carry you and my grand-babies out to the car, Jay and I got the bags."

Sara agreed. Theenda had texted Donovan, to let him know that his parents were in town and they were on their way. He texted back stating he was at Mrs. Paddleton's, he was coming home after the visit. As they waited, Theenda said, "Donovan told me not to come to the Juneteenth Celebration, the Browns are there."

Sara said, "I don't understand."

Theenda explained, "I am going to be a cook at the Brown family house tonight, then free the children"

James said, "you're not going out there alone young lady."

Theenda showed them the map of the Brown mansion and plantation. She had copied the map of the different gates. James continued saying, "I'll open the gates and help with the children escape."

Theenda asked, "how long are you staying, we're leaving at midnight."

Sara said, "as long as it takes."

Eleven O'clock

In Mrs. Paddleton's home was Mrs. Paddleton, Phillipa, Phillip, and Haze. He had a deep scratch from his forehead to the top of his lip. Donovan looked at Haze and asked, "what did you do?"

"I told you, it's not me."

All But One

Phillipa said, "in front of us, she was kind and gentle. And then…"

"Yes," Phillip said, "upstairs away from us, she turned into a loud boorish rough idiot."

Haze said miserably, "this is why I want the divorce. I was fine, no cuts, no bruises, now look at me."

"Okay, you three." Mrs. Paddleton said as she handed Donovan the letter that Charles had written long ago. She continued by saying, "Donovan this young man has been roughed up enough. Get that wild child to sign those divorce papers. I am against that but in this situation, I realized there are times when my belief, needs to be put aside."

Phillip said, "that's right grandma."

Getting back on track, Phillipa surprised Donovan with the news that the Paddleton's knew they were related but the Browns had no idea. Phillip said, "they are a murderous common lot." He pointed to Haze and continued, "his wife belongs with them."

Phillipa said, "not because we think we're better, simply we like people, so we have nothing to do with them."

Mrs. Paddleton said, "back in the 1800s, any distance more than ten miles could take a day or more to travel. To get away from the family Charles came to Ogville which was days away. We know we're related to them because of Charles memoir and this letter." Mrs. Paddleton pointed at the letter Donovan was holding then continued, "put it in the black case, now our cases match seamlessly."

Donovan said, Thank you Mrs. Paddleton." He looked at Haze and said, "man, I'm sorry."

Haze said, "no prob."

"Good," Mrs. Paddleton began then said, "you two remain, friends, through this adventure your about to do, you'll need each other."

Phillipa asked Donovan, "is there anything I can do to help?"

When Phillipa asked the question, an answer to Theenda's suggestion popped in his head. Donovan zoned out for a minute, he remembered Theenda's text saying his parents had come to town. He would ask if his dad would help drive across the country since they were in town.

446

Mrs. Paddleton asked, "Donovan are you with us?"

"Yes ma'am, I just figured out a solution for something." He looked at Phillipa and said, "thank you for asking but for now all is well, it's kind of you to offer."

Phillipa said, "your wife has my number if you need anything…"

Donovan smiled and said, "you're so kind, the whole family is unbelievably great."

Mrs. Paddleton walked Donovan to the door, and said, "Chief Gideon is quietly helping you all he can. It's Stevens the Chief of MacCall and Titleburk that's in the Browns pocket. Go with care young man." She handed him a briefcase filled with cash. "I'm giving you cash again and not a check. For quick use."

Donovan took her hand in both of his and said with a big smile, "thank you Mrs. Paddleton. Without you and your family, I'm not sure we could pull this off."

Haze, Phillip, and Phillipa joined Donovan and Mrs. Paddleton by the door, Phillip said, "I'll bring Haze this evening to the junkyard."

Donovan said, "Mrs. Paddleton maybe you can explain, how did Thee's mother know about the slaves."

Phillip, Phillipa, and Mrs. Paddleton laughed, she said, "It was all planned, one of your church members heard your wife talking to the pastor about her evil mother, pushed down steps, beatings, the list is long. We don't know who in that church enticed Mrs. Carboy here by dangling money. But we all helped once she got her. You didn't know she was here because she was supposed to stay for two weeks, then receive hush money. Luckily, we all knew she would go looking for her daughter, act wild and crazy. We planned well; she went banging at your door. Unknown to you and Mrs. Carboy, she was being watched closely, by us. Chief Stevens already knew she was here, he waited for her to play in our hands."

"How did your group get Mrs. Carboy address?"

Phillipa laughed, "not too many people named Carboy, she was easy to find."

Phillip said, "your wife spoke with the pastor a week before we put the plan motion."

Donovan laughed as he said, "had I not mentioned slaves…"

All But One

Phillip said, "that was the frosting on the cake. We were hoping she would just get violent."

Mrs. Paddleton said, "every time you went out to that plantation you were followed, for your protection. When you took Haze to the airport, how do you think he got a seat so quick?"

Donovan said, "I don't know."

Mrs. Paddleton said, "Felix, who is Chief Gideon's right-hand man, called Thee and told her what to say. Then he called the airport and gave them your name, instructing them to give what you wanted."

Phillip said, "man, you and your boys went out there a lot, delivering stuff."

Donovan said, "digging tools, food, medicine, all black clothes." He stopped talking for a moment then continued, "I saw Mr. Charles Brown today. He's a well-dressed scary looking man."

Mrs. Paddleton answered, "It's because of keeping a secret that's so big. You can't fix him so save them."

Donovan said trying to figure it out, "Mrs. Paddleton, you're like the Underground Railroad."

"Exactly," Mrs. Paddleton confirmed.

Donovan said, "one last question, did my wife know her mother was coming?"

"No, that would have frightened her," Phillip answered.

Haze said to Donovan, "it is such a blessing to be a part of this. Think I'll start going to church."

Donovan asked Haze, "you're becoming a Christian?"

"Naw man, I've had bad dealing with those people. They are mean."

Phillip said, "yea, I've run into a lot that's like that. There is a handful that's nice. When they say I'm a Christian, I run very fast."

Haze said, "I haven't run into a needle full of good Christian."

Mrs. Paddleton said, "yes you did, Donovan and his wife."

Haze paused in mind and soul before he said in a whisper, "that's right. He's my first and true friend."

Donovan said, "I normally say I'm religious, because I've met and worked with Christians."

They laughed.

Becky Lou commented, "the woman I work with at the Library has Bible verses taped to her computer, desk, and listens to Christian music."

Donovan asked, "in the Library?"

"There's an office and break room for us."

Mrs. Paddleton commented, "she wears her religion in public for all to see and not in her heart where it matters with God."

Haze said more to himself, "that's the problem with the world. Look at me, look at me."

Smiling Mrs. Paddleton said, "look at us quietly making a difference."

Donovan said, "we'll never receive an award from humans but from God…"

Becky Lou said, "that's what counts, a reward from God is greater than anything man can give."

Donovan said That's right." He looked at the three and said: "Mrs. Paddleton, it may be a while before we meet again." He reached out and gave her a hug.

She said, "you have my phone number and address, stay in touch."

Donovan said, "the best thing that happened to me outside my wife, is meeting you Mrs. Paddleton." He bowed like a gentleman and kissed the back of her hand. He gave blushing Becky Lou and Phillipa a hug. He shook Haze and Phillip's hand, then said, "see you tonight Haze.

When he pulled off, Mrs. Paddleton cried. Haze said, "he is the man I want to be."

Phillipa said, "the man every woman wants."

Phillip said, "He's a James Bond kind-of-guy."

Mrs. Paddleton said as she wiped her eyes, "yes, James Bond, smooth, easy going, soft spoken, and well dressed."

"And extremely handsome," Becky Lou said dreamily.

Twelve O`clock

Donovan was on his way home; his heart was pounding fifty miles a second. He had seen the devil eyeball to eyeball. He said as he sped home, "God help my Baby Girl, she's cooking for Satan tonight."

****

On the plantation at noon, Lillie and a few of the ladies baked cakes, cookies, and a feast for the evening meal. The women did not mind helping, Lillie told them, "we be celebratin' God fo' a week."

One lady said, "cause He be a 'comin' in da' midnight."

All the women said, "glory be ta' God"

"Dis be a good week," Lillie said smiling.

XXXVIII

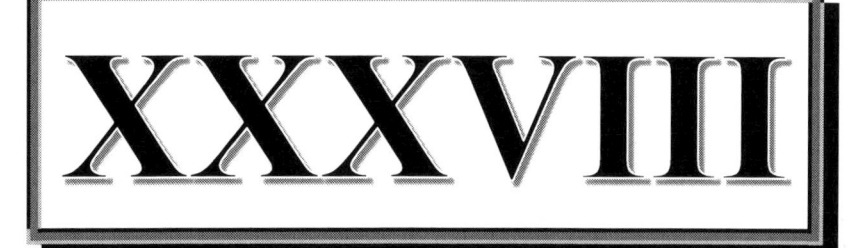

Night Of The Escape

June 17, 2017
Four O'clock

  In the Bright home, Donovan, Theenda, James, and Sara prepared to leave. Donovan and Theenda gloomily rambled through the house, making sure they were not leaving any momentous behind. Theenda carefully wrapped the bride and groom that was on top of their cake, in bubble wrap. They also took pictures, Theenda had kept the tiny velvet box her engagement ring came in, she and Donovan took small items that were dear to their hearts. The couple hugged and cried, they had to leave everything behind, except the objects they were taking. James and Sara sat on the couch holding hands, James said, "we are freeing slaves, I am having a hard time wrapping this around my brain."
  Sara said, "I asked you a question."
  James replied, "yes."
  Donovan and Theenda entered the room carrying book bags filled with memories, Donovan let out a long sigh before he asked, "ready?"
  Before leaving the house, Donovan said, "God be with us."
  James said, "let's pray." The four stood in a circle holding hands as James partitioned God for their safety.
  Leaving out, Donovan said, "we're going to be all right." He kissed Theenda and left going to the junkyard which was an hour and a half drive. But the way Donovan drove his sports car, it took him less than forty minutes, but first, he had to meet with

the panicking committee members. They were anxious about having an event in MacCall. Though Donovan did not say, he knew they were afraid of Charles Brown and his hidden chattels. Ogville residence stayed away from Titleburk and MacCall, but now they were being forced to host a program in the dreaded town.

With James driving, Theenda was in the passenger seat, and Sara in the back, they were going to the Brown's mansion. Theenda to prepare dinner for Charles and Barbara, while James and Sara would quickly tiptoe around the back to save the children, their compound was seven miles from Massa house.

****

The plantation

Jethro had given the overseers water down liquor from the slave store, but Lillie had filled the bottles, Jack Daniels, given to Lee by Donovan. While the slaves enjoyed the food and festivities, the overseers were drunk and sleep in their cabins. Otherwise, the overseers would have raided the food and made a mess of everything. The men set tables up for the ladies to set the food on, the fieldworkers washed up and changed clothes and congregated around the church. One of the women that were helping to serve the food, became ill. Lillie fixed mint tea and stirred and put Aleve in it. The woman guzzled it down and felt better within thirty minutes. She was surprised and in disbelief at how fast she healed. She told everybody about Lillie's tea.

Bo believed he was a cut above the rest, he never attended the service, though a few times he stood outside the church to listen.

Around five o'clock that evening, Bo saw Glaidous talking with several male slaves, he went up to Glaidous and asked, "old man how's the meetin' goin'?"

One of the men said, "it be good preachin' better'n' Massa."

Another man said, "yes Sir, good service."

Bo saw the elderly men through his trained eyes of hate, he said, "I only listen to Massa and Ahe's son preach, nigga' know nothin' bout' God, only Massa know about' God of Heaben."

Glaidous boldly said, "you need to come to the meetings, cause' we know moe' bout' God-den' Massa."

Grumpy Bo smirked, "you be taken' a big chance gettin' smart wid' me old man, I's' report yo' uppity talk ta' Massa, he bring' ya' down a size."

Glaidous and the men headed towards the church, the food was smelling good and it was ready to serve. Bo shyly asked, "dat' food foe' everybody?"

Glaidous said, "come on Bo, join us."

Bo fixed himself two plates, one piled with food the other sweets, he said, "thank you." He left and ate alone in his cabin.

****

In the Junkyard, earlier that morning before anyone arrived, Cole and his employee ran a test on both school buses, the new bus was in good condition. The older bus needed a little work, the two men gave the older bus an oil change, tune-up, new belts, repaired the heating and air conditioning systems, they purchased a new radiator and flushed the engine. Cole had a few city buses that were no longer used, they took the nearly new tires off those buses and put them on the older school bus. When the men completed their work both school buses were in equal condition. They drove both buses to a nearby gas station and filled them up, the buses were ready to go.

Cole said to his employee, "we're doing a good thing."

The employee responded, "a Godly thing."

It was a good thing that Donovan could not take Haze to the junkyard. Phillip needed to talk about something personal, he and Haze had become friends. Phillip shared with Haze that he had met a woman from New Jersey and was going to ask her to marry him. After seeing Tess, Phillip felt he needed advice on what to look for in a woman.

Haze asked Phillip, "is she pretty."

"Beautiful." Was Phillip's reply.

Haze said, "don't go by looks, be honest with what you see and hear her say and do." Haze warned him to steer away from women like Tess, he suggested, "meet her family first, get to know them."

Phillip asked, "did you do that."

"No," Haze answered and continued, "Tess was all over me like bark on a tree. She always had a reason for me not to meet her parents."

Phillip said, "you know, my woman makes excuses about…"

Haze cut him off quickly and said, "don't marry her. If she's refusing to introduce you to her parents, something is wrong." He shook his head and said, "nope, don't do it."

Phillip said, "she's very nice."

Haze said with confidence, "I'm sure great in bed. With the age of computers, look at her parents up, siblings, uncles, aunts. Tess dad killed her mom, he was a police officer. Investigate first, then ask her to marry you if all is well. If not, run for your life."

"Where is Tess father?" Phillip asked.

Haze said, "in prison."

Phillip said, "when I get home this evening, my research began."

When Haze got out the car he said, "let's keep in touch."

Cole walked around to the driver's side of Phillips car and said, "haven't seen you in a few weeks, how's everything going?"

Phillip got out of the car and said, "been busy helping with the escape uncle."

Haze looking confused and said, "so…"

"Phillip said, "my dad's brother, grandma son."

Haze said, "so, you're family," then asked, "your father coming?"

"Dad died a few years ago from cancer." Phillip stayed around for a few more minutes to talk before leaving.

Six PM

Donovan drove into the junkyard straight through to the back where the two school buses were parked. Tess was in her car driving behind Donovan, and KayKay followed Tess in her car. When they arrived in the junkyard, KayKay got out her car yelling at Donovan, "you drive like some crazed maniac."

Donovan calmly replied, "I didn't tell you to follow me. Could have come on your own."

"That's right Kay, you know where this is. I enjoy speeding down those backroads, mind you though, my car is not a speed demon like your sports car." She giggled sweetly and flirted with Donovan.

He paid her no attention.

Haze was already there when they arrived. Cole asked Donovan if he could sell their cars, his employee knew how to switch out the VIN number in the door and light, to give the vehicles new numbers from the cars he had junked. Donovan asked, "are you afraid of going to jail?"

"No, the people I sell these cars to is not your normal everyday folk like yourselves." Laughing Cole said, "remember, my name may be Paddleton, but my blood is from the Brown family who are crooks."

He and Donovan had a good laugh.

Donovan told Cole he could have his car and his wife when she arrived, and I have an Escalade at the house you can have." He gave Cole the key to his house.

KayKay said, "being a Christian woman I will sell you my car and give the money to a charity."

Donovan said, "you can have hers as well."

KayKay argued, "you can't decide what to do with my car.

Haze said, "ah, he just did."

Donovan began taking his and Theenda's things out of his car and put them on the bus he was driving. Haze emptied Tess car and put them on the bus he was driving. He asked if she brought some of his things. Tess rolled her eyes and said, "no."

KayKay got unmad and listened.

Haze said, "no problem."

Donovan asked, "what're you going to ware."

"I washed at Mrs. Paddleton's the clothes I purchased out west." He looked down at what he was wearing then continued, "Phillip gave me some of his things, we're the same size. Besides, I knew Tess was too mean and thoughtless to bring me anything."

When they were finished packing the buses, they talked as they waited for time to pass. Donovan and Haze were going to drive down a back road to avoid the main highway to MacCall. The detour was a two-hour drive to the Brown Plantation. As they were talking Tess asked Haze, "which one of these buses you're driving?"

Haze showed her by standing next to the doorway of the bus he was driving and said, "the one I put your things on."

Tess walked slowly backward for Haze and everyone else to get a full effect as to what she was doing, she stopped and leaned on the bus Donovan was driving. The two junkyard men and KayKay stood watching with anticipation, they could feel something was about to go down

Her tactic had no effect on Haze, when he caught a glimpse of Tess ring finger he asked, "where's your wedding ring?"

Tess got in Haze's face and said, "when I arrived at Mrs. Paddleton's home you were nice in front of her, in the bedroom you slapped me. I went home and took them off."

Haze asked, "does this mean you're going to sign the divorce papers?'

Tess looked around at Donovan, back at Haze and yelled, "hit me again, I will choke the life out of you, I know how I learned from my father." She reached up to slap Haze.

Donovan grabbed her arm and said, "not this time Tess, you're the bully."

KayKay was so into what was going on, she didn't realize that the men had huddle close to her. She was eating up everything that was happening, she was going to have some juicy gossip to share. Then she realized she had no one to tell, all her church gossiping buddies numbers were in the phone that Timpkin destroyed. She slumped. Then she realized the men were too close for her comfort, she snarled, "back off."

Donovan was going back to his bus, Tess shoved him hard out her way as she got on the bus he was driving. Donovan's nose flared, his back straightened as though he had an iron rod for a spine, he seethed in a low baritone voice, "I'm not the one."

Haze walked over to Donovan, put his hand on his shoulder and said, "she's not worth it." He looked at Tess and said, "why don't you stay in Ogville, sign the papers, you can have the house."

Tess screamed, "yes, Haze did hit me at that old woman house, Donovan he's lying."

Donovan said to Haze, "I will talk to mom, she's a lawyer."

KayKay was at her wit's end, she had her phone out, she took pictures of the threear. She found a member of her church and called her, when the woman answered KayKay said, "girl do I have something to tell you."

Donovan walked over snatched the phone, he threw it on the ground, Cole stumped the phone to smithereens, he said, "I want a piece of this," he smashed the cell phone in tiny pieces.

It was time for them to pull off and head to the plantation before they left, Cole told Donovan that the buses were in good condition, he shared with him the work he and his employee had done. He finished saying, "both buses have full tanks."

Donovan thanked Cole for his help and service, he handed him a manila envelope filled with ten thousand dollars. Cole thanked Donovan and told him that the money was more than enough. He said, "giving me the cars was pay." Cole handed the envelope to his employee, he said, "for you."

Donovan said, "when we return with the slaves, you can have my wife car." He kicked a rock then asked, "why are you putting your business in jeopardy."

Cole simple reply was, "this was a front when you came to town my mother knew, you were the one. We opened this junkyard." He looked around for the other man and waved for him to come over when he did, Cold continued, "we're making my friend here the owner. My law firm is in New York, I'm going back home to my wife."

The man said, "Ogville don't have a junkyard." He looked in the bag and said, "thank you for the money."

Flabbergasted Donovan said, "You're welcome," he looked at Cole and asked, "does your mom know how you run the business?"

"The cars will go to men in a shelter," Cole answered.

Coles employee said, "except your car, I am keeping that. I attend Mrs. Paddleton's church even though I am from the shelter. I'll get your Escalade when y'all is on the road."

All But One

Cole said, "men and women are in the shelters, they will use the cars to go to and from work. Mom doesn't mind. Remember she was married to a Brown."

Donovan laughed, he said, "all for a good cause," he shook Coles' hand and said, I saw Charles Brown this morning, he has a different look in his eyes."

Cole's employee said, "the Escalade is mine."

Laughing Cole pat the man on his back and said, "yes, it is you truck."

Donovan gave him the keys and said, "the title is locked in the truck's glove compartment."

Cole said, "we know how to change it over." He strolled over to Haze bus and whispered, "leave her, she's nothing but ghetto trash."

Haze smiled and shook his head in agreement. Before they pulled off Cole said, "when you return, mom will be here to say goodbye."

Donovan said, "good. She'll meet the people she helped."

Cole and the new owner of the junkyard, waved Donovan and Haze off as the buses were pulling out. It was 6:30PM.

Tess was on the bus Donovan was driving, and KayKay was with Haze. Tess said sweetly, "she'll be sorry."

"She's Timpkin's problem," Donovan said still mad, she had pushed him hard enough for him to lose his balance and fell against the bus.

Tess said in a sweet little baby voice, "Don, I am so sorry for pushing and yelling at you. I got caught up in Haze lies."

Donovan said not a word, it was a quiet two-hour ride to the plantation.

KayKay thought Haze wanted to chitchat about what just happened. She was like an eager beaver when she got on the bus. Haze was not in the mood.

James driving Theenda's car followed behind Timpkin to the Brown plantation. Sara asked Theenda, "you're carrying my grandbabies, and about to do what?"

"Burn the house down and save the children," Theenda answered like it was an everyday event. She turned to face Sara and said, "when Charles and his wife run out, we'll catch them and turn them into the Ogville police.

"You can't do all that. James help her."

James was nervous, he wanted her to shut up, he said, "honey, that's the plan."

When they arrived, Timpkin pulled over on the service road, James pulled behind him. Timpkin got out his van, James got out of the car, Timpkin gave directions to the house, Theenda and Sara talked in the car. Sara said, "Thee, James will get the kids, while you're in the house."

Theenda said, "I hope they don't get burned in the fire."

Sara said, "my hands are shaking."

Theenda smiled before saying, "my legs are wobbly."

Sara asked, "how are we getting the kids down here?"

"On the bus, Donovan is meeting us in front of the house. The adult slaves are closer to this road, they are running down through the woods."

James asked Timpkin, "how far is MacCall from here?"

Timpkin answered, "the street you're taking that leads to the house is less than five minutes"

James said, "thanks, Tim."

The two men gripped each other's hand tight; they were extremely nervous.

James got in the car and said, "we're off, this is happening." He let out a long sigh.

Sara said, "is this how the abolitionist felt? Scared stupid. I'm going to pray, Thee bow your head, James drive."

Timpkin covered his van with leaves and branches, and then paced and prayed for their safety, he prayed for the modern-day slaves, he prayed for the driver that had KayKay on his bus, he asked for forgiveness for being a doubtful man.

Earlier that day, Timpkin visited his mother and father to tell them what he was about to do. Both parents were well in their nineties, yet still had good mental and physical health. His mother apologized for scaring him about slaves when he was little. Timpkin laughed and said, "I was teasing, just wanted to see what you'd say."

His dad laughed and said, "silly boy."

Timpkin stayed with his parents until time for him to become an abolitionist. He took his mother shopping for clothes, shoes, and groceries. He went to a hardware store and bought lightbulbs with the lifespan of seven years. After shopping, they picked up a pizza and took it home. They ate and talked, while his mom and dad clean the dishes, Timpkin ran the sweeper throughout the house, even the steps. He changed all the lightbulbs in the house, something he had not done in over a year. He took the drapery down on all the windows, washed them, and hung them back up, he dusted and washed the lamp fixtures, the chandelier, and blinds. When Timpkin finished cleaning, the house sparkled. He said, "Mom, Dad I am going to take a trip, I'm not sure when I can come back to visit. "

His mom looked sad and worried, she said, "is it because I frighten you son about the slaves."

Timpkin sat next to her and said, "no ma'am mama, you know my friends Donovan, and Haze."

His mother said, "yes, I do. Donovan is the one with the petite pretty wife, Haze wife is, woo child, she's wilder than necessary. Lord Lord."

Timpkin and his dad laughed and agreed with her. Timpkin said, "We're taking our wives on a long four-month trip. I'll come as soon as I get back in town." And then he had a bright idea, he said, "let's take selfies so when we talk on the phone, we'll have each other's picture."

With each of their cell phones, Timpkin took several pictures of himself and his parents huddled together. They had so much fun taking those pictures, they made happy faces, funny faces, and crazy faces, they did more laughing than anything. It was a fun way, to go away.

At the base of the plantation, Timpkin leaned against his car, he felt sad, he had lied to his mother. He really didn't know when or if he'd ever return to Ogville. He looked at the pictures, he laughed, he cried.

****

Charles and Barbara stayed the night in the plantation house instead of their castle, they had a plan. Sunday morning at eight o'clock with the slaves in church waiting for him to preach, the husband and wife duo were going to execute the adult slaves, it was going to be quick and easy. After shooting and killing the adults, the children were next.

Charles purchased two machine guns and over a thousand bullets. He said, "soon we will be free of all this mess. I've never been outside these three towns; I've only seen pictures of the rest of the world."

Barbara said, "tomorrow all the slaves, gone."

"Then on to Canada." He chuckled and continued, "Hawaii here we come."

Barbara smiled and said, "where's that cook?"

6:05 PM

Before driving down the long path that led to the plantation mansion, James and Theenda switched drivers. James scooted down in the front seat and Sara laid down as Theenda pulled in front of the house and parked the car. "Theenda said, "the children are around back, Donovan said through a small dense forest." She parked in front of the house, she handed James the keys to the gates, and said, "go left when you're in the first gate and just keep walking until you see a second gate and the cabin."

James asked, "which key is to what gate?"

Theenda said, "the first key is marked outer, the other key is marked, children."

James looked at the keys and said, "got it."

He began to leave then turned around and in a very low voice whispered, "Sara, stay down."

Theenda said, "let me get inside first." Theenda went up to the house and knocked, she sat two bookbags on the porch. Barbara opened the door, when Theenda entered, James quietly slid out the car and whispered to Sara, "Stay in the car, watch for the flairs."

Sara said, "I'm so scared, I've never been this frighten in my life."

"It's going to be okay honey." He turned to leave but first said, "I gotta admit, this is exciting and scary, we're abolitionist, I never in my life thought..."

Sara whispered sternly, "James go."

He left, but came back to the car, reached in the glove compartment and got the flashlight. Sara said, "I'm glad you returned, I'll go to the first gate with you, it's getting dark and creepy out here."

Inside the house, Theenda was shown the locations of everything she needed to prepare supper. Charles and Barbara went down the hall to the sitting room. Theenda got busy cooking. She found a beautiful crystal pitcher in a cupboard. Theenda had purchased a bottle of Everclear alcohol 95% ABV, she mixed the alcohol with MacFuddy Pepper Elixir Soda, orange juice, one-fourth cup of sugar, and a half bottle of knock out drops that Tess had confiscated from the hospital. Theenda had no idea what she was pouring in the punch, Tess had removed the label. She stuck her finger in before adding the drops to taste, she said, "yuck, strong and nasty.

By eight o`clock, supper was ready. She set the table in the dining room and called them to dinner, she put a little bit of ice in their crystal dinner glasses and poured the punch to the rim. Unbelievable to Theenda the couple loved it. They drained the first glass without eating their food. She poured them another, this time they drank and ate. Charles had a third glass. Charles asked pointing at his glass, "what is this I'm drinking, it's delicious."

Theenda showed him the alcohol bottle. He took the bottle and said, "I've never heard of this." Then asked, where did you get it."

Theenda answered, "on eBay."

"What's that?" Charles asked.

"The internet," Theenda answered totally surprised.

Charles looked at Barbara, who said, "I've heard of that, we'll learn about it, our son Harry is always on the internet." She looked at Theenda and smiled.

Theenda said, "if you have a computer, I will show you."

Barbara said, "maybe another time.

Charles winked at Barbara. It was not their intention to let Theenda leave alive.

While Charles and Barbara were eating their supper, the slaves, except Saul and Lillie, were in the church eating the remaining food that the women had cooked earlier that day. Lee stood and announced that they were leaving the plantation. As Lee was explaining their escape to the confused slaves, Saul was in his shack putting knock out drops in Jack Daniel alcohol, the bottles were for Lillie's dinner. She had invited Glaidous, the two overseers, and Bo. Glaidous had not arrived, he was at the church, Glaidous neatly stacked the Bible, two books with the slave's names, and the tin can Moses had buried. He was curious about Paula that wrote she ran away, Glaidous wondered, *where did she go and how?* Glaidous wanted to give the young man that was doing all he could, to get them free, he decided to give the items to Donovan. He looked at the stack of books and tin can and smiled, he mumbled softly, "I's hope he likes dis." He left going to Lillie's, he walked past Lee and patted him on the shoulder, then said to everyone, "I's be back."

Lee had Jethro, Ben, and Cush to bring some of the burlap sacks from the tunnel in the backroom. They laid them on the pulpit, confusion spread throughout the audience. Lee began the explanation of running to freedom.

Earlier that week, Donovan, Timpkin, Cole, his employee, and two male members from Mrs. Paddleton church delivered thirty burlap sacks, and one hundred sandwich bags with a zip top, filled with Potassium Chloride. The Potassium powder was delivered to Cole's junkyard. Donovan, Timpkin, Cole, the two men from the church, and his employee filled the sacks and sandwich bags with potassium. On the day of delivery, the six men piled the sacks on the back of Cole's pickup truck and the two men from church trucks, they drove to the plantation. using three-wheel barrels, they hitched the barrels on the back of mopeds. The men delivered the filled sacks to Lee, Jethro, Saul, Ben, and Glaidous. They were completely dumbfounded at the number of walk-abouts and the mopeds.

Tess had given Theenda two small bottles of what she called, knock out drops. Donovan gave the bottles to Lee and three bottles of Jack Daniel Wine. On the night of the distribution, the men made several trips from the trucks to the gate. when Donovan got home, he did not bother to bathe, he went straight to bed. Theenda slept in another bedroom, his smell made her throw up.

After putting ten drops of the knockout drops in each bottle, Saul delivered the wine to Lillie and ran to the church to help spread the powder.

During this time, Bo, Roy, and Fred were in Lillie's cabin. Around 8:15 Roy asked, "where's Lee and his boy?"
"Right here," Lee said as he entered the cabin. "Cush is wid' his friends."
Bo, Roy, and Fred drunk the wine, ate, laughed, talked, they got tipsy and sleepy. Fred said, "this stuff is strong."
Glaidous stumbled in as though he was drunk, he asked, "whar's da' food. I's hungry."
Lillie got up and fixed him a plate. Lee looked at his mother it was 8:30. She said, "you men fallin' sleep. Y'all go on home now." She handed them each a bottle of the Jack Danial Whisky."
Roy said, "Miss. Lillie, I think you right."
He stumbled to the door with Fred behind him. Bo fell twice before entering his shack.

When the overseers were out of sight, she looked around the cabin one last time and said, "feedom we's comin." She took a quilt that she had made for Theenda, she grabbed the book bag that Donovan had given to Lee, Glaidous had asked her to bring it.
Lillie looked at Lee and said, "let's go."
Lee said, "wait, mama, I's gonna' miss home."
"We all will son, I's been here ova sixty years."
She pushed Lee out the door and said, "we's gotta' go."
Roy and Fred were close to their cabins, Roy said, "you and your woman come over to my cabin."
"Sounds like a party," Fred said cheerfully.

Lee and Lillie entered the church, the slaves were punching holes in the burlap sacks. Lee said, "da' overseer be gone, time ta' spread da' powder." The younger folk spreading the powder, walked around the plantation inside the slave area, while others went around the outside of their gate, others through the tobacco field. The older men carried the sandwich bags and threw one in the doorway of the cabins and between them. The women had gotten pans of water for their men return. At ten o'clock, everyone was in church. Sophie was on a bench sleep when Glaidous entered, he said, "good she finally shut-up."

Lillie looked down at Sophie and said, "naw,' I punched her out."

One of the women said, "iffen' she hadden' I show nuff' would'a."

Lee looked at his mother and said, it's time. With all but Bo, in the church, Lee told the slaves to crawl fast through the tunnel, when they got on the other side of the outer gate, to stand still, keep quiet, and wait for the next instruction.

One of the ladies asked, "wad' about' our thangs' in da' cabin."

Lee simply said, "we's," he cleared his throat and corrected himself, "we don't need them where we be going. We will get new feedom things."

Glaidous said, "Mr. Bright say, out with the old – in with the new." He filled the book bag with the books and tin can.

Jethro lined everyone by the back room, over one hundred years ago Zeek said, "we need ta' build a small room with a dirt floor."

At the time Zeek did not know the reason, but he knew the room had to be built. On the day Harry's hired hands were hoodwinked, the Lord revealed to Zeek the reason for the room with the dirt floor. Zeek's heart was filled with compassion and love, he prayed for the slave's safety. His death was sad and peaceful.

Ben and Saul were the first to go down into the tunnel to lead the slaves to freedom. The frighten slaves came out of the tunnel one by one standing on the outside of the outer gate, looking in. They were amazed. Zeek's work was fulfilled. One of the newly freedmen and women looked all around and up at the sky and said, "da' sky be bigger."

Glaidous and Lillie wanted to stay behind with Lee, he told them they move too slow and would cause him to miss freedom. So, they reluctantly entered the tunnel. When everybody was on the other side of the gate, Ben explained the yellow ribbons tied to the trees. He told them they would be walking fast so keep up, "he said, if you get lost follow the yellow ribbons." He looked at everyone then said, "Let's go."

Cush said, "not without my daddy."
Lillie said, "me either."
"Cush, you stay and wait." Jethro looked at Miss. Lillie and continued, "Miss. Lillie, you will hold Lee up. When he come out da' tunnel he be running."
Cush said, "grandma go."
She said, "I will do no such thang."
Glaidous said, "slow old fool, you's ain't makin' my nephew miss feedom." He went to her and pulled her by the hand, she fought to get loose, she yelled loud, "let me go."
Glaidous said, "sorry sis." He slapped her hard, then said, "now Shut-up and keep up."
"You hit me."
"Shut-up and keep walking."
Sophie said, "she hit me Glaidous."
"Da' two of yous' need ta' keep yo' mouth shut, you be gittin' on my nerve."

9:30 PM

Donovan pulled up next to Timpkin, he uncovered his van. Donovan and Tess got off the bus and joined Timpkin. Donovan told Timpkin, "when Haze arrives set off the first flair. I'm going up to get Thee and the kids."

Before Donovan pulled off in his bus, Haze drove in and next to Donovan. Haze got off the bus first. Timpkin asked, "where's Kay?"

Donovan inquired about Haze pulling over on the highway. Haze said to Timpkin, "I'm so sorry man, she goes on and on none stop asking about things that's none of her business."

KayKay got off the bus trying to hide her face, it didn't work, she wore her hair pulled back in a bun, it was obvious that there was a confutation on Haze bus, the side of KayKay's face was bruised.

KayKay said, "he hit me."

"Did you learn a lesson about keeping your mouth shut?" Timpkin asked in a noncaring tone.

LaVaughn

10:05, Timpkin shot off the first flair. Donovan told him to shoot off the second at 10:30 and 11:00, he said, "we should be on the way to the junkyard."
Timpkin commented, "I hope they follow the ribbons."
Haze asked, "what ribbons?"

The day Donovan and the men made the potassium delivery, they tied yellow ribbons on tree branches for the slaves to follow. Donovan said, "me too." He got on the bus backed out and let to get Theenda.

****

Standing in the doorway of the Church, Lee saw the flair, he thought it was the most beautiful site. He was given a flair and instructions to alert Timpkin that they had left, Lee shot off his flair. The sparkles hit the ground in the slave area igniting the potassium instantly. He said, "wow." He looked around the church one last time. Before leaving he took a mental picture of his uncle standing on the pulpit preaching, the choir singing, and all the slaves saying, Amen. He could hear Charles singing his favorite song, he remembered only a few weeks ago Harry's sermon. He quickly crawled through the tunnel, when he got out, he saw Cush, he grabbed and hugged his son and breathlessly said, "let's go."
As they ran Lee said, "boy you supposed to be wid' da' others."
Cush said, "Daddy I can't leave you." He looked at one of the shacks that caught on fire, he stopped and said, "daddy ain't that pretty."
Lee said, "yes, it is, keep running."
He and Cush ran fast to catch up. The white chemical was on the bottom of the slaves' shoes, they tracked it on the grass and through the forest.

Charles said to Barbara, "let's rest a bit while the girl cleans."
On their way out the dining area, Barbara was drowsy and thought she whispered when she said, "then we kill her before she leaves."

All But One

They laughed. Theenda heard them slowly and clumsy go up the steps, she whispered, "kill me? We'll see about that."

It was time for Theenda to finish her job. On the porch Theenda grabbed the larger bookbag that was filled with potassium salt, she quietly entered the house, got a cup from the cupboard and went upstairs where she spread the chemical in the hallway, a whole cup in front of Charles bedroom doors. She stepped out on the upstairs porch and saw the fire in the slave area, she left a trail of the powder on the porch. Theenda went down the stairs and walked down the long hallway, turned and left through the drawing-room where Harry's H. B. Metropolis plans were developed.

In the corner of the room she saw Harry's hideous gargoyle chair, she laid the bag across the top.

10:15

The frighten slaves were going through the woods, following the yellow ribbons. Sophie said, "I's wanna' go back ta' Massa."

Jethro asked, "is der' an end to da' trees?"

"Maybe we's made a mistake' I's don't wanna lib' in woods," Glaidous complained.

"Shut-up you old, fool," Lillie said still angry.

Ben said, "just keepa' goin,' I gotta' know bout' feedom."

"That's right Ben, gotta' know," Jethro said.

Lee and Cush caught up with the slaves poking along in the woods, he and Cush ran past everyone and went up front with Saul. He asked Saul, "how you doing?"

"I's scared but can't stop now."

Donovan drove to the house, he turned the bus around, so it headed towards MacCall. He parked it, blocking the driveway just in case Charles tried to escape. The bus was so loud he prayed continuously that the owners of the plantation would not hear it. He saw Theenda's car pointing towards the house, he went to the car, Theenda had left the key in the ignition. Donovan turned the car around pointing towards the street for their quick getaway.

XXXIX

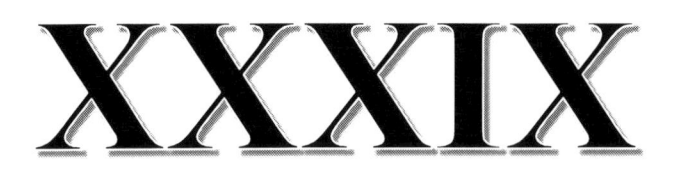

Save The Children

James and Sara got to the outer gate; his hands shook so hard the light from the flashlight was all over the place. Sara said, "let me hold the flashlight."

At first, he could not get the key to fit. When the gate swung open, James fell through and hit the ground, picking himself up he said, "God help me please."

Sara said, "yes, Lord."

They rushed to the children's gate, as he fumbled with the lock, he could see an outline of a house. He said, "Sara shine the light out there"

As Sara shined the light on the cabin, Helen came out, she thought it was a falling star, then she wondered if her Massa was coming. She ran back inside and gather the children in the meeting room. James said to Sara, "stay here."

He ran to the cabin, James busted through the door and said, "let's go." Everybody was together.

One of the thirteen-year-old asked, "who you? And whar's we be goin."

James said, "you're free. Follow me."

A thirteen-year-old girl said, "we's goin' ta' our mom and dads."

James blocked the doorway and said, "follow the light out by the gate."

The older ones made themselves responsible for the young ones, they ran towards the brightest light they had ever seen.

Helen stood on the porch yelling, "chil'ren git back in here."

James said, "you can stay or be free, up to you." He picked up a small child and left with the children. Helen ran back inside the cabin, James yelled, "lady it's your choice."

Helen yelled at the children, "y'all cain't be goin' wid' dat' man."

James and the kids were close to the gate, Helen ran quickly after them. Sara grabbed a child and said, "come on."

Helen saw Sara, she was shocked, it was confusing to her, Charles told his slaves that all coloreds were slaves. She was running confused, questions rumbled in her head, where did these slaves come from? Where was Massa? When they got to the front of the house, Theenda was coming out. James stopped running to inquire about Theenda's wellbeing.

She said, "I'm okay."

Sara said as she put the child down that she was carrying, "follow them."

Theenda spread the smaller bag content on the porch and down the step as the band of slave children ran past. Theenda laid the bag on the steps, she went to the car and leaned against it, she was worn-out. Sara went to her and said, "why don't you get in the car, I'll finish the job."

Helen stopped running when she saw Theenda, she walked up to her and touched her arm, then ran to catch up with the others. Theenda said, "that was the weirdest thing, she rubbed my arm."

Sara said, "be right back." She had seen two small children trailing behind.

Looking at the big yellow loud thing in front of her, Helen refused to get on the bus. She backed away. Donovan said, "I don't have time for this," he yelled, "mom help please."

James had already put several children on the bus and fastened their seatbelts.

Sara stood next to the bus out of breath from carrying the two toddlers that were behind. She pointed at the bus and said in her demanding mom voice, "git-on-the-bus!"

Before obeying, Helen touched Sara's arm then bowed her head low, and got on the bus. Donovan ran to Theenda to see how she was doing. She told him that she was tired and wanted to sleep. Donovan noticed that her voice was sluggish and eyes droopy, he said, "we should have canceled this."

"No, we did the right thing. I'm okay, just tired." She kissed him on the cheek then continued, "let's go."

Donovan gave Theenda a hug.

Looking out the window Helen watched Donovan and Theenda, she could tell he loved her. She smiled and thought I want a man to love me and be kind to me.

James and Sara ran up to Donovan, James said, "let's go."

Donovan asked Theenda to get on the bus with him. His mother said, "she is too tired to ride on that thing."

James said, "boy go."

While they were arguing, Theenda lit a whole book of matches and threw it on the book bag, she lit the second book of matches and threw it on the porch. She ran and got in the back seat; the fire ignited quick. Donovan jumped in the back seat with Theenda, James pulled off. He let Donovan out when they got close to the bus. Donovan jumped on the bus and took off driving fast down the road. The children and Helen yelled.

10:30

Timpkin shot off the second flair. Running through the woods the freedmen and women were in awe of the falling star. Donovan drove fast and parked behind the bus Haze had driven. His dad parked next to Timpkin.

Donovan got off the bus and went straight to Theenda who was asleep. James got out of the car. Sara sitting in the front seat said, "I knew you were coming. "Let her rest."

He left.

Timpkin said, "I hear them coming."

Lee, Cush, and Saul stumbled out the woods, first. Donovan said," I think they left at nine."

Donovan, Timpkin, Haze, and James greeted the men. Then Ben came out of the woods.

10:45

When all the slaves exited the woods, Haze said, "hold on, it's like looking at the United Nations."

James said, "how did Asian, whites, Latino's." He looked at Donovan and asked, "what's going on?"

Donovan said, "when we get settled someplace, I'll let you read all about Harry V. Brown."

Donovan told the kids and Helen to get off the bus, he wanted their parents to collect their children. He was completely surprised when he learned that they had never seen the children before. It was Lillie that explained what happened to the babies. Donovan left it up to KayKay and Tess to figure it out. Timpkin asked all adults sixty and older to follow him, thirteen got in his van that held fifteen.

KayKay thought faster than Tess, she counted seventy-five adults from twenty to over fifty, twenty-six children ranging in the age of two to thirteen, and fifteen children between fourteen and seventeen, there was two eighteen-year-old and one nineteen. The older adults received the children eleven to sixteen, she worked her way down to match the youngest child with the youngest adult, teenagers seventeen and older sat together.

KayKay got in the van with Timpkin, Tess jumped in Donovan's bus, he said, "oh no you won't, when we drop Theenda's car at the junkyard my wife, mom, and dad are riding with me. You need to get on Haze bus."

Tess folded her arms like a pouting child and didn't move. She said flirting, "I'll ride with you sugar,' what your wife doesn't know won't hurt her." And then winked.

Donovan was not having it, he opened the door, got up from the driver's seat, picked Tess up and threw her off the bus, closed the door and drove off.

When KayKay saw Tess flying off the bus and bounce on the ground like an airless basketball, she said, "I need a phone."

Sara saw a body fly in the air, she asked, "did someone fly off Don's bus?"

"No," James answered. "I believe Donovan threw Tess off the bus."

"We raised him better than that. That's no way to treat a lady."

"Tess is not a lady, honey. Haven't you noticed." James replied.

When the bus took off, the slaves screamed, they tried to get off, the little children cried. In Timpkins van, the elderly yelled out for God and Jesus. Glaidous yelled, "dis' be too fast, too fast, oh God save us."

Donovan got on the walkie-talkie and said, "okay people settle down."

When they didn't get quiet even though they were not in Theenda's car, Sara and James could hear them screaming. Sara got on the walkie-talkie and said, "stop the bus, Don." She got out of the car and, on the bus, Donovan was driving, she shouted on the walkie-talkie, "shut-up! if you don't, I personally will yank you off the bus or van and leave you here!" Everyone got quiet. She said softer, "one more scream or cry I will throw you out and let you fend for yourself." She handed Donovan his walkie-talkie, before leaving she asked, "why did you throw that woman off the bus? I didn't raise you like that."

Donovan whispered, "mom, she was trying to take Thee's place."

Sara said, "good job son,"

Haze stopped to let Tess get on the bus he was driving, before she could sit down, he whispered, "you're my relief driver."

They pulled off and no one made a sound, not even the drivers. Helen was sitting in the front seat by the door. When Helen saw James she was frightened, she thought that he was clean and smelt good, but did not understand what was going on. Then she saw Donovan, he was another handsome, clean, smelling good man, he talked differently, but very nice. Helen wanted to get to know Theenda better, she seemed nice.

"How you know I can drive a bus." Tess whispered as she got on the bus, she looked at Helen and said hatefully just below a whisper, "git up, I'm sitting by the window."

Haze looked around at Helen and winked. Her heart fluttered, finally, she got a good-looking man to notice her. She sheepishly smiled at Haze. Helen did not mind sitting on the end, it put her closer to the driver.

In the van was Glaidous, Lillie, Sophie, and ten others. Sophie said, as they were going down the road, "I's miss home and Massa."

Lillie said, "that was home, mean and hateful as it be that was our only home. We'll miss it but not for long." She looked at Glaidous and asked, "What ja' doing with the Bible and books?"

"It's our history, our family, I'm giving dem to Mr. Bright."

Timpkin said, "look the fire has spread in the woods."

All was quiet in the van when Glaidous broke the silence, he said, "I won't miss Massa, I won't miss da' hard work, beatings, threats. Hunger."

Lillie chimed in and said, "being called an animal."

Another woman asked, "Miss Kay, when da' young girls gits' marred' and have a baby, can dey' keep dey' baby?"

"Yes," KayKay replied with sorrow in her voice. She remembered her conversation with Timpkin when she said, they should be left where they were. And Timpkin telling her that they were not animals in a zoo. KayKay said with kindness in her voice, "yes, they will keep their children and raised them until they are grown."

Everyone in the van was satisfied with Miss. Kay's answer.

XL

Harry, It's Over

Midnight

Inside the mansion Charles woke up, looked at the clock on his nightstand, he yelled, "that woman is gone." He got out of bed, grabbed his robe, coughed unceasingly, his eyes burned from the smoke. He shook Barbara to wake her up when she sat up, he asked, "smell smoke?" he went to the door opened it, he heard a crackling noise, Charles looked at Barbara and said, "be back." He went down the hall to the staircase, he saw fire rolling up the steps. He yelled to Barbara, "we have to get out of here, that woman set the house on fire."

As she was getting out of bed, she accidentally flipped Charles pillow over and saw a gun. She grabbed it. The fire was at the top of the steps, Barbara entered the hallway and pointed the gun at Charles and asked, "were you going to shoot me."

"Really, we are about to burn up with the house and you're asking if I was going to shoot you." He looked down the hall the fire was easing towards them, Charles yelled, "no woman! I always sleep with a gun under my pillow. You know that." He ran down the hall to the door that led out to the upstairs porch, it had not caught fire yet. He looked back and said, "come on, here's a way out."

He exited onto the second-floor wrap around porch which was Harry V. Brown favorite spot. It was the porch Harry looked through his telescope to see newly built H. B. Metropolis, joy zipped through him, he had danced.

Standing in Harry's spot, Charles looked towards the slave area and saw purple, red, and yellow flames, it was a beautiful site to see. He turned to Barbara and yelled, "we'll have to jump."

Barbara tossed the gun behind her, it landed in the fire that was coming down the hall. As she ran to Charles the gun got hot and exploded, the bullet hit her in the back, it went through one of her lungs. Barbara fell against the door that led out to the porch. Charles pushed the door open, he pulled Barbara onto the porch. Her last breath she whispered, "it was Donovan." She coughed several times before continuing, "the cook was his wife. Kill them for me." She died; her feet caught fire first.

Had Charles stepped four paces over to his right or left, he would have landed in bushes and possibly saved himself. Charles panicked and jumped dead center, he bounced from one cement step to the next, he landed on the path of the outer gate. Though he should have died instantly, he lingered for sixty seconds, his body was situated so he faced the entranceway to the outer gate. The glow from the fire mingled with the moon, he could see clearly that the gate was opened. A few tears slowly slid on the ground, he said, "Harry, it's over. You didn't win." He tried to move but could not.

Charles laid on the ground, his life unhurriedly deteriorated, he whispered, "my children, my brother, my wife, dear God, I'm sorry." His voice was only a whisper, "please, forgive." Staring at the bright flames, he moaned hard and murmured, "I didn't get to travel." Charles fought to stay alive aslong-as he could, he tried to crawl but to no avail, he wanted to scream but his voice was gone, with all his might he tried to talk, only his lips moved no sound uttered from Charles as he mouth, "young man, you won." The brightness of the fire began to fade, Charles opened his eyes wider, to stop death from taking his life. Lying on the ground in his blood, Charles watched himself die. The fire turned from bright hues of red and yellow to bright gray, dim gray, dark gray, to black. Charles was gone.

H.B. Metropolis gained much richness under Charles as the commander and chief. However, due to Charles boredom and desire to travel, Harry's endlessness of time plantation came to a halt, one hundred fifty-two years after Harry's first meeting, in the drawing room. The person who was Harry's archenemy and ordained by God, completely obliterated Harry Victor Brown plantation, was twenty-three-year-old Donovan Victor Bright.

****

When Donovan and his crew arrived at the junkyard, he jumped off the bus and ran straight to Theenda, he helped her out the car, hugged her tight. All the slaves, Haze, Timpkin, Cole, his helper, and Tess watched the couple, while KayKay stared at Tess. It was as though Tess could feel someone piercing eyes on her back. She was startled when she turned around and saw KayKay's look of evil as she said, "you ain't no friend," she got closer to Tess and whispered, "Haze will one day kill you," she smiled as she continued, "and I will applaud."

Timpkin pulled KayKay back to his van and said, "Kay you have to learn when to speak and when to keep quiet. I am sorry that I did nothing for your eye."
She said, "it's okay, I understand, when we get in our hotel room, I got a lot to talk about, I saw a lot tonight,"
"Is it about the Days?" Timpkin asked.
"Yes."
"Me too. Only when we're in our room."
Kay smiled and nodded in agreement.

Donovan asked Timpkin to join him, Haze, and James, Cole was giving each vehicle a Motorola Professional two-way radio. Cole had his helper to hook the radio's in the three vehicles, while he was working, Mrs. Paddleton said to Donovan, "you did it."

The slaves watched the woman in wonder as she shook Donovan's hand, he went to the bus and asked everyone to get off, they stood in one big cluster. Mrs. Paddleton said, "I am so happy to see you all free and off the plantation. May you have a blessed life, joyous life, a peaceful life, a life filled with the Spirit of God." She went around and shook each one's hand, she gently pinched the baby's cheeks, and hugged the little children. She continued, "I am overjoyed, I love you all."

Donovan had the slaves to get back on the bus. Phillip and Phillipa brought their grandmother to the junkyard, Mrs.

All But One

Paddleton said, "group hug, the Paddleton's, Donovan, Theenda, and Haze joined in the group hug. James, Sara, Timpkin, KayKay, Tess, and the newly freed watched the small group cuddle and laugh. Lillie said from the van, "I's neva thank white folk like us likes dat."

Phillip drove his sister and grandmother home. Cole said, "mama I'll be over when they leave."

Cole's employee taught Donovan, Timpkin, Haze, and James how to use the high-tech radios. Before leaving he had them to try contacting each other, after a few failures, they caught on, he also showed them how to repair the radio if it stopped working.

Donovan, Timpkin, and Haze thanked Cole and shook hands with his helper. Donovan said, "thank you, Mr. Cole. If it were not for you and Mrs. Paddleton, this wouldn't have happened."

Cole said, my pleasure young blood, with the plantation ablaze and the slaves free, my mother can finally rest, and I can go home."

When they were ready to go, Donovan said on the radio, "let's move out!"

Finally, Theenda was on Donovan's bus sitting in the front seat by the door, with a bucket in front of her. His mother and father sat in the seat behind their son. Though his mother kept going to Theenda then back to James, he said. "hone, you stay with Thee."

He noticed that Lee was his son's, right-hand man. He looked around and said, "Lee come sit by me."

Without telling Donovan, his dad had agreed to Sara's question. Sara and James were in their son's home sitting on the couch, holding hands. Sara asked James, "would you want to move out west with our son's caravan? We could put our house up for sale and see if the boys want to move out there."

James said, "yes."

James let Lee sit by the window, being a professor, he wanted to talk to Theenda about the kids' education, she told him that she was working on a curriculum. She said, "my plans are in the car we left behind." They laughed.

Riding on Haze Bus, Tess was offended, she thought Donovan taking up for her pulled them closer together. Her pretense friendship with Theenda was a smokescreen to snatch Donovan away from Theenda's tight grip. He never paid her any attention, after getting thrown off his bus, she decided to leave him alone and be a better wife to Haze. She smiled at Haze, he didn't see her because he and Helen were in a deep conversation about the plantation. The slaves on the bus noticed and whispered about the attention he was giving to one of their own. Tess watched Helen, she noticed that the woman was older but had the same childlike innocence of Theenda.

Tess had a flashback about an argument she had with Haze about Theenda, he said, "she has class, she's beautiful, she has a figure that women dream of, she has a soft sing-song voice, she's innocent." Tess rolled her eyes at Helen and whispered, "she looks like a very poor Theenda."

Tess was pretty but hard, smart but argumentative. Tess sat with her body and face forward, her eyes were cocked sideways at Helen. Tess wondered if Haze was flirting with Helen to make her jealous or was, Haze really interested. After all, he adored Theenda and was always gentle with her just like he was being with Helen. Instead of being kind and tender, Tess got harder. And then she chuckled, H & H, Haze and Helen, it was fate. She whispered to herself, "I don't stand a chance."

****

3:30 AM

They were driving through downtown MacCall to get on the freeway that would take them west. As they passed a furniture store that had bright lights in the windows, in the van Glaidous said, "look yonder Mr. Tim, dat' be the furniture we make."

Timpkin got on the radio and said, "slow way down Donovan and listen to this." He said, "Mr. Glaidous repeat what you said."

He told them again that the furniture in the store and the quilts hanging in the window were made by them. Haze said on the radio, "I bet you that big building in the forest is the holding spot for the furniture."

All But One

Donovan said, "Haze you're right, remember the truck and three men."

Timpkin said, "oh my goodness, the one who shot the two men was Charles, the head honcho."

Donovan and Haze said, "right."

Theenda's soft voice came over the radio, she said, "Sweetie, that's where we purchased our dining and kitchen furniture."

Tess shivered. They drove through MacCall, the whole town smelled of smoke, on the empty freeway everyone saw on top of the mountain a yellowish red glow that lit the sky. Donovan got on the radio and announced, "to all the freedmen and women you are free, that light in the sky is fire, it's destroying the plantation you called home."

Loud applauds and cheering were heard in all three vehicles.

Lillie could be heard as she said tearfully, "Lawd' Lawd', no moe, no moe beatin,' no moe gate. Glory ta' God, we be fee."

Tears of sadness rolled down Theenda and Sara's cheeks. KayKay said, "Glory to God on the highest."

The freedmen and women asked questions regarding the freeway lights, they ask how cars run, and how did Donovan find them. They wanted to know what would happen to the plantation, and if the Browns would find them. Finally, the hum and rocking of the vehicles put the slaves to sleep. Donovan said to Theenda, "baby girl, I am so sleepy." There was no answer, he looked around Theenda and his mom was fast asleep, he smiled, their pillow was each other's head.

James said, "pull over I'll drive."

Donovan said, "thanks dad, a rest stop should be coming up soon, you'll take over then." He reached in his pocket and got the one point nine-ounce energy shot. He continued and said, "I got this, I gave one to the guys, you'll take over at the next stop, is that okay?"

"Sure." James was tired as well, so he sat back and took a nap.

7:00 a.m.

Donovan got on the radio and whispered to the drivers, "hey guys, a rest stop is coming up, it has diesel fuel."

Timpkin replied, "we need to change drivers. I am tired."

"Agreed." Haze said. He looked at Tess who was waking up, he asked her, "can you drive a bus. I claimed you were my relief driver but wasn't sure."

"Yes." Since Tess was thrown off Donovan's bus and embarrassingly got on Haze, this was the first time he acknowledged that she existed. "Yes, I can drive, in school my work-study job was driving campus buses," Tess said ever so sweetly, she smiled at Haze then Helen.

Helen said, "I won't ta' be jest' like you, Miss. Tess."

Haze said calmly, "no you don't." He announced on the radio, "I have a relief driver."

Donovan forgot to cut his radio off, so everyone on his bus heard their conversation.

James woke up and said to Donovan, "I know for a fact Sara will not let Thee drive a bus, that's why we're going with you."

Sara said, "No I won't. She has done enough. Cooked dinner, marched up and downstairs spreading gunpowder, killing folk, running from the degradation of evil, setting fires, she's done enough for a pregnant woman."

Theenda said, "mom, it was potassium salt."

"I don't care what it was Thee, you've done enough."

Laughing James said, "as I said."

"Yes dad, you're driving."

Lillie said, "dat' be' a mouth full. I's wanna' talk likes' dat,' fast, lots of words."

Donovan said, "oops, I left the radio on."

Theenda said, "all I want is a pickle with mustard and some ice cream."

"Son, you're sitting next to your wife while she eats that." Sara looked at Lee and asked, "young man, mind if I sit next to you?"

All But One

"Yes ma'am, you can sit next ta' me," Lee said shyly. He thought all these free people did not mind sitting by him, he beamed with innocent pride.

Theenda got on her phone internet to look up restaurants, she said there's a KFC next to the BP that sales diesel fuel."

Haze said, "yep let's go there."

Theenda asked, "everybody agrees."

"Yes, were the replies."

Theenda said and suggested, "there's a park with benches, swings, and bathrooms, yep, let's eat there."

KayKay suggested, "guys leave the two-ways on, I'll explain what we're doing?" She explained what fuel was, she told them about KFC and the meal they were going to eat. She explained what parks and swings were, she told them about the people they were going to see, she also explained the bathrooms and how they work. She then made a request to Timpkin, James, and Donovan please show the men how to use the urinals and toilets. Ladies, we know what to do."

Theenda and Tess said at the same time, "Roc on."

Since James and Sara were the same age as Timpkin and KayKay, they immediately became friends. They had a lot in common, their children were grown, they were close to their children, they were Christians, they liked gospel music and opera, they were educated, there one difference between the ladies, KayKay liked to gossip, Sara did not, nor tolerate it. Both James and Timpkin liked football, baseball, and chili dog Sundays.

The slaves in the three vehicles were amazed as they listened to the free people jargon, joke, and laugh.

They pulled the two buses and van to the gas and fuel pumps, Donovan went in to pay for the gas, the newly freedmen, women, and children went into the store five at a time, so everyone could utilize the bathroom in a timely manner.

Theenda purchased, in the gas station store, three legal pads, and pens. She gave one to Tess and KayKay, she then told everyone to get back on the bus they were riding and sit next to the same individual, she made the same request of the one's that road in the van. She made Timpkin van the lead, Donovan bus one, and Haze bus two. Theenda asked Tess and KayKay to go to their vehicle, write at the top led, bus one or two, then the individual's names and their seat number, beginning with seat number one upfront. By the time they finished writing who was sitting where and in which vehicle, the tanks were full. Theenda's plan was a good way for them to learn the ex-slave's names. Timpkin drove his van to KFC. Riding with him was Theenda, KayKay, Tess, and Sara, it took the five of them and three KFC employees to help carry the food to the van.

The freedmen and women got on the bus, Donovan and Haze drove them to the park area.

In the park everyone had a great time, they ate, swung, a loud airplane flying over scared them, they all fell to the ground. KayKay got the freedmen and women together and explained what they were hearing and seeing. Donovan said, "the plantation was a no-fly zone."

Haze asked, "people can do that."

Donovan said, "yea if you have enough money, Michael Jackson property was a no-fly zone." He looked at Tess, put his hand on Haze's shoulder and said, "I believe Haze, you're not the violent one."

"Well, except hitting Kay." That was all me, Haze admitted.

Donovan and Haze laughed. Lee joined the men and said, "I like this freedom, Sir."

Donovan put his arm around Lee's shoulder and said, "one-day bro you're going to drop that Sir." Donovan and Haze laughed.

Theenda was pushing a child in the swing when she saw Jethro go over to a young black couple with children, he asked. "you be free?"

Though it was sad and not funny, Theenda chuckled softly.

8:30 a.m.

James called a meeting while the newly freed enjoyed playing in the park. He asked if they could go to New York, he wanted to get all his affairs in order, and get more clothes. Donovan asked, "pops you and mom going with us, how long are you going to stay?"

James said, "your mom and I talked, we're selling our house, we're staying for good.

Donovan said with tears in his voice, "I love you too." He hugged them both, with one arm around his mom, the other his dad.

Sara said, "when we get home, we'll take them to see a doctor." She asked, "how far are we from the plantation?"

Haze answered, "a little under two hundred miles, the buses will only go so fast."

Sara said, "that's far enough," she looked at Donovan and asked and said, "think we can stay the night? I saw a shop down from KFC, let's get them some clothes, they take a shower and leave in the morning."

Donovan asked, "is that okay with everyone?"

KayKay said, "perfect."

Donovan kissed his mom and went to Theenda.

The little girl Theenda was pushing had gone to play ball with other kids, looking on at Donovan and his parents hug, Theenda thought about the mess of hers and burst out crying. Lillie went to Theenda and cuddled her and said, "There now Mr. Bright's baby girl, it gonna' be all right." She took Theenda to one of the benches and rocked Theenda as she hummed a tune the slaves sung on plantation.

Haze watched the two women, his heart softened, he looked at Helen who was talking to one of the children. He smiled; soft Helen reminded him so much of Theenda. Helen had the same cottony kindness in her voice and happy eyes. He looked at the people in the meeting and said, "yes, let's take them across this beautiful magnificent country we live in and call home."

Tess watched Haze and Helen, she said to herself, "I messed up."

Though a man should never hit a woman for any reason, a woman should never push until he's furious, as Tess had. She got mad one time and hit Haze with a baseball bat, she had spit, slapped, kicked, sliced, and argued relentlessly. Defending himself he beat her senseless. She'd go to work where her co-workers felt sorry for her, they told her how much they hated him, some even called the police, Donovan had beat him good for her and now he despised her.

Tess watched Donovan go to Theenda, she had stopped crying. When Donovan approached, Theenda looked up at him and smiled, she stood he kissed her. Haze went to Helen, he gently took the hand of the child she was playing with, Helen looked up at him and smiled, Haze said something that caused her to giggle, Tess thought he's in love. She looked over at James and Sara, Tess smiled because Sara got on her toes and kissed James cheek, they walked away holding hands, Tess said, "like mother like son."

In a distant, Tess saw Glaidous and Sophie arguing, Sophie pushed Glaidous then walked away. Glaidous and Tess eyes met, she could tell he was embarrassed, she looked down at the ground, to herself said, "I need to change, I am Sophie." She sat quietly for a moment and then said, "that's a disgusting attribute to have." She got on bus number two and sat in the driver's seat, she left the door opened.

They entered the store, Rita went to Theenda and asked, Miss. Enda, der' be coloreds and white ta' gather."
Theenda said, "yes they are shopping."
A young black and white couple walked in arms around each other and giggling, the slaves were confused. Ben said, "da women ain't got nuff clothes on."
A few women walked in wearing daisy dukes, and bust popping out their blouse, Lee slobbered on his self. The ex-slave men and women stood in disbelief of how the women customers dressed.
Helen said to no one in particular, "dat' be' how Miss. Becky Lou dress."
The freedmen salivated; they had a hard time trying to focus on choosing new clothes.

Donovan spent over three thousand dollars on purchasing shoes, socks, coats, clothes, and toiletries for all the slaves. The hotel only had four rooms available. They divided the slaves into groups of fours, two rooms for the men and two for the woman. The abolitionist divided themselves into twos, James and Timpkin, Haze and Donovan, Theenda and Tess, lastly Sara and

KayKay, they entered the room with the slaves and showed them how to shower and use the toiletries. The slaves could not believe how clean they could get and how smelly they used to be.

The freedmen and women slept on the bus while Donovan, Haze, Timpkin, and James, the four drivers slept in the rooms. KayKay was in the van with her group, Tess with hers, and Theenda and Sara on the bus with their group.

The following morning, Theenda put Lee, Ben, and Glaidous in charge while the women went into the rooms to shower and change. A MacDonald was down the road, before showering Theenda called and ordered hotcakes, breakfast sandwiches, a bottle of water, and orange juice for everyone.

****

After eating breakfast and before they got on the bus Timpkin looked at James and said, "we're watching the games on Sunday."

James said, "ya betcha, we gotta find some hotdogs and fixings."

They high fived each other and laughed.

Ben and Lee watched the men friendly comradery, Ben whispered to Lee, "I's like freedom."

Jethro stood by himself watching Timpkin and James. He looked over at Donovan with Theenda, he said, "I want to be like him."

Lillie sat on a park bench and listened to a conversation between Sara and Haze. Sara said, "Haze I've noticed you're looking for guidance from my son, he's a twenty-three-year-old man-child that became a leader overnight."

Haze said, "he's normal, I want normal, your family is normal, Helen is normal like Thee. When I was a boy, I was beaten with sticks, belts, extension cords, punched, kicked by my father and mother. As a teen I ran away from home, in my late twenties I moved to Ogville, started my company, I loved the town and people. Age thirty-four I married Tess."

Sara advised Haze, she said, "Haze be you, not Don, you're older and wiser. You have a sweet disposition."

Haze said timidly, "thank you."

Sara continued, "Helen is a sweet girl, end the marriage with the wild one first. Heal emotionally, then if Helen is the woman for you, love her and tell her."

Haze gave Sara a boyish hug and said, "thank you for teaching me how to be normal."

Sara laughed and said, "you're a mess."

James said to Donovan, "when we reach Rochester, I set a meeting with social security, Children Services, the FBI, newspapers, TV news, and your brothers. There are two Asian teens, and no adult that's that race, a Hispanic woman that has had no children, yet four children are of her race, I asked which young person has had a child, only six, yet there are twelve young kids that's too old or too young for any of the slaves to birth. But first let's rest in Columbus, Ohio for a week, I'm tired."

Donovan laughed, and said, "I believe we all can use the rest."

11:00 am

Donovan got on the radio and shouted, "time to move out. Columbus, Ohio here we come."

When Haze was going to bus two, which Tess was driving, Lillie stopped him and said, "Helen is my daughter, if you marry her, you be my son."

Haze laughed and asked, "may I call you mom."

Lillie smiled and answered, "please do." She gave him a motherly hug and kiss on the forehead.

With everyone in their assigned seats, the convoy pulled off.

XLI

All But One

    Bo woke up sniffing the air, he leaped off the porch into muddy water. He stood in disbelief and semi-shock. The night before, while Bo slept in a drunken drugged stupor, the slaves dug a narrow waterway all the way around his shack. Then filled it with water from the thousand-gallon water tanks, plus it had rained hard as Donovan's convoy was going through MacCall. The rain put the fires out and overflowed the waterway. Several of the slave's cabins had burned down, while others were partially standing.

    He jumped off his porch, he slipped and fell in mud and water. He got up and looked for fresh water, there was none. He had a bucket full in his home, he washed up the best he could and changed clothes. He left his cabin slowly, he walked around the plantation calling each slave by their name. He ran to the slave town, the church had completely burned down, not one board or glass was left standing or lying on the ground. The church was nothing but ashes, the hole the slaves dug was filled and covered with dirt. The general store wall that was next to the church had burned off, the items in the store were not touched, and the bar did not receive any damage.

    Bo walked around the plantation, he went to the tobacco field, all the fields were destroyed. The silence made Bo tremble, he thought someway somehow the slaves had gone and left him behind. How will he make it all by himself? Then Bo remembered during the Thursday night service, he had stood outside the church, the title of Glaidous sermon was All But One, Bo heard him say, *"God will save everybody but one, and that one will be left behind."*

Bo said out loud, "they all knew of the escape. How did they get out?" Bo asked himself. He ran to the gate and shook it hoping to find a weak spot. "Glaidous was talking to me." Bo fell on his knees and cried.

Looking up at the sun, it was past time for the slaves to be in the tobacco field, he leaned against the gate and said, "da' ovaseer be gone wid' da' slave."

****

Fred and his woman woke up in Roy's cabin with a serious hangover. Fred asked, "what's dat' smell?"

Roy's woman jumped up and ran outside to vomit, but was startled from the quiet, even the wind was still, the smell of smoke was strong. She said, "guys you may want to come out here."

When they got outside smoke was all around them. "What happened?" Roy asked.

Fred ran back in the cabin and looked at the time, he said, "we gotta wake up da' slaves."

Roy walked around to the back of the cabin, he yelled, "come around here." Roy was looking at the burned trees in the forest between the outer and divider gate.

When they joined him, they could see clearly, with the leaves and most of the trees burned down, the children house looked empty. Roy sent the women back in their cabins to pack, he said, "ladies we are getting out of here today."

He and Fred saddled their horses and galloped to the divider gate when they got there, they saw Charles lying on the pathway, Roy and Fred called out, "Mr. Charles, Help!"

Roy said, "Fred look, the outer gate is opened."

They went to where the divider gate opened and shook hard, but it was fastened tight. They followed the divider gate that had an exit behind the children's area, it was also locked. Fred tried to climb out, but it was impossible.

"Who did this?" Roy asked.

The men said together, "the slaves."

They got back on their horses and began to gallop at top speed from the divider gate to the slave area. The horses stopped at the overseers' cabins, drooling and breathless. They forgot to

All But One

feed and water the horses. Roy asked Fred, "Did you lock the slave gate?"

"After what happened to Bo remember, we stopped lockin' der' gate every night." A confused look was on Fred's face when he asked, "how's Lillie get Jack Danial?"

Roy said, "that's what knocked us out, we're used to drinking watered down liquor from Mr. Brown."

****

The fire had burned to the edge of the service road, where the buses and Timpkins van had parked. No one came to the Browns rescue because the family had done a thorough job concealing the plantation. The Browns had no friends, no visitors, and no one to miss them. The last visitor that was in the plantation house was MacCall's Chief of Police, Stevens.

In town, Stevens had the police to drive around and search for where the smell was coming from. He went to the fire department; they had not received any calls. And then it hit him, he called Charles on his cell, no answer, then Barbara on her cell, no answer, he called both landlines to the plantation mansion and castle, no one answered. He wanted to take an officer with him but realized he was not supposed to know the location of the plantation. So, he went by himself.

****

Confused, Bo searched and searched for the way the slaves had gotten out. He had wandered around the empty plantation for twenty-five minutes. The solitariness and fear smothered Bo's reasoning, he looked up at the whipping tree, it too had suffered through the fire. An idea struck, he ran back to his cabin, in a corner was a rope. Bo grabbed it and went to the whipping tree; he was going to hang himself. He thought about the pain, he had watched Massa Ben hang a slave. Bo dropped the rope and went to the town where he sat at the bar.

In the absence of sound, his mind trundled, like a bowling ball towards pens, the crash was his memories. His two visits to the city with Harry, riding in a car, other coloreds dressed like his

Massa, his Massa saying Sir to a man that was brown, Lillie's beating, the terrible ways he treated the slaves. He remembered unnecessarily yelling at the kids, the overseers rape his wife, her cries for help, he did nothing. Guarding Saul's bloody body to keep the slaves from helping him.

Bo was five years old when Charles father dragged him to the children's area. He yelled, "I's tell my mama and daddy." He never saw his parents again. When he turned fourteen, he was given to an old man that taught Bo how to be a snitch.

Crying, he said, "mom, dad where you be." Unfortunately, he could only hear Lee's voice telling him he's no better than they were, Bo flinched when he remembered Harry raping him. So many slaves had told him that he would die alone and unloved. It had come true, he was alone, and nobody loved him.

Unknown to Bo, his family was very poor and could not care for the evil child. His parents had whipped him and put him on punishments, still, it did not work. When Charles came to their door, Bo was sold for twenty thousand dollars. His parents left town, changed their names, got a job, and were never seen again.

The overseers switched horses, they tried to gallop at top speed to the slave's area, on the unfed thirsty animals. The horses ran for a half mile and stopped. The men got off their horse and tried to pull it, but they would not move. Fred kicked his horse, Roy took his shoe off and slapped his horse on its butt, with the shoe.

The closer Chief Stevens got to the plantation the stronger the smell. When he turned to go down the long driveway the mostly burned down house loomed at him. He ran around the house trying to figure out how to get in. Then he drove around back and saw Charles body lying on the ground. On the porch stairs was Charles blood. Only bits and pieces of the house remained standing. With the forest mostly burned down, he could see more of the plantation, he got back in his truck and drove down the grassy path between the outer gate and the forest. As he drove, he saw two men walking inside the big gate. The Chief was the first human outside the plantation that they had seen in almost thirty years. They yelled out, "HELP!!"

All But One

Chief Stevens was confused, he thought the slaves were black, he continued to drive, he saw the devastation of the slave area. Even though Lee was shaking when he crawled out the tunnel, he took time with Cush and quickly covered the hole over, thus concealing their escape route. When Stevens was driving past and looking at the set up his front tire ran over the hole, but the back tire fell deep into it.

Roy and Haze ran to catch up with Stevens, who was trying hard to free his truck, but the wheel kept spinning. Stevens luck changed when a mule came walking out the woods towards him, around its neck was a rope. The mule had broken out the barn and ran to safety, it was returning hungry and wanted to be fed. Out of breath Roy and Fred caught up with him. They both pleaded, "please help us out," their big mistake was informing the Chief about the Brown family atrocity and when he saved them, they would tell more.

Roy said. "Please help us,"

As Stevens tied the rope to his truck and around the mule's girth, he asked, "you two all right," he turned the truck on and put it in neutral. He pushed while the mule pulled. It took a while, fortunately, man and beast got his truck free.

Fred said, "yes Sir. Officer, we're okay."

Roy asked, "Sir do you have diggin' tools?"

Bo heard the commotion, he ran out of the bar, and saw Roy and Fred, he was going to yell but saw a strange man. Stevens pulled out his gun and shot them both. Bo ran back inside the bar. Stevens got in his truck and drove around the length and width of the plantation. When all was quiet Bo returned outside.

He ran out the slave area over to Roy and Fred by the outer gate, they were dead. Bo had seen the overseers slap the horse backside before getting on, using his fist he punched the horse. The horse was not in the mood, it was hungry, thirsty, and mad, using its hind legs, it bucked. The kick knocked Bo down, before returning to the barn, the horse kicked one last time, Bo was hit in the head. He crawled to the gate, pulled himself up, and saw the hole Stevens truck fell in, he looked around at the church, back at the hole and said, "that's how dey' got out." He died.

****

When Stevens reached home, he took the police car out of the garage and put his truck in. His vehicle was filthy dirty it looked like he had been on a dirt bike trail, he closed the garage door. He took a shower and put on a clean uniform. When he drove up to the police station, several sheriffs' cars were parked around the building. He got out of the car and casually entered the station. One of the sheriffs asked, "where have you been?"

"Driving around trying to find where the smell was coming from," Stevens answered, as unanswered questions juggled through his mind faster than light could travel. Will they find the plantation? Did I drop anything? My tire tracks. And the two guys I shot have the bullets from my gun in them. Big brave confident Chief Stevens was folding.

Stevens was trapped, two sheriffs entered the precinct with Mrs. Paddleton, she was carrying a black case.

****

5:00 pm.

Tess was driving the bus, Kay the van, and James was driving. Theenda got on the two-way radio and said, "my sista's do we need a bathroom break?"

"And we need to switch drivers, Timpkin has been snoring like he's having a hog calling contest," KayKay chuckled as she said, "he won."

"Yes, I could use a break," Tess commented.

James said, "I saw a sign a few miles back for Burger King, Thee, make an order, please. We'll fill up, let everybody stretch. We're almost to Ohio."

Using her cell, Theenda called Burger King and ordered two hundred hamburgers, fries, apple, and cherry fried pies. The order almost wiped the restaurant out of food, the manager had to call for more food to be delivered, he was told to shut down when he ran out.

While they waited for their food Theenda allowed the children to play in the children area. The adults laughed as they watched the kids. Donovan, Timpkin, and Haze took the vehicles to the gas station.

Three employees helped Theenda, Tess, KayKay, and Sara take the food out. The employees gave all the children a toy and placed a crown on their heads. One of the little six-year-old held up his toy and with great big beautiful brown eyes claimed, "dis be feedom toy."

An hour later, everyone returned to their assigned seats and ate on the bus. Donovan cut the two-way radio on, so they could chat. Glaidous said, "glory be I's like dis freedom food."

Jethro said, "dat's right," as he stuffed his mouth.

Lillie said, "I's likes da' indoor toilets, dey' don't stank.'"

Donovan, Haze, and Timpkin were driving. Donovan had download Pandora music app on his pay-as-you-go-phone, when he turned it on, Stevie Wonder song Ribbon In the Sky was playing, "he said Lee this is my jam."

Lee said while chewing on his food, "I like it to, Mr. Bright."

In Timpkins van "Look how big this world is," said Lillie as she chewed on French fries.

"Thank you so very much, Mr. Bright," Sophie cried.

Glaidous stared at Sophie before saying, "I's thought you liked Massa."

"I's like freedom and da' food, dem pannie' cake be, hum good," Sophie answered.

Lee asked, "Mr. Bright if there are no more plantations, where do the babies come from?"

"What babies?" Donovan asked.

Lillie answered, "Massa gib' me Lee to raise, he say I had da' baby, so I da' mama. He act like I's don't know where babies come from, I's delivered lots of babies."

"Miss. Edna," Ben said to Theenda, "Lee say I don't remember gates."

Theenda ask Lillie, "how old was Lee when you got him?"

"Fourteen likes all the others," Lillie replied.

KayKay ask Lee, "Lee, how old were you when you were taken?"

"About four, Mr. Brown go in a thing like this, it be smaller," he pointed outside his window and said, "like those little things."

He was pointing to cars driving past. KayKay being in the van could not see him pointing, Donovan said, "he was taken Kay, to the plantation in a car."

Lee continued to remember, "it be me and some more chil'ren."

"I was one of dem' chil'ren,' I was fo," Jethro commented, from Haze bus.

"There were other chil'ren dey' went to da' other places," Jethro continued to remember.

"I remember that," Lee said. I kind of remember my mom and dad. Not their face, just them."

Donovan said, "this is interesting, why are their memory so clear now?"

Theenda asked KayKay, "Kay, you think it's familiarity, the bus, stores, smells..."

"I believe so Thee."

Glaidous said, "is there a way we can find out, maybe I was adopted, Lillie you may not be my real sister."

"Oh, hush up Glaidous," Lillie said.

Donovan in deep thought said, "Timpkin you may be right about other plantations."

"What?" Timpkin said sternly.

"When all this began you said, driving up and down these freeways what if there are..."

Haze chimed in and said, "don't mean to cut you off Donman, are you telling me that we have to do this all over again"

James said, "not us when we're in New York we are meeting with a few government officials about all this."

Timpkin commented, "good, I'm too old for a repeat."

Soon after their conversation, Haze said over the system, "we're here in Ohio, see the sign."

Before crossing the Cincinnati bridge a huge sign reading, Welcome to Ohio greeted them. As they road high over the Ohio River, many of the slaves lift their legs in their seats.

"Columbus is not far away," Donovan's voice came over the system.

"When we get to the hotel, I want to take a hot bath," Theenda said.

Tess got on the two-way radio and said, "Thee and Kay I am very sorry for how I was acting, Donovan I deserved to be tossed out the bus, please forgive me."

Theenda asked, "Sweetie you threw her out the bus?"

KayKay said laughing, "it's not funny but it was, Thee, you was sleep, girl," KayKay laughed so hard she could hardly breathe, "we were getting ready to drive off, but a superwoman came flying out the bus. Timpkin said, she done gone and went and made Don mad. Girl he said it in the most southern drawl I've ever heard."

"You finished?" Tess said, laughing,

"Yeah." Kay was still laughing.

"Haze I owe you an apology, I am not stupid – Theenda, Donovan, Kay, Timpkin, I started the fights with Haze."

Theenda cut in and said, "yep, we know, do we forgive her everybody?"

They all mumbled, "yes."

"So, moving forward," Theenda said, "Tess apology accepted. We're going shopping for church clothes and stuff, Tess, you in?"

"I'm in. My sister lives in Columbus, I'll text her."

"Sister?" Theenda questioned.

"Yeah, sister," Tess said.

In the van Sophie started humming a song from the plantation, she asked, "Lillie memba' dis' song."

KayKay asked, "Thee what happened to the clothes you bought in town?"

"Hum, at the house in Donovan's office."

Tess asked, "you forgot them?"

"Yep."

Sophie sang louder, Lee said, "Mr. Donovan can I hear your music?"

It was playing softly but Sophie singing drowned it out. When Donovan cut the two-way radio off, Michael Jackson *Beat It* came on, he cut the music up full blast.

Lee said, "I's like this song Mr. Bright." he looked around and asked, "y'all like this.'"

Donovan's bus was rocking, the slaves stood and danced, he looked in the rearview mirror and said to himself, "I will teach them today's steps."

On Haze bus, he said to Tess, "you never said you had a sister."
"Yeah, she ran away when she was sixteen," Tess replied.

Theenda said, "Miss. Lillie and the other's want to attend church. That's the reason I want to go shopping."

In downtown Columbus, the slaves got off the bus in true amazement, they look at the tall buildings, all the cars, the people, and all the black people. Looking at the women in heels, Lillie asked, "Ms. Enda, what kind'a' shoe they wear." She grabbed Theenda's arm and said, "look at all the walk-abouts, and the tall things goin to the sky, will dey' fall?

"No Miss. Lillie, they won't fall, they are tall buildings built well. You are safe here." Theenda answered.

The Hotel knew they were coming, an attendant had them park in the designated area. Theenda reserved rooms in three different hotels in downtown Columbus.

During that week a convention was not in town, nor was it hockey season, the Blue Jackets were not playing, for that reason, the hotel rooms were not full to capacity. In case the freedmen and women had questions, she divided themselves into groups of two's, James and Sara, Timpkin and KayKay, and she and Donovan. Theenda put Haze with her in-laws and Tess with KayKay and Timpkin.

As the freedmen and women entered the hotel, the female freedmen and women stood in awe of the exquisite décor. The men, on the other hand, mouth flopped open, eyes almost popped out as they watched women going to-and-fro in their low-cut tops, short hemlines, and high heels. Lee said to no one in particular, "dey' woman ain't wearin' enough clothes."

Jethro said, "I's like feedom women better than a slave."
Saul asked, "how we meet em."
Ben said, "I's thank we just ask dey name."

Rita stood next to Lee and whispered, "lookie' at da' coloreds and whites be dressed da' same."

Lee was gawking at the women, he ignored her, Rita looked for Theenda,

Theenda looked around for Tess, she called her over and said, "are there any stores opened tonight?"

Rita stood next to Theenda and listened to the women talk.

Tess sister came over to the women, she joined Tess and Theenda and said, "you made it." She and Tess hugged, Tess, said, "my sis," she looked at Theenda and said, "this is my sister Penny," to her sister, Tess said, "this is my friend Theenda." The two women shook hands. Tess looked at Rita and said, "this is Rita."

Theenda said, "tomorrow we want to go shopping for church clothes."

Penny said, "I know exactly the store. It has everything for men women and children."

Tess asked Theenda, "are you getting something for yourself?"

"No, I have enough clothes for the week and a few outfits for church."

Theenda asked Tess, "how about you?"

"I shop at secondhand stores, unlike the Bright's, you all shop at expensive stores, you probably want to go to Sax Fifth Avenue."

Penny said, "sis, you should stay here with me, there's a group here to help with anger issues."

"I'm not angry!" Tess yelled before she stormed off.

Theenda and Penney looked at each other, Rita said, "hum."

Penny asked, "what did she tell you about our family?"

"Your father beat your mother and gave you candy."

"Not even close," Penny said as she watched her sister argue with one of the workers, she continued, "dad beat mom raped us, girls then gave us candy." She began to leave but turned and said, "I'll take you shopping tomorrow." She left to get Tess under control.

XLII

Jeff Brown Return To Ogville

June 19, 2017

    Donovan woke up at five o'clock in the morning, an idea had popped in his head, he looked outside, it was raining. He took his laptop out of its bag, even though he was trying to be quiet, he roused Theenda, she said, "don't bang on that thing the way you normally do. I'm not ready to get up."
    Donovan said, "I'll go in the bathroom."
    Theenda asked, "why don't you get dressed and work in the business center?"
    "I'll run into someone, they will talk and talk, don't have time for that. Go back to sleep Baby Girl."
    He quickly entered the bathroom because he could see that Theenda wanted to talk. In the bathroom was a large countertop, Donovan sat his laptop on the counter and began typing away. Donovan had attended college in New York with a male student, they had become buddies, he was studying journalism and Donovan history. Donovan's friend landed a job as a reporter with a newspaper in Ottawa, Canada. He was looking for a big story to write so that he could move up in the company. Donovan sent his friend an email saying, *man do I have a story for you.* From the documents Donovan received from Mrs. Paddleton, he wrote a ten-page paper about H.B. Metropolis and the slaves escape. He emailed the document to his friend and pictures he had taken, then Donovan called his friend and told him about what he had sent. After the conversation, the newspaper man ran the article. It appeared in the Tuesday morning paper, the caption was, "American Slavery In Twenty-First Century."

Jeff read the article and caught the first flight to America. He rented a car In MacCall and went to the mansion. In the driveway were several government cars and reporters, he got a quick glance of the partially burned down mansion, Jeff turned around and drove off. He returned to downtown MacCall, and drove past the police station, several sheriffs and FBI cars were in front of the building. Jeff went to Ogville.

Jeff casually walked into the Ogville police station, leaned on the counter top and said to the receptionists, "chief in, gorgeous?"

Behind Jeff entered two men wearing black coats.

She said, "yes Sir, I'll get him," she looked at the two men and said, "please have a seat, I'll be right with you." She left to get Chief Gideon of Ogville.

When Chief Gideon came out, he asked, "what can I do for you?"

Jeff said to the Chief, "you don't remember me? I'm Mr. Charles Browns son, Jeff. I am richer and more important than most people in this town."

"Now that you say it," the chief vaguely remembered, "I thought your name was Harry. I believe you're looking for Chief Stevens in MacCall, he knows you and your family well."

Jeff jumped right into the reason he'd returned home, and his revenge on the slaves. "I want to find the bastards who did this to my family," Jeff said in anger.

"Jeff they've been gone for a long time, I don't know where they are." Chief Gideon replied.

Jeff looked at the chief with the attitude of superiority, and the confidence of an arrogant fool, he unknowingly said, "my family paid your family from one generation to the next, to serve as the chief of Police and take care of our biddings. You will find the bastard slaves, or you lose your job."

Chief Gideon said, "you're in the wrong town, you paid Stevens, who was the Chief of MacCall and Titleburk. Not me."

Jeff continued to try and break Ogville's Chief, he said, "that's my great-great grandpa statue sitting in the middle of your downtown."

Gideon tired of Jeff idiocracy said, "just a moment, let me get my deputy, he'll find your human property." He went into his office.

While Chief Gideon was gone, Jeff winked at the secretary, she asked the two men in black coats if she could help them. One of the men said, "we'd like to speak with the Chief."

"I'll let him know."

In the background were two officers, talking on the phone. Jeff looked out the window watching cars drive by, and people slowly walking past the station. To the receptionist, Jeff said, "one day everybody will know that my family is back in control of this town."

Chief Gideon returned and said, "my deputy is making calls now, give him a few minutes."

Jeff said, "I'm going to bring them back."

The chief asked, "have you been home?"

"Yes, I'm looking for my parents, tell me where they are, and I will pay you handsomely."

"Sir, you're in Ogville, my town, not MacCall, I don't want or need your money."

"Your town!" yelled Jeff, "my family owns this town, we own you."

Felix came out to tell the chief the news, "Sir, I think they went back to the plantation."

Jeff yelled unnecessarily loud, "you're not paid to think, I just came from there!"

Chief Gideon said calmly, "if they are not there, one of the men who stole your property worked for the government. They may be on their way to Washington D.C."

Sitting on the counter were two baskets filled with files and papers, Jeff picked up both baskets and slung them across the room, and said, "I'll be back in an hour or two. When I get back, "have my property."

When Jeff stormed out, the receptionist asked, "Sir, he owned slaves, this year?"

"So, he says," said Chief Gideon.

Chief Gideon went back into his office with Felix, another officer named, Hank, followed them. Chief Gideon asked, Did you do it?"

Felix said, "done."

"See that the job is finished." Chief Gideon insisted.

They exited the side door of the Chief office; their police car was parked in the back.

With them gone, Chief Gideon sent an email telling the secretary to send the two men in.

When they entered Gideon's office, he asked, "what can I do for you?"

One of the men said, "we're from Canada, we're here to arrest Jeff, but wanted to speak with you first."

The other man said, "Stevens is in prison."

The men told Chief Gideon about Jeff's falsifying his birth. Gideon laughed, he told them about the Brown family and Stevens.

Jeff sped down the highway on his way to the house in Titleburk, he needed to find his parents and suggest they rebuild H.B. Driving too fast, Jeff turned on the freeway, normally he would have made the turn if his brakes were not tampered with. His car crash through the barrier, the impact caused the tampered gas tank to completely crack. Jeff got out of the car and slipped in the gas that had leaked in the grass. When he stood, gas was on his pants and shirt. Hank and Felix had followed Jeff to do as the Chief had instructed. The officers stopped and blocked traffic, Hank redirected the cars, as Felix call the ambulance and his precinct. The chief called the fire department. Jeff was smoking, Felix said, "your car is leaking gas, put the cigarette out."

Jeff called Felix several unspeakable names, as he was fussing and cursing, he threw the cigarette towards Felix. A spark hit his shirt, Jeff and his car went up in flames as the ambulance and fire truck was parking.

The firemen working at top speed got the fire out, the paramedics saved Jeff life. All though Jeff whole body was burned, the two men from Canada had Jeff discharged, and helicoptered to the Canadian hospital, where Jeff said he was born. Jeff committed an offense in another country, his term in prison was going to belong. Jeff had no family or friend to help, not even the people who worked for his janitorial company or the company he worked for. He reached out to the girl he had purchased the computer and paid three months' rent, she and all others turned their backs on Jeff.

The reporter that wrote the first article about the Brown family, wrote another, the headline read, *Brown Family America's Bad Seed, Captured*. It ran on the front page.

Two weeks after Jeff's admission in the hospital, he was killed during the night shift. The murderer was never caught, search for the person is ongoing.

Donovan's friend got the higher position he wanted, Jeff was not the only person that read the article, so did TV, Newspaper, and Magazine reporters stormed the plantation. In addition, the Canadian Newspaper that Donovan's friend worked for, sold more papers than it had ever.

****

Columbus, Ohio Church day

A busload of freedmen, women, and children exited the buses and entered the church. Pastor Desmoid had told his members about the slaves, he said, "today, we are getting one hundred visitors that just last week, escaped from a plantation located in the deep south. These people have been slaves since their birth." The audience gasped in astonishment. He concluded by saying, "please be kind and remember to welcome them with opened hearts."

Down front, the ushers had saved twelve rows of seats for their visitors.

As Pastor Desmoid finished telling his members about the fugitives, the ushers opened the doors of the sanctuary, Theenda had them to file into the church in twos'. Lillie said to Sophie, who stood next to her, "everythang' in freedom is beautiful."

Sophie replied, "look at the women fancy hats and dresses."

Helen holding onto Faye's arm said, "look at the women's hat. Ain't they fancy."

Faye whispered, "I like dey fancy jewelry."

Once everyone was seated the hostess of the church welcomed them, she said, "on behalf of our Pastor and first lady, Pastor and Mrs. Desmoid, we welcome you to our church. Thank you for worshiping with us today."

The choir stood and sang a foot-stomping high energy gospel. The freedmen and women released pinned up emotions of hate, loneliness, and a lifetime with the deficiency of joy and happiness.

Pastor Desmoid preached on the Love of Jesus, in the middle of his sermon Lillie jumped up and asked, "did God make slave to serve white man, and the white man to serve God?"

For a moment the pastor was taken off guard. It took him a minute to gather his thoughts and recuperate from the blow of Lillie's question. he said, "no ma'am,' ahh hum, God made humans of all race and color to serve Him."

Lillie asked, "where it say dat' in da' Bible?"

He said," turn in your Bibles to Acts 5:29, he read, "we ought to obey God rather than man."

Lillie said, "I knew it, thank you, pastor, thank you." She wept.

After the sermon, Glaidous stood and said, "Sir I's likes ta' sing a song for Jesus if you don't mind."

The pastor said, "I would love to hear your song."

Glaidous stood before the church, closed his eyes, moaned a slow sorrowful rhythmic melody with the flavor of Amazing Grace. It was a song the slaves sang when Glaidous preached. The freedmen and women softly stomp their feet on the carpeted floor, the pounding of their feet vibrated like a heartbeat. The freedmen and women joined Glaidous, as they sang and moaned, the drummer caught on to the beat, as did the church band. And then the members sung with them, they clapped, rocked, and stomped to the gloomiest song they had ever heard, though the words were very powerful. The members reflected on their personal failures, victories, health issues, finances, struggle in their fight to overcome sin.

The church vibrated with everyone praising God. Theenda looked at Donovan and said, "if we were staying in Columbus, I'd make this church my home.

True to James Bright word, when they arrived in Rochester, New York, the FBI and different government departments he contacted, was there to meet the freedmen and women and the modern-day abolitionist. Before James and Sara left for Ogville, the welfare department contacted the Mayor's Office. He had his Legislative person communicate with the owner of their abandoned hotel, they had the company to repair and open the hotel for the freedmen and women temporary housing.

Haze, Timpkin, and KayKay stayed with Sara and James. Donovan and Theenda were at Paul's house.

Tess signed the divorce papers and moved to Ohio with her sister. Unfortunately, she could not get a job.

Tess references from the hospital and her friends in Ogville were damaging to her career. Haze was at the hospital too often from being stabbed, sliced, or hit with a bat, and the fight in the bar sealed her fate as a vicious person. No one in Columbus hired her.

Her luck changed when a manager at a Pittsburg steel factory got Tess resume through an employment site. He called the hospital in Ogville and got a violent report about her, he said to himself, "perfect."

The original nurse was also a hard brute, however, she was killed in a motorcycle accident. As the manager figured, when he saw Tess comradery with the employees, she was textbook fit. She was also, the right choice for his ragged tag rough group of men and women.

Haze first morning in Sara's home, he called Donovan. Theenda and Paul's wife got along well, he left them there with the kids. When Sara entered the kitchen, Donovan and Haze were talking and drinking coffee. Sara said, "good morning fellows." She poured herself a cup of coffee.

Donovan said, "sorry if we woke you mom."

"No, you didn't wake me." She looked at Haze and said, "you are a free man, your healing began, now."

Donovan said, "we were just talking about that."

"I love this family." Haze said.

Sara said, "you're a part of this family." She looked at Donovan and continued, "you're over here early, where's Thee."

"Haze called said he wanted to talk. Thee is with Paul's wife."

"Where's Paul."

"Mom, your son's are so happy about the freedmen and women, that crazy man packed them in a city bus and took them to the hospital, your other son is teaching them history."

Sara laughed as she asked, "how did he get a city bus?"

"No idea."

"And John is doing what?" Sara asked.

"Exactly," was Donovan's reply.

A few days after their arrival, Donovan made copies of Harry's papers that were given to him in the black case, from Mrs. Paddleton. He gave the original copies to the FBI and kept the copy.

Paul had every man, woman, and child ex-slave to get their teeth, eyes, and a full physical exam. Lillie had a tumor in her stomach, she told the doctor, "I's gotta go wid' my people." She refused to have the surgery.

Paul gently talked her into having the surgery, she asked, "you be Mr. Bright brother, I's don't wanna go to da horse-pillo."

Even so, with Paul's assurance, Lillie had the surgery, she was in great pain afterward from the stitches, fortunately, the tumor was not malignant

Their second week in New York, reporters took individual pictures of the freedmen and women and ran them in newspapers and television across America. To claim their child, the parent had to have the child's birth certificate, social security number, hospital records, and pictures.

By the end of July, people traveled to New York to claim a child hoping to get money, even though no one had said anything about cash. Though, Lee's mom and uncle recognized him right away. Lee's dad searched tirelessly for his son; he died a broken man from a heart attack. His mom did not give up on finding her son, even though it took thirty years to see him again. She had the paperwork needed and his tiny footprints from the hospital after he was born.

Lee's mom brought a picture of his dad, he looked just like him and his uncle that came with her. Lee introduced them to Cush, who cried. Lee's mom covered her grandchild face with kisses. Lee told her that he had been a slave for thirty years. He told her all about the plantation. Unfortunately for his mom, Lee did not go home with her. He asked her to go with them, she declined but his uncle said, give us time to take care of things at home. He wrote down their address and said, send us your address. That's when Lee learned that a few years after his dad's death, his dad's brother married his mom. Lee's mom and stepfather/uncle stayed with Lee until the freedmen and women left. Lee introduced Donovan to his parents, Donovan said, "if one day you want to come, there is plenty of room for you and jobs." He told them about the trailers and eventually building houses.

Lee's uncle said, "okay, we'll pack our things and move out there."

His mom was happy, Lee introduced his mom to Lillie.

A great number of parents whose child was small or young came with the proper papers and hospital records. Several of the teen's parents came and identified them and had the correct papers. All the parents had pictures of their child and oftentimes siblings. Several Psychologist was present to talk with the parents and their family.

Faye's mom came, she recognized the woman, her mom had gotten in a bar fight, the man hit her in the head with an empty bottle of wine. A permanent scar in the shape of an eye, formed on her forehead. Faye's mom looked like she had walked from Detroit, Michigan to New York, she was loud, rowdy, and smelt of alcohol. Faye saw her but left out of the building.

Jethro had seen Faye looking at the woman, then left. He followed her and asked, "was that yo' mama?"

Faye answered, "Yes."

"How's come you's say nothin' to her?"

"Did you see her? Did you smell her? She used to tell me when I git's ten I's be a professional streetwalker just like her. So, I was on da' pantation."

"How old you be when dey' take you," Jethro asked.

Faye said, "I was not taken, I was sold at the age of six. I saw Massa gib my mama money, she said ta' me. "go on wid' da' man. Dat be pert' near forty years ago."

From June through mid-September were busy months for everyone in New York. Some news stations ran the news all day long, too many reporters from across America, Canada, and other countries traveled to Ogville, MacCall, and Titleburk. In Ogville Chief Gideon had a meeting with the city's officials and news reporters, he told them all about the Brown family lies and the arrest of Chief Stevens and his precinct.

It took Ogville's residents two weeks to tear down Harry's gigantic statue. In its place, they planted a beautiful flower garden and set decorative benches in the midst of the garden.

Unfortunately, Donovan and Theenda the towns favorite couple were despised by the three town residents. The couple had wiped out a whole family. They blamed Jeff murder on Donovan, the Chief assured the FBI that he had nothing to do with Jeff, he explained, "Jeff returned after the slaves had escaped. He told them that Donovan saved the slaves and was taking them far away.

While in New York, the Bright's met up at Donovan's parents' home to read in the two books and open the wood box that Glaidous had given to Donovan. The family was astonished, Donovan said, "we returned where our family Paula was a slave, and Moses, our grandpa, designed H.B. Metropolis." He looked at John and said, "that's where you get your gift to build."

John said, "little bro' yes, it is, I often wondered where it came from."

James said, "I want to go back before they completely destroy H.B."

"They may have already dad," Donovan replied.

"No, they haven't, it's too early right now they are researching the place, looking for dead bodies, they will want to talk with some of the slaves. No, not yet son, they are still working out how could such a thing happen right under their noses."

Sara said, "you're right honey."

John said, "that's why I like drawing buildings and communities, I am good at it. Mom, dad, I have a confession."

"We already know that you teach architect and design," Sara said.

John asked surprised, "how'd you know."

James said, "we're your parents."

Paul was alarmed, he asked, "he's been lying to the family all these years?"

John claimed, "I'm not that old."

Donovan said, "that's the reason you gave me the wallet, you knew John was not teaching history."

Ignoring Donovan, James said, "the beginning of the Bright's..."

Sara said, "was in the children's cabin at H.B. Metropolis."

Theenda said looking at Donovan, "I called you Moses, Sweetie. Little did I know; you really are Moses Berhanu. Wow!"

Paul, John, and Donovan said together as though rehearsed, "yeah, we're not using that last name."

They laughed.

****

October 2017, The Federal Bureau of Investigation, and Office Of The Inspection General insisted that Donovan with his modern-day abolitionist and a few of the slaves return to the H.B. Metropolis Plantation. The Government Officials had questions about the illegal twenty-first-century slaves. Having no other choice, Donovan, his wife Theenda, Timpkin, and KayKay Linwood, and his sidekick Haze Day, that was divorced from his ex-wife, Tess returned. Including Mrs. Paddleton, who financed the escape, and her twin great-grandchildren, Phillip and Phillipa assisted with the flight to freedom. The freedmen and women that returned were Lee, his uncle Glaidous, Ben, Rita, Helen, Jethro, and Saul.

January 2017, Donovan learned that there were actual slaves hidden by a massive forest and locked within giant gates. His adrenaline catapulted in hyper-overdrive to end slavery in America for good. June 17, 2017, Donovan with his wife, parents, and four friends stole the slaves making them free men and women.

Unfortunately, upon their return home to Ogville, the folk in their hometown were not hospitable. They turned their backs, rolled their eyes, and hissed foul words at the band of modern-day abolitions. Donovan and Theenda went from being the towns favorite young couple to being shunned. They found that their homes and belongings had been destroyed. Donovan and Theenda ran through their home trying to salvage what was not wrecked by the townspeople. Donovan said, "I am going to be so happy to get out of this town."

Theenda replied, "thank God the FBI is near. The town folk is angry with us."

Donovan said, "you'd think they would be happy; the Brown secret is over, and the last member of that family is dead."

Donovan and his wife packed the rental car with things that would be allowed on the airplane. They drove to MacCall, thus forever leaving behind the first house they purchased together.

The day Donovan and his people arrived on the plantation, there were already several FBI agents, people from the Office Of Inspector General, historians, archaeologists, anthropologists, a construction crew with several backhoes, and a host of other people helping to clear the rubble and assist wherever needed. Lastly, Chief Gideon did nothing to stop the townspeople, from looting the Abolitionist homes.

Donovan organized everyone into groups of seven or ten, each group received a slave. Donovan put himself and his people with Lee. The ex-slave were the tour guides, they explained the plantation operations. Though the gates were gone, the freedmen and women knew exactly where everything was once located within the slave compound. Using army jeeps with radios, Donovan with his buddies, and the slaves were driven all over the plantation starting in front of the Brown family mansion. As they drove past, Theenda flinched and lowered her head when she saw the front door. Donovan put his arm around her shoulder, and whispered, "it's all over."

They drove around to the back of the mansion, through where the outer gate once stood, on to the children area, the cabin was still standing. Donovan's father told them about the area, he had helped the children and trainer out the children cabin, through the children gate, past the outer gate, beyond the mansion onto the school bus.

Helen was the children caregiver. She explained how the children system ran and how she took over when the nurse and teacher were escorted out of the children's area, by Mr. Brown. She ended her explanation when she said, "Massa Brown sista' worked wid' da' chil'ren, one day she be gone and neva' come back."

Donovan said, "he killed her."

Helen showed them inside the cabin.

They left the children area and drove through where the divider gate stood, and past the overseers' cabins, "Lee said, "I thank that's whar's the overseer lived."

They got out of the car and entered both overseers cabins.

Everyone on the plantation met where the church once stood, when all was quiet, Glaidous said, "dis' be town. We's escaped from da' church."

The freedmen and women took turns telling Donovan and the government workers about digging their way out the backroom of the church. Lee said, "the last night of the revival I was nervous and happy."

Saul said, "hum-um, I be scared and happy."

The crowd followed the freedmen and women as they talked about the cabins, who lived where, the tobacco field, the whipping tree, and their beatings, they told the crowd about the cruelty they endured.

An agent said, "the gates stood twenty-two feet on top of the land and six feet under."

Another person explained; the gates divided areas."

Theenda asked, "why didn't they climb out?"

Mrs. Paddleton said, "the Browns had the gates greased twice a year by six men. When their work was finished, they were killed."

Donovan said, "can you imagine, over one hundred years of killing twelve men every year."

Mrs. Paddleton said, "when the overseer's, nurses, and teachers turned fifty they were killed."

Timpkin said, "the trees grew away from the gates and not in the slave living quarters, they couldn't climb out."

A construction worker explained, "we dug up thousands of steel plates that directed roots in the opposite direction of the gate."

"Wow," Donovan began then continued, "Harry V. Brown thought of everything."

"His plan was to keep slaves on his property forever." Mrs. Paddleton commented.

Lee said, "had it not been for Mr. Bright, we still be slaves."

A man from The Office Of Inspection General said, "everyone, follow me," he took them where Stevens shot the two overseers and Bo died, he said, "three bodies were found right here, two white men shot, the other looked like something had hit him in the head."

Glaidous spoke up and said, "that was the two overseers and Bo."

Donovan asked, "why didn't they leave with you?"

"Bo was Massa snitch, and da overseers worked for Massa," Ben answered.

Lee said, "they were locked on the plantation with us, and like us could not leave."

An agent pulled Donovan aside and asked, "Mr. Bright, how did you find this place."

Donovan began his explanation when one of the historians went into the area where a construction worker was digging.

Donovan said to the agent, "excuse me." He ran to where the man was digging, he yelled, "Sir! three to four hundred people were buried in that hole!"

Everyone stopped talking and followed Donovan, Jethro said, "Mr. Bright, dat be whar's our vegetables grow."

A historian stood in front of the backhoe to stop the man from digging. Mrs. Paddleton said, "mister stop digging, if Mr. Bright is wrong you can continue, if he's right, the bones will have to be identified and pieced together."

Rita said, "cain't be no dead people in there, our food be planted on dis' here ground."

Donovan asked, "were the plants big, bright, well grown, and healthy every year?"

The seven freedmen and women said in unison, "yaw' Sir."

Helen asked, "whad' dat' got's ta do wid' anything?"

One of the archaeologists said, "oh, I see. The bodies were the fertilizer."

Donovan replied, "exactly, for over one hundred thirty-two years, this has been a burial ground."

The anthropologist said, "dig slow and easy." He said to Donovan, "so far we've found three hundred bodies, some of my men are defining the bones as to age and sex."

The archaeologist said, "yeah, my group and the anthropologist are working together."

An FBI Agent said, "my men are drawing what they could look like." He paused for a moment as though it was hard for him to say, "we found over two hundred children bodies, several were newborn." He looked at Donovan and said, "on top the partial burned second porch a body, the autopsy showed it was a woman, a bullet went through her lungs, and lodge in her ribs. We believe her husband shot her, ablaze from the fire came on the porch and spooked the man, he jumped to his death."

Donovan asked, "where is he?"

The agent said, "in the morgue, his autopsy showed, one side of his face was busted opened, we believe he fell on his chest, four ribs penetrated his lungs. He died instantly."

"Had to," Donovan said.

The man operating the backhoe slowly with caution scooped up dirt, when he got deeper and released the dirt, bones fell out. He was asked to stop digging, the archeologist and anthropologist took over the excavation with their tools.

Ben ran and puked, Rita and Helen, fainted. Lee, Jethro, Glaidous, and Saul were disgusted. The man that began the dig asked, as he pointed to the freedmen and women, "what's wrong with them?"

Haze said, "they ate food grown on top of these bodies."

The group hovered together as they gazed on the grave where thousands of bones laid on top of each other.

Another FBI agent drove to the group, he got out the jeep and said to the other agent, "more bodies in a well not far from the big house was found."

Donovan asked, "did you get the bodies in the woods by that huge building?"

Mrs. Paddleton asked confused, "in the woods?"

Timpkin answered, "yes, I forgot about that. The night we delivered digging tools; we saw truck lights."

Haze said, "yes, four men got out the truck and unpacked it, they put the things in that building."

Donovan said, "we were deep in the woods, so only saw figures, one man shot the three and left."

The FBI Agent standing next to Donovan said in a demanding tone, "Mr. Bright."

Donovan was being constantly distracted; he had not answered the Agent, who was getting on his nerve, question. Mrs. Paddleton looking on said, "the family that harbored free labor from one generation to the next was the Brown family. Harry Brown masterminded and began building this plantation in 1865."

The Agent looked at Mrs. Paddleton and asked, "how do you know that?"

"There were two brothers, Charles and Drew." Mrs. Paddleton began, she continued, "in the late 1800s Drew tried to kill his brother Charles, but he got away and changed his last name from Brown to Paddleton. I know this because, in 1930, I married Charles Paddleton great-grandson, Conley." Mrs. Paddleton looked at her two great-grandchildren and finished by stating, "Drew remained on this plantation and taught the next generation how to run it and keep its secret."

Donovan said, "I learned of the plantation through a student of mine, he found a map in his basement and a message written on a piece of paper. His dad went to MacCall and spoke with the Chief about a plantation that still had slaves, the next day the entire family was killed, the family before they were also killed."

Haze said, "while we planned the slaves escape my best friend was killed, due to his knowledge."

Timpkin said, "from that point on we kept quiet and planned in silence."

Theenda said, "God kept it quiet, and sent us help through Mrs. Paddleton." Theenda went to Donovan and put her arm around his waist.

He looked at her and smiled then said, "I followed the student's map to here, only there were miles and miles of forest to walk through, on the other side of the bushes and trees were miles of the tallest gates I'd ever seen. Using my binoculars, I saw people walking around inside another huge gate."

Theenda said, "he came home and said, "I think I saw slaves today. At first, I didn't believe him." She looked up at Donovan and said, "I'm sorry."

Donovan gave her a little squeeze, then said, "I want to see the castle that Harry V. Brown built."

Mrs. Paddleton said, "in the 1800s going to the castle was a half days journey, in a car we'll get there within a few minutes."

An FBI Agent said, "we've been here two months, we've never seen a castle. Did he have slaves there?"

"No," Mrs. Paddleton said, then completed saying, "the castle was supposed to be Harry's get away, he had planned to move in there after killing his hired hands."

The agent looked at Donovan and asked again, "my last time asking, how did you learn all this, the man barely wrote anything down."

Donovan looked a Mrs. Paddleton and smiled, he said, "I'm a historian, we search until we find what we're looking for, sometimes we find it in a book, other times a friend with a manual." Donovan looked in the agent's eyes for the first time and asked, "would you like to read the manual?"

Mrs. Paddleton said, "Harry's son Charles, wrote everything in his manual, he wrote it after escaping his brother."

The FBI agent answered, "yes, I'd like to read the manual and see the castle," he asked, "when and how did this all start?"

Donovan responded, "in 1825, by a hostile little ten-year-old slave boy named, Moe."

The agent said, "hold up," then he asked, "the man who had slaves was black?"

"No," Donovan began as he looked on the agent's confused face, he continued, "he was a white slave. Most people like to call the whites, indentured servant. Moe's whole family

was owned by the slave master, Jeb. Moe ran from slavery and his drunken mom."
>The agent asked, "how old was he when he ran?"
>Donovan answered, "he was ten years old."

Two agents and an archeologist Outside the outer gate by the building where Charles kept the furniture and tobacco when they arrived there were three bodies. An agent got into the jeep and drove to the crowd, he said to the head agent, "three bodies Sir, with bullet holes."
>Donovan said, "it was Charles Brown that killed them, I remember his face from the Juneteenth celebration."
>The agent said, "I thought you said it was dark."
>Haze said, "it was, he stood in front of the car lights, his face was clear."
>Timpkin said, "we saw him through bushes, still his face was visible."

****

In New York, after the investigation and all the questioning and the officials were satisfied, Donovan's mother and father, with his brothers and Paul's wife and children, sold their homes. They left the Big Apple.
>The American Government reimbursed the money that Donovan used to pay for the trailers and the property. And assured Donovan that if he and his team lived on the property, the tax would be exempted. Donovan asked, "the plan is to get rid of the trailers and build houses, will the taxes still be exempted?"
>The answer was a resounding yes.

Far away in the most North-West town in America, Donovan and his caravan drove from New York to the State of Washington. the freedmen and women were learning trades. Located a few miles from their dwelling place was a glue factory, several of the men were hired there, to do heavy labor. Many of the women were hired to work on the assembly line. The freedmen and women had to get used to working beside White Americans. Due to the brainwashing, they endured behind the iron gates they have limited people skills. Nonetheless, each evening the faithful abolitionist taught them how to respond and enter act with other humans.

At first, the slave children attended the city school with other children, but environmentally, socially, and academically they were behind. The elderly women made quilts, and the elderly men continued to make beautiful wood furniture, Theenda landed a deal with a furniture store that wanted full rights to sell their furniture and quilts. Donovan's mom worked up the paperwork to make it legal. The store purchased the wood and equipment, and built a warehouse, to make furniture and quilts. The freedmen and women loved getting up every morning catching the bus to work.

In the beginning, several city folks were leery about so many blacks being in their neck of the woods. Others were happy for their craftsmanship and their desire to work hard and thorough.

Timpkin, Theenda, Tess, and KayKay joined Donovan who was standing under a tree reading the newspaper from Ogville. Mrs. Paddleton had sent him an article regarding Jeff's death. Theenda said, "we did it, we got away. No more plantation owners."

Donovan looked up from the paper and asked, "what about your sister?"

"She decided to stay in The Big Apple, with mom dead, she and the kids are safe."

Donovan said, "good for her."

Thee said, "with the money, dad left us she attended secretarial school and is an administrative assistant for the FBI in New York Office." She kissed Donovan on the cheek and said, "thank you for talking John into selling sis his home."

"You wouldn't let me give her mom and dad's house."

"Taxes are too high in that Rochester neighborhood."

Changing the subject Timpkin said quietly, "all three of my children are talking about moving here, how do you feel about that?"

Donovan said, "are you kidding me, my whole family is here."

James and Sara had gone to town to get the mail out of their Post Office Box. They had a key to Donovan's box. When they arrived at the trailer's, James saw Donovan and the others, he walked over and handed Donovan a letter from The Office Of The Inspection General.

After reading the letter he said, "they want all the abolitionist and the same freedmen and women to return to the plantation. He looked at his dad and said, "we just came from there, why they want us to come back?"

James said, "I don't know, I'd like to go back."

Donovan replied, "okay, I'll call a meeting and let them know." Donovan asked the church pastor if they could use their recreation room, to meet with the freedmen and women, the pastor granted Donovan permission.

Before the meeting began, Lillie said, "I want to confess."

Glaidous asked, "what did you do, Lillie?"

Lillie stood and came clean when she announced, "Helen is my child when I gave birth to a baby girl, I asked the nurse to name my child after her. The nurse said *I can't do that, I will name her, Helen, after my mother*. I said thank you when she's given to someone else, I will know she's my child."

Helen stood next to her and said, "the nurse told me about the agreement. Even though I was given to another couple, I knew Miss. Lillie was my mom."

Lillie said, "the nurse could have been killed for doing what she did, she said to me that I cain't tell, I told her I won't. Now we be free, I'm telling."

Glaidous said, "Lillie told me about Helen after Massa Tom beat Lillie's husband to death.

Lee said, "my mom wants me to come and live with her. I can't do that. I would like to visit her, get to know her, Miss Lillie be my mom."

Donovan said, "I thought she was moving here."

Lee said, "my uncle won't let her." He looked at Donovan miserably and asked, "can you save her Mr. Bright?"

And ex-slave named Peter said, "my psychologist said we cain't leave each other cause we be brainwashed. That be why Lee cain't live with that woman."

KayKay's daughter stood and said to Donovan, "he's right, on the plantation they were taught to believe, that their lives belonged to their Massa."

Faye said, "Massa say, slave cain't take care of dey' baby, cause we too stupid and dumb. Massa smart, dey care foe' our babies. We were too dumb and stupid." As Faye spoke her voice sounded teary, her shoulders slumped.

KayKay's daughter went to Faye, put her arm around her and said, "the children from age, I'd say eight or nine will never leave the compound structure. It's really a blessing Donovan, that you found a place for all of them to stay together."

Donovan said, "God through Haze got this place."

Theenda said, "They can't leave each other because they are emotionally and mentally depended on each other. Due to brainwashing, they received from the Browns."

Donovan said, "I have the parents phone numbers that kept their child. The children that are six years and older are having a hard time adjusting. One of the parents called me and said, her eleven-year-old daughter killed herself. Her daughter told her that she had to find the nurse and teacher, or Massa would be mad. While everyone was sleeping, the girl left and started walking, she got confused when a truck was rushing down the street, he hit her, she was killed instantly.

Theenda suggested, "the children confusion is happening across board, Donovan and I searched and found a psychiatrist near their homes. The children needed to stay with everyone else. We didn't know, nor did the psychologist in New York prepared or knew."

Lillie said, "when the houses be built. Rita says she be moving in one. Rita tried to leave; she pretends she's happy."

Donovan looked at Lee and said, "flying to H.B., we'll take a detour to Philadelphia, rent a car and go see your mom."

Lee's wife said, "I don't believe they will fly. Jethro and Ben's fiancée and I will drive down, we'll talk to them."

Lee said, "I'm taking driver lessons, Rita gave me the number to the company that taught her how to drive."

Donovan looked at Lee's wife and said, "that's if you have the baby, the agents want us there in a few weeks."

Lee's wife looked at Donovan and said, "please make it four weeks, the baby is due next week."

One of the freedwomen said, "Helen be watchin' yo' twins Mr. Bright, I's watch Lee's baby."

Lillie said, "that sounds like a good plan."

Donovan said, "I'll call the agent, see if I can stretch it to five weeks."

Timpkin went to the front and stood next to Donovan and said, "I looked up on my phone, the Crime & Law Enforcement number of people shot to death by the police in the United States in 2017 and 2018. In 2017 White shot and killed four hundred fifty-seven, Blacks two hundred twenty-three. In 2018, White three hundred eighteen, Blacks one hundred fifty-eight. Though an essay written by a judge discusses the "missing or nonreported police cases, it talks about the inaccuracy of officers involved in the fatal shooting."

Donovan scrolled through google on his phone and said, "a number of hate groups explained over two, three, and this one reads five thousand blacks were killed by police due to our inability to…"

Theenda looking at the expressions on the freedmen and women faces cut Donovan off and said, "we need to withdraw from this conversation it's making some uncomfortable." As she spoke, she discretely used her hands to get Donovan and Timpkin to look at the expression on the freedmen and women faces.

KayKay's daughter caught on and said, "I believe Thee is right, let's change the subject."

XLIII

Freedom Home

    Within the trailer camp the slaves wanted to congregate with each other, but outside was too cold. Every time they had a meeting, the church charged a fee, for that reason, Donovan used his brother's skills to build a place big enough for meetings, have social events, or just congregate to talk. John contacted a company that had steel building kits, with heat and electricity. By February 2018, the building was up and ready to use, it sat in a corner of the trailer park. It had bathrooms, a huge kitchen, a cloakroom, and a large recreation hall. Donovan purchased two hundred fifty chairs and sixty tables that his wife and mom chose. There was enough space to have a party and dance. Theenda and Sara designed the building's interior from the floor to the ceiling, they chose all the appliances, pots, silverware, and dishes.

    Donovan chose a white metal roof to coincide with the snowcapped mountains. He had the men to paint the shutters around the windows glossy black, the building was a metallic gray. When Theenda and Sara finished, the inside was elegantly ornamented and furnished. The metal building was spectacular on the outside and breathtaking inside, so much so, the townspeople held social events in the building.

    In their trailer, Glaidous was reclined next to his wife, they each had a lazy boy. He said, "I's likes my new life, in this world, I would have children."

    "Me to Glaidous," she asked, "does it ever bother you that after I was beaten till I lost our child, we killed our babies before they were born?"

"Yes, but I look at the cuts and scars on my body, I's thank, I's won't no child of mine ta' go through what we did."

"I look at my beat-up body," Sophie said, "I's feel the same, I's remember Cush first beatin,' I felt every lash," she looked sorrowful at Glaidous. She continued, "we would not be allowed to raise our baby."

Glaidous said, "ain't no telling which child we'd receive. Thank God Donovan came when he did," Glaidous looked over at Sophie and continued, "what bothers me, is how you got rid of the baby."

Sophie smiled back and said, "I still miss Massa and da' pantation.' Sometimes I's cry cause I's wonts' ta' go back, Massa smarter den' you."

Glaidous got up, looked down at Sophie and said, "I'm going to sis, I may never be back."

The mountain group had their Thanksgiving Day dinner with church members in the black church fellowship hall. Normally on the plantation, the freedmen and women did not celebrate the holiday. The members fixed a huge meal, with several different cakes and pies. The meal was delicious and beautiful.

Children laughter filled the air with joy, as gospel and Christmas music from the C.D. player enhanced the mood.

At sunset, they all gathered around the piano, and taught each other their songs and shared stories of hardship and good times. Everyone was on one accord, Lillie said, "this day will go down in history as a good and perfect day."

Two days after the feast, Lillie was resting in her living room with the television on, her favorite shows were the soaps. She gathered her quilt about her as she laid back in her lazy boy. Outside was cold and blustery, inside her home was hot.

Rita walked up to Lillie's door and rang the doorbell, Lillie yelled, "come in."

"Miss. Lillie, how are you?" Lee, Cush, and Lillie's trailer home was long wide and roomy. The front door opened to a small hallway on the right was the living room and the kitchen to the left. Miss. Lillie said, "I'm staying out the cold and watching my soaps. Rita entered the exceptionally clean trailer, she sat on the couch. "Good morning Miss. Lillie," Rita began and then continued, "I came to check on you, I got a job at the hospital, they are going to train me to be a nurse aid." Rita beamed from cheek to cheek.

Miss. Lillie sat up and said with joy, "oh baby, that is wonderful, you're going to be a nurse likes' Miss. Tess."

"Not quite like Miss. Tess, she went to college for four years. My training is for a few months at the hospital."

"But you still gonna' be learning.' I am so proud of you young folk." She laid back grimace in pain and held her stomach.

Rita went over to her and said, "I think you ate too much Thanksgiving dinner the other day."

"Child, we all ate too much, I neva' saw so much food in all my life, I neva' knew there was so many different types of meat, I neva saw a bird dat' big."

Lillie frowned this time in serious pain. "I'm going to get Miss. Edna."

Lillie said, "get Mr. Bright brother,' he be a doctor. Miss. Enda need the rest, I's thank she goin' ta' have does' babies early."

Lillie grimaced in pain and passed gas. Rita said, "Miss Lillie, please let me call someone to take you to the hospital." Tears rolled down Rita's cheeks.

"Hush up child, hush your crying, I don't want ta' go ' ta' a horse-pillow,' those nurses wake me up to give me a pill, wake me up and ask how I'm doing. Cain't git no rest."

Rita laughed and said, "okay then," she sat on the couch and continued, "Lee and I's getting hitched, we need you."

"I will be there child," Lillie smiled she reached out for Rita's hand, she gave it a gentle squeeze. Lillie stared at Rita and said, "I love you, child, I love my son, I love everybody here." She frowned in pain.

Rita ran out and got Donovan, Lee, and Cush. Paul Bright came as well, carrying his doctor's bag.

When they all came inside Lillie's trailer she said, "Dr. Bright, thank you for making my last days bearable." She looked at Lee and said, "son he kept me alive ta enjoy freedom." She looked at Cush and continued, "Cush come here baby, it's time for me to go, I want you to grow to be a good man like yo' daddy." She reached out to Donovan, "Mr. Bright, thank you." She squeezed his hand, then said, "thank you for' my freedom."

she looked around the room at everyone and continued, "It's time for' me to go now."

Dr. Bright sent everyone out the trailer when they were gone, he said as he laid her lazy boy back, "Miss. Lillie, I am going to palpate your stomach." When he finished, he continued, "Miss. Lillie, you're going to live, you have a bad case of gas." He gave her Gas X extra strength soft gel.

He told them to come back in, Glaidous had come to see his sister, he was told that she was going to die. Paul said, "no, she's going to live."

Lillie was laughing and passing gas, Glaidous said, "she's smelling up the place."

Paul said, "she has gas." He left.

Glaidous laughed so hard he could not breathe. Lee gaged as he said, "I am going to leave you at it mom." He left.

Glaidous and Lillie laughed even harder, and then he cried.

Lillie asked, "what be wrong?"

He said, "I's neva be happy wid' Sophie." They talked until midnight."

January 5, 2018

Mrs. Paddleton and Timpkins parents died the same month, their funeral was held on the same day two hours apart. Donovan returned to Ogville with Timpkin, to attend portions of both funerals. After the funerals, Donovan met with Phillipa and Phillip.

Timpkins mother died first, instead of calling Timpkin's sister, their dad took both bottles of sleeping pills, seventy in all. He went to sleep and never woke up. They were found lying in bed side by side.

Phillipa told Donovan Mrs. Paddleton left Harry's castle to him. She said, "a buyer offered fifty million."

"Fifty million, that's more than enough to build houses," Donovan asked her about the plantation.

Phillipa said, "The government-owned that, they are setting up offices on a small portion of the land. Harry had over twenty miles of land. The Government is baffled."

"I can only imagine," Donovan said.
Phillipa and Phillip took Donovan to see the castle, he said, "it's just like Mrs. Paddleton."
Phillip said, "yes, it is, and it's yours."
Phillipa commented, "that's the reason great gran gave the house to you. She knew you'd do the right thing."

Phillipa drove Donovan and Timpkin to the airport, she handed Donovan a black attaché case, she said, "grandmothers last donation."
Donovan said, "but the castle. That's more than enough."
"This is your pay, for doing an extraordinary thing. Enjoy." Phillipa said.
Donovan asked her, "what about your grandma's house?"
"The government is allowing us to turn it into a museum, about the Paddleton's and Brown's complete history from 1865 to 2017, how you found the slaves, and the history of Timpkin, Haze, and your wives gave up everything for a group of people you never met."
As he and Timpkin got out of the car, Donovan said, "thank you for Everything, come visit us."

Theenda did not meet them at the airport, she was sick, KayKay picked them up instead. She asked Timpkin about the funeral and how he was holding up. He said, "they lived a long good life. I'm okay." He, his kids, nor sister told KayKay that their father killed himself.

Donovan entered the house to tell Theenda the good news. She said, "we could use some of the money to buy a house."
"No, my sweet, Mrs. Paddleton gave us a case of money just for us."
Theenda smiled weakly and said, "good, I'm ready to get out this trailer. It's too small Sweetie, we have two little people coming."
Donovan said, "yes we do," he paused before continuing, "when you're better, send a letter to the US Government and one to the Paddleton twins, thank them for the money to help build homes for the freedmen and women."

"Sweetie I did already, I made a copy of the letter, I saved it on the disk for you to edit. I sent each twin two cards, a thank you card, and a sympathy card. I'll send another for the castle."

Donovan said, "you're the best."

Before falling asleep Theenda said, "our country came through for us. The President with his demented temper tantrums could have messed up everything, but he allowed the state to handle it. They did well," Theenda said before falling asleep.

Donovan pulled the covers over her shoulders; he kissed her forehead.

Donovan rented a room in the church to have a meeting, they all were present except Theenda. His brother John gave the update on the building construction, he said, "it should be ready the end of February."

The freedmen and women applauded, they piled in the cars and others had to walk the nine blocks to the church, summer was okay, but they did not like the frigid winter. Donovan stood before the group and said, "thank you, John. I will be glad when the building is finished, all we'll have to do is walk across the lot to the building."

Many applauded and others said, "that's right."

Donovan began the meeting, he said, "now that we are settled, I felt the need to quote the words of a Civil Rights leader, Martin Luther King, I have a dream. He gave this speech in our nation's capital, Washington D.C. Last year, I had a dream that one day you would be free from beatings, free from being owned by another human, free to live the way you choose, free to use your skills, free to express yourself, free to be you, free to experience your rights to life, liberty, and pursuit of happiness. Despite all you have gone through, you pressed forward, fought through the brainwashing you received. I appeal to you, believe that you have something to offer this country, yourselves, your families. Don't let nobody interrupt your course of action, your plans, your dreams, say to yourself I have a dream, be a dreamer, be a thinker, but most of all, be a doer." He paused a moment before continuing, "you are religious people, let nothing or no one prevent the union and communion of your soul with Christ."

When Donovan finished everyone applauded and cheered. Lee asked, "where you learn to talk like that?"

Glaidous said, "just thank,' a colored man talk like that, glory be."

Lillie said, "glory ta' God. That be mighty pretty talking Mr. Bright."

Cush said, "Mr. Bright, you make me wanna be a Proud Black American when I grow up, I'm going to be just like you and my daddy,"

Sophie said, "Massa talks pretty likes dat."

One of the slave women rolled her eyes at Sophie, then asked Donovan, "how come we's don't know 'bout freedom? How we be slaves all these years?"

While Donovan told them the history of Harry V. Brown and his H. B. Metropolis, his parents sat proud of their son, Haze said to himself, "I am honored to be his friend."

Rita said to one of the women, "When we left the plantation, Lee and I talked about getting married. Now he's free, he changed his mind, and married someone else."

The woman asked, "what are you goin' ta' do?"

"I can't stay here and see them, no more."

Rita felt the pain of freedom, at first, she did not understand the reason free people got sad. In the end, Rita was feeling the reason.

XLIV

March 2018

Donovan and his brother John traveled to Seattle Washington; they found a construction company that built neighborhoods. They needed two separate areas, one to replace the trailers and one with million-dollar homes away from the freedmen and women. Donovan wanted them to become independent of him.

Paul and Timpkin's son opened a Medical Clinic in town. They also worked for the hospital that was 1950's drab décor and equipment. The two doctors took over and updated the facility inside and out. The hospital electrical system was so outdated it could not handle a computer system. John was also a computer guru, he lived in Europe for two years, to work with a company that built smart homes. He returned home to New York, he taught history, design, and worked at a Computer Technology Company. John called CTC to lay the wiring for the hospital computer system, they worked closely with the electricians.

Philippa and Phillip moved to Washington; they had grown weary of New York and missed their new friends. Phillip went back to Ohio State University, met a girl and her family, they were good people. Phillip joined Paul and Timpkin's son at the hospital, the three worked together to bring the hospital to the twenty-first century. Phillips wife was hired as a supervisor of the nurses. She put out a call for more nurses and doctors to move to the state of Washington, and work in the hospital. Phillipa met a man in New York, he moved with her to the state of Washington. He worked with James on bringing the local college curriculum to the twenty-first century. Later he and Phillipa married.

Donovan, his family, Haze, and the Paddleton's purchased land to build their homes in an affluent community. Donovan's brother, John Bright, was the designer of the houses. He hired the company in Europe to build smart homes. Haze started a janitorial service and named it Then & Now Janitorial Corporation. Sara hung her law degree up and became the Chief Operating Officer and Business Manager for Haze company. She grew the company in the State of Washington and South Western Canada. Donovan's dad became Vice President of the town college.

Most of the freedmen and women were employed in the factory, others worked for Timpkin or Haze. Timpkin did not want to go back to a 9-5 job, he started a lawn care service, he hired several of the freedmen and women. Timpkin hired a woman from town, Sara taught the woman how to grow the business. Timpkin named his company, Linwood Lawn and Garden Care. Lillie asked Timpkin if she could do gardening for him. Timpkin asked around, much to his surprise, several of the residents were interested. Lillie had lost weight, she wanted to get back outside because she felt healthier than ever before. Timpkin hired six of Lillie's friends that were in their sixties to work in teams of two in the gardens. The woman he hired grew Timpkin's company, there were fourteen homes that wanted a garden, and he landed the college and Statehouse lawn and floral contracts.

Sophie did not fare as well, she was diagnosed with Alzheimer, Paul had to put her in the nursing home in town. She had become violent, in the mobile home she broke windows, she scratched Glaidous, she threw pots, lamps, anything she could get her hands on. Glaidous visited her three times a week, Sophie became too violent for the nurses to handle. Sophie had bitten, scratched, kicked the nurses, she threw her bedpan at Dr. Paul Bright. She began to growl her demand to go back to the plantation. Paul sent her to a medical facility in Seattle that could handle her. He thought that Glaidous would be sad and forlorn. Instead, Glaidous beamed with happiness, full of energy, his health got better, Glaidous fell in love with life and his job. He stopped walking around like an old hundred-twenty-year old man, he walked with a bounce in his step. Lillie said to Theenda, "Miss.

All But One

Enda, I's thank Glaidous is happier than he's ever been. I told him not to marry Sophie, she was never good for' him," Lillie smiled before she continued, "Massa put a boy in a cabin, den' put a girl in wid him, we are married. My brother didn't have a chance."

Every one of the freedmen and women attended Donovan and Theenda's Alternative school, though the adults only for six months. KayKay and her daughter opened a mental consulting area in Paul's clinic. The government came through with the restitution, Donovan hired an accountant to teach the freedmen and women about spending and investing their money wisely.

On a weekend day, Donovan, Timpkin, Haze were talking inside the steel building. Donovan said, "Haze you seem happy as a single man."

"Yeah, I've noticed that myself, I often wondered what changed," Timpkin said.

"Don-man," Haze began, "Tess is gone forever, I mean forever."

Timpkin asked, "what're you talking about."

"She got in a fight with the wrong person, her boyfriend allowed her to hit him several times with a baseball bat, he ran in the kitchen with her behind him swinging the bat. She hit him in the face, he grabbed her and sliced her throat"

Donovan asked, "how do you know?"

"The hospital called me about my last hospital bill, I sent a check, the envelope had my P.O. Box number. Tess called them looking for me, they gave her my box number." He stopped and looked at Donovan and Timpkin and said, "can you believe she wanted us to get back together."

Timpkin asked, "how do you know about the fight?"

Haze said, "her boyfriend wrote me a letter and sent a copy of the newspaper article with his picture. She beat him something terrible." He handed them the article.

Donovan said, "I can see why he got off."

Haze said, "yes he did, he sent a note that read, *she'll no longer fight anyone.* He sent me the unsigned divorced papers, he wrote, *no need for this anymore.*

Timpkin chuckled and said, "she was a tough woman,"

Haze agreed, "Yes she was. Helen and I have been talking since we've met. I want to marry her."

"I noticed that," Timpkin smiled then continued, "she came out the woods looking innocent almost childlike. You gently took her to your bus. I wondered, what's Haze doing?"

"I sat her in the front seat, she's quite a talker. When Tess got on the bus she stopped."

"Now we both have wonderful women." Haze said to Donovan.

Donovan and Haze said together, "Happy life, happy wife. Although, Haze, you're not married yet."

Timpkin said, "that line does not work with Kay."

Donovan said, "there's always an exception to the rule."

Timpkin said, "she wants me to build her a million-dollar home where you're building yours, if I don't, she will leave me, she would be intolerable." He scratched his head then continued, "she's unbearable now since we've moved here, she's gotten worse."

"I paid the five of us one and a half million, and divided Tess money evenly between us, use that money to build," Donovan paused for a moment before continuing, "well use the little Uncle Sam left you."

Laughing Haze said, "Yea, man tax killed me."

Timpkin said, "I refuse to live with that woman any longer. She gave me an ultimatum, build her a million-dollar home or she will leave me."

Donovan asked, "what're you going to do?"

"I packed her bags and put her out."

The three men laughed, Timpkin continued, "we're getting a divorce, the children said, it's about time dad. I said, yes, it is. Since mom and dad died, something changed inside of me, I am tired of her bragging, nagging, gossiping, complaining." He shuddered like a chill was in the air, and then continued, "she's using her money to build over there on County Road 299, with those other houses."

Donovan said, "you had me worried, I thought you were going to say next to our houses."

Timpkin laughed and said, "I'm using the money you gave me to build in the mountains. I took a ride up there; the land and homes are beautiful."

Haze said, "Tim the mountain man."

"I can see that," Donovan said agreeing with haze.

While they were talking, Lee, Jethro, Glaidous, and Saul entered the building, Lee asked, "can we join you?"

"Sure," Donovan said.

Jethro said as he sat down, "I can't shake this feeling that, there's no gate." He looked like he was about to cry.

Donovan and Timpkin got uncomfortable, still, Donovan said, "the gates are gone. You were there to see they are gone."

Lee said, "no more gates."

"Yeah," Jethro said.

"It's big out here. Inside the gate, we were protected." Lee said.

Jethro agreed. "Out here we're wide opened."

Timpkin asked, "do you think you'll get used to being in the opening?"

The four men answered in unison, "yes."

Jethro said, "I'll die trying."

Glaidous said, "now that Sophie is gone, I am finally enjoying life. With her, I was still behind the gate."

Haze said, "then it's settled, no more worries."

Glaidous said, "I don't miss the gates, I like the open."

Donovan began, "I read about slavery…"

Jethro said, "you read, Mr. Bright, we lived it."

Glaidous said as he looked at Donovan, "Mr. Bright, I am learnin' since I will be free, a lot of folks hate me cause of my brown skin."

Lillie said, "then there are others, me and a group of women, of multiple races, were makin' quilt sets. I pricked my finger with a needle. A white woman said to another, *if the nigger could sew, she wouldn't get nigger blood on everything*." An angry look scrolled across Lillie's face as she said, "I stood and said really loud, I am a proud black woman that taught you how to sew. If you don't like me because of my brown skin, go tell our brown skin boss that owns this company." Lillie sat down.

Another white woman said, "you tell her Miss. Lillie."

Donovan said, "good for you and her, standing up for what's right."

Glaidous said, "word got around about the incident, the woman was given a choice, leave on her own or get fired. She left."

Lee said, "Mr. Bright we learn what to do at your and Miss. Enda school."

Glaidous said, "I used to' cry when Sophie was with me, she reminded me of the plantation. I stopped crying, I no longer think of where I come from, but where I am and can go."

All the men unanimously said, "amen."

Rita returned to visit everyone; she was driving a canary yellow convertible mustang. She was wearing a long blond wig, she kept flipping it out her face, the way she had seen white women do at her job.

As Rita rolled up in her car, the men were coming out of the steel building, Lee saw her first. He admired the car and was shocked when Rita got out the car, in only a few months she had lost weight, she said, "hi Lee."

The men said, "Hi Rita," and walked away.

Lee asked Rita, "that your car."

"Yes. I came to see Helen and Faye. I'm going to take them for a ride."

Lee said, "have fun."

Rita said, "had we married, this would be our car."

Lee said, "hum, that is interesting."

Lee stood watching Rita strut to Helen's trailer. He called out asking, "going to see mama?"

Rita replied, "I don't have time today, I'm too busy." She swung the hair off her shoulder.

Watching her, Lee said, "I made the right choice."

April 2018

The freedmen and women found a store in the local mall that sold the brightest clothes and shoes they could find. The men discovered that tennis shoes were comfortable, which was fine, though they chose lime green, bright orange or yellow, and the loudest red known to man. The women bought shoes of the same coloreds and hot pink loafers.

One-day Donovan and Theenda took a stroll in the mall, Donovan was pushing his twin boys, in a stroller made for twins. They named the boys Thaddeus and Moses, James said, "two strong names."

On their outing, they saw the store where the newly freedmen and women shopped. They paused for a second and then quickly hurried on their way. When they returned to the trailer park, they saw Lee, his wife, and Cush exited their trailer. Cush was carrying several popsicles; he ran to share and play with the teens. Lee, his wife, and their baby were out for a walk, Lee looked at Donovan and gave him a huge happy smile. Donovan nod and smiled back. Ben walked past holding his wife's hands, they gave a friendly waved and each said, "hello."

He watched the young men in their twenties looking at the girls. Donovan wondered if any of the twenty-year-old were the Janitor's son. He had called the janitor, Donovan purchased tickets for them to fly out. The Janitor said, "my wife is bringing pictures, it may be him, it may not." He thanked Donovan for trying.

Haze and Helen had gone to the justice of Peace and got married. Theenda taught Helen secretary skills, office administration, and typewriter skills. Helen could not grasp how to use the computer; however, she was a whiz on the typewriter.

LaVaughn

EPILOGUE

Sunday, April 15, 2018

    Saul and Jethro had a double wedding, they got married in the black church in town. It was a big production. Their reception was held in the steel building. They wanted the wedding to be held on Easter Sunday, but another wedding was booked in the church. Donovan explained having their wedding on the fifteenth would put them closer to the date they met. Saul said, "that's right, it was on the sixteen-last year."
    Jethro said, "in freedom, Easter Sunday is on the first."
    Donovan wanted to explain the date change but realized he would confuse them even more. The men changed their wedding date to the fifteenth.

    One cool day in March, Lillie visited Donovan and Theenda in their trailer. Only Donovan was home, Theenda was out shopping with Sara and Rita for the wedding. Lillie said to Donovan, "Mr. Bright, I want to show the Essence you gave us slaves."
    Confused Donovan asked, "show it where."
    Lillie answered, "at Saul and Jethro wedding, we can celebrate our one-year freedom, because of the Essence Magazine you put in the gate."
    Donovan said, "you want to showcase the magazine. Okay, I'll make that happen." He went to an art store and purchased a gold painted easel.

    For the reception, Glaidous had drawn on six feet paper a picture of Donovan, Haze, and Timpkin, his drawings resembled the three men perfectly. Written underneath the drawing read, *Easter Sunday 2017 we met Mr. Bright as slaves. Easter Sunday 2018 we are free.*

    Lillie wanted to write something, she asked Sara to write it for her. On four-feet paper Sara wrote a sign, Lillie chose a thick red marker, it read, *All us slaves thank Donovan Bright, Haze Day, Timpkin Linwood, Ben Bright, and their wives, for their unwavering courage and tenacity, despite death threats to emancipate us, slaves. From slave to Freedmen and women. Thank you.*

    Theenda had the men to hang both signs on the wall.

    Sitting under and between the signs on an easel, was the Essence Magazine in the freezer bag that Donovan had left between the gates prong. As they were putting the signs on the wall, KayKay stood next to Theenda and asked, "does it bother you that our names are not on the list. We helped; we were there."

    Theenda coolly replied, "no, we didn't trample through the woods to meet them, deliver heavy supplies, take food and meds, teach them how to use the equipment. No, I am not offended, while they worked and received death threats, we sat comfortably in our homes talking about it."

    Rita attended the wedding, she had helped Theenda, Sara, and Lee's wife decorate. Lee's wife was a secretary for the manager at the factory, where the couple worked. Rita got rid of the wig and over Lee breaking up with her, she became herself again. After all, she had her apartment, car, a job, and a male orderly that was interested in her, and Rita him. Still, Rita felt something was missing, she talked to Miss. Lillie about the emptiness in her life. Miss. Lillie said, they are building our houses, pick one."

    Rita replied, "I will on Monday." She walked away smiling, knowing one day soon she would be back with her friends.

    Donovan and Theenda stood in front of the Essence magazine, she said, "that's my favorite magazine, President Barack Obama."

    "Baby Girl, look at the lives it saved."

    Lillie watched Donovan and Theenda glare at the magazine display before she went to them. She said as she pointed at the Essence Magazine, "Mr. Bright, Miss. Enda, that magazine saved our lives, thank you very much." She smiled before continuing, "I learned how to speak correctly, because of you two. Thank you."

A tall handsome man that was Lillie's age, from the city, took her hand and led her onto the dance floor.

Theenda's eyes followed the couple, she saw Glaidous dancing with a woman fifteen years younger than him, she too was from the city. He was having a good time. Sophie died in Seattle Washington, Glaidous was free and wanted to take his time getting married again. The Browns had put Sophie in his cabin when he was seventeen years old, he was sixty-six when they escaped. It was Sophie that would ram a stick up her to get rid of the baby, after the third time, he stopped sleeping with his wife and Faye became his once a week relief.

Looking around the room, Theenda giggled and said, "yes it did."

"Yes, what did Baby Girl."

Theenda said, "at first I was furious with you, but now, not at all." She looked up at Donovan and said, "look around the room, listen to the laughter, see joy, all because of The Essence Magazine you left."

Glaidous did not like the loud colors the others wore, he dressed more like Timpkin use to. Dress pants, matching tie and shirt, and jackets with a patch on the elbow. At work, he wore khakis and plaid shirts, with brown loafers. He went to Timpkin's barber to get his hair and beard professionally cut, he materialized into a handsome man. Timpkin transformed into a striking gentleman, he hired a stylist from Seattle to help him with his wardrobe and looks. Theenda said to Donovan, "have you noticed that Timpkin dress better, look taller, handsome even."

KayKay and her daughter heard Theenda comment about Timpkin, his daughter, smiled. KayKay said to her daughter, "Glaidous and your father is like a blind person telling a blind person the color of his shirt." She laughed.

Her daughter looked at her mom and said, "that's why dad put you out," she walked away.

KayKay looked at Donovan and Theenda, sucked her teeth, rolled her eyes at the couple and angrily left the building.

Theenda said, "ignore her."

Donovan did not see KayKay or hear his wife, he was watching the townspeople couple themselves with the freedmen

All But One

and women, he said to Theenda, "have you noticed the locals dating and marrying the freedmen and women, quick like they are in a hurry."

"Yep, and then there is Haze who did the same."

Donovan stated, "I wonder if there's a psychological meaning behind it."

"I believe so," Theenda stopped then continued, "it's called, a small town with not enough men or women, and then here we come."

Donovan said, "we brought a smorgasbord."

They laughed.

Theenda said, "from twenty-year-old to sixty."

The babies and children were in an additional room, which was added two weeks after the steel building was erected. Helen and a few other women watched the children. Helen loved the twins, she had never seen two babies born, from one person. She was amazed at how they looked just alike. She kept baby Thaddeus and Moses close to her while watching the children play and listening to their laughter. Helen had sad memories when she remembered the children compound, they played quiet and were not allowed to run inside or outside. She thought in freedom, kids run, laugh, play hard, and had fun, she smiled. Haze walked in; Helen smiled even bigger. Cush ran up to her, and said, "Miss. Helen, I like freedom." he ran off to play.

Never having an opportunity to be a kid, the teenagers played as hard as the young children.

Haze put his arm around Helen and said, "how are you doing Mrs. Day?"

She said, "just fine Mr. Day," she kissed him on the cheek.

In the reception room, Jethro and his wife danced across the floor. Saul's wife didn't know how to dance, they sat, talked, and laughed. The freedmen and women only spoked about H.B. if asked, otherwise, it did not exist.

Luther Vandross song, *A House Is Not A Home*, played, James and Sara went on the dance floor. Sara asked, "did you give them that CD?"

Most of the slaves stopped dancing, they liked fast songs.

James said, "you know I did Honey; this song was playing when we met, this is my jam."

Sara laughed and said, "yes it was."

Donovan escorted Theenda on to the dance floor and said, "A House Is Not a Home is dad's favorite song," He bowed waist down and asked, "may I have this dance beautiful lady."

Theenda curtesy and answered, "yes you may." Theenda looked up at Donovan, their eyes met.

Donovan said a little above a whisper, "Hello Baby Girl, I think I saw slaves today."

Theenda smiled, she laid her head against his shoulder.

Luther Vandross flawless velvet voice created an atmosphere of pure romance. Donovan and Theenda held each other close and tight, as they danced slow and smooth.

The End